Praise for

NEW
YORK

"What makes this novel so entertaining is the riotous, multilayered portrait of a whole metropolis. Rutherfurd offers the reader a chance to watch a rural outcrop grow into one of the world's greatest cities in a mere 350 years. He delivers magnificently on the challenge; it is hard to imagine any other writer combining such astonishing depth of research with the imagination and ingenuity to hold it all together."

—*The Washington Post*

"[A] lush, lavish tribute to the Big Apple. Sweeping in scope . . . fascinating . . . Although it is hard to do justice to a city with such a throbbing pulse, Rutherfurd's homage is compulsively readable."

—*Booklist*

"Edward Rutherfurd has tackled big subjects in his fiction before. London, Russia, Ireland, to name but three. Now he turns his keen academic eye toward the city that never sleeps. . . . An heir to James Michener . . . Rutherfurd's research is exhaustive."

—*USA Today*

"A history lesson, well researched . . . entertaining and . . . will make you feel like a bit of a brain."

—*The Times* (UK)

"In the tradition of James Michener, Rutherfurd unfurls more than three centuries of the city's history as seen through the eyes of the descendants of Van Dyck and Master—and the many other colorful characters he introduces along the way. . . . As accessible to the casual reader as it is to the history buff."

—Associated Press

ALSO BY EDWARD RUTHERFURD

Sarum

Russka

London

The Forest

Dublin

The Princes of Ireland

The Rebels of Ireland

New York

THE NOVEL

Edward Rutherfurd

Anchor Canada

This book is dedicated, with a lifetime of thanks,
to Eleanor Janet Wintle

Library and Archives Canada Cataloguing in Publication

Rutherfurd, Edward
New York : the novel / Edward Rutherfurd.

ISBN 978-0-385-66427-1

1. New York--Fiction. I. Title.

PR6068.U88N49 2010   823.914   C2010-902554-7

Printed and bound in the USA

Published in Canada by Anchor Canada,
a division of Random House of Canada Limited

Visit Random House of Canada Limited's website: www.randomhouse.ca

10 9 8 7 6 5 4 3 2 1

Contents

Maps

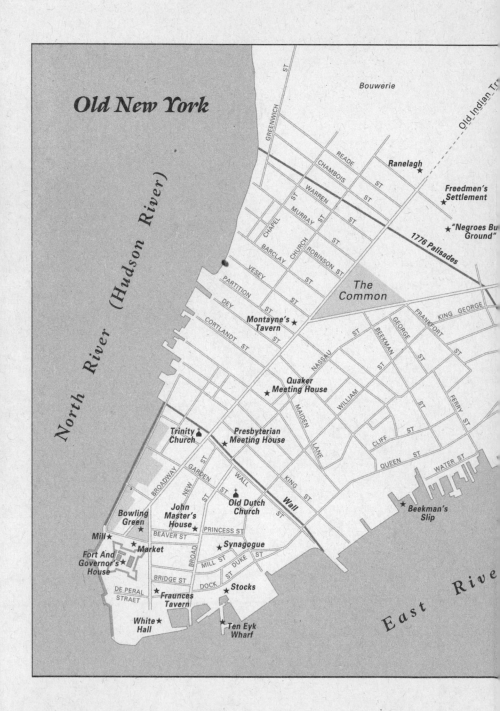

Old New York

Bouwerie

Old Indian Tr...

GREENWICH ST

READE ST
CHAMBOIS ST

Ranelagh ★

Freedmen's
★ Settlement

WARREN ST
MURRAY ST

ST

★ "Negroes Bu
Ground"

CHAPEL ST

1776 Palisades

BARCLAY ST

CHURCH ST

ROBINSON ST

VESEY ST

ST

PARTITION ST

The
Common

DEY ST

ST

Montayne's ★
Tavern

CORTLANDT ST

ST

KING GEORGE

FRANKFORT

GEORGE ST

BEEKMAN ST

ST

NASSAU ST

North River (Hudson River)

Quaker ★
Meeting House

WILLIAM ST

FERRY ST

MAIDEN LANE

ST

CLIFF ST

Trinity ♟
Church

Presbyterian ♟
Meeting House

ST

QUEEN ST

WATER ST

BROADWAY

GARDEN ST

NEW ST

WALL ST

KING ST

Wall

Bowling
Green ★

John
Master's
House ★

Old Dutch
Church ♟

ST

★ Beekman's
Slip

Mill ★

BEAVER ST

PRINCESS ST

Fort And
Governor's ★
House

★ Market

★ Synagogue

BROAD

MILL ST

DUKE ST

ST

BRIDGE ST

DOCK

DE PERAL
STRAET

★ Fraunces
Tavern

★ Stocks

White ★
Hall

★ Ten Eyk
Wharf

East River

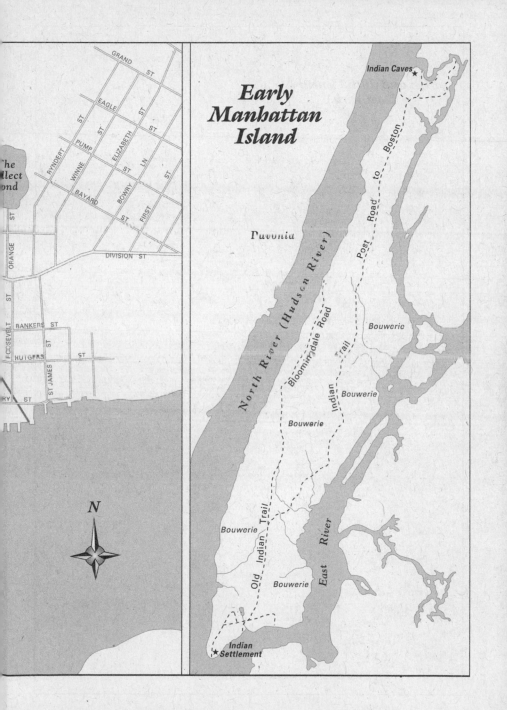

GRAND ST

EAGLE

ST

ST

RYNDEPT ST

PUMP

WINNE

ELIZABETH ST

LN

ST

BAYARD

BOWRY

ST

FIRST ST

DIVISION ST

The Collect Pond

ST

ORANGE ST

ST

ROOSEVELT ST

BANKERS ST

RUTGERS ST

ST

ST JAMES

ST

RY ST

*Early
Manhattan
Island*

Indian Caves

Pavonia

North River (Hudson River)

Post Road to Boston

Bloomingdale Road

Indian Trail

Bouwerie

Bouwerie

Bouwerie

Old Indian Trail

Bouwerie

East River

Bouwerie

N

Indian
Settlement

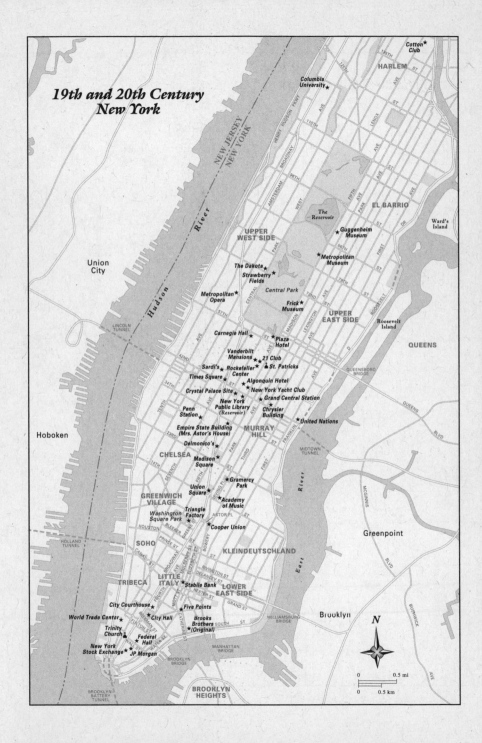

19th and 20th Century New York

Cotton Club ★

HARLEM

Columbia University ★

NEW JERSEY
NEW YORK

EL BARRIO

The Reservoir

Ward's Island

UPPER WEST SIDE

Guggenheim Museum ★

Metropolitan Museum ★

Union City

The Dakota ★
Strawberry Fields ★

Central Park

Frick Museum ★

UPPER EAST SIDE

Roosevelt Island

Metropolitan Opera ★

QUEENS

Carnegie Hall ★

Plaza Hotel ★

Hudson River

Vanderbilt Mansions ★
★ 21 Club

Queensboro Bridge

Sardi's ★
Times Square ★

Rockefeller Center ★
Algonquin Hotel ★

★ St. Patricks

★ New York Yacht Club

Crystal Palace Site ★

★ Grand Central Station

Penn Station ★

New York Public Library (Reservoir) ★

Chrysler Building ★

★ United Nations

Empire State Building (Mrs. Astor's House) ★

MURRAY HILL

Hoboken

Delmonico's ★

CHELSEA

MIDTOWN TUNNEL

Madison Square ★

★ Gramercy Park

Union Square ★

GREENWICH VILLAGE

★ Academy of Music

Washington Square Park ★

Triangle Factory ★

Greenpoint

★ Cooper Union

SOHO

KLEINDEUTSCHLAND

East River

LINCOLN TUNNEL

HOLLAND TUNNEL

TRIBECA

LITTLE ITALY

★ Stabile Bank

LOWER EAST SIDE

City Courthouse ★

★ Five Points

World Trade Center ★

★ City Hall

Brooks Brothers (Original) ★

WILLIAMSBURG BRIDGE

Brooklyn

Trinity Church ★

Federal Hall ★

New York Stock Exchange ★

★ JP Morgan

MANHATTAN BRIDGE

BROOKLYN BRIDGE

BROOKLYN BATTERY TUNNEL

BROOKLYN HEIGHTS

N

0   0.5 mi

0   0.5 km

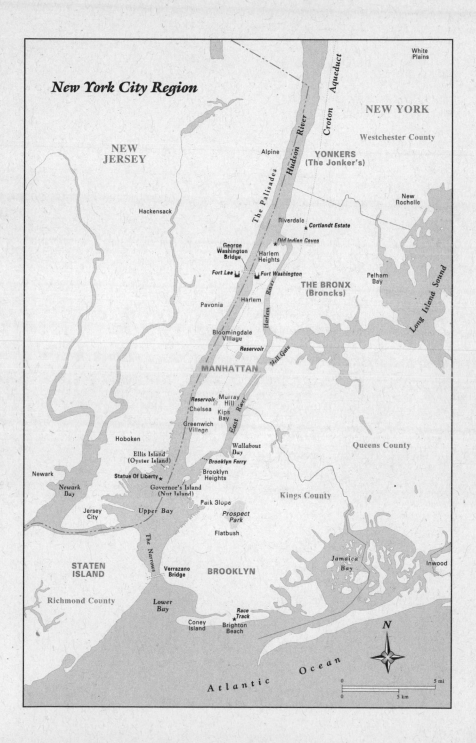

New York City Region

White
Plains

NEW YORK

Westchester County

NEW
JERSEY

Alpine

YONKERS
(The Jonker's)

New
Rochelle

Hackensack

Riverdale

Cortlandt Estate

Old Indian Caves

George
Washington
Bridge

Harlem
Heights

Fort Lee

Fort Washington

Pelham
Bay

THE BRONX
(Broncks)

Pavonia

Harlem

Bloomingdale
Village

Reservoir

Hell Gate

MANHATTAN

Reservoir

Murray
Hill

Chelsea

Kips
Bay

Greenwich
Village

Hoboken

Wallabout
Bay

Ellis Island
(Oyster Island)

Brooklyn Ferry

Queens County

Statue Of Liberty

Brooklyn
Heights

Newark

Governor's Island
(Nut Island)

Park Slope

Kings County

Newark
Bay

Prospect
Park

Jersey
City

Upper Bay

Flatbush

The Narrows

STATEN
ISLAND

Verrazano
Bridge

BROOKLYN

Jamaica
Bay

Inwood

Richmond County

Lower
Bay

Race
Track

Coney
Island

Brighton
Beach

Long Island Sound

The Palisades

Hudson River

Croton Aqueduct

Harlem River

East River

Atlantic   Ocean

N

0   5 mi

0   5 km

Preface

*N*EW YORK IS, first and foremost, a novel. All the families whose fortunes the story follows are fictional, as are their parts in the historical events described. But in following the stories of these imaginary families down the centuries, I have tried to set them among people and events that either did exist, or might have done.

The names of the principal families in this book have been chosen to represent the traditions from which they come. Van Dyck is a common and easily remembered Dutch name. Master is a fairly common English name, though I confess that while considering the family's destiny as merchants and Wall Street men, the phrase "Master of the Universe" sprang naturally into my mind. White is another typical English name. Keller is the fiftieth most popular German name, meaning a "Cellar Man." O'Donnell is a well-known Irish name, Caruso a famous Southern Italian name, and Adler, meaning "Eagle" in German, is found all over Middle Europe. In the case of characters who make brief appearances, the Rivers family are invented; the family of Albion appeared in my book *The Forest.* My choice of the name Juan Campos was inspired by the famous Puerto Rican composer Juan Morel Campos. The name Humblay does not, so far as I am aware, exist, but is an old spelling of "humbly" to be found in sixteenth-century prayer books. For the origins of the names Vorpal and Bandersnatch, readers are directed to Lewis Carroll's poem: *Jabberwocky.*

It has been necessary to invent very little in terms of historical event during the course of this narrative. Here and there, to maintain the narra-

tive flow, there are a few simplifications of complex historical sequence or
detail, but none, I believe, that misrepresent the general historical record.
A few words, however, are needed as to historical interpretation.

American Indian tribes. While I have made reference to certain local
tribes, such as the Tappan and the Hackensack, whose names are still to be
found in local topography, the New York region contained such a multi-
plicity of tribal groups that I have not wished to confuse the reader by using
too many. Instead, I have often followed the common practice of referring
to these tribes by the name of their shared language group, which was
Algonquin. Similarly, the tribes to the north are often called Iroquois—
which was their language—although where appropriate, individual tribes
like the Mohawks are so named. Readers may be surprised that in the early
part of the story I have not used the name of Lenape to denote the native
people of the Manhattan region. But in fact, this name was only applied to
these groups at a later historical period, and so I have preferred not to make
use of it when it would have signified nothing to the people described.

Some recent histories, in particular *The Island at the Center of the
World*, Russell Shorto's admirable book on New Amsterdam, stress the
tradition of personal and civic freedom bequeathed to New York by the
Dutch. I have tried to incorporate this work into my story, with the slight
proviso that civic independence had a history dating back into the Middle
Ages in England and much of Europe, as well.

My view in my original draft, that the English were harsher slaveowners
than the Dutch, has been modified in conversations with Professor Graham Hodges, whose book *Root & Branch* covers this subject thoroughly.

I have chosen to believe that the English governor, Lord Cornbury, was
indeed a cross-dresser. Several distinguished historians have been kind
enough to agree that this is a good choice.

My view of the changing relations between Englishmen and Americans
evolved considerably during the course of this narrative thanks to my
conversations with Professor Edwin G. Burrows, the distinguished co-
author of *Gotham*, whose book on this subject, *Forgotten Patriots*, came
out during the the writing of this novel.

New York is a vast subject, and one of the most complex cities in the
world. Any novelist covering its rich history will have to make many
choices. I can only hope that the reader may find that this book conveys
something, at least, of the history and spirit of what is, for me, a much-
loved city.

New York

New Amsterdam

S O THIS WAS freedom.

The canoe went with the river's tide, water bumping against the bow. Dirk van Dyck looked at the little girl and wondered: Was this journey a terrible mistake?

Big river, calling him to the north. Big sky, calling him to the west. Land of many rivers, land of many mountains, land of many forests. How far did it continue? Nobody knew. Not for certain. High above the eagles, only the sun on its huge journey westward could ever see the whole of it.

Yes, he had found freedom here, and love, in the wilderness. Van Dyck was a large man. He wore Dutch pantaloons, boots with turnover tops, and a leather jerkin over his shirt. Now they were approaching the port, he had put on a wide-brimmed hat with a feather in it. He gazed at the girl.

His daughter. Child of his sin. His sin for which, religion said, he must be punished.

How old was she? Ten, eleven? She had been so excited when he'd agreed to take her downriver. She had her mother's eyes. A lovely Indian child. Pale Feather, her people called her. Only her pale skin betrayed the rest of her story.

"Soon we shall be there." The Dutchman spoke in Algonquin, the language of the local tribes.

New Amsterdam. A trading post. A fort and little town behind a palisade. But it was important, all the same, in the worldwide commercial empire of the Dutch.

Van Dyck was proud to be Dutch. Their country might be small, but the indomitable Netherlanders had stood up to the mighty, occupying Spanish Empire, and won their independence. It was his people who had constructed the great dykes to reclaim huge tracts of fertile land from the rage of the sea. It was the maritime Dutch who had built up a trading empire that was the envy of the nations. Their cities—Amsterdam, Delft, Antwerp—where the rows of tall, gabled houses lined stately canals and waterways, were havens for artists, scholars and freethinkers from all over Europe, in this, the golden age of Rembrandt and Vermeer. Yes, he was proud to be Dutch.

In its lower reaches, the great river was tidal. This morning it was flowing down toward the ocean. During the afternoon, it would reverse itself and flow back toward the north.

The girl was looking forward, downstream. Van Dyck sat facing her, his back resting against a large pile of skins, beaver mostly, that filled the center of the canoe. The canoe was large and broad, its sides made of tree bark, sturdy but light. Four Indians paddled, two fore, two aft. Just behind them, a second boat, manned by his own men, followed them down the stream. He'd needed to take on this Indian canoe to carry all the cargo he had bought. Upriver, the late-spring sky was thunderous; above them, gray clouds. But ahead, the water was bright.

A sudden shaft of sunlight flashed from behind a cloud. The river made a tapping sound on the side of the boat, like a native drum giving him warning. The breeze on his face tingled, light as sparkling wine. He spoke again. He did not want to hurt her, but it had to be done.

"You must not say I am your father."

The girl glanced down at the little stone pendant that hung around her neck. A tiny carved face, painted red and black. The face hung upside down, Indian fashion. Logical, in fact: when you lifted the pendant to look at it, the face would be staring at you the right way up. A lucky charm. The Masked One, Lord of the Forest, the keeper of nature's balance.

Pale Feather did not answer him, but only gazed down at the face of her Indian god. What was she thinking? Did she understand? He could not tell.

From behind the rocky cliffs that stretched up the western bank like high, stone palisades, there now came a distant rumble of thunder. The little girl smiled. His own people, the Dutchman thought, as men of the sea, had no liking for thunder. To them it brought harms and fears. But the Indians were wiser. They knew what it meant when the thunder spoke: the gods who dwelt in the lowest of the twelve heavens were protecting the world from evil.

The sound echoed down the river, and dissolved in space. Pale Feather let the pendant fall, a tiny gesture full of grace. Then she looked up.

"Shall I meet your wife?"

Dirk van Dyck gave a little intake of breath. His wife Margaretha had no idea he was so near. He'd sent no word ahead of his return. But could he really hope to bring the girl ashore and conceal her from his wife? He must have been mad. He twisted round, awkwardly, and stared down the river. They had already reached the northern end of the narrow territory called Manhattan, and they were running with the tide. It was too late to turn back now.

⁘

Margaretha de Groot took a slow draw on the clay pipe in her sensual mouth, looked at the man with the wooden leg in a considering kind of way, and wondered what it would be like to sleep with him.

Tall, upright, determined, with piercing eyes, he might be gray, and well into middle age now, but he was still indomitable. As for the peg leg, it was a badge of honor, a reminder of his battles. That wound might have killed some men, but not Peter Stuyvesant. He was walking down the street with surprising speed. As she gazed at the hard, polished wood, she felt herself give a tiny shudder, though he did not see it.

What did he think of her? He liked her, she was sure of that. And why shouldn't he? She was a fine, full-bosomed woman in her thirties with a broad face and long blonde hair. But she hadn't run to fat, like many Dutchwomen. She was still in good trim, and there was something quite voluptuous about her. As for her liking for a pipe, most of the Dutch smoked pipes, men and women alike.

He saw her, stopped, and smiled.

"Good morning, Greet." Greet. A familiar form of address. Like most Dutchwomen, Margaretha van Dyck was normally known by her maiden name, Margaretha de Groot; and that is how she had expected him to address her. Of course, he'd known her since she was a girl. But even so . . . He was normally such a formal man. She almost blushed. "You are still alone?"

She was standing in front of her house. It was a typical Dutch town house, a simple, rectangular dwelling, two stories high, with wooden sides and its narrow, gabled end turned to the street. This end displayed a handsome pattern of black and yellow brick. A short stairway led up to the street door, which was large and protected by a porch. This was the Dutch "stoop." The windows were not large, but the ensemble was made impressive by the high, stepped gable that the Dutch favored, and the roof ridge was crowned with a weathervane.

"Your husband is still upriver?" Stuyvesant repeated. She nodded. "When will he return?"

"Who knows?" She shrugged. She could hardly complain that her husband's business took him north. The trade in furs, especially the all-important beaver pelts, had been so great that the local Indians had hunted their animals almost to extinction. Van Dyck often had to go far north into the hinterland to get his supplies from the Iroquois. And he was remarkably successful.

But did he have to stay away so long? In the early days of their marriage, his journeys had only taken a couple of weeks. But gradually his absences had extended. He was a good husband when he was at home, attentive to her and loving to his children. Yet she couldn't help feeling neglected. Only that morning her little daughter had asked her when her father would be home. "As soon as he can," she had answered with a smile. "You may be sure of that." But was he avoiding her? Were there other women in his life?

Loyalty was important to Margaretha de Groot. So it was not surprising if, fearing her husband might be unfaithful, she told herself that he was morally weak and, dreaming of solace in more righteous arms, allowed a voice within her to whisper: "If only he were a man like Governor Stuyvesant."

"These are difficult times, Greet." Stuyvesant's face did not show it, but she could hear the sadness in his voice. "You know I have enemies."

He was confiding in her. She felt a little rush of emotion. She wanted to put her hand on his arm, but didn't dare.

"Those cursed English."

She nodded.

If the trading empire of the Dutch extended from the Orient to the Americas, the English merchants were not far behind. Sometimes the two

Protestant nations acted together against their common enemies, the Catholic empires of Spain and Portugal; but most of the time they were rivals. Fifteen years ago, when Oliver Cromwell and his godly army took away King Charles of England's crown—and his head—the rivalry had intensified. The Dutch had a lucrative slave trade between Africa and the Caribbean. Cromwell's mission was clear.

"The slave trade must belong to England."

Many honest Dutchmen wondered if this brutal trafficking in humans was moral; the good Puritans of England had no such doubts. And soon Cromwell had taken Jamaica from the Spanish, to use as a slaving base. When Cromwell had died four years ago, and a second King Charles had been restored to the English throne, the same policy had continued. Word had already reached New Amsterdam that the English had attacked the Dutch slaving ports on the Guinea coast of Africa. And the rumor across the ocean was that they wanted not only the Dutchman's slave trade, but his port of New Amsterdam as well.

New Amsterdam might not be large: a fort, a couple of windmills, a church with a pointed spire; there was one small attempt at a canal, more like a large ditch really, and some streets of step-gabled houses which, together with some modest orchards and allotments, were enclosed within a wall that ran from west to east across Manhattan's southern tip. Yet it had a history. Ten years before even the *Mayflower* sailed, the Dutch West India Company, seeing the value of the vast natural harbor, had set up a trading post there. And now, after half a century of fits and starts, it had developed into a busy port with outlying settlements scattered for dozens of miles around—a territory which the Dutch called the New Netherland.

It already had character. For two generations the Dutch and their neighbors, the Protestant, French-speaking Walloons, had been fighting for independence from their master, Catholic Spain. And they had won. Dutch and Walloons together had settled in New Amsterdam. It was a Walloon, Pierre Minuit—a name that was still pronounced in French, "Minwee"—who had bargained with the native Indians, four decades ago, to purchase the right to settle on Manhattan. From its birth, the tough, independent spirit of these mixed Protestant merchants had infused the place.

But above all, it had position. The fort, to a soldier's eye, might not be impressive, but it dominated the southern tip of Manhattan Island where it jutted out into the wide waters of a magnificent, sheltered harbor. It guarded the entrance to the big North River.

And Peter Stuyvesant was its ruler.

The English enemy was already close. The New England men of Massachusetts, and especially of Connecticut with their devious governor, Winthrop, were always trying to poach territory from the outlying Dutch settlements. When Stuyvesant built up the stout wall and palisade across the northern side of the town, the New Englanders were politely told: "The wall is to keep the Indians out." But nobody was fooled. The wall was to keep out the English.

The governor was still gazing at her.

"I wish that the English were my only enemy."

Ah, the poor man. He was far too good for them, the worthless people of New Amsterdam.

The town contained some fifteen hundred people. About six hundred Dutch and Walloons, three hundred Germans and almost as many English who'd chosen to live under Dutch rule. The rest came from all parts of the world. There were even some Jews. And among them all, how many upright, righteous men? Not many, in her opinion.

Margaretha was not a religious woman. The Dutch Reform Church was stern and Calvinistic; she didn't always abide by its rules. But she admired the few strong men who did—men like Bogard, the old dominie preacher, and Stuyvesant. At least they stood for order.

When Stuyvesant clamped down on the excessive drinking in the town, or forbade some of the more obviously pagan folk festivals, or tried to keep the town free of the foolish Quakers or wretched Anabaptists, did any of the merchants support him? Hardly any. Not even the Dutch West India Company, whose servant he was, could be relied upon. When a parcel of Sephardic Jews arrived from Brazil, and Stuyvesant told them to go elsewhere, the company ordered him: "Let them in. They're good for business."

No one could deny that he'd been a fine governor. The men who came before him had mostly been corrupt buffoons. One idiot had even started an unnecessary war with the Indians that had nearly destroyed the colony. But Stuyvesant had learned to rule wisely. To the north, he kept the English at bay. To the south, he had made short work of an upstart Swedish colony on the Schuylkill River when it had become an irritation. He'd encouraged the sugar trade, and started to bring in more slaves. Every ship from Holland brought, as ballast, the best Dutch bricks to build the city's houses. The streets were clean, there was a little hospital now, and the school had a Latin master.

Yet were the people grateful? Of course not. They resented his rule. They even thought they could govern themselves, the fools. Were these men capable of governing? She doubted it.

The worst of them had been a two-faced lawyer, van der Donck. The Jonker, they'd called him: the squire. He was the one who went behind the governor's back, who composed letters to the West India Company and published complaints—all to bring down Stuyvesant. And for what? "The Jonker is a lover of liberty," her husband used to tell her. "You're all fools," she would cry. "He loves only himself. He'll rule you in Stuyvesant's place if you give him half the chance."

Fortunately the Jonker had failed to destroy Stuyvesant, but he'd managed to get his hands on a big estate north of the city. He'd even written a book on New Netherland which her husband assured her was fine. The wretch was dead and gone now—thank God! But the people of New Amsterdam still called his big estate "The Jonker's Land," as if the fellow were still there. And his example had so infected the merchants that, in her opinion, Stuyvesant shouldn't trust any of them.

The governor's hard eyes were fixed on her.

"Can I count upon you, Greet?"

Her heart missed a beat. She couldn't help it.

"Oh yes."

He was happily married, of course. At least, she supposed he was. He and Judith Bayard lived up at their bouwerie, as the Dutch called their farms, with every appearance of contentment. Judith was older than Peter. It was she who'd nursed him back to health after he lost his leg, and married him afterward. So far as Margaretha knew, he'd only once had an affair, and that had been when he was a young man, long before he met Judith. A small scandal. She thought the better of him for it. If it hadn't been for that little scandal, he might have become a Calvinist minister like his father, instead of joining the West India Company and going to seek his fortune on the high seas.

"And your husband? Can I count on him?"

"My husband?" Wherever he might be. Avoiding her.

Well, that was about to change. While he'd been away, she had given the matter some thought and formulated a plan for his future that would be more satisfactory. It was lucky that Dutch custom gave women far more freedom—and power—than the women of most other nations. And thank God for Dutch prenuptial agreements. She had some very definite plans for Dirk van Dyck, when he came home.

"Oh yes," she said. "He'll do as I say."

"I am going down to the fort," Stuyvesant said. "Will you walk with me?"

✣

London. A cheerful spring day. The River Thames was crowded with ships. Thomas Master gazed at the vessel before him and tried to decide.

In his hand was the letter from his brother Eliot, telling him that their father was dead. Tom was too honest to pretend he was sorry. He was twenty-two, and now he was free.

So which should it be? England or America?

On his left lay the great, gray mass of the Tower of London, silent, giving nothing away. Behind him, as he glanced back, the long, high roof of Old St. Paul's suggested disapproval. But of what? Of himself, no doubt. After all, he'd been sent to London in disgrace.

Thirty years ago, when Adam Master from England's East Coast and Abigail Eliot from the West Country had first met in London, these two earnest young Puritans had agreed that England's capital was a shocking place. King Charles I was on the throne; he had a French Catholic wife; he was trying to rule England like a despot, and his new henchman, Archbishop Laud, was determined to make all Englishmen conform to the high ceremonies and haughty authority of an Anglican Church that was papist in all but name. After they married, Adam and Abigail had stuck it out in London for a few years, in the hope that things might get better. But for Puritans the times had only got worse. So Adam and Abigail Master had joined the great migration to America.

Englishmen had been going to Virginia for two generations. By the time Shakespeare's Globe Theater was performing his plays on the Thames's south bank, half the population of London were smoking clay pipes of Virginia tobacco. But the number who'd actually left for Virginia was still modest. A few hardy souls had ventured to Massachusetts; other settlements had also started. But it was hardly a migration.

In the second half of King Charles's reign, however, something completely different occurred. The Puritans of England started leaving. From the south, the east, the west, they gathered in groups, sometimes families, sometimes whole communities, and took ship across the Atlantic. There was hardly a week when a vessel wasn't sailing from somewhere. From the mid-1630s, King Charles of England lost about a fiftieth of all his subjects in this manner. Gentlemen like Winthrop, young men of means like Harvard, merchants and craftsmen, laborers and preachers, with their wives and children and servants—they all took ship for America, to avoid King Charles and his Archbishop. This was the first real peopling of the American colonies, and it took place in little more than a decade.

King Charles never seemed to have felt any embarrassment at this loss. Indeed, it wasn't a loss; more of a gain. Rather than give him trouble at home, where he was trying to establish his authoritarian rule, they had obligingly gone to settle a huge new extension to his kingdom. Wherever they went on this huge, uncharted American continent, the land was England's; for they were still all his subjects, every one. As for the freedom of worship they enjoyed, it was out of sight, and could probably be corrected, later on.

Adam and Abigail Master had gone to Boston. There they had found the harsh, sometimes cruel godliness of the congregation to their liking. They were not, after all, seeking tolerance; they were setting up God's kingdom. And their elder son Eliot had followed them closely in this regard. Studious, cautious, determined, Eliot was everything a Boston father could wish for. But Tom had been another matter.

Tom Master was a fair-haired, blue-eyed fellow. Though he had slightly protruding teeth, women found him attractive. As a little boy, he was slim, always on the move, inventive. By the time he approached manhood, his whole demeanor suggested a quick, good-humored sharpness. He was full of vigor. But his behavior and his choice of friends left much to be desired.

For even in those early days, it had to be confessed, there were those—seafarers and fishermen, merchants and farmers, to speak nothing of the meaner sort—who were more concerned with the money to be made in Massachusetts than the saving of their souls. The congregation imposed its will as much as possible, but there were many backsliders.

And young Tom, to the great regret of his parents and of his brother Eliot, seemed destined to be heading straight for hell. He did not work at his lessons. He had the ability, but he would not apply himself. He got drunk. He kept bad company. Once, he even missed Sunday worship. And though his father had not spared the rod, he could see after a while that it was not a question of discipline, or precept. There was something deep in Tom that his father did not know how to change.

Adam Master had built up a good, sound practice as a lawyer. He'd bought a farm. He owned a ship. Eliot had studied law, but wanted to preach. Tom had been apprenticed to a merchant, and shown an aptitude for business. That was something, at least.

But two events had broken his father's heart. The first had been when Abigail lay dying. She had sent for her second son and, in the presence of his father, begged him to reform his life. For his own sake, and to help her depart in peace, she begged him to promise her that he would never drink another drop of liquor in his life. By that first step, she hoped, he might yet turn to better ways. And what had he said?

"Aw, hell, Ma. You know I can't promise that." To his mother on her deathbed. Adam could never forgive his son for this incident. He did not quarrel with Tom. He knew it was not what Abigail would have wished. He was polite. He did all that a father should. But he knew that Tom was no good.

So when Tom, at the age of nineteen, had enjoyed his first affair with the wife of a sea captain while that worthy man was away on a voyage— the captain of the very ship that Adam owned—his father managed to keep it quiet, for Eliot's sake. But he told young Tom that he was to leave Massachusetts at once. He had sent him, with a somewhat bleak letter of introduction, to a merchant he knew in London. And with instructions not to return.

Tom had been exiled back to the Old World. He was not good enough for the New.

Tom had liked London. It suited him. Though Cromwell and the Puritans had ruled England for a decade, the great experiment in ruling without a king had finally descended into confusion and martial law. By the time Tom arrived, the English had restored the dead king's son, a second King Charles, to the throne. And King Charles II was a merry fellow. His younger brother James, the Duke of York, might be proud and stiff, but the King himself was flexible and cautious. He had no wish to be turfed out like his father. After years of exile, he wanted to have fun, and was glad if his subjects did too. He loved chasing women, racing horses and visiting the theater. He also took a genuine interest in science.

The London Tom encountered was on the cusp between two worlds: the medieval and the modern. With Britain's overseas domains expanding, London's busy merchants had many opportunities to make their fortunes. Rich aristocrats and gentlemen set the tone of fashion. There were all kinds of entertainment. For a year Tom had been very happy.

And yet, after a while, he'd begun to yearn for America. Not for Boston or his Puritan family, but for other things that were harder to define. A sense of space, of new frontiers, of making the world anew. A longing for freedom. The freedom of the wilderness, perhaps. He couldn't have put it into words.

And now, with his father dead, he supposed there was nothing to stop him returning.

There was another development, also, to be considered. Here in London, there were rumors that King Charles II and his brother James were taking a new interest in the American colonies. If so, that would be all the more reason for an ambitious young fellow like himself to look toward America again.

So what should he do? Should he stay and enjoy the amusements of London, or venture across the ocean? It would be easy enough to tell the merchant he worked for that with his father dead, Eliot had summoned him home. It certainly wouldn't take him long to pack his few possessions. The ship in front of him was leaving tomorrow for Boston. The captain had a berth for him. Should he take it?

He paused, laughed to himself, took out a coin and tossed it. Heads: Boston. Tails: London.

⁜

Up in the north, the thunder spoke. But ahead, as the big river reached the open waters of the harbor, was a lake of liquid gold.

Van Dyck had tried to show Pale Feather the significance of the place the night before, using a map he had made himself. Pointing with the stem of his pipe he had explained.

"This line, which runs straight from top to bottom, is the North River. Many days upriver there are big lakes and waterways that extend all the way up to the regions of ice. To the left of the river"—he swept his pipe across the paper—"lies the whole continent of America. To the right," and here he indicated a huge, triangular wedge of land, with its point down and its wide base sweeping out into the Atlantic, "are the territories of Connecticut, Massachusetts and many other places. And here beside them is the great ocean that my people crossed." Tracing his pipe down to the southern tip of the wedge, he indicated another striking feature. For here a long island, about twenty miles across and a hundred miles from end to end, lay moored as it were, alongside the wedge in the Atlantic. Between this island and the mainland coast there was a long, sheltered sound. "All round this area"—he indicated the bottom of the wedge and the neighboring end of the island—"your people dwelt for many generations. And this"—he tapped the southernmost point of the wedge—"is Manhattan."

Manna hata: it was an Indian name. So far as he knew, it just meant "the Island." The place was a narrow peninsula, really; except that at its northern tip, a small, steep gorge allowed a channel of water from the North River to snake round into the long island's sound, converting the peninsula of Manhattan, technically, into an island.

Had it not been for the great breakwater of the long island protecting its ocean side, Manhattan would have been exposed to the full force of the Atlantic. But thanks to this happy circumstance, as the North River came down to the tip of Manhattan, it entered a splendid, sheltered harbor about four miles wide and seven long—a spacious anchorage known to mariners as the Upper Bay. Better yet, as one passed through the narrows at the harbor's southern end to encounter the Atlantic, two huge sandbars, one on each side, served as outer breakwaters against the ocean swell, creating the calm waters of the Lower Bay, so vast that all the ships in the world could well have lain at anchor there.

"It's the gateway to the north," he had explained. But Pale Feather had not understood. And though he had spoken to her further of trade and transport, he could see that she did not grasp the significance of the white man's map.

White men had been coming there since the days of Christopher Columbus. At first they had been seeking gold, or trying to find a route to the Orient. One, Verrazano, who arrived in 1524, was known by name; others had been forgotten. And not always white men either: the Portuguese sea captain Gomez had been black. He'd come, grabbed nearly sixty of the local Indians to sell as slaves, then disappeared over the horizon. But it was the arrival of another man which had changed everything for the people of the great North River and its harbor.

Henry Hudson had been an Englishman, employed by the rival

Dutch, to find a shorter route to China by sailing east. Having had a look for this fabled North-East passage above Russia and decided it was useless, he'd ignored all his orders, doubled back across the Atlantic, and looked for a passage round the North-West instead. It was Hudson who had ventured into the bay below Manhattan, and gone up the big river for several days before concluding: "It isn't the way to China."

"It may not lead to China," he'd told his Dutch employers upon his return, "but the land is magnificent. And full of beavers."

And the people of northern Europe had an insatiable greed for beavers.

"The beaver," van Dyck would tell his children, "is a most useful creature. Beaver oil cures rheumatism, toothache and stomach pains. A beaver's testicles, powdered and dissolved in water, can restore an idiot to sanity. Its fur is thick and warm." But it was the soft pelt under the outer fur that men really desired. And why? Because it could be made into felt.

Hats. Everyone wanted a felt hat, though only the richer souls could afford one. It was the height of fashion. The hatters who made them sometimes went mad, poisoned by the mercury that used to separate the felt from the fur. And perhaps, van Dyck admitted to himself, there was a certain madness in this — that a whole colony, an empire perhaps, could be founded, men risk their lives and kill in turn—all on account of a fashionable hat. But such was the way of the world. The coast of north-eastern America might have been colonized for the Atlantic fishing trade, but the great harbor of New Amsterdam and its big North River were settled because of the felt hat.

And it was in gratitude to the intrepid explorer that van Dyck and fur traders like him would often refer to the big river not as the North, but as Hudson's River.

✛

"There it is. New Amsterdam." The Dutchman smiled to see his daughter's shiver of excitement. Ahead, the southern tip of Manhattan jutted out into the harbor's watery immensity. Seabirds wheeled over the small waves. There was a bracing saltiness in the air.

Pale Feather gazed at the big sails of the windmill and the squat mass of the fort which presided over the open waterfront. As they rounded the tip of Manhattan, where the merchants' gabled houses had gathered themselves, more or less, into rows, van Dyck pointed out some sights to her.

"You see those houses near the fort? Your people had a camp there before the White Men came. They left such piles of oyster shells behind that we called it De Peral Straet—the street of pearls. That pale house belongs to Stuyvesant. It's called the White Hall."

Passing the southern point, they turned into the long, broad channel that ran up the eastern side of Manhattan. Though not really a river, this waterway was known as the East River. Van Dyck indicated the land on the opposite bank.

"Brooklyn." The Dutch had named it after a place near Amsterdam.

"My people's land," the girl said.

"It was."

The wharf had been built on the east side of the point. The canoe made toward it. Several ships lay at anchor in the East River nearby. As they reached the landing, curious eyes were turned upon them.

It did not take long to arrange for the pelts to be carried in a pair of large handcarts to the West India Company's big storehouse. Van Dyck walked beside the carts, with Pale Feather moving lightly beside him. He nodded briefly to men he knew. There were all kinds of folk by the waterfront: sailors in open shirts, merchants in broad pantaloons, even a dominie, dressed in black and wearing a tall, conical, wide-brimmed hat. As they left the shore, he met a pair of Dutch merchants, Springsteen and Steenburgen, men of some substance, with whom it was necessary to pause for a moment to exchange greetings.

"Your wife was talking to Stuyvesant by the fort, Meinheer van Dyck," remarked Springsteen.

"You may meet her any minute," said Steenburgen.

Van Dyck cursed inwardly. Yesterday the plan had seemed easy enough. His men would unload his boat and the Indian canoe. The Indians would wait to return with the tide. That would give him time to show Pale Feather around the little town and give her some Dutch cookies— the happy culmination of the brief time they'd spent together. Then the Indians would take her safely back upstream, and he'd go home to his wife and children.

Normally, even if Margaretha heard that he was at the wharf, she'd know he needed to deal with business at the warehouse first, and she'd wait for him at the house. He hadn't counted on her being down at the fort.

Well, he'd keep his promise to his daughter, but he'd have to be careful.

"Come, Pale Feather," he said.

It wasn't easy keeping an eye out for his wife while he showed Pale Feather around. But she seemed quite happy. He found he was quite proud of the town. You couldn't deny that Stuyvesant had improved the place. The broad, muddy bankside had been partly cobbled. Even in the busiest area, close to the market, the houses with their high, stepped gables had spacious, well-tended gardens behind. Moving up the east side, they crossed over the small canal and came to the city hall, the Stadt Huys. This was a big building with a central doorway, three rows of windows, another two in the steep mansard roof, and a widow's walk on the roof above. It stood together with a group of other buildings, like so many Dutch merchants, gazing stolidly out at the East River. In front of the Stadt Huys was a double stocks for punishing malefactors. He had to explain to Pale Feather how people were locked in the stocks to be humiliated.

"Over there," he pointed along the bank, "we also have a gallows where people are choked to death with a rope for more serious offenses."

"My people have no such custom," she said.

"I know," he answered kindly. "But we do."

They had just paused in front of a tavern where some sailors were drinking when from round the corner, strolling toward them in her loose gown, and with a pipe in her hand, came Margaretha van Dyck.

⁘

Margaretha gazed at her husband and the little girl. It was only a few minutes since Meinheer Steenburgen's wife had told her that van Dyck was in town. It might have been her imagination, but when the woman had imparted this news, Margaretha thought she'd seen a little glint in her eye—the sort of look one might give to a wife whose husband has been seen with another woman—and this had put her on her guard.

Would Dirk do such a thing to her, in public? A sudden cold fear had seized her, but she had controlled herself, and smiled at the woman as though she'd been quite expecting her husband that day anyway.

And here he was with an Indian girl. Not a mistress, anyway. But a girl who looked . . . a little pale for a pure Indian, perhaps.

"You're back," she said, and embraced him briefly. Then she stepped back.

"Yes. We were unloading at the storehouse."

Did he look nervous? Perhaps.

"Your trip was successful?"

"Very. So many pelts I needed an Indian canoe as well, to get them all back."

"That's good." She stared at Pale Feather. "Who's the girl?"

Dirk van Dyck glanced at Pale Feather and wondered: Did she understand what they were saying? He suddenly realized that he did not know. Some of the Indians spoke Dutch, but he had always spoken to his daughter in her native tongue. He said a silent prayer.

"She came with the Indians in the canoe," he answered coolly. "One of the Turtle clan." Among the local Indians, the clan, or phratry, passed down the female line. You belonged to your mother's clan. "I am friendly with the Turtle clan."

Margaretha eyed Pale Feather thoughtfully.

"You know the mother?"

"No." Van Dyck shook his head. "She's dead."

"The child looks half-caste."

Had she guessed? He felt a stab of fear, and quickly fought it down.

"I think so too."

"The father?"

"Who knows?" He shrugged.

His wife sucked on her pipe.

"These Indian women are all the same."

It was strange, van Dyck considered. Despite their Calvinistic Church, Dutch women quite often had lovers before they were married, and it was tolerated. But because some of the Indian women, whose people had been dispossessed by the white man, had been reduced to selling their bodies at the trading ports for small sums of a currency they did not understand, his wife could believe that every Indian woman was a common whore.

"Not all," he said quietly.

"She's a pretty little thing." Margaretha blew smoke out of the side of her mouth. "It's a pity their looks never last."

Was she right? Would his little daughter's looks fade away even in his own lifetime?

He saw that Pale Feather was staring ahead, looking numb. Dear God, had she understood what they were saying? Or had she divined their meaning from their tone of voice?

Dirk van Dyck loved his wife. Not as much as he should, perhaps, but she was a good woman in her way, and a fine mother to their children. He supposed that no marriage was perfect, and whatever the shortcomings of his own, they were as much his fault as hers. He had been faithful to her, mostly—apart from Pale Feather's mother, whom he regarded as a special case.

Anyway, there was no reason why Margaretha should guess that Pale Feather was his daughter. No reason, except her woman's instinct.

"Don't bring her to the house," said Margaretha quietly.

"Of course not," he heard himself say.

She'd guessed. He was almost certain of it. Was she going to accuse him when he got home? Was she going to make a scene? Perhaps. But then quite likely he'd deny it, and that would leave her looking like a fool. She was too proud for that.

He wished he had not hurt her though.

"Send her away," said Margaretha firmly. "Your children are waiting for you." She turned to go.

He certainly couldn't blame her. Indeed, he admired her. She was behaving with dignity, holding her family together. But then he looked at Pale Feather.

She was still staring ahead, but the blank shock on her face said it all. She did not need to understand their words. Their tones and their looks said it all. The magical time he'd promised her was turning into hurt and misery. He hadn't meant to, but he'd betrayed her. A great wave of remorse washed over him. He couldn't leave her like this.

Margaretha was moving away. Whatever pain he'd caused his wife, it was already done. Besides, she was a grown woman, and strong. Whereas the girl at his side was an innocent child. He thought quickly.

"I still have business to finish, Greet, after the Indians go," he called after her. "I have to go up to Smit's bouwerie. You remember, a quarter of the pelts are for him." It was quite true that he had to ride up to see the farmer, though he hadn't been planning to go today. "Tell the children I shall be home tomorrow."

"And when do you plan to leave again?" She had turned.

"Leave?" He smiled. "Not for months."

Margaretha nodded. Was she mollified?

"Until tomorrow, then," she said.

For a little while, neither he nor Pale Feather spoke. He wanted to put his arm round her, to comfort her, but did not dare. So they walked along the street in silence, until she asked: "That is your wife?"

"Yes."

"Is she a good woman?"

"Yes. A good woman."

They went on a few paces.

"Are you sending me back now?"

"No." He smiled at her. "Come with me, my daughter," he said.

⋅⋔⋅

It took him less than an hour to get ready. He sent one of his men to get his horse. He also bought some food, and two blankets. Then, after giving the Indian men their instructions, he and Pale Feather set out.

The main route out of New Amsterdam was a broad thoroughfare that began at the market in front of the fort and ran up the western half of the town to the wall.

Van Dyck rode slowly. Pale Feather was content to walk along beside him. The Dutch houses soon gave way to pleasant allotments and orchards. They reached the town's wall and went out through the gate with its stone bastion. The broad way continued straight for a few hundred yards, past a cemetery and a mill. The track then led to the right. On the East River side they passed a small tobacco plantation and a swamp. Soon after, on their left, they came to a big pond. And from there the track led north all the way to the top of the island.

Manhattan Island was a strange place: only a mile or two across, but thirteen long miles from top to toe. A wilderness of marsh, meadow and woodland, dotted with hillocks and outcrops of bedrock, it had been a magnificent Indian hunting ground. Indeed, the very track they were taking had long been an Indian trail.

The Manates had been the name of the Indians who'd occupied the island. But they were just one of so many groups of Algonquin-speaking people who had settlements in the region. There were the Canarsee Indians over the East River in Brooklyn; across the harbor, by the broad piece of land the Dutch called Staten Island, dwelt the Raritan. Starting up the great river to the north one encountered the Hackensack and the Tappan. There were a score of names. From the start, the White Men had noticed that all these folk were handsome: the men tall and graceful, the women with finely cut features. As van Dyck gazed down at the girl walking beside him, he felt proud.

But few of the White Men bothered to study the Indians. Would he have done so himself, he wondered, if it hadn't been for the girl's mother? Even the settlement on Manhattan had been born of confusion. When the local Indians had taken a parcel of goods from Pierre Minuit, their understanding had been clear: the White Men were giving the usual gift for the right to share their hunting grounds for a season or two. In European terms, it might be thought of as a rent. Since Indians did not personally own land, the idea that Minuit was buying the land in perpetuity would never have occurred to them. Not that the good burghers of New Amsterdam would have cared if they had understood, van Dyck considered wryly. The Dutch idea of land entitlement was practical: if you settled it, you owned it.

No wonder there had been friction down the years. Aggrieved Indians had attacked. Outlying settlements upriver had been abandoned. Even here on Manhattan, two Dutch hamlets—Bloomingdale, a few miles up the west side, and Harlem in the north—had suffered severe damage.

But always, in the end, the White Man took more land. Vast tracts upriver were granted to Dutch patroons. A Dane called Bronck had paid the local Indians to vacate his huge parcel just north of Manhattan. Some small Indian groups were still eking out an existence on Bronck's land and the wilder parts of Manhattan. That was all.

They had gone about five miles along the trail, and reached an area of woodland in the center of the island, when van Dyck decided it was time to eat. Taking a small path that led westward, they went past dells and outcrops of bedrock until they came to a glade where wild strawberries sprinkled the grass. There van Dyck dismounted, and tethered his horse to a sapling. Tossing a blanket on the ground, he told Pale Feather to sit.

"Now," he smiled, "let us see what your father has brought."

It had been easy enough to buy corn porridge, dried raisins, hickory nuts and some pieces of smoked meat—the mixture that the Indians called "pimekan." Also, Dutch coleslaw and rye bread. But he had also bought some Dutch treats—chocolates and cookies—which would please any child. Sitting side by side, father and daughter shared their meal contentedly. She had just eaten her first cookie when she turned to him and asked: "Do you think I should get a tattoo?"

Van Dyck paused. What an enchanting figure she was. Her little feet were encased in moccasins, her long, dark hair tied back with a thong.

Like most Indian girls of her age, in the warm months of the year, she covered only the lower part of her body with a deerskin skirt that reached to her knees. Her chest was bare, except for the little hanging pendant; her breasts had not started to grow yet. Her skin—protected from the sun and from mosquitoes by a light smearing of raccoon oil—was perfect. When she was older, she'd probably put a little red paint on her cheeks and darken the area round her eyes. But until then, he hoped she would remain exactly as the perfect little girl she was. Not that the Indian women went in for big tattoos like the men. But even so . . .

"I think you should wait," he said carefully, "until you are married, and then choose a tattoo that will be pleasing to your husband."

She considered, and nodded.

"I will wait."

She sat quietly, but it seemed to him that she was thinking about something. After a while she looked up at him.

"Did you ever kill a bear?"

The rite of passage. To become a man, among her people, every boy had to kill a deer—and rightly so. It was proof that he could feed a family. But to prove that he was truly a brave, he must accomplish the far more difficult and dangerous task of killing a bear. When a man had done that, he was truly a warrior.

"I have," he answered. Seven years ago, out in Iroquois territory, the local Indians had warned him that some men had been attacked recently on the mountain path he was to travel. Bears did not usually attack, but when they did, they were formidable. He had gone prepared. But when the beast suddenly appeared and came at him with a rush, he had been lucky to kill it outright with a single shot from his musket. "It was a black bear," he told her, "in the mountains."

"You killed it alone?"

"Yes."

She said nothing, but he could see that she was pleased that her father was a proper warrior.

It was still early afternoon. The sunlight was cascading through the leaves onto the grassy banks where the wild strawberries grew. He felt at peace, and leaned his head back. The plan that he had so suddenly formed was to spend all day with her. In the morning, the Indians and the canoe would meet them at the north end of the island and take Pale Feather back upriver. Then he could go back by Smit's bouwerie and be home long before dark. It was a good plan, and they had plenty of time. He closed his eyes.

He might have dozed a few minutes when, sitting up, he realized that Pale Feather had disappeared.

He looked around. No sign of her. He frowned. Just for a foolish moment, he felt a little pang of fear. What if something had happened to her? He was about to call her name when a tiny movement caught his eye. About a hundred yards away in the trees, a deer had raised its head. Instinctively, he kept still, and silent. The deer stared in his direction, but did not see him. The deer lowered its head.

And then he saw Pale Feather. She was away on the right, upwind of the deer, standing behind a tree. She put her finger to her lips, signaling: Silence. Then she stepped out from her concealment.

Van Dyck had often seen the stalking of the deer; he'd done it himself. But never like this. As she carefully slipped between the trees, she seemed lighter than a shadow. He listened for the softest sound of moccasin on moss. Nothing. As she worked her way closer, she sank down almost to a cat's crouch—slower and slower, each pace forward hovering, weightless as a whisker, over the ground. She was behind the deer now, only fifteen yards away . . . then ten . . . five. Still the deer did not sense her. He couldn't believe it. She was behind a tree, three paces from the animal, which was cropping the grass, head down. She waited. The deer raised her head, paused, lowered her head again. And Pale Feather sprang. She went through the air like a flash. The deer started, leaped, and raced away through the trees—but not before, with a cry of joy, the girl had touched her.

Then, laughing, she ran over to her father, who scooped her up into his arms. And Dirk van Dyck the Dutchman realized that he never had been, and never would be, as proud of any child as he was of his elegant little Indian daughter at that moment.

"I touched her," she cried with glee.

"You did." He hugged her. To think that he should be the father of a child who was perfect. He shook his head in wonderment.

They sat together for a little while after that. He did not say much, and she did not seem to mind. He was wondering whether it was time to move on when she turned to him.

"Tell me about my mother."

"Well," he considered. "She was beautiful. You are like her."

He thought of their first meeting at the camp on the sound where her people used to collect shellfish in summer. Instead of the usual long-houses, her people pitched wigwams by the shore. They would dry the shellfish, scrape them out of their shells, bury the shells and store the dried oysters, mussels and clams to be made into soup at a later date. Why should he have been so struck by this particular young woman? Because she was unattached? Perhaps. She had been married but lost her husband and her child. Or was it something, a special light of curiosity in her eyes? That too. He had stayed two days there, spent a whole evening talking with her. The attraction had been mutual; but he had business to attend to and nothing more than conversation had passed between them before he had continued on his way.

A week later, he had come back.

It was during the time he had spent with her that he had truly come to know the Indians. He came to understand also why some of the first Dutch settlers, having no women of their own, had married Indian women and afterward refused even the most powerful religious persuasion to give them up. She was lithe as a wild animal, yet if he was tired, or angry, she would be gentle as a dove.

"You loved her very much?"

"Yes. I did." It was true.

"And then you had me."

It was the custom of her people that there was always a place for such extra children in the extended family of the mother's clan.

"If you had not had a wife in the White Man's trading post, you would have married my mother, wouldn't you?"

"Of course." A lie. But a kindly one.

"You always came to see her."

Until that terrible spring, three years ago, when he arrived at the village and learned that Pale Feather's mother was sick. "She was in the sweat lodge yesterday," they told him, "but it did no good. Now the medicine men are with her."

He knew their customs. Even for a severe fever, an Indian would retire to a little cabin heated with red-hot stones until it was like an oven. Sitting there until he was pouring with sweat, the sick one would emerge, plunge into the cold river, then wrap himself in a blanket and dry out by the fire. The treatment often worked. If not, there were the medicine men, skilled with herbs.

As van Dyck approached the house where she lay, an old man had come out. "Only the *meteinu* can help her now," the old fellow said sadly. The *meteinu* had skills beyond the ordinary medicine men. They communed with the spirit world and knew the secret spells. If they alone could help her, she must be close to death.

"What kind of sickness has she?" van Dyck asked.

"A fever." The old man seemed uncertain, but grimaced. "Her skin . . ." He seemed to be indicating pockmarks. He walked quietly away.

Pockmarks. The Dutchman gave a shiver of fear. The greatest curse the White Man had brought to America was disease. Influenza, measles, chickenpox—the common maladies of the Old World, against which the Indians had no resistance. Whole villages had died. Perhaps half the native population of the region had already faded away. Malaria had come with the White Men's ships, and syphilis too. But the most fearsome import of all had been smallpox. Only last year, that terrible scourge had wiped out nearly a whole tribe south of New Netherland, and then appeared even in New Amsterdam.

Could it be smallpox?

Then he had done a terrible thing. He could explain it, of course. He had to think of himself, his wife and children, the good people of New Amsterdam. The dominie would have told him: consider the greater good. Oh yes, he was justified. He had done the right thing when he hesitated and then, avoiding even Pale Feather, hurried back to his boat, and gone downriver.

But couldn't he have waited, instead of running like a coward? At a time when her family were preparing to be at her side, he'd deserted his Indian woman. Couldn't he at least have seen the child? The pain, the awful, cold shame of it, haunted him still. Several times a year he awoke in the middle of the night, crying out at the horror of what he had done.

A month later, he'd returned, to find Pale Feather safe in the bosom of her extended family, and to learn that her mother had died the day after he had fled, not of smallpox, but the measles.

He'd tried to make it up to his daughter. Every year, when her people celebrated the feast of the dead, he had arrived. Normally one did not speak of the dead, but at this yearly feast, it was appropriate to do so, and to pray for their souls. This was what he had been doing for the last few days, before taking Pale Feather downriver.

"Tell me what you remember about me when I was little," she said.

"We should move on," he answered, "but I will tell you as we go."

So they left the glade where the wild strawberries grew, and found the old Indian trail again, and as he rode slowly along, he did his best to call to mind all the little incidents he could remember from her childhood, of days he had spent together with her and her mother; and this seemed to please Pale Feather. After a time, though she was not tired, he put her up on the horse in front of him.

They reached the top of Manhattan well before dusk and camped on high ground above some Indian caves. Wrapping themselves in two blankets, they lay staring up at the sky, which was clear and full of stars.

"Do you know where my mother is now?" she asked him.

"Yes." He knew what the Indians believed. He pointed his arm along the line of the Milky Way. "Her spirit has traveled along the path of stars to the twelfth heaven. She is with the Maker of all things."

She was silent for a long time, and he wondered if she were still awake. But then, in a sleepy voice, she said: "I think of you often."

"I think of you too."

"If you cannot see me, you can always hear me."

"Tell me how."

"When there is a little breeze, listen to the voice of the wind sighing in the pine trees. Then you will hear me."

"I will listen," he said.

The next morning they made their way down to the water and found the two Indians with the big canoe. There they parted and Dirk van Dyck went home.

⁓⁓⁓

Margaretha van Dyck waited three weeks. It was a Sunday afternoon. Her husband had been reading a story to their children, and Quash the slave boy, in the parlor while she sat in a chair watching. These were the times she liked him best. Their son Jan was thirteen, a strong boy with a mop of brown hair, who admired his father and who wanted to follow in his footsteps. Dirk would take him to the company warehouse, explain the workings of the ships, the ports they called at, and the trade winds their captains had to follow. But Jan also reminded her of her own father. He had less waywardness of spirit than Dirk, more love of the counting house. She thought he'd do well.

They had lost two other children a few years ago to a fever. That had been a terrible blow. But the compensation had been the arrival of little Clara. Fair-haired and blue-eyed, she was now five years old, and looked like an angel. A wonderfully sweet-natured child. Her father adored her.

As for Quash the slave boy, he was coming along very well. He was about the same age as Jan, and had been allowed to play with him when he was younger. He was very good with Clara, too. But Quash knew his place.

And watching her husband contentedly reading to his family, Margaretha thought that perhaps her marriage might still become a very happy one, if she could make some small adjustments.

So after the reading was over and the children had gone to a neighbor's, and her husband had remarked that he'd need to make another trip upriver soon, she nodded quietly. Then she sprang her trap.

"I was thinking, Dirk, that it's time you joined a syndicate."

He looked up quickly, then shrugged.

"Can't afford it."

But she knew he was paying attention.

Dirk van Dyck had a talent for the fur business. A quarter-century ago, when the West India Company still monopolized the trade of the port, he would have been a more significant figure. But since then, the economy of New Amsterdam had opened up and expanded hugely; and it was the golden circle of leading families—Beekmans, van Rensselaers, van Cortlandts and a score of others—who formed the syndicates to finance the shipping of tobacco, sugar, slaves and other growing commodities. This was where a man could make a fortune. If he had the price of entry.

"We may have more money than you think," she said quietly. We: a team, husband and wife. She made it sound as if they shared the money jointly, but they both knew it wasn't so. When her father had died six months ago, Margaretha had inherited; and under the terms of her prenuptial agreement, her husband had no control over her fortune. Nor had she let him discover how large that fortune was. "I think we could invest a little in a syndicate," she added.

"There is risk," he warned.

She knew. Some of the largest investors in the colony were rich widows and wives. She had consulted them all.

"No doubt. But I trust your judgment." She watched him consider. Had he guessed her plan? Probably. But it was hardly an offer to be refused. He thought, then smiled.

"My dear wife," he answered in an affectionate voice, "I am honored by your trust and I will do whatever I can for our family."

It had been the richest woman in the colony, a widow who'd just taken her third young husband, who'd given her the advice. "Don't rule your husband. But arrange the conditions in which he will make his choices." It would not take long, Margaretha judged, for van Dyck to get a taste for larger transactions. And for the busy social life that went with them. He'd soon be too occupied in New Amsterdam to go running after Indian women in the wilderness. And once he became accustomed to his new life, he'd also be too afraid of her cutting off the funds, even if he were tempted to stray.

"I shall still need to go upriver," he remarked.

"Oh?" She frowned.

"I can't abandon the fur business I have. Not yet, anyway. We still need that income, don't we?"

She hesitated. Actually, his earnings were useful; and unless she was willing to tell him how much money she really had, his argument was sound. But she saw his game. He was trying to slip off the hook. Damn him.

Did he have a woman out there in the wilderness? Or several? That Indian child, she was sure, had been his. Strictly speaking, he could be in serious trouble. In his passion for moral order, Stuyvesant had actually made it illegal to have sexual relations with Indians. But whatever her feelings, bringing her husband before the governor's court was hardly going to solve anything. No, she'd remain calm. Let him wriggle as much as he liked, she could still outwit him. She'd keep him so busy that he wouldn't have time to go upriver for long.

"You are right," she said sweetly. Let him think he was winning.

⁕

The next few weeks went well for Dirk van Dyck. He soon became involved with a group of large merchants who were shipping tobacco to the great blending and flavoring factories across the Atlantic in old Amsterdam. He and Margaretha found themselves being entertained in some big merchant houses where he'd hardly set foot before. He'd bought a new hat and even some pairs of fine silk stockings. In the parlor, the chimney piece had been decorated with handsome, blue-and-white delft tiles. Margaretha had even taken Quash the slave boy, who had run about the place doing the odd jobs, dressed him up, and taught him to wait at table. When the old dominie had done them the honor of calling, he had particularly complimented them upon the smartness of the slave boy.

One day in June, when van Dyck was leaving a game of ninepins in a tavern, a young Dutch merchant had addressed him as Boss. And when a Dutchman called you "Baas," it meant you were a big man, a man of respect. He walked with a new confidence; his wife seemed delighted with him.

So the quarrel, when it came, took him by surprise.

It was an evening in July. He was due to go upriver the next morning. Margaretha had known this for some time. So it seemed hardly reasonable to him when she suddenly said: "I think you should not go tomorrow."

"Why ever not? The arrangements are made."

"Because you shouldn't leave your family when there is so much danger."

"What danger?"

"You know very well. The English."

"Oh." He shrugged. "The English."

She had a point of course. Springsteen the merchant, whose opinions he respected, had put it to him very well the other day. "The English want our fur and slave trade, of course. The tobacco that's shipped through this port would be worth ten thousand pounds a year to them. But above all, my friend, if they have New Amsterdam, they have the river, and then they control the whole of the north."

English aggression had been growing. Out on the long island, the English who controlled the far end had always left the territory nearer Manhattan to the Dutch. In the last year, however, Governor Winthrop of Connecticut had been demanding taxes from some of the Dutch settlements too; and not all had dared to refuse.

An even bigger scare had come more recently.

If King Charles II of England was an amusing rogue, his younger brother James, the Duke of York, was another matter. Not many people liked James. They thought him proud, inflexible and ambitious. So it had come as a shock when news arrived: "The king has given the American colonies to his brother, from Massachusetts almost down to Maryland." That territory included the Dutch New Netherland. And the Duke of York was sending a fleet to America, to make good his claim.

Stuyvesant had been beside himself. He'd started strengthening defenses, posted lookouts. The West India Company, though they sent no troops or money, had ordered him to defend the colony. And the gallant governor was determined, at least, to hold New Amsterdam itself.

But then another message came from Holland. The British government had promised the Dutch—with absolute and categorical assurances—that they had no designs on their colony. The fleet was going to Boston. Soon after that came comforting news. The fleet had arrived at Boston, and was staying there. The crisis was over. Stuyvesant was already on his way upriver to deal with some problems with the Mohawk Indians up there.

So when Margaretha used this threat of the English to tell him not to go upriver, van Dyck saw her ploy for what it was: an attempt to control him. And which he did not intend to allow.

"And my business?" he asked.

"It can wait."

"I think not." He paused while she eyed him. "You and the children will be in no danger," he continued.

"So you say."

"Because it's true."

"Does this mean you refuse to remain here?"

"Even the Muscovy Duke thinks it's safe now," he remarked easily. The people of New Amsterdam, who often resented Stuyvesant's dictatorial ways, would call him that behind his back.

"There's no need to refer to the governor by that stupid name," she said angrily.

"As you like." He shrugged. "Peg Leg then."

The fact was that few of the merchants, including his wife's rich friends, had much love for Stuyvesant, or even the West India Company, come to that. Some of them, van Dyck reckoned, couldn't care less what nation claimed the colony, so long as their trade wasn't disturbed. It amused him, faintly, that his wife's friends shared his own view rather than hers.

"He's worth ten of any of you," she cried furiously.

"My God," he laughed, "I believe you're in love with him."

He had gone too far. She exploded.

"Is that all you can think of? Perhaps you should not judge others by yourself. As for your own visits to Indians . . ." She let the words fall with a bitter contempt—there could be no mistaking her meaning. "You had

better return in three weeks, if you want to use my money any more."
This last threat was shouted as she rose to her feet. Her eyes were blazing
with rage.

"I shall return," he said with icy quietness, "when my business is
done." But she had already stormed out of the room.

He left the house at dawn the next day, without having seen her again.

···

It was a lovely summer morning as the broad, clinker-built boat, rowed by
four oarsmen, made its way northward. Instead of taking Hudson's great
river, however, van Dyck's journey today began the other side of Manhattan, on the East River. In the center of the boat was a great pile of the
thick, tough Dutch cloth known as duffel. This legitimate cargo would
satisfy any prying eyes.

It was a peaceful scene. After a time, they inched past a long, low slip of
land that lay midstream and then, having come nearly eight miles from
the wharf at New Amsterdam, they swung across to their right, to a small
jetty on the eastern side where a group of men with a wagonload of casks
was awaiting them. For this was their real cargo.

It took some time to load all the casks. The foreman, a corpulent
Dutch farmer, asked if he wished to test the goods.

"Is it the same as before?" van Dyck inquired.

"Exactly."

"I'll trust you." They'd done business many times.

Brandy. The Indians couldn't get enough of it. Selling brandy to the
Indians was, strictly speaking, illegal. "But the crime is less," the foreman
had genially informed van Dyck, "because I've watered it." Only a little—
the Indians couldn't tell the difference—but enough to add ten extra percentage points to van Dyck's profits. When the casks were all loaded, the
boat pulled away into the stream.

There was only one problem with this operation: the cargo had to be
loaded up the East River. Unless he returned all the way back past New
Amsterdam, it would be necessary to continue up the eastern side of
Manhattan in order to join Hudson's great North River. And that
involved dangers.

For at the top of the East River, the waterway forked. On the left, a narrow channel led around the northern tip of Manhattan. On the right, a
broader channel led eastward to the huge sound whose placid waters, shel-

tered from the ocean by the long island, stretched for nearly a hundred miles. The danger lay at the fork. For even if all three waterways seemed calm, they were secretly pushed or pulled by subtly different tides and currents so that, at their meeting, a complex hydraulic churning took place, made even harder to read by the positioning of several small islands in the intersection. Even on the calmest day when, out in the sound, the soft waters scarcely seemed to stir the reeds, any unpracticed waterman coming to the fork could suddenly find his boat sucked into eddies and whirlpools and smashed uncontrollably into a wall of water that seemed to have arisen like an angry god from the deep. "Hell Gate" they called this place. You avoided it if you could.

Cautiously, therefore, keeping close to the Manhattan side, they entered the narrow channel on the left; and though buffeted, they came through safely.

On their left lay the little settlement of Harlem. Though the northernmost part of Manhattan was only a mile across, it rose to impressive heights. On their right was the beginning of Bronck's land. The narrow channel continued for a few miles until, passing some ancient Indian caves and encampments, it led through a steep and winding gorge into the great North River. Here, too, there was another place of dangerous cross-currents to be negotiated. Once out into the big river, van Dyck gave a sigh of relief.

From here the going was easy. When the Atlantic tide came in through the harbor, and gently pushed the river into reverse, the current flowed back upstream for many miles. The tide was in their favor. With only a light exertion from the oarsmen, therefore, the laden boat moved swiftly northward. On their right they passed the Jonker's estate. On their left, the tall stone palisades of the western bank continued, until at last they gave way to a hump-backed hill. And now, to his right, Van Dyck saw his destination, the Indian village on the slope of the eastern bank. "We shall rest here," he told the oarsmen, "until the morning."

❖

She was so pleased to see him, and she happily led him round the little village so that he could greet all the families. The houses, made of saplings bent, tied and covered with bark, were arranged, without any protective palisade, on a pleasant shelf of land above the water. The largest house, a long, narrow dwelling, provided quarters for five families. There were two walnut trees near this house and, in the bushes behind, clusters of wild grapes. On the riverbank below, huge fishing nets were folded on frames. Swans and mallard ducks fed in the shallows by the reeds.

Poor though she is, van Dyck thought, my daughter lives no worse than I.

They ate in the early evening, succulent fish from the river. There were still hours of daylight left when Pale Feather asked him to walk up the slope with her to an outcrop with a fine view over the water. He noticed that she was carrying a small object with her, wrapped in leaves. They sat together very comfortably in the evening sun and watched the eagles that circled high above. After a little while she said: "I have a gift for you. I made it myself."

"May I see it?"

She handed him the little package. He unwrapped the leaves. And then he smiled in delight.

"Wampum," he cried. "It is beautiful." God knows how many hours it had taken her to make it.

Wampum. Tiny slices of seashell drilled through the center and strung in strands. White from the periwinkle; purple or black from the hard shell clam. Woven together the strands became belts, headbands, all kinds of adornment.

And currency. Among the Indians, strings of wampum paid for goods, marriage proposals, tribute. And since it represented wealth, the wise men of the tribe always made sure that wampum was distributed among the various families.

But it was more than adornment and currency. Wampum often had meaning. White signified peace and life; black meant war and death. But in wearing wampum it was also easy to make elaborate patterns and little geometric pictograms which could be read. Huge, ceremonial belts many feet long might signify important events or treaties. Holy men wore wampum bearing symbols deep in significance.

It had not taken the Dutch long to learn that they could buy fur with wampum—which they called sewan. But the English Puritans up in Massachusetts had gone one better. Traditionally, the Indians had dug the shells from the sand in summer and done the tedious work of piercing them with a stone drill in winter. But, using steel drills that speeded production, the English had started to manufacture their own wampum, cutting out the local Indians. Worse, as the supply of wampum rose and demand for goods grew also, it took more wampum to buy the same goods. To the Dutch and English merchants, this inflation was normal; but to the Indians, accustomed to thinking of wampum's beauty and intrinsic worth, it seemed the White Men were cheating them.

What van Dyck now held in his hands was a belt. It was less than three inches wide, but six feet long, so that it would go more than twice round his waist. On a background of white shells were some little geometric figures picked out in purple. The girl pointed to them proudly.

"Do you know what it says?" she asked.

"I don't," he confessed.

"It says"—she ran her finger along it—" 'Father of Pale Feather.' " She smiled. "Will you wear it?"

"Always," he promised.

"That is good." She watched happily as he put it on. Then they sat together for a long time, watching the sun as it slowly grew red and sank over the forests across the river.

In the morning, when he was leaving, he promised that he would come in to see her again on his return.

⁌⁌⁍

Dirk van Dyck's journey that summer was a pleasant one. The weather was fine. On the western bank stretched the vast, forested regions that were still controlled by the Algonquin-speaking tribes like his daughter's people. He passed creeks he knew well. And he traveled, as he liked to say, as the guest of the river. That mighty tidal flow from the ocean could send its pulse up Hudson's River for a hundred and fifty miles, all the way to Fort Orange. In summer, even the salt seawater came upstream nearly sixty miles. So, for the most part, he let the current take him in a leisurely fashion toward his destination up in Mohawk territory.

Many people feared the Mohawks. The Indians who dwelt in the regions around Manhattan all spoke Algonquin, but the powerful tribes like the Mohawks who controlled the vast tracts of land to the north of them spoke Iroquois. And the Iroquois Mohawks had no love for the Algonquin. It was forty years, now, since they had started to press down upon them. They raided the Algonquin and took tribute. But despite the Mohawks' fearsome reputation, the attitude of the Dutch had been simple and pragmatic.

"If the Mohawks raid the Algonquin, so much the better. With luck, that'll mean the Algonquin are too busy fighting the Mohawks to give trouble to us." The Dutch had even sold guns to the Mohawks.

In van Dyck's view, this policy had some risk. The northern outposts of New Netherland, up at Fort Orange and Schenectady, lay in Mohawk territory. Sometimes the Mohawks up there gave trouble. It was just such trouble that had called Stuyvesant up to Fort Orange the other day. Little as he liked Stuyvesant, van Dyck had no doubt that the tough old governor would cope with the Mohawks. They might be warlike, but they'd negotiate, because it was in their self-interest.

As for himself, van Dyck wasn't afraid of the Mohawks. He spoke Iroquois and he knew their ways. In any case, he wasn't going as far as Fort Orange, but to a trading post on a small river about a day to the south of the fort. In his own experience, whatever was passing in the world, traders were always welcome. He'd go into the wilderness and sell the Mohawks adulterated brandy, and return with a fine cargo of pelts.

"Put your trust in trade," he liked to say. "Kingdoms may rise and fall, but trade goes on forever."

It was a pity, of course, that he needed to trade with the Mohawks. For he liked his daughter's Algonquin people better. But what could you do? The White Man's eagerness for pelts and the Indians' eagerness to supply them had wiped out so many of the beavers in the lower reaches of Hudson's River that the Algonquin hadn't enough to sell. Even the Mohawks had to raid up into the territory of the Huron, still further to the north, to satisfy the White Man's endless demands. But the Mohawks supplied. That was the point. So they were his main trading partners now.

His journey took ten days. Venturing into the interior, he encountered no trouble. The Mohawk trading post, unlike most Algonquin villages, was a permanent affair with a stout palisade around it. The Mohawks there were tough and brisk, but they accepted his brandy. "Though it would have been better," they told him, "if you had brought guns." He returned with one of the largest loads of pelts he had ever brought downriver. Yet despite the valuable cargo he now carried, he was still in no hurry to return to Manhattan. He considered ways of delaying, a day here, a day there.

He intended to keep Margaretha waiting.

Not too long. He'd calculated carefully. She had set a deadline, so he was going to break it. He'd tell her of course that the business had taken longer than anticipated. She'd suspect he was lying, but what could she do about it? Leave her with a little uncertainty: that was the way. He loved his wife, but he had to let her know that she couldn't order him around. An extra week or so should do it. So, on his orders, the oarsmen did not exert themselves too much as they journeyed slowly south; and van Dyck counted the days, and kept a cool head.

There was only one thing that troubled him—one thing he had failed to do. A small matter perhaps, but it never left his mind.

He had no present for his daughter.

The wampum belt she'd given him. It had a price, of course. But it was beyond all price. His little daughter had made it for him with her own hands, threaded the beads, sewn them, hour after hour, into this single, simple message of love.

And how could he respond? What to give her in return? He had no skill with his hands. I cannot carve, or carpenter, or weave, he thought. I am without these ancient skills. I can only buy and sell. How can I show my love, except with costly gifts?

He'd nearly bought a coat, made by the Mohawks. But she might not like a Mohawk coat. Besides, he wanted to give her something from his own people, whose blood, at least, she shared. Try as he might, he had not been able to decide what to do, and the problem remained unsolved.

They had come back into Algonquin territory when he directed his men to pull over to the western bank, to a village where he'd done business before. He liked to keep up his contacts, and it was a good way of delaying his return a little more.

He received a friendly welcome. The people of the village were busy, because it was harvest time. Like most of the local Indians, they had planted maize in March, then kidney beans, which served as useful props for the tall maize plants, in May. Now both were being harvested. For two days, van Dyck and his men remained in the village, helping with the harvest. It was hard work in the hot sun, but he enjoyed it. Though they had little fur to sell, the Algonquin were still able to trade maize to the White Man, and van Dyck promised he would return in a month to take a cargo of maize downriver for them.

The harvest went well. On the third day they had all sat down for the evening meal, and the women were bringing out the food, when a small boat came in sight. It was paddled by a single man.

As the boat drew near, van Dyck watched. When it reached the shore, the man stepped out and dragged the boat up the bank. He was a fair-haired young fellow, still in his early twenties, with slightly protruding teeth. His face was pleasing, but quite hard. Despite the warm weather, he was wearing riding boots and a black coat that was splashed with mud. His blue eyes were keen. From the boat he lifted a leather bag, which he slung over his shoulder.

The Indians looked at him suspiciously. When one of them addressed him, it was clear that he did not speak Algonquin. But by an easy gesture he made clear that he was asking for food and shelter; and it was not the custom of the Algonquin to refuse. Van Dyck motioned the stranger to sit beside him.

It took only a few moments to discover that the young man did not speak Dutch either. He was English, which van Dyck could speak well enough. But the fair-haired man in the dark coat seemed cautious about saying much in that language also.

"Where are you from?" van Dyck asked.

"Boston."

"What's your business?"

"Merchant."

"What brings you here?"

"I was in Connecticut. Got robbed. Lost my horse. Thought I'd go downriver." He took the bowl of corn he'd been offered and started to eat, avoiding further questions.

There were two kinds of men van Dyck knew in Boston. The first were the godly men, the stern Puritans whose congregations lived in the light of the Lord. It was a harsh light, though. If Stuyvesant was intolerant of outsiders like the Quakers, and kicked them out when he could, that was nothing to what the people of Massachusetts did to them. Flogged them half to death, from all accounts. It did not seem to him that the stranger was one of the godly, though. The second kind were the men who'd come to New England for the money to be made in fishing and trading. Tough, hard men. Maybe the young stranger fell into this category.

But his story seemed unlikely. Was he a fugitive of some kind who'd gone west to shake off his pursuers? Stolen the boat too, maybe. He resolved to keep a careful eye on him.

❖

Tom Master had not been having a very good time. His voyage to Boston with the English fleet had encountered storms. When he had reached

Boston and gone to the family house, now occupied by his brother, Eliot had greeted him with a look of horror, followed by hours of silence that, Tom decided, were even more unpleasant than the storms at sea. His brother did not actually throw him out of the house, but he made it clear in his quiet, serious way that, dead or not, their father should be obeyed; and that Tom had violated every rule of decency by attempting to re-enter the family circle.

At first Tom had been hurt, then angry. The third day, he'd decided to treat the whole business as a joke; out of sight of his brother, he had laughed.

But finding employment in Boston proved to be no laughing matter. Whether he had a bad reputation, or whether Eliot had been busy warning everybody about him, he could find no encouragement from any of the merchants he knew. Evidently, if he remained in Boston, life was going to be difficult.

He also wondered if his father had made any provision for him in his will. But when he asked his brother, and Eliot told him, "Only under certain conditions, which you do not fulfill," he had no doubt that his brother was telling the truth.

So what was he to do? Should he return to London? Eliot would probably pay for his passage, if that would remove him permanently from Boston. But it irked him to be run out of town by his own brother.

Besides, there was still the other consideration that had brought him here.

The Duke of York's fleet remained in Boston harbor. The commander was making a show of attending to the Duke's affairs in Boston. But a conversation with a young officer had soon confirmed what Tom had suspected all along. The fleet was going down to New Amsterdam, and soon. "If the Duke can take New Netherland from the Dutch, he'll be master of an empire here," the officer told him. "We're carrying enough cannonballs and powder to blow New Amsterdam to bits." The King of England's assurance to the Dutch had been that amusing monarch's favorite tactic: a brazen lie.

And if this was the case, then the opportunities for a young Englishman in the American colonies were about to improve. It would be foolishness on his part to return to England now. What he needed was a plan.

The idea came to him the next day. Like many of Tom's ideas, it was outrageous, but not without humor. He'd met a girl he remembered, in a tavern—a girl of no good reputation—and talked to her for a while. The day after that, he returned to talk to her again. When he told her what he wanted, and named the price he'd pay, she laughed, and agreed.

That evening, he spoke to his brother.

He started with an apology. He told Eliot that he felt repentance for his past misdeeds. This was greeted by silence. Tom then explained that he wanted to settle down, no matter how humbly, and try to lead a better life.

"Not here, I hope," his brother said.

Indeed that was his plan, Tom told him. And not only that, he thought he'd found a wife. At this news, Eliot had gazed at him in blank astonishment.

There was a woman he had known before, Tom explained, a woman who had also led a less than perfect life, but who was ready to repent. What better way of showing Christian forgiveness and humility than to save her?

"What woman?" demanded Eliot coldly.

Tom gave the girl's name and the tavern where she worked. "I was hoping," he said, "that you would help us."

By noon the next day, Eliot had discovered enough. The girl was nothing less than a common whore. Yes, she had told him, she'd be glad to marry Tom, and be saved, and live here in Boston no matter how humbly. For anything was better than her present, fallen condition. Though Eliot saw at once that this might be a hoax, he did not see the humor of it. Nor did it matter whether the thing was true or not. Clearly Tom was prepared to make trouble, and embarrass him. Alternatively, Eliot assumed, Tom would be prepared to leave—for a price. That evening they spoke again.

The interview was conducted in the spirit of mournfulness in which Eliot seemed to specialize. It took place in the small, square room he used as an office. On the desk between them was an inkwell, a Bible, a book of law, a paper cutter and a little pine box containing a newly minted silver dollar.

The offer Eliot made was the inheritance that Adam Master had left for his younger son if, and only if, he showed evidence that he had joined the community of the godly. With perfect truth, Eliot informed his brother: "I am disobeying our father by giving you this."

"Blessed are the merciful," said Tom, solemnly.

"You refuse to return to England?"

"I do."

"This letter, then, will give you credit with a merchant in Hartford, Connecticut. They are more tolerant," Eliot said drily, "of people like you down there. The condition is that you are never, ever to return to Massachusetts. Not even for a day."

"In the Gospels, the Prodigal Son returned and was welcomed," Tom remarked pleasantly.

"He returned once, as you have already done. Not twice."

"I shall need money for the journey. Your letter gives me nothing until I reach Hartford."

"Will that be enough?" Eliot handed him a quantity of wampum and a purse containing several shillings. Some of those shillings would pay the girl in the tavern and the rest, Tom reckoned, would be enough for his journey.

"Thank you."

"I fear for your soul."

"I know."

"Swear that you will not return."

"I swear."

"I shall pray for you," his brother added, though evidently without much conviction it would do any good.

Tom rode away early the next morning. Before he left the house, he slipped into his brother's office, and stole the silver dollar in the box. Just to annoy him.

He had taken his time, riding westward across Massachusetts, staying at farms along the way. When he came to the Connecticut River, he should have turned south. That would have brought him to Hartford. But it irked him to take orders from his brother, and so, for no particular reason, he had continued westward for a few days. He was in no hurry. The money, which he kept in a small satchel, would last him a while. He'd always heard that the great North River was a noble sight. Perhaps he'd go as far as that before turning back to Hartford.

Leaving Connecticut, he'd passed into Dutch territory. But he saw no one and, keeping an eye out for Indians, proceeded cautiously for a couple of days. On the evening of the second day, the land began to slope down, and soon he saw the sweep of the big river. On the terrace above the riverbank he came to a Dutch farmstead. It was small: a single-story

cabin with a wide porch, a barn on one side, a stable and a low outbuilding on the other. A meadow ran down to the riverbank, where there was a
wooden dock and a boat.

He was met at the door by a thin, sour-faced man of maybe sixty, who
spoke no English. When Tom made clear that he was seeking shelter for
the night, the farmer grudgingly indicated he might sup in the house, but
that he must sleep in the barn.

After stabling his horse, Tom entered the cabin to find the farmer, two
men he took to be indentured workers, and a black man he assumed was
a slave, all gathering for supper. The mistress of the house, a short, fair-
haired woman a good deal younger than the farmer, ordered the men to
table, and pointed to where he should sit. He didn't see any sign of children. Tom had heard that the Dutch farmers ate with their slaves, and certainly everyone sat together at this table.

The woman was an excellent cook. The stew was delicious, washed
down with ale. It was followed by a large fruit pie. Conversation, however,
was limited, and since he spoke no Dutch, he could contribute nothing
himself.

He wondered about the woman. Was the farmer a widower who'd married again? Could she be his daughter? Or was she a housekeeper of some
kind? Though small, she was full-breasted, and there was something
decidedly sensual about her. The gray-haired farmer addressed her as
Annetie. The men treated her with respect, but between the farmer and
herself there seemed to be a kind of tension. When he addressed the men,
he appeared to ignore her. When she brought the bowl of stew toward
him, Tom noticed that he leaned away from her. And though she sat quietly listening to the conversation, Tom noticed a look of suppressed irritation on her face. Once or twice, however, he had the impression that she'd
been watching him. Just once, when their eyes met, she gave him a smile.

When the meal was over, the hired hands and the slave retired to the
outbuilding to sleep, and Tom went out to the barn. Dusk was falling, but
he found some bales of straw in the barn and spread his coat on them.
And he was about to settle down when he saw a figure with a lamp coming toward him.

It was Annetie. In her hand she held a jug of water and a napkin containing some cookies. As she gave them to him, she touched his arm.

Tom looked at her with surprise. He was no stranger to the advances of women, and there was no mistaking what this was. He looked at her in the lamplight. How old was she? Thirty-five? She was really quite attractive. He looked into her eyes and smiled. She gave his arm a light squeeze, then turned; and he watched the lamp as it crossed the yard back to the house. After this he ate the cookies, drank a little water, and lay down. The night was warm. The door of the barn was open. Through it he could see light coming through the shutters of the farmhouse window. After a time the light went out.

He wasn't sure how long he'd been dozing when he was awakened by a sound. It was coming from the farmhouse and it was loud. The farmer was snoring. It could probably be heard all the way across the river. Tom stopped his ears and tried to sleep again, and he had almost succeeded when he became aware that he was not alone. The door of the barn had been closed. Annetie was lying down beside him. And her body was warm. From the house, the snores of the farmer still rang out.

Dawn was almost breaking when he awoke. He could see a faint paleness under the barn door. Annetie was still beside him, asleep. There was no sound of snoring coming from the house. Was the farmer awake? He nudged Annetie, and she stirred. And as she did so, the barn door creaked and a pale, cold light fell across them.

The old farmer was standing in the doorway. He had a flintlock. It was pointed at Tom.

Annetie was gazing at the old man blankly. But the farmer was intent upon Tom. He indicated to Tom that he should get up. Pulling on his clothes, Tom did so, picking up his coat and his satchel. The farmer motioned him toward the door. Was he going to shoot him outside? But once in the yard, the farmer pointed to the track that led back up the slope. His message was clear: Get out.

Tom in turn pointed to the stable where his horse was. The farmer cocked his gun. Tom made another step. The farmer took aim. Would the old Dutchman really shoot him? They were miles from anywhere. Who would do anything about it if he disappeared? Reluctantly, Tom turned toward the track and made his way up into the woods.

But once out of sight, he paused. After waiting a while, he crept back toward the farmstead. The place was silent. Whatever had passed between the farmer and Annetie, there was no sign of any activity now. Skirting the house, he stole toward the stable door.

The bang almost made him jump out of his skin. The shot passed over his head and smacked into the stable door in front of him. He turned and saw the old farmer. He was standing on the porch, reloading his flintlock.

Tom looked for an escape. He started to run down toward the river. He made for the little dock and the boat. It was only the work of a moment to untie it. Thank God there was a paddle in the boat. But he'd hardly clambered in before another shot rang out, and a splash in the water told him that the old man had only missed him by a foot or two. Seizing the paddle, he pushed off and paddled furiously downstream. He didn't pause or even look back until he'd gone a quarter-mile. He'd gone downstream with the tide after that, pulling into the bank and resting when it turned.

During his rest, however, it had occurred to him that he still didn't know whether Annetie was the old man's wife, daughter, or had some other relationship entirely. Only one thing was certain. The farmer had his horse, which was worth a lot more than the boat he'd taken.

The thought had bothered him.

✦

Van Dyck let Tom eat in silence. But after a while he asked him whether he'd seen the English fleet in Boston. At this, Tom seemed to hesitate for a moment, but then allowed that he had. "And what's the fleet doing, exactly?" van Dyck asked. Again the young man hesitated, then he shrugged.

"They were busy in Boston when I left." He took a corncake and chewed on it for a few moments, staring down at the ground. But van Dyck had a feeling he knew more than he was telling. The Indians asked him if the stranger was a good man. "I don't know," he answered in Algonquin. "You should watch him."

The Indians told van Dyck he should return to them when the summer was over, to join in the hunt. Van Dyck had hunted with them before. The big hunts were enjoyable, but ruthless. Locating the deer, a huge party would fan out in a great arc—the more people the better—and come through the forest beating the trees, driving the deer toward the river. Once the deer were slowed up in the water, it was easy to kill them. So long as there were deer, these Algonquin lived well. Van Dyck promised he would come. And he continued to talk and laugh with them for some time.

It was clear that his obvious friendship with the Indians intrigued the young Englishman. For after a while he asked van Dyck if it was usual for the Dutch to be so friendly with the natives.

"You English do not care to know the Indian customs?" the Dutchman asked.

The young man shook his head.

"The Boston men are busy getting rid of their Indians. It isn't difficult. They just need one thing."

"What's that?"

"Wampum." The young man gave a wry smile. "The Boston men make the Indians pay tribute in wampum, according to how many men, women and children there are. But usually the Indians can't manufacture the wampum quickly enough. So then they make them give us land instead. The Indian population shrinks, every year."

"And if they do pay?"

"Then our English magistrates fine them, for their crimes."

"What crimes?"

"It depends." Tom shrugged. "Massachusetts can always think of something that's a crime. The Indians there will all be gone one day."

"I see." Van Dyck looked at the young Englishman with disgust. He'd have liked to strike him. Until it occurred to him: Was the conduct of his own Dutch people any better? Every year the number of Algonquin in New Netherland diminished. The hunting grounds on Manhattan were already nearly gone. On the Bronck's and Jonker's estates, the Indians were being purchased and pushed off their grounds. It was the same out on Long Island. In due course, no doubt, up here across the great river, where so far the Dutch only had a few outposts, the Algonquin would also be forced back. Add to that the ravages of European diseases— measles, smallpox and the like. No, he thought sadly, it matters not from which quarter we come, the White Man destroys the Indian sooner or later.

If these reflections tempered his feelings, van Dyck felt a desire to put this young fellow in his place. And when Tom observed that although wampum was considered good enough for the Indians, all reckoning in Boston was nowadays done in English pounds, he saw his chance.

"The trouble with you English," he said, "is that you talk of pounds, but you have nothing a man can put his hands on. At least the Indians have wampum. It seems to me," he added coolly, "that the Indians are ahead of you in that regard." He paused to watch the fellow take this in.

For it was absolutely true. Back in England, you could find the traditional pennies, shillings and gold florins. But the higher coinage was in short supply. And out in the colonies, the situation was downright primitive. In Virginia, for instance, the currency was still tobacco, and business was often done by barter. In New England, though merchants would keep the reckonings between them in pounds sterling, and write their own bills of credit, there was practically no English silver or gold coinage to be had.

But if he aimed to embarrass the young Englishman, it didn't seem to work. Tom laughed.

"I can't deny it," he acknowledged. "Here's the only money I trust." And from inside his black coat he took out a little flat box which he tapped lightly and handed to van Dyck. The box was made of pine and sat in the palm of the Dutchman's hand. He slid back the lid. The inside was padded with cloth, and contained a single coin, which gleamed in the fading light.

It was the silver dollar he'd stolen from his brother.

Daalders, the Dutch called them, but the word sounded more like the German "Thaler"—dollar. Merchants had been using dollars for nearly a century and a half now, and the Dutch made most of the dollars found in the New World. There were three kinds. There was the ducatoon, better known as the ducat, which had a horse and rider stamped upon it and was worth six English shillings. Next came the rijksdaalder, which the English called the rix dollar, worth five shillings—or eight Spanish real, if you were sailing south. But most common of all was the lion dollar.

It was actually worth a bit less than the other dollars, but it was the most handsome. Its face was larger. On the obverse it showed a standing knight, holding a shield which bore the image of a lion rampant; and on the reverse, the same lion splendidly filled the whole face. The coin had a small fault: it was not always well struck. But that hardly mattered. The handsome Dutch lion dollar was used from New England to the Spanish Main.

"Dutch money," Tom said with a grin, as van Dyck took the coin out of the box and inspected it.

Lion dollars were usually worn, but this one hadn't even a scratch. It was new-minted; it shone splendidly. And as the Dutchman gazed at it, a thought suddenly came to him.

Getting up, he went over to where two Indian girls, about the same age as Pale Feather, were sitting. He showed them the coin, letting them hold it. As they turned the shining disk over in their hands, examined the images and the way the falling sun reflected upon it, their faces lit up. Why was it, van Dyck wondered, that gold and silver objects seemed to fascinate both men and women alike? "It is beautiful," they said. Returning to the young fellow from Boston, van Dyck told him: "I'll buy it."

"It will cost you," Tom considered, "a ducat and a beaver pelt."

"What? That's robbery."

"I'll throw in the box," Tom added cheerfully.

"You're a young rogue," the Dutchman said, with amusement. "But I'll take it." He didn't bother to bargain. He had just solved his problem. The pelt was a sacrifice he almost felt better for making. For now he had a present for his daughter.

That night, to make sure Tom didn't steal anything, he slept in his boat. And as he lay back on the pelts, and felt the little wooden box with its silver dollar safe in the pouch on his belt, and listened to the faint breeze in the trees, he imagined that, as she had promised, he could hear his daughter's voice. And he smiled with contentment.

❖

Van Dyck left the young Englishman in the morning. He'd be at Pale Feather's village before evening, stay there with his daughter all through tomorrow, and continue to Manhattan the day after that.

The weather was warm. He wore an open shirt. Around his waist, he had changed his usual leather belt and put on the wampum belt she'd given him. A little pouch containing the silver dollar hung from it.

The river was almost free of traffic. Occasionally they saw an Indian canoe in the shallows; but as they slipped downstream with the tide, they had the great waterway to themselves. The high western banks protected the river from the light breeze. The water was still. They seemed to be traveling in an almost unearthly quiet. After a time, they came past a bend where, from the west bank, a high point jutted out above the water, looking like a sentinel. Van Dyck had his own names for these landmarks. This one he called West Point. A while later, the river curved again to pass around the small mountain whose flattened hump had caused van Dyck to name it Bear Mountain. After that, the river opened out into a wider flow, two or three miles from bank to bank, which would extend southward fifteen miles until it narrowed into the great, long channel that ran down past Manhattan to the mighty harbor.

Time passed, and they were still some miles above the channel when one of the oarsmen nodded to him and van Dyck, turning to look back up the river, saw that some five miles back, another boat was visible, following them. As he stared he realized that the boat was gaining on them fast. "They must be in a hurry about something," he remarked. But he wasn't much interested.

Half an hour later, approaching the entrance to the channel, he glanced back again, and was astonished to discover how far the other vessel had come. It was much bigger than his own, with a mast for a sail; but as the breeze was from the south, the men were rowing. It had halved the distance between them and was advancing rapidly. He couldn't see how many oars it carried, but one thing was certain.

"Those boys," he said, "are rowing like fury."

They were entering the narrow channel now, and van Dyck let the oarsmen take it easy. They were coming down the west side of the stream. Above them, the gray stone palisade of cliffs were catching the rays of the afternoon sun. A slight choppiness now appeared in the water. He glanced back, but the curve of the river now hid the boat that, he assumed, must be following him into the channel.

And then, suddenly, the boat was upon them. It was coming fast and he could see every detail of the vessel now: a big, clinker-built longboat, with a covered section in the middle from which the mast rose. Eight men were rowing four pairs of oars. It was high in the water, so it could not be carrying any cargo. Why should this empty vessel be in such a hurry? There was a figure standing in the stern, but he couldn't see what sort of man it was.

The vessel pulled closer. It was only a few lengths behind them, then a length. Now it was level. Curious, he looked across at the figure in the stern.

To find himself staring into a face he knew only too well. A face which, some instinct told him, he did not wish to encounter. And the man was staring straight back at him.

Stuyvesant.

He quickly looked away, but it was too late.

"Dirk van Dyck." The harsh voice came ringing over the water.

"Good day, Governor," he called back. What else could he say?

"Hurry, man! Why aren't you hurrying?" Stuyvesant was level with him now. Then, without waiting for a reply, Stuyvesant turned to van Dyck's oarsmen. "Row faster," he shouted. "Pull." And the oarsmen, recognizing the fearsome governor, obeyed at once and sent the boat hurtling through the water. "That's it," he yelled. "Well done. Keep up with me. We'll go down together, Dirk van Dyck."

"But why?" called van Dyck. The governor had already gone a little past him, but his men were managing to keep up the same pace now, so that the two of them could continue their shouted conversation downstream.

"You don't know? The English are in Manhattan harbor. The whole fleet."

So the English fleet had come after all. He'd heard nothing, but that wasn't surprising. The people at New Amsterdam would have sent a swift rider up to Fort Orange to tell the governor, who was now racing downriver with the benefit of the tide. No doubt word would spread among the Indians soon, but it would take some time.

Clearly the English had lied. He thought of the young fellow from Boston. Had Tom known they were coming? He must have. That's why he'd hesitated when asked about the English fleet.

"What are we going to do?" van Dyck shouted downstream to Stuyvesant.

"Fight, van Dyck. Fight. We'll need every man."

The governor's face was set hard as flint. Standing tall and erect on his peg leg, he had never looked more indomitable. You had to admire the man. But if the whole English fleet had come down from Boston, it would be a powerful force. The ships would be carrying cannon. Despite all Stuyvesant's recent efforts, van Dyck couldn't imagine the shore defenses of New Amsterdam holding up for long. If Stuyvesant meant to fight, it would be a bloody and unrewarding business.

As though in tune with his thoughts, a cloud crossed the sun and the high stone palisades above them suddenly turned to a sullen gray that seemed grim and threatening.

Whatever Stuyvesant might be saying, another thought quickly occurred to van Dyck. If I can see the danger of this course, he realized, so can every other merchant in the place. Would the men of New Amsterdam support their governor against the English? Probably not, if the English came in force. Was his family in danger? Unlikely. Would the English want to blow the place to bits and make enemies of the Dutch merchants? He didn't think so. The English wanted a rich port, not an angry ruin. They had every incentive to offer generous terms. It was politics and religion, in van Dyck's private view, that made men dangerous. Trade made them wise. Despite Stuyvesant, he guessed, there would be a deal.

So did he want to blow into Manhattan with Stuyvesant, like an avenging angel?

He looked at the river ahead. Another hour at this rate and they'd be at the northern tip of Manhattan. He glanced at his oarsmen. Would they be able to keep up this pace? Probably not. And so much the better. If he could discreetly fall behind, then he should be able to separate himself from Peg Leg before reaching New Amsterdam.

He waited. The governor's boat was already a couple of lengths ahead.

"Keep up," Stuyvesant cried. He had turned completely round to watch them.

"I'm with you, my General," van Dyck called back. Hearing this, his men pulled harder still, and for a little while kept pace with the bigger boat. So much the better. Let them wear themselves out. If he could just satisfy the governor for the time being.

The prow of the boat hit a tiny wave, rising and smacking down on the water, causing him to lean forward. He straightened up, and as he did so, the pouch on his belt tapped lightly against the top of his thigh. He glanced down, thought of the silver dollar in its box, safely secreted in the pouch, and realized with a shock: they were almost at Pale Feather's village. This unexpected business with Stuyvesant had caused him to forget his daughter. The tap on his leg had been a reminder.

Pale Feather. What was he going to do?

Stuyvesant was still watching him intently. He dare not pull across to the village now. For all he knew, the governor would turn and drag him downriver by force. The man was quite capable of such a thing.

Minutes passed. The two boats, held in place by the invisible force of Stuyvesant's will, sped together down the stream. They were coming past the village now, away on the eastern bank. Van Dyck could see the Indians with fishing nets in the shallows. Other figures, women probably, were watching from higher up the bank. Was Pale Feather among them?

He could not tell. Was she looking at him now? Did she know he was going past her, not stopping even for a moment, despite his promise? Would she suppose her father had turned his back on her?

He stared across the river, then looked away. If his daughter was there, he did not want her to see his face. A foolish gesture. Even with her keen eyes, she could not see his face from there. He lowered his head, gazed at the pelts at his feet, and felt ashamed. Away on the far bank, the little Indian village began to fall behind. He glanced back. He could still see the line of women, but they were becoming blurred and indistinct.

They slipped downstream another hundred yards. Then another.

"Pull across stream." He gave the order. The oarsmen looked astonished.

"But, Boss—" said one.

"Pull across." He pointed to the eastern bank. He was the Boss, after all. Unwillingly, they obeyed him.

As the boat began to turn, Stuyvesant saw at once.

"What the devil are you doing?" he shouted over the water.

Van Dyck hesitated. Should he reply? He thought quickly.

"I'll follow," he cried, in a voice which, he hoped, suggested that his only desire was to be with the governor. "We'll catch up shortly."

"Maintain your course," Stuyvesant bellowed back. A second later, Stuyvesant's voice came over the water again. "Never mind your Indian bastard, van Dyck. Think of your country."

How did he know about Pale Feather? Van Dyck cursed the governor under his breath. It had been a mistake to take the girl to New Amsterdam. He should never have done it.

"Follow me, Dirk van Dyck," Stuyvesant's voice rang out again. "Forget your half-breed and follow me, or your wife shall hear of this, I promise you."

Van Dyck cursed again. Had the governor and his wife discussed the girl? What was the relationship between Stuyvesant and his wife anyway? Who knew? But the threat to tell Margaretha was serious. It was one thing to leave her in doubt about where he was. But to have her know that he'd defied the governor, failed to protect his family—for that was what she'd say—all for the sake of his half-breed daughter . . . Such an accusation would be a serious matter. Margaretha wouldn't let this go. God knows what it would do to his business, and his family life. Curse Peg Leg. Damn him. He nodded to his men.

"We'll follow," he said, resignedly.

The prow of the boat swung round, pointing once again down the flow of the stream.

Van Dyck stared ahead. What an exercise in futility! Was he condemned to follow Peg Leg all the way, now? The very thing he had been trying to avoid.

His hesitation had caused quite a distance to open up between his boat and the governor's. He thought of the English fleet ahead, of the determined, wrong-headed governor, and of his wife's hurt and angry face. He thought of his innocent, defenseless little daughter who had waited for him. The gray palisade of rock above him seemed to echo with a soundless lament as the water rushed by. He glanced back again. The village was out of sight, hidden by the trees. He had come to his daughter, then passed by on the other side.

"Turn back."

"Boss?"

"We're going back. Turn round," he ordered them. The men were looking at each other, hesitating. "Do you want to fight the English, then?" he cried. The men glanced at each other again. And obeyed. The prow swung round toward the eastern bank.

Stuyvesant was still watching. He saw, and understood. And now his voice came up the stream in a great cry.

"Traitor!" The word reached van Dyck like a clap of thunder. And for all he knew, it went echoing up the great river, all the way to its origins in the distant north. "Traitor."

He gazed toward the governor's boat, but he did not alter his course. It was a parting of the ways, and they both knew it, as the great river swept Stuyvesant southward in its mighty current, and he, free for a moment at least, turned back to give the shining dollar to his daughter.

New York

M Y NAME IS Quash, which signifies that I was born on a Sunday. For I have learned that in Africa, from where my people come, a child is often named for the day on which it is born. In Africa, I have been told, my name would be Kwasi. If I had been born on a Friday, it would be Kofi, which in English is Cuffe. Monday's child is Kojo, which in English they say Cudjo; and there are other similar names.

I believe I was born around the year of Our Lord 1650. My father and my mother were both sold out of Africa as slaves, to work in the Barbadoes. When I was about five years old, my mother and I were taken from my father to be sold again. In the market, my mother and I were separated. From that moment, I have never known what became of her; but I was bought by a Dutch sea captain; and this was fortunate for me, because the Dutch captain brought me to New Amsterdam, as it was then called; whereas if I had remained where I was, it is not likely I should be alive today. In New Amsterdam, the Dutch captain sold me, and I became the property of Meinheer Dirk van Dyck. I was then about six years old. My father I do not remember at all, and my mother only slightly; they are certainly long since dead.

From an early age, I always had the dream that I might one day be free.

I came by this notion on account of an old black man I met when I was aged eight years old or nine. At this time there were in the province of New Netherland only maybe six hundred slaves, half of them in the city. Some were owned by families, others by the Dutch West India Company.

And one day in the market I saw an old black man. He was sitting in a cart, wearing a big straw hat, and he was smiling and looking pleased with himself. So I went up to him, being somewhat forward at that age, and said: "You look happy, Old Man. Who is your master?" And he said: "I have no master. I am free." And then he explained to me how it was.

For the Dutch West India Company, having brought in parcels of slaves some years before, and used them in many public works such as building up the fort, paving streets, and suchlike, had given land to some of those who had worked longest and best, and worshipped at their Church, and upon certain further conditions of service had made them free. They were termed freedmen. I asked him if there were many such people.

"No," he told me, "just a few." Some lived a little way above the wall, others further up the island on the east side, and some more across the north river, in the area they call Pavonia. I could see small hope of such a thing for myself, but it seemed to me a fine thing that a man should be free.

I was fortunate, however, to be in a kindly household. Meinheer van Dyck was a vigorous man who liked to trade and go upriver. His wife was a large, handsome lady. She was strong for the Dutch Reformed Church and the dominies and Governor Stuyvesant. She had a low opinion of the Indians, and was never happy when her husband was away among them.

When I first arrived in that house, there was a cook, and an indentured servant called Anna. They had paid for her to cross the ocean, in return for which she was to give them seven years of work, after which time they were to give her a certain sum of money, and her freedom. I was the only slave.

Meinheer van Dyck and his wife were always mindful of their family. If they ever had angry words, we seldom saw it, and their greatest delight was to have their family all around them. As I was working in the house, I was often with their children, and because of that I came to speak the Dutch language almost as they did.

Their son Jan and I were about the same age. He was a handsome boy with a mop of brown hair. He looked like his father, but he was more heavily built, which he took from his mother, I think. When we were young, we often played together, and we always stayed friends. As for his baby sister Clara, that was the prettiest child you ever saw, with golden hair and bright blue eyes. When she was little, I would carry her on my shoulders, and she would go on making me do this even when she was ten or eleven, laughing all the while, just to vex me, she said. I loved that child.

I was always very fast at running. Sometimes Meinheer van Dyck would set myself and Jan and little Clara in a race, with Jan well in front of me and Clara near the finishing line. I would usually pass Jan, but when I came up with Clara I'd hold back just behind her so she could win, which used to delight her very much.

Some Dutch masters were cruel to their slaves, but Meinheer van Dyck and the Mistress always showed me kindness in those years. As a young boy I was only given light work. As I grew a little older, Meinheer van Dyck would give me many tasks to do. I always seemed to be fetching and carrying something. But the only time he ever whipped me was after Jan and I had broken a window, and then he took a strap to us both, each getting the same.

✦

When I was about fourteen years of age, Meinheer van Dyck became a more important man of business than he was before, and everyone started to call him Boss, including myself. So from now on I shall call him by that name. And about this time it entered into the mistress's mind that I should look well dressed up in livery like a servant in a big house. The Boss laughed, but he let her do it, and I looked very well in that livery, which was blue. I was very proud of myself. And the mistress taught me to open the door for guests and wait at table, which pleased me greatly. And she said, "Quash, you have a beautiful smile." So I made sure to smile all the time, and I was in high favor with her, and the Boss too. One day, the old Dominie Cornelius came to the house. He was a man of great consequence. He was tall, and always dressed in black, and despite his age, he was still very upright. And even he remarked to the Boss's wife upon my smart appearance. After that, I could do no wrong with her. So I suppose that on account of all this good treatment, I had too great a conceit of myself. Indeed, I believe I thought myself more like an indentured servant than a slave, for a time. And I often thought about what I could do that would cause that family to hold me in higher regard.

It was about a month after his visit to the house that, on an errand for the Mistress, I saw that old dominie in the street, dressed in black and wearing a big pointed black hat with a wide brim. Now it happened that just a few days before, I had conceived a notion of how I might raise myself in the estimation of the Boss and his family; for I remembered that old black man telling me how the freedmen had been allowed to become Christians in the Dutch Church. And so when I saw the old dominie, I went up to him and said, very respectful: "Good morning, sir." And he gave me a somewhat stern look, because I was interrupting him in his thoughts, but he recognized me and said: "You're the van Dycks' slave boy."

"I am, sir," I said. "And I was wondering," I went on, "if I might ask Your Reverence something."

"Oh? What's that?" he said.

"I was wondering," I said, "if I might join the Church."

He looked at me for a moment as if he'd been struck by a thunderbolt.

"You wish to become a member of my congregation?"

"Yessir," I said.

Well, he didn't speak for a while, but he just stood there looking at me, in a cold, considering kind of way. When he did answer, his voice was quiet.

"I see you for what you are," he said. And I, being young and foolish, supposed that this might mean something good for me. "You seek," he asked me, "to better yourself?"

"Yessir," I said, very hopeful, and giving him my best smile.

"As I thought," he murmured, more to himself than to me. And he nodded. "Those who join the congregation," he said, "do so for love of God, not in hope of any reward."

Now, on account of living with the van Dyck family, and knowing how their children were raised, I reckoned that I knew a little of the Christian religion. And, forgetting I was only a slave and that he was the dominie, I was disposed to argue.

"But they do it to escape hellfire," I said.

"No." It seemed to me that he did not want to have any conversation with me, but being a dominie, he was obliged to give instruction, even to a slave. "It is already predestined who shall go to hell and who shall be saved," he said. "The godly serve the Lord for His sake, not for their own." Then he pointed his finger at me. "Submission, young man, is the price of entry to the Church. Do you understand?"

"Yessir," I said.

"You are not the first slave to imagine that by worshipping at our

Church you may open a path to freedom. But it will not be tolerated. We submit to God because He is good. Not to better ourselves." And now his voice was getting louder, so that a man passing in the street turned to look. "God is not mocked, young man," he cried to me then, and fairly glared at me before he strode away.

A few days later, the Boss turned to me and said: "I hear that you had conversation with Dominie Cornelius." And he gave me a strange look.

"Yes, Boss," I said. But I took care not to speak of religion again, after that.

❖

And soon there were more important things to concern me than the saving of my soul. For that summer, while the Boss was away upriver, the English came.

I was working in the kitchen when Jan came running in with the news. "Come quickly, Quash," he calls. "Down to the water. Come and see."

I was wondering if the mistress would give me permission, but a moment later she was there too, with little Clara. Clara's little round face was flushed with excitement, I remember. So we all went down to the waterside by the fort. It was a clear day and you could see right across the harbor. And there in the distance you could see the two English sails. They were riding out in the entrance to the harbor, so that no ships could get in or out to the sea. By and by, we saw a puff of white smoke. Then there was a long pause until we heard the sound of the guns, like a little rumble; for they were maybe seven miles away. And the people by the water cried out. Word came that the English settlers out past Brooklyn were mustering and taking up arms, though nobody knew for sure. The men on the walls of the fort had a cannon pointed out at the harbor, but the governor not being there, nobody was taking charge, which greatly disgusted the Mistress. I think she'd have been glad to take charge herself.

They had already sent messengers upriver to warn the governor. But it was a day or two before he came back. During that time, the English ships stayed where they were and didn't come any closer.

Then one evening the governor arrived to take charge, and as soon as she heard this, the Mistress went to see him. When she got back, she was looking very angry, but she didn't say why. The next morning, the Boss came home too.

When the Boss walked in the door, the Mistress remarked that he had been gone a long time. And he replied that he had come back as soon as he could. That was not what the governor said, she answered. She heard he'd made a stop upriver. And she gave him a black look. Made a stop when the English were attacking his own family, she said.

"Indeed I did," says he, with a big smile. "And you should be glad of it."

She looked at him somewhat hard when he said that. But he paid no mind. "Consider," he says, "when Stuyvesant told me the English had come, I had no means of knowing how matters stood here. For all I knew, they had already entered the town, seized all our goods and driven you out of house and home. Was I to see our cargo—a rich one, by the way—stolen by the English too? It might be all the fortune we had left. So I thought to take it to a place of safe keeping. It is lodged with the Indian chief in the village to which Stuyvesant saw me going. I have known this Indian many years, Greet. He's one of the few I can trust. And there it should remain, I think you'll agree, until this business is over."

Well, the Mistress didn't say a word more, but it showed me plainly the good character of the Boss, to be thinking always of his family.

All that day New Amsterdam was in much confusion. There were boats taking messages from the English commander, Colonel Nicolls, to Governor Stuyvesant, and back; but no one knew what was in those messages, and the governor, he said nothing. But the English gunships stayed down by the narrows.

The next day, when I went down to the waterfront with the Boss and Jan, we came upon a crowd of people. They were pointing across to Brooklyn, on our left. And sure enough, you could see the glint of weapons where English troops were gathering by the ferry. And somebody pointed down toward the narrows, and said that to the west of them, on the big hump of land the Dutch call Staten Island, the English had landed more troops.

Meinheer Springsteen was there.

"We've a hundred and fifty men in the fort," he said to the Boss, "and we can muster maybe two hundred and fifty capable of fighting in the town. Even with some slaves, that's five hundred, maximum. The English colonel has twice that number of trained troops. And they say the English settlers on the long island have mustered troops as well."

"We've cannon in the fort," said the Boss.

"Short of powder. And ammunition," he says. "If the English gunships come close, they'll blast us to bits." He took the Boss by the arm. "The word is, they've demanded we give them the town, and that Stuyvesant won't budge."

After Meinheer Springsteen moved on, Jan asked the Boss if the English would destroy us.

"I doubt it, my son," he said. "We're worth far more to them alive." Then he laughed. "But you never know." Then he went to talk to some of the other merchants.

When we got home, he told the Mistress that none of the merchants wanted to make a fight of it, and she was angry and said that they were cowards.

The following day, Governor Winthrop of Connecticut arrived in a boat. I saw him. He was a small, dark-featured man. And he had another letter from Colonel Nicolls. He and Governor Stuyvesant went into a tavern to discuss it. By now all the merchants were down by the waterfront wanting to know what was going on and the Boss went there too. When he came back he said that some of the merchants had discovered from Governor Winthrop's men that the English were offering very easy terms if Governor Stuyvesant would give them the town; so after Winthrop left, they demanded of Governor Stuyvesant that he show them the English letter. But instead of showing the letter, Governor Stuyvesant tore it up in their faces; and they were mighty angry. But they took the pieces of that letter and they put them together again. Whereat they found the English were ready to let them keep all their Dutch customs and all their wealth, and let everything go on just exactly the same as before, so long as Governor Stuyvesant would give them the town without any trouble. So that's what they all wanted to do. Except Governor Stuyvesant, that is.

The Mistress was all for Governor Stuyvesant.

"He did right," she cried. "He's the only man among you all." And she called the merchants a pack of mongrel dogs and some other things I won't repeat.

Just then someone in the street started shouting, "The English are coming." And we all ran out and sure enough down at the waterfront we saw the English gunships coming across the harbor toward us. And by and by they lay off the town, with their cannon pointing at us; and they stayed there, just letting us know what they could do if they had a mind to.

Well, the next morning the merchants all signed a petition to the governor telling him to surrender. The Mistress asked the Boss, did he mean to sign, and he said, "I do." Even Governor Stuyvesant's own son signed it, which must have been a bitter blow to his father. But still he wasn't giving in. And we all went down to the fort, and we saw the governor up on the ramparts alone, standing by one of the cannons, with his white hair flying in the wind, and the Boss said: "Damn it, I think he means to fire the cannon himself." And just then we saw two of the dominies go up and plead with him not to do it, for fear of destroying us all. And finally, being men of God, they persuaded him to come down. So that was how the English got the place.

⁙

Back across the ocean, the English were so pleased with their victory that they declared war on the Dutch, hoping to get more of their possessions. But soon the Dutch paid them back by taking some of their rich places in the tropics. The next year they had a terrible plague in London, and then that city burned down in a great fire; and the year after that, the Dutch sailed right up the River Thames to London, and took the King's best fighting ship and towed it away, and the English were so weakened, there was nothing they could do about it. So then they agreed to a peace. The Dutch took back the places the English had taken from them in the tropics, on account of the slaves and the sugar trade. And the English kept Manhattan. The Mistress wasn't pleased, but the Boss didn't mind.

"We're just pawns in a bigger game, Greet," he said.

When Colonel Nicolls became the new governor, he told the Dutch people they were free to leave if they desired, but promised them they should never be asked to fight against the Netherlands if they stayed, no matter what the quarrel. He changed the name of the town to New York, on account of the Duke of York owning it, and the territory around he called Yorkshire. Then he gave the city a mayor and aldermen, like an English town. But most of the men on that body were the Dutch merchants anyway, so they were better pleased than they had been when Governor Stuyvesant was ruling them, for Colonel Nicolls was always asking their counsel. He was a friendly man; he'd raise his hat whenever he saw the Mistress in the street. He also started the racing of horses, which was liked.

And by and by, after Governor Stuyvesant had crossed the ocean to the Netherlands, to explain himself for losing the city, the old man came back to his bouwerie here; and Colonel Nicolls treated him very respectful, and the two of them became the best of friends. The English governor was always going out to spend time with the old man at his farm. The Mistress still had no love for the English. "But I won't deny," she would say, "that Nicolls is polite."

The next governor was like Colonel Nicolls. He started the mail service to Boston. He took plenty of profit for himself as well. The rich merchants didn't care, but the poorer part of the Dutch people, which was the greatest number, were not so pleased with the English rule after a while, on account of the English troops in the city, that gave them trouble and expense.

✣

When I was a boy, most of the slaves owned by the West India Company were engaged in building works. The merchants' slaves were mostly gardening, or loading and unloading the boats at the wharfs. Some were used as extra crew on the ships. But there were women slaves too. They were mostly employed in laundry and the heavier housework; though a few of them were cooking. The men would often be passing in the street, and especially in the evening, you would see them talking to the slave women over the fences as the dusk fell. As you might imagine, children were sometimes the result of this conversing. But although it was against their religion, the owners did not seem to mind that these children were born. And I believe the reason for this was plain enough.

For the trade in slaves is very profitable. A slave bought fresh out of Africa in those days might fetch more than ten times his purchase price if he was brought to the wharf at Manhattan, and in other places even more. So that even if a good part of the cargo was lost upon the way, a merchant might do uncommonly well in the selling of slaves. It was surely for this reason that both old Governor Stuyvesant and our new ruler, the Duke of York, had had such hopes of making Manhattan a big slave market. And indeed, many hundreds of slaves were brought to New Amsterdam in the days of Governor Stuyvesant and, after, some directly from Africa. Many slaves remained in this region, and others were sold to the English plantations in Virginia and other places. So if a slave in New York had children, their master might wait until the children came to a certain age, and sell them; or sometimes he would keep the children and train them for work, while he sold their mother, so that she wouldn't be spoiling them with too much attention.

There being quite a number of young women around the town, therefore, my interest in them grew, and by the time the English came, I was
getting very eager to make myself a man in that regard. And I was always
looking out around the town for a slave girl that might be agreeable to
giving me some experience in that way. On Sundays, when the Boss and
all the other families were in church, the black people would come out
into the streets to enjoy themselves; and at these times I was able to meet
slave girls from other parts of the town. But the two or three I had found
were not easy to spend any time with. Twice I was chased down the street
for trying to come into the house of the owner of one of them; and
another was whipped for talking to me. So I was in some difficulty.

There were women in the town, of course—it being a port—who
would give a man all he wanted so long as he paid. And I had a little
money. For from time to time, the Boss would give me small coin for
spending, if he was pleased with me. Or if he hired me out for a day, as
was often done, he would give me a little of what he received. And I had
been putting this money by in a safe place. So I was thinking it might be
necessary to expend some of this money on a lady of that kind in order to
become a man.

One evening I slipped out in the company of some other slaves, and
they took me along the Bowery road to a place some distance above the
town, where most of the free black people had their dwellings.

We went to a wooden house, which was larger than the others, that was
like an inn. The man who owned that house was a tall man, and he gave
us some sweet cakes and rum to drink. There were about a dozen black
people there, and some of them were slaves. And we had only been there
a little while when I noticed an old man asleep in the corner, and wearing
a straw hat, and realized that it was the old man I had met in the market
when I was a boy, that told me I could be free. So I asked the tall man that
owned that house who the old man was, and he said, "That is my father."
He talked to me for a while. I was very impressed with him. He owned
the house and some land besides, and he had people working for him,
too. He was free as any white man, and had no shortage of money. His
name was Cudjo.

After I had been talking to him and drinking rum for a while, I noticed
a girl of about my own age come into the house. She sat quietly in the corner near where the old man was asleep, and nobody seemed to pay heed
to her. But I glanced at her several times, and wondered if she'd noticed

me. Finally, she turned her head and looked right at me. And when she
did I saw that her eyes seemed to be laughing, and her smile was warm.

I was about to go over to her, when I felt Cudjo's hand grip my arm.

"You'd best leave that girl alone," he said quietly.

"Why's that?" I asked. "Is she your woman?"

"No," he answered.

"You're her father?"

"No." He shook his head. "I own her. She is my slave."

At first I didn't believe him. I did not know that a black man could
have a slave. And it seemed strange to me that a man whose own father
had obtained his freedom would own a slave himself. But it was so.

"You're looking for a woman, young man?" Cudjo then asked me, and
I said I was. "You ever have a lady friend before?" he inquired, and I said I
had not.

"Wait here a while," he told me, and he went out.

By and by he returned with a young woman. She was somewhere
between twenty and twenty-five years old, I guessed. She was almost as
tall as I was, and her slow, easy way of walking seemed to say that, however other folks might feel, *she* was comfortable with the world. She came
over to the bench where I was and sat down beside me and asked me my
name. We chatted a while and drank together. Then she glanced over at
Cudjo and gave him a small nod.

"Why don't you come with me, honey," she said.

So I left with her. As we went out, Cudjo smiled at me and said, "You're
going to be all right."

And I became a man that night.

In the years that followed I became friendly with a number of slave
women in the town. Several times the Boss said to me that one of the
meinheers was complaining his slave girl was with child and that it was
my doing. Some of his neighbors said the Boss should send me to work
on a farm out of town. But he never did so.

※

It was always my aim to please both the Boss and the Mistress equally. But
sometimes it was not so easy, on account of them not always agreeing
between themselves.

For instance, the Mistress did not always like the Boss's friends. The
first she took a dislike to was Meinheer Philipse. You'd have thought she

would have liked him, because he was Dutch, and his wife and the Mistress had always been close. They were rich, too. But the Mistress said Meinheer Philipse was getting too English for her liking, and forgetting he was Dutch. The Boss seemed to like him well enough, though.

The second came into our lives the following way.

The Boss loved to be on the water. He was always looking for an excuse. Sometimes he would take the family out to some place in a boat. One time we went to the little island just off the tip of Manhattan, that they called Nut Island, with a big basket of food and drink, and passed the whole afternoon there. Another time we went further across the harbor, to the place they call Oyster Island.

One day the Boss said that he was going to a place out on the long island, and that Jan and I were to accompany him.

We set out from the dock and went up the East River. When we came to where the river divides and we entered the channel that leads eastward, the waters began to churn and rush so violently that I was full of fear. Even Jan looked pale, though he didn't want to show it. But the Boss just laughed and said: "This is Hell Gate, boys. Don't be scared."

Once we passed through, the waters grew calm, and after a while he turned to me and said: "This is the Sound, Quash. On this side," he pointed to the left, "the coast runs all the way up Connecticut and Massachusetts. On that side," and he pointed to the right, "Long Island runs out for a hundred miles. Now are you glad you came?"

For that was the most beautiful place I ever saw in my life. There was a clear blue sky above, and I could feel the sun on me. Everywhere you looked, the water was calm, and the land rose so gently, with beaches and great banks of reeds, and there were seabirds skimming over the waves. I thought I was in paradise.

We sailed for some hours until we came to a small village on the island side of the Sound, with a wharf where we loaded the boat with supplies that the Boss was going to sell in the city. But toward the time we were finishing, a man came to inspect us. He was an English merchant. Soon he was looking thoughtfully at the Boss, and the Boss looked at him, and the man said: "Did I once sell you a silver dollar?"

"I believe you did," said the Boss.

And after that they fell into conversation for half an hour. I did not hear all of it, but I was standing near them when the Englishman said that he'd married a couple of years ago, and that he was mighty glad he'd come back across the ocean from London. Finally, as we were leaving, I heard the Boss say that the man should come to live in New York, where he might do very well; and the Englishman said he reckoned he would.

That man's name was Master. And he was going to cause plenty of trouble with the Mistress.

❖

I had one chance to please the Mistress very much.

In the American colonies, everyone knew their lives depended on the disputes of our masters across the ocean. Five years after the last dispute between the English and the Dutch had ended, trouble started again. Only this time it was more of a family business.

King Charles II of England was close to his cousin King Louis XIV of France, and he hadn't forgotten the drubbing he got from the Dutch. So in 1672, when King Louis attacked the Netherlands, King Charles joined in. But things still didn't go too well for them, because when the French with all their troops came into the Netherlands, the Dutch opened their dykes and flooded the land so the French couldn't cross. The next summer we heard that Dutch ships were coming up the coast, burning the English tobacco ships off Virginia and causing all kinds of trouble. And at the end of July, we saw the Dutch warships anchoring off Staten Island.

Now there was a young gentleman in the city then, by the name of Leisler. He was a German, I believe, but he had come to Manhattan and married a rich Dutch widow and done well for himself in business. He was all for everything Dutch, and the Mistress for that reason had quite a liking for him. While the Boss was out, he came round to the house, and I heard him telling the Mistress that many people were wondering whether to welcome the Dutch and tell them they could throw the English out of Manhattan again, if they had a mind to.

"Some of the merchants think a deputation should go out to Staten Island," he said. "But I'm worried about those guns in the fort. There's forty-six cannon there which could do harm to the Dutch ships."

When Leisler had left, the Mistress looked thoughtful. When the Boss came back, she told him what Leisler had said. The Boss already knew about the rumors, and he told everyone to stay in the house. Then he went out again to find out more.

He hadn't been gone long before the Mistress called: "Have you got a hammer, Quash?" Well, I did have a hammer, in the workroom at the back. So she looked around the workroom and saw some big metal pegs that the Boss had used for securing a tent. "Take those too," she said. "You come with me."

I was afraid to go, on account of what the Boss had said, but I daren't say no to her either. So we went to the fort.

The sun was getting low, but there were a lot of people about. The captain of the fort was in charge. He had some soldiers, but he was trying to muster the volunteers, who were mostly standing around on the area they call the Bowling Green, just in front of the fort. The Mistress didn't take any notice of the captain. She just walked into the fort with me, and she called to some of the volunteers to come with her. I suppose about twenty of us went in together. Then the Mistress went straight to the gun emplacements, and before anyone realized what she was doing, she took a spike and the hammer from me, and she starts hammering the spike into the powder hole of one of the cannon, so that it can't be fired. Some of the soldiers saw it, and they started to shout, and try to interfere with her, but she didn't take any notice, and she hammered that spike down into that cannon so hard that it was stuck fast. Spiking the guns, they call that.

The soldiers were getting very excited now. They were not well trained. They started to run toward us, and shouted to the volunteers to stop the Mistress. But being all Dutch, those volunteers weren't volunteering. And by now the Mistress had moved on to the next gun.

Just then, one of the soldiers got to the Mistress, and he started to swing at her with his musket. There was nothing for me to do but throw myself at him, and before he could strike her, I knocked him down, and hit his head on the ground hard enough for him to stay down. But another soldier was close by me now, and he had a big pistol which he pointed straight at me, and pulled the trigger. I supposed I was about to die. But luckily for me the pistol was not well primed, and it did not fire. The Mistress turned and saw all this, and she called for the volunteers to keep the soldiers off, which they did.

Well, there was a lot of confusion after that, with the soldiers being uncertain what to do, and more volunteers coming into the fort to help the Mistress, and the captain being at his wits' end when he found out what was going on. The Mistress kept spiking guns until she ran out of spikes. Then she left the hammer with the volunteers and told them to get on with it.

The next day, the Dutch landed with six hundred troops on the open ground above the wall. They marched to the fort, with quite a few of the Dutch people cheering them on, and the English captain had to surrender. There wasn't anything he could do about it.

I was in high favor with the Mistress after that. I had been afraid the Boss might be angry with me for disobeying his orders, and going to the fort; but the day after it all happened, he says to me: "The Mistress says you saved her life."

"Yessir," I said.

Then he just laughed.

"I suppose I should be grateful," he says. And he didn't give me any trouble about it.

✤

So the Dutch had New York again. This time they called it New Orange. But that only lasted a year. Sure enough, across the ocean, our masters made another treaty and we were given back to the English again, which didn't please the Mistress.

For a while after that, things were pretty quiet. Manhattan was called New York once more, but the new English governor, whose name was Andros, spoke Dutch and helped the merchants—especially the rich ones. He filled in the canal that ran across town. The Mistress said he did it because it reminded people of Amsterdam. But that old ditch used to stink, and I reckon that's why he did it. They made a fine street called Broad Street over the top.

And it was at this time that Mr. Master, that we had met on Long Island, came to live in New York. He and the Boss did a good deal of business together. The Boss liked the old fur trade up the river, but the trade down the coast with the West Indies sugar plantations was growing now, and that was the business Mr. Master did. The Boss would take a share in his voyages sometimes, and so would Meinheer Philipse.

But the Boss did one thing that gave the Mistress great delight. Jan was getting of an age to take a wife, and the Boss arranged a marriage for him with a girl from a good Dutch family. Her name was Lysbet Petersen and she had a considerable fortune. I had seen her in the town, but never spoken to her before the day she came to the house when the betrothal was announced.

"This is Quash," Jan told her, giving me a friendly smile, at which the young lady gave me a nod. So I was glad when Miss Clara added: "Quash has been with us all our lives, Lysbet. He's my best friend."

The young lady gave me a warm smile after that, to show she understood I should be treated kindly.

And it was a pleasure indeed to be at that wedding, and see the dominie smiling, and the Boss and the Mistress arm in arm looking so pleased.

❖

It was the next year that I was able to do the Boss a service that would change my life.

In the year 1675, there was a terrible rising among the Indians. The Indian chief that led it was named Metacom, though some folk called him King Philip. I scarcely know what quarrel started it off, but it wasn't long before all the bitterness in the Indians' hearts against the White Men, for taking their land, caused them to rise up in Massachusetts and the farther parts of Connecticut; and soon the Indians and the White Men were killing each other in great numbers. And the people in New York were terrified.

For these tribes that were fighting were all speakers of Algonquin. So it seemed natural that the tribes around New York might start in too. For though much weakened there were still considerable numbers of them upriver and out on Long Island.

But Governor Andros knew what to do. He gathered all those Indians and made them swear not to fight; and a good many he brought to camp near the city, where he could keep an eye on them. Then he went upriver to the Mohawk Indians, and he promised them plenty of trade and supplies on condition that, if the Algonquin around New York gave any trouble, the Mohawks would come and smash them. And it certainly worked, because there was no trouble around Manhattan.

One day during this time, the Boss took me to a place in the middle of Manhattan island where some of the Indians had been ordered to camp. He told me that he knew these people from a long way back when he used to trade with them. They had pitched several of their wigwams beside a clearing. It was a good place. Wild strawberries were growing in the grass. The Boss spent a while talking to the Indians in their own tongue, and you could tell they were glad to see him; but I could see that some of them were sick. By and by the Boss came and said to me: "Are you afraid of the fever, Quash?"

From time to time the fever had come to the town. When I was about eighteen years of age, I remembered it being very bad, and quite a few children and older folk dying. But the fever never seemed to trouble me.

"No, Boss," I said.

"Good," he says. "Then I want you to stay with these people a while, and see they have everything they need. Any food or medicine they lack, you come to town and tell me."

So I stayed in that place for nearly a month. And several of those families took the fever badly. One of their women especially, that was paler than the rest, she lost her husband, and her children were nearly gone. But I helped her carry those children over to the river, where we cooled them down, and afterward I went to town for oatmeal and suchlike. I believe that if I hadn't helped her she might have lost those children too. Anyway, I told the Boss about it, and he said I had done well.

But when it was all over, and I returned home, I was hardly through the door when the Mistress turned on me.

"You're wasting time saving those Indians," she shouted at me. "Now get on about your work and clean this house that you've neglected for a month." I knew she had a low opinion of Indians, but it wasn't my fault that I helped them. The Boss told me not to worry about it, but she seemed to forget about my saving her life after that, and was cold toward me for quite a time.

And this made me realize that you can live with people all your life, yet not be sure you know them.

÷

But I had certainly earned the gratitude of the Boss. It was about a month later that he called me to the room where he used to work and told me to close the door. He was smoking his pipe, and he looked at me thoughtfully, so that I wondered if I was in some kind of trouble.

"Quash," he said quietly after a minute or so, "no man lives forever. One day I shall die, and I have been thinking about what shall be done with you at that time."

I wondered if maybe he had in mind that I should work for his son Jan. But I kept my mouth shut and just listened respectfully.

"So I have decided," he said, "that you shall be free."

When I heard those words I could scarcely believe it. The freedmen I knew had all worked for the Dutch West India Company long ago. I had hardly heard of any private owners in New York freeing their slaves. So when he said that, I was overcome.

"Thank you, Boss," I said.

He sucked on his pipe for a while. "I'll need you as long as I'm alive, though," he added, and I must have given him a pretty careful look, because he started laughing. "Now you're wondering how long I'll last, aren't you?"

"No, Boss," I said, but we both knew it was true, and that made him laugh more.

"Well," he said, "I'm in no hurry to die yet." Then he gave me a kindly smile. "You may have to wait a long time, Quash, but I won't forget you."

It seemed that my dream of freedom was one day to come true.

❖

So I certainly wasn't expecting an even greater joy to come into my life just then.

After the Indian troubles, New York was quiet again. Some rich English planters had come there from the Barbadoes and such places. They mostly lived in big houses down by the East River waterfront, and some of them didn't trouble to speak Dutch. But many of the Dutch families in the town were still bringing their relations over. So with all the Dutch houses, and Dutch being mostly spoken in the streets, you'd almost have thought Governor Stuyvesant was still in charge.

Meinheer Leisler was becoming quite an important figure in the town these days, and the lesser Dutch folk all liked him. He'd often come to see the Mistress too, always very polite and neatly dressed, with a feather in his hat. And this attention was most pleasing to her. For the Mistress, though still a handsome woman, was now approaching the end of her childbearing years, and was sometimes a little depressed. The Boss, understanding this, was always considerate toward her, and did his best to find ways to please her too.

If only the same could have been said for Miss Clara. For since the time of her brother's marriage, that little girl I had loved had turned into a monster. I could hardly believe it. To look at, she was the same sweet-faced, golden-haired girl I had always known. She was still kind to me and respectful, mostly, to her father. But to her mother she was like the devil. If her mother asked her to help the cook or go to the market, she'd be sure to complain that her mother knew very well she'd promised to go to visit a friend just then, and that her mother was inconsiderate. If the Mistress said anything, Miss Clara said it wasn't so. Whatever was amiss, she said it was her mother's fault until at times the Mistress could stand it no more. The Boss would reason with Clara and threaten to punish her. But soon she'd be complaining again. I truly felt sorry for the Mistress at those times.

One day Mr. Master came by the house in the company of one of the English planters. And they and the Boss were talking in English together. I was there also. By that time I had learned some words of English, enough to understand some of what they said.

Just after they had started, the Boss asked me in Dutch to find him something, which I did. And when I brought it he asked me something else, which I answered easily enough, saying something that made him laugh, before I went back to my place. But I saw that English planter staring at me, and then in English he told the Boss to mind being so friendly to me, because they had had plenty of trouble with black slaves down on the plantations, and the only way to deal with us was to keep well armed and to whip us if we tried to be saucy. I just looked at the floor and pretended I didn't understand, and the Boss laughed and said he'd remember that.

The subject of their conversation, as it happened, was slaves. For Mr. Master had just returned to New York with a cargo of slaves, and some of these were Indians. On account of complaints from other countries about the taking of their people to be sold, Governor Andros had ordered that only black people might be sold as slaves in the market—for all the nations of the world agreed that Negroes should be slaves—and this was an inconvenience to Mr. Master.

"I'm aiming to sell these Indians privately," he said. "I have a nice young Indian girl, and I was wondering if you'd like to buy her."

Well at that moment in walked the Mistress looking upset, so I guessed that Miss Clara had been causing her grief again. The Mistress would sometimes pretend she didn't understand English, but she didn't bother with that now, because she shouted: "I'm not having any stinking Indians in this house." But then she turned to the Boss and said: "I need a slave girl to help here, though. You could buy me a black one."

And the Boss was so glad to do something to please her that he went out to purchase a slave girl the very next day. Her name was Naomi.

·⁝·

By this time I was about thirty years old. Naomi was ten years younger. But she was wise for her years. She was quite small, with a round face, and a little plumpness to her, which was pleasing to me. At first, being in a strange house, she was quiet; but we would talk together. As the days went by, we came to get acquainted better, and we told each other about our lives. She had lived on a plantation, but she had been fortunate to work as a servant in the house. When the owner of that house lost his wife and married again, the new wife said she wanted all new slaves in the house, and the old ones were to be sold off. So her owner sold her to a dealer who had taken her up to New York, where the prices were good.

I told Naomi that this was a kindly house, which seemed to comfort her a little.

Naomi and I got along together very easily. Sometimes I would help her if she had heavy tasks, and when I was tired, she would help me. For a few days I was sick, and she looked after me. So as the time went by, I began to feel a great affection for Naomi, on account of her kindness.

And I began to have thoughts of making her my wife.

I had never had a shortage of lady friends. Besides the women in the town, there was a girl I liked to see. She lived up at a little village on the East River just below Hog Island, and her name was Violet. On a summer evening, when the Boss told me he wouldn't be needing me any more, I used to slip up there. Violet had several children, some of which may have been mine.

But Naomi was different from those other women. I felt protective toward her. If I was to enter into relations with her, it would be to settle down, and I had not considered doing that before. So for quite a time I tried just to stay friends with Naomi but keep her at a distance from me. After a while I could see that she was wondering what I meant by my behavior; but she never said anything, and I did not tell her my thoughts.

Then one evening, in the middle of her first winter, I found Naomi sitting alone and shivering. For having always lived in warm places, she had never known the cold of New York. So I sat beside her and put my arm round her. And by and by, one thing led to another; and after that it wasn't long before we were living together like man and wife.

The Boss and the Mistress must have known it, but they didn't say anything.

✦

It was spring when the Boss told me I was to go up the Hudson with him. I had always been curious to see that great river, so, although it meant that I would be parted from Naomi for a little while, I was pleased to be going. Usually the Boss would have made this journey a few weeks later, but Clara and the Mistress had been quarreling so much, I believe he was glad to get away from them.

Just before we left, he and the Mistress had some hard words. The Mistress was never too happy when he was going upriver, and then she started blaming him for Clara's behavior. They closed the door, so I didn't hear it all, but when we set out, the Boss was looking down and he didn't say much.

He was wearing a wampum belt. I had noticed that he always put that belt on when he was going upriver. I believe one of the Indian chiefs must have given it to him.

There were four oarsmen, and the Boss let me take the tiller. By the time we were out on the water an hour, he was looking more cheerful again. The tide and the wind being against us, we made slow headway that day; but the Boss didn't seem to care. I think he was just happy to be out on the river. We were still in sight of Manhattan when we pulled over to make camp.

The next morning, we hadn't gone far when he gives me a look and says: "So, Quash, I reckon you've made Naomi your wife. Didn't you know you have to ask my permission?"

"I don't know as she's my wife, exactly, Boss," I said. "To take a wife you have to go to church." I wondered what he'd say to this.

"The English have words for it," he told me. "Under English law—which we are supposed to use—since she lives in the house with you as though you were married, she would be called your 'common-law wife.' So," he gave me a smile, "you be good to her."

"You aren't angry with me, Boss?" I asked. He just smiled and shook his head. "And the Mistress?" I said.

"Don't worry." He sighed. "On that, at least, we are agreed."

He was gazing up the river for a while after this, the breeze in his face,

and I was watching him to see if he was still in a good temper. Then he
turned and gave me a smile.

"Can I ask you something, Boss?" I requested.

"Go on," he said.

"Well, Boss," I said, "it's like this. You told me that one day I might
have my freedom. But even if Naomi is my common-law wife, that won't
do her any good. She'll still be a slave."

He didn't answer.

"You see, Boss," I said, "I'm thinking about what happens if we have
children."

For I had made sure to understand the law. And Dutch or English, it
didn't make a difference. The child of a slave belongs to the master. And if
the master frees the slave, the child is still owned by him, unless he frees
that child by name also. That is the law.

He still didn't reply for a moment, and then he nodded to himself.

"Well, Quash," he said, "I'll have to think about that, but not yet
awhile." And I could tell that he didn't want to talk about that subject any
more.

⁜

During that afternoon, we pulled over to the bank where there was an
Indian village and the Boss told me to wait in the boat while he went to
talk to the Indians. He was gone a long time, and when he came back, he
got into the boat and told the oarsmen to pull upstream. He seemed to
have something on his mind, so I kept quiet and minded the tiller.

We went for maybe half an hour, round a bend in the river, when he
said to me: "You remember those Indian children you saved?"

"Yes, Boss," I said.

"Well," he said, "their mother died. Fever."

I didn't mind so much about the mother, but I had worked hard to save
those children, so I asked him if they were all right.

"Yes," he said, "the children live."

"That's good, Boss," I said.

⁜

That evening, we made camp. We ate round the campfire, the Boss, me
and the four oarsmen. The Boss was always good with the men. They

respected him; but he knew how to sit and joke with them. And even if maybe he had other things on his mind, he would always give the men his time.

The Boss had brought good provisions and a keg of beer. After we had all eaten and drunk a bit, the men were laughing, and teasing me about the women they said I'd had; and the talk fell to women in general. Then one of the men laughed and said that he was afraid of the Mistress. "I wouldn't want to get on the wrong side of her, Boss," he said. And knowing that the Boss and the Mistress had had a falling-out, I wished he hadn't said that. And I could see a cloud pass over the Boss's face. But then he just smiled and said, "I wouldn't want to get on the wrong side of any woman." So the men all agreed about that. But soon after, he said, "Well, I reckon it's time to sleep." And it wasn't long before the men were dozing; and I lay down too.

But the Boss didn't sleep. He sat by the fire staring out over the river, very thoughtful, and I reckoned he was thinking about his hard words with the Mistress. So I kept quiet.

He stayed like that a long time. The fire was getting low. The stars over the river were fine, but there were some clouds passing across them; and then after a time, a light breeze came and started to stir the trees, just a little, like a whisper. It was peaceful as a lullaby, and as I listened to it I started to feel sleepy. But the Boss wasn't getting to sleep.

So by and by, thinking maybe to take his mind off whatever was concerning him, and help him get to sleep, I said: "Listen to the breeze, Boss."

"Oh," says he. "You still awake?"

"Maybe it'll help you get to sleep, Boss," I said.

"Maybe, Quash," he answered.

"That breeze is so soft, Boss," I said. "It's like a voice in the pine trees. You can hear it if you try."

Well, he didn't say anything. But after a moment I saw his head bend down, so I supposed he might be listening. When he didn't move for a while, I reckoned maybe he'd gone to sleep. But then he got up slowly, and glanced across at me. And I pretended to be asleep.

Then he moved away and started walking along the riverbank in the dark.

I lay still a long time, waiting for him to come back, but he didn't. And by and by I began to wonder if he was all right. There are plenty of bears in the woods, though you'd expect to hear a shout if one of them attacked him. But when he still didn't come, I got up, and I started to move along the riverbank after him. I went very carefully, and I never made a sound. But there was no sign of him. I didn't want to call out, so I just went on. And I must have gone nearly half a mile when I did see him.

He was sitting on a little patch of grass by the water, under the stars. He had his knees drawn up with his back bent, and his shoulders hunched over his knees. And he was weeping. His whole body was shaking, and he was almost choking. I never saw a man weep so. And I daren't go forward, but I didn't like to leave him there. So I stopped there awhile, and he went on weeping as if his heart would break. I was there a long time, and the breeze grew a little stronger, but he never noticed. And then after a while the breeze died, and there was just a big silence under the stars. And he was a little quieter. And not wanting him to find me there, I stole away.

When I got back to the fire, I tried to sleep, but I kept listening as well, on account of him. And it was nearly dawn when he came back.

⁂

We went for days up that great Hudson River, and we saw the big Mohawk villages with their wooden houses and palisades. And the Boss bought a great quantity of furs. And when we returned, and I ran in to see Naomi, she gave me a curious smile. Then she told me that she was expecting a child, which caused me greatly to rejoice. And soon after the idea came to me that if it was a boy, I should call him Hudson, on account of my journey at that time.

But Naomi also told me the Mistress and Clara had quarreled that morning and that Miss Clara had run out of the house. "The Mistress is in a black mood," she said.

I was going by the parlor door just after the Boss came in. The door was open, and I could hear the Boss telling the Mistress about the pelts we bought from the Mohawks, but she didn't seem to be saying anything.

"Where's Clara?" he asked.

"Out," she answered. Then after a little pause: "I suppose you spent time with your other Indian friends too."

"Only briefly," he replied. "They had no furs."

The Mistress didn't respond.

"By the way," he said, "Pale Feather is dead."

I'd been listening by the door a little while now, and was thinking I'd better move away, when I heard the Mistress's voice.

"Why tell me?" she said. "What's a stinking Indian more or less?"

The Boss was silent for a moment after she said that. When he answered her, his voice was quiet.

"You are cruel," he said. "Her mother was a better woman than you." Then I heard him starting to walk out of the room, and I got away quick.

And after that time, it seemed to me, there was a coldness between him and the Mistress, as if something had died.

◈

I often thought about those words after that, and I reckoned I understood what they must mean. But I didn't care too much. For now I had my own family to think about.

With every year that went by, I came to realize my good fortune in being married to Naomi. She would do all her work about the house for the Mistress, even when she was big with child, but she never complained. I knew how much she had to do and helped her all I could. At the end of the day, she always had a smile for me. We shared everything, and grew to have such an affection between us that, as the years went by, I could hardly imagine what it had been like to live without her.

My little Hudson was the most lively little baby you ever saw. I delighted to play with that child, and the Boss would come and play with him too. I believe for a time Hudson thought the Boss was his grandfather or something. When he was two years old, Naomi had another child, a girl; but that baby wasn't strong, and she died. Two years later, though, we had another little girl, and we named her Martha. She had a round face like her mother, and as she grew up, I could see she had her mother's nature.

In no time, it seemed, Hudson was a boy of five. He could run and scuttle about. The Boss said he couldn't catch him. And Naomi said Hudson looked just like me. I used to put him on my shoulders and take him with me on my errands around the town. But always, if there was time, I would take him down to the waterside, for he loved to look at the ships. And the thing that really excited him was to see them unfurl their sails so they would make a great slap and a bang in the wind.

One day, when Mr. Master was visiting, he asked Hudson what he liked to do. And Hudson piped up and told him that he wanted to be a sailor.

"Ha," said Mr. Master to the Boss. "Maybe he should come to work for me." And the Boss laughed. But when I thought of all the cargoes of slaves that Mr. Master was carrying up to New York, I didn't want my son to sail in any ship like that.

As for Martha, she was a most affectionate child. She would throw herself into my arms if I'd been out for a while, and cling on to me round the neck, and say she wouldn't let go unless I told her a story. And I didn't know any stories, so I had to make them up. It wasn't long before I was telling her stories about a great hunter called Hudson, who lived up the river of that name, who was free, and who had a sister Martha who was very loving and wise. It was amazing the adventures they had with the animals up in that wilderness.

∙┼∙

During this time, the Boss also found a good husband for Miss Clara. I think he and the Mistress were both glad to get her out of the house. Once again the Boss pleased the Mistress very much by finding a good Dutch family, so that she was married by the dominie in the Dutch church just like her brother Jan. Her husband did not live in town, but out on Long Island, so we did not see her often. But the Mistress would go out to stay at Clara's house from time to time, and from all accounts they got on much better now that Clara was married.

As for the Boss and the Mistress, they lived together, but without any quarreling they seemed to go their separate ways.

The Boss and Mr. Master became very close. Mr. Master was one of those men who never seem to look any older. With his narrow face, and his shock of yellow hair, those hard, blue eyes he had, and the stringy build of his body, he hardly changed at all apart from some lines on his face. He had a pleasant manner, and he was always busy with something. Whenever he came by, he'd say, "Good day, Quash," and when he left, "You're a good man, Quash," and he'd give me a quick look with those blue eyes of his. Sometimes he'd say to the Boss, "Quash here is my friend. Is that right, Quash?" And I'd say, "Yessir."

In these years, wishing to keep the rich Dutch families on their side, and to profit by their friendship, the English governors were giving out huge grants of land to them. And English merchants did well too. And Mr. Master was eager that the Boss should get himself some land. Because in England, he said, you couldn't be considered a gentleman unless you had plenty of land. And the important men like Meinheer Philipse and the van Cortlandts, who had a big place north of the city, were all becoming gentlemen as fast as they could. And their women were piling up their hair and dressing in fine dresses that pulled in their bellies and pushed out their breasts.

Well, I could see the Boss was taking to this idea. Jan was liking it as well, and sometimes Jan would say they should buy some land. But not the Mistress. She went on wearing a plain round cap on her head and a loose Dutch gown, like the other Dutchwomen. But those Dutchwomen loved jewelry even more than the English. She liked having big jewels hanging from her ears, and I reckon she had a jeweled ring on every finger. And most of the time she would be sucking on her clay pipe.

As for being impressed with anything that was English, she was further from that than ever.

"That is a contemptible nation," she used to say. "They let themselves be ruled by the papists."

For it turned out that our owner the Duke of York had been a secret Catholic all along. People reckoned King Charles II might be a secret Catholic too, but he denied it. The Duke of York didn't hide it though. He was all for the Catholics, and he even sent a Catholic governor to New York. You can follow almost any religion in New York, or none. For they say half the people here don't believe in any religion at all. But almost everyone is afraid of the Catholics.

That Catholic governor made a charter giving free elections in the province and promising there should be no taxes raised without the men who were elected having a say. So even some of the religious Dutch said he wasn't so bad. But the Mistress wasn't impressed.

"Never trust an Englishman," she would say, "and never trust a papist."

⁂

The winter that ended the year 1684 was uncommonly cold. The big pond north of the town was frozen solid for three months. Like most Dutch people, the Boss liked to skate on the ice; and one morning we all went up there together with Jan and his two little daughters too.

Jan worked with his father, but in those years the business of distilling rum from molasses had been greatly increasing. There had been a distillery across the harbor on Staten Island for quite a while, but Jan had set up another in the town with Mr. Master. He was trading in the spirits that came from Holland as well, like the gin they call Genever.

And the Mistress came with Miss Clara and her husband. They hadn't any children yet, but I had never seen her look more beautiful. The Boss showed all the children, including my son Hudson, how to skate, and the Mistress was all smiles and said to see all the people skating on that big pond was just like a Dutch painting. She didn't even seem to mind when Mr. Master and his family showed up.

Now Mr. Master had a son named Henry, who must have been about eighteen years old at this time. He looked just like his father. And when that young man saw Miss Clara looking so pretty and flushed with the exercise and the cold air, he couldn't take his eyes off her. And they skated together. Even the Mistress was amused and said, "The boy's in love with you."

That day would always stay in my mind as a very happy one.

✧

The blow fell in 1685. The news broke over New York like a thunderclap. King Charles II was dead and his brother the Duke of York was king in his place. King James II, the Catholic.

New York had a Catholic king. In no time at all, he was giving Catholics the running of things. Then he tore up the charter that gave elections to the province here. "I told you so," the Mistress said. "I told you never to trust a Catholic."

That wasn't the worst of it. Over in France, King Louis XIV suddenly decided to throw all the Protestants out of his kingdom. There were a huge number of these folk, and they had to take what possessions they could and run. Some went to the Netherlands, and before long they were arriving in New York as well. Huguenots, people called them.

One day Meinheer Leisler came to see the Mistress in the company of one of these Huguenots, a very stately man called Monsieur Jay. And Monsieur Jay said that King James had written and congratulated King Louis for throwing all those Protestants out of his kingdom. They said that there was much discontent in England about the Catholic king. The Boss was shocked; as for the Mistress, from that time she would talk of nothing else. She said the English should revolt and throw the king out.

That's what the Dutch had done when they were under the Catholic Spanish king. The Boss said that the English were prepared to wait. For King James had no son, and his two daughters were both Protestant. In time, he said, things would return to normal. That didn't satisfy her, though.

And for the next two years, everyone in New York was complaining about the king.

It was a spring day in the year 1689 when the Mistress came hurrying to the house with a big smile on her face and told us that the English had kicked King James II out of his kingdom.

"God's will is done," she cried.

The cause was a child. After years of having no more children, King James suddenly had a son, that was to be a Catholic. "Even the English wouldn't stand for that," she said. It seemed that in no time they'd kicked him out, and sent for his elder daughter Mary. The Glorious Revolution, they called it.

"Not only is Mary a Protestant," said the Mistress, "but she is married to our own William, ruler of the Netherlands. And William and Mary are to rule England together." She was almost dancing for joy, to think that we should be under Dutch rule again.

Soon after the Glorious Revolution came news that the Dutch and English had declared war on Catholic King Louis of France. King William's War, they called it. We were all afraid that the Catholic French up in the far north would join the Iroquois Indians and come all the way down to New York. And the French and the Indians did attack some of the Dutch settlers far upriver. But for merchants like the Boss and Mr. Master, a war can also be a big opportunity.

I shall always remember the sunny day when the Boss told us we were to come with him down to the waterfront. So we all went. The Boss and the Mistress; I was allowed to bring Hudson. When we got there, Jan and Mr. Master and his son Henry were waiting for us. And we were all rowed out to a ship at anchor in the East River. That was a fine ship, with tall masts and several cannon. Mr. Master took us all around. Hudson was looking at everything on board; I never saw him so excited. Several merchants had invested in that ship making a voyage to attack the French merchantmen, now that we were at war with them, and take their cargoes. Mr. Master had taken an eighth share, and the Boss and Jan had taken another eighth. I could see that the vessel was well built for speed. "She'll outrun anything the French can bring against us," Mr. Master said. He was very pleased with himself. "And the captain's a first-rate privateer. With luck she'll make a fortune."

Just then Hudson started to pull my sleeve, wanting to ask a question. I told him to keep quiet, but Mr. Master said, "No, let him ask." So then Hudson says: "Please, Boss, what's the difference between a privateer and a pirate?"

The Boss and Mr. Master looked at each other and laughed.

"If the ship's stealing from us," says the Boss, "it's a pirate. But if it's stealing from the enemy, it's a privateer."

✢

A little while after the ship left, Miss Clara's husband became sickly and died. She had no children, and so she returned to live in the house with her parents for a while. I wondered if there was going to be trouble, but the years had passed and she and her mother got along fine. Naturally Miss Clara was grieving for a while, but I heard the Mistress say to the Boss, "We must find her another husband." For the time being though, I think the Mistress was glad of her company.

My Naomi was good with a needle, and used to do all the mending needed in the house. She'd also started to teach little Martha how to sew. And it wasn't long before Miss Clara noticed Martha's skill. Being so young, her fingers were so supple and quick, it was amazing what that child could do. Soon she was saying, "That child is a treasure." She used to take Martha for walks. The Mistress didn't seem to mind.

✢

It was one thing to send out privateers against the enemy, but it was another to rule the province. And for a while there was all kind of confusion. Up in Boston, they'd thrown King James's governor in jail. In New York, nobody knew who was supposed to be in charge. And this was where Meinheer Leisler stepped into history. For since he was one of the leaders of the city militia, the city fathers asked him to take charge until things were sorted out.

You can imagine how pleased the Mistress was. Some of the prominent Dutchmen supported him, like Doctor Beekman and some of the Stuyvesants. The Dutch small traders and craftsmen and all of the poorest Dutch were for him, because he was Dutch. The Huguenots that were arriving by almost every ship all liked him; and he helped them to have a Huguenot settlement out at the place they named New Rochelle, after one of the French towns they'd been kicked out of. And many of the English, especially out on Long Island, liked him, because they hated Catholics in general, and he was a good Protestant. Some of the most religious ones were even saying the Glorious Revolution was a sign that the Kingdom of God was at hand.

So Meinheer Leisler was ruler of New York for a while. But it wasn't easy for him. I remember him coming by to see the Mistress one time and saying how hard it was to keep good order. "And I shall have to raise taxes," he said. "They aren't going to like me after that." I could see that his face, which was always so jaunty, was looking tired and strained. "But one thing," he said, "I promise you I'll never give this town over to any Catholics again." And Meinheer Leisler was running the town for about a year and a half.

But if the Mistress was all for him, the Boss was more cautious.

I first came to understand what was in the Boss's mind one day when we were walking down the main street that runs from the fort up to the gateway, that the English were calling Broadway. That part of the town was mostly occupied by the lesser Dutch folk—carpenters, carmen, brickmakers, cordwainers and mariners. They all loved Leisler. And I remarked to the Boss how popular Meinheer Leisler was.

"Hmm," he said. "It won't do him much good, though."

"How's that, Boss?" I asked. But he didn't say.

Soon enough, however, you could see what the trouble was. For Meinheer Leisler started putting ordinary folk into city offices and giving them power. Even the big Dutch merchants didn't like that. Some of the dominies started complaining about him too.

The Mistress took no account of this complaining. She spoke up for Leisler all the time. "He is Dutch, and we have a Dutch king now," she would say.

"But he is also an English king," I heard the Master warn her once, "and his court is in London. The big merchants have friends in the English court, which Leisler does not." He told her to be careful what she said.

Well, as the months went by, there was so much opposition from the leading men that Meinheer Leisler started to strike at them. He arrested Meinheer Bayard; and he had warrants out for van Cortlandt and several others. The ordinary Dutch folk who loved Meinheer Leisler even attacked some of those big men's houses. Because he was rich, the Boss was even afraid they might come and burn his. One evening he came home saying there was going to be trouble in the streets, and when I told him the Mistress was out, he said, "Come with me, Quash. We'd better make sure she's safe." So we went round the town. And we were just coming along Beaver Street to the bottom of Broadway when we saw more than a hundred women marching to the fort to show their support for Meinheer Leisler. And there in the front row was the Mistress. For a moment the Boss looked so angry that I thought he was going to drag her out. But then he suddenly laughed. "Well, Quash," he said, "I reckon this means they won't be attacking our house."

In the end, though, it all turned out as the Boss had warned. A ship arrived from London with troops to take over the city. Meinheer Leisler, knowing about all his enemies, held out in the fort saying he wouldn't give over the city without direction from King William himself. But finally that came too. And then they arrested him, because the king had been told he was a dangerous rebel. "It's your friends who engineered this," the Mistress told the Boss.

"Just be glad they haven't arrested you too," he answered. Though when he heard the city fathers were asking King William if they could execute Meinheer Leisler, he said that would be a shame.

⁜

Just after this, the Boss and Mr. Master's privateer came home. It had taken a small prize, but not enough to show much profit. They also had some slaves. But I didn't like the look of those slaves.

"I don't think they're healthy," Mr. Master said. "We'd better sell 'em quick." And he sold them the next day.

All this time, poor Meinheer Leisler was locked up waiting to know his fate. Most of the people in the city were shocked. In our house, there was a terrible gloom. The Mistress was hardly speaking to anyone. Early in May, when one of the women that had been marching with the Mistress asked to borrow Naomi for a few days to do some needlework at her farm, the Mistress lent her; and I think Naomi was glad to get out. The house was so sad that I told her, "Take little Martha too." So they went to that bouwerie, which was just a couple of miles north of the city, and they stayed there ten days.

During that time, the weather became very changeable. Some days it was hot and sultry, and the dung from the horses and the other animals was stinking in the streets; then there would be a day of cold and rain. Everybody seemed to feel it. My spirits are usually even, but I felt down. I could hardly do my work. Finally Naomi and little Martha returned late one evening. We didn't talk much. They were so tired that they both went straight to sleep.

The next morning, I went out with the Boss to the waterfront. Mr. Master and the other merchants were settling accounts on the privateer, and discussing whether to send out another one. After that, we went by the fort, because the Boss and Mr. Master wanted news of Meinheer Leisler. When they came out, the Boss was shaking his head.

"Bayard's determined to destroy him," he said to Mr. Master. "I don't believe they'll even wait for King William."

And they were just going into an inn, when we saw young Hudson running toward us.

"What is it, boy?" says the Boss.

"It's Martha, sir," he cried. "I think she's dying."

✢

That poor child was burning up with fever. It was terrible to see her. And Naomi was looking sick and starting to shiver too.

"It was those slaves from the Boss's ship," she told me. "They'd been sold to the bouwerie we were at. They were sick when we arrived, and one of them died. I'm sure we did catch something from them."

But nobody knew what the sickness was. All that night my little Martha was burning up, and by morning she could hardly breathe. Naomi and I were tending her, but around the middle of the night Naomi started taking the same way too. So I bathed them with cold water to try to take the fever down, but it didn't seem to do much good.

Then in the morning, Miss Clara came to the door.

"You mustn't come in, Miss Clara," I said. "I don't want you to get sick."

"I know that, Quash," she said. "But I want to tend to her."

I almost choked when she said that. But I called to the Mistress at once to warn her to keep Miss Clara away. And the Mistress told her she mustn't go in. But Miss Clara had a will of her own. She wouldn't give in, even to the Boss and the Mistress. She said she wasn't leaving until she'd given Martha some herbal drink that'd be good for her, that she'd brought. And the Boss said, "Give the drink to Quash then," but she wouldn't. And she stood there holding Martha's hand, and gave her the drink. Martha could hardly swallow it, but maybe it did her some good, for she was quieter then. I managed to get her out of the room after that.

Well, about dusk, my little Martha died. Her mother being so exhausted had fallen into a fitful sleep a little while before. And not wanting the child's body to be dead in the room with her, I picked Martha up and stole quietly down into the yard. And the Boss said I could put her in the stable for the time being, and that maybe I should bury her that night.

When I got back to Naomi, she was trying to sit up and looking for Martha.

"Where is she?" she cried.

"It's cooler down below," I said. I couldn't bear to tell her the truth just then. "She's resting there a while." But at that moment through the window we heard Clara weeping. So they must have told her.

"She's dead, isn't she?" says Naomi. "My little Martha's dead."

And I don't know what came over me, but I couldn't answer her. And then Naomi just fell back on her bed and closed her eyes.

Later that night she began to take the fever really bad. She was shivering and burning.

"I'm going, Quash," she said to me. "I'm going tonight."

"You've got to hold on if you can," I said. "We need you, Hudson and me."

"I know," she said.

The next morning it began to rain. Just a slow, steady rain. I was tending Naomi, so I had no thought of what else was passing in the world that day. But in the afternoon, the Boss came into the yard and asked after Naomi.

"Have you heard the news?" he said to me then. "They executed poor Leisler today."

"I'm sorry, Boss," I said.

"The Mistress is taking it very hard," he told me. "They gave him a traitor's death."

I knew what that meant. They hang you, but not long enough to kill you. Then they tear out your bowels and cut your head off. It was hard to think of such a thing happening to a gentleman like Meinheer Leisler.

"He was no more a traitor than I am," said the Boss. "The people are taking pieces of his clothes as relics. They say he's a martyr." He sighed. "By the way, Hudson should remain in the kitchen tonight, I think."

"Yes, Boss," I said.

That night, the rain continued. I wondered if the coolness would help Naomi, but it didn't seem to. Up to the middle of the night, the fever was causing her to toss and turn, and cry out. Then she grew quieter. Her eyes were closed, and I couldn't tell if she was getting better or losing the fight. Toward dawn, I realized that the rain had stopped. Naomi's breathing was shallow and she seemed very weak. Then she opened her eyes.

"Where's Hudson?" she said.

"He's fine," I told her.

"I want to see him," she whispered.

"You mustn't," I said.

She seemed to sink after that. About dawn I got up and went outside for a moment, to breathe some fresh air and look at the sky. It was clear. The morning star was in the east.

When I came back in, Naomi had gone.

❖

The days after the funeral, the Boss and the Mistress were very good to me. The Boss made sure I had things to keep me busy, and he made sure that Hudson was working too. He was right to do that. As for the Mistress, she didn't say much, but you could see that she was very shocked about the killing of Meinheer Leisler.

One day, as I was working in the yard, the Mistress came and stood beside me. She was looking sad. After a while, she said: "You and Naomi were happy together, weren't you?" So I said, yes. "You didn't quarrel?"

"We never had a cross word," I answered.

She was quiet for a moment or two. Then she said: "Cruel words are a terrible thing, Quash. Sometimes you regret them. But what's been said cannot be unsaid."

I hardly knew how to answer that, so I kept working. After another moment or two, she nodded to herself, and went indoors.

❖

Late that year, the Mistress got another slave woman to take the place of Naomi, and I believe she thought maybe I'd take up with her instead. But although she wasn't a bad woman, we didn't get along so well; and truth to tell, I don't think anyone could have replaced Naomi.

Young Hudson was a great consolation to me. There being just the two of us, we spent a lot of time together. He was a handsome boy, and a good son. He never got tired of being at the waterfront. He'd get the sailors to teach him knots. I believe he knew every way to tie a rope there was. He could even make patterns with them. I taught him all I could, and I did tell him that I hoped that one day, if the Boss allowed it, we might both be free. But I did not speak of that much, for I did not want to raise his hopes too high, or for him to suffer disappointment if I was not able to get our freedom yet awhile. It always gave me joy to have him walking at my side. Often, as I was walking and talking to him, I'd rest my hand on his shoulder; and as he grew taller, sometimes he'd reach up and rest his hand on mine.

Those were difficult times for the Mistress, though. She was still a handsome woman. Her yellow hair had gone gray, but her face hadn't changed so much. In these years, however, the lines started crowding her face, and when she was sad, she started to look old. It seemed that nothing was going her way. For although most people were still speaking Dutch in the city, every year there seemed to be more English laws.

Then the English wanted their Church—the Anglican Church as they call it—to be the leading religion of the place. And the governor said that no matter what church you went to, you still had to pay money to support the Anglican priests. That made a lot of people angry, especially the Mistress. But some of the dominies were so anxious to please the governor that they didn't complain, and even offered to share their churches with the Anglicans until they could build their own.

She had her family at least. But the Boss, although he was more than sixty years of age, was always busy. Since King William's War against the French was still continuing, there were plenty of privateers going out; and the Boss and Mr. Master were busy with those. Sometimes he'd go upriver for furs. Once he went away with Mr. Master down the coast to Virginia.

She would be often at Jan's house, which was not far off, seeing her grandchildren. And Clara was a comfort to her. But Clara was often out of the house, and I reckon the Mistress was lonely.

❖

It was a summer afternoon soon after the Boss and Mr. Master had returned from Virginia that the family all gathered in the house for dinner. Jan and his wife Lysbet were there and their daughters, and Miss Clara. Hudson and I were serving at table. Everybody was cheerful. And we had just brought in the Madeira at the end of the meal when Miss Clara stood up and told them she had an announcement to make.

"I have good news," she said, looking around at them all. "I am to be married."

The Mistress looked quite astonished, and asked whom she was wanting to marry.

"I'm going to marry young Henry Master," she said.

Well, I had a plate in my hand, and I almost dropped it. As for the Mistress, she looked at Miss Clara, disbelieving.

"The Master boy," she cried. "He's not even Dutch."

"I know," said Miss Clara.

"He's much younger than you," the Mistress said.

"Plenty of women in this town have married younger men," Miss Clara countered. And she named a rich Dutch lady who'd had three young husbands.

"Have you spoken to the dominie?"

"It's no use the dominie saying anything. We are to be married in the Anglican church, by Mr. Smith."

"Anglican?" The Mistress made a sort of gasping sound. "His family dares to demand that?"

"It was my idea."

The Mistress just sat there staring at her as if she couldn't believe it. Then she looked at the Boss.

"You knew of this?"

"I heard something. But Clara's more than thirty now, and a widow. She'll make up her own mind."

Then the Mistress turned to her son and asked him if he had known.

"I had a notion of it," he said.

After he said that, the Mistress seemed to sag in her chair.

"It would have been kinder," she said quietly, "if somebody had told me."

"We didn't know for sure," said Jan.

"It's not so bad, Greet," said the Boss cheerfully. "Henry's a nice boy."

"So, Clara," the Mistress continued, "you are happy to marry an Englishman, and desert your Church. This means nothing to you?"

"I love him," Clara replied.

"That will pass," said the Mistress. "You realize that in an English marriage, you will have few rights."

"I know the law."

"You must never belong to your husband, Clara. Dutchwomen are free."

"I am not worried, Mother."

Nobody said anything for a moment. The Mistress looked down at the table.

"I see," she said at last, "that my family cares nothing for me." She nodded. "You are all in league with Master." She turned to Miss Clara. "I wish you joy of it."

Later that year, Mr. Smith, the English clergyman, married them. The Mistress refused to attend the service. People weren't surprised. Many of her Dutch friends would have felt the same. When the Boss came back afterward, she was sitting in the parlor looking like a thundercloud. He was looking quite contented, and I could see he'd had a few drinks.

"Don't worry, my dear," he said. "You weren't missed."

᛭

I'd have been happy enough myself, if only my son Hudson hadn't wanted to go to sea. He was always pestering me about it, and the Boss was all in favor. Mr. Master said he'd take him any time, and it was only because the Boss knew I didn't wish it, and that Hudson was all I had, that he didn't hire him to Mr. Master. "You're costing me money, Quash," he told me, and he wasn't joking.

One day Mr. Master came to the house with a Scottish gentleman named Captain Kidd. He'd been a privateer and married a rich Dutch widow. He was a well-set man, very upright. He had a weather-beaten face, but he always wore a fine wig, and a spotless cravat and a rich coat of blue or red. The Mistress called him a pirate; but having so much money now, he was very respectable and was friends with the governor and all the best families. Mr. Master told him how young Hudson could tie all kinds of knots, and made Hudson show him, and the captain was very impressed.

"That slave laddie o' yours belongs at sea, van Dyck," he said in his Scottish voice. "Ye should make him a mariner." Then he sat in the parlor telling the Boss tales of his adventures in front of Hudson, and for a month after that I had a terrible time with my son wanting to go to sea.

✦

All my life in that household, I'd been accustomed to hearing the family talk among themselves freely. If there was something that had to be said privately, the Boss and the Mistress would make sure they were alone and close the door before they discussed it. But people spoke their thoughts, especially at mealtimes when I was serving them. So as the years went by, there wasn't much of the family's business or their opinions about what was passing in the world that I didn't know.

But once I heard something that I should not have heard.

It wasn't my fault. There was a pleasant little garden behind the house. The room the Boss used as an office gave on to it. Like all the Dutch gardens, it was very neat. There was a pear tree in that garden, and a bed of tulips. There was a patch where cabbages, onions, carrots and endive were grown, together with a stand of Indian corn. Against one sheltered wall there were peaches growing. I never liked to work in that garden when I was young, but I had come to like tending to the plants there now.

On a warm spring day I was quietly working there, not far from the window of the Boss's office, which was open. I didn't even know he was in there when I heard the voice of his son Jan.

"I hear that Meinheer Philipse has made an English will," he said.

"Oh." I heard the Boss's voice.

"It's the right thing for a gentleman to do," says Jan. "You should consider it."

There was a big difference between the English and the Dutch when it came to dying. When a Dutchman died, his widow continued owning his house and all his business until she died herself; and then everything was split between the children, boys and girls alike. But the Englishwomen are not given such respect. For when an Englishwoman marries, her wealth all belongs to the husband, as if she was a slave. And she isn't supposed to transact any business. And if her husband dies, the eldest son gets almost everything, except a portion set aside for the upkeep of the widow. And the English were even passing a law that the son could kick his mother out of the house after forty days.

The big English landowners liked this way of arranging matters, because by keeping all the estate together, the family would keep its power. And some of the Dutch, after becoming gentlemen, wanted to have an English will for the same reason; but most of the Dutch didn't take any notice of that English law. Their wives wouldn't stand for it, I reckon. And I didn't imagine the Boss would take any notice, either.

"We've a Dutch will that goes back to the time of our marriage," the Boss said. "It's held by old Schermerhorn, your mother's lawyer. She'd have a fit if I altered it."

"She wouldn't have to know. A new English one would supersede it."

"Why do you mind?"

"Truthfully, Father, I don't trust her judgment. The way she carried on over the Leisler business. I don't think she's the right person to manage our money. Clara's well provided for. She had a generous dowry, and she got money from her first husband too, and God knows Henry Master's not short of money. Under his father's English will he'll get almost all the Master fortune, you can be sure. She's far richer than I am."

"I see what you mean," said the Boss.

"You know I'll always look after Mother. So would Clara."

"No doubt."

"I just think you should protect me. And the van Dyck family. That's all."

"I'll consider it, Jan, I promise you. But this had better stay between us."

"Absolutely," said Jan.

I moved quietly to the other end of the garden after that, and when I went back into the house, I never said a word about what I'd heard, not even to Hudson.

⁙

From the year 1696, I remember two events. The old wall across the north of the town was falling to bits and some years back a street had been laid along its line, which they called Wall Street. And in that year, the Anglicans began the foundations for a fine new church where the new Wall Street met Broadway. Trinity Church, they were calling it.

The second event was the final voyage of Captain Kidd.

King William's War with the French was still continuing. Two hundred miles upriver, a Dutch settlement called Schenectady had been attacked by French and Indians, and out on the ocean the French and their pirates were still giving so much trouble that the English begged Captain Kidd to go and deal with them. The captain was retired, as I have said, and a respectable man. In fact, he was helping at that very time with the building of Trinity, Wall Street. But he agreed to do it. "Though I don't think it took much to persuade him," said the Boss. "Those old sea dogs always get restless on dry land."

I was on my way home one afternoon when Hudson came up to me. I thought he was looking excited, but he didn't say anything. He just started walking along beside me, very companionable, the way he often did. And I put my arm on his shoulder, the way I often did. And we walked along side by side. Then by and by he said: "Captain Kidd wants to take me to sea."

I felt my heart sinking, like a ship going under.

"You're too young to be thinking of that," I said.

"I'm near sixteen. There are ship's boys far younger than that."

"The Boss won't allow it," I said. And I prayed it might be so. "Are you in such a hurry to leave your father?" I asked him.

"No," he cried. And he put his arm round my neck. "It isn't that. But at sea, I could learn to be a sailor."

"You could learn to be a pirate," I answered. For I had often seen the crews of these privateers, and I trembled to think of Hudson living among such men.

We were scarcely in the house before the Boss sent for me.

"Well, Quash," said the Boss, "Captain Kidd wants to buy Hudson. He's made a very good offer."

I just looked from one of them to the other. I didn't know what to say. Then I went down on my knees. It was all I could do.

"Don't send him away to sea, Boss," I said. "He's all I have."

"He wants to go, you know," said the Boss.

"I know," I told him. "But he don't understand. Captain Kidd's a fine gentleman, I expect, but his crew . . . Some of the men he's collecting are just pirates."

"You can't keep him forever, Quash," said the Boss.

I was thinking as fast as I could. As well as losing Hudson to the perils of the sea, I was mightily afraid of what Captain Kidd might do if he owned him. What if he decided to sell my son in some distant port? What would become of Hudson then? I was still hoping the Boss might set him free as well, one day.

"Maybe Captain Kidd would pay you for the service of Hudson without buying him," I said. "You'd be renting him out. But the captain would still have to return him to you. He'd be worth more, trained as a sailor," I said. I was just trying to think of anything. But I saw that the Boss was looking thoughtful.

"That'll do, Quash," he said. "You go along now, and we'll talk tomorrow."

The next day it was decided that Hudson should be rented out to Captain Kidd. I was grateful for that at least. It was many weeks before the ship was ready, and that time was very precious to me, because I thought I might never see my son again. But I didn't tell him what I was thinking, and he was so excited that he was down at the waterside whenever he could get away from me.

Certainly, many people had high hopes of making money from that voyage. Not only the governor, but several great English lords had put money into it. People said even King William had a secret share. The ship was called the *Adventure Galley*, on account of the fact that it carried oars, so that it could attack other vessels even if there was no wind. It carried a hundred and fifty crew and thirty-four cannon.

As the time approached when the ship was due to sail, I made Hudson sit with me, and I told him: "Now you obey Captain Kidd in all things, because he's your boss for now. But some of these men you're sailing with are very bad men, Hudson. So you just tend to your business and keep yourself to yourself, and maybe they won't bother you. But just remember what your father and mother taught you, and you won't come to no harm."

Finally, in September of that year of 1696, the *Adventure Galley* sailed out of New York harbor, and I watched Hudson till he was out of sight.

⁕

Months passed and there was no word. I knew that if he didn't find any prizes nearer, Captain Kidd would most likely head across the ocean, toward southern Africa and the Cape of Good Hope. For round the Cape toward the island of Madagascar, there'd be French merchantmen and pirates to be found.

One day a ship put into port that had been in those parts, with news that Captain Kidd had lost a third of his crew to cholera near Madagascar. But whether it was true, or whether my Hudson was dead or alive, I had no means of knowing.

That spring Miss Clara gave birth to a son. So far, Jan had only daughters, so this little boy pleased the Boss very much. They called the boy Dirk, after him.

"I have a grandson, Quash," he said, "and with luck I may even live to see him grow up. Isn't that a fine thing?"

"Yes, Boss," I said. "You're a lucky man."

But although Miss Clara brought the baby round to show to her mother, the Mistress still wasn't pleased to have an Anglican grandson.

⁘

And then, just when I wasn't expecting it, came the news I'd been waiting for all my life. The Mistress was out that day, when the Boss called me into the parlor.

"Quash," he said, "you know I promised you that when I die, you shall be free."

"Yes, Boss," I said.

"Well," he said, "being free may not be all you think. But anyway, in my will you'll be given your freedom, and some money too."

"I'm getting old myself, Boss," I said, secretly praying. "May Hudson also be free?"

"Yes," said the Boss, "he will also be freed. If he lives."

"Thank you, Boss," I said.

"You are to tell no one about this, Quash," said the Boss severely. "Don't speak of it to Hudson, or any of the family. For reasons you do not need to know, this is between you and me. Do you understand?"

"Yes, Boss," I said.

So I reckoned that he must have made an English will.

"There's one more thing," he said. "You have to promise to do something for me, after I'm gone." He took out a little bundle of cloth and unwrapped it. And inside I saw the wampum belt he was wearing the time we went upriver.

"You've seen this before?"

"Yes, Boss," I said.

"This is a very special belt, Quash," he told me. "It has great significance and value. In fact, this is more precious to me than anything else that I possess. And I keep it wrapped up and hidden in a place which I will show to you. When I die, Quash, I want you to go and fetch this belt. Don't tell anyone what you're doing, not even the Mistress. But I want you to take this belt to Miss Clara's house, and tell her that this is my particular gift to little Dirk. And he is to have it, and keep it, and give it to his son one day, if he has one, or pass it down to my descendants in memory of me. Will you promise to do this for me, Quash?"

"Yes, Boss," I said. "I promise."

"Good," he said. Then he showed me the hiding place; and we put the wampum belt there, so that it would be safe.

❖

The rumors about Captain Kidd started the following spring. Ships came into the port saying instead of hunting down pirates, he'd turned pirate himself. I asked the Boss what he thought.

"Who knows," he said with a shrug, "what happens at sea?"

I thought of my Hudson, but I didn't say more. The rumors continued, but we heard nothing definite all the next year. In the spring of 1699, we heard that English naval vessels were out looking for him. And finally, Captain Kidd turned up in Boston that summer, and word came that he'd been arrested.

And that was where, it seemed to me, the Boss showed at his best. Because within the hour of this news arriving, he was on his way to Boston to find out about Hudson. I tried to thank him as he left, but he gave me a grin and told me he was just checking on his property.

There was a fast vessel going up to Boston that day. But two weeks passed. And then, one afternoon, I saw two men walking down the street toward the house. One was the Boss. The other was a black man, a little taller than me, a powerful-looking fellow. And then, to my amazement, he started running toward me, and took me in his arms, and I saw that it was my son Hudson.

❖

In the days that followed Hudson told me all kinds of things about that voyage, about the cholera, and how they couldn't find any French vessels. He said the captain was following his commission, but so many of the crew were pirates that he could hardly stop them attacking even the

Dutch ships. They were bad people, he told me. In the end they took a French ship, but its captain turned out to be English, and that was the start of the trouble.

"I was arrested too, in Boston," Hudson told me. "But when the Boss turned up and said I was only a slave that he rented to Captain Kidd, believing him to be a privateer, they reckoned I was of no account, so they let me go. I think the Boss may have paid them something too."

But Captain Kidd wasn't so lucky. For a long time he was held in Boston, and then they sent him to be tried in England.

The only thing people in New York went on talking about was the money Captain Kidd must have made from that voyage. Those that invested never saw any—except for the governor. Captain Kidd had buried some treasure on a place called Gardiner's Island, but he told the governor where it was, and so the governor collected that. But people said there was more buried treasure somewhere, maybe out on Long Island. I asked Hudson if it was true, but he just shook his head; though I did wonder if maybe there was something he knew that he wasn't telling.

Truth to tell, none of this was important to me. The only thing I cared about was that I had my son back and that one day he'd have his freedom. Though I did what the Boss said, and never told him that.

✦

I was grateful for something else too. After being with those pirates, my Hudson was not so anxious to go to sea for a while. He was happy enough to live in the house with me; for many months we were quite content. New York was tranquil enough. The Boss used to go often to the houses of Jan and Miss Clara, but in particular I could see that he took a delight in his little grandson Dirk.

In the year 1701, we heard that Captain Kidd had been executed in London for piracy. Hudson said that the trial must have been rigged, though he did allow that the captain had killed a man. I was sorry for the captain, but I was still relieved that the idea of privateering looked more dangerous than ever to my son.

Quite often the Boss would hire Hudson out to people to work for them a while, and since I had trained him well, they would pay the Boss quite a good fee. Each time the Boss would give Hudson a share of this, so that he was getting to put by a little money of his own now.

It was one morning in October that the Boss sent me over with a message for the man that ran the rum distillery on Staten Island. I seldom went to that place, and was glad to go. There was a boat going there from the wharf, and we made a pleasant journey across the harbor to the dock by the village that they call the old town. The English call the island Richmond. I knew there were two big estates there, and I could see farms dotted about on the little hills. It seemed to me a very pleasant place.

I didn't get back from there until halfway through the afternoon. I walked along the waterfront and was making my way to the house when I saw Hudson running toward me.

"Come quickly," he cried. "The Boss is dying." So we ran into the house. And they told me there that the Boss had been struck by a terrible crisis not long after I had left, and that he wasn't like to live. And they took me in to see the Boss at once.

There was a doctor there, and some of the family, including Clara. The Boss was looking very gray, and I saw that his breathing was shallow. But he recognized me, and when I went to his side, he tried to smile.

"I'm safe back, Boss," I said. "And I'm sorry not to see you looking better." Then he tried to say something to me, though it just came out like a strange noise. But I knew what he was saying. He was telling me, "You're free, Quash. You're free." And although nobody could understand him, I smiled and said: "I know, Boss. I know." After a moment, his head fell back and I said: "Don't you worry yourself about that now, Boss." And I took his hand. Then he frowned, and he seemed to be trying to shake my arm; then he stared very hard into my eyes. And I knew what he wanted. "I ain't forgotten my promise, Boss," I said. "I remember what you told me to do." And although he couldn't speak, he squeezed my hand.

The Boss lived through most of that day. Early in the evening, I was in the yard with Hudson when Clara came out with tears in her eyes and told me that the Boss had another huge seizure, and that he was gone.

"I know you loved him, Quash," she said.

"Yes, Miss Clara," I said. And part of me was sad because, as the life of a slave goes, the Boss certainly treated me as well as any slave can hope for. But part of me was just thinking about my freedom. I didn't know if the Boss had told the family I was free, but I knew it was in his will, so I wasn't worried.

❖

The Boss's funeral was a big affair. Half of the city of New York was there, I reckon, Dutch and English alike. And everyone was very kind and respectful to the Mistress. That evening she went over to Jan's house for a while. And while she was gone, it occurred to me that this would be a good time to get the Boss's Indian belt from its hiding place. So I went and did that, and keeping it wrapped up, I took it to where I slept, and hid it there; and nobody was the wiser.

The next day, during the morning, the Mistress said she was going out to see about some business concerning the Boss's affairs. And I was wondering if maybe it would soon be time to speak to her about my freedom. And I thought that when she returned, depending on her mood, I might mention it. In the meantime, while she was out, I reckoned I would carry out my promise to the Boss concerning the Indian belt, and get that done with. So I took the belt all wrapped up, and I started for Miss Clara's house, which was down on Bridge Street.

Well, I had got halfway there, just past the end of Mill Street, when I heard a voice behind me.

"What've you got there, Quash?"

It was the Mistress. I was thinking maybe I'd pretend I didn't hear her, and I glanced around quick to see if I could avoid her, but before I could do anything, I felt her hand on my shoulder. So I turned and smiled, and asked, "Anything I can do for you, ma'am?"

"No," she says, "but you can show me what you got there."

"Just some things of mine," I said. "It ain't nothing."

"Then show me," she said.

She can't surely think I'm stealing from her, I thought, after all this time. I didn't want to show her that belt, because the Boss had told me to keep it a secret. But she had her hand on the thing, and there wasn't much I could do. So I started to unwrap it. And for a moment she looked puzzled, but then as she saw what it was, her face grew dark.

"You give me that," she said.

"The Boss told me to take it," I answered. I didn't want to tell her where I was going with it, so I let her think he gave it to me.

"And I'm telling you to give it to me," she shouted. She had suddenly started to tremble with rage. I had an idea why the sight of that belt made her so angry, but there was nothing I could do about it.

Well, just then I had to think mighty fast. I knew I must do what I promised the Boss. Also, if I did what he said and gave that belt to Miss

Clara for her son, then no one could say I'd stolen it. And I reckoned that
if the Mistress was angry, it didn't really signify, because I knew I was
already free. So instead of obeying her, I turned, and before she could get
her hands on it, I ran as fast as I could, and dodged behind some carts,
and then made my way to Miss Clara's house.

When I got there, I found Miss Clara, and I gave her the message from
the Boss, exactly as he'd said, and told her that belt was to be kept by
young Dirk and by his sons after him for as long as there was family,
because that was what the Boss wanted. Then I explained about the Mistress, and she told me not to worry, and that if there was trouble she'd
speak to the Mistress about it. So then I left her, but I waited until early
afternoon before I went home, to give the Mistress time to calm down.

✦

There was no sign of the Mistress when I entered the house. But Hudson
told me that Jan and a lawyer had arrived a short while ago and that they
were with her in the parlor. So I reckoned they must have come about
the will.

I went into the hallway to see if I could hear anything. The parlor door
was closed. But then I heard the Mistress's voice, very loud.

"Damn your English will. I don't care when it was made. I have a good
Dutch will."

You can imagine I went close to the door after that. I could hear the
lawyer speaking, though not what he was saying; but I heard the Mistress
shouting back at him clear enough.

"What do you mean, I may stay here a year? This is my house. I'll stay
here a lifetime if I please." Then, after the lawyer spoke some more: "Free
Hudson? That's for me to decide. Hudson belongs to me." I could hear
the lawyer's voice, still very quiet. Then the Mistress exploded again. "I
see what's going on, you traitor. I don't even believe my husband signed
this English will. Show me his signature. Give it to me."

There was a pause for a moment. Then I heard Jan shout.

I had my ear so close to the door now that, when it flew open, I nearly
fell into the room. At the same moment, the Mistress burst past me. She
was staring straight ahead. I'm not sure she even saw me. She had a document in her hand and she was making for the kitchen. The next thing I
knew, I was colliding with Jan, who was rushing after her. By the time I
got my balance, she'd already gone through the kitchen door with a bang,

and I heard her bolt the door behind her. Jan was too late to catch her. He started shouting and hammering on that door, but it wasn't any use.

Hudson was in the kitchen, and he told me what happened next. The Mistress went straight to the kitchen fire, and she threw that will onto the flames and stood there watching it until it was burned to a cinder. Then she took a fire iron and poked it until it was just ashes. Then, quite calm, she opened the kitchen door, where both Jan and the lawyer were standing by now.

"Where's the will?" said the lawyer.

"What will?" she answered. "The only will I know is in a strongbox at my lawyer's."

"You can't do this," says Jan. "The will was witnessed. I can take you to court."

"Do it," she said. "But you may not win. And if you don't, then I'll see to it that, even though you're my flesh and blood, you'll get nothing. I'll spend it all. In the meantime, until a judge tells me otherwise, this house and all that is in it is mine."

They went away after that, saying she should hear from them. And I supposed it was my turn to face her anger now. But to my surprise, she turned to me very calmly and said: "Quash, will you fetch me a glass of Genever?" And when I brought it to her she said: "I am tired now, Quash, but we shall discuss your freedom and Hudson's tomorrow."

"Yes'm," I said.

❖

The next morning she was up early and went out, telling us to mind the house until she got back, and not to let anyone in.

Late in the morning, she sent word to Hudson that she needed help at the market; so he went down there. After a while she came back, ahead of him, and she told me to come into the parlor, where she sat down.

"Well, Quash," she said to me, "the last few days have been sad."

"I'm very sorry about the Boss," I said.

"I'm sure you are," she answered. She was quiet for a moment, as if she was thinking. "It was sad for me, Quash, to discover that my husband meant to dispossess me and turn me out of my home; and that my own family were party to it." She gave me a cold stare. Then she looked down. "It was sad for me too, Quash, when you disobeyed me yesterday, and ran off with that Indian belt. Perhaps you knew about that English will, and you supposed that since you and your son would be free, you could now insult me as you pleased."

"The Boss just told me that Hudson and I should be free when he died," I said. For that was true.

"Well," she said, and her voice was calm, "I have decided otherwise. Hudson is already sold."

I just stared at her, trying to take in her meaning.

"Sold?" I said.

"Yes," she said. "To a ship's captain. He is already on board."

"I'd like to see him," I said.

"No," she answered me.

Just then there was a tap on the door, and a gray-haired gentleman came in and bowed to the Mistress. I knew I'd seen him before, and then I remembered—it was the English planter that Mr. Master had brought to the house one time, years ago. The Mistress nodded to him and turned to me.

"Since I am now the owner of everything that was my husband's—unless a judge can tell me otherwise—you also belong to me, Quash. And whatever my husband may have said, since you have disobeyed me, I have decided to sell you. This gentleman happened to be in the market today, and he has bought you. You will go with him at once."

I was so shocked I couldn't speak a word. I must have looked round, as though I was wanting to escape.

"I have two men with me," the planter said sharply. "Don't try any of that."

I still couldn't believe the Mistress would do such a thing to me.

"Mistress," I cried, "after all these years . . ."

But she just turned her head away.

"That's it. Bring him now," the planter called out; and two men came into the room. One was about my size, but I could tell he was very strong. The other was a giant of a man.

"I got to get my things," I mumbled.

"Hurry," said the planter. "Go with him," he told the two men.

So I collected my possessions, including my little store of money that I'd always hidden away safe. And I was afraid they would take that, but they didn't. I was still in a daze as they led me out to a cart and drove me away.

✦

The planter had a farm about ten miles north of Manhattan. The building was a Dutch farmhouse with a hip roof. But the English planter had added a wide covered veranda all around it. He had half a dozen slaves, who were kept in a low wooden shed near the cow pen.

When we arrived, the planter said I should take my shirt off, so he could inspect me; and he did so. "Well," he said, "you ain't young, but you look strong enough. I dare say we shall get some years of work out of you." They were leading me toward the slave shed when he said: "Stop." There was a big post in the ground just there, and suddenly his two men took my arms and put my wrists in a pair of manacles hanging in chains from the top of the post.

"Now then, nigger," the planter said to me. "Your mistress tells me that you stole from her and that you tried to run off. Well, that kind of thing won't be allowed here, you understand?" And he nodded to the shorter man, who was the foreman. And the foreman went into the house through the veranda, and he came out with a terrible-looking whip. "So now you are going to learn some good behavior," said the planter. And I was looking around, unable to believe this was happening. "Turn your face back," the planter said.

And then the foreman gave me the first lash.

I had never been struck with a whip before. That only time the Boss had given me a whipping, when I was a boy, had been with his belt. But the whip is nothing like that at all.

When that whip lashed across my back, it was like a terrible fire, and a tearing of flesh, and I was so surprised and shocked by it that I screamed out.

Then I heard the whip whistle and crack again. But this lash was worse than the first. And I leaped half out of my skin. And as I did so, I saw the planter watching me to see how I was taking it. The third lash was so terrible I thought I was going to burst with the pain of it; my head jerked back so hard, and I felt my eyes starting out of my head. And they paused for a moment, and my whole body was shaking, and I thought maybe they'd done with it. And then I saw the planter nod to the foreman as if to say, "That's about right."

"I never stole," I cried out. "I don' deserve this."

But the lash fell again, and after that again, and again. I was on fire. My body was straining and slamming into the post in agony. My hands were clenching so hard on the manacles that the blood was coming from my fingers. By the time he had given me a dozen lashes I thought I was going to die; but still he went on until he had given me twenty lashes.

Then the planter came close and stared at me.

"Well, nigger boy," he said, "what have you got to say?"

And I was just hanging there against that post, at over fifty years of age, whipped for the first time in my life. And all my dignity was gone.

"I'm sorry, Boss," I cried. "I'll do whatever you say."

"Don't call me Boss," he said. "I'm not a damn Dutchman."

"No, sir," I whispered. And if I had anger in me, that whipping was so terrible that I would have licked up the dust if he'd told me to. And as I looked into his eyes, I was so desperate.

"Don't speak to me," he said, "unless I tell you to. And when you speak to me, you thieving buck nigger son of a bitch, you look down at the ground. Don't you ever dare look me in the face again. Will you remember that?" Then, as I looked down at the ground, he called to the foreman: "Give him something to make him remember that."

Then the foreman gave me ten more lashes. At the end I believe I fainted, for I do not remember being taken down and thrown into the shed.

⁜

I worked half a year at that farm. The work was hard. During the winter when the snows came, the planter had a forge and we slaves were taught to make nails, which we did for ten hours a day; and those nails were sold. We were always put to work earning him money in some way. He fed us enough and kept us warm, so we could work. And even if we'd thought of it, we were too tired by the end of the day to give any trouble. I wasn't whipped again; but I knew that if I gave him any cause, he'd do it, and more.

And all this made me consider how fortunate I had been during the years when I was owned by the Boss—when every year men like Mr. Master were taking maybe thousands of Negroes to the plantations, where conditions would be similar, or worse. And it filled me with sadness to think that this was the lonely life, without their children, that my parents must have known.

In the spring, we were put back to work in the fields again, digging and plowing. And I was at work about noon one day, all caked in mud, when I saw a light covered cart rolling up the lane, and a man and a woman get out and go into the house. Some time later the planter came out and shouted to me to come over, so I hurried to him. And as I stood in front of him, taking care to look down at the ground, I heard a rustle of a dress on the veranda; but I daren't look up to see who it was, and then I heard a voice I knew saying: "Why, Quash, don't you know me?" And I realized it was Miss Clara.

❖

"You've changed, Quash," Miss Clara said to me, as she and Mr. Master brought me back to New York. "Did he mistreat you?"

I was still too ashamed of being whipped to tell her, so I said: "I'm all right, Miss Clara."

"It took us a while to find out where you were," she told me. "My mother refused to tell who she sold you to. I had people asking all over town. We only found out the other day."

I asked if they knew anything of Hudson.

"He was sold to a sea captain, but we don't know who. He could be anywhere. I'm sorry, Quash," she said. "You may have lost him."

I couldn't speak for a moment.

"It was good of you to come for me," I said.

"I had to pay quite a price for you," said young Henry Master with a laugh. "The old planter knew we wanted you, so he did me no favors."

"We know you were supposed to have your freedom," said Miss Clara.

"Hmm," said her husband. "I don't know about that. Not after what I just had to pay. But we still have to decide what to do with you, Quash."

It seemed that the difficulty was the Mistress. Recently she had gone upriver all the way to Schenectady, intending to live there. She chose that place on account of the fact that it had a strong Dutch church and a town with hardly any English in it. "So long as she stays up there, we can keep you with us, or at my brother's," explained Miss Clara. "But my brother doesn't want her coming back and finding you back. It might make her angry, and she still controls everything at present. I'm sorry you can't be free," she added.

"It don't matter, Miss Clara," I said. For I was better off with them than with that planter. And besides, what was freedom to me now, if my son was still a slave?

❖

Through that spring and summer I worked for Miss Clara and her family. And since I knew how to do most everything about the house, I was very helpful to them.

In particular, I took pleasure in her son Dirk. He was a mischievous little boy, full of life, and I thought I could see something of the Boss in him. He had fair hair and blue eyes like his mother, but you could see already that he had a quickness in him; though when it came to his lessons, he was a little bit lazy. And how that child loved to go by the waterside. He reminded me of my own son. I'd take him down there and let him look at the boats and talk to the sailors. But above all, he liked to go round past the fort so he could look up the river. That river seemed to draw him somehow. For his birthday, which fell in the summer, he was asked what he would like, and he asked if he could go upriver in a boat. So on a fine day young Henry Master and the little boy and me all set out on a big sailing boat; and we went up that mighty river, running before the wind and with the tide, all the way up past the stone palisades. We camped for the night before returning. And during that journey, Dirk was allowed to wear the Indian wampum belt, which we passed round his body three times.

"This belt is important, isn't it, Quash?" Dirk said to me.

"Your grandfather attached great value to it," I answered, "and he gave it to you special, to keep all your life and to pass on in the family."

"I like the patterns on it," he said.

"They say those wampum patterns have a special meaning," I told him, "telling how the Boss was a great man and suchlike. I believe they were given to him by Indians who held him in particular affection. But that's all I know."

I could tell that boy loved to be on the river. He felt at home there. And I hoped that he would make his living on the river rather than with the slaving ships.

And it may be, as it happened, that I was able to affect his life in that regard. For one day, when I was washing in my room in the attic, and thinking myself alone, I heard little Dirk's voice behind me.

"What are all those marks on your back, Quash?"

The whipping at the farm had left terrible scars all over my back, which I always concealed, and I would not have had the boy see them for all the world.

"Something that happened a long time ago," I told him. "You just put it out of your mind, now." And I made him go back downstairs.

But later that day, Miss Clara came by when I was tending some flowers in the garden, and she touched my arm and said, "Oh Quash, I'm so sorry." A couple of days after that I was serving the family at table when little Dirk pipes up, "Father, is it ever right to whip a slave?" And his father looked awkward and muttered, "Well, it all depends." But Miss Clara just said, very quiet, "No, it is never right." And with her character, I knew she wouldn't be changing her mind about that.

Indeed, I heard her say to her husband once that she wouldn't be sorry if the whole business of slavery came to an end. But he answered that as things stood, he reckoned a good part of the wealth of the British Empire depended on the slaves in the sugar plantations, so it wouldn't be ended any time soon.

❖

I stayed with Miss Clara and her husband through that year. During that time there was an outbreak of yellow fever in the city, but fortunately it didn't touch our house. And I remained with them most of the next.

Back in England, both Queen Mary and her husband, Dutch King William, had now died, and so the throne was given to Mary's sister, Anne. And the government at this time thought so highly of the importance of America that they sent out a great gentleman that was cousin to the queen herself, and his name was Lord Cornbury. So Lord Cornbury came to live in New York.

None of this would have affected me if it hadn't been for the Mistress. Nobody knew why—Jan said he reckoned she'd probably quarreled with somebody—but in October she sent a letter, saying she might be returning to New York, and Miss Clara called her brother round to her house to decide what they should do. I was in the parlor with them. "But you'd better not be here, Quash," they both told me, "if she comes."

"We are looking after Quash," said Miss Clara.

"Of course we are," said Jan. "And I think I have the answer. A place where his duties would be light, and he'd be well taken care of." He nodded and gave me a smile. "For I have just been with the governor himself."

"Lord Cornbury?" says Miss Clara.

"No less. It seems that His Lordship is looking for a personal manser-

vant. I told him all about Quash, and he was most interested." He turned
to me. "If you work for him, Quash, you'll be well treated. Not only that.
Governors only stay a few years, then they return to England. If you
please His Lordship, as I know you will, then at the end of his stay, he has
agreed that he'll give you your freedom."

"But what if Lord Cornbury changes his mind and decides to sell
Quash?" Miss Clara objected.

"I thought of that. I have Lord Cornbury's word that if he were not satisfied, he would sell Quash back to us for the price he paid."

"You're sure Quash would be comfortable?" Miss Clara asked.

"Comfortable?" Mr. Master laughed. "He'd live better than we do."

"Quash," said Miss Clara, "if you're not happy, you come straight back
here to me."

"Well," said Jan, "Lord Cornbury hasn't seen Quash yet. But if it goes
well, Quash, I shall be grateful to you, for this will certainly put me in
good standing with the governor."

"I'll do my best," I said.

And so it was that in the space of only a year and a half, I passed from
the ownership of that cruel planter into the household of the governor
himself.

⁜

His Lordship belonged to the ancient family of Hyde, and was the son
and heir of the Earl of Clarendon, the queen's uncle. So he was one of the
royal family. But there was nothing proud about him. He was always gracious, even to a slave like me. He was somewhat tall, of a good build, with
dark hair and large brown eyes. He would have been swarthy if he had not
been carefully shaved each day—and it was one of my duties to shave
him. I had never lived in the house of an aristocrat, and so I was often
observing him, both to study how I could please him, and to see what he
would do next.

I soon learned why Jan was anxious to please Lord Cornbury. "I am a
Tory," His Lordship would say with a smile. "I favor the queen and her
court. How could it be otherwise when I am her cousin?" He was partial
to the greater families who were English in their manners and favored
them with offices, contracts, and land. On this account, the many lesser
Dutch in the city who still remembered poor Meinheer Leisler did not
like Lord Cornbury. And I think he had no great liking for them. But for-

tunately I spoke English well enough, and after so many years close to the Boss, I knew how to make a master feel comfortable with me.

His Lordship and his wife had had five children, but only two were still living: Edward, who was a boy of twelve when I arrived, and a handsome, dark-haired girl of eight named Theodosia. Edward was mostly with his tutor, and Theodosia with her mother; my duties concerned His Lordship only. He was an easy master, for though he insisted upon good order, he always explained what he wanted, and he told me if he was pleased. He was always polite with the people who came to see him; yet I could tell that behind his good manners, he was ambitious.

"A governor should leave his mark," I once heard him say.

In particular, he was anxious to build up the Anglican Church. The vestrymen of Trinity, who included some of the greatest merchants, were often with him, and he gave that church a big stretch of land running up the west side of the city. And he had Broadway paved with fine cobble-stones all the way from Trinity to Bowling Green, in front of the fort. He also put Anglican clergymen into some of the churches of the Presbyterians and the Dutch—which those people did not like at all. But that didn't trouble him. "Gentlemen," he told them, "I am sorry, but it's what the queen wants." It was all part of his plan. I was in the room one day when he addressed the Trinity vestrymen. "New York is English in name," he said, "and we look to you and to the Anglican clergy to make it so in fact."

He wasn't proud, but he liked to do things in style. The governor's residence in the fort had some good rooms, but it wasn't elegant. "This house really won't do," he would say. One day we took a boat across to Nut Island, which is only a short distance from the tip of Manhattan, and as he walked about among the chestnut trees there, he said to me, "This is a delightful place, Quash. Delightful." And in no time at all, he had them building a beautiful house on a knoll out there. Soon they were calling it Governor's Island after that.

Of course, it had to be paid for. But a tax for the city defenses had just brought in over a thousand pounds; so he used that. Some of the merchants that paid the taxes were angry, but he didn't care. "No one is attacking us at present," he said.

During this time, I would still see Miss Clara and the family now and then, but there was no further word about the Mistress—until one day in Wall Street I saw Jan. "She came back, Quash," he told me. "She came

back and discovered all the governor's been doing for the Anglicans
against the Dutch, and in three days she was gone to Schenectady again
and says she'll never return." He was laughing. "God bless Lord Cornbury," he says.

And I had reason to be grateful to His Lordship too. For one day, seeing me looking sad, he asked me what was the matter, and I told him I
was wondering what became of my Hudson. And what did he do, but
cause letters to be sent to every port in the world where the English
traded, and every English naval vessel, to make inquiries for him. "It will
take time, and I promise you nothing," he said, "but we can try." He was
a kindly man.

⁘

I had been with him more than a year when he surprised me.

Lady Cornbury was a slim, elegant lady. She and I did not have occasion to speak much, but she was always polite with me. I knew she gave
His Lordship some anxiety. I'd find him standing by a table piled with her
unpaid bills, muttering: "How are these to be settled?" For His Lordship
was not as rich as people supposed. But when he and Her Ladyship were
alone, you could hear them laughing together.

One day His Lordship told me that he and Her Ladyship would be
supping alone with two friends who were just arrived from London. That
evening, after I had shaved him carefully and laid out his clothes, he told
me: "I shan't need you now, Quash. I want you to go down to open the
door for the guests, and wait at table." Accordingly I opened the door to
the English gentleman and his wife, and took them into the main reception room where Her Ladyship was waiting, before His Lordship was yet
down. After a while, Her Ladyship informed me that there was to be
another, secret guest, a great personage, and that I was to open the door
and announce her. And when she told me who I must announce, I almost
fainted. But I did as she said, and opened the door, and sure enough the
great personage was there, so I turned and announced loudly: "Her
Majesty, the Queen."

And before my eyes, in walked Queen Anne. Except, as she passed me,
I realized it was His Lordship.

He was wearing a dress that belonged to Her Ladyship. It was somewhat tight, but he carried it very well. And I must say he moved grace-

fully. He was wearing a woman's wig. And after I had shaved him, he had so powdered, rouged, and painted his face that he really might have passed for a very handsome woman.

"By God, Corny!" cried the English gentleman. "You gave me a start. Your height gives you away, but you do look uncommonly like her. Astounding!"

"She is my cousin german, you know," said His Lordship, very pleased with himself.

"Show us your leg," demanded the English lady. And so His Lordship lifted his skirts and showed us his leg which, in silk stocking, looked very fine. And then he moved his leg about in a manner which almost made me blush. "Why, Corny," she laughed, "you could have been a woman."

"Sometimes," said Her Ladyship quietly, "he is."

Now His Lordship moved around the room, curtsied to his guests, and was applauded.

I served them supper, and they were all very merry, His Lordship taking off his wig, saying it was damnable hot, and telling stories about the people they all knew at the English court. And I was glad to see them happy, for I guessed that, although they had a great position in New York, the governor and his lady must miss the theater and the court and their friends in London.

⁘

It seemed that His Lordship was pleased with the evening. For a month later, he arranged another. I helped him prepare, and he struggled considerably with Her Ladyship's dress, which was too tight for him. "We shall have to do something about this," he said to me.

This time he had two gentlemen from the great Dutch families of the English party, a van Cortlandt and a Philipse. They were much astonished when the queen entered, and neither of them having seen that lady, for a minute or two they did not realize the jest. I don't think they enjoyed His Lordship's performance, though, being polite, they didn't say so.

As before, this took place in the governor's house in the fort; and after the guests were gone, His Lordship had a desire to take the air, and told me to come with him up on the battlement of the fort that looked over the harbor.

It was a fine night, with the stars sparkling in the sky over the water.

There was one sentry up there. He glanced at us, supposing that it must be Her Ladyship; and then, realizing it was not, he stared harder, but he couldn't make out who this tall lady was, in the dark.

"It must have been here," His Lordship remarked to me, "that Stuyvesant stood when the English came to take the city."

"I believe so, My Lord," I said.

He stayed there a while, and then we walked back. As we passed the sentry, the governor said, "Goodnight." And hearing a man's voice, I saw that sentry almost jump out of his skin. He was certainly staring after us as we departed. And after we came down, I said to His Lordship that the sentry had been astonished hearing a man's voice coming from a lady, and that I wondered if he would realize who it was. But His Lordship just laughed and said, "Did we give him a fright?" And then I understood that in his heart, being such an aristocrat, the governor didn't think it mattered what the sentry thought. And I realized this was a weakness in him.

From these evenings I also understood two other things. The first, that it pleased His Lordship to remind people that the queen was his cousin and that he looked like her. The second, that, as Queen Anne or not, he liked to dress as a woman.

✦

Anyway, I was in favor with the governor after this; and he had not forgotten that it was through the van Dyck family that I had come to him. For one day he summoned Jan to the fort. I was serving in the room when Jan came in. There were a number of government contracts to be given out at that time, and His Lordship calmly picked up one of them, and handed it to him.

"You served me well in selling me Quash," he said. "Perhaps you could supply Her Majesty's government these goods."

As Jan read the contract, I saw his eyes open wide.

"Your Lordship is very kind," he answered. "I am in your debt."

"Then perhaps," said His Lordship, "you'd like to do something for me." And he waited.

"I should like very much," said Jan warmly, "to give Your Lordship fifty pounds, if Your Lordship would do me the honor of accepting it."

So His Lordship graciously said he would. And all this was very interesting to me, as explaining how the business of government is done.

✤

I continued to study His Lordship carefully, as to how I might please him; and soon after this I had a lucky chance when, passing one of the tailors in Dock Street, I saw in a store a large silk petticoat which I estimated might fit His Lordship very well. Having always kept any money which came my way, I had no difficulty buying it; and that very evening when we were alone, I gave it to His Lordship. "It's for the next time Your Lordship should be Her Majesty," I said.

He was very delighted, and tried it on at once. "All I need," he said, "is a dress as big."

I had noticed that each time he had dressed as the queen, his children were out of the house. So I guessed that His Lordship still had some fears as to what people might think of his habit. I was careful therefore never to let him see any trace of mockery in my own manner toward him. A week after I gave him the petticoat, he wore it under a dress for supper alone with Her Ladyship, and as I was helping him dress beforehand, he asked me: "Do you find it strange I dress like this?"

"In Africa, My Lord," I said, "where my people come from, in certain tribes, the great chiefs sometimes dress as women. But only they are allowed to do it. We count that a sign of special distinction." I invented this, but His Lordship didn't know it.

"Oh," he said; and he looked very pleased.

Some months passed; and from time to time His Lordship would perform as the queen, or occasionally he would just choose to walk about in women's clothes.

It was during this year that Her Ladyship started to be unwell. The doctors did not know what was wrong with her, so they bled her, and gave her herbal cures, and said that she must rest. The business of the household went on much the same. His Lordship would often attend to his son's studies, or keep Theodosia company by reading to her in the evenings. But I did notice that, with Her Ladyship being unwell, His Lordship would sometimes be restless at night, and walk about in his room alone; and I know that when he did so, he would often be dressed as a woman.

✤

I had for some time been wondering if there was a way I might put this situation to my use; and one day when I was in the market, who should I see but Violet, the mulatto woman from the East River that I used to go with. She looked a lot older now, but I recognized her, and she knew me. She had a little girl with her, of maybe nine years old, that was her grand-daughter. "Would she be my granddaughter too?" I asked her quietly. And she laughed and said, "Maybe." This little girl's name was Rose.

Well, it seemed that this Rose was wonderfully quick with the needle, and Violet was looking for someone to give her regular work. And when I told her I belonged to the governor now, she was wondering if I couldn't do something for her.

"Wait a while," I said, "and I'll see."

·:·

I started my work the next day. Using a framework of thin sticks, like wickerwork, I began to make a rough model of the governor's body. Fortunately, having always been good with my hands, the task was easy enough. Taking one of his shirts, I was able to adjust this to make it perfect. Then I bought lengths of silk and of lining. This cost me a good deal of my savings, but I was confident of getting a return. After this, I borrowed an old dress of Her Ladyship's, which I knew she never used. Then I loaded all these items onto a cart and took them up to Violet's.

"Her Ladyship wishes to give a dress to a friend out on Long Island," I told her. "This is the shape of her body, but we are not sure of her height, so the dress must be left long, and we can hem it later." Then I showed her the dress I'd borrowed, to use as a model for the design, and told her that if Rose could do it she'd be well paid. "She can do it," said Violet. So I told them I'd be back in two weeks.

And sure enough, when I returned, it was done. And I returned to His Lordship, and told him I had a dress which I thought would fit him better. When he saw the dress, he stared at the material and ran his hand over the silk, and said I had chosen very well. The fit was perfect. I hemmed it then and there myself, and His Lordship was delighted.

"It cost a bit, My Lord," I told him, and named a figure that was less than any of the dressmakers in the town would have charged. He gave me the money on the spot. The next day, I paid Rose for her work—a small amount, but enough to please her. And then I waited.

As it happened, Her Ladyship seemed to get better at this time. His Lordship and she resumed their normal life. Several times he wore that dress at supper, and remained entirely satisfied. But after a while, as I had expected, he asked me if I couldn't get him another. I said I reckoned I could. But the next day I came in with a long face.

"There's a difficulty, Your Lordship," I told him. I explained that the dressmaker where I'd got the dress was getting suspicious. Wasn't I the governor's slave, she had asked, and told me that if Her Ladyship wanted a dress, they would not give her credit. His Lordship groaned when I said that. "But they were wanting to know who the dress would be for," I told him, "and I did not like the look in the dressmaker's eye, so I said I would have to consult Her Ladyship," I said.

Now although I had invented this tale, His Lordship knew that he was becoming more and more unpopular among the Dutch and the Presbyterians, and many others. He had enemies. So did Her Ladyship, on account of the unpaid bills. And there had also been a few rumors about His Lordship's strange dressing, enough to make even a proud man like His Lordship cautious.

"You did right," he said to me. "I suppose we'd better leave this for a while." I could see he was disappointed, though.

So I waited another few days. Then, one evening when he was looking a little sad, I made my move.

"I've been thinking, Your Lordship," I said. "There might be an answer to our problem."

"Oh?" he said.

"Yes," I said. For I had always considered, I told him, that if ever I became free, I might open a little store in the town, to sell all kinds of goods for ladies, and make dresses as well. I believed that Jan and Miss Clara would stake me and send me customers; and I already had a seamstress in mind that I could employ. "If I had that business," I said, "I could make Your Lordship any dresses you want, and there'd be no one to ask questions. For people wouldn't see me as Your Lordship's slave any more. Nobody except me would know I was even supplying you. I could supply Her Ladyship too. And naturally, where Your Lordship is concerned, I wouldn't be looking for profit. I'd supply Your Lordship and Her Ladyship at cost."

"At cost?" he said, and I nodded.

"Not only dresses, Your Lordship. Petticoats, silk stockings, anything you and Your Ladyship might like," I said.

"Hmm," said His Lordship. "And the price for this is to give you your freedom?"

"I couldn't do it otherwise," I said.

"I will consider it," he said.

Now you may think I was taking a risk in offering to supply Her Lady-ship, given that her bills were not always paid. But I reckoned that His Lordship would take good care to pay my bills, if he wanted any more dresses.

⁜

The next day, I get a summons to go to the small sitting room. I was expecting to find His Lordship there. But it was Her Ladyship. She was sitting in a chair, and she gave me a thoughtful look.

"His Lordship has told me about your conversation," she said. "And I have one concern."

"Your Ladyship?" I asked.

"Yes. By making you free, His Lordship would have no sanction against you if you were to talk. You know what I mean." And she looked me straight in the eye. "I must protect him," she said.

She was right, of course. His Lordship was placing himself in my power. And I admired her for saying it. So I was silent for a moment. Then I took my shirt off. I saw her eyes open wide when I did that. But then I turned round, and I heard her give a little gasp as she saw the scars on my back.

"That is what a planter did to me, Your Ladyship," I said, "before I came here. And truth to tell, My Lady, I would kill that planter, if I could do it."

"Oh," she said.

"But in this house," I continued, "I have received nothing but kind-ness." And I said this with some emotion, because it was true. "And if His Lordship gives me my freedom, which I have been wanting all my life, I'd rather be whipped again than repay him with treachery."

Well, she gave me a long look, and then she said: "Thank you, Quash." And I put on my shirt again, and bowed to her, and left.

⁜

So that is how, in the year 1705, at around the age of fifty-five, I finally obtained my freedom. It all worked out as I expected. Jan was good to me, and helped me rent a store on Queen Street, which is a good part of the town, and he showed me how to buy the best goods; and Miss Clara was sending me so many customers that I had my hands full. Not only did I employ little Rose, but soon I had two more like her as well. Their being young, I didn't have to pay them much, but they were glad of the regular work, and soon I was making good money.

And from this and all that went before, I learned that, if you give people what they want, it can make you free.

The following year, Her Ladyship died. And I was sorry for that. The year afterward, His Lordship's party fell from office in London. And as soon as they learned this, all His Lordship's enemies in New York sent urgently to London begging to have His Lordship removed from office on account of all the debts he still owed. They also said that he was dressing in women's clothes, for those rumors were growing too—though no one ever heard any word of that from me. They even threw His Lordship in the debtors' jail.

Fortunately for him, his father died, and he became the Earl of Clarendon, which being a full peerage of England means, under English law, that he cannot be prosecuted—which is a fine trick, I must say. And he is safe back in England now.

Jan and Miss Clara continued to be helpful to me, letting me know if cargoes of silk fabrics or other goods arrived in the port, and helping me get some pieces at cost price. So I wasn't surprised, soon after His Lordship had left for England, when I got a message that Jan had some goods for me if I would come round to his house that day.

As it happened, Miss Clara was also there when I arrived, and we went into the parlor.

"I've bought some goods I think might interest you, Quash," he said. "And Clara thinks you'll like them too."

I knew she had a good eye, so I was eager to see them.

"Well, here they are," he said. And I heard the parlor door open, and I turned. And in walked my son Hudson.

"The captain of one of Mr. Master's privateers bought him off a ship down in Jamaica," explained Mr. Jan. "Do you want him?"

Hudson was looking so fine and strong, and he was smiling. And I think Miss Clara was smiling too, or she may have been crying; but I'm not sure, because suddenly my eyes were full of tears and so I couldn't see too well.

But after we had embraced, I had to make sure I understood.

"So now Hudson belongs to . . . ?"

"Hudson is free," said Miss Clara. "We bought him and now we're giving him to you."

"He's free, then," I said, and for a moment or two I couldn't speak.

But then—I don't know why—the idea came into my mind that I wasn't satisfied. I knew that they meant kindly to me and to Hudson. I also knew, from all that I had lived through in my own life, that this traffic in human beings in which Mr. Master was engaged was a terrible thing. In my heart I considered that neither he nor any man should have the ownership of another; and if he gave up even one slave, so much the better. And I knew that I wanted my Hudson's freedom more than I had ever wanted even my own. Yet despite all these considerations, I knew that in my mind I was not satisfied with this transaction.

"I thank you for your kindness," I said to Mr. Master. "But I am his father, and I should like to buy the freedom of my son."

I saw Jan glance at Miss Clara.

"He cost me five pounds," he said. I was sure that this was too low a figure, but I said he should have it, and I gave him the first part of the payment that very evening.

"Now your father has bought your freedom," I told my son. I don't know if it was right or wrong, but that purchase meant a lot to me.

⁙

That was two years ago. I am sixty years of age now, which is older than many men live, and far older than most slaves. Recently, my health has not been so good, but I think I have some time remaining to me yet, and my business thrives. My son Hudson has a little inn just above Wall Street, and he does well. I know he would rather go to sea, but he stays here to please me; and he has a wife and a little son now, so maybe they will keep him here. Each year, we go to Miss Clara's house for the birthday of young Dirk, and I see him put on the wampum belt.

The Boston Girl

T HE TRIAL WOULD begin tomorrow. The jury had been rigged
by the governor. Handpicked stooges of his own. Conviction guaranteed. The first jury, that is.

For when the two judges saw it—though they were friends of Governor Cosby themselves—they threw the stooges out and started again. The
new jury was not rigged. The trial would be honest. British fair play. New
York might be a long way from London, but it was English, after all.

The whole colony was waiting with baited breath.

Not that it mattered. The defendant hadn't a hope.

✦

The third day of August, the year of Our Lord 1735. The British Empire
was enjoying the Georgian age. For after Queen Anne, her equally Protestant kinsman, George of Hanover, had been asked to take the throne; and
soon been followed by his son, a second George, who was ruler of the
empire now. It was an age of confidence, and elegance, and reason.

The third day of August 1735: New York, on a hot and humid afternoon.

Seen from across the East River, it might have been a landscape by Vermeer. The long, low line of the distant wharfs, which still bore names like
Beekman and Ten Eyck—the step-gabled rooftops, squat storehouses and
sailing ships at anchor—made a peaceful picture in the watery silence. In
the panorama's center, Trinity Church's graceful little steeple seemed to
offer a pinprick to the sky.

In the streets, however, the scene was far from peaceful. Ten thousand people lived in New York now, and the place was growing bigger every year. Wall Street, on the line of the former ramparts, was only halfway up the waterfront. West of Broadway, orchards and neat Dutch gardens remained, but on the eastern side, the brick and wooden houses were tightly crammed together. Pedestrians had to thread between stoops and stalls, water barrels and swinging shutters, and dodge the wheels of the carts churning their way over the dirt or cobbled roadway to the noisy market.

But above all, for anyone in the streets, the wretchedness came from the fetid air. Horse droppings, cowpats, slops from the houses, and garbage and grime, dead cats and birds, excrement of every kind, lay strewn on the ground, waiting for the rain to wash it all away, or the sun to bake it to powder. And on a hot and steamy day, from this putrid mess, a soupy stench arose, fermented by the sun, creeping up wooden walls and fences, impregnating brick and mortar, choking every ventricle, stinging the eyes, rising to the roof gables.

This was the smell of summer in New York.

But by God it was British. A man gazing at it across the East River might be near the village of Brooklyn where Dutch was still spoken, but he was situated in Kings County nonetheless, and the next county upriver was Queens. Behind Manhattan island, he would see the mainland across the Hudson River. And for that territory, Charles II of England himself had chosen the name New Jersey.

Within the city, the Dutch, step-gabled houses of New Amsterdam were still charmingly to be seen, especially below Wall Street; but the newer houses were in the simple, English Georgian style. The old Dutch City Hall had also been succeeded by a classical building that sat on Wall and gazed complacently down Broad Street. One might hear Dutch spoken by the market stalls, but not in the merchants' houses.

With English language went English liberties. The city had a royal charter, with the king's own seal on it. True, a former governor had demanded a bribe to procure this royal recognition, but you expected that sort of thing. And once such a charter was granted and sealed, the free men of the city could point to it for the rest of time. They elected their city councillors; they were free-born Englishmen.

Some people in New York might have said that this English freedom was less than perfect. The ever-growing number of slaves sold in the market at the foot of Wall Street might have said so; but they were Negroes who, New Yorkers were now generally agreed, were an inferior people. The women of New York—those who still remembered the old Dutch laws which made them equal to their menfolk—may also have regretted their inferior status under British law. But honest Englishmen were well assured that such complaints from the weaker sex were unseemly.

No: what mattered was escaping the tyranny of kings. Puritans and Huguenots were equally agreed. No Louis, King of France; no Catholic James. The Glorious Revolution of 1688 had established that the Protestant British Parliament would oversee the king. As for English common law, the right to trial by jury, and to assemblies that could refuse oppressive taxes, why some of those ancient rights went back five hundred years, to Magna Carta or before. In short, the men of New York were just as free as the good fellows back in England who had cut their king's head off, not a century ago, when he tried to be a tyrant.

That was why the trial, taking place tomorrow, was so important.

·÷·

The two men walked along the road together. The man in the tightly buttoned brown coat seemed uncomfortable. Perhaps it was just the heat. Or perhaps something else was worrying him.

Mr. Eliot Master of Boston was a good man, who cared about his children. He was also a cautious lawyer. He would smile, certainly, when it was appropriate; and laugh when it was called for, though not too loud and not too long. So it was unusual for him to worry that he might have made a terrible mistake.

He had only just met his New York cousin for the first time, but already he had reservations about Dirk Master. He'd always known that their grandfathers, his namesake Eliot and Dirk's grandfather Tom, had gone their separate ways. The Boston Masters had never had any contact with the Masters of New York. But as he was going to visit New York, Eliot had wondered whether enough time had passed to reestablish relations. Before writing to his kinsman, however, he had made some inquiries about these people, and ascertained that the merchant was a man of fortune. That was a relief, for Eliot would have been disappointed to have a kinsman who did not do well. But as to his character, well, that remained to be seen.

As it was a hot day, the merchant was wearing the light and simple coat called a banyan: sober enough. But the silk vest under it had concerned the lawyer. Too colorful. His periwig was too flamboyant, his cravat too loosely tied. Did these things suggest a character lacking in gravitas? Though his kinsman had warmly invited him to stay at his house while he attended the trial in New York, Eliot Master had instead made arrangements to stay with a reliable lawyer he knew; and seeing his cousin's silk vest, he considered the choice had been wise.

You wouldn't have guessed they were cousins. Dirk was large, and fair, with prominent teeth, and an air of genial confidence. Eliot was of medium size, his hair brown, his face broad and serious.

In Boston, the Master family lived on Purchase Street. Eliot was a deacon of the Old South Congregation Church, and a selectman. He was familiar with business. How could you not be, among the wharfs and watermills of Boston? His wife's brother was a brewer—a good, solid enterprise, fortunately. But, as a graduate of the Boston Latin School and Harvard University, it was education and sound ethics that Eliot valued.

He wasn't sure that his New York cousin possessed either.

Cautious though he was, Eliot Master was ready to stand up for principle. About slavery, for instance, he was firm. "Slavery is wrong," he told his children. The fact that, even in Boston, about one person in ten was now a slave, made no difference to him at all. There were none in his house. Unlike many of the stern Boston men of the past, he would tolerate freedom in religion, so long as it was Protestant. Above all, like his Puritan ancestors before him, he was vigilant against any attempt at tyranny by the king. This was why he was here in New York, to witness the trial.

✢

It had been proper of his cousin to ask him and his daughter to dinner that day, and useful that, while Kate rested at their lodgings, Dirk was showing him round the town. The merchant was certainly well informed; and clearly proud of his city. Having walked up Broadway and admired Trinity Church, they had taken the road north as it followed the line of the ancient Indian track, until they were nearing the old pond.

"The land to the east was all swamp a couple of years ago," the merchant told him. "But my friend Roosevelt bought it, and look at it now." The area had been drained and laid out as handsome streets.

Such development was impressive, the lawyer remarked, when he'd heard how New York's trade had been suffering in recent years.

"Trade is bad at present," the merchant acknowledged. "The sugar planters in the West Indies were too greedy and overproduced. Many have gone under, so that our own trade, which lies chiefly in supplying them, has been badly hit. Then those damn fellows in Philadelphia are supplying flour at lower prices than we can." He shook his head. "Not good."

Since New York had been stealing away Boston's trade for half a century, the Bostonian could not entirely suppress a smile at New York's present discomfort.

"You still do well, though?" he asked.

"I'm a general trader," said his cousin. "The slave trade's still good."

Eliot Master was silent.

On their way back, they passed by Mill Street, and Dirk Master indicated a building there.

"That's the synagogue," he said, easily. "Not a bad building. They have two communities, you know: the Sephardics, who came here first from Brazil—rather gentlemanly; and the Ashkenazim, Germans—not gentlemen, but more of them. So they elect an Ashkenazi as president of the congregation, but the services are Sephardic. God knows if the Germans understand them. Funny really, don't you think?"

"I do not think a man's religion is a laughing matter," said the lawyer, quietly.

"No. Of course. Wasn't quite what I meant."

It might not have been. But the Boston man thought he detected in the merchant's manner a hint of moral carelessness—confirmation that he'd been right to have reservations about that silk vest.

They were about to part, when Dirk Master suddenly stopped, and pointed.

"There he is," he cried. And seeing Eliot look puzzled, he smiled. "That young devil," he explained, "is my son."

The lawyer stared in horror.

Eliot Master would never admit to having a favorite, but of his five children, he loved his daughter Kate the best. She had the most brains—though he thought it a pity they should be wasted on a girl. He liked his women to read and think, but only to the degree that would be considered appropriate. She also had a sweet nature, almost to a fault. At the age of five, she had been distressed by the poor folk she had seen in Boston. Well and good. But it had taken him three years of patient explaining to make her understand there was a difference between the deserving and the undeserving poor.

He was anxious, therefore, to find the right husband for Kate. A man intelligent, kind and firm. At one time, he had considered his respected neighbor's son, young Samuel Adams, although the boy was a few years younger than Kate. But he had soon seen that there was a waywardness and lack of application in the boy that ruled him out. As Kate was now eighteen, her father was all the more careful that she should never be taken to any place where she might form an unfortunate attachment.

Naturally, therefore, he had hesitated to bring her to New York, where the presence of these cousins, about whom he knew little, might add to the risk.

But she had begged to come. She wanted to attend the trial, and she certainly understood the legal issues far better than the rest of his children. She would be safely with him all the time, and he had to admit he was always glad of her company. So he'd agreed.

Before him, not fifty yards away, he now saw a tall fair-haired youth, accompanied by three common sailors, coming out of a tavern. He saw one of the sailors laugh, and slap the youth on the back. Far from objecting, the young man, who was wearing a shirt that was none too clean, made some cheerful jibe and laughed in turn. As he did so, he half turned, allowing the lawyer a clear sight of his face. He was handsome. He was more than handsome.

He looked like a young Greek god.

"Your daughter must be about the same age," the merchant said cheerfully. "I expect they'll get on. We'll expect you for dinner then, at three."

❖

Kate Master looked at herself in the glass. Some of the girls she knew got little dressmaker's dolls with the latest fashions from Paris and London. Her father would never have allowed such vanities in the house. But if she dressed more simply, she was still pleased with the result. Her figure was good. Her breasts were pretty—not that anyone would see them, because a lace modesty piece covered all but the tops. The material of her bodice and skirt was a russet silk, worn over a creamy chemise, that suited her coloring. Her brown hair was arranged simply and naturally; her shoes had heels, but not too high, and round toes, because her father did not approve of the new pointed shoes that were the latest fashion. Kate had a fresh complexion; and she'd used powder so lightly, she didn't think her father would notice.

She wanted to look well for these New York cousins. She wondered if there would be any young men of her age.

⁕

When they arrived at the house in the fashionable South Ward near the old fort, Kate and her father were both impressed. The house was handsome. Above a basement were two floors, five bays across, simple and classical. A gentleman's house. As they went in, they noticed a big oak cupboard in the hall, obviously Dutch, and two upright chairs from the time of Charles II. In the parlor, there were solemn pictures of Dirk's parents, some shelves holding a black-and-gold tea set from China, and several elegant walnut chairs with tapestry seats, in the Queen Anne style. It all proclaimed that the New York Masters had had their money a good, long time.

Dirk greeted them warmly. His wife was a tall, elegant lady, whose soft voice gently let them know that she was confident of her place in society. And then there was their son, John.

Her father hadn't told Kate about the boy. Though she tried not to do so, she found herself stealing glances at him. He was wearing a spotless white shirt of the best linen, and a green-and-gold silk vest. He wore no wig—and why would he, with his magnificent mane of wavy golden hair? He was the most beautiful young man she had ever seen in her life. He said a few polite words when they were introduced, though she hardly heard them. But he contented himself with listening to his father speak, so she could only wonder what he was thinking.

Before dinner, the conversation was confined to family inquiries. She learned that John had two sisters, both away, but no brothers. He was the heir, then.

The dinner was excellent. The food plentiful, the wine good. Kate was placed on the merchant's right, between him and John. The conversation was general and cordial, but she could tell that everyone was being cautious, anxious not to offend the other party. Mrs. Master remarked that she knew the lawyer they were staying with. And her husband said that he hoped his cousin would find some good legal minds among the members of the New York Bar.

"There are fine minds in New York outside the legal profession," Eliot responded politely. "The fame of Governor Hunter's circle still resounds in Boston, I assure you."

Governor Hunter, who had come after the eccentric Lord Cornbury, had gathered a notable circle of friends, mostly Scots like himself, into a sort of intellectual club. Two decades later, this circle was still reverently spoken of by men of culture in other cities. Kate had often heard her father refer to them. She glanced at the boy on her right. He was looking blank. Beyond him, his mother's stare was vague.

"Ah, Hunter," said their host firmly. "I wish we were always so lucky with our governors."

Hoping to draw young John into the conversation, Kate remarked to him that she noticed more Negroes in New York than Boston. Yes, he answered quietly, about one in five of the city's population were slaves.

"My father does not approve of slavery," she said brightly, and received a warning look from Eliot. But their host intervened in his easy manner.

"You may have noticed that the servants in this house are not Negro slaves, Miss Kate, but Irish servants working out their indentures—to pay for their voyage mostly. However, it's true that I'm in the slave trade. Some of the best Boston families, like the Waldos and Faneuils, are in it too. A Boston merchant I know said his three main lines are Irish butter, Italian wine and slaves."

"My daughter meant no discourtesy, cousin," Eliot said quickly, "and few people in Boston agree with me." Clearly he was determined that the dinner should pass off easily. "Though I do confess," he could not help adding, "that as an Englishman, I can't ignore the fact that a senior British judge has ruled that slavery should not be legal in England."

Dirk Master looked at his Boston cousin thoughtfully. He'd been quite curious to meet him. He himself was the only Master in the male line in New York. His van Dyck cousins had been women who'd married and moved out of the city. So he'd few relations to call his own. This Boston lawyer was certainly a very different kind of man, but he didn't dislike him. That, at least, was a start. His daughter seemed pleasant enough, too. He leaned back in his chair, and considered his words.

"Forty years ago," he said, "my Dutch grandfather was a fur trader. The fur trade still continues, but it's not so important now. My other grandfather, Tom Master, was in the West Indies trade. And that trade has now grown so huge that three-quarters of all the business of this city derives

from supplying the sugar plantations. And sugar plantations need slaves."
He paused. "As to the morality of the slave trade, cousin, I respect your
opinion. My Dutch grandfather intended to free the only two slaves
he had."

Eliot bowed his head noncommittally.

A mischievous twinkle came into the merchant's eye.

"But at the same time, cousin," he continued, "you may acknowledge
that we British are also guilty of a mighty hypocrisy in this matter. For we
say that slavery is monstrous, yet only if it takes place on the island of
Britain. Everywhere else in the British Empire, it's allowed. The sugar
trade, so valuable to England, entirely depends upon slaves; and British
vessels carry thousands every year."

"It cannot be denied," Eliot politely acknowledged.

"Does it concern you, sir," Kate now ventured, "that New York is so
dependent upon a single trade?"

The merchant's blue eyes rested upon her, approvingly.

"Not too much," he answered. "You've heard of the Sugar Interest, I've
no doubt. The big sugar planters have formed a group to influence the
London Parliament. They have huge wealth, so they can do it. They and
their friends sit in the legislature; other Members of Parliament are persuaded or paid. The system reaches into the highest quarters. And this
lobbying, as we may call it, of Parliament has been entirely successful.
During the last few years, while the sugar trade has been down, the British
Parliament has passed two measures to protect it. The greatest is the Rum
Ration. Every man serving aboard a British Navy vessel is now given half
a pint of rum per day. I do not know what this costs the government, but
multiplied across the entire navy and through the whole year, it is a truly
astounding quantity of rum—and therefore of molasses from the plantations." He smiled. "And not only is the Rum Ration their salvation, but
that salvation is eternal. For once you give a sailor the expectation of rum
as his right, he will not be weaned from it. Stop the rum and you'll start a
mutiny. Better still, as the navy grows, so does the rum ration and the fortunes of the sugar planters. So you see, Miss Kate, New York's sure foundation is actually the English Sugar Interest."

Kate glanced at her father. She knew this cynical use of religious words
could not be pleasing to him, though she secretly rather enjoyed the
tough frankness of the merchant's mind.

"You said there was a second measure, sir," she said.

"Yes. The Molasses Act. It says we may only buy molasses from English traders and English ships. That keeps the price of molasses high and protects the English planters. I do not like it so well, because I also manufacture rum here in New York. I could buy my molasses far cheaper from the French traders, if it were allowed." He shrugged.

It was now that young John Master chose to speak.

"Except that we do." He turned to Kate and grinned. "We get molasses from the Frenchies outside the port and smuggle 'em in. 'Tain't legal, of course, but it's what Pa does. I go out on those runs," he assured her, with some pride.

The merchant looked at his son with exasperation.

"That's enough, John," he said loudly. "Now what we should all like to hear," he bowed toward Eliot, "is my cousin's opinion of tomorrow's trial."

Eliot Master looked down at the table. The truth was, he felt a sense of relief. If, before arriving at the house, his secret terror had been that his daughter might take a liking to her handsome cousin, upon entering the house, seeing the young man cleaned up, and realizing that he must be heir to a fortune far larger than his own in Boston, he had been faced with an uncomfortable proposition: whatever his feelings about these New Yorkers and their business, would he really have the right to deny her, if Kate should wish to marry such a rich kinsman? So far, he had been struggling. But now, by his foolish intervention, this boy had just exposed himself and his family for what they were. Not only slavers, but smugglers as well. Their fortune, so much greater than his own, was explained. He would be polite to them, naturally. But as far as Eliot Master was concerned, they were no better than criminals. His duty as a father, therefore, required him only to ensure that his daughter saw this young scoundrel for what he was.

Thus satisfied, he turned his mind to the trial of John Peter Zenger.

If tomorrow's trial was of great consequence for the American colonies, its origins lay in England. Political events in London never took long to affect Boston and New York. As Dirk Master liked to say: "London gives us laws, wars and whores." By "whores," however, he meant the royal governors.

Though there were honorable exceptions, like Governor Hunter, most of these men came to America only to line their pockets, and the colonist knew it. And the present governor was among the worst. Governor Cosby was venal. In no time he had made illegal grabs for money, rigged courts and elections, and thrown out judges who did not give him what he wanted. The only newspaper in the city being under the governor's control, some of the merchants had started another of their own, to attack Cosby and expose his abuses. They'd hired a printer named John Peter Zenger to produce it. The governor was determined to close it down. And to this end, last year, he had thrown Zenger in jail, and was now about to try him for seditious libel.

Eliot Master placed his fingers together. As a lawyer, he saw several issues. "My first comment," he began, "refers to the manner of Zenger's arrest. I understand that he is not a rich man."

"He's a poor immigrant from Palatine Germany," said the merchant. "Trained here as a printer. Though he's turned out to have quite a talent for writing."

"And having arrested him, the governor arranged for his bail to be set at an outrageous sum, which Zenger could in no way afford? And as a result, he has languished in jail for eight months?"

"That's correct."

"Then there is a point of principle here," the Boston lawyer said, "concerning excessive bail. It should not be allowed. But the main issue," he continued, "is that the royal governor has been offended."

"We're all ready to offend this royal governor," his host remarked, "but because poor Zenger printed the paper, he's being used as the scapegoat. Our people are determined to provide him with a good defense. And the new jury are quite decent fellows. I believe seven of them are even Dutch, so no friends of the governor's. Has the fellow a chance?"

"I think not," answered Eliot. "If it can be shown that Zenger did in fact print the offending articles, the law says that the jury must find him guilty."

"There's not much doubt that he printed the piece," said the merchant. "And he's continued to put out new issues of his journal by passing fresh articles to his wife under the door of his cell. But what about the fact that every word he printed about Governor Cosby is true? Shouldn't that count for something?"

"Our British law of libel says that's no defense," the lawyer answered. "And if the words insult the king's representative, they are seditious libel. True or false, it makes no difference."

"That is monstrous," said the merchant.

"Perhaps." Eliot nodded. "My present concern is that the law is being misused. And that is why I am so anxious to see this trial."

"You must be," his cousin remarked, "to come all the way from Boston to see it."

"I will tell you plainly," Eliot Master continued, "I think this no small matter. The Zenger trial, in my opinion, goes to the very root of our English liberties." He paused a moment. "A century ago, our ancestors left England because King Charles I was setting up a tyranny. When Members of Parliament challenged his right, he tried to arrest them; when honest Puritans printed complaints of his sins, he cut off their ears, branded them and threw them in prison—using this very same charge, we should note, of seditious libel. Eighty-five years ago the tyranny of King Charles was ended when Parliament cut off his head. But that did not end all future abuses. And now, in the little tyranny of this governor, we see the same process at work. This trial is sent to us, I believe, as a test of how we value liberty." During this speech, he had raised his voice considerably.

"Well, cousin," said the merchant with a new respect, "I see you are quite an orator."

It was not often that Kate heard her cautious father speak with such passion. It made her feel proud of him. Hoping he would approve, she joined the conversation now.

"So when Locke speaks of natural law, and the natural right to life and liberty, would that not include the liberty to speak one's mind?" she asked.

"I think so," said her father.

"Locke?" queried Mrs. Master, looking bemused.

"Ah, Locke," said their host. "Philosopher," he said to his wife, as he tried to remember something about the thinker whose doctrines, he knew, were inspiring freedom-loving men on both sides of the Atlantic.

"You read philosophy?" Mrs. Master asked Kate, in some perplexity.

"Just the famous bits," said Kate cheerfully, with a smile toward the boy who, she supposed, had done the same. But young John Master only gazed at the table and shook his head.

It was now that Kate decided that the Greek god by her side might be shy. It rather increased her interest. She wondered what she could say to encourage him. But raised in the literary Boston household of her father, she still had not quite comprehended that she was in alien territory.

"Last summer," she remarked to him, "we saw some of the Harvard men perform an act of Addison's *Cato*. I have heard that the whole play is to be given later this year in our American colonies. Do you know if it's coming to New York?" The question was pertinent to the Zenger trial. For Addison, founder of England's *Spectator* magazine, and model for every civilized English gentleman, had scored a huge success with his account of how a noble Roman republican had opposed the tyranny of Caesar. The play's reputation had long since crossed the Atlantic, and she felt sure her companion would have read of it in the newspapers. But all she got was a "Don't know."

"You must forgive us, Miss Kate, if we concern ourselves more with trade than literature in this house," the merchant remarked; though he felt bound to add, with a hint of reproach: "I believe, John, you've heard of Addison's *Cato*."

"Trade holds the key to liberty," the Boston lawyer added firmly, coming to their aid. "Trade spreads wealth, and in so doing, it promotes freedom and equality. That's what Daniel Defoe says."

At last young John looked up with a ray of hope.

"The man that wrote *Robinson Crusoe*?"

"The very same."

"I read that."

"Well then," said the lawyer, "that is something."

⁘

They made no further attempts at literary conversation, but for a time devoted their attention to the three handsome fruit pies that had just been brought in. Yet as he glanced round the table, Eliot Master was not unhappy. He had been quite pleased with his own little oration, and he meant every word of it. His cousin had been quite right that he would not have come here, all the way from Boston, if he was not passionate about the matter. As for his cousin Dirk's character, he might be a rogue, but he evidently wasn't a fool. That at least was something. The merchant's wife, he privately discounted. That left the boy.

It was entirely clear, he thought, that this boy, however good-looking, was of slight intelligence. Good enough for the company of rough sailors and smugglers, but otherwise a lout. There was no possibility, he felt sure, that his Kate, who had acquitted herself so well in the conversation, could have any interest in such a fellow. His mind at rest, he took a second slice of apple pie.

So he was even more gratified by the brief exchange that ended the dinner.

It was nearly time to leave. Kate had done her best to entertain her cousin John. She'd asked him about how he passed his time, and discovered that he liked best to be down at the waterside, or better yet on a ship. By gentle probing, she had learned something more of his family's business. Like other merchants of their kind, the New York Masters engaged in a wide range of activities. Besides owning several vessels, they had a thriving store, they made rum, albeit with illegal molasses, and even undertook to insure other merchant ships. He did not use many words, and spoke quietly, but once or twice he looked at her directly, and it was all she could do not to blush as she gazed into his eyes, which were as blue as the sky. Whether he liked her, however, she had no idea.

Before they rose from the table, Dirk Master made her father promise that he would come to visit them again while in New York, and she was glad that her father politely said that he would.

"You'll be at the court for the whole trial?" the merchant asked.

"From the beginning to the end."

"And Miss Kate?" their host inquired.

"Oh, indeed," she said enthusiastically. "My father is concerned with royal tyranny, but I have come to support the freedom of the press."

Her father smiled.

"My daughter is of the same opinion as the poet: 'As good almost kill a man as kill a good book.'"

It was the sort of quotation that, in their Boston household, might be heard on any day of the week.

"'He who destroys a good book, kills reason itself,'" Kate immediately chimed in.

Their host looked at them both, and shook his head.

"It sounds familiar, but what are you quoting?" he asked genially.

Kate was surprised he would need reminding. The words came from John Milton, author of *Paradise Lost*. Not from a poem, but a pamphlet, the greatest defense of Free Speech and the freedom of the press that was ever penned.

"It's from Milton's *Areopagitica*," she said.

"Ah, Milton," said her host.

But young John's face contracted into a frown.

"Harry who?" he asked.

It came unbidden. She did not even have time to think. She burst out laughing.

And young John Master blushed, and looked ashamed.

⁜

"Well," said her father cheerfully, as they walked back to their lodgings, "the dinner could have been worse. Though I'm sorry your New York kinsmen turn out to be smugglers."

"Mr. Master seems well informed," she suggested.

"Hmm. In his way, I dare say. The boy, I'm afraid," he added confidently, "is beyond redemption."

"Perhaps," she ventured, "you are too harsh."

"I think not."

"I liked him, Father," she said, "very much."

⁜

The court was on the main floor of the City Hall on Wall Street. The courtroom was a light-filled, lofty space. The two judges, Philipse and Delancey, wigged and robed in scarlet, sat enthroned upon a dais. The jury sat together on two benches to their left. The crowd of people, of all sorts, were seated around the sides, and on the floor of the hall. It might have been a Protestant congregation about to hear a preacher. In the center, before the judges, was the dock, like a box pew, for the accused. He had not far to come, for the cells were in the basement of the building.

Kate and her father had secured good seats in the front row. She looked around the hall eagerly, taking in the scene. But most interesting of all to her was to witness the change in her father. To the outside observer, he looked the quiet, careful lawyer that he was; but to Kate, his unwonted paleness, the alertness in his eye, and the taut nervousness of his face told a different story. She'd never seen her father so eager in her life.

Bradley, the Attorney General, in wig and long black gown, plump and confident, was nodding briskly to people here and there. The court had appointed a lawyer named Chambers, competent enough, to defend the printer. The Attorney General nodded to Chambers, too, as though to say: "It is not your fault, sir, that you are about to be crushed."

And now there was a stir. Through a small door at the back of the court, two officers like huge, black bumblebees were bringing Zenger in. How small he seemed between them, a neat little fellow in a blue coat, who nonetheless kept his head up bravely as they led him to his box, and shut him in.

The charge was read. The Attorney General rose.

Kate had been to trials before. She knew what to expect. It did not take the lawyer long to say that Zenger was a "seditious person" guilty of libels designed to scandalise and vilify the good Governor Cosby. The jury listened. She could not tell what they thought.

Then Chambers rose and said a few lackluster words in the printer's defense. She saw her father frown. "You'd have thought," he whispered in her ear, "that Zenger's backers would have given him better help than this."

But just then, something strange occurred. An old gentleman, who had been sitting quietly near the back, suddenly stood up and made his way stiffly forward.

"If it please Your Honors, I am retained to represent the accused."

"And who are you?" one of the judges asked irritably.

"The name's Hamilton, Your Honor. Andrew Hamilton. Of Philadelphia."

And now Kate saw her father start, and lean forward excitedly.

"Who is he?" she asked.

"The finest trial lawyer in America," he answered in a low voice, while the whole court buzzed.

It was clear that the judges and the Attorney General had been completely taken by surprise, but there was nothing they could do about it. They were still more astonished when the Philadelphia lawyer calmly told them: "My client does not deny that he published the offending articles." The Attorney, therefore, had no need to call any witnesses. This was followed by a long silence, until, looking rather puzzled now, Attorney Bradley stood to declare that if indeed the accused did not deny publishing the libels, then the jury must find him guilty. Glancing a little nervously at Hamilton, he also reminded the jury that it didn't matter whether the newspaper articles were true or false. It was libel anyway. Then, for a considerable time, citing law, custom and the Bible, the Attorney explained to the jury why libel was so serious a crime, and why, under law, they had no choice but to pronounce Zenger guilty. Finally, he sat down.

"Hamilton's lost it already," Kate whispered to her father, but he only answered, "Wait."

The old man from Philadelphia seemed to be in no hurry.

He waited while Chambers said a few words for the defense, then, having shuffled his papers, he slowly rose. Though he addressed the court politely, the look on his face seemed to suggest that he was slightly puzzled by the whole proceedings.

For it was hard for him, he told them, to see why they were all here. If a reasonable complaint about a bad administration was a libel, it was news to him. Indeed—he gave the jury a wry, sideways glance—he wouldn't even have realized that the articles in Zenger's paper referred to the governor personally, if the prosecutor hadn't assured the court that they did. At this, several of the jurymen grinned.

Moreover, he pointed out, the legal authority for the prosecutor's idea of libel came from the tyrannical Star Chamber court of fifteenth-century England. Hardly encouraging. And besides, wasn't it possible that a law made in England, centuries ago, might have become inappropriate for the American colonies today?

It seemed to Kate that this sounded disloyal to England, and she glanced at her father; but he leaned across and whispered: "Seven of the jurors have Dutch names."

Yet for some reason, the old man suddenly seemed to wander. It was just like the case of American farmers, being subject to English laws that were designed for a different kind of landholding system, he declared. He seemed to have a particular interest in farming. He talked of horses and cattle, and was just warming to the subject of fencing livestock, when the prosecutor rose to point out that all this had nothing to do with the case. And Kate might have concluded that the old man from Philadelphia had indeed lost the thread of his argument, if she had not noticed that three of the jurors, who looked like farmers, gave the prosecutor a black look.

The prosecutor would not be denied, however. The charge was libel, he reminded them, and the defense had already admitted it. But now old Andrew Hamilton was shaking his head.

"We are charged with printing and publishing 'a certain false, malicious, seditious and scandalous libel,'" he pointed out. It was up to the Attorney now to prove that Zenger's complaints about the evil governor were false. For in fact, he offered, he'd be happy to prove that every word was true,

The faces of the jurors lit up. They were looking forward to this. But Kate saw her father shake his head.

"It won't wash," he muttered. And sure enough, for several minutes, though the old lawyer struggled with might and main, the Attorney and the judge interrupted him again and again to deny him his point. The law was the law. Truth made no difference. He had no defense. The prosecutor looked satisfied; the jury did not. Old Andrew Hamilton stood by his chair. His face was strained. He seemed to be in pain, and about to sit down.

It was over, then. By a monstrous law, poor Zenger was to be doomed. Kate looked at the printer, who was still very pale and upright in his box, and felt not only sympathy for him, but shame at the system that was about to condemn him. She was most surprised, therefore, to see her father suddenly gaze at old Hamilton with admiration.

"By God," he murmured to himself. "The cunning old fox." And before he could explain it to her, they saw the Philadelphia lawyer turn.

The change was remarkable. His face had cleared. He stood tall. It was as if, like a magician, he had suddenly transformed himself. There was a new light of fire in his eyes. As he started to speak, his voice rang out with a new authority. And this time, no one dared interrupt him.

For his summing-up was as masterful as it was simple. The jury, he reminded them, was the arbiter in this court. Lawyers could argue, the judge could direct them how to find; but they had the power to choose. And the duty. This wretched law of libel was as uncertain as it was bad. Almost anything you said could be twisted and turned into libel. Even a complaint against abuse, which was every man's natural right.

By this means, a governor who did not wish to be criticized could use the law as a weapon, and place himself above the law. It was a legally sanctioned abuse of power. And what stood between this tyranny and the liberties of a free people? They, the jury. Nothing else.

"The loss of liberty, to a generous mind, is worse than death," he proclaimed. The case was not about a printer in New York, it was about their right, and their duty, to protect free men against arbitrary power, as many other brave men had done before them.

Now, he told the jury, it was up to them. The choice was in their hands. And with that, he sat down.

The judge was not pleased. He told the jury that despite anything the Philadelphia lawyer said, they should find the printer guilty. The jury retired.

As the court broke out into a hum of conversation, and Zenger continued to sit upright in his box, Kate's father explained to her.

"I did not realize myself what he was up to. He made the jury furious that the common-sense defense of Zenger—that the poor devil did no more than say the truth—was to be disallowed. And then he played the card he had intended to play all along. It's called Jury Nullification. A jury has the right to decide a case, notwithstanding anything they have heard regarding a defendant's guilt, or the state of the law. It is the last and only defense against bad laws. After a jury has refused to convict, the law does not change, but few prosecutors want to bring a similar action, for fear that future juries will do the same thing. That is the tactic old Hamilton has just deployed. And brilliantly."

"Will it work?"

"We're about to find out, I think."

For the jury was already returning. They filed into place. The judge asked if they had a verdict. The foreman said that they had. He was told to give it.

"Not guilty, Your Honor," he said firmly.

The judge cast his eyes to heaven. And the people in the courtroom erupted with glee.

Eliot Master looked so happy as they left the court that Kate put her arm through his—a familiarity she would not have attempted normally, but one which was accepted.

"This has been an important day in our history," her father remarked. "I am glad, Kate, that you were here to see it. I think that tomorrow, we may safely depart for Boston. Indeed," he continued, with a wry smile, "I have only one regret."

"What is it, Father?"

"That tonight, we must sup with our cousins."

⁜

Young John Master turned into Broadway. He passed several people he knew, but gave them the briefest nod he could and kept his head down. As he passed Trinity Church, he glanced up. Its handsome Anglican tower seemed to look down on him with contempt. He wished he'd come up some other street.

He didn't need reminding he was worthless.

The buttoned-up man from Boston had made that pretty clear yesterday. Politely, of course. But when the lawyer had learned that he'd read *Robinson Crusoe*, his patronizing "Well then, that is something" had said it all. The Boston man thought he was an idiot. John was used to it. The vicar at their church, the principal of his school, they were all the same.

His father had always let him work in the business and enjoy the company of the mariners with whom he was comfortable. But only because he was kind, and accepted him as he was.

His father and his teachers would have been surprised to know that, secretly, John had sometimes tried to study. If he could acquire some knowledge, he'd thought, one day he'd surprise them all. But it was no good. He would stare at the book, but the words would arise from the page in a meaningless blur; he would fidget, glance out of the window, look at the page again; try as he might, nothing ever seemed to make sense. Even when he did read a few pages, he'd find that soon afterward, he could remember nothing of what he'd read.

God knows his father was no scholar either. John had watched him bluffing the Boston lawyer and his daughter as they talked about philosophers and the like. But at least his father knew enough to bluff. And even his father had been embarrassed when he hadn't heard of Addison's *Cato*. The note of reproach in his father's voice had made him so ashamed.

It wasn't as if these people from Boston were from another world. He couldn't just say: "These are lawyers, men of the cloth, nothing to do with a family like ours." They were his own kith and kin. Close cousins. Kate was a girl of his own age. What must they think of their relations in New York?

Not only that they were stupid and uneducated, but that they were common smugglers. Yes, he'd gone and blurted that out too, in his stupidity, to embarrass his father even more.

But the worst moment, the memory that made him cringe, had been with the girl.

The truth was that although he was pretty familiar with the girls he met with the sailors around the town, he'd always been rather shy with the girls from families like his own. They all knew that at school he'd been a fool. His manners were unpolished. Even with his fortune, he wasn't considered much of a catch; and the knowledge that this was the case made him avoid the fashionable girls even more.

But this girl from Boston was different. He'd seen that at once. She was nice-looking, but she was unaffected, and simple. And kind. He'd watched her efforts to draw him out of his shyness, and been grateful. Even if he hadn't read the books she had, the way she spoke with her

father, and her affection toward the lawyer, impressed him. She was everything, he supposed, that one day he'd like in a wife. While they talked,
he'd even found himself thinking, was it possible that he could hope to
marry someone like this? She was his second cousin. There was that
between them. The thought of it was strangely exciting. Could it be that,
despite his roughness, she might like him? Though Kate did not realize it,
he was observing her closely. Each time the conversation exposed his
ignorance, he told himself he was a fool even to think of her. Each time
she was kind to him, he felt a new hope rising.

Until she had laughed at him. He knew she hadn't meant to—which
made it even worse. "Harry who?" he'd asked, and despite herself, she had
burst out laughing. He couldn't blame her. He had made an utter fool of
himself. In her eyes, he could never be anything but an oaf. And she was
right. That's all he was. It was useless.

Now she and her father were coming to the house to sup with them
again, and his father had told him not to be late.

At the corner of the street ahead, there was a tavern. He went in.

❖

The mood at supper was festive. The whole city was rejoicing. Zenger the
printer was free. Hamilton was the toast of the town. That very evening
began the saying that would be repeated for generations to come: "If
you're in a tight spot, get a Philadelphia lawyer."

Dirk Master had produced his best wine; and Eliot, in a mellow mood,
was glad to drink it. Though the evening supper was normally a much
lighter meal than the formal afternoon dinner, the sideboard and table
were soon piled with oysters, baked clams, cooked hams, cold cuts, sweetmeats, and more besides. Mrs. Master seemed less reserved than before.
Though hardly a lover of literature, she discovered that Kate, like her, was
an avid reader of popular women's novellas, so they found plenty to talk
about.

There was only one puzzle. Where was young John Master?

Kate had given much thought to their second meeting. She had so
much regretted her thoughtless laugh before; as well as being hurtful, it
was also rude. It had always been part of her upbringing that a mistake,
however regrettable, can usually be corrected. She was determined, therefore, both to make a better impression this time, and to make amends.

For an hour before coming, she had carefully prepared herself. She'd rehearsed subjects of conversation that she thought he might like; she had thought hard about anything she could say to overcome the bad impression she must have made; and she had put on a simple dress with a small brown-and-white check that suited her very well.

For to her own surprise, she found that young John Master's lack of learning hardly troubled her at all. It was not just that he looked like a Greek god—though that, she confessed to herself with some amusement, was a factor. There was something else about him, an inner strength and honesty she thought she divined, and an intelligence too—different from her father's, but not to be scorned. And, strangely touching and appealing in a way that was new to her, was another realisation: the Greek god was vulnerable.

So from the moment they arrived, she had been waiting for him to appear. She could see that the boy's father was looking out for him too, with a hint of perplexity: and when they sat down to sup, she ventured to ask her host if his son would be joining them.

"He'll be along, Miss Kate," the merchant answered, with a look of slight embarrassment. "I can't think where the boy's got to."

But the fish was removed, and the meat too, and still he did not come. And perhaps it was the hope of seeing him again, as much as politeness, that made her say to her host, in her father's hearing, that she hoped he and his family would all come to visit them in Boston before long.

It was not often that her father lost control of his manners. The look of horror that crossed his face lasted only a second. But it was visible to all. Though he corrected himself quickly, it was not quite in time.

"Indeed!" he cried warmly. "You must dine with us. Dine with us, when you come to Boston."

"How kind," said his New York cousin, a little drily.

"We shall await—" Eliot hastened to say. But what he would await was not revealed. For at this moment, the door was thrown open, and young John Master lurched into the room.

He was not a pretty sight. If his shirt had been as white as his face, it might have been better. But it was filthy. His hair was tousled. His eyes were glazed as he stared round the room, trying to focus. He swayed unsteadily. He looked sodden.

"By God, sir . . ." his father broke out.

"Good evening." He did not seem to have heard his father. "Am I late?" Even from the doorway, the smell of stale beer on his breath and on his shirt was now filling the room.

"Out! Leave us, sir," the merchant shouted. But John remained oblivious.

"Ah." His eyes now rested on Kate, who, since he was behind her, had turned around to look at him. "Miss Kate." He nodded to himself. "My cousin. The lovely, I say the lovely, Miss Kate."

"Sir?" she replied, scarcely knowing what it would be best to say. But she needn't have worried, for her cousin had acquired a momentum of his own. He took a step forward, seemed about to topple, righted himself, and then cannoned into the back of her chair, against which he steadied himself for a moment as he lolled over her shoulder.

"What a pretty dress, cousin," he cried. "You are beautiful tonight. You are always beautiful," he cried out. "My beautiful cousin Kate. I kiss your hand." And leaning over the back of her chair, he reached his hand down over her shoulder, attempting to take her hand in his. And then threw up.

He threw up over her hair, over her shoulder, over her arm, and all over her brown-and-white check dress.

He was still throwing up a moment later, as his enraged father dragged him from the room, leaving behind a scene of some confusion.

❖

It was a bright, clear August morning, somewhat cooler than the days before, as the small carriage carrying Kate and her father rolled up the Boston road. Behind them the sound of cannon boomed out. The people of New York, whether their governor liked it or not, were giving a formal salute to Andrew Hamilton as he set out, in the other direction, for Philadelphia.

"Ha," said her father, with satisfaction. "A salute deserved. It has been a visit worth making, Kate, despite the unfortunate incident last night. I am truly sorry, my child, that you should have suffered such a thing."

"I did not mind, Father," she answered. "I have known my brother and sisters to be sick in the past."

"Not like that," he answered firmly.

"He is young, Father. I think he is shy."

"Pah," said her father.

"I did not dislike him," she said. "In fact—"

"There is no reason," said her father decidedly, "for us to encounter those people any more."

And since Boston was far away, and her father in control of her fate, she knew that she would never, in all her life, see her cousin John again.

٭

As the salute of the cannon echoed over New York harbor, and old Andrew Hamilton took his leave, the townspeople could enjoy not only their triumph over a venal governor, but something more profound. Eliot Master's statement had been correct. The Zenger trial did not change the law of libel, but it told every future governor that the citizens of New York, and every other town in the American colonies, would exercise what, without being philosophers, they believed to be their natural right to say and write what they pleased. The trial was never forgotten. It became a milestone in the history of America. And the people at the time sensed correctly that it was so.

There was one other feature of the trial that was little remarked upon, however.

The rights that Eliot Master believed in, the rights claimed by Andrew Hamilton and exercised by the jury, came from the common law of England. It was Englishmen, alone in Europe, who had executed their king for being a tyrant; it was England's great poet, Milton, who had defined the freedom of the press; it was an English philosopher, Locke, who had argued for the existence of men's natural rights. The men who fired the cannon knew they were British, and they were proud of it.

Yet when old Hamilton addressed the jury, he had made one other point that they had liked. An ancient law, he told them, might have been a good law long ago, in England; but it could also become a bad law centuries later, in America. Though no one particularly remarked upon this statement, the idea had been sown. And it would put down roots, and propagate, in the huge American land.

The Philadelphia Girl

THE BOY MOVED cautiously. A May evening. Late shadows were falling, and nothing was safe. Not a street, not a house. If only he had known what was going on when he arrived, he might have acted differently. But he'd only found out an hour ago, when a slave in the tavern had explained: "Ain't nowhere safe for a nigger in New York. Not now. You take care."

He was fifteen years old, and the way things were going, this would be the worst year of his life.

Things had been bad when he was ten. That was the year his father had died, and his mother had taken up with another man and left, together with his brothers and sisters. He wasn't even sure where they were now. He'd stayed behind with his grandfather in New York, where the old man ran a tavern frequented by sailors. He and his grandfather had understood each other. They both loved the harbor, and the ships, and everything to do with the sea. Maybe fate had been the guiding hand at his birth, when his parents had given him the same name as the old man: Hudson.

But fate had been cruel this year. The winter had been colder than anyone could remember. The harbor was frozen solid. On the last day of January, a young fellow arrived at the tavern after skating down the frozen river from a village seventy miles to the north, for a wager. Everyone in the tavern had bought him a drink. That had been a cheerful day; but it was the only one. The weather had grown even colder after that. Food had become scarce. His grandfather had fallen sick.

Then his grandfather had died, and left him all alone in the world. There'd been no big family funeral. People were being buried quietly that winter. A few of the neighbors and the patrons of the tavern came to mourn. Then he'd had to decide what to do.

That choice, at least, had been easy. His grandfather had talked to him about it before he died. It was no use trying to run a tavern at his age. And he knew what he wanted, anyway.

"You want to go away to sea?" the old man had said with a sigh. "Well, I reckon I wanted the same thing at your age." And he'd given the boy the names of two sea captains. "They know me. Jus' you tell them who you are, and they'll look after you."

That was where he'd made his mistake. Been too impatient. It hadn't taken long to dispose of the tavern, for the premises was only rented. And there was nothing else to hold him in the city. So as soon as the weather turned at the start of March, he'd wanted to be off. His grandfather had kept his modest savings and a few items of value in a small chest. Hudson had taken the chest and left it for safe keeping with his grandfather's best friend, a baker who lived near the tavern. Then he was free.

Neither of the captains were in port, so he'd signed on with another, and sailed out of New York on the seventeenth of the month, St. Patrick's Day. The voyage had gone well enough. They had reached Jamaica, sold their cargo, and started their return by way of the Leeward Islands. But at that point, the ship had needed repairs. He'd been paid, and taken on by another ship's master, to sail up the coast to New York and Boston.

He'd learned his lesson there. The captain was a useless drunkard. Twice the ship had nearly been lost in storms before they even reached the Chesapeake. The crew wouldn't be paid until they reached Boston, but long before they reached New York, he'd decided to cut his losses and jump ship. He had his pay from the last voyage, and he reckoned he could stay in New York until one of his grandfather's captains turned up.

He'd slipped away from the ship that morning. All he needed to do was to avoid the waterfront for a few days until his present ship and her drunken master had gone. He might be a Negro, but he was a free man, after all.

It had been mid-afternoon when he went to the baker's. The baker's son, a boy of about his own age, had been there. For some reason, the boy had given him an awkward look. He'd asked for the baker, but the boy had shaken his head.

"He's been dead a month. Mother's running the business."

Hudson expressed his sorrow, and explained that he had come for his chest. But when he said that, the boy just shrugged. "Don't know anything about a chest." It seemed to Hudson that the boy was lying. He asked where the baker's widow was. Away until the next day. Could he look for the chest? No. And then the strangest thing had happened. He'd never been particular friends with the baker's son, but they'd known each other most of their lives. Yet now the boy had suddenly turned on him as if the past had never been.

"You'd better be careful, nigger," he said viciously, "if I were you." Then he waved him away. Hudson had still been in a state of astonishment when he went into the tavern, and met the slave who explained what was going on.

The best thing might have been to go back to the waterside, but he didn't want to encounter the captain, who'd be looking for him by now. In the worst case, he could head out of the town, and sleep in the open. But he didn't want to do that. The thought that the baker's family might have stolen his money worried him considerably.

He was moving cautiously, therefore, as he made his way through the streets.

❖

The trouble had started on March 18. A mysterious fire broke out in the governor's house, and the fort had been burned down. Nobody knew who'd done it. Exactly a week later, another fire had started. Seven days after that, van Zant's warehouse had burst into flames.

It was arson, clearly. But what was its purpose? Thefts had also taken place. Were the gangs of burglars in the town starting the fires as diversions for their activities? Or could the papists be behind it? The British were at war with Catholic Spain again, and most of the garrison at the fort had been sent to attack Spanish Cuba. Were Spanish Jesuits organizing mayhem in the British colonies? The fires multiplied.

And then a black slave named Cuffee was caught, running from one of them.

A slave revolt: the fear of every slave-owning colonist. The city had experienced one back in 1712—quickly put down, but terrifying while it lasted. More recently there had been revolts on the West Indies plantations, and Carolina. Only last year mobs of slaves had tried to burn down Charleston.

So when the city recorder had taken over the investigation, suspicion soon focused on the Negroes. And it wasn't long before he'd found a seedy tavern, run by an Irishman known to be a fence for stolen goods, and frequented by Negroes. Soon the tavern's prostitute was talking. Money was offered for testimony. Testimony came.

There was an easy way of getting slaves to confess. Build a bonfire in a public place, put the Negro on it, light the bonfire and ask him questions. Slaves were soon being accused and questioned, even the slaves of respectable people, in this manner. Two slaves, one belonging to John Roosevelt the butcher, gave the desired confessions as they were put to the fire, and, hoping to escape at the last moment, started naming others. Fifty names came thus, in the twinkling of an eye; and the recorder would have spared their lives for such useful testimony; except that the crowd, moved by their natural feelings, threatened to riot themselves, if they could not watch the black men fry.

But now the business of justice was truly begun. Accusations came thick and fast. Any black man doing anything that looked the least suspicious was thrown in jail. By late May, almost half the Negro men in the city were behind bars, waiting to be tried for something.

⁂

John Master looked at the Indian belt thoughtfully. He'd always liked that belt, ever since he was a child. "It was my van Dyck grandfather's dying wish that I should have this belt," his father had often told him. "He set great store by it." So when his father had given it to him on his twenty-first birthday, and said, "May it bring you good fortune," John had been touched, and kept it safely in his big oak press ever since. Sometimes he would take it out and look at the pleasing pattern of the wampum shells, but he hardly ever put it on. This evening was a special occasion, though. And he hoped it might bring him luck.

Tonight he was going to ask Mercy Brewster to be his wife.

The last five years had seen a remarkable change in young John Master. Though he'd kept his good looks, he'd filled out into a large and sturdy figure. He no longer thought that he was worthless. The visit of his Boston cousins had proved to be a turning point. The morning after the humiliating incident with Kate had been the only time he'd ever seen his father truly angry, and it had done him good. He'd been so shaken that he'd tried to pull himself together. With a new determination, he had applied himself to the one thing he seemed to have a talent for, and he'd worked hard, as never before, at the family's business.

His father Dirk had been astounded, but delighted. The gift of the wampum belt had been his signal to his son that he had faith in him. John had kept on his path and gone from strength to strength, and by now he was generally regarded as an accomplished merchant. But he knew his own weaknesses. He knew that his mind was inclined to be lazy; and he had to take care how much he drank. Having no illusions about his own shortcomings, however, he could accept those of others with good grace. As he approached his mid-twenties, John Master had a view of human nature that was broad and balanced.

There had even been talk of him running for political office. But he wasn't keen to do it. For the last few years of the city's life had also taught him much.

After the Zenger trial, the venal Governor Cosby had died, and there had been a move for reform in New York. New men had come into the city government—lesser merchants, craftsmen, men of the people. One might have thought the corrupt regime of the past had been replaced. But not a bit of it. In no time at all, most of the new people had been corrupted themselves, with high offices, high salaries and the chance of riches. In New York, as in London, it seemed the dictum of the old British prime minister held good: "Every man has his price."

"I'll stick to making money like an honest rogue," John told his father, genially.

As he strode along that evening, with a silver-topped walking stick in one hand, he looked every inch the respectable citizen. The streets after dark could be dangerous, but he wasn't concerned. Not many footpads would care to take him on.

As for this Negro conspiracy, he didn't believe a word of it. He knew every tavern keeper in the city, and the fellow accused was the biggest villain of them all. It was entirely possible that he'd started some fires, and he might have got a gang of discontented slaves and others working for him. But beyond that, John Master believed nothing. The prostitute would say anything if you paid her. As for the slaves who'd started naming people when the fire was put to their feet, their testimony was worthless. People would say anything under torture. He'd seen the city recorder eagerly taking down the names they screamed out, and felt only disgust. Everyone knew about the Salem Witch Trials up in Massachusetts, the previous century. In his opinion, that was where this sort of thing led—to endless accusations, executions and tragic absurdity. He just hoped it would be over soon.

Thank God that tonight he had happier things he could think about.

⁘

When he'd first told his father he wanted to marry Mercy Brewster, Dirk Master had been astonished.

"The Quaker girl? Are you sure? In heaven's name, why?"

As for his mother, she had looked very doubtful.

"I don't think, Johnny, you will make each other happy."

But John Master knew his own mind, and his parents were wrong. Entirely wrong.

"In fact, she's not a Quaker," he'd told them. He'd supposed she must be, when they first met. After all, her family was recently arrived from Philadelphia, and she addressed people as "thee" and "thou." But before long, he had learned that though her father had been a Quaker once, he had been read out of the meeting for marrying a member of the Anglican Church. He was a member of no congregation now. But though he let his Anglican wife take their children to that church, he insisted that at home, the family use most of the Quaker customs that he loved.

"Thee is talking to a Quaker in all but name," Mercy had told John with a smile. "Philadelphia has many mixed families like ours. We never let ideas disturb us too much, down there."

The first thing John had noticed was that this Quaker girl paid no attention to his looks. Most girls did. Since he had become more successful, his earlier awkwardness with young women of his own class had disappeared. When he entered a room, most female eyes were upon him. Sometimes when young women met him, they blushed. But Mercy Brewster didn't. She just looked him calmly in the eye and spoke to him naturally.

She seemed to have no particular sense of her own looks, either. She was just an ordinary girl, somewhat short, with curly hair parted in the middle, and brown eyes set wide apart. She was matter-of-fact, at peace with herself. He had never met anyone like this before.

There had been one anxious moment.

"I like to read," she had said, the first time he had called on her, and his heart sank. It was not any book of philosophy she showed him, however, but the jolly *Almanack* of Ben Franklin, the Philadelphia printer. Even he could dip into that book of stories and jokes with pleasure.

For months he'd just thought of her as a friend. He'd call at her house, in an easy, familiar manner. If they met at someone else's house, he'd chat with her, and scarcely realize that he'd spent more time in her company than with anyone else. Their conversations were never romantic. They talked of everyday things, and business matters. Like most Quaker girls she was brought up, in a quiet way, to be the equal of any man; and she certainly had a good head for business. When she asked him about shipping, she showed a quick and intelligent grasp of anything he told her. She did not flirt with him; and he did not flirt with her. She did not challenge him; she seemed content to accept him exactly as he was. He felt easy, and happy in her presence.

Once or twice, he had found himself giving her an affectionate smile, or touching her shoulder lightly, in a way that might have invited a response. But she had always chosen to treat these as signs of friendship, and nothing more. Indeed, he'd even wondered recently if she might deliberately be keeping him at a distance.

It was when they went to the preaching that everything changed.

⁂

Many times in Christianity's history there have been charismatic preachers: men who gather others to them and inspire more, so that a movement begins—each movement, like a river in flood, leaving a rich deposit of fertile soil for future generations.

John Master had heard of the Wesley brothers some years ago. Inspired by an intense faith and a desire to preach, they and some Oxford friends had begun an evangelical movement within the Anglican Church. In 1736, John Wesley had arrived in the American colonies, at Savannah, Georgia, hoping to convert the native American Indians there. And although he'd returned somewhat disappointed after a couple of years, he had immediately been replaced in Georgia by his Oxford friend George Whitefield. Meanwhile, the Wesleys' evangelical mission in England was quietly growing. Texts of their sermons had crossed the Atlantic to Philadelphia, Boston and New York. Some churchmen thought the movement unseemly, and contemptuously referred to these earnest young men as "Methodists." But many more were inspired by their fervent preaching.

In the summer of 1739, after a visit to consult with the Wesleys in England, George Whitefield had returned to spread the word more widely in the colonies. His first stop had been in Philadelphia.

"He is quite remarkable, you know," Mercy told John Master.

"You went to hear him preach?"

"Of course I did. I went with Ben Franklin, who is a friend of his. For you may be sure," she added with a smile, "that Mr. Franklin does not allow any person of celebrity to remain a day in Philadelphia without his making their acquaintance."

"He impressed you?"

"Very much. His voice is powerful, and has such clarity of tone that they say he can be heard a mile away—like Our Lord at the Sermon on the Mount, I suppose. And though the words themselves are such as other preachers use, he has a way of describing scenes so that you feel you see them directly before your eyes. It is very affecting. He spoke in the open to a crowd of thousands. Many were quite overcome."

"Was Mr. Franklin overcome?"

"Before we set off, he said to me: 'Whitefield is a good fellow, but I shall not allow myself to be led by the nose. So you see, I have taken all the money out of my pocket. Then I cannot be tempted to give him anything until my head is cool.'"

"Franklin gave him nothing, then?"

"Quite the contrary. Mr. Whitefield was collecting for the orphans in Georgia, and by the end of the preaching, Mr. Franklin was so excited he made me lend him money to put in the collection. He paid me back, of course," she added.

Whitefield had come to New York twice. The Anglicans and the Dutch Reform dominies would not let him speak in their churches. But a Presbyterian minister welcomed him. He also preached out of doors. Not everyone cared for his message. When he spoke of the need to minister to the slaves, some thought he was stirring up trouble. Then, last November, he had come to the city again.

"Won't you come to hear him?" Mercy asked.

"I don't think I care to," John replied.

"I should like to see him preach out of doors again," she said. "But I can't go out in that crowd all alone. It would be kind if you would accompany me," she added, a little reproachfully.

John could hardly refuse after that.

✧

It was a chilly autumn day as they walked up Broadway. They passed Trinity Church and the Presbyterian Meeting House. A few streets more, and they went by the Quakers' Meeting House. Some way further, where the old Indian road forked away to the right, the big, triangular space of the Common began. And it was out onto the Common, despite the cold, that streams of people were flowing. By the time John and Mercy arrived, they found a huge crowd already assembled.

A high wooden platform had been set up in the middle of the Common. There were all kinds of folk there: respectable merchants and their families, craftsmen, apprentices, sailors, laborers, slaves. Looking about, John reckoned over five thousand had already gathered, with more arriving all the time.

Though they waited more than half an hour, the crowd was well behaved and remarkably quiet. The sense of anticipation was keen. Then at last, a group of half a dozen men was seen walking toward the platform; and when they reached it, one of them mounted the steps and faced the crowd. John had expected some sort of introduction, but there was nothing. No hymns, no prayers. In a loud voice, proclaiming a passage from the scripture, the preacher went straight to his work.

George Whitefield was dressed in a simple black robe with white clerical tabs. He wore a long wig. Yet even from where they stood, John could see that the preacher was still in his twenties.

But with what confidence he preached the word. He told them of the story of Lazarus, who was raised from the dead. He cited the scripture and other authorities at some length, but in a manner that was easy to follow. The crowd listened intently, respectful of his learning. Then he painted the scene, graphically. He did not hold back. Imagine the body, he told them, not only dead in the tomb, but stinking. Imagine that they were there. Again, he went over the scene, so vividly that it seemed to John Master that he, too, could smell that rotting body.

Yet consider the spiritual message of the episode, Whitefield urged them—not only that a miracle was wrought. For was not Lazarus like every one of them? Stinking in sin, and dead to God, unless they let

Christ raise them up again. And John, despite himself, could not help thinking of his own, dissolute past, and sensing the deep emotional truth in what the preacher said.

Next, Whitefield chided them—for their sin, and for their sloth, in failing to turn from evil. He raised every objection that could be thought of, as to why a man might not come to God, and answered them, every one. And then, having left his audience moved, shamed and with nowhere to hide, he began his exhortation.

"Come," his voice started to rise, "haste ye away and walk with God. Stop," he boomed in a mighty voice, full of emotion, "stop, oh sinner. Turn ye, turn ye, oh ye unconverted man. Make no longer tarrying, I say, step not one step further in your present walk." The crowd was with him now. He had them in his hand. "Farewell, lust of the flesh," he cried, "I will no more walk with thee. Farewell, pride of life. Oh, that there may be in you such a mind! God will set His mighty hand to it. Yes He will." And now his voice was rising into an ecstasy, and all around the crowd, faces were looking up, some shining, some with tears in their eyes. "The judge is before the door. He that cometh will come and will not tarry." Now he called to them, now was the time, now the very hour that should lead to their salvation. "And we shall all shine as stars in the firmament in the kingdom of Our heavenly Father, forever and ever . . ."

Had he summoned them to come forward to him at that moment, had he told them to fall to their knees, most of them would have done it.

And against his will John Master, too, had tears in his eyes; and a great, warm tide of emotion swept through him. And he glanced down at Mercy beside him, and saw in her face such a radiant goodness, such a calm certainty, that it seemed to him that if he could only be with her all his life, he should know a love, and happiness, and peace that he had never known before.

That was when he had decided to marry her.

⁙

His parents had begged him to wait before declaring his love. Come to know her better, and be certain, they counseled. They had some idea that the emotions stirred by Whitefield's preaching had had a part in this, were glad when the evangelist left the city soon afterward, and gladder still, this spring, that he had not returned.

Meanwhile, John had continued to see Mercy as usual.

But even if he had been careful not to declare himself, she couldn't have failed to be aware, by the spring, that the growing affection on his side might lead to more than friendship. For him, this cautious courtship was a new experience. His affairs with women had so far tended to be straightforward, and to resolve themselves speedily, one way or the other. But this gradual evolution, during which he studied her, and came to appreciate her qualities more each day, led him into a realm where he had not been before. By Easter, he was deeply in love, and she must know it. Only the general turbulence in the city had delayed him from declaring his love already. That, and one other thing.

He was not sure his affection was returned.

There was nothing coy about Mercy Brewster; and she knew her own mind. Yet he did not know how she felt about him. She had given him no sign. All he could tell was that she loved him as a friend, and that there was something, whatever it might be, that made her hesitant about encouraging him further. Recently, he had made his intentions very clear. He had given her signs of affection, let his arm slip around her waist, given her chaste kisses, and nearly more than that. But, though not entirely discouraging these advances, there had been a subtle reluctance, a quiet distancing of herself, that was more than merely Quaker propriety.

Well, it was time to bring matters to a head. He had let her know that he meant to call that evening, and that he desired a private interview with her, so she knew what must be coming. But he wasn't sure what her answer was going to be.

No wonder then if, under his silk waistcoat, he put on the wampum belt, to bring him luck.

❖

Mercy Brewster waited. She was neatly dressed and she looked well enough. And that, she had decided, would have to do.

She'd talked to her parents about John Master long ago. After all, her father would have to give his permission. Mr. Brewster was uncertain about the young man's morals, but not too much against him. Her mother knew John's parents and, besides their wealth, of which no one could be unaware, considered them respectable.

If John Master felt easy in the company of Mercy Brewster, it was not so surprising. She'd been raised in a city of comfortable charm. Though only founded late in the seventeenth century, Philadelphia was so well placed to serve the markets of the south, and so ready to welcome new-comers of different creeds and nations, that it had already surpassed both Boston and New York in size. And perhaps because, unlike the poor, rock-strewn land of Massachusetts, Philadelphia lay in some of the richest pasture in America, it was an easy-going place. Religion had also played a part. The Quakers who were so prominent in the city were by avocation gentle, private folk—quite unlike the harsh Puritans who had founded Boston, and who had always considered it their calling to judge and order the lives of others.

If a man in Philadelphia cared to read, well enough, so long as he didn't seek to impose his books on you. Too much learning, too much attain-ment, too much success, too much of anything that might disturb the leafy quiet and genteel comfort of its deep pastures and broad valleys was, from its beginnings, anathema to happy Philadelphia. If John Master knew his business, and came from a good family, and was a friendly sort of fellow, then that was all a nice Philadelphia girl required.

John Master was wrong about one thing, though. He thought Mercy hadn't noticed that he looked like a Greek god. Of course she had! The very first time he spoke to her, it had taken all Mercy's sound Quaker upbringing to keep a calm countenance. I must see the inner man, not the outer show, she had reminded herself, again and again. Yet how was it possible, she wondered, that this divine-looking being wants to spend time with a plain little person like me? For a long time, she had assumed that he saw her as a harmless friend. No one could suppose there was more to it than that. When, once or twice, he had given hints of some-thing further, she had wondered whether he might be trifling with her. But even when it seemed his feelings might be stronger, there was still one thing that worried Mercy Brewster.

She was not sure that he was kind. Oh, he was kind enough in a gen-eral, everyday sort of way. He loved his parents. He seemed to have some honest friends. But in this regard, the Quaker girl was more demanding than John knew. Had he shown, she asked herself, true thought for oth-ers, anywhere in his life? He was young, of course, and the young are self-ish; but on this point she must be satisfied.

This doubt was not something she could let him know. If he suspected her concern, it would have been too easy for him to contrive some gesture that would satisfy her. All she could do was to watch, and wait, and hope. For without this reassurance, she could not love him.

He never guessed it, but the preaching they had attended on the Common had been a test. If he'd refused to go, she would have quietly withdrawn herself, secretly closed an inner door, remained a friend, but nothing more. During Whitefield's sermon, though John had not noticed, she had been watching him. She had seen how he was moved, seen the tears in his eyes, and been pleased. He is good, she had told herself. His heart is warm. But was this only when he was moved by Whitefield's preaching, or was it something more serious and solid? She continued to observe him. Even after it became plain that he was ready to confess his love for her, she would not allow herself to be moved from this point, and she continued to be uncertain, and to maintain her distance from him.

And this was not easy for her since, for some months now, she had been completely, and agonizingly, in love.

This evening he was coming. She knew what he was going to say. But she still was not sure what she was going to answer.

✥

Young Hudson hadn't been having any luck. He'd tried a few inns, but been told there was no room. There were some disreputable places where he knew he could stay, but he'd avoided those so far. He'd gone to the house of a tailor he knew, hoping to get a berth there, but the man had left the city because times were bad. Another friend, a free black man like himself, had been thrown in jail. He'd been on his way to a ropemaker he knew when, passing by Vesey Street, he'd made a terrible mistake.

He'd noticed the smoking chimney at once. It belonged to a house a few doors down the street. Even in the gathering darkness, he could see the thick black smoke coming out of it, although he saw no sign of any flames. Somebody had better take a look at that, he'd thought, but not wanting to get involved, he'd been going on his way when the two watchmen came round the corner.

They saw the smoke too. And they saw a black man. And they stared at him. They were staring at him hard.

And then he'd panicked.

He knew what they were thinking. Was he a black man starting a fire? He could stay where he was, of course, and protest he was innocent. But would they believe him? In any case, with the ship's captain looking for him, he hardly wanted to be questioned by the authorities. There was only one thing to do. He took to his heels and ran. The watchmen shouted and came after him, but he was faster than they were. A quick turn down an alley, over a wall, down another alleyway, and he'd lost them.

He was halfway along Ferry Street now, hoping he was safe, when he heard the footsteps hurrying behind him, and turned to see the two watchmen.

For a moment, he wondered what to do. Should he run? He might get away, but if he didn't, then running would confirm his guilt. Could they even be sure, in the darkness, that he was the black man they'd seen in the other street? Probably not. But they mightn't care about that. He hesitated, and was on the point of fleeing again, when he saw that another man was now coming toward him, from the other end of the street. Quite a big, fit-looking man, carrying a silver-topped stick. If he fled, and the watchmen gave chase, the man with the stick would probably catch him. There was nothing to do but stand his ground, with what dignity he could.

The two watchmen reached him. Although he wasn't moving, one of them grabbed him by the collar.

"Gotcha." The fellow shook him. "We saw you."

"Saw what?"

"Back in Vesey Street. Startin' a fire."

"A what? I wasn't in Vesey Street."

"Don't answer back, nigger. You're goin' to jail."

The man with the stick had reached them now.

"What's this?" he asked.

"We saw this nigger boy tryin' to burn down a house in Vesey Street," said one of the watchmen. "Right, Herman?"

"Could be," the other man answered. But Hudson noticed that he looked a little doubtful.

"Not me, it wasn't," Hudson protested. "I wasn't even in that part of town."

"And when was this?" asked the stranger.

"Maybe ten minutes ago, wasn't it, Jack?" said Herman.

"The nigger belongs in jail," said Jack.

"Not this one," said the stranger, coolly. "Because until I sent him on an errand five minutes ago, he was with me." He looked Hudson straight in the eye, then turned back to the watchmen. "My name's John Master. Dirk Master's my father. And this slave boy belongs to me."

"He does?" Jack looked suspicious. But Herman was ready to capitulate.

"That'd explain it," he said. "I thought he looked different."

"Goddammit," said Jack.

The stranger waited until the two watchmen had turned the corner before he spoke.

"You didn't light a fire, did you?"

"No, sir," said Hudson.

"Because if you did, I'm in trouble. Who do you belong to?"

"Nobody, sir. I'm free."

"That so? Where do you live?"

"My grandfather had a tavern near the waterfront, but he died. He was called Hudson."

"I know it. I've drunk there."

"I don't remember you, sir."

"Only went there once or twice. But I've been in all the taverns. Been drunk in most of them. What's your name?"

"I'm called Hudson too, sir."

"Hmm. So where d'you live now?"

"Nowhere at present. I was at sea."

"Hmm." His rescuer considered him. "Jumped ship?"

Hudson was silent.

"There was a drunken captain down by the docks today, hollering for a Negro boy that jumped ship. Can't say I liked the look of him. Drunk on board, too, I should guess."

Hudson considered. The stranger, for whatever reason, seemed to be on his side.

"He nearly lost the ship twice, sir," he confessed.

"Well, you'd better stick with me for the moment," said John Master. "You can act as my slave until something better turns up."

"I'm free, sir," Hudson reminded him.

"You want to come with me or not?" asked his benefactor.

And seeing that he had nowhere else to go, Hudson accepted the offer. At least he'd be safe for a while.

✢

Mercy Brewster was rather surprised when John arrived with a new slave. It only took a few moments for him to explain what had happened, after which Hudson was sent down to the kitchen.

"My guess is he's telling the truth," John said when Hudson was out of earshot. "If not, I've made a horrible mistake." He smiled. "I'm afraid I lied, Mercy. You won't approve of that."

"But you lied to save him from being wrongly arrested. You may even have saved his life."

"I suppose so. I couldn't leave the poor fellow like that."

"No," she said quietly. "I see you couldn't."

"Hope you don't mind me bringing him here."

"Oh no," she said, a little breathlessly, "I don't mind at all." She looked at him for a long moment, and decided. Yes, he was kind. He could not have done such a thing, if he were not kind. And then, with her heart secretly in a terrible flutter, she asked: "Was there something you wished to say to me, John?"

Montayne's Tavern

IT WAS GUY Fawkes Night, and they were burning the Pope in New York.

In England, the Fifth of November was an important day. A century and a half had passed since Catholic Guy Fawkes had tried to blow up the Protestant Parliament, and they'd been burning his effigy on bonfires on that day ever since. Indeed, it being the same season, the celebrations had pretty much taken over the ancient rites of Halloween. And Guy Fawkes Night had come to New York, too. But by and by, the New Yorkers had decided to improve on the old English model and get to the heart of the matter. So they carried an effigy of the Pope himself through the streets, and burned him on a great bonfire in the evening, and everybody celebrated. At least, pretty much everybody. The Catholics in the town may have objected; but there weren't too many of them, and they had the sense to keep quiet.

When John Master saw Charlie White through the crowd on Broadway that evening, he waved and smiled. And Charlie nodded, but he didn't smile. And John realized it was years since they'd spoken. So he started toward him.

And maybe John Master felt a tad awkward when he said, "It's good to see you, Charlie." And he almost said, "I was thinking about you the other day," but he didn't because it would have been a damn lie, and they both knew it. Then fortunately he realized that they were right outside Montayne's Tavern, so he said, "Let's have a drink." Like it was old times.

✢

Old times. Charlie remembered old times, all right. Those had been the days, when he and John Master had been boys together.

Happy times mostly. Fishing in the river. Walking up Broadway arm in arm. Sleeping out in the woods, and thinking they heard a bear. Taking a boat out to Governor's Island and spending all day there, when John was supposed to be at school. Getting into mischief in the town. Once or twice John had let him come in one of his father's longboats to run the molasses in from the French vessels at night. And John's father had given Charlie a handsome tip, to keep quiet about it, though Charlie would rather have died than breathe a word.

He'd been almost one of the family. That was friendship.

As John had got older, they'd gone to the taverns too. But Charlie couldn't get drunk the way John did, because he had to work. So John mostly got drunk with the sailors, and Charlie got him home afterward.

When John had turned away from all that, and started to work, he hadn't seen so much of Charlie, and Charlie had understood. He doesn't want to see me, Charlie thought, because I remind him of what he's trying to get away from. I remind him of what he used to be. He understood it, but he was still hurt. They'd see each other from time to time, even go for a drink. But it wasn't the same any more.

Charlie had made a small mistake once. He'd been in the market place, and happened to see John standing near the entrance to the fort, talking to a merchant. He'd gone over and greeted his friend, as he usually would, and John had given him a cold look, because he was interrupting him. The merchant hadn't been too pleased either that a fellow like him would interrupt them. So Charlie had gone away quickly, feeling a bit of a fool.

The next day John had come round to his house first thing in the morning.

"Sorry about yesterday, Charlie," he'd said. "You took me by surprise. I'd never done business with that fellow before. I was trying to understand what he wanted."

"That's all right, John. It's nothing."

"Are you free this evening? We could have a drink."

"Not this evening, John. I'll come by soon."

But of course, he hadn't. There was no point. They were moving in different worlds now.

John hadn't forgotten him though. About a year later, he'd come by again. Charlie was a laboring man, but he also had a cart, and was engaged part-time in the carrying business. John had asked him if he could engage with the Master family to transport goods up to some local farms. It was a regular contract, a full day every week, and the terms were good. Charlie had been glad of it, and the arrangement had continued for quite a while. John had put other business his way when he could, down the years.

But by the nature of things, it was a case of a rich man giving work to a poor one. The last time the Masters had given Charlie work, it hadn't been John, but a clerk who'd come to make the arrangements.

They'd both married, John to the Quaker from Philadelphia, Charlie to the daughter of a carter. They both had families. John wouldn't have known the names of Charlie's children. But Charlie knew all about John's.

For the fact was, Charlie often thought of John. He'd often pass by Master's handsome house. He knew what Mercy Master looked like, and her children. He picked up gossip about them in the taverns. A curiosity, which may have been a little morbid, made him do it. But John Master would have been surprised to know what a close watch Charlie White kept on his affairs.

✢

They sat down at a wooden table in the corner and nursed their drinks.

"How's your family, Charlie? You doing all right?"

Charlie needed a shave, and his face was getting furrowed. Under the mess of his black hair, his eyes narrowed.

"They're well," he admitted. "They say you've been doing well."

"I have, Charlie." There was no point in denying it. "The war's been good for a lot of people."

It was three years since John's mother had died and his father Dirk had retired from business and gone to live on a little farm he'd bought north of Manhattan, up in Westchester County. He lived there very contentedly, looked after by a housekeeper. "You're like an old Dutchman," his son would tell him affectionately, "who's retired to his bouwerie." And though Dirk liked to be told about what was going on, it was John Master who was entirely in control of the family business now. And thanks to the war, business had been booming as never before.

For the old rivalry between France and Britain had taken a new turn. If the two powers had been struggling since the previous century for control of the subcontinent of India, the rich sugar trade in the West Indies, and the fur trade of the north, their conflicts in America had mostly been skirmishes, conducted with the aid of the Iroquois, on the upper Hudson or St. Lawrence rivers, far to the north of New York. Recently, however, both powers had tried to grab control of the Ohio Valley to the west, which joined France's vast, Mississippi River territory of Louisiana to her holdings in the north. In 1754, a rather inexperienced young Virginian officer in the British Army, named George Washington, had made an incursion into the Ohio Valley, set up a small fort and promptly been kicked out of it by the French. In itself, the incident was minor. But back in London, it had caused the British government to come to a decision. It was time to drive their traditional enemy out of the North-East once and for all. They'd gone to war in earnest.

"I should thank George Washington," John Master would cheerfully say, "for making me a fortune."

War had meant privateering, and John Master had done well out of that. It was a high-risk business, but he'd figured it out. Most voyages made a loss; but the profits from the few captured were spectacular. By taking shares in about a dozen ships at a time, and averaging his risk, his profits had more than paid for the losses. In fact, he'd been able to double or triple his investment every year. It was a rich man's game. But he could afford to play.

The real benefit to New York, however, was the British Army. Before long, ten, twenty and soon twenty-five thousand redcoats had arrived from England to fight the French, together with a huge fleet and nearly fifteen thousand sailors. They came to New York and Boston.

Armies and fleets need provisioning. Not only that: the officers wanted houses built, and services of every kind. In addition to his regular trade supplying the Caribbean, John Master was getting huge government contracts for grain, timber, cloth and rum; and so were most of the other merchants he knew. Modest craftsmen, swamped with demand, were upping their prices. True, some laboring men complained that off-duty soldiers were taking part-time jobs and stealing work from them. But by and large, laboring families like Charlie's could get unheard-of wages. Most people in New York with anything to sell could say with feeling: "God bless the redcoats."

"I get a lot of building work," said Charlie. "Can't complain."

They talked of their families, and of old times, and they drank through the evening. And remembering his youth, it seemed to John that it hadn't been such a bad thing that he'd spent time with fellows like Charlie. I may be a rich man of forty now, living in comfort, he thought, but I know the life of the streets, the wharfs, and the taverns, and I run my business better because of it. He knew what men like Charlie were thinking, knew when they were lying, knew how to handle them. He thought of his own son, James. James was a good fellow. He loved the boy, and there was nothing much wrong with him. He'd taken pains with his general education, always explaining things about the trade of the city, things to watch out for. Putting him on the right path. But the fact was, John considered, that the next generation was being brought up too genteel. What James needed, his father was thinking, was to learn a few of the lessons that he'd learned himself.

So when, late in the evening, Charlie remarked that his son Sam was thirteen, exactly the same age as James, John suddenly leaned over to him and said: "You know what, Charlie, your Sam and my James should get together. What do you think?"

"I'd like that, John."

"Why don't I send him over?"

"You know where to find me."

"Day after tomorrow, then. Noon."

"We'll be waiting."

"He'll be there. Let's have a last drink."

The Pope had been burned to a cinder by the time they parted.

⁂

The following morning, John Master told his son James about Charlie White and that he was to go to visit him the next day. He reminded him again that evening. Early on the day in question, before he went out, he gave James precise directions for finding Charlie's house, and told him not to be late. James promised he'd be punctual.

⁂

Mercy Master had a visitor of her own that afternoon. She'd chosen a time carefully. Both her son James and his elder sister Susan were out. Her husband wouldn't be home for a long time yet. When the architect arrived, he was ushered by Hudson into her parlor, where she had cleared a little table, and soon the drawings were laid out upon it.

She was preparing her husband's tomb.

Not that she wanted John dead. Far from it. Indeed, it was part of her passion that John should be well cared for, dead or alive. And so, as a Quaker, she was being practical.

Mercy's passion for her husband had only grown with the years. If she saw a new wig, or a fine coat in the latest London fashion, or a splendid carriage, why then she would immediately think: My John would look well in that. If she saw a fine silk dress, she would imagine how it might please him to see her wearing it, and how well they might look together. If she saw a Chippendale chair in a neighbor's handsome house, or some beautiful wallpaper, or a handsome silver service, she would want to buy them too, to make their own house more elegant and worthy of her husband. She'd even had his portrait painted, along with her own, by fashionable Mr. Copley.

Her passion was innocent. She had never cut herself off from her Quaker roots. Her love of such finery was not to make a worldly show at the expense of others. But since her husband was a good man, who had been blessed with success in his business, there seemed no harm in enjoying the good things that God had provided. In this, she certainly had the example of other Quakers before her. In Philadelphia, the Quaker oligarchs ran the city like Venetian nobles; just above New York, it was a rich Quaker named Murray who had built the magnificent country villa called Murray Hill.

And here in the city, God had never provided such opportunities for elegance before. If the cultivated classes of Boston and Europe had found New York somewhat coarse in John's youth, things were changing fast. The rich classes were drawing ever further apart from the hurly-burly of the streets. Tidy Georgian streets and squares were closing themselves off into a genteel quiet. In front of the old fort, a discreet and pleasant park, called the Bowling Green, after the fashion of Vauxhall or Ranelagh Gardens in London, now provided a haven where respectable people could promenade. The theater might be limited, and concerts few, but the aristocratic British officers who had recently arrived in the city could find themselves in houses quite as fine as their own at home. The town house of one rich merchant family—the Waltons—with its oak paneling and marble foyer, put even the British governor to shame.

England. England was the thing. If the British shipping laws ensured that few goods from Continental Europe could get into American ports, it hardly mattered. England supplied everything that elegance required. China and glass, silver and silks, all manner of luxuries, dainty or robust, were being shipped from England to New York, along with easy credit terms to induce people to buy. Mercy Master bought them all. Truth to tell, she would dearly have loved to cross the ocean to London to make sure that she wasn't missing anything. But that was not to be thought of, with all the business that her husband had to do.

There was only one thing that John Master had denied her. A country house. Not a farm, like the old bouweries of the Stuyvesants and their like. A country house might have a few hundred acres of farmland, but that wasn't really the point. It was also a place to escape the unhealthy city in the hot and humid summer. But above all it was a trophy—a villa in a park—a place for a gentleman to show off his good taste. It was a fine old tradition: rich gentlemen had set up these parks in the Renaissance, the Middle Ages and in the Roman Empire. Now it was New York's turn. Some were on Manhattan; there was the Watts house at Rose Hill; and Murray Hill of course; and others with names taken from London, like Greenwich and Chelsea. Some were a little further north, like the van Cortlandts' estate in the Bronx. How well her husband would look in such a place. He could well afford it. But he had adamantly refused.

"There's always my father's farm to go to," he told her. Further north, he'd already bought two thousand acres up in Dutchess County, which he was clearing. "Westchester and Dutchess counties will be the breadbaskets of the North," he said. "And I'll grow grain on every yard of land I own." And if she sighed, the Quaker in her knew he was right.

But from time to time she'd continued to wonder, what else could she do for her husband, within the city's bounds? They had their house, their furniture, their portraits: what more remained?

Why, a tomb. A mausoleum. If you couldn't build a house in which to live a few years, you could, for far less expense, build a tomb in which to rest for all eternity. The mausoleum would honor her husband; she could be buried beside him; and their descendants after them. It was a project. You could employ an architect. You could show people the designs. For a month, now, she had been engaged on the business, but in secret. She meant to surprise her husband with it on New Year's Day.

And so when, at three o'clock that afternoon, her husband came home earlier than expected and discovered her with the architect and the plans, she was much put out.

⁜

John Master gazed at the plan for his tomb. It was fit for a Roman emperor. He knew very well that some of the old landed families of the region—especially if they were Presbyterian—laughed at the pretensions of the New York merchants, and he didn't entirely blame them. But as he gazed affectionately at his wife, he only remarked: "Why, Mercy, I'm little more than forty and you want to bury me already." Then, since his loving wife's only failing was that she did not always see a joke, and the preposterous magnificence of the tomb struck him once more, he sat down on a Chippendale chair and burst out laughing.

But soon he got up and kissed his wife and told her he was grateful. And he smiled to himself at the discovery of her plan. For as it happened, he also had been preparing a surprise, for her. But of his secret, he thought with satisfaction, she still knew nothing at all.

"Did James get back from Charlie White's, by the way?" he asked; and was told he hadn't. "Good," he said. That probably meant the meeting was going well.

⁜

At noon that day, Charlie White and his son were ready in front of their yard. The street on which they lived lay on the west side of Broadway, not far from Montayne's Tavern, and about half a mile north of Trinity Church, which owned the land. If the streets in the fashionable quarters of the city were neatly cobbled and the houses made of brick, the streets up near the Common where Charlie lived were dirt, and the ramshackle houses made of unpainted clapboard. But the area was cheerful enough.

In the yard behind them stood Charlie's cart, with its number painted on it in red. Charlie had three boys and two girls. The oldest boy was a sailor, the next was a fireman, who rode proudly on one of the new fire engines sent over from London. Young Sam helped his father. Sam wasn't sure what he felt about James Master coming to visit.

"What am I supposed to do—take him with me selling oysters in the street?" he asked. Oysters, the poor man's food. Sam often earned some extra money selling oysters.

"Just be yourself," replied his father. There was no need to say more. If rich young James Master should become Sam's friend . . . Well, you never knew what a friendship like that might lead to.

The fact was, Charlie White had become quite excited about this visit.

After all these years, his childhood friendship with the Masters was to be renewed. Was it back to the old days?

Last night, he'd told his family stories about the times he and John Master used to spend together. He'd had a few drinks during the evening. He may have boasted a little. His children had always known there had once been a friendship, but it had never seemed to amount to much, and their father seldom spoke of it. Hearing him that evening, therefore, they'd been a bit surprised, and quite impressed.

His wife was less impressed. Mrs. White was a plump, comfortable woman. She loved Charlie, but after years of marriage, she knew his weaknesses. His carting business had never been as good as her father's had been. He didn't always concentrate on the work in hand. She was afraid that he was going to be disappointed with this encounter, and she certainly didn't want their children getting any foolish ideas. Years of marriage to Charlie had left her skeptical.

"So you had a few drinks with John Master, and invited his son round."

"Wasn't my idea," said Charlie. "It was his."

"When he was drunk."

"I've seen him drunk. He wasn't drunk."

"You think rich young Master's going to show up?"

"I know he is. His father told me."

"Well, maybe he will, and maybe he won't," said his wife. "But I'll tell you one thing, Charlie. John Master wants something. I don't know what he wants, but when he's got it, he'll forget about you again, just like he did before."

"You don't understand," said Charlie. "He's my friend."

His children were all looking at him. His wife said nothing.

"You'll see," Charlie said.

So now Charlie and Sam waited. The street was busy. Once in a while, a respectable person came by, but no sign of young James Master. A quarter of an hour passed. Sam glanced at his father.

"He'll come," said Charlie.

Another quarter-hour passed.

At one o'clock, Charlie said to his son: "You can go in now, Sam."

But he himself remained, for a long time, staring up the street.

✣

At six o'clock that evening, James Master walked toward his home, and hoped his father was not there. He was still working out what he was going to say.

He'd meant to go to Charlie White's house. In a way, when you came to think of it, he'd almost done so. At least he'd set out for the place in good time. But something had held him back. He hadn't really wanted to meet Sam White. Not that he looked down on poor people. It wasn't that. But if only his father wouldn't make all these arrangements for him.

For he knew what this was, of course. It was another of his father's plans for improving him. He thinks I need friends like Sam White, so I'll understand the world and grow up like he did, he thought.

And then, if only his father hadn't kept reminding him about it, and giving him directions. You couldn't tell him, of course, but it seemed to James, right now, that it was really his father's fault more than his own that he hadn't turned up.

Perhaps it was just fate. He'd been on his way when he'd met a friend, which had caused a necessary delay. And after that, he'd still almost gone; but he realized that the delay with his friend had been so long, that it was too late to go now, anyway.

So maybe the best thing to do was say that he couldn't find the place and that he'd go back the next day. And he'd pretty much decided that was what he'd do, when he met his father just a minute sooner than he expected, in front of the house.

"Well, James, did it go well?" His father was smiling expectantly. "Charlie's quite a character, eh? And what's Sam like? A chip off the old block?"

"Well . . ." James looked at his father's eager countenance. "No. He's pretty quiet, I guess."

"But he was friendly, I hope. And you were too?"

"Yes . . . Yes, I was." He was getting in so deep now, where he hadn't meant to. Should he break down and confess? His father would probably take a strap to him, but he didn't mind that. It was the sense of disappointment the whole thing would create. He just wished he could get his father off his back.

"So you'll meet again?" his father said hopefully.

"I reckon so. Don't worry, Father, we'll see each other if we want to."

"Oh."

"You should just leave it between us, Father."

"Yes. Yes, of course. Don't worry, my boy. I won't interfere." And with that, his father let him escape into the house.

⁜

Had he got away with it? He wasn't sure. He knew his father didn't see Charlie White too often, but they were sure to see each other, all the same. The best thing, he reckoned, would be to go round to Charlie White's house the very next day, say he got the date wrong, and spend time with Sam. That would cover his tracks, pretty much, and make everything all right. And he very nearly did. But he put it off until so far into the afternoon that unfortunately, he realized, it was too late again. Same thing the next day. The third day, he was starting to put the whole thing behind him, when in the middle of the street, a cart with a red number painted on it stopped and the driver, a thickset man with a few days' stubble, and a heavy leather coat, leaned down and asked him: "Would you be James Master?"

"I might. Who's asking?"

"Name's Charlie White. I had an idea you were coming round to my place the other day."

It was his chance. He could say he was just going round. Make his excuse. Make everything right. The work of a moment. Why didn't he take it? Because some inner resistance to the whole thing, or maybe a stupid panic at being caught, suddenly intervened. He hardly knew what it was, or why it happened. Yet he heard himself say: "Not that I know of, Mr. White. Can I do something for you?" And it was said so politely, with a voice and expression of such perfect innocence, that Charlie White was taken in.

"Nothing, young gentleman. My mistake. I must've gotten the wrong person." And he whipped up his horse and drove his cart away.

⁜

So his wife had been right, Charlie thought. After all his hopes had been raised, after he'd thought his so-called friend had felt some affection for him, Master hadn't even told the boy at all. Just left him to look like a fool in front of Sam, and humiliated him in front of his family. He'd already had to endure his wife's studied silence on the subject. He'd seen his children looking at him with a mixture of pity and mockery. Maybe John had forgotten, or changed his mind. Whatever the cause, it showed one thing. At the end of the day, a poor man's feelings were of no account. There was no friendship, no respect, nothing but a rich man's contempt. There was no other explanation. And from that day, though he never knew it, John Master had a secret enemy.

᛭

John Master didn't see Charlie White in the next couple of weeks. He once again asked James if he and Sam were meeting, but James had mumbled something evasive, so he'd let the matter drop. But he still might have looked in to see Charlie, if a small incident hadn't occurred.

His son James at the age of thirteen might be somewhat diffident, but his daughter Susan, who was three years older, and possessed his own striking blond good looks, was already a confident and popular young woman who was attracting the interest of the men of New York. Susan had a cheerful, easy-going character, but she already knew exactly what she wanted—which was to marry a man with a good-sized estate in Westchester or Dutchess county. And given her looks and fortune, there was no reason why she shouldn't.

So when the two young New Yorkers, both Yale men, came to dine at the house, Master had assumed that, with his daughter's favor in prospect, they'd be equally anxious to get into his own good graces.

If only the conversation had not turned to the subject of universities.

If Massachusetts possessed Harvard College, and Connecticut had followed with Yale, New Yorkers came to think that they, too, should have a place of higher learning. So King's College had been set up. It was only a small establishment, in the poor section of town where Charlie White lived—though it had pleasant gardens down to the Hudson River. Since Trinity Church had given the land for the college, the Trinity vestry reckoned it should be an Anglican foundation, and the English governor had agreed. But this had brought howls of rage from the other churches, especially the Presbyterians.

Most of the rich city merchants like Master belonged to the Anglican Church. The Trinity crowd, some called them. And it was true that the Trinity crowd dominated the Assembly and most of the best appointments. So this attempt to control the new seat of learning as well was seen by all the other congregations as a monstrous abuse. Presbyterians said it was a conspiracy. Even poor folk, who might have small interest in the university, hurled insults at the privileged Anglicans. Tempers had run high. Master considered the whole thing was blown out of all proportion. And a compromise had been reached. But the business exposed much bad feeling in the city, and the rumblings could still be heard.

The young Yale men had been Presbyterians. The discussion had become quite heated. And the young men had dared to insult him and call him a lackey of the governor—in his own house! He'd thrown them out after that, and Mercy and Susan had supported him. But for days afterward, John Master had felt irritable and ill at ease.

And because Charlie White, who mightn't have cared about the university himself, belonged to the class that had abused the Anglicans, John Master had experienced an unconscious aversion to seeing the carter and his family just then. It was quite unfair, and he was scarcely aware of it. But he hadn't gone over to Charlie's house, even by the year's end.

❖

It was New Year's Day when John Master announced his surprise. He led up to it gradually.

"You know, Mercy," he said, "the unpleasantness of those two Yale men and all the bad feeling over the university has been making me think, I wouldn't mind getting away from the city for a while."

"We could stay in the country, John," she suggested. "Or we could go to some of my relations in Philadelphia, if you like."

"There's another problem though, which prevents my going away to either of those places," he continued. "I'm concerned about all the business we have going through Albion's, when I don't really know them."

Five years ago, when his father's old London agent had retired, he'd recommended that the Masters transfer the agency to the firm of Albion. The arrangement had worked well so far, but the relationship had been conducted entirely by letter; and with the London shipments increasing every year, John considered it was time he got to know the Albions personally, and assess them against the other trading houses.

"What do you mean to do then?" she asked.

"I thought," and now his handsome face broke into a grin, "that I'd better go to London. And I wondered whether perhaps you'd like to come."

London

⊰1759⊱

O H TO BE in England. And here she was. On the very Thames
itself, at the heart of Britain's empire.

Ships, towers, domes and church steeples lay crowded under the glittering sky. On the waterfront, the old gray Tower of London spoke for antiquity. On the ridge above, the great dome of Protestant St. Paul's looked so stately, majestic and dependable. With joy and excitement Mercy prepared to set foot, at last, on dry land.

And for all its faults—the sooty fogs from five centuries of coalfires, an underclass addicted to cheap gin, the vast discrepancies between rich and poor—London was a glorious place. It was by far the largest city in Europe. The crooked, rat-infested alleys of the medieval city had mostly disappeared in the Great Fire of the previous century—though magnificent gothic halls and churches still remained—to be replaced by the splendid streets and squares of Georgian houses that spread in a huge sweep from the city to Westminster. To think that it was all, for months, to be hers. Why she hadn't a care in the world.

Except for young James, that was.

✢

The arrangements John Master had made before leaving New York had been simple. He had a clerk he trusted to take care of his regular business at the warehouse. The rum distillery foreman was likewise a good man.

The land in Dutchess County was under the tight control of an agent, who also collected the numerous property rents in the city. As for the family house, that was no trouble at all. Hudson would look after that. But nonetheless, he needed someone to oversee the whole, and also to keep track of the various interest payments due from a number of reputable businesses in the city. For since, unlike London, New York still had no banks, Master and other merchants of his kind made most of the loans necessary to the business of the place.

So his father Dirk had agreed to come back to the city, and live in the house while John was away. John wasn't sure that his father particularly wanted to do it, but he'd agreed with good grace, and there was certainly no one better fitted for the task.

It had also solved one other problem.

Mercy had been disappointed when her daughter Susan had not wanted to accompany them to London, but she had understood it. It was not that Susan was lacking in affection for her parents or interest in the world. But everything she already wanted was in the New York colony—her friends, the man, whomever he might be, that she would one day marry. The ocean crossing to London was not a small undertaking and it might be a year before they were back. To a girl of Susan's age that seemed a long time, a year of her life given up for no future purpose, and that could have been better spent in America. To argue with her was pointless. They could force her to go, but at the end of the day, for what purpose? She wasn't going to change her mind. And the presence of her grandfather in the house meant that she could be safely left there under his care.

But James was another matter. When he'd confessed to his mother that he had no desire to go to London either, she'd told him frankly: "Your father is quite decided that you should come, James." And seeing her son look vexed: "It would break his heart if you didn't, you know."

She wasn't surprised. Boys of that age were often moody. It made it worse that he was the only son and that his father's hopes were centered on him. It was only natural that John was forever making plans for the boy, and just as natural that James should feel oppressed. But she really couldn't see what was to be done. "Your father loves you, and means only for your good," she would remind her son. And in her opinion, her husband was right. James should certainly come to London; and she told him so herself.

But the voyage had been a trial. Summer had already begun before they took the packet which sailed, in company with several other ships and a naval escort to protect them against French privateers, across the Atlantic to London. Her husband was a wonderful sailor. The weeks on the ship didn't seem to bother him at all. Whether it was drinking in the great silence of the night sky under the stars, or weathering a squall while the ship pitched and tossed, she'd never seen him happier. James, on the other hand, would sit for hours on deck, staring gloomily at the Atlantic Ocean as if it were his personal enemy; and in rough seas, while his father was cheerfully up on deck, James would stay miserably below and think bitterly that if he drowned, it would all be his father's fault for dragging him uselessly on a journey where he never belonged in the first place. To her husband, when he complained that their son wouldn't speak, she said: "It's just his age, John, and being cooped up on a ship."

"I think he blames me," John remarked sadly.

"Not at all," she lied. But she hoped very much that James might cheer up in London.

⁓

They had no sooner arrived at the London waterside than a pleasant, middle-aged man, with the bluest eyes she'd ever seen, came forward with hand outstretched to greet them.

"Mr. Master? I am Arthur Albion, sir, at your service." And within moments, he had them all in his carriage, with two boys loading their luggage into a cart behind. "I have taken the liberty of procuring you some lodgings," he announced, "not far from those occupied by another distinguished gentleman from the American colonies, though he is away from London at present."

"Indeed?" said John Master. "And who might that be?"

"Mr. Benjamin Franklin, sir. I dare say he'll be back in London soon."

But if there was no sign of Ben Franklin in the weeks that followed, it hardly seemed to matter. For London was all that Mercy had hoped, and more.

It wasn't long before John told her he was satisfied that Albion's were one of the best trading houses in London. They were solid, and well trusted. Arthur Albion was a member of one of the best city guilds. "As for our friend Albion," John declared with a laugh, "he's a most gentlemanly fellow. But if there's a chance to turn a pretty penny, I've never seen a man move quicker in my life."

He proved to be a perfect guide. Though he was a merchant and a city man, Albion came from an old family of landed gentry down in the New Forest, and through family connections, and his own courtly manners, he had access to a number of London's aristocratic houses. His wife came from an old family of French Huguenots. "Silk merchants and jewelers," she told Mercy cheerfully. What better person could there be to guide her round the fashionable shops? They were fast friends within a week. Hats and ribbons, silk dresses and shoes, not to mention the daily delicacies to be found in Fortnum & Mason the grocers—they sampled them all. Since servants were needed to wait upon them in their handsome lodgings, the two ladies interviewed them together.

Best of all, Mercy could buy things for her husband.

She could see at once that Mr. Albion, though he dressed quietly, had a perfect sense of fashion. John dressed well. And London fashions reached New York quite quickly. But there was a certain style, a special look, hard to define but unmistakable, in a London tailor. She had Mr. Albion take John to his tailor and his wigmaker before they'd been there a week.

Then there were the other things, that she and Mrs. Albion could buy for him together. The silver buckles for his shoes, a fine new watch, a sword, a sword knot, linen for his shirts. She even bought him a silver snuffbox. The fashion for snuff had come to New York, of course, and several American tobacco merchants had started manufacturing it. But if John Master smoked a pipe now and then, he drew the line at the snuffbox. "If I start snorting snuff, I'll sneeze over you all day—and all night too," he promised cheerfully.

⁘

John Master was enjoying London very much indeed. Albion had chosen their lodgings wisely—just off the Strand, in the thick of everything. In no time, John was frequenting some of the best coffee houses, where you could find the newspapers and the *Gentlemen's Magazine*, and strike up conversations with all kinds of interesting fellows. The theaters showed comedies that were to his taste. To please Mercy, he even sat through a concert of Handel's music—and quite enjoyed it.

But their great relief was James.

John Master could remember his own youth only too well and what a disappointment he'd been to his own father. So if he often made plans for James, it was only because he hoped that his son might do a little better than he had himself. If in New York he'd thought James should learn about fellows like Charlie White, here in London, the opportunity seemed entirely different. Here was a chance to acquire, at the empire's fountainhead, all the history, knowledge of law and manners that a gentleman should know. Before they had sailed, he'd written to Albion, asking him to find James a tutor. He hoped this wasn't going to make James even more morose. But to his great relief, it was soon clear that Albion had chosen well: a bright young fellow recently down from Oxford, who could give James some companionship as well.

"The first few days," the young fellow announced, "I think I'd better show James round the town. I can give him some history lessons as we go." And it seemed to work. A week later, when Master went across to Westminster with his son, he was quite astonished at how much of the history of the British Parliament James knew. A few days after that, James even corrected him, politely but firmly, upon a point of grammar. "Damn your impudence," his father cried. But he didn't mind at all.

James was getting along famously with his young tutor. When the Albions introduced him to rich London boys of his own age, he found them not so different. Indeed, the young bloods of New York had taken up the nasal drawl of London's upper class when they spoke, and James knew how to do it. It was agreeable to find that these English boys accepted him as a good fellow like themselves. Albion's own son Grey, who was three years younger than James, obviously looked up to him, which raised his spirits further, and soon the Albions' house by Lincoln's Inn became his second home.

And flushed with this new confidence, James also began to seek out his father.

John Master knew that boys of this age needed the company of their father, and he had been wanting to take his son about in London. What he had not foreseen was that it would be James who took him.

Every day or two they'd set off from their lodgings near the Strand to explore the wonders of London. A short walk to the east lay the lovely site of the old Knights Templar, where the lawyers had their quarters now. Beyond that, the busy printers and newspapermen of Fleet Street worked under the shadow of St. Paul's on the city's ancient hill. They went to the Tower. And Albion took them both, together with Grey, to the Royal Exchange and the port.

Or turning west along the Strand, they'd saunter down Whitehall to Westminster, or enter the Mall on their way to the royal palace of St. James, and stroll up to Piccadilly. At least once a week, James would come eagerly to his father with a suggestion of some kind. Should his father like to go to Tyburn, where they'd hanged a highwayman last week? Or the pleasure gardens at Ranelagh, or take a boat downriver to Greenwich, or up to Chelsea?

It touched John so much that his son wanted to share these things, and although he didn't tell the boy so, these were some of the happiest days of his life.

⁘

Strangely enough, it was Mercy who became uncomfortable.

Arthur Albion had invited the Masters to dine with a number of merchants, lawyers and clergymen. He knew men of learning, writers and artists too, but he'd correctly judged that John Master was not anxious to discuss the merits of Pope the poet, or even Fielding the novelist, or meet the formidable Dr. Johnson, who was preparing his great dictionary nearby in his house off the Strand. He had introduced them to several Members of Parliament, though, and before the month of September was out, they had attended dinners or small receptions in a number of handsome houses. But there was one other class of person whom his visitors had yet to encounter. This was to change in the first week of October.

"My dear," John announced to Mercy one day, "we are invited to Burlington House."

Mercy had seen the great houses of London from the outside. She passed the huge facade of Northumberland House on the Strand every day; and there were at least a dozen other great establishments that had been pointed out to her. She knew that these great enclaves, closed off behind their gateways and walls, belonged to the highest noblemen in England. But since some of these buildings extended a hundred yards or more along the street, she had assumed that they contained all kinds of places of business, or possibly government offices, around their internal courtyards.

As they all went together in his carriage to the evening reception, Albion explained what they were about to see.

"It's not really a private party," he said with a smile. "I should think the nearest thing in New York would be a governor's reception. There will be a great crowd of people there; we may, or may not, have the honor of meeting our host. But you'll have the chance of seeing the greatest people in England."

Burlington House stood on Piccadilly, not far from Fortnum & Mason. Mercy and Mrs. Albion had used the same dressmaker and hairdresser; and a quick inspection had assured her that John was perfectly turned out in a similar manner to Albion. But as they entered the huge courtyard, glanced at the massive colonnades and saw the great sweep of steps to the doorway ahead of them, she couldn't help feeling a trace of nervousness. The front facade of the Palladian mansion resembled nothing so much as a Roman palazzo. Flanking the impressive doorway were rows of liveried footmen. She heard her husband ask a very reasonable question.

"What's this huge place used for—its daily business, I mean?"

"You do not understand, my friend." Albion smiled. "This is a private residence."

And then, for the first time, Mercy felt afraid.

She had never seen anything like it before. The great rooms and halls with their coffered ceilings were so large and so high that the biggest mansion in New York could have fitted into any one of them. Even the scale of a church like Trinity looked puny by comparison. America had nothing like this, imagined nothing like this, and would not have known what to do with it. How modest, how insignificant, how provincial even New York's greatest mansions must look to the men who lived in such palaces. All over Europe, an entire class was accustomed to live in this way—a class of whose very existence, she suddenly realized, she was almost entirely ignorant.

"Such wealth," she heard her husband remark to Albion, "must confer enormous power."

"It does. The Duke of Northumberland, for instance—whose London house is bigger than this—comes from a feudal family who ruled like kings in the north for centuries. Today, the Duke has dozens of Members of Parliament who vote exactly as he tells them to. Other powerful magnates do the same thing."

"We have no feudal families like that in the colonies."

"The proprietors of Maryland and Pennsylvania still possess land grants which give them feudal powers," Albion pointed out.

It was perfectly true that the seventeenth-century grants made to a few families like the Penns, and indeed the land grants of the great patroons up the Hudson River—grants given them to develop what was then empty territory—had left these magnates with almost feudal powers.

"They don't build palaces, though," John said.

Meanwhile, Mrs. Albion was whispering in Mercy's ear.

"There's the Duchess of Devonshire. They have another house like this just along the street. There's Lord Granville. And oh my, there's Lady Suffolk. You don't often get the chance to see her."

"Who's Lady Suffolk?"

"Why, the king's old mistress. A very kind lady, much respected. And look over there." She indicated a handsome lady to whom everyone was bowing. "That's Lady Yarmouth, the king's present mistress. The most important lady at the court."

"The king's mistress is important?"

"Of course. After the queen died she became, you might say, the royal consort."

"And before she died, what did the queen think of her husband's mistress?" Mercy asked wryly.

"Oh, they were great friends. They say the king consulted the queen closely on how to woo Lady Yarmouth. See to her left, that's Lord Mansfield, very influential."

But Mercy didn't look at Lord Mansfield. She was still grappling with the notion of the royal mistress. How could it be that the ruler of the country, the head of the Established Church, could not only take mistresses, but that these women were honored like honest wives? New Yorkers, heaven knows, were no strangers to immorality, but her Quaker soul was offended by this official acceptance of public vice.

"Does everyone at court keep a mistress?" she asked.

"Not at all. Lord Bute, the king's closest adviser, is a religious man of unimpeachable morals."

"I am glad to hear it. Doesn't private vice make a man unworthy of public office?"

And now kindly Mrs. Albion looked at Mercy with genuine astonishment.

"Well," she laughed, "if it did, there'd be no one to govern the land."

Mercy said nothing.

And now, by the door, there was a stir. A name had been announced and the crowd was parting. She looked to see who it was.

The young man was about twenty. A big, ungainly boy, with bulging eyes and a small head. He looked a little shy. But as people bowed, she realized who this must be.

Prince George was the king's grandson. But since his own father's early death, he'd become the heir to the throne. Mercy had heard that he took a keen interest in agriculture, and that he meant well. From the smiles that accompanied the bows and curtsies, it seemed that people liked him. So this was the Prince of Wales.

But as she watched his progress round the room that evening, and observed his simplicity of manners, she wondered whether when he became king, he would do anything to change this world of aristocratic excess and immorality. Somehow, she doubted it.

⁂

Ten days later, the Albions took them on a journey to the west. James came too, and young Grey Albion. It was a pleasant party, all the more so as Mercy had the chance to observe her son and the Albion boy. Young Grey had a very sweet nature, and it was clear that James quite enjoyed acting the elder brother to him. They went down to the New Forest, where the Albion family came from, and across to Sarum and Stonehenge. They enjoyed the ancient intimacy of the forest, and admired the huge agricultural estates around Sarum. Albion also told them much about the improved farming methods and machinery that were bringing England an ever increasing prosperity. From Stonehenge they had gone to Bath, and spent several delightful days in the fashionable Roman spa.

It was here, in the pump room one morning, that Albion encountered a friend. Captain Stanton Rivers came from an important family. The captain was a slim, graceful man in his late thirties, and his father was a lord. But it was his older brother who would inherit the title and estate, and so the captain had to make his way in the world. "Any officer in the British Navy longs for war," he told them with a pleasant smile, "for it brings the hope of prize money. We navy men are just glorified privateers, you know. And here at Bath," he added frankly, "there are always plenty of officers like myself hoping to find an heiress or a rich widow. But at present," he announced, "I have another prospect in mind. I'm thinking of going to America."

"And what do you mean to do there?" Albion asked with some amusement.

"I've received word, Arthur, from a friend in Carolina that there's a widow there, without heirs but of childbearing age, who possesses two excellent plantations, and who hopes to marry again. She wants a gentleman of good family. He sent me a miniature of her, and assures me that despite telling her every fault in my character that he can think of, he has not been able to deter the lady from considering me."

"You mean to go to Carolina?"

"I have already discovered what I can about plantations. I believe I could learn to manage one. I intend to make a tour of the colonies, and visit New York as well," he said. "Carolina widow or not, I mean to learn as much about our American colonies as I can."

A glance from Albion indicated to John Master that his host would like him to oblige his friend. He needed no further hint.

"Then I hope you'll do me the honor of staying with us in New York," he said. "I should be delighted to be of service to you."

From Bath they went to Oxford. Here their journey took them on smooth turnpike roads—a far cry, Mercy was forced to admit, from the rutted tracks of New England—and they made the seventy-mile journey in a single day. Oxford, with its cloistered colleges and dreaming spires, charmed her. But before returning to London, Albion had taken them to see the country house of the Churchill family, at nearby Blenheim Palace.

And here, as she had at Burlington House, Mercy received another shock. The country villas she knew back at home were handsome houses. But nothing could have prepared her for this. A park that stretched as far as the eye could see. A vast mansion, stone wings outstretched, that was half a mile across. It was a quarter-mile from the kitchen to the dining room. The library, which to her should be an intimate haven, was sixty yards long. The cold, baroque magnificence of the mansion was stupefying. And while Albion took them proudly round, and her husband and the two boys stared at everything in awe, her quiet Quaker intelligence saw the grandeur for what it was. This was not the pride of wealth; nor even the arrogance of power. The message of the Churchills was as simple as it was outrageous: "We are not mortal men at all. We are gods. Bow down." The crime of Lucifer. And Mercy felt a sinking of the heart.

"I suppose," John remarked to her that evening, "that to an English lord America must look as provincial Britain did to a senator of imperial Rome."

It was not a thought that brought her any comfort. From that day, though she did not tell her husband, Mercy was ready to return to America.

✦

They met Ben Franklin in December. His lodgings were quite close, in Craven Street, off the Strand. He lived modestly but comfortably in a pleasant Georgian house, of which he occupied the best floor, looked after by a devoted landlady and a couple of hired servants. John was eager that young James should have a sight of the great man, and urged him to take careful note of everything Franklin said.

Mercy also was excited. Though she knew that Ben Franklin's experiments with electricity and his other inventions had brought him world renown, her memory of him from Philadelphia was as the author of *Poor Richard's Almanack*: the jolly friend who'd gone with her to the preaching. The man with the round, spectacled face, like a kindly storekeeper; the thin brown hair falling to his shoulders; the twinkling eyes.

When the two Masters and their son were ushered in, the man who rose to greet them was still the man she knew. And yet he was different.

Mr. Benjamin Franklin was now in his early fifties. He was fashionably dressed in a rich blue coat with big gold buttons. He wore a spotless white stock round his neck, and a powdered wig. His face was somewhat leaner than she'd expected. His eyes did not twinkle. They were intelligent and alert. He might have been a successful lawyer. There was also in his manner a faint hint that, though ready to welcome fellow colonists, his time was limited.

"Remember, Franklin made a fortune in business before he entered public life," John had remarked to her the day before. "And whatever he does, he always makes sure he is paid. The British government pays him a large salary as Postmaster of the Colonies—even though he's three thousand miles away from his duties. And the people of Pennsylvania are paying him a second salary to represent them here in London." He'd grinned. "Your friend Mr. Franklin is a very cunning fellow."

Franklin bade them welcome though, remembered Mercy, and made young James sit beside him. Apologizing for his poor hospitality, he explained that he'd been on a tour of the Scottish universities, where he'd met Adam Smith and other Scottish men of genius. "Six weeks of the greatest contentment in my life," he declared. But he'd returned to find all manner of business awaiting him.

He chatted to them very amiably. But it soon became clear that the Masters were not acquainted with any of the London printers, writers and scientific men whose company Franklin enjoyed, and John was afraid the great man might become a little bored with them; so, hoping to keep him talking, he ventured to ask him about his mission for the people of Pennsylvania.

The Pennsylvanians might be paying Ben Franklin handsomely to represent them in London, but they hadn't given him an easy task. If William Penn in the last century had devoutly desired to establish a Quaker colony in America, his descendants, who lived in England, desired only to receive their tax-free income from the huge Pennsylvania land grants they'd inherited. The people of Pennsylvania were sick of them and their proprietorial rights, and wanted a charter like other colonies.

But the Penns had friends at court, Franklin now explained. And if the Pennsylvania grant was disturbed, then Maryland and other proprietorships might also be called in question. The British government was unwilling to upset the apple cart. It seemed like too much trouble.

"The further difficulty, which I had not foreseen," he continued, "is that in the minds of many government ministers, the administration of the colonies is a special department, where the views of the colonial assemblies, beyond local matters, are not strictly relevant. They think that the colonies should be ruled either through proprietors like the Penns, or directly by the king and his council."

It was now that young James interposed.

"Would not that leave the colonies, sir, in the same position as England was under Charles I, where the king was free to rule as he pleased?"

"You have studied history," Franklin said to the boy with a smile. "But not quite, I think, for the Parliament in London still keeps watch over the king." He paused. "It is true that there are some, even friends of mine in the London Parliament, who fear that one day the American colonists will want to separate from the mother country, though I assured them that I had never heard such a sentiment expressed in America."

"I should hope not," said John Master.

But it was now that Mercy suddenly spoke.

"It would be a good thing if they did." The words burst from her almost before she knew she was uttering them, and they were said with vehe-

mence. The men all stared at her in astonishment. "I have seen enough of
our English rulers," she added, more quietly, but with no less feeling.

Ben Franklin looked surprised, but thoughtful. After a short pause, he
continued.

"Well, I am of the contrary opinion," he said. "Indeed, Mrs. Master, I
should go further. I believe that in the future, America will be the central
foundation of the British Empire. And I shall tell you why. We have the
English language, English laws. Unlike the French, we have denied the
rule of tyrant kings. And I have high hopes that the young Prince of Wales
will be an excellent king when his turn comes. Our government is by no
means perfect, but taken all in all, I thank the Lord for British freedoms."

"I agree with every word," said John.

"But consider this also," Franklin went on. "The vast territories of
America lie across an ocean; yet what is America if not the western frontier of our freedom-loving empire?" He gazed at them all. There was a
light of enthusiasm in his eye. "Did you know, Master, that in America
we marry earlier and produce twice as many healthy children as people
do in Europe? The population of the American colonies is doubling
every twenty years, yet there is enough land to settle for centuries. The
farmlands of America will provide an ever-expanding market for British
manufacture. Together, Britain and her American colonies may grow,
regardless of other nations, for generations. I believe that is our destiny."

This was Ben Franklin's prescription. There could be no doubt that he
passionately believed it.

"It is a noble vision," said John.

"Indeed," and now Franklin grinned, "there is only one thing needed
to perfect our English-speaking empire."

"What's that?" asked John.

"Kick the French out of Canada and have the whole place to ourselves," the great man said cheerfully.

He had just spoken these words when a serving maid came into the
room with a tray of refreshments. It seemed to be a signal to end the serious part of their conversation, for their host's mood lightened, as he
insisted they all have tea with him before they left.

As they walked back to their lodgings afterward, Master turned to
Mercy a little reproachfully.

"I had not known you felt such aversion for the English. I thought you
were contented with our visit."

She felt an instant remorse. She had no wish to bring unhappiness to her dear husband, who tried so hard to please her.

"I scarcely know what came over me," she said. "I expect Mr. Franklin is right. But the English way of thinking is sometimes hard for me, John, for I am still a Quaker at heart." And she resolved that, as long as they remained in London, she would do her best to make her husband happy.

Satisfied with this half-truth, John Master asked young James what he thought.

"I think Mr. Franklin is a great man, Father," he answered.

"You like his views on America's destiny?"

"Oh yes."

"So do I." And as he thought of his son's liking for London, and the huge possibilities Franklin had outlined for the British Empire, it seemed to John Master that the future looked bright.

That evening as they were eating supper, and they were all in a cheerful mood, Mercy remarked upon something else.

"Did you notice what happened," she asked, "when the maid was serving tea?"

"I don't think so," said John.

"He thought no one saw, but Mr. Franklin patted the girl's bottom as she passed."

"The old devil."

"They say, you know," she smiled, "that he's quite incorrigible."

✣

But if Mercy kept her feelings about the British to herself after that, her sense of displeasure remained, and was heightened just before Christmas.

It seemed that their offer of kindness to Captain Rivers, when they'd met him in Bath, had not been forgotten. For in mid-December they received an invitation to dine with his father, Lord Riverdale, the very next week.

Riverdale House was not a palace, but a substantial mansion near Hanover Square. From the two-story hall, they mounted a grand staircase to the *piano nobile,* where a grand saloon ran from the front to the back of the house. The company was not large. His Lordship, who appeared to be an older, stouter version of his son, was a widower. His sister acted as hostess. Captain Rivers had invited a couple of his military friends. Mercy was placed on His Lordship's right, where he made much of her, thanked her for their kind invitation to his son, and talked interestingly about the capital's affairs.

There was plenty to talk about. News had arrived in the morning that across the Atlantic, British forces had defeated the French up at Quebec. Though the daring young British general, Wolfe, had tragically been killed, it seemed that Ben Franklin's wish was about to be realized, and the French kicked out of the north. When Mercy told Lord Riverdale about their visit to Franklin and his views on the empire's destiny, he seemed delighted, and begged her to repeat it to the whole company.

Yet if the old aristocrat was charming, the colonel on her right did not please her so much. He was a military man. She did not mind, therefore, that he was proud of British arms. "A well-trained redcoat is a match for even the best French troops, Mrs. Master," he declared. "I think we've just proved that. As for the lesser breeds . . ."

"The lesser breeds, Colonel?" she queried. He smiled.

"I was out in Forty-five, you know."

The Forty-five. It was not fifteen years since Bonnie Prince Charlie had landed in Scotland and tried to take back the old kingdom from the Hanoverian rulers in London. It had been a wild, romantic business. And utterly tragic. The redcoats had moved against the ill-equipped and untrained Scotsmen and smashed them.

"Untrained men can't stand against a regular army, Mrs. Master," the colonel continued calmly. "It can't be done. As for the Highland Scots . . ." He smiled. "They're little more than savages, you know."

Mercy had seen plenty of Scots arriving in Philadelphia and New York. They didn't seem like savages to her, but it was clear that the colonel believed what he said, and this didn't seem the time and place to argue with him.

A little later on, however, the conversation turned to Irish affairs.

"The native Irish," the colonel said emphatically, "is little better than an animal." And though she knew that this was not to be taken too literally, the Quaker in her found such judgments arrogant and unseemly. But no one at the table disagreed with him, she noticed.

"Ireland has to be ruled firmly," Lord Riverdale said quietly. "I'm sure we all agree."

"They're certainly not capable of governing themselves," the colonel remarked, "not even the Protestant Irish."

"Yet they have an Irish Parliament, surely?" Mercy asked.

"You are quite right, Mrs. Master," Lord Riverdale said with a smile. "But the truth is, we make quite sure that the Irish Parliament has no power."

Mercy said no more. She smiled politely, and the evening continued pleasantly. But this she knew: she had seen the heart of the empire, and she did not like it.

⁑

Young James Master didn't know what to do. He loved his parents. As the new year began, he had talked to his father, but not his mother.

Since coming to London, he'd grown in confidence, and also in height. For he was already an inch and a half taller than when he arrived, and the fine new coat his father had bought him was in full retreat up his arms.

"I believe you'll be taller than I am," his father laughed.

It was not surprising that James had fallen in love with London. It was, indisputably, the capital of the English-speaking world. The city was so full of activity that, as the great Doctor Johnson was to say: "A man who is tired of London is tired of life." In his tutor, James had gained a guide; in young Grey Albion, an admiring younger brother. The English fellows of his age accepted him as one of themselves. What more could a boy of rising fifteen want?

One thing. He wanted to go to Oxford. He was still too young. But under the clever handling of his tutor, he was making huge strides in his studies. "There's no reason why he shouldn't be ready to go to Oxford in a few years," his tutor told his father. And truth to tell, John Master had been delighted by the idea. "You'd be doing far better than I did," he confessed very frankly to James. Indeed, when he remembered the humiliation he'd felt at the hands of his Boston cousins, he couldn't restrain a smile. Harvard and Yale were fine places; but to have a son who'd been to Oxford—that would be one in the eye for the Masters of Boston!

There was also another consideration. He knew the men in the provincial Assembly, and the New Yorkers close to the governor; and a surprising number of these fellows had been educated in England. An Oxford degree might be a useful asset for the family in the future.

Master talked to Albion about it, and the London man agreed.

"If James goes to Oxford," Albion told him, "he should live with us in London during the vacations. We already think of him as one of the family."

There was only one problem.

It was New Year's Day when Mercy gave John the unexpected news.

"John, I'm with child."

After so many years it had come as quite a surprise, but it seemed there was no doubt. And with the news had come one other request.

"John, I want to return to New York. I want my child born in my home, not in England."

He waited a day before he brought up the subject of James and Oxford. He was prepared for her not to like the idea, but not for her dismay.

"Let him go to Harvard, John, but do not leave him here. I beg you." And even after he had pointed out the advantages of the thing, she had only become more distressed. "I could not bear to lose my son to this accursed place."

When he informed the boy of his mother's feelings, James said nothing. But he looked so unhappy that John told him to wait a few more days, while he considered.

And for several more days, John Master did consider the matter, most carefully. He could understand Mercy's feelings. The thought that he and his son should be parted by three thousand miles, quite possibly for years, was just as painful for him as it was for his mother. Especially after their growing companionship in London, it would probably hurt him even more. On the other hand, James had clearly set his heart on it, and Master had no doubt in his mind that Oxford would be good for his son.

Set against that, however, must be the condition of his mother. A pregnancy was always dangerous, and as a woman got older, he believed it was more so. Should he and James cause her acute distress at such a time? What if, God forbid, things were to go wrong? A vision came into his mind of Mercy on her sickbed, calling for her son, three thousand miles away. Of Mercy's silent reproach. Of poor young James's subsequent guilt.

He broached the subject gently with Mercy one more time. Her feelings were as strong as ever. And so there was only one decision, he concluded, to be made.

"You shall return with us to America," he told James. "And there you'll remain for some months. But after that time, if you have not changed your mind, we'll consider the question of Oxford again. I promise you nothing, but we'll consider it. In the meantime, my boy, you must make the best of it, put on a cheerful face, and take care not to distress your mother. For if you complain, and distress her," he added ominously, "then I'll close the subject forever."

He did not tell his son that he had every intention of sending him back to England within the year.

And whether James guessed this, or whether he simply heeded his words, John Master was greatly pleased that for the remaining weeks of the winter, James was as kind and obliging as any parent could wish their son to be. They continued to enjoy great happiness in London. And finally, after a fond parting from the Albions, the three Masters took ship in the first fine weather of the spring, to make the long voyage back to New York.

Abigail

M ANY NATIONS HAD followed the imperial dream. But by the 1760s, no reasonable person could doubt that Britain was destined for glory. Soon after the Masters got back to New York, news came that the old king had died, and the modest, well-meaning young Prince of Wales had come to the throne as George III. And every year, new blessings were heaped upon his empire.

In America, Britain's armies had driven the rival French from Canada. In 1763, at the Peace of Paris, the French abandoned all their claims to the vast American hinterland, and were allowed only the modest town of New Orleans down in the Mississippi marshes; while their Catholic allies the Spanish had to give up their huge domains in Florida.

The whole eastern American seaboard was now Britain's. Except for the presence of the Indians, of course. Recently, when a leader of the Ottawa Indians, named Pontiac, had started a rebellion that had terrified the colonists of Massachusetts, the British Army, aided by local sharpshooters, had smashed the Indians soon enough—a valuable reminder to the colonists of their need for the mother country. But beyond such necessary firmness, the British believed their policy was generous and wise. Let the Indians fear English power, but don't stir them up. There was still plenty of empty land in the east. Any drive westward into the hinterland could wait for a generation or two. Cultivate the huge garden of the eastern seaboard, therefore, and enjoy its fruits.

Ben Franklin himself would not have disagreed. Indeed, thanks to his indefatigable lobbying, the prudent British government had even given him a valuable stake in the great enterprise. For his son William Franklin, with a law degree, but no administrative experience, was now made governor of the colony of New Jersey.

As for the rest of her far-flung empire and her rivalry with France, Britain now controlled the fabulous riches of India and the rich sugar island of Jamaica. Her navy dominated every ocean. Britannia ruled the waves.

Such was the enlightened, happy empire of Britain's well-meaning young king.

But not everyone was happy.

⊹

The way Charlie White saw it, things were going from bad to worse, and no mistake. As he walked up Broadway, a sharp north wind was coming down the Hudson River, slicing through the January dusk like a knife. There was a thin, frozen crust of snow on the streets. And Charlie's mood was black.

It was Twelfth Night. He'd been planning to give his wife a present, but he had nothing.

Well, almost nothing. A pair of mittens he'd found going cheap in the market. He'd been lucky there. But that was all.

"I wanted to buy you a new dress," he'd told her sadly, "but it's all I can do to put food on the table."

"It's all right, Charlie," she said. "It's the thought that counts."

It was the same for most of their neighbors. It had been like this ever since the damned British Army had gone.

The war was over. That was the trouble. Gone were the redcoats who needed provisions; gone were the officers who wanted houses, and furniture, and servants. Naval ships came in but only briefly, and were gone. The whole place was in recession. Money was tight. Merchants in London were shipping their excess stocks across the ocean, selling them off at bargain prices in New York, so that honest craftsmen couldn't make a living. Yet farmers in the market, having fewer customers to sell to, were marking their prices up, to compensate.

"England uses this place to fight the French," he told his family, "but once that's done, they leave us in the lurch."

The only people who weren't suffering were the rich. They lived in another world. The theater was full. Pleasure gardens with London names like Ranelagh were being opened. "London in New York," people called it. Everything was fine for men like John Master.

Charlie had steered clear of Master since the merchant's return from London. He knew all about young James being sent to Oxford, for he still, bitterly, followed the family's every move. But if his contemptuous former friend had come to his house now, Charlie would have spat in his face.

Things had got so bad in the White household that Charlie's wife had started going to church. Not the Anglican church, of course. You could leave that, Charlie thought, to the Trinity crowd. She preferred the Dissenters. Sometimes, to keep her happy, he'd even go with her to a service or a preaching. But he hadn't any faith himself.

"Your mother's took to religion, son," he had told Sam. "I reckon it's poverty that's drove her to it."

But where the devil was young Sam? That was why he was walking up Broadway in the freezing dusk. Looking for his favorite son. He'd been out since noon. What the devil was he up to?

Charlie had a pretty good idea, of course. Sam was seventeen, and Charlie had noticed, not without a touch of pride, that his son was starting to make headway with the girls. There was a pretty young serving girl he'd spotted him with last week. The young scamp was probably off somewhere with her.

But it was Twelfth Night, and the family was celebrating together. Sam should have more consideration. Charlie was going to give his son a piece of his mind when he found him.

An hour passed. Charlie visited all the taverns on the West Side, but no one had seen his son. Irritated, he went back to the house. The rest of the family was there, waiting to eat. So they ate without Sam. And his wife said she didn't mind, so long as Sam was all right, which was a damn lie.

So after it was all over, Charlie went out again. His wife said there was no point and he knew it. But he couldn't just sit there. It was a dark night now, and the wind had a vicious bite to it. The clouds in the sky were ragged, and through their tatters, you could see the faint, cold glimmer of a star or two. The streets were almost empty.

He walked down Broadway, called in at a few taverns, but had no luck. He passed Trinity Church and continued southward. He was entering the area he hated now.

The Court area, they called it these days. The old fort had become Fort George. In front of it, the small park of Bowling Green had been neatly railed off into a fashionable enclave, with street lamps at each corner to deter any vagrants from loitering. The governor's house was here. Even the taverns had royal names.

Rich mansions loomed in the darkness all around. It mattered not to their owners—families like Livingston, Bayard, van Cortlandt, De Lancey, Morris—whether the city was going through boom or bust. They were impregnable, in their inherited security. Charlie turned east, into Beaver Street. At the end of it, he came to some railings, and a pair of handsome iron gates, surmounted by lamps. These protected a wide cobbled path and steps leading up to a large classical house. The shutters had not been closed; the warm light from the tall windows streamed out into the yard.

John Master's house. He'd built it soon after his return from London.

Charlie continued across the southern end of Manhattan until he came to the East River. The long waterfront of docks and warehouses was quiet now, the ships so many shadows in the water. He walked along the wharfs a little way, then turned up Queen Street. There were lighted windows here, taverns still open.

He'd gone fifty yards when he came upon the shape on the ground. It was a black man, huddled in a blanket, against a warehouse wall. He glanced up at Charlie and, without much hope, held out his hand.

"Boss?"

Charlie looked down at him. Another sign of the times. All over the city, the smaller masters, short of cash, had been freeing their household slaves. It was cheaper than feeding them. They were everywhere: free blacks, with nothing to do but beg. Or starve. Charlie gave him a penny. Just after Schemmerhorn's Wharf, he came to a large tavern, and went in.

There was quite a crowd in there, mariners mostly. Over at a table, he caught sight of a carter he knew. Big fellow, red hair. Never liked him much. If he could remember his name, he supposed he might speak to him, though he didn't really want to. But the carter had got up and was coming toward him. Well, no need to be rude. Charlie gave him a nod.

But the next thing he knew, the fellow was taking his arm. Bill. That was his name.

"I'm sorry about your boy, Charlie," he said.

"My boy? You mean Sam?" Charlie felt himself going pale. "What's wrong with him?"

"You don't know?" Bill looked concerned. "He ain't dead, Charlie," he explained hurriedly. "Nothing like that. But the press gang took him and a dozen others late this afternoon."

"Press gang?"

"They were here and gone so quick you wouldn't believe it. The ship's already sailed. Your Sam's in the Royal Navy now, serving His Majesty."

Charlie felt a strong arm round him before he even realized he was falling. "Sit down here, Charlie. Give him rum!" He felt the rough hot liquid searing his throat and warming his stomach. He sat helplessly, while the big red-headed fellow sat beside him.

And then Charlie White cursed. He cursed the British Navy which had stolen his son, the British government which had ruined his city; he cursed the governor, and the congregation of Trinity, and John Master and his big house, and his son at Oxford. He cursed them all to hell.

⁘

It was some weeks later, on a damp spring day, that Hudson looked in upon his employer in the small library of his house, and found John Master trying to finish some paperwork, but somewhat hampered by the five-year-old girl who was sitting on his knee. His wife was out.

"Can we go now, Papa?" the little girl asked.

"Soon, Abby," answered Master.

So Hudson stepped forward and quietly took the child from her father's knee.

"I'll mind her until you're ready," he said softly, and Master smiled at him gratefully. With the child clinging to his neck, Hudson retreated toward the kitchen. "We'll find you a cookie, Miss Abby," he promised.

Abigail didn't object. She and Hudson had been friends since her birth. In fact, he'd almost had to deliver her.

In the quarter-century since John Master had rescued him, Hudson had always worked for the Master family. He had done so of his own free will. After that first evening, Master had never questioned Hudson's claim that he was not a slave. He'd employed him at a reasonable wage, and Hudson had always been free to go. Five times, when the urge had come upon him, Hudson had gone to sea in one of the Masters' ships; but with the passing of the years, his desire for roaming had grown less. In the house, John had employed him first as a handyman, then in other capacities. Nowadays, he ran the entire household. When the family had gone to London, Master had not hesitated to leave the place in his care.

Fifteen years ago, he had married. His wife was a slave in the Masters' house. Her name was Cleopatra. At least, it had been when she arrived, until Mercy, thinking the name inappropriate, had made her change it to Ruth. Hudson and she had a daughter, then a son. When Hudson called his son Solomon, and Mercy asked him why he chose this biblical name, he told her it was because King Solomon was wise. But to his wife afterward he'd added quietly: "And old King Solomon was a rich man too." Since his wife was a slave, his children were slaves too. But Master had made a straightforward arrangement.

"You can buy them out for a fair price now, Hudson, or they can be mine until they're twenty-five. After that, I'll set them and their mother free." Since the children were fed and clothed, and Master saw to it that Solomon was taught to read, write and figure, this wasn't a bad deal.

"For it ain't so good to be free and black in New York," Hudson reminded Ruth. "Not these days, anyhow."

There were still black freedmen in the city. But the last half-century had certainly been bad for Negroes. The old days of the Dutch, when white farmers and their black slaves might work in the fields side by side, was not even a memory. As England's mighty sugar trade had grown larger than ever, so the numbers of slaves being sold in the markets had risen. Since the days when Hudson's grandfather was a boy, the West Indies had sucked in almost a million slaves, and the whole African slave trade was now in British hands. With such vast numbers in the market, the unit price of a human being dropped. Most city tradesmen and craftsmen could afford to go down Wall Street to the slave market by the river, to buy a household slave or two. Farmers came across the Brooklyn ferry from Kings County to buy workers for their fields. There were more slaves as a percentage of population in the New York region than anywhere north of Virginia.

And if all these black people were chattels, why then—most people nowadays agreed—it must be that God had created them inferior. And if they were inferior, then it stood to reason that they shouldn't be free. Besides, people hadn't forgotten the slave disturbances, like the burnings of 1741. Blacks were dangerous.

So if most people assumed that he was John Master's slave, Hudson didn't much care. "At least that way," he pointed out, "people don't give me no trouble." All he could do was count himself lucky and hope, one day, for better times.

He'd run the house smoothly for old Dirk Master while John and Mercy had been in England. Hudson and John's father had always got along well, and Dirk had sent a letter full of praise for him to London. Had Hudson sent a report on Dirk Master, however, it wouldn't have been so glowing. The trouble was young Miss Susan.

Susan Master had not only grown up into a beautiful young woman; she was even-tempered, practical, and knew her own mind. As her grandfather remarked to Hudson, "At least I don't have to worry about her."

But Hudson wasn't so sure about that. When young Mr. Meadows had begun to court her, it was clear that Susan liked his advances very well. He was a handsome young fellow, with a strong face, a splendid horse, and heir to one of the best farms in Dutchess County. In short, although she was still very young, he was just what she wanted.

Just so long as things didn't go too far before they were married. And they might. There had been times when the two young people had been left alone in the house for far too long. "You have to tell her," Hudson urged his wife, "to take care." And he himself had summoned the courage, to remark gently to old Dirk that the young people were spending a lot of time unsupervised together. "If she gets into trouble, and maybe young Mr. Meadows changes his mind . . ." he'd lamented to Ruth.

"I reckon the Masters would make him marry her," Ruth assured him.

"Maybe," he'd answered, "but it won't look right." And again he'd tried to warn her grandfather.

But old Dirk Master had refused to be worried. He was enjoying his time in New York. The burden of the business was light. It seemed that he was unwilling to allow anything to disturb his peace of mind. And indeed, Susan's cheerful face and sensible character seemed to give the lie to Hudson's worries. But when his son Solomon came running into the house, one summer morning, to tell him that the Masters had returned and that he was wanted at the waterfront right away, he'd experienced a huge sense of relief.

To be followed, instantly, by panic. For when he got the cart to the waterfront, he'd found Mercy almost giving birth to a child. He and Master had helped her into the cart, Solomon had been sent running to the doctor, the midwife had been summoned, and Hudson and Master had carried her into the house and up to her bedroom, both wondering if the child would be born before they even got her upstairs.

What a day that had been. But what joy it had brought. For not two hours later, little Abigail had been born.

Hudson loved Abigail. Everybody did. She had rich brown curls and hazel eyes. She was a little plump. As a baby, she seldom cried, and as a little girl, she seemed to love everyone around her. "That's the most sweet-natured child I ever saw," he'd say to Ruth. His own face wreathed in smiles, he'd play with her whenever he could, as if she were his own.

The presence of Abigail had also compensated Mercy for the departure of her other children. Later that year, Susan had been married. The following summer, James had been allowed to return to England, to prepare himself for Oxford. "But Abigail's here," Master would say to Hudson with a smile, "to keep us all young."

For nearly half an hour, now, Hudson happily kept her occupied in the kitchen, until her father was ready.

✦

John Master looked at the two letters before him and sighed. He knew he'd been right to let James return to England, but he missed him, and he wished that he were back.

The first was from Captain Rivers. They had kept in touch since their meeting in London. As promised, Rivers had visited New York, where they'd spent a pleasant week. Then he'd gone down to Carolina and married his rich widow. They already had two children. By all accounts, the captain had done well with his plantations, and Master knew that he had an excellent account with Albion. Many of his neighbors, however, Rivers told him, complained of their English creditors. They'd lived easy for years, buying all manner of goods on credit—which the London merchants were happy to grant them. "Now times are harder," he wrote, "they can't pay." Rivers had the sense to live within his means.

He also described a visit to Virginia. His host had been George Washington, the former British officer, who had large landholdings there. Washington, too, had complaints against the mother country, but of a different kind. "He dislikes the government's restraints on trade, especially the iron trade from which his wife's large fortune comes," Rivers wrote. But a deeper complaint concerned the western frontier. After serving in the army, Washington had been granted bounty lands in Indian territory. Yet now the ministry in London, wanting to maintain peace with the Indians, had told him he couldn't claim his lands and kick the Indians out. "I met many Virginians in the same position," Rivers wrote. "They were hoping to make fortunes out of those land grants, and now they're furious—though Washington tells them to be patient."

On the whole, Master considered the British view was right. There was still plenty of available land in the east. Every year thousands of families from the mother country were arriving—English, Scots and Irish—in search of cheap land. And they were finding it. Washington and his friends would have to be patient.

But the other letter worried him. It was from Albion.

It started cheerfully enough. James was happy at Oxford. He was tall and handsome, and quite a hero to young Grey Albion. In London, a fellow called Wilkes had written articles against the government, and been thrown in jail for it. But the whole city had risen in protest, and now Wilkes was a national hero. It reminded Master of the Zenger trial of his youth; and he was glad, though not surprised, that good Englishmen were defending free speech.

But then Albion came to the main point of his letter.

Britain's finances were in a mess. The years of war had left her with a great empire, but huge debts. Credit was tight. The government was struggling to raise taxes where it could, but the English were now taxed higher than any nation in Europe. A recent attempt to impose a cider tax down in the West Country had caused riots. Worse, having been promised some lowering of the high wartime land taxes, the Parliament men were clamoring to pay less taxes, not more.

Britain's greatest cost was America. Pontiac's revolt had shown that the colonies still required expensive garrisons to defend them, but who was going to pay?

"It's hardly surprising therefore," Albion wrote, "that the ministry should look to the American colonies, who so far have paid almost nothing, to contribute to the cost of their own defense. The new duty on sugar imposed last year only covers about an eighth of what's needed."

Master shook his head. The Sugar Act of the previous year had been a badly drafted mass of irritating regulations. The New Yorkers had been furious. However, it was at least the custom for the government to receive duties on trade, and he reckoned the grumbling would subside.

"So that is why it was proposed," Albion continued, "that the tax upon stamps, which as you know we all pay here, should be extended to the colonies also."

But a Stamp Act would not be a duty on trade. It was a tax. The tax itself was simple enough. Every legal document, every commercial contract and all printed matter in England required a payment to the government. The amount was not large. But it was still a tax.

If there was one principle that every good Englishman understood, it was that the king could not tax the people without their consent. And the colonists had not been asked.

"Nor was it very intelligent of the king's ministers," John had remarked to his wife, "to choose the one tax best calculated to irritate the merchants, lawyers and printers who run this place."

When the first rumor of this proposal had reached America, a mass of complaints and petitions had been dispatched to London. In New York, Mayor Cruger had announced that the city council couldn't afford the usual supplies of firewood for the English troops in the barracks. "We'll let 'em freeze," he had gleefully told Master. "That'll make 'em think." Moderate colonists like John Master had agreed that money had to be raised. "But let our proper representatives, the assemblies in each colony, work out how to do it," they suggested. Ben Franklin thought that the colonies should meet together in a congress to devise a common solution. In London, the government then announced that the matter would be reviewed for a year. And there, Master had supposed, the matter rested. Until he read the rest of Albion's letter.

> I am concerned that your last letter speaks of consultation between the colonies and the ministry. For the king has placed the whole matter in the hands of the Prime Minister, Grenville; and though Grenville is honest and thorough, his nature is impatient and somewhat obstinate. I should caution you, therefore, that I have it on the best authority that Grenville has no thought of waiting for the colonies to propose anything. The Stamp Act will be law by Easter.

And that, John Master thought grimly, will put the cat among the pigeons. But having read the letter over again and thought about its implications, he decided that there was nothing more for him to do just then but take his daughter out for her walk, as he had promised her. He could consider the business further as he walked.

Having found her in the kitchen with Hudson, he told her to put on her coat, and when she asked very sweetly if Hudson might come too, he smiled and answered: "By all means, Abby. The exercise will do him good."

⁘

Hudson was glad to be out. The wind was damp, but the sun was bright as they reached Broadway. He'd supposed they'd all go into Bowling Green, where Abigail could play; but today she said she wanted to walk instead. Hudson kept a couple of paces behind them. It gave him pleasure to see the tall, handsome man holding his little girl by the hand and to watch people smile as they greeted them. Abigail was dressed in a little gray cloak, and a pointed hat she'd been given, in the old Dutch style, of which she was very proud. Master was wearing a brown, homespun coat, well cut of course, but plain.

If John Master dressed plainly, nowadays, Hudson knew it was by design. Some months ago, word had arrived of a new group of dandies in London. Macaronis, they called themselves. They had taken to parading round London's West End and their extravagant plumed hats and jeweled swords had caused quite a scandal. "Since every London fashion comes to New York by the next boat," John had warned his friends, "we'd better be careful." Such public extravagance could only be an offense to most people in hard-pressed New York. "Don't let any of your family dress up like a Macaroni," he had urged. "It's not the time."

John Master had been one of a group who'd taken the lead in promoting local cloth and linen manufacture in the city; and in recent months, instead of the fashionable cloths and bright silk waistcoats he had always favored before, he'd made a point of wearing good American-made homespun whenever he went out.

By the time they got to Trinity, he thought they'd turn back, but little Abigail said she wanted to go further. I'll have to carry her back, Hudson thought with a smile. They were coming into the poorer quarter of the town now, toward the Common. Hudson wondered if it was wise to go up here. He decided to walk beside them. A little way ahead was Montayne's Tavern.

There was quite a crowd of fellows—mariners, laborers and small craftsmen—drinking in the street by the tavern doors. Seeing this crowd, Abigail glanced up at Hudson uncertainly. He smiled. "They won't do you no harm," he told her.

"I used to go into places like that all the time, when I was young," Master remarked cheerfully. And they had just come level with the door, when he saw a face that made him exclaim: "Why, it's Charlie White." And taking Abby by the hand, he told her: "Come, Abby, you shall meet an old friend of mine." And he strode across and called out: "Charlie!"

Hudson was maybe twenty feet away while he watched what happened next.

Charlie White turned and stared.

"Charlie. You haven't forgotten me?"

Charlie went on staring.

"Charlie, this is my little girl, Abigail. Say how d'ye do, Abby, to my friend Mr. White."

Charlie hardly glanced at Abigail. Then, deliberately, he spat on the ground in front of Master. Hudson saw Master going red. Charlie was turning to the men in front of the tavern.

"This here is Mr. Master," he called out. "Neighbor of the governor's. Son's in England. At Oxford University. Whadda ya think of that?"

The men were giving Master ugly looks. Someone made a rude noise. Hudson tensed.

"What's this about, Charlie?" cried Master. But Charlie White seemed to ignore the question. Then, suddenly, he thrust his face, contorted with hatred, into Master's.

"I ain't your friend, you two-faced Englishman. You get outta here." He glanced down at Abigail in her tall hat. "And take your little witch with you."

Abigail was looking up at them both, wide-eyed. She began to cry. Hudson started to move forward.

But with a shrug of disgust, Master turned away. Moments later, they were walking rapidly down Broadway. Hudson picked Abby up and let her cling to his neck. Master was stony-faced, and wasn't speaking.

"Who was that wicked man?" Abby whispered to Hudson.

"Don' you mind him," he told her softly. "He's a little crazy."

⁙

For some days after this humiliation, John Master was in a state of anger. If it hadn't been for the number of Charlie's friends, who might have joined in, and the fact that his little daughter was there, he would probably have struck Charlie. As it was, his little girl had been frightened, and his dignity had suffered considerably.

He was also mystified. Why should his old friend hate him so much? What did Charlie's anger mean? Several times in the next couple of weeks he wondered whether to go round and have it out with Charlie. And had he done so, perhaps he might have discovered the truth. But a lifetime's experience—that it was better to leave trouble alone—and his own wounded pride prevented him.

One thing was clear, however. The mood in the city was uglier than he'd thought. He'd seen the faces of the men with Charlie at the tavern, and their venomous looks had shaken him. He knew of course that men like Charlie had no love for the rich, Anglican, Trinity crowd, especially when times were hard. He understood if they despised corrupt royal governors. So did he. But when Charlie had called him an Englishman, and used the term with such hatred, he'd been taken aback. After all, the way he saw it, Charlie and he were both English colonists, the same as each other.

He'd always prided himself on his knowledge of men like Charlie. Had he allowed himself, in the years since his return from London, to get out of touch with the city streets? He realized that perhaps he had, and decided he'd better do something about it. In the following weeks, he spent more time talking to the men at the warehouse. He chatted to stall-holders in the market, went into the taverns near his house and listened to what people were saying. He soon ascertained that the bad feeling was more widespread than he'd supposed. Everyone seemed discontented. Whatever was wrong with their lives, people were blaming the government. And the government was in London.

So he was greatly concerned, late that spring, when news arrived that the Stamp Act was law.

Even then, the protests surprised him. Down in Virginia, a young lawyer named Patrick Henry had set the assembly there ablaze when he called King George a tyrant. A furious councilman Master met in the street told him: "So now we know, John. Those damned fellows in London mean us to be slaves." And it seemed that the poor folk were just as furious about the measure. It was strange in a way, Master considered. It was true that newspapers and almanacs would be taxed, but he suspected it would be his own class who'd pay most of the stamp duty, rather than fellows like Charlie. But it seemed that the tax was a symbol: an imposition from London, levied without consent; proof positive that the British government thought it could treat the colonies as it liked.

The act was due to go into effect at the start of November. Meanwhile, shipments of officially stamped paper were being sent from England.

If New Yorkers were angry, they certainly weren't alone. Word came that in Boston a mob had burned the stamp distributor's house. His counterparts in Rhode Island and Connecticut were threatened. The New York distributor didn't wait for trouble. He quit.

New York had an acting governor at present. Cadwallader Colden was an old Scottish physician with a farm on Long Island. Years ago, his research into yellow fever had helped produce the first sanitation measures in the city, but that was of no account now. An angry crowd gathered to protest outside his city house. Colden might be seventy-seven, but he was a tough old Scot. He summoned British troops from upriver, and put more guns in Fort George. But that didn't stop the protests.

One day, Master caught sight of Charlie leading a crowd of angry men by the fort. Remembering Charlie's angry words, he told Mercy: "Keep Abby indoors. I'm afraid there could be trouble."

That afternoon, he gathered the household together. Besides Mercy and Abigail, there was Hudson of course, and Ruth. Hudson's daughter Hannah was a quiet girl who worked in the house with her mother. Young Solomon was quite a different character, a lively youth who liked it when Master hired him out and gave him some of the proceeds. Three other hired servants made up the rest.

Calmly and quietly, Master told them that he wanted everyone to be careful while there was trouble in the streets, and to stay safely in the house during the coming days, and not go out without permission. Only afterward did Hudson come to him and ask if he might go out to see if he could learn a little more. To this he agreed. And when Hudson returned at dusk, the black man warned him: "After dark, Boss, I think we better close the shutters and bolt the doors."

That evening, down in the cellar, he and Hudson looked over the household's defenses. Master had two fowling pieces, which fired shot, a flintlock and three pistols. He had dry powder and ammunition. But none of these guns had been used for a long time, and so they spent an hour or more cleaning and oiling them. Master could only hope they would never be needed.

One ray of hope came from New York's Provincial Assembly. There were still sensible fellows leading the colony, and Master was relieved when one of the Assembly men came to him in late summer and told him: "We've agreed that a congress of all the colonies shall meet in New York."

⁘

The congress met in October. Twenty-seven men from nine of the colonies stayed in various lodgings in the town and met together for two weeks. He would see them in the street each day. They all seemed to be sober fellows. When they had completed their work, their conclusion was carefully framed but unequivocal. In petitions to Parliament, and to the king himself, they declared: "The Stamp Act is against the British Constitution."

If John Master had hoped this would calm the situation, however, he was soon disappointed. Many of the merchants still weren't satisfied, and Charlie White and his sort were spoiling for trouble. It didn't help that the very day the congress finished, a ship arrived in the harbor carrying the first two tons of stamped paper to be used under the act. Old Governor Colden wisely smuggled the cargo into the fort under cover of darkness, but that didn't get rid of the problem. Crowds swirled round the fort, threatening leaflets were printed, people hung flags at half mast all round the town. There was only a week to go before the act came into force and the stamped paper would be used. God knows what would happen then.

At the end of the month, Master attended a meeting of two hundred of the city's leading merchants. Some, like himself, counseled patience, but the mood of the meeting was clean against them. When he got back he told Mercy: "They've decided on a non-importation agreement. We'll refuse to import any more goods from Britain. That's clever, of course, because it will hit the London merchants like Albion, and they in turn will put pressure on Parliament. But I wish we hadn't done it, all the same."

On the last night of October, he stood by the water's edge under the stars. At the tip of Manhattan, the squat, black mass of Fort George, now armed with ninety cannon, silently guarded the stamped papers from England. Tomorrow those papers were due to be distributed. In five days' time, it would be the Fifth of November—Pope's Day, with its usual bonfires, no doubt. But what larger conflagration, he wondered, might be about to engulf the city before then?

⁑

The day began. The sky was clear. A faint, cold breeze crossed the harbor. He walked over to Bowling Green. All was quiet. He returned to the house, had breakfast with Mercy and Abigail, then attended to business for some hours.

At noon, he went out again. There were people about, but no sign of trouble. He went to the fort. There was no word that old Governor Colden was attempting to distribute any of the stamped papers. Thank God for that at least. He went back to his house, and settled down to work again.

There was much to do. The non-importation agreement would hit his business with London, of course. But it also opened up opportunities. Like any sensible businessman, Master had been listing the goods that would no longer be obtainable in New York. Which of these could be manufactured locally? What were the likely substitutes? What should he do, meanwhile, with the balance of credit held for him by Albion in London? These were interesting questions. In the middle of the afternoon, Hudson came in to inquire if he wanted anything. Master asked for tea, and told Hudson to send the boy out, to see if anything was happening in the town. Then he went back to work. He did not know how long he had been working when Hudson entered the room again.

"Solomon's back, Boss. He says something's happening up on the Common."

Master strode swiftly up Broadway. The November afternoon was already turning into dusk. In his right hand, he held his silver-topped walking stick. He strode past Trinity Church. He could see Montayne's Tavern ahead, and the Common beyond. But he got no farther.

The crowd that was streaming toward him must have numbered a couple of thousand people. By the look of it, they were mostly the poorer sort—small craftsmen, sailors, freed slaves and laborers. In the middle of this procession, he saw a large cart like a carnival float. He drew to one side, to let them pass.

It was hard to gauge their mood. They looked truculent, rather than angry, he thought. Many were laughing and joking. As for the carnival float, in its way it was a work of art.

For anticipating Pope's Day, they had constructed a splendid mock gallows. Except that, instead of the Pope, they had made a large, and really very lifelike, dummy of Governor Colden, with another dummy of the devil sitting beside him. The governor held a huge sheaf of stamped papers in his hand, and he also carried a drum. Despite himself, John acknowledged the grim humor of the thing. Obviously they intended to burn the governor instead of the Pope this year. The question was, what else did they mean to do? Joining the throng of spectators who were moving along beside the procession, he kept pace with the float as it went down Broadway.

He had gone about a quarter-mile when he heard the roars. They were coming from a side street, and they were rapidly getting louder. Something was approaching, but he couldn't see what.

The hideous crowd that suddenly debouched into Broadway from the west side must have been several hundred strong. They, too, had an effigy, but of a different kind. Lurching wildly about on a pile of wood was a huge and obscene-looking dummy of the governor, looking more like a pirate than a pope. With Indian whoops and cries, this second procession, like a stream in spate meeting a river, crashed into the main body, causing a massive eddy. The first float rolled like a vessel that has been struck amidships, though it righted itself.

Many of the new crowd were carrying lanterns and torches. Some had clubs. Whatever they were going to do, they clearly meant business. And now, with the pressure of this new addition, the tide of the procession picked up speed so that John Master, even with his long legs, had to stride as fast as he could to keep up.

As the two effigies of the old governor passed Trinity almost side by side, he was able to get a good look at the second cart—and realized to his horror that it was not an ordinary cart at all. The wood on which the dummy sat had been piled up in no less a vehicle than the governor's carriage. God knows how the mob had managed to steal it. He saw a figure clamber up into the carriage. The figure was waving a cocked hat and shouting wildly to the crowd. It was Charlie White. And there was no doubt where they were headed. Reaching the southern end of Broadway, they made straight for the fort.

From the edge of Bowling Green, Master watched them. With torches lighted in the gathering dusk, they yelled abuse at the governor. He saw a party of them run forward and nail a message on the fort's big wooden door. Then, surging all around the fort, the crowd started throwing sticks, stones, anything they could lay their hands on, at the walls of Fort George, fairly daring the governor to fire upon them.

If the troops fire on them now, thought Master, they'll burn the whole place down. But the garrison remained silent, behind their stout walls.

The crowd wanted action though, and they meant to have it. With whoops and shouts, a large group began to drag the two effigies of the governor back onto Bowling Green. Another party was bringing bales of straw to the green; moments later, he saw flames starting to rise. They were setting fire to the effigies, burning the float, governor's carriage and all. Almost forgetting the danger, he found himself watching the bonfires, fascinated like a child. Until he heard a voice hiss by his side.

"Enjoying the bonfire?" It was Charlie. His face, gleaming menacingly in the light of the flames, contorted into a snarl. "After the fort, we're coming for you."

Master was so horrified that for a moment he could not speak; and by the time he said, "But Charlie . . ." it was too late. Charlie had gone.

He was glad to see, when he reached his house, that all the shutters were closed. Once inside, he told Hudson to bolt the doors. Everyone knew what was passing at the fort nearby, and Mercy looked at him anxiously. "I got the guns ready, Boss," Hudson whispered to him. But he shook his head, and murmured: "There's too many. Better not provoke 'em. But if they come, you and Solomon take all the women down to the cellar." The worst moment was when Abigail, her eyes wide and round, asked him: "Is the bad man who hates you coming to kill us?"

"No such thing, child." He smiled. "We'll all go into the parlor now, and I'll read you a story."

So he and Mercy and Hudson's wife and the other household servants all went and sat in the parlor. And John read to them from the children's tales that Abigail liked. But Hudson and young Solomon kept watch on the street from the windows upstairs.

An hour passed, and more. From time to time they heard roars from the direction of the fort, but the crowds did not seem to be coming in their direction. Eventually, Hudson came down, and said: "Sounds like they're going away. Maybe I'll take a look." But Master wasn't sure whether to let him.

"I don't want you getting hurt," he objected.

"It ain't the black men, Boss, that they're after tonight," Hudson answered quietly. A few moments later he slipped out into the street.

An hour passed before he returned. The news he brought was not good. After burning the effigies of the governor, the crowd had swung back up Broadway to the house of Major James, the fort's English artillery commander. "They took everything out of his house—china, furniture, books. Smashed all they could and burned the rest. You never saw such destruction."

Things quietened down in the next few days. Old Colden had the stock of stamped paper transferred to the City Hall, where it remained. But before Christmas, a new force arose. Its leaders were a mixed group. Some, Master considered, were just troublemakers like Charlie. One, to his certain knowledge, had originally been a convict. But others were more formidable. Two of them, Sears and McDougall, were fellows who'd worked their way up in the privateering trade from poverty to modest wealth, but were still close enough to their roots to carry the mob with them. They made their headquarters at Montayne's Tavern. And they had a program. "First we'll make a union with all the other colonies. Then to hell with London—we'll repeal the Stamp Act ourselves!" They had a stirring name for their movement, too: the Sons of Liberty.

The Liberty Boys, John Master called them. Sometimes they used reason, sometimes they used force. One night when John and Mercy were at a play, a crowd of Liberty Boys came and broke up the theater, telling the astonished patrons that they shouldn't be enjoying themselves when the rest of the city was suffering. At other times, they patrolled the docks to make sure that no one was receiving any goods from England.

The Provincial Assembly was horrified by the trouble in the streets, voted generous compensation to Major James for the destruction of his property, and did its best to control the mobs. Though the Assembly was divided into two main factions, the two faction leaders, Livingston and De Lancey, were both rich gentlemen and friendly with John Master. And each told him: "We gentlemen have got to stop these Liberty Boys getting out of hand." But it wasn't easy.

Master received some small hope from Albion. In London, the English merchant told him, the obstinate Grenville had been replaced by a new prime minister, Lord Rockingham, who was sympathetic to the colonies and wanted to get rid of the Stamp Act. Others felt the same. "But they are so troubled by the radicals and our own London mob at present, that they fear to make concessions which might look like weakness. Be patient therefore."

Try telling that, John thought, to the Liberty Boys.

He had to endure another six weeks before a ship finally arrived with the news: Parliament had repealed the act.

The city was jubilant. The Sons of Liberty called it a triumph. The Assembly voted that a new and splendid statue of King George should be erected on Bowling Green. The merchants rejoiced that trade could resume once more. Master was astonished at how suddenly the mood of the population could swing.

But though he was glad of this news, John Master could not rejoice with a full heart. For the same ship had brought another letter. It was from James.

My dear Father,

As I shall shortly complete my studies at Oxford, the question arises as to what I should do. Mr. Albion has suggested that, if I wish, and if you are agreeable, I might learn something of our business by working for him for a while. As you know, he has extensive trade not only with the American colonies, but with India too, and most parts of the empire. Though I long to return to the bosom of my family and be with you all again, I cannot help reflect that it would be greatly to our advantage if I were to remain here for a while. I could lodge, for the time being, with Mr. Albion. But of course, I shall in all things be guided by your wishes.

Your obedient son,
James

Having read the letter to himself, alone in his office, Master kept it with him for several days before sharing its contents with his wife. He wanted to think about it first.

It was one evening almost a week later that he came into the parlor where his dear Mercy and little Abigail were sitting. He had just been perusing the letter again, and now he gazed at them thoughtfully. It would be hard, he considered, for any man to love his wife and daughter more than he did. Yet only now did he realize how greatly he had been looking forward to the return of his son.

It hadn't occurred to him that James wouldn't want to come home. You couldn't blame the boy, of course. He obviously loved London. And even with the Stamp Act repealed, it remained to be seen how matters would shape themselves in New York. James might be better off in London.

So what should he do? Should he consult Mercy? What if she demanded James come home, when the boy so obviously didn't want to? No, that would do no good. James might return unwillingly, and then be resentful of his mother. Better, it seemed to John Master, to take the decision himself. If Mercy blamed him, well, so be it.

But he could not help wondering, as he looked sadly at his wife and daughter: Would he ever see his son again?

The Loyalist

YOUNG GREY ALBION stood at the door of the room. James Master smiled at him. Besides the fact that Grey was like a younger brother, it always amused him that young Albion's hair was always a mess.

"You aren't coming out, James?"

"I must write a letter."

As Grey departed, James sighed. The letter wasn't going to be easy. Though he always added a brief note to the regular reports Albion sent his father, he realized with shame that he hadn't written a proper letter to his parents in over a year. The letter he must now compose had better be long, and he hoped it would give them pleasure. The real reason for writing, however, he would save until the end.

He wasn't sure they were going to like it.

"My dear parents," he wrote, then paused. How should he begin?

⁂

John Master had never had a quarrel with his wife. Yet on this bright spring day, he was very close to it. How could she think of such a thing? His look signaled reproach, but in fact he was furious.

"I beg you not to go!" he protested.

"Thee cannot mean such a thing, John," she answered.

"Can't you see it makes me look a damn fool?"

How could she not understand? Last year, when they'd invited him to be a vestryman at Trinity, he'd been flattered. The appointment carried prestige, but also obligations—one of which, quite certainly, was not to have your wife openly attending a meeting with a mob of Dissenters. Five years ago, it mightn't have been so bad, but times had changed. Dissenters were trouble.

"Please do not blaspheme, John."

"You are my wife," he burst out. "I demand that you obey me."

She paused, looking down, weighing her words carefully.

"I am sorry, John," she said quietly, "but there is a higher authority than thee. Do not forbid me to hear the word of God."

"And you want to take Abigail?"

"I do."

He shook his head. He knew better than to argue with his wife's conscience. He had enough on his mind without dealing with that.

"Go then," he cried in exasperation. "But not with my blessing." Or my thanks, he added under his breath. And he turned his back on her until she left.

As John Master surveyed his world in the spring of 1770, he was sure of one thing. There had never been a time when the colony had greater need of good men, with good will, and cool heads. Five years ago, when Livingston and De Lancey from the Assembly had spoken of the need for the gentlemen to control the Liberty Boys, they'd been right. But they hadn't managed to do it.

The main factions in the Provincial Assembly had divided on more or less English political lines for a long time now. De Lancey and his rich Anglican crowd were generally called Tories, and they reckoned that Master, as a vestryman of Trinity with a son at Oxford, was one of them. The Whigs, led by Livingston and a group of Presbyterian lawyers, might stand up for the common man and oppose anything they considered an abuse of royal authority, but they were still level-headed gentlemen. As a moderate, non-partisan fellow, John Master had plenty of friends among them too.

So surely, he'd felt, if decent men like himself used common sense, the affairs of the colonies could be set in good order. But it hadn't happened. The last five years had been a disaster.

For a short time, when the Stamp Act had been repealed, he had hoped that good sense might prevail. He'd been one of those who'd urged the Assembly to supply provisions to the British troops again.

"God knows," he'd pointed out to one of the Assembly Whigs, "we need the troops, and they have to be fed and paid."

"Can't do it, John," was the reply. "Point of principle. It's a tax we haven't agreed to."

"So why don't we just agree to it?" he'd asked.

But if he could see why the ministers in London felt the colonies were being obstructive, why did the London men, in turn, have to be so arrogant?

For their next move had been an insult. It had come from a new minister, named Townshend: a series of duties, slapped on a whole range of items including paper, glass and tea. "New minister, new tax," Master sighed. "Can't they play any other tune?" But the sting was in the tail. The money raised wasn't only to pay for the troops. It would be used to pay the salaries of the provincial governors and their officials too.

And, of course, the New York Whigs were furious.

"The governors have always been paid by our elected Assembly," they protested. "It's the one thing that gives us some control over them. If the governors are all paid from London, they can ignore us entirely."

"It's obvious, John," a fellow merchant told him. "London wants to destroy us." And then he had added: "So to hell with them."

In no time, the merchants were refusing to trade with London again. The Assembly, it seemed to Master, was losing its way. But worst of all had been the damned Sons of Liberty. Charlie White and his friends. They'd practically taken over the streets.

They'd erected a huge Liberty Pole, tall as a ship's mast, on the Bowling Green, right in front of the fort. They were always having fights with the redcoats there. If the soldiers took the pole down, the Liberty Boys would raise another one, even bigger, a totem of triumph and defiance. And the Assembly men were now so frightened that they pandered to them. Some of the Liberty boys were even standing for election themselves. "If we're not careful," Master warned, "this city will be governed by the mob."

On top of all this had come the trouble with the Dissenters.

Master didn't mind Dissenters. There had always been plenty in New York: respectable Presbyterians, the Huguenot congregation of the French church, and the Dutch of course. Then there were Lutherans and Moravians, Methodists and Quakers. A fellow called Dodge had started a group of Baptists. Beyond even the Dissenters, for that matter, there had always been a community of New York Jews.

The trouble had started with a simple, legal issue. Trinity Church was a corporation. Corporate status brought legal and financial benefits. So then the Presbyterian churches had decided that they ought to be corporations too. The issue, however, was delicate. The king's coronation oath, and much historic legislation, obliged the government to uphold the Church of England. To incorporate a Dissenting Church might be a legal and certainly a political problem. As soon as the Presbyterians raised the issue, however, all the other churches wanted to incorporate too. The government had not agreed. The Dissenters were disappointed.

But alas, he had to admit, it was his own Church which had thrown fuel onto the fire when a truculent Anglican bishop had publicly announced: "The American colonists are infidels and barbarians."

After that, what could you expect? The outraged Dissenters were at daggers drawn with the whole British establishment. Respectable Presbyterian Assembly men found themselves in the same camp as Liberty Boys. Just when cool heads were needed, some of the best men in the city were making common cause with some of the worst.

As for today's preaching, Master could understand why Mercy wanted to go. The great Whitefield himself had returned to the city. The word was that the preacher was unwell, but a huge crowd was gathering to hear him. It wasn't that John objected to Whitefield himself, or his message. No doubt there'd be some members of the Anglican congregation in the crowd. People who, as Mercy would say, were coming to the light.

But it was still a mistake. These meetings only excited the passions. Good God, he thought, next we'll have Charlie White burning down my house and saying he's doing the work of the Lord.

These were the melancholy thoughts that occupied him after Mercy and Abigail had gone. He felt depressed, and lonely.

✣

The preacher's face was broad, and when he looked upward at the sky, the sun seemed to bless him with a special radiance. As he was helped up to the platform he had looked unwell; yet once his melodious voice rang out over the crowd on the Common, he seemed to draw new life from the inspiration of the day. The crowd was enraptured.

But Mercy could not concentrate.

Abigail was by her side. At ten years old, she was old enough to understand. At the moment, she was dutifully staring at the preacher, but

Mercy suspected that Abby was not listening either. Several times already, she had seen her daughter glance around.

She had lied to the child when she told her that her father could not come, and she could see that she had been disappointed. She suspected that Abby had heard them arguing. What was the child secretly thinking? Mercy almost wished she hadn't come. But it was too late to do anything about that now. Though they were at the fringe of the crowd, she couldn't very well walk away from the preaching. How would that look? Besides, she had her pride.

Minutes passed. Then, suddenly, Abby was tugging at her arm.

"Look. Papa's coming."

He was striding toward them. Dear God, had he ever looked more splendid and more handsome? And he was smiling. She could scarcely believe it. He reached her, and took her hand.

"We went together to a preaching once," he said softly. "So I thought we'd go again."

She did not reply. She squeezed his hand. She knew what this had cost him. But after a minute or two she whispered: "Let's go home, John."

As they walked back arm in arm, little Abby was skipping ahead, joyful to see her parents united again.

"I have a confession, John," said Mercy, after a while.

"What is that?" he asked affectionately.

"I think I went to the preaching because I have been angry with you, for many years."

"Why?"

"Because I blamed you for letting James remain in London. It is five years now since I have seen my only son. I wish he were here."

John nodded. Then kissed her hand.

"I shall write to him today, and tell him he is to return at once."

⁘

The letter from James, together with one from Albion, was brought to the house early that evening. Hudson took them to Master in his library. Mercy and Abigail were reading in the parlor. He read them alone.

If the disorders in the colonies have been bad, you would scarcely believe what we have witnessed here in London. You may recall the fellow Wilkes, whose libel of the government and subsequent trial were somewhat like our famous Zenger affair in New York. Since then Wilkes, while in jail, had himself elected to Parliament. When this was disallowed, the radicals of London whipped up the mob, and they have almost taken over control of the streets of London. They cry "Wilkes and Liberty" just like your Liberty Boys of New York. Whatever the rights and wrongs of the business, it's a shameful thing to see the mob so passionate and out of control, and the government is not inclined to give in to these disorders, here or in the colonies—nor would the gentlemen of Parliament stand for it if they did. Good sense and order must prevail.

As for the American colony, the refusal of American merchants to trade with England, besides being disloyal, does less to harm the mother country than they suppose. There are two reasons. First, the Boston and New York men may observe these embargoes, but the southern colonies privately ignore them. Even Philadelphia is trading with London. Second, merchants like Albion are more than making up for the shortfall in their trade with India and the other countries of Europe. But in any case, I think that the present quarrel with the colonies will end before long. The new prime minister, Lord North, is well disposed toward the American colony, and it's thought that he will do all he can to end the quarrels. All that is needed is a little patience and good sense which, I have no doubt, the better sort in New York can provide.

And now, my dear parents, I have joyful tidings . . .

As Master read the rest of the letter, he groaned. For several minutes afterward, he stared straight ahead. Then he read the letter once more. Having done this, he put it aside and turned to the letter from Albion. It contained a number of business matters. Then it turned to the subject of James.

You will have learned from James that he is to be married. Normally I should never have allowed him to enter into such an engagement, while living under my roof, without his first obtaining your blessing. But I must tell you frankly that the young lady's circumstances do not permit such a delay. A child will be born this summer. I must now tell you something of his wife—as she will be by the time you receive this letter.

Miss Vanessa Wardour—for so I call her, although she was briefly married to Lord Rockbourne before he died in a hunting accident—is a young lady of considerable fortune. She is also, it will interest you to know, a cousin to Captain Rivers, on his mother's side. She has a handsome house of her own in Mount Street, Mayfair, where she and·James will live. As you may surmise, she is a few years older than James, but besides her wealth and many fine connections, she is generally accounted a beauty.

I will not say that I am without reservations in this matter, nor did I promote it—I understand James first met the lady at the house of Lord Riverdale—but most of London would certainly say that your son had made a brilliant match.

John Master put the letter down. It was some time before he could bring himself to show it to Mercy.

⊰1773⊱

No one could remember a worse winter. The East River was frozen solid. But it wasn't just the awful fact of the cold. It was the misery that went with it. And the deaths. Darkness was falling, but Charlie White was nearly home. His hat was pulled down, his scarf was wrapped round his face. He'd driven his cart across the frozen river to Brooklyn to buy a hundredweight of flour from a Dutch farmer he was friendly with. At least his family would have bread for a while.

Sometimes in the last couple of years Charlie had felt angry, sometimes just discouraged. If his personal feelings against John Master were as keen as ever, they were mixed with an outrage and a grief that was more general.

He knew the troubles of the poor, because his family often suffered them. And it seemed to him that there must be a better way in which the world could be arranged. Surely with a vast, fertile continent stretching westward, southward and northward, it could not be right that working folk in New York were starving. It could not be right that rich men like Master, backed by the British Church and British arms, could profit hugely when ordinary folk could not find work. Something must be wrong. Something needed to change.

Surely, if free men like himself were running the city, instead of the rich, and if their elected representatives ruled the land, instead of royal governors who cared nothing for the wishes of the colonists, then life would have to get better.

The protests against the Stamp Act had worked. The new prime minister, Lord North, had removed Townshend's taxes—except, just to save his face, the tax on tea. And that was just the moment, in Charlie's opinion, for the Sons of Liberty to continue the fight. But influenced by the old guard like John Master, the city authorities had turned against them. The statue of King George had been set up on Bowling Green. Everyone said, "God save the king." There was a tough new English governor called Tryon now, and more British troops under General Gage. It was back to business as usual. Why, Montayne had even told the Liberty Boys not to meet in his tavern any more.

Well, to hell with Montayne. The boys had got their own meeting place now. Hampden Hall they called it, after the hero who'd stood up to the tyrant Charles I in the English Parliament. As for John Master and his crowd, and Tryon, and General Gage—let them remember what happened to King Charles. It might be quiet on the streets, but Sears and the Sons of Liberty had a large faction in the Assembly, now, who listened to them. "Change will come," Charlie would say grimly to his friends, over a drink in the tavern. "And when it does . . ."

Not this winter, though. Last year, there had been a collapse of credit in London. Soon all the colonies were suffering—and that was before this terrible winter hit. The poorest were starving. The city authorities were doing their best to feed them, but it was hard to keep pace.

Charlie had just got to the southern end of the Common, where it met Broadway, when he saw the woman and her daughter coming out of the dingy old Poor House.

The woman paused for a moment, glancing anxiously up at the darkening sky. By the look of it, she'd been in the Poor House longer than she realized, and the darkness had taken her by surprise. Then she took off her shawl and wrapped it round her daughter, for the wind was starting to bite.

The street was nearly empty. He drew level. She looked up.

"Are you going down Broadway?" She had no idea who he was. He didn't answer. "Would you take us down Broadway? I'd be glad to pay. With my daughter, here . . ."

She was right, of course. In the last few months, with the times being

so hard, the streets had become unsafe. Women he knew had taken to selling their bodies for extra cash. He knew men who'd been robbed. The
woman and her daughter shouldn't be walking home alone when it was
getting dark.

"How d'you know I won't rob you?" he muttered through his scarf.

She looked up, only able to see his eyes. Her face was kind.

"You would not harm us, sir, I am sure."

"You'd better get up," Charlie grunted. He indicated the space on the
seat beside him, then nodded to the back of the cart. "The young lady can
sit on the sack."

He turned the horse's head down Broadway.

So this was the wife of John Master. He'd recognized her at once, of
course, though she didn't know him. And she thought he wouldn't harm
her. Well, I dare say I wouldn't, he thought, once I'd burned your house
down.

As they started down Broadway, he gave her a sharp look.

"You don't look as if you belong in the Poor House," he remarked in a
less than friendly tone.

"I go there each day," she said simply.

"What do you do there?"

"If we have them to spare, we take a load of provisions up there in our
cart. Sometimes blankets, other things. We give them money to buy
food." She glanced back at the sack of flour. "We do what we can."

"You take your daughter?"

"Yes. She should know what kind of city we live in. There's much for
any good Christian to do."

They were just coming level with Trinity Church. He glanced at it with
dislike.

"Would that be a Trinity Christian?"

"Any Christian I should hope. My father was a Quaker."

Charlie knew that too, but he said nothing.

"My daughter talks to the old ones," she continued quietly. "They like
to talk to a child. It comforts them." She glanced at him. "Have you been
in the Poor House?"

"Can't say I have."

"There are many children in there, and some of them are sick. I was
tending one of them today. That's what I chiefly fear now. Some have died
in the cold, but most will be fed. They are weak, though. The old ones

and the children are starting to fall sick. It's disease that will carry them off."

"You could fall sick yourself, going in there," he muttered.

"Only if it's God's will. Anyway, I'm not in their weakened condition. I don't think of it."

They had just gone down Broadway another hundred yards when they saw a cart being driven by a black man coming swiftly toward them.

"Why, there's Hudson," she remarked. "Hello, Hudson," she called. As the two carts met, Hudson looked relieved.

"The Boss sent me to bring you safe home," Hudson said.

"Well, this kind man has brought us down, as you see. But we'll come with you now." She turned to Charlie. "I don't know your name," she said.

"Don't matter," said Charlie.

"Well, let me give you something for going out of your way."

"No." He shook his head. "I reckon you were doing the Lord's work."

"Well, then, God bless you, sir," she said, as she and Abigail got down.

"And God bless you, too," he answered. And he was level with Trinity before he silently cursed himself. Dammit, he thought, why did he have to say that?

✤

If John Master hadn't come out to fetch Mercy himself, it was because he'd received an unexpected visit. Captain Rivers had called to see him. He'd arrived by ship from Carolina that very morning, and informed Master that he'd already taken lodgings in the town. He looked older. He had some gray hairs. But John had to admire the straightforward, manly way that Rivers explained the reason for his visit. Namely, that he was broke.

Well, not entirely. If, during the last ten years, many Southern landowners had got themselves in trouble with their London creditors, the recent collapse of the London credit markets had made matters much worse. Captain Rivers himself had always dealt with Albion, and his credit there was good. But his wife was another matter.

"She's had dealings with other London merchants going back to the time before our marriage. I wasn't even aware of the extent of them until recently. It seems we owe far more than I realized."

"Can you retrench?" Master asked.

"We've done so. And the plantations still provide a good income. But the London creditors are pressing. And they're so far away. They've no way of seeing how we run things. To them, we're just another damned colonial plantation in trouble. What I want is to pay them all off, and raise a new debt to someone here in the colonies. The plantations provide ample security. If you came down to Carolina, you could see for yourself that we are sound. You could leave a clerk to work with us, if you please. I've nothing to hide."

On the whole, John was inclined to consider the proposition. His instincts told him Rivers would perform. And he had just told him, "Before I commit, I'd like to do as you suggest, and see the place for myself," when he heard his wife and daughter come into the house, and smiled. "We'll dine at once," he said. "I hope you will join us."

❖

The dinner was a pleasant family affair. Nothing was said of Captain Rivers's business. Mercy, who'd liked him when they'd met before, was pleased to see him. He also knew how to talk easily and draw Abigail out. At thirteen, she was just starting to turn into a young woman; and Master, watching her in animated conversation with the Englishman, thought with some satisfaction that she was really becoming very pretty.

He was also glad to use the opportunity to probe Rivers on another subject.

James had written regularly since his marriage. He had a son called Weston, aged two. Albion had taken him into partnership. His last letter told them that a little girl had been born, but died at once. The letters spoke of his wife Vanessa, and from time to time he gave them dutiful messages from her. "But we know very little of your cousin," John told Captain Rivers. "What can you tell us?"

If Rivers hesitated, it was only for a moment.

"Vanessa? I've known her since she was a child, of course, and she was beautiful even then. After her parents died, she was brought up, so to speak, by an uncle. She has neither brother nor sister, so she inherited a considerable fortune." He paused. "Though she'd never miss the season in London, she loves the country too." He laughed. "I dare say she'll make James into a country squire, one of these days. He'll have to learn to hunt."

"Is she a godly woman?" asked Mercy.

"Godly?" Captain Rivers almost looked puzzled, then collected himself. "Absolutely. A staunch supporter of the Church, to be sure."

"Well," said Mercy quietly, "I hope that James will not wait too long before he brings her home."

"Indeed," said Rivers, noncommittally.

✥

It wasn't until he was sitting alone with the captain, after the ladies had retired, that Master returned to the subject of Vanessa and his son.

"I'm thinking of what you said about your cousin, and remembering my time in London," John began quietly. "I should think she'd want her husband to be a fashionable man."

"Probably," Rivers answered.

"So she can't like the fact that he's in trade."

"I couldn't say."

"From what I saw in London," Master continued, "the English don't consider a man a gentleman if he's in trade. A man may belong to a gentry family and engage in trade because he has to—like our friend Albion. But once an Englishman makes his fortune in trade, he'll probably sell up his business, buy an estate in the country, and set himself up as a gentleman there. Trade and being a gentleman don't mix. But why is that, would you say?"

"It is true," said Rivers, "that in England, a gentleman goes into Parliament, or the army, but avoids the counting house if he can." He laughed. "They're supposed to be the old warrior nobility. Knights in armor, you know. In theory at least."

"It's different in America."

"A man like Washington in Virginia, say—an officer in the army, with a country house and huge estates—he'd be called a gentleman in England, without a doubt. Even Ben Franklin," Rivers added with a smile, "is entirely retired from trade nowadays. He's quite the gentleman in London."

"And what does that make me?" asked Master wryly.

For just a moment, he saw a look of worry cross the aristocrat's face. My God, Master realized, Rivers is wondering if he's insulted me and I'll refuse him a loan.

"In Carolina," Rivers answered simply, "I work in my own storehouse, and I'll sell you goods across the counter at my trading post. And you shouldn't lend me a penny if I were too proud to do it. Here in New York, sir, you live in a far higher style than I. You have ships and businesses which others manage for you. Your landholdings are large. Should you ever consider returning to England, you would live as a very considerable gentleman indeed." He gave Master a curious glance. "With your son there, I wonder if you think of it. You'd have many friends, including, I can assure you, the Riverdales."

It was cleverly said, and kindly meant. But it also came as a shock. Return to England? After the Masters had been rich in New York for more than a century? The thought had never crossed his mind.

Yet later that night, thinking it over, he had to admit Rivers's question was natural. His son was gone. He had an English wife. James was English. He was blind if he didn't see it. And his English wife was only waiting, presumably, for James to inherit a fortune and retire from business.

And then John Master realized something else. He was determined to stop her. He wanted James back, here, in America. But how the devil was he to do it?

✤

As the Master household entered the spring of 1773, Hudson had several things on his mind. He could count himself fortunate that he and his family were warm and well fed in one of the kindest houses in New York. That was a blessing. But there was still plenty to worry about. His first concern was Mercy Master.

Early in March, John Master had taken a ship down the coast to Carolina, intending to spend some time inspecting the Rivers plantation. He had not been gone three days when Mercy fell sick. Hudson reckoned it must be something she had caught on one of her visits to the Poor House. A physician was called, but she lay in her bed with a fever for days on end, and though his wife and Hannah nursed her constantly, Ruth confided to Hudson that she wasn't sure that their mistress would live. A letter was sent after John Master, but who knew when it would catch up with him. Meanwhile, Solomon was dispatched to Dutchess County to summon Susan from her farm.

But most touching to Hudson was the behavior of Abigail. She was only thirteen, yet she was quite as calm as any adult. Perhaps the visits to the sick that she'd made with her mother had prepared her. During the worst of her mother's fever, she had quietly taken turns with Hannah to help at the bedside. By the time her elder sister arrived from Dutchess County, Mercy's fever had somewhat subsided, and Abigail would sit by her bed, wipe her brow and talk to her gently, keeping her company by the hour.

Susan was a brisk, practical woman with two children of her own now, and another on the way. She stayed in the house for a week, and was pleasant company, but once she was sure that her mother was out of danger, she said that she must get back to her family. And as she truly remarked, nobody could be a better help to her mother than Abigail already was.

Nearly a month elapsed before John Master returned, looking distraught. Only to find, upon entering the bedroom, that his wife was propped up in bed, pale but clearly no longer in danger, and listening with a smile as Abigail read to her. Even so, for weeks after that, Mercy had been pale and listless, and Hudson was sorry to see the strained and worried look on the face of John Master too.

But if Hudson was concerned about the Master family, he also had worries of his own. He wasn't sure exactly when it had started, but it was that spring when he began to notice a change in Solomon. Why was his son suddenly becoming defiant toward him? He questioned his wife. "Solomon gives me no trouble," Ruth told him. "But I dare say a young man of his age will often rile his father." That might be so, but he had also taken to disappearing. At first Hudson supposed the boy was out chasing girls, but one evening he heard Solomon boasting to his sister Hannah of some escapade in the town with Sam White and a group of other young Liberty Boys.

Hudson could guess where his son had met them. Master would sometimes send Solomon to work at the warehouse by the wharfs, and there were all kinds of men working down on the waterfront.

"You stay away from those Liberty Boys," he commanded his son. "What'll Mr. Master say if he hears about that?"

"Maybe Mr. Master'll be run out of town one day," Solomon answered cheekily. "Then it won't signify what he thinks."

"Don' ever speak like that again," his father told him. "And don' you go talking about Mr. Master's business either."

He hadn't wanted to tell Master about the incident, but he wondered if there was some way of getting Solomon away from such dangerous friends. Early in April he suggested to Master that perhaps Solomon might go up to Dutchess County and work for his daughter Susan for a while. Master said he'd consider it, but that he couldn't spare Solomon at present.

So there wasn't much more that Hudson could do.

∻

One of the first things that John Master had done when he returned was to write a letter to James. He informed him about his mother's sickness. As she lay in her room, Mercy would wonder aloud to her husband, almost every day, when she would see her son again. John told James plainly that, at the least, it was time he made a visit. There was nothing else he could do. It would be many weeks before he could expect a reply from London.

Meanwhile, nothing stood still in the colony. Ironically, it was Ben Franklin who caused the next crisis. Still more ironically, he did so by trying to calm things down.

A few years ago, a royal official named Hutchinson had written to a friend from Massachusetts. Incensed by the difficulties he was encountering, he told his friend it would be better to curb English liberties in the colonies, to make sure that America was kept firmly under Britain's thumb. By chance, Franklin saw the letters in London. And because he still believed in Britain's grand imperial destiny, he sent them privately to friends in America—not to cause trouble, but to warn them of the sort of reaction their intransigence was stirring up. It was a horrible miscalculation. His friends in Massachusetts published the Hutchinson letters that summer.

The colonies were in an uproar. Here was proof positive that the English wanted to destroy American liberties. And almost as if on cue, the British government was able to supply a measure on which their rage could focus.

The problem was simple enough. It concerned another part of the empire. The mighty East India Company had got itself into a mess.

"They have huge overstocks of tea," Albion wrote to Master, "and they can't shift them." As usual, when huge trading enterprises mismanage their affairs, the company turned to the government to bail them out. The solution suggested was to dump the tea on the large American market. "Until the overstocks are cleared, this will be bad for merchants like yourself, who'll be cut out," Albion wrote. "But there's no doubt that the American market can absorb the tea."

The problem was that the tea still carried the duty that was so disliked.

"It is sure to be seen," Master sighed to Mercy, "as a government conspiracy."

There was one intelligent solution, Albion explained, and it was suggested by Ben Franklin. Dump the tea, he was telling his friends in London, but take off the duty. The overstocks would be cleared, the colonists would get cheap tea. Merchants like Master would suffer, but only for a short while, and everyone else would be happy.

"Will they do it, John?" Mercy asked him.

"I shouldn't think so. They'd see it as giving in." Master had shaken his head. "I'm afraid there's nothing to do but take the tea, and hope for wiser statesmen in the future."

"You think there'll be trouble?"

"Probably."

⁌⁌⁌

There was trouble. When news of the new Tea Act arrived that summer, Sears and the Liberty Boys were out on the streets in no time. Anyone accepting the tea would be a traitor, they said, and Master was disappointed that many of the merchants agreed with them.

"This is going to be just like the Stamp Act again," he said sadly. He could only hope the shipments of tea would be delayed as long as possible.

At the end of the summer, a letter came from James. He sent tender words to his mother. He and Vanessa were discussing when they could make a journey across to New York, he told his father, and he would make arrangements as soon as he could. The letter was full of affection, but Master found it unsatisfactory. He hoped that James's next communication would contain more definite plans.

Through the autumn the city's mood grew uglier. By November, some of the Liberty Boys were saying that when the tea ships arrived, they'd destroy the cargo and kill the governor too. The East India Company agents in the town were so scared they started resigning. New York waited tensely.

But it was from Massachusetts that word finally came. In December, a man came riding down the old Boston road. He was a silversmith who enjoyed the excitement of being a courier. His name was Paul Revere. The news he brought was startling. The first tea ships had arrived in Boston, and a party of men, some of them quite respectable citizens, had boarded the ships dressed as Indians, and dumped the tea into Boston harbor. The Sons of Liberty were delighted.

"We'll do the same when the tea ships get to New York," they declared.

But no tea ships appeared. The new year began. Mercy caught a cold, and was confined to her bed for a while. John Master fretted that he had not heard from James, and wrote to him again. Then word came from Philadelphia that the tea ships had arrived there, but had been turned away without violence. By March John told Mercy, "I don't think the tea ships are coming here, thank God."

⁘

It was in April that Hudson was sent up to Dutchess County. He had a wagonload of goods that John Master wanted to send his elder daughter, together with some fine old family chairs and a quantity of china that Mercy thought Susan might like to have.

He had a pleasant journey. The weather was fine. The rutted roads might make for slow going, but it was pleasant to make one's way northward from the great coastal sweep of New York and the long ridges of Westchester up into the more intimate scenery of hills and dales where Susan and her husband had their farm.

The house was handsome. Its outside was of rough limestone masonry; it had a gambrel roof, and blue-and-white tiles round the fireplaces. But to these homely Dutch features were added a handsome facade with a double row of five Georgian windows, a center hall, high ceilings and panelled rooms, which proclaimed a certain English sense of propriety and importance. Hudson spent two nights there with Susan and her family, who treated him in a most friendly manner, and he considered once again that this would be a fine place where his son could keep out of trouble.

He learned about the tea ships as he crossed onto Manhattan.

"Two came. The first turned back. But the captain of the second said he'd unload his tea and the Liberty Boys be damned. They nearly hanged him."

"And then?"

"They had themselves a tea party. It's been quite a day."

It was dark when he got back to the house. Going to the kitchen door, he found Ruth alone. She embraced him warmly and whispered, "Thank the Lord you came back." But when he asked, "Where's Solomon?" she put her finger to her lips.

"The Boss was asking for him too. I told him Solomon's sick, an' sleeping. But the truth is he went out in the morning and I ain't seen him since. Oh Hudson, I don' know where he went."

With a curse, Hudson went back into the yard. He could guess where Solomon had gone. He went across to the Bowling Green, then started up Broadway. Like as not Solomon would be in one of the taverns by now.

But he'd only visited two of these when he caught sight of a figure, dressed as an Indian, flitting down a side street. A figure that he recognized at once. And moments later the Indian found himself held against a wall, in a grip of iron.

"What you been doin', son? What kept you so busy all day? Dumpin' tea, maybe?"

"Maybe."

The next few moments between Hudson and his son were unpleasant. But even when Hudson had done, his son was not abashed. What would Master say, if he knew, Hudson asked.

"What do you know?" Solomon cried. "Everyone's with the Liberty Boys now. Even the merchants. I told Sam White that the Boss says we ought to take the tea," he continued. "And Sam says the Boss is a traitor. The Liberty Boys are going to throw the redcoats and the traitors out of the colony."

"And where will that leave you and me?" his father demanded. "You think the Liberty Boys are goin' to do anything for the black man?" It was true that, together with small craftsmen, sailors, laborers and all kinds of poorer folk, the ranks of the Sons of Liberty contained a number of freedmen. But what did that signify? Besides, there was another consideration. "You better remember," he told his son ominously, "that you're a slave, Solomon. If the Boss wants to sell you, ain't nobody goin' to stop him. So you be careful."

⁜

During that summer of '74, the conflict seemed to take on a life of its own. When news of the Boston Tea Party had reached London, the reaction had been predictable. "Such insolence and disobedience must be crushed," the British Parliament declared. General Gage was sent from New York up to Boston to govern the place, firmly. By May, the port of

Boston was virtually shut down. The Coercive Acts, Parliament called this tough legislation. "The Intolerable Acts," the colonies called them.

Again, Paul Revere rode down to New York, this time to seek support. Naturally, Sears and the Sons of Liberty were up in arms for the Boston men. But many of the merchants were now enraged at London's harsh measures. The Sons of Liberty were getting support from all quarters. One day, Master saw a large parade of women coming down Broadway, calling for a trade embargo. Tempers continued to rise. A British officer caught Sears in the street and put the flat of his sword across his back.

Yet despite all this, Master was glad to see, there were powerful voices in the American colonies who saw the need for moderation. Toward the end of summer the other colonies called for a general congress to meet at Philadelphia, and the New York Assembly agreed to send delegates. The men chosen, thank God, were solid, educated gentlemen: Livingston the Presbyterian, John Jay the lawyer, a rich Irish merchant named Duane, and others. The congress was to meet in September.

In the meantime, Master did what he could to encourage a return to sanity. He made his house a meeting place for men of moderate opinion. Sometimes his guests were members of the old, grandee Tory families— Watts, Bayard, De Lancey, Philipse. But often they were merchants whose sympathies might be wavering, but whom he hoped to keep on the right path—men like Beekman, or Roosevelt the distiller. But despite these modest efforts, he knew it was the men who had powers of argument and oratory who really mattered. He had particular hope in John Jay the lawyer—tall, handsome, persuasive, and related to so many of the great old families of the province.

"It's Jay and men like him," he told Mercy, "who'll make them see sense."

❖

At the end of August, a cavalcade rode into town. This was the Massachusetts delegates and their party. Riding down the Post Road, they had also picked up the Connecticut delegates along the way. Their second day in town, Master was in Wall Street, talking to one of the Assembly men who'd dined with them the night before, when a small group came down the street.

"See the fellow with the big head, wearing the bright red coat?" the Assembly man murmured. "That's Sam Adams. And the pink-faced,

balding fellow in black just behind him is his cousin John Adams. A
lawyer. Clever, they say, and talkative—though he didn't say much at dinner. Don't think he likes New York. Probably isn't used to being interrupted!"

It was a little while later, returning home, that Master caught sight of
the elderly man. He was walking stiffly, but with great firmness of purpose. His brown coat was buttoned tight. He looked vaguely familiar.
John tried to think where he'd seen him.

And then he realized. It was his cousin Eliot. He was a little shrunken
and his face was thinner. But then, John thought, he must be over eighty.
He went up to him.

"Mr. Eliot Master? You may not recognize me, sir, but I am your
cousin John."

"I know who you are." It was said without enthusiasm.

"You have come with the Boston delegates?"

"I intend to watch events in Philadelphia."

"I remember your daughter Kate."

"I expect you do. She's a grandmother now."

John decided to change the subject.

"This congress is a serious business, sir. Let us hope that moderation
will prevail."

"Oh?" Old Eliot looked at him sharply. "Why?"

Even after forty years, John Master felt himself fumbling for his words
under the lawyer's stern eye.

"I mean . . . there's a need for cool heads . . ." He nodded. "Compromise."

The Bostonian snorted.

"New York," he said drily. "Typical."

"Just a minute," cried John. Dammit, he thought, I'm not a drunken
boy any more, and my Boston cousin isn't going to put me down. "The
quarrel is about tax without representation, is it not?"

"It is."

"Well, we are not entirely without representation."

"Is that so? Our Assembly has been stripped of all power." Old Eliot
paused a moment. "Or are you referring to the doctrine of *virtual representation*?" He spoke the last words with wonderful contempt.

John Master was aware that some in London had argued that, since the
British Parliament had the interests of the colonists at heart, then

although the colonists had no actual representation in the British legislature, they were *virtually* represented. He could just imagine the ridicule to
which the Boston lawyer would easily subject that notion.

"I am not referring to that foolish doctrine," he declared. "But at least
our voice is heard in London. Wouldn't it be wiser to seek a better understanding with the king's ministers, rather than merely provoke them?"

For a moment or two, the Boston man was silent, and John even wondered if he might have gained a point. But no such luck.

"When we met before," the lawyer finally said, making it clear the
memory gave him no pleasure, "it was the time of the Zenger trial."

"I remember Zenger."

"That was a question of principle."

"Indeed."

"Well, so is this." Eliot Master began to turn away.

"Will you call upon us before you leave?" John offered. "My wife
would be—"

But Eliot was already in motion.

"I don't think so," he said.

⁜

The Philadelphia congress went speedily to its work. But if John Master
had hoped for judicious compromise, he was sadly disappointed.

"They've gone mad," he cried, when he heard what they had decided.
"Boston is to take up arms against the mother country? What became of
moderation and good sense?" And when the men supporting the congress
called themselves Patriots, he said: "How can you be a Patriot when you're
disloyal to your king and country?"

It was at this time that he began consciously to refer to himself by
another term he'd heard.

"If they are Patriots," he declared, "then I'm a Loyalist."

But the tide was against him. Decent men like Beekman and Roosevelt
were taking the Patriot side. Even John Jay, a man of good sense, who'd
always declared that those who own the country ought to run it, had been
convinced. "I don't like it any more than you," he told Master on his
return, "but I don't think we can do anything else."

In the city, the Assembly was getting weaker by the day. The Sons of
Liberty were triumphant. The smaller craftsmen had formed their own
Mechanics Committee. Master heard that Charlie White was on it. And

now they and the Liberty Boys told the Assembly: "We'll make sure the congress is obeyed in New York. Not you."

"Do you really want to exchange a Parliament—which I grant you is inept—for an illegal congress and the tyranny of the mob?" Master demanded of John Jay. "You can't have the city run by men like Charlie White."

Besides this, there was also another, obvious consideration. If the colonies moved toward rebellion, London would have to react. With force.

⁘

John Master was walking up Broadway toward Trinity one day when he saw a clergyman he knew. The clergyman was a scholarly gentleman who taught at King's College. The previous week this learned divine had published a firm but reasoned statement of the Loyalist case that John had considered admirable, and so he went up to thank him. The clergyman was clearly delighted, but taking John by the arm he also told him: "You must do your part too, you know."

"In what way?"

"You must lead, Master. You're a respected man in the city. Jay and his like are going to the dogs. If sound men like you don't take the lead, then who will?"

"But apart from Trinity vestry, I've never taken any public position," John objected.

"So much the better. You can step forward as an honest man, impelled only by a sense of duty. Tell me this, how many of the larger city merchants would you say are loyal, at present?"

"Perhaps half, I'd guess."

"And the smaller traders and better sort of craftsman?"

"Harder to say. Less than half—but many of those may be persuadable."

"Precisely. Somebody has to give them backbone. You could do it—if you have the courage." And seeing Master look uncertain, he went on eagerly: "There are farmers upriver and out on Long Island who would rally to the cause. Most of the Queens County men, to my knowledge, are Loyalists. Even the poorer sort in the city can be led back to reason. All is not lost. I urge you, Master, search your conscience and do your duty."

John returned home, somewhat flattered, but uncertain. He discussed it with Mercy.

"Thee must follow what thy conscience tells thee," she said. "And I shall be at thy side."

He thought about it for a week. Then he went to work. He started inviting not only merchants to his house, but spread the net wider, to any honest traders and craftsmen whom he thought might like a return to order. He took the Brooklyn ferry, and rode out to solid Dutch farmers who had no patience with the radicals. He even, with no small courage, went into the city taverns and discussed the issues with laboring men and sailors. On one of these occasions he saw Charlie White standing near. Charlie eyed him with disgust, but didn't interfere.

❖

And perhaps it was because he was so busy with all these activities that he did not take sufficient notice, at first, when his wife started to look tired.

He supposed it was a small malady. Abigail thought so too. Mercy was not feverish. She went about her daily life as usual. In recent years she had liked to rest a little in the afternoons. But several times she remarked to Abigail, "I think I'll rest a little longer this afternoon." As the November days grew shorter, the declining light seemed to sap her energy further. But whenever her husband came in, she would rouse herself from her lethargy, and made him tell her all that he had been doing. And when he inquired tenderly if she was unwell, she would answer: "Why no, John. I think it is the weather that is making me feel a little quiet today." And if he suggested, as he several times did, that he should stay at home with her for the day, she would not hear of it.

Her paleness they ascribed to the weather. Whenever the sun was out in the morning, Abigail would persuade her to walk with her to the Bowling Green, or even to the waterfront, and her mother said these walks were a pleasure to her. In the middle of the day, Ruth and Hannah would serve her hot broth, or cutlets, in the hope that these would give her more strength—a regime the doctor commented on with favor when once or twice he called. "A glass of red wine at midday, and brandy in the evening," he also recommended.

At the end of November, since there was a ship crossing to London despite the winter weather, John sent his son a letter telling him that, though there was no cause for alarm, his mother was down in spirit and that it was more than time that he should come.

But it was not until mid-December, when he was just about to make his first public speech, in the upper room of a tavern, that Solomon appeared at the door and came quickly to his side.

"You'd better come quickly, Boss," he whispered. "The mistress is sick. She's real bad."

·✥·

There had been some blood. Then she had fainted. She was lying in bed and looking very drained. It seemed she had bled before, but concealed the fact. The doctor was summoned. He was noncommittal.

For nearly a month, John thought that Mercy was going to get better. Perhaps because she said she was, perhaps because he wished to believe it. She was going to get better. But when another vessel left for England at the end of December, he sent a letter to James. "Your mother is dying. I cannot tell you how long she will last, but I urge you, if you can, to come now."

He curtailed his political activities after that. Abigail was her nurse, but he could not let her bear all the burden. Each day he would make Abigail go out for an hour or two, and sit by Mercy's side. Sometimes she liked him to read to her, from the Gospels, more often than not. And as he read their magnificent language, their power and peace brought some comfort to him also. But not enough. Sometimes, when Mercy was in pain, he suffered almost as much as she did herself.

As the weeks passed, and she grew paler and thinner, he followed the events of the world, of course. In February, the moderates carried the day, and the New York Assembly refused to select any delegates to attend a second congress in Philadelphia. He applauded their good sense, and hoped that his own efforts in the early winter had contributed to their strength of purpose. But it was to no avail. The Patriots responded with rallies in the streets, and set up a new committee of their own. The Assembly, unable to control events, was slowly becoming irrelevant.

By March, it seemed to John Master that it could not be long before Mercy sank away from him. But a little flame of determination kept her there.

"Do you think James will come?" she would sometimes ask.

"I wrote in December," he told her truthfully. "But the journey takes time."

"I shall wait for him as long as I can."

When Abigail sat with her mother, she would sometimes sing to her. She did not have a large voice, but it was tuneful, and pleasant. She would sing very quietly, and it seemed to soothe her mother.

Every evening, John Master would eat with Abigail. Hudson would serve them. Master would try to talk to her of other things. He would describe to her the great network of trade that linked New York to the south, the West Indies and to Europe. Sometimes they would discuss the political situation. She liked him to tell her about England, and all that he had seen there, about the Albions and, of course, James. Sometimes she'd ask him questions about his childhood and youth. But if he did his best to distract her, he soon came to realize that she too, in her quiet way, was deliberately asking him questions in order to take his mind off their troubles, and he was grateful for her thoughtfulness.

If Abigail was a support to him, he had to say that Hudson's son Solomon had also come into his own. Hudson was always finding ways to keep the boy busy in the house. When a leak appeared in the roof after a storm, the young fellow was up there fixing it in no time, and did the job thoroughly. Twice, in the early months of the new year, Hudson had asked if Solomon mightn't be sent to work for Susan for a while up in Dutchess County. But the young man was making himself so useful here in New York that Master had refused to think of it.

By mid-March, Mercy was getting very thin and her face was gaunt. But nature in her kindness seemed to be taking her away into a realm of increasing sleepiness. If John worried about Abigail, who was looking tired and wan, he scarcely realized how strained he looked himself. Just before the end of March, when he was sitting with Mercy one night, she put her thin hand in his and murmured: "I can't hold out any longer, John."

"Don't go," he said.

"It's time," she answered. "Thee has suffered enough."

She faded away at dawn.

✦

It was three weeks later that one of the warehouse men came running to the door with the news from Boston.

"There's been a fight. The British redcoats have been licked by the Patriots at Lexington."

John Master rushed out of his house at once. For an hour he gathered all the news he could. As he came by the waterfront, he noticed that a ship had just come in from England. But his attention was drawn to a crowd of men by another ship that was about to leave. The men, with whoops and cries, were busy unloading its cargo onto the dock.

"What on earth are they doing?" he asked a waterman.

"It's a cargo of provisions for the English troops. The Liberty Boys are making sure they don't get them," the waterman told him. "There's another party gone up to the arsenal to take all the guns and ammunition." He grinned. "If the troops come down from Boston, they'll find our boys ready for them."

"But this is revolution," Master protested.

"Reckon it is."

And Master was just wondering what to do when young Solomon found him.

"Miss Abigail said to come home at once, Boss."

"Oh? What's happened?"

"Mister James just arrived from London."

"James?"

"Yes, Boss. An' he have a little boy with him."

"I'll come at once," cried Master. "And his wife?"

"No, Boss. No wife. They came alone."

The Patriot

T HEY DINED EARLY, James and his father, Abigail, and Weston, the little boy. Hudson and Solomon waited at table.

As James gazed at his family, he felt many emotions. The first hours after his arrival had been a melancholy time. After the shock of discovering that his mother had gone he'd reproached himself bitterly for not coming sooner. But now, looking at his family, he suddenly experienced a great wave of affection. There was his father, still handsome as ever. And Abigail, the baby sister he hardly knew, almost fifteen already, and turning into a young woman. With what joy and hope she'd greeted him. How protective he felt toward her.

And then there was Weston. James had watched his father's face soften and his eyes light up at the sight of the little boy. With his fair hair and blue eyes, Weston looked like a tiny version of his grandfather.

There was so much to say. James wanted to know about his sister Susan and her family, and it was agreed that he should go up to Dutchess County to see them as soon as possible. He gave them news of the Albions, and recent events in London. There was only one person who had not yet been discussed.

"We are sorry not to have the pleasure of welcoming your wife," his father said at last.

"Indeed." Vanessa. On his arrival, James had told them briefly that, because of the need for a hasty departure, it had not been possible for his wife to accompany him. It was an imperfect explanation. But now, with a glance at his little son, he smiled cheerfully, as if her absence were the most natural thing in the world. "Vanessa looks forward to that pleasure in the future."

There was a pause. They were waiting for him to say more. He didn't.

"Do you mean to stay long, James?" Abigail inquired.

"I am uncertain."

"So are the times," his father replied grimly.

James steered the conversation to lighter topics after that. He wanted to know all about Abigail's life, what pastimes she enjoyed, what books she liked to read. Everyone made much of little Weston.

It was only some time later, when Abigail had taken Weston off to bed, and James could sit alone with his father, that they could talk seriously about the colony's affairs.

John Master gave him a full account of the recent events up at Lexington. Whatever the Boston men might think, he pointed out, this had only been a skirmish between the Patriots and a small body of troops, and had no bearing on what the full might of well-trained British troops would do to the Patriots in a real encounter. As for the raiding of the supplies and the seizing of arms in New York, they were rebellious acts for which a price would surely be paid.

"But let me explain the background of these events," he continued. Going over the last few years of the colony's history, John Master described very frankly the ineptitude of the royal governors, and the effects of London's failure to compromise, as well as the obstinacy of the Boston men. He told James about the decline of the Assembly, the rise of the Sons of Liberty and the riots, and about his encounters with old Eliot Master, Captain Rivers and Charlie White. His account was careful, clear and balanced.

Yet underneath his measured manner, James could sense his father's pain. Everything John Master believed in was under attack. The vicious way that his old friend Charlie White had turned upon him seemed to have hurt his father especially. In the midst of all this turmoil, and without his wife for comfort, John was obviously lonely, and even afraid.

"So I'm glad to have you here," the older man concluded. "As a loyal family, we have to decide what to do."

"What do you have in mind?"

His father looked thoughtful for a moment, then sighed.

"I'll tell you something," he answered. "When Captain Rivers came here, he asked me if I thought of going to live in England. At the time, I was astonished he should say such a thing. God knows, we've been here for generations. Yet if matters don't improve, then, for your sister's sake, I confess I almost wonder if perhaps we shouldn't all return to London."

James did not express an opinion, but he asked his father several questions, gave him what comfort he could, and promised they should discuss all these matters in the days to come.

As they were retiring to their bedchambers, however, his father suddenly stopped him.

"I do not wish to pry, James, but I was surprised that you and Weston came without his mother. Is all well with your wife? Is there anything you wish to tell me?"

"No, Father, there is nothing to say at present."

"As you wish." Though he looked concerned, John did not press him further. And James, having wished his father goodnight, was glad to escape to his room, and avoid further questions for the present.

But it was not only the subject of Vanessa he wished to avoid. There was something else he had concealed from his father.

✤

They were just finishing breakfast the next morning when Hudson announced: "Solomon says there's a lot of people going up to Wall Street."

By the time James and his father got there, a crowd of thousands already blocked the street. The focus of interest seemed to be City Hall. They had only been there a few moments when two men approached them, and James found himself being introduced to John Jay, the lawyer, and a robust figure wearing a bright waistcoat, who he learned was Duane, the merchant.

"What's going on?" John Master demanded.

"They want us to arm the city against the British," said Jay.

"An outrage!" cried Master.

"What'll you do?" James asked.

"Give them what they want, I think," Jay answered calmly.

"You'd condone armed rebellion?" Master cried again. He looked at James as if to say, "This is what we have come to." Then turning back to Jay, he indicated the crowd. "Is that what you and your people want?"

James watched the Patriot lawyer carefully, wondering what his attitude would be. Just then, a roar broke out from the crowd.

"My people?" John Jay looked at the crowd with disdain. "A disgusting mob," he said coldly.

"Yet you're prepared to lead them," Master protested.

"There are larger issues at stake," the lawyer replied.

"We have to do it, Master," Duane interposed. "It's the only way to control 'em."

Master shook his head in disbelief. "Let's go home, James," he said.

But James did not want to return just yet. Telling his father he'd come home in a while, he lingered in the area for some time, watching the people in the street. He walked around the town, pausing now and then to talk to storekeepers and others he encountered—a rope-maker, a flower seller, a couple of mariners, one or two merchants. In the middle of the morning, he went into a tavern and sat, listening to the conversation. By the end of the morning, he was certain that the plan he had already formed was correct.

It was mid-afternoon when he entered the tavern known as Hampden Hall. Inquiring of the innkeeper, he was directed to a table, where two men were sitting. Striding over to it, he addressed the elder of the two.

"Mr. White? Mr. Charlie White?"

"Who's asking?"

"Name's James Master. I think you know my father."

Charlie raised his wrinkled brow in surprise. "And what would you want with me?" he asked suspiciously.

"A word." James glanced at the other man, who was about his own age. "You'd be Sam?" The man indicated that he probably was. James nodded. "Fact is, gentlemen, I believe I owe you both an apology. Mind if I sit down?"

It did not take James long to tell them how, all those years ago, his father had instructed him to go to Charlie's house to meet Sam. He related how he'd meant to come, how he'd procrastinated, failed to show up, and then lied to his father. "The sort of thing," he admitted sadly, "that boys are apt to do. My father always supposed I'd been to see you," he continued. "And when I met you afterward, Mr. White, I let you think he never told me to go at all." He shrugged. "So, as I said, I reckon I owe you an apology," he concluded, "and my poor father too."

Sam was looking at his father. Charlie said nothing.

"I don't seem to be doing much better now that I'm older," James went on. "My father summoned me home again and again, to see my mother. I didn't come. Now I'm here at last, and I find that I'm too late. She died while I was on my way."

"Your mother was a kind lady," Charlie said quietly. "I'm sorry she's gone." He paused for a moment. "This don't make me your father's friend, though."

"I know."

"You and him will always be Loyalists. Me and Sam will be Patriots. Way I see it, we'll probably be fighting each other before long."

"Perhaps, Mr. White. But maybe not. There's something else you don't know."

"What's that?"

"I'm not a Loyalist, Mr. White. I'm a Patriot."

Vanessa

JAMES MASTER COULD never have imagined, when he first came to London, that he would marry Vanessa Wardour.

Indeed, when it happened, all London was astounded. The young colonist was a handsome young fellow, certainly, and heir to a considerable fortune. But the lovely Vanessa Wardour was at the pinnacle of aristocratic society. No doubt, they supposed, she'd turn him into a country gentleman, or a man of fashion. But whatever she did with him, young Master could count himself exceedingly lucky to be taken, in almost a single step, from colonial obscurity to the innermost circles at the apex of the empire.

James was very proud of being British. It was how he'd been brought up. With what rapture, when his parents had first taken him to London, he'd listened to Ben Franklin as the great man described Britain's imperial destiny. How overjoyed he'd been to go to Oxford, to enjoy its stately quadrangles and dreaming spires, and to imbibe the knowledge of ancient Greece and Rome that was proper to an English gentleman.

For when Englishmen walked through London's classical streets and squares, or took the waters at Bath, when aristocrats made the Grand Tour to Italy and commissioned Palladian country houses back at home, or when politicians made fine speeches full of Latin tags, how did they see themselves, if not as the honest, sturdy heirs of ancient Rome? To be an English gentleman, in an age when Britain's empire was expanding, was a fine thing indeed; and young men in such a position might be forgiven for feeling a sense of superiority.

It was natural, too, when Englishmen considered how to manage their widespread territories, that they should look to the Roman Empire for a model. And how was the mighty Roman Empire governed? Why, it was ruled from Rome, of course. Provinces were conquered, Roman peace established and governors sent out to rule them. The barbarians were given the benefits of civilization, and they were grateful for them. What more could they want? As for laws and taxes, they were decided by the emperor, the senate and people of Rome.

It was a splendid thing for young James Master to join such an elite.

True, now and then, he was reminded that his status was in question. A lighthearted remark from some fellow Oxford undergraduate: "Come on, Master, you damned provincial." Or an expression of friendship: "Don't mind that James is a colonist—we count him as one of us." Words spoken in jest, and not intended seriously—yet proving all the same that, in their hearts, young British gentlemen did not consider an American their equal. James took such occasional teasing in good part. If anything, it made him all the more determined to join the exclusive British club.

Back in London after university, James had been happy. The Albions had long been his second family. He and Grey had been together at Oxford for a year, and it had been pleasant for him to act as mentor to the younger fellow. In London, too, he led the way. Especially when it came to women.

James was very attractive to the gentler sex. With his tall good looks, his undoubted fortune, and pleasant, easy manners, he was much in favor with young ladies looking for a husband, and with older women looking for something less permanent. True, the younger ladies might acknowledge, it was a pity his fortune was in the colonies. But perhaps he would stay in London, or at least do as a number of other rich New York merchants did, and maintain a house in both cities. Besides his Oxford education, his views on life seemed to be sound. He loved London, was strong for the empire, and when it came to the radical mobs that troubled both London and New York, he was quite decided. "They must be dealt with firmly," he would say. "They are a threat to good order."

Unsurprisingly, in these circumstances, James Master had a very agreeable time.

It was one day in summer when Grey Albion suggested that James join him and his friend Hughes for dinner. James met them at a tavern off the Strand. The two friends made an interesting pair: Albion, the privileged young man with his untidy hair, and laughing blue eyes; Hughes, the son of a humble candle-maker, working his way up in a law office, always neatly dressed. But behind his quiet and respectable manner, Grey told James, lay a mind that was surprisingly bold and daring.

During the meal, the young men enjoyed a general chat. They had ordered roast beef, and the innkeeper had brought them his best red wine. They all drank freely, though James noticed that the young law clerk only drank one glass to his two. He learned that Hughes had no hand in politics, but that his father was a radical. Hughes, for his part, asked James questions about his family and childhood in New York, and professed the hope that he might go there one day.

"And do you intend to return to America yourself?" he asked.

"Yes. In due course," James answered.

"May I ask what side will you take in the present dispute when you do?"

"My family is loyal," James said.

"Very loyal," Grey Albion added with a grin.

Hughes nodded thoughtfully. His narrow face, with its thin, hooked nose and bead-like eyes, reminded James of a small bird.

"My family would certainly be on the other side," he remarked. "As you know, many of London's artisans and radicals think that the colonists' complaints are just. And it isn't just humble folk like my family. Some of the great Whigs, even solid country gentlemen, say that the colonists are only demanding the same thing that their own ancestors did before they cut off King Charles's head. No tax without representation. It's the birthright of every Englishman."

"No cause to rebel, though," said Grey Albion.

"We rebelled in England, last century."

Grey turned to James with a laugh. "I told you my friend had a mind of his own."

"But do you not fear disorder?" said James.

"So did the royalists when we complained of the tyranny of the king. All governments fear disorder."

"But the empire . . ."

"Ah." Hughes stared at James. There was a little light of danger in his eye. "You think that, like the Roman Empire, the British Empire must be governed from the center. London is to be the new Rome."

"I suppose I do," said James.

"Nearly everyone does," Hughes agreed. "And that is why, in the case of America, we run into a difficulty. More than a difficulty. A plain contradiction."

"How so?"

"Because the colonists believe they are Englishmen. Does your father believe he's an Englishman?"

"Certainly. A loyal one."

"But because he lives in America, your father cannot have the very rights that make him English, and therefore loyal. The system of empire doesn't permit it. Your father is not a freeborn Englishman. He is a colonist. He may be grateful to be ruled by freeborn Englishmen in London—and that, I grant, is better than being ruled by a tyrant—but that is all he can have. If your father is loyal to the king and to the empire because he thinks he is an Englishman, then he deceives himself. And all because no one can think of how else to run an empire. Therefore, I say, there must sooner or later be conflict. If your loyal father has any sense, he will rebel." This bleak paradox seemed to give Hughes a certain satisfaction. He looked at them both triumphantly.

James laughed.

"I don't think I shall tell my father what you say of him. But tell me this: how else could the empire be governed? How could the American colonists be represented?"

"There are two alternatives. There could be American representatives in the London Parliament. An unwieldy arrangement perhaps, with America being an ocean away from London, but it might do the trick."

"And have colonists voting on English concerns?" said Grey Albion. "I can't see any government standing for that."

"You see," said Hughes, with a sly smile to James, "what you colonists are up against. In fact," he turned to Albion, "if governments were wise, they would think even larger thoughts. Were the American colonies to have representation in London, then as they grew, so might the number of their representatives, and in a century or two, I dare say, we should have an imperial parliament in which the American members made up the majority. Who knows, the king might even abandon London and keep his court in New York!"

Grey Albion burst out laughing. James shook his head, amused, but thoughtful also.

"You said there were two alternatives," he reminded Hughes.

"Indeed. The other would be to let the Americans govern themselves—at least to approve the taxes they must pay."

"If they are willing to pay taxes at all."

"That may be a difficulty. But they should pay for their defense. However, it is a hard thing for ministers in London to give up any power."

Here, Grey Albion interposed.

"You omit one difficulty, Hughes. Our ministers fear that if they give in to radical American demands, then other parts of the empire, especially Ireland, will want more liberty, and the whole British Empire could collapse."

"I think they'll have even more trouble if they don't," said Hughes.

"You do not consider then," James asked, "that the present arrangement for America can last?"

"I think that men like Ben Franklin and your father may find tempo rary compromises. But the system is fundamentally flawed."

When the evening was over, and James and Grey Albion walked home together, Grey was full of amusement.

"Isn't Hughes a character? He always has an opinion on everything. Some people think he's a little mad, but I relish him."

James nodded silently. He didn't think Hughes was mad in the least. But what the legal clerk had said made him uneasy, and he wanted to think about it further.

⁘

It was the next evening that he met Vanessa for the first time. It was at Lord Riverdale's house and he was wearing a splendid new blue coat in which he knew he looked handsome. Since Vanessa was introduced as Lady Rockbourne, he assumed that she was married. They talked for some time, and he certainly noticed that she was very beautiful. She was fair, and slim, with pale blue eyes that seemed to be focused in the middle distance. But he thought no more about his encounter until toward the end of the evening, when one of the other ladies of the party declared to him that Vanessa had been much impressed with him. James remarked that he had not met her husband.

"You didn't know? She is a widow." The lady gave him a meaningful look. "And quite unattached."

A few days later, he received an embossed invitation to a reception at Lady Rockbourne's house in Mayfair.

It took a month for them to become lovers. During that time, he was aware that she was both arranging for them to meet frequently, and taking stock of him. He was certain, quite soon, that she was physically attracted to him; but obviously that was not enough. When the signal was finally given, therefore, he felt rather complimented. Not that he was sure, even then, why she had chosen him. And when he asked, she gave him only a lighthearted and evasive answer.

James had never had an intimate relationship with an aristocrat before. Indeed, he admitted to himself, part of Vanessa's attraction for him was her class. Not because he was a social snob, but because he was curious. There was, in her attitude to the world, a bland assumption of superiority that, had it been turned against him, he would have found shocking, but, because he was in her favor, he found amusing. He observed the elegant way she did things, the amazing lightness with which she moved, the subtle inflection by which she could alter the meaning of a single word, or indicate an irony; and by contrast, the astounding frankness she could sometimes employ when lesser mortals might prefer to be less direct. All these were new to James, and fascinating. And yet at the same time, he sensed in her an inner nervousness, a dark place of the soul, and his sense of this vulnerability made him feel protective toward her. Perhaps, he thought, it was his strong yet tender arm that she secretly craved.

As the months went by, he was in her company more and more. If she did not see him for a day or two, her footman would appear at the Albions' house with a note to summon him. She had become quite dependent. And for his part, he had become so fascinated by her that when she told him she was pregnant, it did not seem strange to him that he should suggest they marry.

She did not answer at once; she took a week to consider. And he well understood—he had, after all, no great title or estate. It was one thing to have an intimate friendship, another to marry. To have a child without a husband was certainly a serious affair, even for a widow in her invincible social position, though she could probably get away with it by leaving speedily for the European Continent and not returning until after the child was born and safely given away into foster care. But for whatever reason, after a week, she told him she would marry him.

The marriage was performed quietly, with just the Albions, the Riverdales and a few close friends for witnesses, at the fashionable church of St. George's, Hanover Square. And six months later, little Weston was born.

James was very proud of little Weston. Even as an infant, he looked like John Master. And James couldn't help also feeling proud that for the first time, so far as he knew, the Master family had married into the aristocracy. Future generations would carry in their veins the blood of nobility, even royalty, stretching back to time immemorial.

Vanessa seemed happy too. If she was now only plain Mrs. Master, her very presence gave the name a new luster, and the fact that the baby was universally admired was also gratifying. Indeed, there had been little friction between her and James in the first year of their marriage, except for one minor matter.

He continued to work. He spent less time at the Albion trading house than he had before—which Albion himself well understood—but he by no means neglected business.

"Must you be such a tradesman, James?" his wife would remark. But he would only laugh.

"It's not as if I lived at the warehouse," he'd reply. "Albion's a gentleman, with a perfectly respectable place of business in the city, and I go there to keep an eye on my family's affairs—which are considerable," he'd remind her.

"Perhaps, James," she'd suggest, "we should buy an estate in the country. You could manage that. I'd like to see you in Parliament, I think."

"I've no objection to either," he said. "But the family business must still be attended to."

He realized that, like many women, she planned to refashion the man she loved, and it quite amused him. But he hadn't the least intention of neglecting his affairs, all the same.

He also remarked several times that they must think of crossing the Atlantic to visit his family, who would be anxious to meet her. To this she replied, "Not yet, James. Not with little Weston so young." And as this seemed reasonable, he did not argue.

When she became pregnant again, he was delighted. He'd rather hoped for a girl this time. Then she lost the baby and he was very sad. But for Vanessa, the loss took a greater toll.

She became depressed. For weeks she remained in the house, going out little, staring lifelessly through the window at the sky. She seemed to do everything listlessly. He tried to comfort her, persuade her to amusements, but mostly in vain. She seemed to shrink from intimacy. Even Weston seemed to bring her little joy. After a short time playing with him, she would hand him back to the nursemaid and motion them away.

Gradually she returned to her normal state, or something like it. But there was a change. Though she allowed him into her bed, it was plain to James that she did not really welcome his embraces. He tried to be tender, and hoped for better times. Almost more difficult for him to understand was her attitude to Weston.

He had assumed that all women were maternal. It was, he thought, their natural instinct. It was strange indeed to him, therefore, that even after she had recovered, Vanessa did not seem to care for her son. To outside eyes, she was a perfect mother, but she was going through the motions, and in her attentions to the child, there was little warmth. Once, with the little boy on her knee, she gazed at Weston's face and remarked to James: "He looks just like you."

"He's the image of my father, actually," James replied.

"Oh," she said sadly. "Is that it?" And she put little Weston down, without enthusiasm, so that James could only wonder whether she had affection for either him or for his son.

It was shortly after this incident that James encountered Benjamin Franklin in the Strand. When he introduced himself and explained who he was, the great man was friendly. "Come back to my lodgings," he said, "and let us talk."

As always, Franklin was enlightening. They spoke of the Patriot cause, and James related the conversation he'd had with young Hughes.

"I confess," he told Franklin, "that I have often pondered his words since, and wondered whether he may be right. Perhaps a fundamental agreement between the British government and the American colonies can never be reached."

But Franklin was more sanguine.

"I cannot fault your young friend's logic," he said cheerfully. "But the political art uses negotiation and compromise rather than logic. The question is not whether the British Empire makes sense, but whether men can live together in it. That's the thing. I am still hopeful that we can, and I trust you will be too."

It was in a happier mood that James walked back from the Strand to Piccadilly. Turning up into Mayfair and arriving at the house, he was let in by the butler, who informed him that his wife had a lady visitor, and that they were in the small drawing room. Ascending the stairs, James came to the drawing-room door, and was just about to let himself in when he heard his wife's voice.

"I can scarcely bear it. Every day under this roof has become a torture."

"It cannot be so bad," he heard the visitor say gently.

"It is. I am trapped in a marriage with a colonial. A colonial who wants to drag me to his cursed colony. I tremble that if we go there he might want to stay."

"Stay in America, when he has the chance to live in London? I cannot think it."

"You do not know him. You cannot imagine what he's like."

"You told me that as a husband he is . . ."

"Oh, I do not complain of his manhood. For a time I even loved him, I think. But now . . . I cannot bear his touch."

"These things are not so uncommon in a marriage. They may pass."

"They will not. Oh, how could I have been such a fool, to trap myself with him? And all because of his cursed child."

"Do not say such things, Vanessa. Does he know your feelings?"

"He? The colonial? Know? He knows nothing."

James turned silently from the door. He knows now, he thought grimly. Going downstairs, he told the butler that there was no need to mention to his wife that he had been there, because he had just remembered that he had an errand to run. He did not return for over an hour.

❖

In the year that followed, James went about his business as usual. He watched carefully for signs from his wife—either of the loathing she had concealed, or of any improvement in her feelings toward him. He could detect neither. Knowing her feelings kept him, for the most part, from her bed, and she made no complaint of this. Occasionally she gave indications that she expected his attentions, and as she was an attractive woman, and he a vigorous man, he was able to satisfy her when she wished. For the rest, he patronized a certain discreet establishment in Mayfair where the girls were reputed to be clean. And truth to tell, he sometimes wondered if he would even keep up the miserable pretense of his marriage, if it were not for little Weston.

As news of one outrage after another came from the American colonies, as the cause of the Patriots rose, and the Congress met in Philadelphia—and as the British government remained obtuse in meeting every challenge—James often thought of his dear family in New York, and his little son in London, and wondered: Did he really want little Weston to be part of his mother's world, or to live in the cleaner, more simple world in which he had been raised himself?

How he longed to take Weston over to meet his grandparents. With what agony he answered his father's letters that begged him to return. When once or twice he had raised the issue with Vanessa, even promising her that their visit would be brief, she had refused to countenance the voyage.

Strangely, the quarrel that finally brought matters to a head did not begin over his own family, but over Ben Franklin. It took place at the start of December 1774.

When his well-meaning intervention in the affair of the Hutchinson Letters had so badly backfired, Franklin had not only caused outrage in the colonies. Many in London concluded that he'd stirred up trouble deliberately, and he was roundly cursed. In retaliation, Franklin had written a couple of pieces pointing out some of the errors of the London government in turn. This exacerbated the situation further, and though he still had influential friends in Parliament, Franklin was now unpopular.

James and Vanessa were returning in their carriage from a dinner, through the frosty night-time streets, when James unwisely remarked that he'd been sorry to hear Franklin so roundly abused at the party.

"No doubt," Vanessa murmured.

"He means well," James said. And for no particular reason, except no doubt it had been pent up for so long, this triggered Vanessa's outburst.

"Franklin is a damned colonial. A dirty little traitor, masquerading as a gentleman."

"I think that's a little unfair."

"He came to London. He promised to make himself useful. We treated him like an Englishman. We even sent his bastard son out to govern New Jersey. There's only one thing for the upstart to do, if he *is* a gentleman.

Keep his mouth shut unless he's told to open it. As far as I'm concerned, he and all the other colonial traitors should be taken out into a field and shot. That would reduce the colonies to order."

"Well, now we know what you think."

"I know nobody who thinks otherwise, you accursed colonial," she cried. "Be grateful that you have a son who is born in a civilized country. I pray to God he may never set foot in your damned colony."

James called to the coachman, who must surely have heard most of this, to stop the carriage. He stepped out. Vanessa said not a word.

As he walked home, James felt neither sorrow, nor even anger, but disgust. When he reached the house, he went quietly to his bureau, and took out the last letter from his father. As he read over its urgent plea that he should come to see his mother, he was overcome with shame. If not with his family, he resolved to take ship as soon as possible. Then he retired to his dressing room, where he slept alone.

He rose late, and breakfasted by himself. He was about to leave for Albion's office when the butler gave him a letter. It was written in Vanessa's bold hand. It announced that she had left, early that morning, that she was going to the Continent, and that she could not say when she would return.

✦

It was just before Christmas that James went to see Ben Franklin. To his surprise, when he told the old man his decision, Franklin did not try to dissuade him.

"The fact is," Franklin confessed, "I have come to the same conclusion. I have been knocking upon every door I know in London. Some still open to me, and those that do, all tell me the same story. The British government will not budge. I always believed that compromise was possible. Now, I no longer believe it." He smiled. "Your young lawyer friend was right, it seems. I expect to be following you shortly."

"I had not realized how much we colonials are despised."

"The British are angry. When people are angry, any insult will do; and prejudice is magnified into a cause."

"I had not understood British arrogance, either."

"All empires become arrogant. It is their nature."

James parted from the old man with warm expressions of goodwill. It only remained to prepare for his journey, and, since his mother was gone, to take little Weston with him. This at least was a blessing: Weston would see his grandparents after all.

As he took the little fellow's hand to board the ship, he made only one private vow: the little boy must never know that his mother did not love him.

War

Outside, the sky was blue. Hudson had already told her that the streets were quiet. Abigail handed the letter back to her father, stepped into the hall where little Weston was waiting, and took the child by the hand.

"Come, Weston," she said, "we'll go for our walk."

The boy was like her own child now. He was such a dear little fellow. She'd have given her life rather than let any harm come to him.

A year after James's return, how the world had changed. For a while, the voices of moderation had still been heard. The Continental Congress had sworn they only wanted justice from Britain. In New York, men like John Jay had managed to restrain the Liberty Boys. But not for long.

The rebellion had taken on a life of its own. First, after the skirmishes of Lexington and Concord, when General Howe and his redcoats had tried to break out of Boston, the Patriots had inflicted terrible casualties on them at Bunker Hill. Then, up in the northern reaches of the Hudson River, Ethan Allen and his Green Mountain Boys took the redcoats by surprise and seized the little fort of Ticonderoga, with all its heavy cannon. After this, the Congress had been so emboldened that they even tried a sortie into Canada.

Down in Virginia, the British governor had offered freedom to any slaves who cared to run away to join the British Army—which had made the Southern planters furious. In England, King George had declared the

American colonies in a state of rebellion—which by now was the truth—
and ordered their ports closed.

"The king's declared war on us," the Liberty Boys announced.

But the thing that had stirred people most was not a military engagement at all. In January 1776 an anonymous pamphlet had appeared.
Soon it became known that the author was an Englishman named
Thomas Paine, who'd recently arrived in Philadelphia. The pamphlet was
entitled "Common Sense." "Damned sedition," John Master had called
it, but as a piece of writing it was brilliant.

For not only did Paine argue for an independent America—God's
country, where fugitive Freedom could find a safe haven from Europe's
ancient evils—but he used phrases that echoed in the mind. King George
became "the royal brute of Britain." Of British rule he remarked: "There
is something very absurd in supposing a continent to be governed by
an island." And of independence, simply and memorably: "'Tis time
to part." Within weeks "Common Sense" was being read all over the
colonies.

By now it seemed unavoidable: it was war. New York, with its mighty
harbor and control of the northern river route to Canada, would be a key
point. Washington of Virginia, chosen by the Congress as commander-
in-chief, had already inspected the city. Early in 1776, he'd sent Lee, his
trusted general, to strengthen it.

If General Charles Lee had any connection with the notable Lees of
Virginia, it must have been distant. For he turned out to be an eccentric
Englishman. He'd served in America in the French and Indian War, and
taken an Indian wife before returning to fight in Europe. Recently, however, he'd returned to America to settle. Passionate for the colonists' cause,
this hot-tempered military man strode around the city with his pack of
dogs, usually followed by a crowd of curious children. He knew his business, though. In a month, he had laid the solid groundwork for the city's
defenses.

His presence in the city had had one other consequence for the Master
family. When James went to offer his services, he had much impressed the
peppery general, who had soon sent him up to Boston to join Washington.

As Abigail walked along Beaver Street, her mind turned to her dear
brother, and she wondered how long it would be before she saw him

again. She crossed the street to Bowling Green. Little Weston was tugging at her hand. She let him run ahead.

✦

John Master looked at the letter again. It was not easy to get letters from England at the moment—and as a well-known Tory, he had to be cautious. Many of his Tory friends had left the city during the last months. Tryon, the royal governor, was safely on a ship in the harbor now. For Loyalists who dared to remain, it was wisest not to draw attention to oneself. A man who corresponded with England might be taken for a spy. But Albion had cleverly sent his letter through Boston, and a messenger had handed it to Solomon at the door of the house last night.

The letter was clear, concise, and not very encouraging.

A huge army was being gathered. So large, that British redcoats would not be enough. The government was hiring German mercenaries. They had even tried to get troops from Russia, but the Empress Catherine had refused them. There was no drawing back now.

There had been many in England whose sympathies lay with the rebels, he reminded Master. The Londoners, in particular, were the colonists' friends. Even Lord North, the prime minister, was minded to be conciliatory, until the fighting started. In the House of Commons, Burke, Charles James Fox and other fine orators were still speaking out for the colonists' cause. In the Lords, both the great Chatham, who had led England to victory over the French in the last war, and Franklin's friend Lord Dartmouth were still prepared to urge compromise. A few army officers had even refused to serve against the colonists.

But once British soldiers were being killed, public sympathy had swung toward the government. It was only to be expected. Above all, King George, with all his honest heart, believed it was his duty not to give way. The majority in Parliament agreed with him. And even if they hadn't, so many Members of Parliament had public offices which paid fine salaries for no work, or held military commissions where promotion depended on the government, or had friends with government contracts, or could, quite simply, be bribed, that Lord North could be certain of securing a majority.

Was there still hope? Yes, Albion said, for two reasons. The first was the vast expense of sending armies so far. The second was that France, seeing

British power engaged in America, would probably attack other parts of the empire, and try to snatch back what they lost in the last war. Once the Patriots had seen what they were up against, and been thoroughly terrified, perhaps they would temper the more extreme of their demands, and a compromise might be reached.

He ended his letter on a lighter note.

> Did James tell you, the rumor has always been that Lord North's mother cuckolded her husband with the king's father? And that King George and his prime minister are thus half-brothers? (They look so alike, I'm sure 'tis true.) If the prime minister should ever grow weary of chastising the colonists, therefore, his royal brother, believing God to be on his side, will be sure to make him stick to his purpose.

Master had watched Abigail carefully as she read the letter. He had been amused at her shock when she came to the passage about the king and his brother.

"I never imagined, Papa," she had said, "that Lord North was the king's bastard brother. Are such things often done in England?"

"They have been known," he had answered with a smile, "even in America."

But the real point, he thought now, as he read the letter again, the real point was that there was still hope. There would probably have to be fighting, but once the Patriots discovered what they had done—despite Charlie White and the Liberty Boys, despite General Lee and his fortifications, despite the tragic folly of his own son James—a settlement of some kind would be negotiated. There was still hope for himself, and Abigail, and little Weston.

He sat for some time, contemplating the situation, until he was interrupted by a commotion at the door. In some surprise, he went into the hall, to find Hudson struggling to close the door upon two large men. A moment later, the door burst inward.

And he stared in horror.

✣

There were only a few people on Bowling Green, and it was easy to entertain little Weston. James had taught him to throw and catch a ball, and all you had to do was throw the ball to him by the hour.

"Throw higher," he would cry, or, "Further away." He loved to show how he could jump, or dive for a catch. He was remarkable, she thought, for his age. Abigail always worried that he must long for his mother, and hoped she was able to make up for some of that lack. So although she found it quite boring to play catch for hours, that was more than made up for by the joy of seeing the little fellow so happy and proud of himself. She only wished that James were here to see it.

How excited she'd been when James had first returned. How tall and handsome he was. What joy she had felt to see him sitting at the family table. And what relief. With James there, she'd been sure, things would go better.

It had been on the third day that he had broken the news. He and his father were closeted together nearly an hour. She'd heard her father's cry of pain, then raised voices, then a long rumble of conversation before her father had emerged, looking pale and grave.

"Your brother has decided to support the Patriot cause," he told her. "I understand his reasons, though I do not agree with them. Now, Abby," he had continued gently, "we must keep the family together, you and I. Discuss the subject with James as little as possible. On no account argue with him. He is your brother, and you must love and support him. Above all, little Weston must hear no cross word in this house."

And that was what they had done. No one entering the house would ever suppose that James and his father were on different sides. The news of the day was discussed calmly. Master might offer an opinion on the competence of Washington, or the incompetence of the troops he was raising. James might shake his head over some unwise or arrogant decision made in London. But their discussions were always polite.

Not long after his return, they had all gone up into Dutchess County. Abigail had happy memories of visits to her grandfather, old Dirk Master, at his farm when she was a little girl. After he had died, John Master had kept the farmhouse, which they would use from time to time in the summer. The family's sizable landholding in the county was managed by her sister Susan's husband, along with his own estate.

On this occasion, they had stayed with Susan. It had been pleasant enough. Susan was becoming quite matronly now, and though happy to see her family, was more preoccupied with her children and running her farm than with the great affairs of the outside world. Her husband, a brisk, cheerful man, put it bluntly.

"We aim to stay out of trouble here, if we can." He and James seemed to get on well enough, but Abigail could tell that, family loyalty aside, they had not much in common.

Just before they left, however, Susan did take her brother by the arm in an affectionate manner, and urge him: "Come to see us again, James, and do not wait too long. I am glad, after all these years, to know my brother again." And James promised that he would.

As for her own relationship with her brother, Abigail could hardly have asked for anything better. He would often sit with her, tell her about the things he'd seen. Though his appearance was dignified, he could regale her with funny stories about his student days to make her laugh. He soon discovered the things she liked, and even with the port closed to English trade, he'd manage to find her something—some lace or ribbons, a book, or even a little posy of flowers that would please her. As for his son, he was a model father. When she watched him playing with Weston, or teaching him to read, or took the little boy for walks, she felt so proud of James.

And so, thank God, it was possible for her to love and respect both her father and her brother. She ran the house now, pretty well she thought. Hudson and his wife consulted with her on all day-to-day matters. She did her best to be a comfort to her father, a companion to James and a mother to Weston.

But why was James alone? Where was his wife? Soon after his arrival, Abigail had tried to ask him, but he had given her a vague answer and gently discouraged her from inquiring again. Her father knew no more than she did. Three weeks had passed before James could bring himself to tell them that he and Vanessa had had a serious falling-out.

"I still hope for a reconciliation," he said, "but I cannot count upon it." In the meantime, it was agreed that there was no need to say anything to little Weston. He was told that his mother would be coming to join them when she could, and though he clearly missed her, he seemed to accept her absence as some unexplained necessity of the adult world.

After several months, a letter came from Vanessa. It was written on thick paper, in a bold, firm hand. With messages of love for little Weston, she spoke of her concern about the rebellion, and asked when James meant to return, clearly giving no indication that she meant to join him.

Meanwhile, as the rebellion grew, James's presence in the house seemed to afford them a measure of protection. Many of the Tory Loyalists were leaving, some sailing to England, others retiring to their farms, where they hoped they would not be troubled. Some went to Loyalist Kings or Queens counties on Long Island, though the Patriots would make occasional sweeps to harass them. As long as James was in the city, though, the Master house was considered a Patriot place.

Abigail had been playing with Weston for a little while when she carelessly threw the ball a bit too wide. Diving to one side, the boy hit his knee against a small rock, grazing it. She ran to him as he got up, his small face puckering. Apart from the trickle of blood, she could see that he'd soon have quite a bruise. She was expecting him to cry. "Shall we go home now?" she asked, as she started to wrap her handkerchief around the bloody knee. But he shook his head. And understanding that boys don't cry, she went back to her former place, and threw him an easy catch, feeling sorry for him and proud of him at the same time.

They'd continued in this way for a minute or two more when she heard shouting coming from the street behind her. She paused to listen, but after a moment it seemed to die down. The ball passed back and forth a few more times when she became aware that people at the end of the green were starting to hurry in the direction the noise had come from, as though drawn to a spectacle of some kind. She hesitated, wondering what to do. "Throw, Abby," called Weston as he tossed the ball to her.

Pretending to miss her catch, and turning to retrieve the ball, she went back a little way, trying to see what was happening—only to catch sight of Solomon, running toward her.

"You gotta stay here, Miss Abigail," he told her breathlessly, as soon as he reached her.

"What is it?"

"The Boss," he whispered to her, so that Weston should not hear. "They come for him. They sayin' he's a spy, on account of his gettin' letters from England. Don' you go back there," he added urgently. But she wasn't listening.

"Stay with Weston," she commanded. She thrust the ball into his hand. "Keep him here." And she began to run.

There was quite a crowd in front of the house. They were waiting expectantly. She tried to push through them, but before she could get to the gate, the front door of the house opened and the crowd let out a roar.

They had stripped her father to the waist, and his feet were bare. He was still a large and powerful man who could have put up a fight, but at least a dozen men were coming through the doorway with him, too many to resist. He was trying to maintain his dignity, yet his face was ashen. She had never seen her father at a disadvantage before. The men were jostling him.

The shouts from the crowd rose. By the sound of it, they wanted entertainment as much as revenge. On the steps in front of the door, her father was made to stop. One of the men was carrying a bucket of tar.

And now Abigail understood. It was no use trying to intervene; she knew she could do nothing. She had to think quickly. She turned, and started to run. Where should she go? Up to Wall Street? The City Hall was there, and people with authority. But the fort was closer. There was so little time. How long did it take, to tar and feather a man?

It was a cruel custom. A ritual humiliation. Strip a man, paint him with tar, then throw feathers all over him, which would stick to the tar. There was the shame of nakedness, the blistering pain of the hot tar, the suggestion that he were dark-skinned like a native or a slave, and feathered like a chicken, ready for the pot. When they'd done their work, they led the man through the streets, for all the town to mock. Afterward he had to scrape and scrub his blistered skin. Men had been known to die of it.

She ran as fast as she could, looking wildly about her as she went, in the hope that there might be somebody in the street with authority to stop the appalling business. Reaching the gate of the fort, she rushed to the sentry.

"Where is your officer?" she cried. "I need an officer."

"None here," he answered.

"My father—they're going to tar and feather him."

"Try City Hall, maybe," he said with a shrug.

"Damn you," she cried, and turning in desperation, she began to run up Broadway.

She had gone a hundred yards when she saw the cart. It was standing at the side of the street, while the carter chatted to a passer-by. Abigail didn't hesitate. "Help," she called out to the carter. And the fellow turned.

"City Hall," she panted. "Please take me. They're going to tar and feather my father."

Thank God the carter didn't hesitate. A strong arm pulled her up. Glancing at his face, she thought she might have seen him before, but she didn't know where. Without a word, he whipped up his horse, and the cart moved briskly to the middle of Broadway. But then, instead of going north, it veered round.

"To City Hall," she cried. "For God's sake, go to City Hall."

But the carter took no notice, and then unexpectedly said: "If you want to save him, Miss Abigail, then sit tight."

Before she could understand what was happening, they were entering Beaver Street. Seeing the crowd, the carter didn't slow down at all, but drove straight at them, so that they scattered. Her father was still at the top of the steps. The men had already daubed his chest and back, and they were just about to tar his feet. They looked up in surprise at the interruption.

"Stop that!" the carter shouted in a gruff voice. He clearly expected to be obeyed.

The man with the tar brush hesitated, but his companion holding the bucket cursed and protested: "He's a damn Tory spy."

The carter's whip snaked out so fast that Abigail hardly saw it. An instant later, the man with the bucket let out a howl, as the whiplash caught his hand, and he dropped the bucket, spreading tar all over the steps.

"Are you arguing with me?" the carter inquired.

"No, Charlie," the man with the tar brush replied. "We ain't arguing."

"Good," said Charlie White. "Cos this here's the house of James Master, the Patriot officer, and it's under protection. Anyone interfering with the people in this house . . ." He did not need to finish the sentence.

"All right, Charlie," said the man with the tar brush, "whatever you say. Come on, boys." And he led his men out to the street.

Charlie looked round the crowd, and meditatively cracked his whip over their heads. They began to disperse.

"You'd best go tend to your father, Miss Abigail," Charlie said to her quietly, and gave her a hand down. By the time she reached the top of the steps, the cart was already moving away. He didn't look back.

✢

They were not troubled after that, though her father was greatly astonished by Charlie White's protection. Seeing Charlie in the street two days later, Abigail stopped the carter and told him, "My father wants to thank you." But Charlie shook his head. "It ain't about him anyhow," he said gruffly, and turned away.

A month after that, thank God, James came back from Boston, very pleased with himself. General Howe and his redcoats had been obliged to evacuate Boston and leave for Nova Scotia. And Washington had made him a captain. But the memory of her father's humiliation never left Abigail's mind, and made her all the more anxious to preserve and defend the family. One day, when James lightheartedly asked her, "Well, Abby, are you a Tory or a Patriot now?" she didn't answer. "I think Weston is starting a cold," she said. "He shouldn't go out today."

It was hard at times to say exactly who was in charge of New York. The royal governor and the old Assembly were a dead letter. There was usually a Patriot Provincial Congress in existence, run by men like Livingston of the old elite. Still moderate, the New York Congress continued to hope for a settlement. But in the streets of New York, it was the Liberty Boys who decided what should happen.

The preparations for war continued. The British might be up in Nova Scotia, but everyone knew they'd be back. Patriot troops were pouring in, and the Liberty Boys took a gleeful pleasure in finding the houses of departed Loyalists in which to quarter them. The Tory stronghold of King's College was practically turned into a barracks. On the common above Charlie White's home, a field of tents appeared. When Charlie White and his men insisted that every spare man be sent to help build the new ramparts along the river, even John Master, after some protest, agreed to send Solomon.

"If it makes you feel any better," James told him, "General Lee doesn't believe we can hold the city. The British ships can enter the harbor and blow us to bits if they choose. But he thinks we should put up a damn good fight first."

"And Washington?" his father asked.

"His instructions are to hold out."

"The word is," John told Abigail with some amusement, "that the Provincial Congress is planning to leave the city as soon as the British appear."

"Where will they go?"

"White Plains, probably. That's twenty-five miles north." He grinned. "From there, I should think, they could safely jump either way."

❖

In mid-June another letter arrived from Albion, this time carried on a merchantman from the West Indies. He gave details of the huge force now approaching, and some brief words on the British commanders: General Howe in command, with his brother, Admiral Howe, in charge of the navy; General Clinton, raised in New York as a boy, an able commander; Cornwallis, also able, though hot-headed. He also gave Master an interesting piece of information. The Howe brothers would in addition be paid a huge stipend to negotiate a satisfactory peace. "So they are to pursue both war and peace at the same time."

Did I ever mention another curious circumstance, that the Howe brothers are also cousins to the king? This comes about because the king's great-grandfather had a bastard half-sister—to whom he was so close that many said she was his mistress too. However that may be, this lady married and her daughter, having become Lady Howe, gave birth to our general and admiral. The king likes them and calls them cousins. So you may say that this American expedition is quite a family business.

His letter assured Master that the force would be so overwhelming that victory would be speedy, and that, for whatever reason, it was generally assumed in England that the American colonists would be too soft to fight. His letter ended with a surprising piece of news.

I must also tell you that my son Grey accompanies the forces coming to America. Somewhat against my better judgment, he has prevailed upon me to buy him a commission in the army. I pray he will come through safely, and hope that he may have the opportunity of calling upon you. Who knows, perhaps he and James may even serve together, side by side.

When her father showed her the letter, Abigail read it with some astonishment.

"It seems, Papa," she remarked, "that Mr. Albion does not know that James has become a Patriot. Yet you have written to him several times since that occurred. Did you not tell him?"

"I must have forgot." He smiled at her a little ruefully. "I was hoping that James might change his mind."

"Oh Papa," she said, and kissed him.

✣

It was in the last week of June that she witnessed a conversation between her father and her brother that made her feel proud of both of them.

Since May, the Continental Congress in Philadelphia had been meeting to discuss a general declaration of the reasons for their actions, and their future intentions. When all Thirteen Colonies had been asked to send delegates, the moderates of the New York Congress had done so, without great enthusiasm. Yet in the event, the men who gathered to consider the question were no wild radicals, but a sober group of merchants, farmers and lawyers, often with personal ties to Britain. Many were graduates of America's finest universities—Harvard, William and Mary, Yale and the College of New Jersey at Princeton. One southern gentleman had been educated by the Jesuits in France. But three delegates had been at the Scottish universities of Edinburgh and St. Andrews; two more were graduates of Cambridge, one of Oxford; and six others had either been to school, or studied in England. Added to these was Ben Franklin, the former imperialist, who had been living in England for almost the whole of the last twenty years.

True, their leading lights were now committed to independence. John Hancock, the richest man in Boston, had long ago fallen out with the British government, though more on account of his stupendous smuggling activities than any profound point of principle. Jefferson, that glorious inheritor of the European enlightenment, and John Adams, the scholar lawyer, had both concluded that independence was necessary—though only after long periods of soul-searching. But many of the other delegates remained uncertain, and the word from Philadelphia late in June was that the colonies had still not reached agreement.

The conversation took place after dinner.

"Forgive me, my dear son," Master began gently, "but as the British Army is soon expected, I must ask you this. If they come in huge force and defeat Washington utterly, will that not be the end of the whole matter? Aren't you staking a great deal upon a most dangerous chance?"

"No, Father," James answered. "We may lose the battle, but even British generals have warned the government that no army can hold down forever a people that wants to be free."

"A quarter of the population is probably still Loyalist, and many others will go with the prevailing wind. The Howe brothers may also be able to offer a compromise that will satisfy most of the Patriots."

"It's possible. But there is every indication that Britain will never give us the real independence we seek."

"What is it you want to create? A republic?"

"Yes. A free republic."

"Be careful what you wish for, James. You have been to Oxford and know more history than I. Didn't the stern Roman Republic fall into decadence? And in England, after they cut off King Charles's head, Cromwell's rule turned into such a dictatorship that the English brought back the monarchy again."

"We shall have to do better."

"A fine claim, my boy, but no country of any size has ever managed it."

"Have faith, Father."

"I haven't, but never mind. Another question. The purpose of the present meeting in Philadelphia is to produce a document declaring the colonies' intention to be independent, is it not?"

"Certainly."

"Why is it so important?"

"Do you want my honest answer?"

"Of course."

"Because, if we don't, the French won't take us seriously."

"The French? This is for the French?"

"No. For ourselves as well. But for the French, it's essential. Consider, the British have a navy which controls the seas. We colonists have only privateers. Against the Royal Navy, we haven't a chance. But the French maintain a powerful navy, and they are a huge supplier of arms—down in the South, they are already supplying the Patriots, though in secret. But we cannot prevail over Britain, unless we have the French and their fleet. And much as they'd like to strike a blow against Britain, it will be expensive for them, and they won't risk much unless they know that we truly mean business. That's why we need a declaration. To show the French that we're serious."

"Then you are truly the enemies of Britain," his father sighed, "to entangle yourselves with her greatest enemy." John Master shook his head. "Not only that, James. The kingdom of France is a papist tyranny. It represents everything you say you're against."

"Necessity, Father."

"Well, I'm not sure it will work. I don't believe the colonies will hold together. The differences, especially between North and South, are too great. They haven't managed to agree in Philadelphia yet. Georgia didn't even send proper delegates."

"You may be right. I can't deny it."

His father nodded sadly, then poured more wine into James's glass. And for some time longer, the two men discussed these desperate issues, without a cross word passing between them. And knowing how much pain her father must be suffering, Abigail could only admire his restraint.

Yet James too, she thought, must have made a sacrifice. For he could surely have remained in England and argued the colonists' cause, without any risk to himself.

✢

On the twenty-ninth day of June, the British fleet began to arrive. Abigail and her father watched from the fort. A hundred ships, carrying nine thousand redcoats, sailed up through the Narrows and anchored off Staten Island. It was an impressive sight. The British disembarked, but took no immediate action. Evidently they were waiting for more reinforcements. The city trembled. Two days later, James grimly confessed: "The Staten Island militia has gone over to the British. There are boatloads of Loyalists crossing from Long Island too."

His father said nothing. But that evening, when they thought she had retired to her room, she heard her father quietly say: "It's not too late for you to go to Staten Island too, James. I'd come to vouch for you."

"I can't, Father," James replied.

✢

On the eighth of July, James came in looking excited.

"The Philadelphia Congress has agreed to a Declaration of Independence."

"All the colonies agreed?" his father asked.

"Almost all, though only at the last minute. New York abstained, but they'll ratify."

The next day, to her father's disgust, a large number then swept down Broadway to Bowling Green, knocked down the bronze statue of King George, tore off his head, and carted the torso away. "We'll melt it for bullets to shoot at the redcoats," they declared. That evening, James brought a printed copy of the Declaration to show his father.

"Jefferson of Virginia wrote most of it, though Ben Franklin made corrections. You must confess, it's rather fine."

His father read it skeptically.

"'Life, Liberty, and the Pursuit of Happiness.' Novel idea, that last. Sounds like one of Tom Paine's effusions to me."

"Actually," James corrected, "it's adapted from the philosopher Locke. Except he said 'property' instead of 'happiness.'"

"Well," said his father, "property sounds a better investment to me."

Declaration or not, the Patriot cause hardly looked promising. Although, in the South, the Patriots were still holding on to redcoats, up in Canada, they were getting nowhere. And in New York, on July 12, the British at Staten Island finally made a move. Abigail, her father and James went down to the waterfront to watch.

Two British ships were making their way across the harbor. The Patriots had a battery ready at the fort on Governor's Island, a short distance out in the harbor, as well as the usual battery at the old fort, and another at Whitehall Dock, to guard the entrance to the Hudson River. As the British ships moved easily toward the Hudson, all the batteries began to blaze at them.

"They're still out of range," James remarked irritably. "What are those fools doing?" Gradually the ships drew closer. The shore batteries should have been able to pound the ships now, but their aim was hopelessly misdirected. The British ships, which could have annihilated them, didn't even trouble to return fire. Then there was a loud explosion from one of the shore batteries. "It seems," said John Master drily, "they've managed to blow themselves up." James said nothing, as the British ships sailed into the Hudson and continued northward.

It was in the quiet of the evening, as the glow of sunset spread across the harbor, that Abigail and James, who had gone down to the waterfront again, caught sight of the masts approaching from the ocean. As the minutes passed, they saw ship after ship move in from the ocean, and draw toward the Narrows. They remained there, watching, as the red sun sank, and the whole mighty fleet swept in toward the anchorage.

"Dear God," James murmured, "there must be a hundred and fifty of them." And in the twilight, Abigail could see that her brother's brave face was tense.

✢

Yet still the British waited. They waited over a month. Admiral Howe, whose fleet this was, seemed as content as his brother to take his time. Washington, meanwhile, lodging up at the commandeered mansion of the Morris family overlooking the Harlem River, supervised the defenses of the city, New Jersey and Long Island with a calm and stately dignity that was to be admired.

By the time he was done, any ships trying to go up the Hudson would have had to pass between a pair of forts with batteries—Fort Washington up on Harlem Heights and Fort Lee on the opposite New Jersey shore—plus a further string of small forts which had been constructed across the East River on Brooklyn Heights, to protect the city from an attack across Long Island.

At the start of August, a flotilla arrived bearing Clinton and Cornwallis from the south, with eight more regiments. A few days later came another twenty-two ships, with yet more regiments from Britain. On August 12, the New Yorkers were astonished to witness a third huge fleet—a hundred ships this time—sail in with the Hessian mercenaries.

The superiority of the force across the water was total. Some thirty-two thousand of Europe's finest troops against Washington's untrained volunteers. One thousand two hundred naval cannon, against some small shore batteries that hadn't hit two ships directly in front of them. If Admiral Howe chose, his gunners could reduce New York City to rubble. As for the Patriot forces, James reported that some of the troops in the camp were falling sick.

But Howe didn't blast the city to bits. He tried to talk to Washington. He had no luck. Washington sent his first letter back, with the message: "You failed to address me as General." Then he told the admiral: "Talk to Congress, not to me."

"Is Washington foolish, Papa, to hold out?" Abigail asked one day.

Many people in New York clearly thought so. Families were loading their possessions onto carts every day, and taking the road north, out of the city. In some of the streets, every house was now empty.

"It's a game of bluff," Master answered. "Howe hopes to frighten us into submission. What's passing in Washington's mind, I do not know. If he truly supposes he can withstand the British, then he's a fool. But I'm not sure that's his game. Howe wants to weaken Patriot resistance by offering peace. Washington has to take that offer away from him. So he must force Howe to attack, and shed American blood."

"That's cruel, Papa."

"It's a gamble. If the Patriots panic, or if Washington is annihilated, then it's all over. But if Washington can survive, then the Patriots' moral cause is strengthened. As for the British, that huge fleet and those thousands of men are costing the government a fortune, every day." He smiled. "If the British wanted to bombard New York, they'd have done it by now."

There remained the question of which way the British would come. Would they come straight across the harbor and, supported by the huge firepower of their ships, dare a landing on Manhattan? Or would they come the other way, across the western end of Long Island to Brooklyn, and make the short crossing over the East River from there? Opinion was divided. So the Patriot militias were being split between the city and Brooklyn Heights.

Abigail watched some of them crossing to Brooklyn. To her eye, they did not seem very impressive. They marched untidily; many of them, having no proper uniforms, had made do with sprigs of greenery stuck into their hats.

In the third week of August, Washington ordered all civilians to quit the city. Assuming that they'd go up to the farm in Dutchess County, Abigail started making preparations to leave. But to her surprise, John Master told her they were staying. "You'd keep little Weston here?" she asked.

"I am convinced he's as safe here as anywhere else," he said.

That afternoon, a party of soldiers started to chop down a cherry tree that grew in front of the house. Most of the orchards in the city had already been cut down for firewood, but this seemed absurd. Her father had just gone out to remonstrate with them, and she was watching from the door, when, to her surprise, James walked by. To her even greater surprise, he was in the company of a very tall, upright man, whom she recognized immediately.

It was General Washington.

He was an impressive figure. If James Master stood six foot tall, the general was almost three inches taller. He stood ramrod-straight, and she had the sense that he was very strong. James, seeing his father, indicated him to the general.

"This is my father, sir. John Master. Father, this is General Washington."

The general turned his gray-blue eyes toward John Master, and bowed gravely. He had a quiet dignity, and with his great height adding to the effect, it was easy to see why men regarded him as their leader. Abigail expected her father to bow his head politely in return.

But it seemed that John Master, for once, was determined to dispense with his usual good manners. Granting the great man only the minimum nod that courtesy demanded, he gestured toward the soldier with the axe and said: "What the devil's the point in chopping down this tree?"

Washington stared at him. "I told all civilians they should leave the city," he said coldly, ignoring the question.

"I'm staying," said her father.

"Waiting for the British, no doubt."

"Perhaps."

Abigail was open-mouthed, wondering what was going to happen next. Would Washington have her father locked up? James was looking horrified.

But the great man only stared at Master impassively. He gave no sign of emotion at all. Then, without another word, he walked on. He had only gone a few yards, when he paused briefly next to James.

"Typical Yankee," Abigail heard him say quietly. But whether her father also heard she could not tell. The tree, meanwhile, came down.

+

Five days later, the action began. Abigail could not see much from the waterfront. Ships were moving from their anchorage by Staten Island, but the operation was taking place round the southern end of Long Island, below Brooklyn, and was mostly out of sight. With her father's small brass telescope, however, she did manage to pick out a dozen flatboats full of redcoats. Evidently they meant to advance across Flatbush to Brooklyn and the East River. Lying across their path, however, was a line of ridges where the Patriots were already digging in.

The next morning, while the British were ferrying still more troops to Long Island, Washington went over to Brooklyn, taking James with him. That evening, James returned with more detailed information.

"The British forces are huge. We think they'll ship the Hessians across tomorrow. And then you have to add their American contingents, too."

"You mean Loyalists?" said his father.

"Certainly. When Governor Tryon fled the city, he busied himself elsewhere, collecting Loyalist militia. And there are two regiments of New York and Long Island volunteers, besides. Washington will be fighting against Americans as well as British in Brooklyn. Oh, and there are eight hundred runaway slaves on the British side, too."

"What does Washington mean to do?"

"We're dug in along the ridges. The British will have to go through the passes under our fire, or try to march up steep slopes, which cost Howe so dearly when he tried it at Bunker Hill. So we think we can hold them."

The next morning, when he left, James gave little Weston and Abigail a kiss, and shook his father's hand warmly. Abigail knew what it meant.

✤

Yet still the British took their time. Three more days passed. Abigail occupied herself with little Weston. Her father claimed he had things to attend to in the town, but she knew very well that he was down at the waterfront, hour after hour, telescope in hand, trying to see what was happening. The night of the twenty-sixth of August was surprisingly cold. A gibbous moon hung in the sky.

Then, early in the morning, they heard the guns begin to stir.

All morning the roar of cannon and the distant crackle of musket fire came across the water. Smoke rose from the hills of Brooklyn. But it was impossible to tell what was happening. Soon after noon, the sounds died down. Before evening, the news was clear. The British had smashed Washington, though the Patriots were still holding out on Brooklyn Heights, just across the river. Then it started to rain.

Abigail found her father at the waterfront the next morning. She had brought him a flask of hot chocolate. He was standing in the rain, wrapped in a greatcoat and wearing a large three-cornered hat. His telescope was sticking out of his pocket. She hoped he wasn't going to catch a cold, but she knew he wouldn't come home.

"There was a break in the clouds," he said. "I could see our boys. The British have come round the side of the hill. They have Washington trapped against the river. He can't escape. So it's over. He'll have to surrender." He sighed. "Just as well."

"You think James . . ."

"We can only hope."

The rain continued all day. When her father came in at last, she had

Hudson draw him a hot bath. That evening little Weston asked her: "Is my father killed, do you think?"

"Of course not," she said. "They just moved to a safer place."

The next day was the same, and her father mostly stayed indoors. But at noon, the rain ceased, and he rushed down to the waterside again. She went to him an hour later.

"What the devil are they waiting for?" he said irritably. "The British will have them now, as soon as their powder's dry. Why in God's name doesn't Washington surrender?"

But nothing happened. At supper that evening he was tense, and scowled at everybody. That night he went out again, but soon returned.

"There's a damn fog," he growled. "Can't see a thing."

⁘

The hammering on the door came at midnight. It woke the whole house. Abigail rose from her bed hastily and hurried down, to find her father with a primed pistol in his hand and Hudson at the door. At a nod from Master, Hudson opened it.

And Charlie White walked in. He glanced at the pistol.

"Evening, John. Need your keys."

"What keys, Charlie?"

"To your damn boats. Broke into your warehouse easy enough, but you've got so many padlocks, it's wastin' time."

"What do you want with my boats, Charlie?"

"We're gettin' the boys back from Brooklyn. Hurry up, will you?"

"Dear God," cried Master. "I'm coming."

He was back an hour later. Abigail was waiting for him.

"I've never seen anything like it," he told her excitedly. "They've got a whole fleet of boats. Barges, canoes, anything that'll float. They're trying to ferry the whole army across during the night."

"Will it work?"

"As long as the British don't realize what's going on. Thank God for the fog."

"And James?"

"No sign of him yet. I want you to wake up Hudson and Ruth, and start preparing hot broth, stew, whatever you can. The men I saw coming off the boats are in terrible shape."

NEW YORK271

"We're to feed Patriots?" she said in astonishment.

He shrugged. "They're soaked to the skin, poor devils. I'm going back now."

She did as he asked, and was in the kitchen with Hudson and his wife an hour later when her father entered again. This time he was grinning like a boy.

"James is back—he'll be coming here shortly. I told him to bring his men. Have we got stew and broth?"

"Soon, Father. How many men is he bringing?"

"About two hundred. Is that a problem?"

The two women looked at each other.

"Of course not," said Abigail.

⁘

As the men crowded into the house, James took Abigail and his father aside, and gave them a brief account of what had happened.

"We hadn't properly secured our left flank. The Long Island Loyalists saw it and told the British. A force of British and Long Island men came round by Jamaica Pass during the night and attacked our rear in the morning. Then the whole line rolled up. We must have lost twelve hundred men—that's killed, not counting the wounded. It was a disaster. If Howe had followed up and attacked us on Brooklyn Heights, then it would all be over. As it is . . ." He gave a despairing gesture. "We live to fight another day. Perhaps."

Judging by the dispirited looks and haggard faces of his men, the remains of Washington's army was not in much condition to fight.

The house became an impromptu camp for the rest of that day. In the yards, on fences and clothes lines, or laid on the ground, sodden tents and uniforms were spread out to dry, so that when the sun finally broke through steam rose all around the house. Hudson placed a big tub by the front gate, which Abigail repeatedly refilled with broth, to be served to any soldiers that passed.

Around noon, as Master himself was ladling out broth to some passing men, Washington rode by. His face was tired and drawn, but looked with surprise at the Loyalist merchant with his ladle.

Without a word, Washington raised a finger to his hat, and rode on.

⁘

But in the days that followed, things only got worse.

"Three-quarters of the Connecticut militia—that's six thousand men—have upped sticks and left," James reported. "Nobody thinks we can hold New York. Except maybe Washington. Who knows?"

If the British had the upper hand tactically, their strategy remained the same. They wanted to parlay. On September 11, John Adams, Rutledge and Ben Franklin himself arrived at Staten Island to talk with the Howes.

"The British offered to pardon everybody if we'd just drop the Declaration of Independence," James said. "The delegation had to tell them no."

His father said nothing. "Though it'd make a damn sight more sense to say yes, in my opinion," he confided later to Abigail.

The next day the Patriot leaders had a war council.

"Washington was completely outvoted," James told them. "We can't hold the city. But there is another way of denying New York to the British."

"What's that?" asked his father.

"Burn it down."

"Destroy New York? No sane man would do that."

"John Jay wanted to." James smiled. "But don't worry, Father. Congress has forbidden it."

Two days later, Washington moved his forces north to the rocky natural fortress of Harlem Heights, near his headquarters. But he still left five thousand men in the city under old General Putnam. He wouldn't abandon New York without making a stand.

"I'm to stay here with Putnam," James told them.

"Spend what time you can with Weston," Abigail urged him. They might, she thought, be the last days the little boy would see his father for quite a while.

✛

But there wasn't any time. The British came the next morning. They came across the East River at Kips Bay, about three miles above the city ramparts, near the Murray Hill estate. Everyone watched from the waterfront, and by all accounts, it was an awesome sight.

Five warships, at point-blank range, emptied salvo after salvo onto the shore, in a massive bombardment, while a fleet of flatboats, bearing four thousand redcoats, skimmed quickly across the river. As the redcoats charged onto the Manhattan shore, the defending militiamen, understandably, fled for their lives.

Abigail and her father stayed with little Weston at the house. There was nothing else to do. Hudson told them the Patriot forces were on the Bloomingdale road that led up the west side of Manhattan. Would they try to engage the redcoats, or slip past them? She didn't know where James was. Her father was outside by the gate, listening for gunfire.

If the Patriot troops were heading out, so were the remaining Patriot civilians. It was a strange scene. Families with their possessions laden on wagons, or just handcarts, were going by. When she went out to her father, he told her he'd seen Charlie White ride past in a hurry. Did he say anything? she asked.

"No. But he waved."

An hour passed. Then another. The silence was eerie. At last, her father heard the rattle of muskets. But in a few minutes, it stopped, and silence resumed. Twenty minutes went by. Then a lone horseman cantered into the street.

It was James. He rushed indoors.

"It's over. I have to leave."

"Was there a fight?"

"Fight? Hardly. The British started to come across the island. Our men were to make a stand above Murray Hill, and Washington came down to supervise. But at the first shots, our men bolted. Washington was like a madman, beating them with the flat of his sword, cursing them for cowards and worse. But they paid no heed. They ran like rabbits. It was shameful."

"I thought Washington was a dry fellow."

"No. He has a fearful temper. But he controls it, mostly."

"Where are the British now?"

"On their way here. Howe moves at a snail's pace—it's almost as if he's letting us get away. Perhaps he is. Who knows? But I have to leave now, Father. I only came to bid farewell."

"My son." Master put his hands on James's shoulders. "You see how it goes with the Patriots. I implore you, for your own sake, for the sake of your family, give this business up. It's not too late. Take off your uniform. Remain here at the house. I hardly think the British will give you any trouble if you do so."

"I cannot. I must go." He embraced Abigail, went to where little

Weston was watching wide-eyed, picked him up and kissed him. Then he turned back to his father.

"There is one more thing I have to say to you, Father."

"Tell me quickly."

"In all the world you are the man I would soonest trust with my son." With that, he embraced him, and was gone.

They watched James until he was out of sight. After that, they turned indoors, and her father went into his office and closed the door. A moment later, through the door, Abigail heard him burst into tears.

"Come, Weston," she said to the little boy, "let us go to Bowling Green."

✢

The entry of the British was like the entry of every conquering army. Whether out of joy, or fear, people waved and shouted with delight. Her father hoisted a Union Jack above the door. Since much of the city was empty, the army could have their pick of quarters. "Though no doubt," her father warned her, "some colonel will want to commandeer this house."

The British were moving quite swiftly now, to take over most of Manhattan Island. But the next day the Patriots, having fled so ignominiously before, suddenly put on a show.

Up in the north of the island, just below the Patriot encampments on Harlem Heights, a party of several hundred redcoats, chasing some Connecticut Rangers away, suddenly saw a swarm of Patriots sweeping down upon them from the high ground. There was a sharp exchange, but the Patriots pressed bravely forward, and this time the redcoats had to flee.

No doubt this put some heart into the Patriots. But strangely, Abigail noticed, it seemed to please her father too. "At least the Americans gave some account of themselves," he remarked.

It was at eleven o'clock precisely the following morning, while her father was out, that Hudson came to inform her that an English officer was at the door. "No doubt he wants to commandeer the house," she said with a sigh, and went to the door.

And found there an officer, a little younger than her brother, whose hair was a mess, but who looked down at her with the most beautiful blue eyes.

"Miss Abigail?" he inquired. "I am Grey Albion."

Fire

T HE GREAT FIRE of New York began at midnight on September 30.

Hudson saw the flames when he went to shutter the upper windows. They weren't far off, down below the fort on Whitehall Dock, he guessed. "Wind's blowing this way," he told his wife Ruth. "I'd best go and take a look."

It was only a few yards from the door of the house to the corner of Broad Street. Turning down Broad Street, he went swiftly toward the waterfront. The wind was blowing briskly in across the East River from Brooklyn, and he felt it in his face. At the Dock Street crossing, he saw the fire. It was at the far end of the street where it met Whitehall. He could see that the Fighting Cocks Tavern was already a mass of flame, and the fire seemed to be spreading fast. He wondered how it could have happened so quickly. People from the area were standing and staring, but almost all the firemen, being Patriots, had fled the city, so nobody was doing anything. The house beside the tavern was already well ablaze. Just south of the tavern, a small warehouse suddenly began to burn.

He frowned. That was odd. The wind was blowing the other way.

Then he noticed something.

❖

By the time Hudson got home, the blaze had spread over a whole block. He found Master and the rest of the household already up. "Breeze'll bring it this way, Boss," he announced, "an' there's no firemen."

"Not much we can do, then," said Master grimly.

But that was when young Mr. Albion spoke up.

"I think, sir," he said, "we could try."

When Mr. Albion had first arrived at the house, the Boss had been quick to see his opportunity. Within a day, he had Albion and two other young officers quartered there. "Mr. Albion's our personal friend, Hudson," he'd explained. "And I'd rather house some junior officers here as guests, than have to move out for some colonel." Undoubtedly young Mr. Albion seemed very gentlemanly, and the two other officers gave no trouble.

That night, certainly, they were splendid. In no time they had the household filling every available container with water. Solomon had appeared in the kitchen, and Hudson made him go out and man the water pump. Before long there were buckets and troughs of water up on the top floor, and by all the windows on the south-west side. Albion had prepared a station for himself up on the roof, from which he had already stopped the drainpipes and filled the gutters with water. "Luckily the roof's slate," he told them. "That'll help."

"I'm afraid he'll get trapped up there," Abigail confided to Hudson, but he told her, "Don' you worry, Miss Abigail, I reckon he can look after himself."

Meanwhile, the fire was coming toward them. The breeze was carrying it in a broad swathe, two blocks wide. Its spread was assisted by the fact that, over the decades, the old Dutch ceramic tiles on the roofs had been replaced with wooden shingles. From the waterfront, it moved up the blocks between Whitehall and Broad Street, and its progress was rapid. By one o'clock, it was less than two blocks away. Half an hour later, looking from the front door along Beaver Street toward Bowling Green, Hudson saw the flames catch the roof of the last house.

A great black cloud was towering over the southern side of the street now, filled with glowing embers. He could hear the embers pattering down on the roofs of houses nearby. A house on the other side of the street was catching fire. The huge roar of the moving furnace was getting louder. Master called down to him to close the door, and he went quickly back inside.

Young Albion was very busy now. The other officers had rigged up a pulley to carry buckets of water up to him. He also had a brush with a long pole with which he could push embers off the roof. As the walls of the house were solidly built of brick, the key was to douse the woodwork and the shutters. With luck, the gutters full of water would put out the embers before they set fire to the eaves, but one of the young men had gone into the attic, with more buckets of water, to try to stop the roof timbers catching fire. Abigail had joined her father at one of the windows. Solomon was still busy at the pump.

"If I give the word," Master ordered, "everyone must leave the house at once." Hudson wondered if they would. The young men seemed to be enjoying themselves too much. A message came from Albion that more than half of Beaver Street was already alight.

It was almost two o'clock when flames began to crackle from the house next door. Up on the roof, Albion was exerting himself wildly. Hudson went up to help him. Flames were licking one side of the house. They poured buckets of water on that part of the roof so that the gutter would overflow down that wall. The heat was getting fierce. Albion's face was streaked with black, and seeing tiny embers in his tangled hair, Hudson poured a bucket of water over his head, and the young man laughed. Below, they heard Master's voice, calling out for them to leave. Hudson looked at Albion. The young officer grinned.

"I can't hear a thing, Hudson, can you?"

"No, sir."

And they were just pushing some more embers off the roof when Hudson noticed something. He pointed to the smoke. Albion stared, then let out a shout of triumph.

"Quick, Hudson. Tell 'em to get back. We can still save the house."

The wind had changed.

⁘

The Master house escaped the Great Fire of New York that night. The huge charred line of destruction ran along the entire southern side of Beaver Street, but on the northern side the last two houses, next to Broad Street, were spared. The rest of the city was not so lucky. For as the wind shifted toward the eastern quarter, it carried the fire across to Broadway. A little later, shifting back again, it carried the conflagration straight up the great thoroughfare. There was nothing anyone could do to stop it. Trinity Church, with its noble spire, went up in flames and was a blackened hulk by morning. In the poor quarter to the north and east of it, the modest timber houses went up like kindling wood. On and on the fire swept, all that night and the following morning, from Broadway to the Hudson, until at last, some time after Charlie White's dwelling had gone up in a single flash, it came to an end, only because, reaching empty lots, it ran out of houses to burn.

What had started the fire? Was it an accident, or deliberate arson? If arson, it must have been the Patriots. Inquiries were made. Nothing was established. One Patriot officer was caught in the city. He admitted he came there to spy, but denied that he'd started the fire. General Howe had to hang him, as a spy out of uniform—the rules of war demanded it. But the cause of the fire remained a mystery.

⁙

Hudson waited a week before he spoke to his son Solomon.

"When I was out by the fire," he said quietly, "I saw something funny. I saw two people running away from a warehouse near the tavern. One of them looked like Charlie White."

"That so?"

"Man with him was black. Younger. In fact, I could'a swore it was you."

"I was at the house when you got back."

"And before?"

"Didn' you tell me you was once accused of starting a fire in the dark?"

"You stay out of trouble," said Hudson, with a furious look.

Love

ABIGAIL WAS SITTING on a folding stool, with a parasol over her head. Her father stood behind her. Weston was cross-legged on the grass. There was quite a crowd around the edge of Bowling Green: ladies, gentlemen, officers and men.

"Oh, well hit!" cried her father, as the ball soared over the heads of the crowd, and everybody applauded. "Grey's having quite an inning," he remarked with a smile to his daughter. Indeed, Albion had nearly fifty runs.

They were playing cricket.

There were two teams in New York now, one in Greenwich Village, just above the city, the other out at Brooklyn. But you could see children playing with bat and ball on any street in the fashionable quarter. Albion had already taught Weston how to bat and bowl. "Though I've nothing to teach him about fielding," he'd laugh. "I'd hate to be batting if Weston were on the other team."

Grey Albion had been in high favor with John Master since the night of the fire. Indeed, as the months went by he'd become like a second son to John and a favorite uncle to Weston. Though he was in his late twenties, almost as old as James, there was something boyish about him, with his handsome face and unruly hair. He would romp with Weston, make the other young officers join in a game of blind man's buff, like so many children, or once in a while organize some outrageous practical joke upon Abigail herself that kept the household laughing for days.

She knew that other girls thought him attractive. "It's so unfair," they cried, "that you should have him living in your house." But if his blue eyes melted the other girls, she had long ago decided that she was not so impressed herself. Besides, he treated her entirely as a little sister. Indeed, at times she found him almost infuriating—not because of anything he did, but on account of his assumption of superiority.

"This business with the rebels will soon be over," he'd assure her. "Another battle or two against a real army and they'll run like rabbits to their holes. They're just a rabble led by men who aren't gentlemen—I exclude James of course."

Not that the other young officers she met thought any differently. They all had the same easy contempt for the rebels, as they always called the Patriots. For even if they understood that the colonists might have had complaints, once a man took up arms against the king, he was a rebel, and rebels must be put down. There was nothing more to say.

Indeed, when it came to James's choice to be a Patriot, Albion was honestly mystified. Abigail seldom spoke of James in his presence. But although, if his name came up, Albion only spoke to her about James with respect and affection, she once overheard him telling her father: "To tell you the truth, sir, I cannot imagine what made him do it. If he walked into the room now, I don't know what I'd say to him."

Once she had tried to question him about her brother's wife. Around the turn of the year, John Master had received a letter from Vanessa. In it she told him that she had received a communication from James, letting her know that he was with the Patriots, and that Weston was in New York. She did not disguise her feelings. In her bold hand, the words stood out in capitals: SHAMEFUL, TRAITOR, VILLAIN. She thanked God, at least, that her little son was in such safe and loyal hands, and hoped that the time would soon come when she and Weston should be reunited. Though when this was to be, and in what manner, she did not say.

"What is Vanessa like?" she'd asked Albion.

"Oh, a very handsome lady," he'd answered.

"I mean her character."

"Well . . ." He had seemed to hesitate. "I do not often move in such high circles, so I don't know her well. But when we met, she was always very civil to me. She has a fine wit. She's known for it."

"Does she love Weston?"

"I think every mother loves her child, Miss Abigail." He'd paused before adding, somewhat enigmatically, "But a fashionable lady cannot always spare a lot of time for her children."

"And does she love my brother?"

"I'm sure she would not have married without love." He'd paused again. "Though she cannot approve his becoming a rebel."

"Why does she not come here?"

"Ah." He had looked a little flummoxed. "She knows that Weston is safe with your father. I expect she'll have him sent to England in due course. She probably thinks the crossing is too dangerous at present, with Patriot privateers upon the sea."

Since Patriot privateers were no match for British convoys, this last excuse was weak. But Albion had seemed reluctant to say more, and she hadn't pressed him.

As for news of James, the last autumn had been the most worrying time. Even moving at his usual snail's pace, it had not taken General Howe long to drive Washington and his army across the Hudson River. Harlem Heights, White Plains, and the rebel strongholds on the river, Fort Washington and Fort Lee, all fell. Huge numbers of Patriots were killed, thousands taken prisoner. Then General Cornwallis had chased Washington south, past Princeton and over the Delaware River into Pennsylvania. "These are the times that try men's souls," Tom Paine had declared.

At Christmas, Washington had led a daring raid across the Delaware and struck at the British and Hessian garrisons. It was a brave gesture. Then he'd been able to dodge Cornwallis, and lead his army to camp at Morristown from where, thank God, James had managed to send a letter to let them know that he was alive. But John Master did not think much of the Patriots' chances.

"Washington took one trick, but the British still hold all the good cards."

✦

In New York, however, Abigail had watched as the new British regime set in. For in the mind of General Howe, she now learned, the conduct of war assumed an aristocratic pattern. Summer was for fighting, winter for resting, and enjoying yourself—at least if you were a gentleman. And General Howe, it was soon clear, meant to enjoy himself.

Admittedly, New York was not exactly a resort. In fact, it was a confounded mess. For a start, a vast swathe of the western side of the city had been burned down in the fire. In place of block after block of charming Georgian, Dutch-gabled or wooden-frame houses, there was now a charred wasteland, almost three-quarters of a mile from end to end—a sea of freezing mud in the cold weather, and a stinking morass when it got warmer. This had become a huge bivouac, so disgusting that Master wryly confessed, "I prefer not to be on Broadway when the wind's coming from the western side." Besides this, the troops were crowded into a couple of barracks, and another permanent camp up on the Common. But for the British officers, and the Loyalists arriving from all quarters, there wasn't enough proper accommodation, and hardly enough food to go round.

As for the unfortunate Patriot prisoners, who'd been taken in large numbers, they were being crammed into the almshouse, the Nonconformist churches or any secure space that could be found, and fed scraps if they were lucky.

For landlords, however, the shortage had benefits. "I've just been offered three times the old rent for that pair of row houses we own on Maiden Lane," her father told Abigail in the spring.

Indeed, John Master was soon in high favor with the British command. A Loyalist merchant with huge experience, a fellow who'd lived in London, and who believed in compromise—he was exactly what they thought an American ought to be. General Howe took a particular liking to him, and several times invited him to dine. Wisely, Master was entirely frank with him about James, and the general seemed to trust him all the better for it: "William Franklin has the same problem with his father Ben as you do with your son James," he genially remarked. In no time Master had contracts for supplying grain and meat from anywhere he could find them. This included the produce from the farmlands up in Dutchess County, and with a pass procured by her father, Susan was able to come into the city with supplies. Business was resumed with Albion in London. The army officers wanted any luxuries and comforts that he could supply. "I've never been busier," he confessed.

Meanwhile, despite the conditions, the British officers were doing their best to re-create the pleasures of London. They opened a theater and, there being no troupe to perform, put on the plays themselves. As the spring of 1777 progressed, there were races, dances, cricket. And then, of course, there were the women.

"Armies always attract women," her father remarked to Abigail, and she could see why. The streets might be filthy, but the officers parading through them in their bright uniforms were like so many gorgeous birds in plumage. Nor were the married ladies of the city indifferent to the brave showing of the officers, or to their power. Mrs. Loring, the wife of the Commissar of Prisoners, was so often seen with General Howe that it was assumed she was his woman.

"Is she his mistress?" Abigail asked her father.

"I can only say," he answered, "that she is always at his side."

Indeed, an air of agreeable sensuality, warmly encouraged by the commander, descended upon the richer part of the town.

Every so often, Abigail would be aware that Grey Albion had gone out in the evening and not returned by the time Hudson locked the house. Several times, curious, she had seen him quietly enter the house after Hudson had opened it up again soon after dawn. Reflecting on this to Ruth in the kitchen, one morning in May, she'd received from that lady an amused smile.

"Ain't nothin' lackin' in that young man, Miss Abigail, you can be sure."

But as summer approached, everyone knew that the British would make their move. Although the colonies, from Boston and New Hampshire in the North down to the plantation states of the South, were nominally under Patriot control, the only organized Patriot army was still the ill-trained and much depleted force commanded by George Washington, down in New Jersey, barring the road to Philadelphia.

In June, General Howe had made a sortie toward Washington, and Grey Albion and his fellow officers had been gone for a while. Though he believed, like his fresh young officers, that his regular troops would destroy the Patriots in open battle, Howe had learned at Bunker Hill that, with good cover, the Patriot sharpshooters could inflict terrible damage. When he couldn't get the battle he wanted, therefore, he was back in New York by the end of the month. So the question now was, what would he do next?

It was just the previous day that Abigail's father had been asked to supper with Howe. On a whim, he had taken her too.

She'd found it strange to be sitting so close to the general. The only other guests were Mrs. Loring and a couple of other officers. Knowing

what she knew, each time the general turned his big fleshy face and protruding eyes toward her, Abigail could not help imagining that she was
gazing into the face of King George III himself.

The meal was simple, but enjoyable. Howe was in a friendly mood,
and she could see that he liked her father, but it was also clear that the
general had something he wished to discuss.

"Tell me, Master," he said after a while, "have you any knowledge of
the terrain up the Hudson?" When her father said he had, Howe continued. "You've never met General Burgoyne, I think. Gentleman Johnnie,
they call him. A dashing fellow. Gambling man. Writes plays in his spare
time." The general sniffed. This last, Abigail could see, was no compliment.

"I heard that he did well up in Canada, but that he's headstrong," her
father said frankly.

"All sail and no ballast, though I grant he's brave and daring. He has
the ear of the ministry, though, especially Lord George Germain, and as
you know he now means to come down the Hudson Valley from Canada,
take Albany, hold Ticonderoga and the other forts, and thus cut Washington off from the whole north-east. Daring plan. Wants to make a great
name for himself. Thinks it will be easy."

"How will he travel?"

"I'm not sure. Perhaps along the forest trails."

"He'll find it tough going. Trails can be blocked. He's a sitting duck for
sharpshooters."

"Germain suggests I go up to join him, then we'd come down together.
But he doesn't insist upon it." Howe glanced meaningfully at Abigail. "I
know you are loyal, Master, but this must be in confidence." He paused.

Her father turned to her. "Abby, you must promise me now, upon your
love for me as your father, that you will never repeat any word that passes
in this room tonight, to a living soul. May I have your promise?"

"Yes, Father, I promise."

"Good." Howe gave a brief nod, and continued. "In the coming days,
the ships here will be loaded. Any spy will be able to see that. But they
won't know where we are going. We might be going upriver to Burgoyne,
or down the coast to the South, where the Loyalists may rise to help us.
Or, I could sail round into the Chesapeake Bay and up toward Philadelphia."

"Where Congress is."

"Precisely. If we took their great base from them, cut Washington off from the South, and trapped him between New York and Philadelphia, then I think his position would be desperate. There would still be a large garrison here in New York. When Burgoyne arrives, it'll be even stronger. Then Washington would have to fight in the open between two proper armies. With luck it wouldn't come to that, and he'd have the sense to give up." He stared at John Master. "My own staff are divided. You know the terrain—do you think it could be done?"

"Yes," Master said slowly, "I think it could."

They talked of other things after that, but Abigail could see that her father was deeply thoughtful. As they parted from Howe that night, Master turned to him. He sighed. "I think your plan would work, General," he said sadly, "but tell me this: how would I get a pardon for my poor son?"

Howe shook his hand understandingly, but gave him no answer.

⁘

Now, on this sunny day in July, the activity at the docks told Abigail that the process of loading the ships had already begun. This might be the last cricket match Grey Albion and his friends took part in for a long time.

Like the other players, he was dressed in a white cotton shirt and breeches. He was wearing a peaked hat to protect his eyes from the sun. He was certainly graceful and athletic, as he raised the bat to strike.

The ball soared over their heads. He'd scored the winning run. Weston jumped up and clapped wildly. There was applause from all around Bowling Green, as the players were walking off. He was coming toward them, pulling off his cap, and as he came close, she realized that, beneath his curly hair, little beads of sweat were dripping from his brow.

"Well played, Grey," said her father.

"Thank you, sir," he answered, then smiled down at her. "Did you enjoy the game, Miss Abigail?" he asked. And as he did so, a tiny drop of sweat fell from his brow upon her wrist.

"Oh yes," she said. "I liked it well enough."

⁘

James Master sat on his horse with a spyglass to his eye. From where he was on the New Jersey shore, he had a perfect view across the huge waters of the harbor. And if he did not see the cricket ball that had just soared into the air behind the fort, he could see something a lot more interesting. A ship at dock, being loaded with supplies. He had already been there three hours, and this was the second loading he had seen. Behind him, a dozen troopers waited for their captain patiently.

Captain James Master had changed in the last year. His outlook and beliefs were the same, but he was a battle-hardened and experienced officer now. Something more, perhaps. If his unhappy marriage in London had given him his share of private bitterness, the last year had taught him much about the limits of human trust in general. And he had learned that not in the heat of battle, but by studying the cold endurance of the man he had come to revere.

Last December, after his untrained troops had been chased out of New Jersey by the redcoats, George Washington could have been forgiven if he'd despaired. Two of his fellow generals—Lee, to whom he had entrusted the fortification of New York, and Gates, up the Hudson Valley, both of them British army officers who reckoned they knew more than he did—had lobbied hard to replace him. Even the untrained troops he had, having enlisted only for the calendar year, were likely to leave by the month's end. Others weren't even waiting, but deserting. Apart from a brief skirmish or two, his army had been humiliated, captured or chased away in every place. As the campaign season ended, what was left of his army were camped beyond the Delaware River, which was stoutly guarded on the other side by tough Hessian soldiers. Not appreciating Howe's views on the aristocratic season for war, Washington feared that if the Delaware froze solid, the British commander might sweep south to cross it with his whole army.

"Whatever Howe does," he told James, "we have to give some account of ourselves before our men depart." Something had to be done to lift Patriot morale.

At least the Patriots had a talent for mounting raids. James had gone on several. They harassed the enemy, but they also provided information. There were plenty of American Loyalists in the area, aiding the Hessians. Without his having to do anything, the sight of James's tall figure holding a pistol was enough to frighten most of these into talking, and one cowering farmer told him: "The Hessians have moved into Trenton now. About fourteen hundred of them. It's quite open, no ramparts. Your own deserters have told them you mean to strike at them, but their commander refuses to build ramparts because he despises you."

They hadn't many troops—some five thousand men left, a third of them unfit for duty. But early in December two thousand of Lee's men turned up, thank God, followed by five hundred from Gates, and a thousand more from Philadelphia. Still a modest force, but enough. Yet hardly well equipped. There was ammunition—every man had at least sixty rounds, and enough powder—but their uniforms were in a pitiful state. And many of the troops no longer had boots, and were marching through snow and ice with their feet wrapped only in cloth.

Notwithstanding these difficulties, the plan Washington hatched was daring. They would strike across the river—in midwinter and at night—and take the Hessians by surprise.

"We'll make three crossings," he explained to James. "One as a diversion, a second to bring reinforcements. But the main body of nearly two and a half thousand men will cross with me, then sweep down on Trenton and hit them before dawn. We'll outnumber the Hessians, so I think we have a chance. With luck, all three forces can then unite and strike against Princeton too."

What a night it had been. They'd assembled on the afternoon of Christmas Day. At dusk, the transports had been brought from their hiding places to the riverbank: large, open ferries for the cannon and horses, high-sided Durham boats for the men. To recognize each other in the darkness, there was a password: "Victory or Death." The river was narrow, though there were ice floes everywhere. As the darkness deepened, the wind whipped up choppy waves. Then sleet began to fall, then hail.

Washington took the first boat across to secure the landing. James was at his side. Rather than attempt to sit down in the boat, which was filling with rainwater, they all stood. With the darkness and the storm, James could hardly see his hand in front of his face. All he could hear was the rattle of hailstones and the bumping of ice on the high sides of the Durham.

"Terrible conditions, Master," Washington muttered.

"There's one good thing, sir," James said. "The Hessians will never believe we'd cross in such weather."

Clambering, sodden, onto the far bank at last, they sent the boat back, and waited for the next batch of men to come over. Though it could not have taken so very long, it felt to James as if their crossing had lasted an eternity. And indeed, although Washington had planned to have his entire force, horses and cannon all across by midnight, it was three in the morning before his daring crossing of the Delaware was completed and the two thousand four hundred men were finally able to form into two columns for their march, through the remainder of the night, down to the little open town of Trenton.

As they began their march, James could not help reflecting grimly: if he lived through this adventure, and his grandchildren ever asked him what it was like to cross the Delaware with Washington, he'd have in all honesty to answer: "We couldn't see a thing."

The sleet had turned to snow. Riding beside the column, James realized that the bleeding feet of the men without boots were leaving dark little trails of blood in the snow. But on they pressed, with Washington going up and down the line, murmuring words of encouragement in the darkness. It was dawn as they approached the outposts of the encampment at Trenton.

Memories of battles are often confused. But certain things about that morning's engagement remained very clearly in James's mind: Washington leading the attack in person on the outposts; the well-trained Hessians, caught by surprise, falling back in good order, firing as they went. The sight of Trenton in the gray early morning—two wide streets, a scattered collection of timber houses, looking so strangely peaceful, despite the sudden commotion.

In the excitement of the moment, he hardly noticed the danger as the bullets zipped past him, but he did notice with pride that the Patriots were fighting well. With surprising speed, they had field cannon set up at the head of the main streets, raking the Hessians with grapeshot. A detachment had swiftly cut off the enemy's retreat on the Princeton road. After a spirited engagement, the main body of Hessians had been trapped in an orchard, and nine hundred men surrendered.

By mid-morning, it was all over. Learning that his other two commanders had failed to bring their forces across the River Delaware the night before, Washington had wisely gone back to safety across the river by noon the same day.

But they had defeated the Hessians. They'd taken hundreds of prisoners. In no time, news of Washington's success had spread all over the Thirteen Colonies, delighting the Congress, and putting heart into every Patriot.

✢

The following months had been hard, but bearable. James had grown steadily closer to General Washington, and he had come to appreciate not only the external difficulties his leader faced—with supplies, deserters, spies and the problems of yearly enlistment—but also that, behind his aloof manner, his commander was secretly troubled by doubt and melancholia. And the fact that the general had to overcome these inner conflicts, also, made James admire him all the more.

In March, Mrs. Washington had come from Virginia to join her husband in camp, and this led to a lightening of everyone's spirits. For if the general was inclined to seem cold and distant, Martha Washington was warm and comfortable. She would invite even the most junior officers to eat with them, as if they were all part of a large, extended family. She might, in her own right, be one of the richest women in Virginia, but she'd tend the sick and wounded men by the hour. Come the spring of 1777, James was so devoted to his commander that Washington might have been his second father. And the general clearly liked and trusted him in turn.

There was one thing about their relationship that amused James Master—as a young Yankee officer had complained to him that Easter.

"You have an unfair advantage over me, Master, with the general."

"What's that?"

"He likes you because he thinks you're a gentleman. And he doesn't really like me, because he reckons I'm not."

"He thinks very highly of you," James assured him.

"Oh, he treats me well. He's the fairest man I have ever met, and I'd follow him to the gates of Hell. But it's the same with all us Yankees from the north-east—he doesn't like our manners."

In fact, James had noticed the same thing himself. As well as being born a Southern gentleman, Washington's marriage to Martha had brought him into the highest social circles in Virginia, whose style of life was closer to that of the English landed gentry than to a Yankee merchant from Massachusetts or Connecticut.

"I always use my best London manners in his presence," James confessed with a laugh. "But it wouldn't count for a thing if I failed in my duties."

More subtly, however, James suspected the great man considered that his years in London made him useful. Washington would often ask him about how he thought the English might react to one situation or another. He was also impressed that James had known Ben Franklin, and asked many questions about how he had conducted himself in London. When news came that Congress had sent Franklin to Paris to get French support, the general had remarked to James frankly: "What we do here is of great importance, but in the long run, the outcome of this war may be decided in Paris. I am glad you give me such a good account of Franklin's abilities as a diplomatist."

If Washington liked what he considered the gentlemanly manners of the Old World, there was one aspect of British behavior, however, that gave him great concern. This was the terrible treatment given to American prisoners. James disapproved no less, but understood it better.

"The British don't consider us soldiers, even now. They see us as rebels, and to call us anything better would be to admit the legitimacy of our cause. So as far as they're concerned, our Patriots captured at Brooklyn are not prisoners of war at all. They are traitors, sir, and lucky not to be hung."

This Washington could never accept.

"I have reports of prisoners being treated worse than animals," he exploded. And he gave particular instructions that any rough punishment his men might have been tempted to use toward the captured Hessians must be disallowed. He'd been writing personally in protest to the British generals ever since he took command. But there was no sign that the British took the slightest notice. "Have they no humanity?" he once cried to James.

"To us, sir, humanity trumps legality," James answered. "In England, it's the other way round."

But though he knew that nothing would temper Washington's honest outrage, James could not help reflecting that these continuing stories of British cruelty to American prisoners were having an effect all over the colonies that the British surely did not intend. A farmer bringing a cartload of fresh vegetables into the camp one day had said it all.

"My son was taken prisoner. Why would I want to be ruled by people who treat him like an animal?"

Meanwhile, despite the winter success against the Hessians, the Patriots' position was still perilous. When Howe had recently tempted Washington to open battle in June, Washington had avoided the trap, but one large engagement could still destroy the Patriot army at any time. Above

all, Washington needed to discover what Howe's next move would be. He
was trying to employ spies. But he'd also sent James to reconnoiter around
New York, and James was determined not to fail him.

So now, after a while, he put his spyglass down and sighed. The loading
of ships told him that something was afoot, but he needed to find out
much more than that. It was time to try other measures.

⁘

Abigail was just leaving Bowling Green with young Weston the next
morning when a man came up to her. He looked like a farmer, delivering
goods to the market no doubt, so she was rather surprised that he should
quietly address her by her name.

Then she realized—it was Charlie White.

It did not take her long to leave Weston back at the house and return to
Broadway. By the time she got there, her heart was beating fast. She was
not sure what this meant, but she thought she could guess. Without a
word, Charlie took her up Broadway. At Wall Street, they turned eastward
and crossed to the East River. Then they walked northward up the wharfs
for ten minutes until they were almost at the palisade at the top of the
town. Coming to a small storehouse, she followed Charlie in. And there,
sitting on a barrel in the shadows, she saw a tall figure in a greatcoat, who
rose and came toward her.

A moment later, she fell into her brother's arms.

He was wearing his uniform under his coat. The combination of the
two, she thought, must have made him terribly hot. But it was important
he should be in uniform, he explained, for otherwise if he were caught, he
could be shot as a spy. He explained that Charlie had smuggled him into
the city in a cart full of goods, but said little else about his movements. He
was anxious to know all about Weston and his father, and most astonished when she told him that Grey Albion was in the house.

"Alas," he said, "how I wish that you could tell my dear father and little Weston that you have seen me, and that I think of them every day, but
I fear that you cannot do so."

At last, however, he came to the business at hand.

"Charlie has already listened in the marketplace. It is evident that General Howe is starting to put supplies in his ships, but the townspeople
don't seem to know where he is going."

"I shouldn't imagine many people have been told," she answered.

"You have no idea yourself?"

Abigail's heart missed a beat. She looked down. Then she gazed back into his face.

"Brother, why would the general tell a girl like me such a thing?" It sounded so reasonable. And it was not a lie.

"No." He frowned thoughtfully. "Do you think Albion knows?"

"Perhaps, James, but he is only a junior officer. He hasn't said so."

"Our father?"

She hesitated a moment. What could she say? "If Father knows, then he certainly hasn't confided the information to me." This also was, strictly speaking, true.

He nodded, and looked sad.

And as Abigail watched him, she too was overcome by feelings of great sadness. She knew that her brother loved her. She knew that he longed to see her father, and his little son, and that he could not. Yet she could not help feeling a stab of pain that he had come to see her only to question her, to get information which, if given, would make her a traitor.

At the same time, how she longed to tell him. He must be risking his life to come here. And perhaps, despite her promise to her father and to General Howe, she might have told him, if the information could have saved his life. But it wouldn't. It would only give help to Washington and his Patriots, so that they could prolong this unhappy business even fur- ther. James was doing his duty, she was doing hers. Nothing could be altered. She wanted to weep, but knew that she must not.

"I am sorry that Grey Albion is here," he said at last.

She supposed her brother meant he should not wish to have to fight his friend.

"Father likes him," she said.

"And you?"

"I admit that he is agreeable," she answered. "But there seems to me to be a fault in his character. I think he is arrogant."

Her brother nodded. "Such arrogance is to be expected in an English officer, I fear." He paused. "We were friends formerly, God knows, and his father could not have been kinder to me."

"It's the war that makes you enemies."

"Yes, but it's more than that, Abby. My feelings toward England, and what Grey represents, have changed. To tell the truth, I am not sure I'd

care to see him now." He gave her a searching look. "I should be sorry if
you liked him too well."

"Then to tell you the truth, I like him very little."

Satisfied on this account, her brother said she should not tarry long.
And a few minutes later, she was walking back through the town alone.

⁘

It was later that month that General Howe finally sailed out of the harbor
with a great fleet, and began to make his way down the coast. With him
went Grey Albion, and the other young officers in the house. Though she
and her father went to the dock with little Weston to see Albion off, Abigail did not believe she was especially sorry to see him go.

When news of the expedition finally came back, it was encouraging.
General Howe's short voyage down to the Chesapeake had been hit with
bad weather, but all the same, his plan had worked. Washington, having
been wrong-footed, had to double-back from the north. And although he
made a brave stand at Brandywine Creek, the redcoats had taken
Philadelphia. A letter came from Grey Albion to her father to say he'd be
in Philadelphia with Howe for the winter.

And at first, the news from the North seemed equally good for the Loyalist cause. As planned, Johnnie Burgoyne had struck south from Canada
and soon taken back the fort of Ticonderoga. He'd got the Indians with
him too. Four of the six Iroquois nations had agreed to join the British
side.

"The Patriots will love us for that," John Master remarked drily.

"Are the Indians so cruel?" Abigail asked.

"They have their customs. In King George's War, thirty years ago, the
British colonel of the Northern militias paid the Iroquois for every French
scalp they brought him, women and children included."

"I hope we would not do such a thing now."

"Don't count on it."

By September they expected to hear that Burgoyne had secured Albany
and was on his way down the Hudson River to New York. But then other
rumors began. The local Patriot militias with their sharpshooters were
slowing him down. He was stuck in the northern wilderness. The Indians
were leaving him. A force of redcoats was sent up the Hudson to see if
they could help him.

Then, late in October, a swift boat came down the great river bearing an astounding message. Her father brought the news to the house.

"Burgoyne's surrendered. Upriver. The Patriots have taken five thousand men."

"Where?" she asked.

"Saratoga."

The news of the British defeat at Saratoga burst upon the British like a thunderclap. Her father, however, though grave, was not surprised.

"Just as I warned Howe," he said grimly. "An overconfident general, in terrain he does not understand." The Patriots' woodsmen's tactics of felling trees in his path, driving away livestock and removing any food had left his men demoralized up in the huge wilderness. The two Patriot generals, Gates and Benedict Arnold, had, after two engagements at Saratoga, worn him down. And though Burgoyne's British and Hessian troops had fought bravely, without reinforcements from the South they'd been hugely outnumbered by the seventeen thousand men of the Patriot militias.

"Saratoga sends the signal," John Master judged. "It shows that, however many troops the British field, there will always be local militias to outnumber them. And still more important, it tells the only people who really matter, that the Americans can prevail."

"What people are those?" Abigail asked.

"The French."

✢

If Saratoga was a cause for Patriot rejoicing, James could see little sign of it in Washington's army that December. Congress had moved out of Philadelphia, Howe had moved in, and the Patriot army, now reduced to twelve thousand men, was out in the open countryside as winter descended. Washington had already chosen their quarters, however.

Valley Forge. The place had its merits. With the high grounds named Mount Joy and Mount Misery close by, and the Schuylkill River below, Valley Forge was defensible, and at under twenty miles from Philadelphia, it was a good place from which to keep an eye on British movements.

The Patriot army had started building the camp right away. Stout log cabins, more than a thousand of them in the end, stood in clusters as a sprawling city of huts emerged. At least this activity kept all the men busy, and they soon became rather proud of their efforts. But James often had to take parties of men for miles to find the timber to chop down. The key, Washington insisted, was to ensure that the roof was well sealed.

"For it's a Philadelphia winter we have to contend with," he reminded them, "not a northern one."

It wasn't long before Yankee troops discovered what he meant. For instead of a covering of northern snow, which seals in everything it falls upon, Valley Forge was suffering through a different kind of winter. Snow there was, from time to time, and freezing sleet, but it would soon melt. Then it would rain, so that the water seeped its way through every crack and crevice, before it froze again. The dry cold of the North might kill a man who had no shelter, but the cold, damp winds and clinging chills of Valley Forge seemed to seep into the marrow of men's bones.

Log cabins or not, their clothes were in tatters, many still had no boots, and everyone was half starving. The commissary did a magnificent job. There was fish from the river. Occasionally there was meat. Most days, every man was given a pound of decent bread. Most days. But sometimes there would be only firecake, as they grimly called the tasteless husks of flour and water the cooks might have to give them. And sometimes there was nothing. James had even seen men trying to make soup out of grass and leaves. Some weeks, a third of the army was unfit for any duties at all. Their horses looked like skeletons and frequently died. There was nothing left to forage, not a cow within miles. And when James was sent out to the small towns of the region to see if he could buy more provisions, the only money he had to offer were the paper notes offered by Congress, which most traders were suspicious of.

Each day, they buried more men. As time passed, the deaths mounted into hundreds, passed a thousand, reached two thousand. Sometimes James wondered if they'd ever have made it at all without the camp followers—about five hundred of them, mostly wives or female relations of the men. They were given half-rations and half-pay, and they did their best to care for their menfolk. In February, they were joined by Martha Washington. Washington always put on a brave face to his men, but James spent enough time in his company to see that in private he was close to despair. Though he and the other junior officers did all they could to support their chief, he remarked to Mrs. Washington once: "The general's saved the army, and you've saved the general."

One other person gave Washington comfort. A young man sent from France by the indefatigable Ben Franklin. He'd arrived some months before. Though only twenty years old, he had several years of service in the Musketeers. Arriving in America, he was immediately made a major general.

Marie-Joseph Paul Yves Roch Gilbert du Motier, Marquis de Lafayette, was a rich young aristocrat, with a fine ancestral estate. His young wife, whom he left behind in France, was the daughter of a duke. An ancestor had served with Joan of Arc. And he had slipped out of France in search of one thing, and one thing only. *La Gloire*. He wanted to be famous.

Believing that this might further good relations with the French, Washington had taken him onto his staff. And then discovered to his surprise that he had acquired a second son.

Lafayette had no illusions about his own lack of experience. He'd take on anything asked of him. He also proved to be competent and intelligent. At Brandywine, he'd fought well and been wounded. But in addition to all this, his aristocratic upbringing and his sense of honor had given him the very qualities that Washington most admired. Slim and elegant, he had exquisite manners, was completely fearless—and he was loyal to his chief, which was more than could be said for most of the other Patriot commanders. When Gates and other generals schemed against Washington behind his back, the young Frenchman came to know of it, and warned Washington at once. They tried to get him out of the way by sending him up to Canada, but he soon got out of that, and rejoined Washington at Valley Forge, where his Gallic charm helped to lighten the grim realities of daily life.

James liked Lafayette. In London, since an educated gentleman was supposed to speak the language of diplomacy, he'd learned to speak a little French. Now, with plenty of time on their hands at Valley Forge, Lafayette helped James improve his mastery of the language considerably.

But Lafayette was not the only man Ben Franklin sent across. His other and still greater gift arrived in the new year. And if Lafayette had brought a touch of Gallic charm to Washington's army, the Baron von Steuben was to change it entirely.

Baron von Steuben was a middle-aged Prussian officer and aristocrat. He'd served under Frederick the Great. A lifelong bachelor, he turned up with an Italian greyhound, a letter from Franklin, and an offer to give the ragged Patriot troops the same training as the finest army in all Europe. And in his own eccentric way, he was as good as his word.

For now at Valley Forge, first in the snow and slush, then the mud, then in sight of the snowdrops and finally during the sunny days when the green buds appeared on the trees, he drilled them as they had never been drilled before. Instead of the motley collection of manuals from different militias, he produced a single, classic drill book for the whole Continental army. Next he trained a cadre of men who would act as instructors. Then, in full dress, he would stride from one training ground to another, supervising and encouraging them all with a stream of curses in German or French, which his orderlies would precisely translate—so that by the end of their training, every soldier in the Patriot army possessed a broad vocabulary of profanities in three languages.

At first they thought him mad. Soon they came to respect him. By the end of spring, they loved him. He taught them to drill, to march, to maneuver in battle, to rapid-fire. Finding that hardly a man knew how to use a bayonet, except to roast meat over the fire, he taught them the bayonet charge and told them: "I will teach you how to win a battle without any ammunition at all."

By the time he was finished, they were good, by any standards. Very good.

"We needed a German to teach us how to fight the Hessians," Washington remarked wryly to James one day in spring.

"The British can employ Germans, sir," James answered with a smile, "but we're the real thing."

"I'm getting word," Washington told him, "that we may soon expect fresh recruits who'll sign on for three years."

But the news that really ended the agony of Valley Forge came soon after this conversation.

Ben Franklin had done it. The French had declared war on Britain. At Valley Forge, on Washington's instructions, Baron von Steuben organized a huge parade.

⁂

Grey Albion's invitation to Abigail came on the first day of May, in a letter to her father from Philadelphia.

"He confirms the rumor I've been hearing. General Howe's been recalled." Master shook his head. "It's a shameful business. When London heard about the Saratoga surrender, Parliament was so furious that the ministry employed newspaper writers to blame it all on Howe. So now he's recalled. It seems that Howe's young officers in Philadelphia are determined to honor him before he goes. There's to be a ball, and I don't know what else. Even a joust. Albion's one of the knights. He wonders if you'd like to go."

The invitation was so unexpected that she hardly knew what to say. With all the pretty girls in Philadelphia to choose from, she was surprised that he should have thought of her, but she had to acknowledge that it was kind of him. And indeed, when she thought of the festivities, and the joust, and the chance to be in gracious Philadelphia, she decided that perhaps there would be no harm in going.

But by the next day, her father had had second thoughts.

"It's a long way, Abby, and you never know who may be out there on the road. I can't easily go myself. Who'd go with you? If you encountered Patriot soldiers, I don't think they'd do you any harm, but I can't be sure. No," he concluded, "it's kind of young Grey to think of you, but it won't do."

"I expect you're right, Papa," she said. If Mr. Grey Albion wants to ask me to a ball, she thought to herself, he'll just have to do it again, some other time.

⊹

If the catastrophe at Saratoga the previous October, and the entry of the French against them this spring, caused despondency among the British, for loyal John Master, the world began to change during that long summer of 1778. It was a subtle change. He did not even see it coming. It took place in his mind and heart.

The war seemed to have entered a period of stagnation. Down in Philadelphia, after the departure of poor Howe, General Clinton had taken over, and now that there was danger of invasion from a French fleet, the British decided to pull out and return to New York. It wasn't only the troops. Several thousand Loyalists had to ship out too. "Poor devils," Master remarked to Abigail. "The British ask for Loyalist support, but then they can't protect them."

As the main British force returned by land, Washington shadowed them. News came that there had been an engagement at Monmouth—a Patriot force under Lee and Lafayette had attacked the British rearguard under Cornwallis, with considerable success, and might have done more damage if Lee had not pulled back. But the British had eventually returned safely to New York, and young Albion with them.

So once again, Congress was back in Philadelphia, and New York, under General Clinton now, remained a British base, but with huge territories, from White Plains above the city, to the tracts of New Jersey across the Hudson, dominated by the Patriots. In July, Washington moved up the Hudson Valley to the great lookout fortress of West Point, fifty miles upriver. An affectionate letter came from James, delivered through Susan in Dutchess County, to let the family know that he was safe at West Point, and to ask his father to attend to some small matters for him. But he gave them no other news.

Soon after that, as if to confirm how the military situation had changed, Admiral d'Estaing arrived with a powerful French fleet at the entrance to the harbor. For a while he stayed there, blocking off the ocean. Then British naval reinforcements arrived and he moved, for the time being, to safe anchorage up the coast at Newport, Rhode Island. But the message was clear. The French were in the war, and the British no longer controlled the sea either.

Two other vexations depressed John Master. In August, another fire broke out in the city and destroyed a pair of houses he was renting out. More worrying was a threat to his land in Dutchess County.

It was a curiosity of New York that year: the city was now ruled by the British General Clinton, while the great New York hinterland, under Patriot control, had a Patriot governor of the same name—though certainly no relation. And Patriot Governor Clinton was eager to confiscate the lands of any and all known Loyalists in his territory. "Since we manage it, we've given out that we own the land," Susan told him. But it seemed to Master that it would only be a matter of time before the Patriot governor took his land away.

⁙

At the end of August, an unexpected visitor came to the house: Captain Rivers. But the news he brought was bleak. He was giving up.

"South Carolina has been in Patriot hands for two years now, but in North Carolina, many Loyalists like myself have held on. Since spring, however, life's become impossible. My wife and children have already left for England. And there's nothing I can do except surrender my plantation into your hands, in the hope that you can recover your debt one day."

"The slaves?"

"The main value lies there, of course. I've transferred them to the estate

of a friend, who's in a safer area. But how long he'll be able to stay I don't
know." He gave Master a detailed inventory of the slaves. "Many are
skilled, and therefore valuable. If you can find a buyer for them, they're
yours to sell."

"You can't hold out a little longer?" Master asked. "Relief may be at
hand."

For with Philadelphia abandoned, the latest British talk was of a big
strike against the South. General Clinton had already announced he was
sending an expedition to seize one of the French Caribbean islands, and
another to Georgia, where the Patriot garrisons were small, and the Loyalists many. But Rivers shook his head.

"Diversions, Master. We can split our forces as many ways as we like,
and run around in the huge wilderness of America, but in my opinion,
we'll never tame it. Not now."

At dinner that evening the conversation was frank. They were all old
friends—John Master and Abigail, Rivers and Grey Albion. At one point,
Rivers turned to Master and asked: "I once asked if you'd think of retiring
to England. You weren't interested then, I think. But might you consider
it now?"

"My father will gladly serve you, sir," Albion chipped in, "if you care to
send funds to England for safe keeping. He already holds balances of
yours."

"Let's not think of that yet," Master replied. But it was significant to
him that both Rivers and young Albion should be suggesting such an
abandonment. It was discouraging.

Yet his real agony of mind came not from causes military or financial.
It was moral.

In the spring, the British government, alarmed by the entry of France
into the war, had sent commissioners to New York to try once more to
reach a settlement with the colonists. Master had met them before they
went down to try their luck with the Congress. The best of them, in his
opinion, was a man called Eden. Yet having enjoyed a lengthy talk with
him, Master had returned home shaking his head.

"It seems," he told Abigail, "that their instructions from King George
are to bribe the members of the Congress. I had to tell him, 'They aren't
the British Parliament, you know.'"

Only a day or two afterward did he reflect with some irony that, without even considering the matter, he had rightly assumed that the Con-

gress he opposed would have higher moral standards than the government he loyally supported.

But the discovery that shook him came at the end of August.

James's letter from West Point had asked him to perform one service which his father had put off for some weeks now—only because he feared it might be time-consuming. At the end of August, feeling a little guilty, he decided he really must attend to it.

One of James's men had a brother who had been captured by the British. The family having received no word of him for more than a year, but believing he was in prison in New York, James asked if his father could discover what had become of the fellow. His name was Sam Flower.

It took Master a whole day to find out that the unit to which Flower belonged had first been kept in a church building in the city, but then they had been sent across the East River. No other information was available.

The next day was hot and sultry, so Master was quite glad to escape the unpleasantness of the city streets and take the ferry across the water to Brooklyn. The ferry dock lay across the water from the northern part of the town. From this point, the river made a turn eastward. On the Manhattan side, the buildings along the waterfront petered out. On the Brooklyn side, one came around the river's corner to a great sweep of salt meadows, cordgrass, open water and mudflats whose Dutch name had long ago been transmogrified to Wallabout Bay. And there in Wallabout Bay lay the prisons Master was looking for.

The hulks. Disused ships. Animal transports mostly. Huge, blackened, decrepit, dismasted, anchored with great chain cables in the muddy shallows, the hulks lay not a mile and a half from the city yet, thanks to the river bend, out of sight. There was the *Jersey*, a hospital ship, so-called. And the *Whitby*, an empty carcass since it had burned last year, its charred and broken ribs pointing sadly to the sky. But there were several others, and they were all crammed with prisoners.

It was easy enough to hire a waterman to take him out to the ships. At the first vessel the fellow in charge, a burly, heavy-jowled man, was reluctant to allow him on board, but a gold coin changed his mind, and soon Master was standing with him on the deck.

With the bright morning sun, and the line of Manhattan Island less than a mile away across the water, the outlook from the deck might have been pleasant. But despite the gold coin, the attitude of the custodian was so suspicious and surly that, as soon as he set foot on deck, Master felt as if a grim cloud had suddenly settled over the day. When Master asked for Sam Flower by name, the fellow shrugged contemptuously.

"I've two hundred rebel dogs below," he answered. "That's all I know." When Master asked if he might go below to make inquiries, the fellow looked at him as if he were insane. He took him to a hatch, though, and opened it. "You want to go down there?" he said. "Go." But as Master moved forward he was assailed by such a stench of urine, filth and rottenness that he staggered back.

At this moment, from another hatch, an ill-kempt soldier with a musket appeared, followed by two figures. As soon as these two were on deck, the soldier banged the hatch closed behind them.

"We let 'em up two at a time," their custodian remarked. "Never more than two."

But Master hardly heard. He was staring at the men. They were not just thin, they were walking skeletons. Both were deathly pale; but one of them, with sunken eyes, looked feverish and seemed about to fall at any moment.

"These men are starving," said Master.

"Course they're starving," said the custodian. And with the first trace of a change of expression since their conversation began, he actually smiled. "That's because I don't feed 'em."

"I think that man is sick," Master said.

"Sick? I hope he's dying."

"You wish this man to die?"

"Makes room for the next one."

"But are you not given money to feed these men?" Master demanded.

"I am given money. They live or die as they please. Mostly die."

"How can you deal in such a manner, sir, with prisoners under your charge?"

"These?" A look of disgust formed on the man's face. "Vermin, I call them. Traitors that should've been hung." The fellow nodded toward the city. "You think it's any better over there?"

"I wonder, sir, what your superiors would say about this," Master said threateningly.

"My superiors?" The man put his face very close to Master's, so that the merchant could smell his stinking breath. "My superiors, sir, would say: 'Well done, thou good and faithful servant.' Why don't you go and ask them, sir, if you really want to know?" And with that he told Master to get off his ship.

At the next hulk, a young officer poked his head over the side and informed Master, politely enough, that he could not come aboard because half the prisoners had yellow fever.

At the third, however, he had more luck. The hulk itself appeared to be rotting away, but the tall, thin, hard-faced man who allowed him up was dressed as an officer, and responded to his inquiries precisely. Yes, he had a record of every prisoner who had been on the ship. Sam Flower had been one of them.

"He died, sir, six months ago."

When asked where Flower was buried, the officer waved in the direction of the salt meadows. The bodies were tipped into trenches there and all around, he explained. There were so many of them, and besides, they were only criminals.

Master said nothing. At least he had his information. Before leaving the vessel, however, he noticed signs that there had recently been a fire in the fo'c'sle. It clearly hadn't spread far, and he couldn't imagine the stern officer at his side letting such a thing get out of hand, but he thought to ask: "However would you get the prisoners off, if a fire were to take hold?"

"I shouldn't, sir."

"You'd let them get to the water, though, surely?"

"No, sir. I'd batten down the hatches and let them burn. Those are my orders."

John Master returned to the city in a somber mood. In the first place, he was shocked that Englishmen, his fellow countrymen, could behave in such a way. The Patriots might or might not be legal prisoners of war, there was an honest legal quarrel over that—but whatever their status, what did it say of the humanity of his own government that they could treat these men in such a way? You may call a man a rebel, he thought, you may call him a criminal, you may say he should be hung—especially when he is a stranger and not your own son. But faced with farmers, small traders, honest laborers, decent men as the Patriots so clearly were, what kind of blindness, what prejudice or, God save us, what cruelty could induce the British authorities to lock them up in hulks and murder them like that?

Of course, he told himself, he had not known such things were going on. The hulks were out of sight. True, Susan on her visits had told him of

Patriot newspapers that railed against the prisoners' treatment. But these were gross exaggerations, he had assured her, stoutly denied by such men as his good friend General Howe.

Yet had he ever gone into the city prisons, only a few hundred yards from his door? No, he had not. And as he considered this circumstance another, and most unpleasant, phrase began to echo in his mind: the words of the loathsome fellow on the first hulk. "You think it's any better over there?"

During the next week, he began to make his own discreet inquiries. He said nothing to Albion—it might put him in a difficult position—but there were plenty of people in the town from whom he could get information. A friendly chat with a prison guard; a conspiratorial word or two with an officer. Quietly and patiently, using all the skills at drawing people out that he'd mastered in the taverns of the town so long ago, he gradually found out all he wanted.

The guard from the hulk was right: the city prisons were practically the same. Behind the walls of converted churches and sugar houses, the prisoners had been dying like flies, their bodies loaded on carts and, often as not, taken away in the darkness. Loring, whose wife had been old General Howe's companion, had stolen their possessions and the money for their food. And for all his denials, there could be no question: genial General Howe, with whom he had so often dined, had known about it all.

He felt sadness, shame, disgust. Yet what could he do? Others might raise the issue, but if *he* did, what would people say? Master has a Patriot son—his loyalty would be in question. There was nothing he could do. For the sake of Abigail and little Weston, he must keep silent.

It was no small agony to him therefore when, early in September, his grandson came to ask for guidance. To give him company, they had sent Weston to a small school nearby, where he was taught with other Loyalist children. Foreseeing that the subject of his father James must sooner or later arise, Master had told the little boy most carefully what to say. And now it had come up.

"So what did you say?" his grandfather asked.

"That my father was persuaded by the Patriots that they were still loyal to the king, and that we hope he will now return."

"Good." It was a mediocre argument, but the best Master could come up with.

"They say he is a traitor."

"No. Your father has an honest disagreement, but he is not a traitor."

"But the Loyalists are right, aren't they?"

"They believe so. But the quarrel is complex."

"But one side must be right and the other wrong," said Weston, looking confused.

Master sighed. What could one say to a little boy?

"I am a Loyalist, Grandfather, aren't I?" Weston pursued. "You told me so."

"Yes." Master smiled. "You are very loyal."

"And you are a Loyalist, Grandfather, aren't you?" asked Weston, wanting confirmation.

"Of course," Master replied. "I am a Loyalist."

Only he could not say the truth. That he was a Loyalist who'd lost his heart.

✦

But he was still a businessman. General Clinton liked him. And so, that September, when Master suggested it might be time to fit out another privateer, Clinton was delighted. "Take from the French and the Patriots as much as you like," the general encouraged him, "and I shall be vastly obliged to you."

The preparations for the voyage were advancing well when a small incident occurred which took him by surprise. He was working quietly in his little library one morning when Hudson entered and requested a private interview.

"I was wanting, Boss," he began, "to speak about Solomon. He's been twenty-five a while now."

Of course. Master felt a pang of guilt. He had always promised that Solomon should be free when he was twenty-five, and the distraction of the war was no excuse for his omitting to deliver on his promise.

"He shall be free today," he told Hudson at once. But to his amazement, Hudson shook his head.

"I was hoping, Boss," he said, "that you'd keep him a slave for a while."

"Oh?" Master looked at him with some bewilderment.

"The fact is," Hudson confessed, "he's been keeping some bad company."

There was no need, Hudson considered, to tell Master about the arguments he and Solomon had been having. And certainly no need to allude to his suspicions as to what his son might have got up to with Sam and Charlie White. Solomon was just an impatient young fellow in search of adventure. His father understood that well enough. But he also understood something else equally clearly.

If you were a black man, there was nobody you could trust. Yes, the British offered slaves their freedom, but they only did it to weaken the Patriot slave owners of the South. If the British won this war, he doubted they'd be helping the black man any more. As for the Patriots, if they could beat the British, they'd be wanting to get as many slaves back as they could.

Nothing was certain, but it seemed to Hudson that the nearest thing to security that his family had, whether slave or free, was the protection of John Master. So the last threat Solomon had uttered had filled his father with horror.

"I'm due my freedom now," he'd said, "and when I get it, maybe I'll be going off to join Captain Master." And if he didn't get his freedom, Hudson had inquired sarcastically, what then? "Then maybe I'll run away to join the British Army and get it that way." Whichever of these harebrained solutions his son attempted, Hudson could see nothing but trouble.

"Solomon don't mean any harm, Boss," he told Master, "but you might say he's restless, and I'm afraid of him getting into all kinds of trouble if he's free. Fact is," he admitted mournfully, "I don't know what to do with him."

"In that case," Master suggested with a smile, "I may have a solution. Let him serve on board the new privateer. That should give him some adventure and keep him out of trouble. Any prizes they take, as crew he may have his share. And the day this present conflict is over, he shall be free. Will that do?"

"Why, yes, Boss," Hudson said, "I reckon it would."

Soon afterward, when Solomon sailed away in the handsome ship, the merchant turned to Hudson and remarked with a grin: "I've every confidence that he'll make an excellent New York pirate!"

✛

In the month of October, John Master received another letter from Vanessa in London. He read it several times to satisfy himself that he had understood what it really meant.

Whatever her words, Master considered, it was very clear from her actions that James's wife had little interest in either her husband or her son. To him such a thing might be inexplicable, but the evidence was plain to see. "If Vanessa loved her little boy," he'd remarked to Abigail, "she'd have turned up here by now."

Her latest letter contained the usual pious hopes for little Weston's welfare, a pained inquiry as to whether her husband had yet had the decency to abandon the rebel cause, and asked him whether he was planning to stay in New York or, as her cousin Captain Rivers had told her he might, depart for civilization with his family and her little son. In short, was little Weston about to return to London? And as he perused her letter, and read between the lines, Master reckoned he saw what was on her mind.

She needed to know if she would have to look after her little son, or whether she might remain undisturbed. And the most likely reason for her wanting to know, Master surmised, must be that she had taken up with another man. If she has a lover in her house, he thought, the little boy would be a decided inconvenience. Almost as bad as a husband.

With some care, therefore, he composed a letter back in terms of equal insincerity. He knew, he said, how she must long to see her son, but at present, with Patriot pirates out on the high seas, he felt it was better to keep the boy here in New York.

He wondered whether to convey the contents of the letter to James, but decided there was no point. He did not even pass on Vanessa's expressions of affection to little Weston. The boy seldom spoke of his mother now, and perhaps it was better that way.

✦

For Abigail, the months that followed were quiet enough. She had plenty to do with running the house. She would take charge of Weston when he was not attending school, and every few weeks she would write out a detailed report of Weston's activities, together with a little family news, and convey it through Susan to James. And though these letters took some time to reach West Point, she knew that he received them gratefully.

Grey Albion and his fellow officers were back in the house. For a short time, it had seemed that Grey would be sent down to Georgia, but General Clinton had changed his mind and kept him in New York. But he was so busy that she saw less of him now. As winter approached, Clinton had put him in charge of ensuring that all the troops were kept warm.

"I'm afraid," Albion remarked one December day, "that we're going to have to cut down some fine stands of trees on the estates north of the city. I hate to do it, but there's no choice." Often he was away for days. Abigail didn't take particular notice of his comings and goings, but she had to admit that when he went off in his greatcoat, wearing a fur hat and carrying an axe, he looked quite handsome.

When he was in the house, he'd play with little Weston just as before, and accompany her on walks with the boy, and make himself agreeable. But she noticed a certain change in his manner. The easy arrogance that· had sometimes irritated her before seemed to be muted now. The brief skirmish with the Patriots on the way back from Philadelphia in the spring had given him more respect for them. "They acquit themselves like proper troops now," he admitted. "We shall get some hard knocks at the next engagement."

She noted also that his tone toward herself had changed. If he had treated her as a little sister before, he would talk to her now of more serious things—the progress of the war, the chances for peace, and the future of the colonies. Not only that, he would ask her what she thought, and seemed to give her opinion quite equal weight with his own.

"I wish I could show you London, Miss Abigail," he once remarked.

To make conversation, she asked him what he liked best about London. She knew about the great sights from her father, but he spoke of more intimate things, of handsome old parks by the river, of ancient churches where Crusaders had prayed, or narrow city streets with timbered houses and haunting echoes. And when he did so, his handsome face took on a tender look.

On another day, he spoke about his family. "You'd like them, Miss Abigail, I think. My father is very courtly. I'm a clumsy fellow compared to him." And once, he spoke of his old nanny. "She lives in our house still, though she is nearly eighty now. I like to sit with her and keep her company, when I can." Abigail was glad to think of him showing such solicitude.

As the spring of 1779 began, encouraging news came from the South. Down in Georgia, Savannah had fallen to the British redcoats, then Augusta. Soon the whole of Georgia was back under British rule. In New York, there was talk of an expedition up the River Hudson. Albion mentioned these plans to her in passing, but her father told her: "He's pleaded with Clinton to let him go. He wants to see some action." And some time later he said, "Albion's got his wish."

It was not until the end of May that the little flotilla of boats were ready to set off. Abigail stood with her father on the wharf to watch. The men, in their scarlet tunics and white crossbands, looked very smart. Grey Albion was going briskly about his business, and Abigail realized that she had never seen him like this before—hard, stern-eyed, giving crisp orders to the men. And far too busy, naturally, to take any notice of her.

As the boats went out into midstream and started up the great river, she turned to her father.

"James is up there, Papa. What if he and Grey . . ."

"I know, Abby," he answered quietly. "Let's not think about it."

--:--

Some time passed before they heard news. The redcoats were doing well; Washington was holding West Point, but they'd taken two of his smaller forts. Word also came that there had been casualties.

Grey Albion was brought back a day later. Abigail was told to take Weston to a friend's house while the surgeon performed his work.

"Nothing to worry about," her father said firmly. "A musket ball in the leg. The surgeon'll have it out in no time." But when they returned later that day, John was looking solemn. "All's well. He's sleeping," he told Weston. But to Abigail he confessed, "He's lost a lot of blood."

When she saw him in the morning, his eyes were half closed, but he recognized her, and smiled weakly. The next day she went in to him several times. In the evening, she noticed that he was shivering. By late that night, he was running a high fever.

The wound was infected. The doctor, who knew them well, was brisk. "I suggest you nurse him, Miss Abigail," he told her after he had cleaned the wound. "You'll do quite as well as any nurse I can provide. Let's pray the infection doesn't spread," he added, "and I don't have to take his leg. You must do the best you can to cool the fever. That's the greatest enemy."

In the days that followed, Albion's condition varied. Sometimes he was feverish and delirious, and she could only do her best to cool his brow and his body with damp towels. At other times he was lucid, but he worried.

"Will they take my leg off?" he'd ask.

"No," she lied to him, "there's no fear of that."

And thank God, the infection did not spread—though ten days passed before he began to mend, and more than a month until he began to hobble about on a crutch, and look like himself again.

It was the day before he first began to walk that a tiny incident occurred. If, that is, it occurred at all. She had been sitting in a wing chair in his room while he slept. The afternoon sun was coming in pleasantly through the open window. The room was quiet. And she must have fallen asleep herself. For in her sleep, she dreamed that they were walking together down by the waterside, when suddenly he had turned to her, and remarked in a soft voice, but with great feeling: "You are still so young. Yet where would I ever find another, such as you?"

Then she had awoken, to find him awake and gazing at her thoughtfully. And she had wondered whether he might actually have spoken the words, or whether she had only imagined them in her sleep.

⁘

A curious feature of Master's business at this period concerned the visits of Susan from Dutchess County. Every so often she would appear with two or three carts of produce. Master would arrange for their sale, and the British were only too delighted to buy whatever she had to offer. This business had become even more profitable than usual in recent months, for until then, the Iroquois in the North had been shipping boatloads of corn downriver to the city. But now the Patriots had intercepted this traffic. The last time Susan had brought down two wagonloads of corn, Master had been able to sell it for five times the price he'd have gotten before the war.

As far as the ethics of these transactions, when Abigail had once asked her sister which side she was on, Susan's reply had been simple.

"The same side as my neighbors, Abby," she'd said. "And plenty of others. The Patriots control Dutchess County, so I'm a Patriot. But if the British will buy my corn, for good money, I'll sure as hell sell it to them. As for the silks, and the tea and the wine I'll be taking back from New York, there's plenty of Patriots where I live that'll be glad to buy them, and they won't be asking where they came from."

"How would Washington feel about your selling us corn?" Abigail asked.

"He'd be mad as hell. But he won't know."

"And James?"

"The same, I guess, but he won't know either."

As far as the British authorities were concerned, the return traffic was illegal. Loyalist merchants in New York were not supposed to supply the rebels with anything, but nobody took much notice. British merchants were cheerfully supplying the upstate Patriots with any luxuries they could pay for. It was illegal if one were caught, so few people were. Susan simply paid the guards at the checkpoint when she left the city.

But here Master had shown his own old-fashioned sense of loyalty. For although he knew perfectly well what Susan was doing, he had always refused to take part in supplying the Patriots himself. So Abigail was greatly surprised by a conversation that took place in her father's library one day in September.

Grey Albion was out. The day before, as thanks for all that she had done in nursing him, he had given Abigail two beautiful presents. One was a silk shawl, carefully chosen to go with one of her favorite dresses; the other a handsomely bound edition of *Gulliver's Travels*, which she had once told him she enjoyed. And she had been pleased and touched by the evident trouble to which he'd gone. That morning he had left the house to see General Clinton at the fort, and was not expected back until later. Weston was at school, so Abigail and her father had been alone when Susan arrived at the house.

She had come into the town with three carts that day. Her father agreed to come with her at once to arrange the sale of the goods. But then, to Abigail's amazement, he remarked: "I've a quantity of silk, and some excellent wines and brandy in the warehouse. Do you think you could dispose of them for me on your return?"

"Of course," Susan laughed. But Abigail was shocked.

"Father! You're surely not going to supply the Patriots?"

Her father shrugged. "No point in leaving goods in the warehouse."

"But what if General Clinton found out?"

"Let's hope he doesn't." And something in Master's tone of voice told her that, for whatever reason, some change must have taken place in her father's soul.

She had just left her father and Susan in the library and stepped into the hall, when she saw Grey Albion. She had not heard him return. He was standing still, looking thoughtful. Afraid he could have heard what had just been said, she blushed, then, murmuring some excuse, went back into the library to warn her father that he was there. When she came into the hall again, Albion was gone.

During the rest of that day, she wondered what Albion would do if he had heard them. Would he feel obliged to inform General Clinton? Would he pretend he knew nothing? There was nothing she could do but wait and see.

So she was quite nervous in the evening when she heard him ask her father for a private audience alone. The two men went into the library, closed the door and remained there, speaking in low voices, for some time. When Albion came out, he looked serious, but said nothing. When she asked her father if Grey had raised the matter of the illegal shipments he only replied: "Don't ask."

And as no complaints seemed to be raised against her father in the days that followed, she assumed that the issue had been resolved.

⁙

Soon afterward, Albion resumed his duties. General Clinton used him on his staff now, and he was busier than ever. Perhaps it was just that he was preoccupied, but it seemed to Abigail that Albion, having thanked her for her care so gracefully, was putting a tiny distance between them now. And although she knew it was unfair, she could not help a feeling of irritation.

The mood in the house was somewhat somber too. News came that the Patriot governor had taken away Master's farms. Anticipated though this was, it was a blow to them all.

The news from across the ocean was worse.

"It seems," Albion told them, "that all Europe is taking the chance to strike at Britain's empire now. France has persuaded Spain to join them. The French and Spanish fleets are in the English Channel, and it's fully expected they'll attack Gibraltar. The Spanish will surely move against us in Florida. The Dutch are against us, too, and as for the Germans and Russians, they're standing by, happy to watch us lose." To add insult to injury, the American privateer, John Paul Jones, using ships supplied by France, had the cheek to raid the coasts of Britain herself.

A new contingent of British troops arrived. "But half of them are diseased," Albion reported. "Now we have to keep them from infecting the others." Abigail hardly saw him in the two weeks after that.

❖

It was early in October when, finding her in the parlor one evening, Grey
Albion modestly announced: "Some of the other officers and I are going
to a ball, Miss Abigail. I wondered whether we might have the honor of
your company in our party." The Garrison Assemblies, as they were
known, usually took place twice a month in the big assembly room at the
City Tavern on Broadway, and her father had taken her to some of these.
The invitation coming directly from him, though, she was taken by surprise, and hesitated. "I should perhaps warn you," he added quickly, "that
this ball might not be to your taste."

"Oh? How so?"

"It is what they call an Ethiopian Ball."

And Abigail stared at him in surprise.

The last six months had seen one other development in New York. It
had begun when General Clinton, looking for ways to undermine the
Patriots, had proclaimed that any Negroes serving with the Patriot forces,
if they deserted to New York City, might live there as free men and follow
any trade or occupation that they chose. The response had been greater
than he had expected—so great that he'd confessed to Master, "We may
have to limit the tide."

It had certainly enraged the Patriots. Long Island Patriots had already
suffered when runaway slaves had told British raiding parties where to
find their hidden valuables. Just across from Staten Island, in Monmouth
County, a brigade under the daring black officer, Colonel Tye, had been
terrorizing the Patriot forces. "These cursed British are stirring up slave
revolts yet again," they protested. In the city, however, the results had
been interesting. "I've found a carpenter and a warehouseman I needed,"
Master had announced with satisfaction. "And we got some welcome new
troops," Albion had reported. An extra barracks had been set up for them
on Broadway.

But perhaps the most unusual development had been in the city's
social life. For it remained a curious feature of the empire that while
Britain led the world in trading slaves, and used huge numbers on the
sugar plantations, slaves were now hardly known in Britain itself. To
Albion and other young bloods like him, the free blacks of New York
seemed a delightful curiosity. So they set up dances, with black bands
playing the fiddle and the banjo. And to make it more intriguing, they

opened these dances to the black people too. It was all great fun, they thought, and rather exotic.

"I am not sure your father would approve."

It was true that some Tory Loyalists had expressed great displeasure at the influx of free blacks into their city. But Master was a vestryman of Trinity, and the Trinity vestry had stuck with their former tradition in providing schooling for the black community.

"I shall be glad to join your party," Abigail said, with just a hint of reproof.

It was her father who suggested that Hudson and his wife should accompany the young people. The gathering was only a short distance away, so they all decided to walk there together.

There was a large crowd. About half of them were black, a sprinkling were civilians from the city, the rest were British officers and their guests. A thousand candles lit the room brightly. Notwithstanding the difficulties of getting food, splendid refreshments had been provided. The band was excellent, and the dancing was conducted in the usual manner, except that the formal opening minuet was dispensed with, nor was anyone in the mood to attempt a French cotillion. Instead the company got straight down to jigs, reels, square and country dances. The tunes were popular and lively: "Sweet Richard," "Fisher's Hornpipe," "Derry Down." And Abigail was pleased to observe that, lively though the occasion certainly was, everything was done with a charming decorum.

Hudson was in his element. She realized that, in all her life, she had never seen him perform in such a setting. Several times, she found herself paired with him for a moment or two, as, with a kindly smile, he whirled her round. She caught sight of Albion doing the same with Hudson's wife. And she of course was often on his arm.

They all sat down together, Albion and his friends, the Hudsons and two other black couples they had encountered. The conversation was very merry. She complimented Hudson on his dancing, for which he gravely thanked her.

"And how do I dance, Mrs. Hudson?" Albion cheerfully inquired. She paused, only for a moment.

"Why, mighty fine . . . for a man with only one good leg!"

This was greeted with roars of approval, and laughter.

"His leg's good enough to go into action soon," one of his fellow officers remarked.

"True," Albion said with a smile.

"Oh?" Abigail said. "You are leaving?"

"Yes," he confirmed. "I only received the news today, but General Clinton is going to join the forces down in the South, and he is taking me with him. So I may see some action again."

"When do you leave?" she asked.

"At the end of the month, I think."

"Come," cried one of the others. "It's time to dance again."

They all walked back together afterward. It was past midnight. Though the city was under a military curfew—which, for some reason, General Clinton insisted upon—this was relaxed for certain social events. Here and there, street lamps gave them enough light to make their way along. The two Hudsons walked together, she and Albion a little way behind. He had given her his arm.

"You must try not to get shot again, in the South," she said. "I cannot undertake to nurse you twice."

"I'll do my best," he answered. "It'll probably be very dull. No fighting at all."

"Then you'll have to chase those beautiful Southern girls, instead," she suggested.

"Perhaps." He was silent for a moment. "But where would I ever find another such as you?" he said quietly.

Her heart missed a beat. The exact words. It had not been a dream, then, after all.

She wanted to make some easy reply. None came. They continued to walk.

When they reached the house, Hudson opened the front door and ushered them into the parlor. It was quiet. Obviously, the rest of the household had gone to sleep.

"I expec' the gentleman would like a glass of brandy before retirin'," Hudson said softly. "If you jus' give me a minute or two."

The room was warm. There was still the remains of a fire glowing in the grate. Albion stirred it for a moment. She took off her cloak. He turned.

"I can't believe you're leaving," she said.

"I have no wish to do so." He was gazing at her with an affection that could not be mistaken.

She looked up at him, her lips parting, as he stepped forward and took her in his arms.

As the minutes passed, there was no sign of Hudson. She heard only the faint crackle of the fire in the grate as they kissed and, pressing more passionately against each other, kissed again until she would, she knew, have given herself to him there and then, had not the door opened and her father's voice, coming from the hallway, caused them to spring apart.

"Ah," her father said easily as, taking his time, he entered the room, "you're back. Splendid. I hope the party was a success."

"Yes, sir, I think it was," said Albion.

And after a few polite exchanges, he went off to his bed.

⁘

In the remaining time before his departure, he was kept very busy. General Clinton was planning to sail down the coast to Georgia with eight thousand troops. As well as being occupied around the port, Albion was often away, spending days on Long Island and the various outposts around the city.

All too soon, the day of departure was upon them. He was to bid farewell to the family at the house, before going out to march to the ships with his men. But before doing so, he drew her into the parlor with him alone. And there he took her hand and looked into her eyes with great sincerity and affection.

"Dear Abigail. How can I ever thank you enough for all that you have done for me? Or for the happiness of being in your company?" He paused a moment. "I hope so much that we shall meet again. But war is uncertain. So if, perchance, we should not, I must tell you that I shall carry the memory of our time together as the best and the brightest days of my life."

Then he kissed her gently upon the cheek.

It was said with much warmth, and she bowed her head in acknowledgment of the great compliment he was paying her.

But she had hoped for something—she was not sure what—something more.

Later, she and her father took Weston down to the waterfront to watch the ships sail out of the harbor.

⁘

The Christmas season came and went. They heard from Susan that James had moved with Washington to winter camp. The weather by now had turned bitterly cold. Snowstorms came, again and again, burying the streets. Not only the Hudson River, but even the harbor froze. No one could remember anything like it, and Abigail wondered with some anxiety how her brother was faring. Down the coast there were big storms. No word came of Clinton and his fleet. "Remember, they have to pass New Jersey, Virginia and both the Carolinas," her father reminded her, soothingly. "It's eight hundred miles even as the crow flies."

At last news came that the ships, after suffering badly, had finally arrived at the mouth of the Savannah River. She waited for a letter from Albion. Not until late February did it appear. It was addressed to her father, and announced that he was safe and that the army, under Clinton and Cornwallis, was preparing to move up the coast into the Patriot country of South Carolina. "Our object, without a doubt, will be the city of Charleston." He sent his greetings to the family, with a lighthearted message to Weston, telling him to start preparing for the cricket season, as soon as the weather allowed. To Abigail, he sent his warmest remembrances.

"I shall reply, of course," her father said, and wrote the next day, to which she added a letter of her own.

Abigail did not find it easy to write her letter. She kept it short, gave Albion some report of life in the city, and her walks with Weston. But how should she finish? Did she dare commit her affections to paper? How would that expose her? And how might they be received? Or should she instead write something lighthearted, letting him guess the tenderness that lay beneath? She couldn't decide.

In the end she wrote only that both she and Weston hoped he would be returned to them safely, "so that you and he may play cricket, and we, perhaps, may dance." It wasn't perfect, but it would have to do.

⁂

The spring passed quietly. She occupied herself with Weston and wrote her usual accounts to James. News arrived from the South from time to time. A vigorous young cavalry commander named Tarleton was making a name for himself chasing down Patriots. Then in May came a hasty dispatch: Charleston had fallen.

New York erupted with joy. There were parades, banquets and, soon, a letter from Grey Albion.

"This quite changes the position," her father remarked. "If we smash the south, and then turn all our forces on Washington, even with his better-trained men, he may find it hard to survive." Her father gave her a summary of Albion's letter. "It seems young Tarleton cut Charleston off completely from the north. His methods are brutal but effective, according to Albion. A huge surrender, he says. The whole of South Carolina will soon be in British hands again. The Patriot troops in North Carolina are in poor shape too. Perhaps our friend Rivers gave up too early." She hadn't seen her father look this pleased in months. "General Clinton is so satisfied that he plans to return to New York and leave Cornwallis in charge down there," he concluded.

"Is Albion returning also then?" she asked.

"Not yet. He wants to stay with Cornwallis. Hoping to make a name for himself, I expect."

"I see. Does he enclose any letter for me?"

"No. But he thanks you for yours, and sends you his warmest good wishes." Her father smiled. "I'll give you the letter. You can read it for yourself."

"I'll read it later, Papa," she said, and left the room.

For the next few days, New York continued to celebrate. But Abigail did not. In truth, she hardly knew what to feel. She told herself that she was being foolish. A young man going to war had kissed her. He must have kissed a score of girls before. He said he had tender feelings for her. Perhaps he had. But that, she supposed, might pass. And what did she feel for him? She scarcely knew.

Her world seemed bathed in a sunless light that left the landscape uncertain.

She felt sure that Albion had acquitted himself with distinction, so why had he declined to return with General Clinton? And mightn't he at least have replied to her letter in person? Surely he'd have done so, if he cared for her? Two more days of this silent moping followed, until her father, who could bear it no longer, took her aside and asked her frankly: "My child, have I done something to cause you unhappiness?"

"Nothing, Papa, I promise you."

He paused, as if considering something. "Might this have any connection with Grey Albion?"

"No, Papa. None at all."

"I think, Abby, that it has." He sighed. "I wish your mother were still alive. It must be hard for you talk to your father about such a matter."

She gave in. "I thought at least he'd write to me." She shrugged. "If he cared."

Her father nodded, seemed to reach a decision of some kind, and put his arm around her shoulder.

"Well then, I'll tell you, Abby. Do you remember the day that Susan came and I sent goods to the Patriots? Albion came to me that evening. He spoke of you . . . in the most tender terms."

"He did?"

"He expressed his feelings plainly. Indeed, nobly." Her father nodded at the recollection. "But you are still young, Abby, and with this war continuing . . . and so much uncertainty . . . He and I decided it was best to wait. Wait until the war is over. Who knows how matters may stand then? In the meantime, for his sake as well as your own, you should think of him as a friend. A dear friend."

Abigail stared at her father. "Did he ask for my hand in marriage?"

Her father hesitated. "He may have mentioned the possibility."

"Oh, Papa," she said, reproachfully.

"You care for him, then?" he asked.

"Yes, Papa."

"Well, I like him too," he now declared.

"He would want to take me to England, I suppose?"

"I'm sure of it. I'd miss you, Abby. Should you wish to go?"

"Would you go also?"

"I might have to, Abby, if the Patriots recoup and win."

"Then, Papa," she smiled, "I'd tell him, 'I'll go if my papa comes too.'"

✥

Solomon was happy. It was a beautiful June day and the sea was sparkling. They were off the coast of Virginia and running north toward New York, under the bright blue sky and a breeze coming from the south-east.

The vessel was French. They'd taken her off the coast of Martinique, with a fine cargo of French silks, wine and brandy, and even a small chest of gold. The captain had split the crew, sending the mate to take the prize to New York with a dozen of their own crew, including four slaves, and six of the captured Frenchmen.

Though he was still waiting for his freedom, Solomon enjoyed being at sea. Life aboard a privateer, especially one owned by Master, wasn't so bad. And since he was the merchant's personal property, neither the captain nor the mate were going to give him any trouble, as long as he performed his duties well. In any case, he'd long since become a valued member of the crew. The last time they'd hit bad weather, and the mate had needed assistance, he'd called out: "Take the wheel, Solomon," and afterward told him: "I knew you'd keep her steady."

But he was looking forward to seeing his father and mother again, back in New York. And with such a rich prize, he could be quite certain that Master would put down some money to his account.

When they saw the other vessel, it was coming from the mouth of the Chesapeake, and it was gaining on them fast. The mate put a spyglass to his eye and cursed. "Pirates," he said. "They're flying the Stars and Stripes."

Solomon reckoned afterward that the mate probably saved his life that day. Thrusting a pistol into his hand he told him: "Take the damn Frenchies below. We can't trust 'em on deck. Shoot any one of 'em that tries to move."

So he was below deck a while later when he heard the rattle of musket fire followed by the roar of cannon sweeping the deck with grapeshot. After this, there was a series of bumps, followed by a loud knocking on the hatch and a rough voice telling him to open up. Reluctantly he did so, and clambered on deck.

The scene before him was grim. Most of the New York crew were dead, or close to it. The mate had blood all over one leg, but was alive. A dozen Patriots had boarded the ship, including a thickset, red-haired man who carried a bullwhip and had two pistols stuffed into his belt. Solomon assumed he was their captain. As the Frenchmen emerged, and saw the Patriots, they broke out into a voluble welcome in their native tongue. The red-haired captain quickly moved them to one side of the deck and sent two fellows to search below. Two of the blacks were lying dead already, but the other slave was the cook, and they soon found him and brought him up. "That's all, Cap'n," they reported.

The captain turned to the wounded mate. "So this is a French prize you took?" The mate nodded. "You outta New York?" The mate nodded again. "So these"—he indicated the Frenchmen—"are the French crew?"

"Right," said the mate.

"Hmm. These Frenchies are our friends, boys," he called to his men.

"Treat 'em nice." He turned his attention to the cook. "He a slave?" At the mate's nod, "Galley?"

"Cooks good."

"I can use him. And this one?" He turned to Solomon.

"Crew. Good hand," said the mate, "very."

The red-haired captain fixed Solomon with a pair of fierce blue eyes. "What're you, boy?" he demanded. "Slave or free?"

And now Solomon had to think fast.

"I's a slave, Boss," he said eagerly. "I belongs to the Patriot Captain James Master, sir, that is serving with General Washington."

"How so?"

"I was forced upon this vessel to prevent me joinin' Captain Master, sir. An' if you make inquiries of him, he will answer for me."

It was a good try, and the pirate considered it, but not for long.

"Captain James Master. Don't know the name. But it don't signify, anyhow. If you're his slave, then you must've run away to the damn British to get your freedom. Which makes you the enemy, far as I'm concerned. An' you sure as hell are a slave again now, boy. An' you're a lyin', thievin' treacherous slave too, that needs a whippin'." But before dealing with Solomon further, he turned to glance around the deck and, indicating the bodies that were lying there, he called to his men. "Over the side with all these." Then he went across to the mate. "You don't look good, my friend," he remarked.

"I'll live," said the mate.

"I don't think so," said the captain. And pulling out one of his pistols, he shot the mate in the head. "Throw him over too," he ordered.

Having completed this business, he came back to Solomon again and, standing with his legs wide apart, eyed him, fingering the bullwhip thoughtfully as he did so.

"Like I said, you need a whippin'." He paused, considering, then nodded to himself. "But though I should, I reckon I ain't goin' to whip you. No, I believe I'm goin' to lie instead. I'm goin' to say that you never been whipped because you are the most humble, obedient, hard-workin', God-fearin' nigger that ever walked the face of the earth. That's what I'm goin' to say." He nodded. "An' you know why?"

"No, Boss."

"Because, you lyin' Loyalist, son-of-a-bitch runaway, I'm goin' to sell you."

❖

It was only when her father's captain returned, expecting to find the French vessel already in New York, that Master realized that he had lost his prize, and had to tell Hudson that his son was missing. "I don't think our French ship sank," her father told them all. "More likely it was taken. Solomon may still be out there somewhere, and we shouldn't give up hope." If the ship was still afloat, news of it would come across the high seas, sooner or later.

Meanwhile, word was coming from the South of continuing British successes. Patriot heroes like Rutledge, Pickens and Marion "the Swamp" Fox were still doing their best to harass the redcoats and their supporters; but the southern Patriot army was not in good shape. Congress sent General Gates down into South Carolina, but Cornwallis soon smashed him at Camden.

Perhaps to distract their thoughts from their private worries, Master kept his household busy. General Clinton, back in New York, dined several times at the house, and Abigail and Ruth made sure that these dinners were excellent. From the general, and his officers, Abigail received the impression that they now considered the war might be won. Her father thought so too.

"I'm damn sure Clinton's hatching a new plan of some kind," he told her. "But whatever it is, he's keeping it under his hat."

Of particular pleasure to Abigail was a dinner to which General Clinton brought two extra guests. One was Governor William Franklin, whom the Patriots had kicked out of New Jersey and who was living in the city now.

It was interesting to observe Ben Franklin's son at close quarters. You could see that he had many of the lineaments of his father's face. But where the father cultivated features that were round and merry, the son's were thinner, more patrician, and somewhat sour. As for his views on the Patriots, he explained them to her precisely.

"I can say so in this house, Miss Abigail, because, as well as your brother, my own father is a Patriot. But while there are of course men of principle on the Patriot side, I consider most of them to be rebels and bandits. I still have a band of good men hunting Patriots down in New Jersey. And I personally should be well content to hang any we can catch."

She didn't think she liked him.

But young Major André was a very different matter. He was about her brother's age, a Swiss Huguenot, whose faint French accent gave his conversation a special charm. What really delighted her, however, was that, serving on Clinton's staff, he knew Grey Albion well. They spoke of him all evening.

"I must confess, Miss Abigail," he told her, "that I had heard of you from Albion, who spoke about you with admiration."

"He did?" She could not help a faint blush of pleasure.

He gave her a kindly smile. "If it is not indiscreet, Miss Abigail, I could say that he spoke of you in terms of the highest regard. And equally, if it is not impertinent, I have the impression that you think well of him too."

"I do, Major André," she confessed. "Very well."

"In my judgment, you could not bestow your regard on a better fellow." He paused. "He told me also that he had been a close friend of your brother, James . . ."

"I hope that one day their friendship may be resumed."

"We shall all hope for that day," he agreed.

"Well, Abby," her father asked, when the guests had departed, "was that a good evening?"

"A very good evening indeed," she answered happily.

✣

So it came as a great shock ten days later, when her father told her: "Major André is taken, and like to be hanged."

"How? Where?"

"Up the Hudson. Toward West Point."

Master had the full story from Clinton the following day.

"It's the devil of a business," her father said. "Now I know what Clinton was up to, though he couldn't tell me before. He's been planning it for over a year, and young André was acting as go-between."

"Planning what, Papa?"

"To get control of West Point. For whoever holds West Point controls the River Hudson. Get West Point from Washington, and we deal him a mortal blow. It might have been the end of the war."

"We were going to capture West Point?"

"No. Buy it. Benedict Arnold, who's one of Washington's best commanders, had control of the fort. Clinton's been working on him for more than a year, negotiating over the money, mostly, he tells me. Arnold was going to hand the place over to us."

"A traitor."

Her father shrugged. "A man of mixed loyalties. Unhappy with the commands the Patriots had given him. Disapproved of their bringing in the French. Wanted the money for his family. But yes, a traitor."

"To Washington. General Clinton must like him, though."

"Actually, Clinton despises him. But to get West Point, he says, he'd have paid the devil himself."

"What happened?"

"Our friend André had gone up to make the final arrangements. Then he got caught, and the Patriots discovered the plan. So Washington still has West Point and Arnold's fled to our camp."

"And André?"

"It's a wretched affair. Like a fool, he'd taken off his uniform, which makes him a spy. Under the rules of war, Washington and his people are supposed to hang him. But they don't want to do it—seems they like him—so they're trying to work out a deal."

"I wonder if he and James have met."

"Perhaps. I shouldn't be surprised."

The final report from her father came a few days later.

"André's hanged, I'm afraid. Clinton was almost in tears. 'They wanted Arnold for him,' he told me. 'But if I give them Arnold, I'll never get another Patriot to come over. So they've hanged my poor André.'"

For a moment, she wondered if James had been at the execution, then decided not to think about it.

❖

When James Master had approached the stone house where the condemned man was being held, he hadn't expected to be there long. Washington himself had sent him on this brief errand of mercy. He meant to accomplish it quickly and courteously, and then to be gone. He was sorry for the fellow, of course—it was a wretched business—but James Master hadn't much time for sentiment these days.

Anyone who hadn't seen James Master for a couple of years would have been struck by the change. His face was much thinner, for a start. But there was something else, a hardness in the set of his jaw, a strain in the muscles of his cheek, which could be signaling pain, or sourness, depending on his mood. Worse even than these, to anyone who loved him, would have been the look in his eyes. Iron determination resided in them, certainly, but also disillusion, anger and disgust.

None of this was surprising. The last two years had been terrible.

Getting the French into the war, though crucially important, had always been a cynical arrangement. But Washington had still hoped for a little more than he got. Admiral d'Estaing had frightened the British most effectively, but when Washington had tried to persuade him to a big joint operation to take New York, he'd refused, and he and his fleet now spent most of the time down in the West Indies, doing all they could to weaken the rich British interests there. This July General Rochambeau had arrived at Newport, Rhode Island with six thousand French troops. But he'd insisted he stay with the French ships that had been bottled up there by the British Navy, so until he moved, he and his troops might as well not have come. As far as James could see, the French regarded the American colonies as a sideshow. If the Patriots were looking for moral support, they were almost as alone as when they'd started.

Then there had been the behavior of the British themselves. Every Patriot newspaper in the colonies had been voicing outrage at the cruel treatment of American prisoners, and Washington tirelessly took the British commanders to task. But perhaps, despite all this, James himself had not quite wanted to believe that the people among whom he had lived, and that he thought he knew, would actually be guilty of such atrocities. It was the letter he'd received from his father that had finally told him everything. The letter itself had been brief. It informed him that Sam Flower had died of disease on a prison ship, that there was no grave for his family to visit, and had ended with these words: "More than this, my dear son, I cannot say, and would not wish to say." James knew his father. What those words said, and what they did not say, told him the worst. A tide of rage and disgust had arisen within him and had set, over the long months, into a hardened, bitter hatred.

The last winter had been terrible. Washington's camp at Morristown had been well constructed and perfectly laid out. Their log cabins had been sealed with clay, and Washington himself had occupied a sturdy house nearby. But no one could have predicted the weather. Twenty-eight snowstorms buried them almost up to the roofs of the cabins. Sometimes they ate nothing for days at a time. Washington had been an inspiration—he'd even held an officers' dance in a local tavern, though they'd needed sledges to get there. But by the end of winter, the Continental army was exhausted.

Spring and summer had only brought news of awful defeats in the South. Two and a half thousand Continentals taken prisoner at Charleston, not counting local militias as well. Yet still the Patriots held on, and hoped for better things—partly because men like James Master were quite determined that, having gone so far against an enemy they had come to hate, they would never turn back.

It was a grim-faced, iron man, therefore, who now strode into the stone house where poor Major André was awaiting execution.

Above, the sun was shining down on the general's camp at Tappan. The northern end of Manhattan was only ten miles away down the Hudson River. Ten miles, however, that the luckless prisoner had not managed to negotiate. Certainly André had been unlucky, but also foolish, after parting from the traitor Arnold, to have taken off his uniform to get away in disguise. Having done that, he'd made himself a spy. Washington had insisted that he be given a proper, formal trial, and he'd been able to argue his case. But the verdict could hardly be otherwise, and tomorrow he was due to hang.

André was sitting quietly in the room where he was housed. He had been writing letters. On a sideboard were the remains of a meal he'd been sent from Washington's table. James had seen him at a distance several times in recent days, but not spoken to him yet. At his entry the young Swiss courteously arose, and James informed him of his purpose in being there.

"I am instructed by the general to ensure that you have everything you need. Any letters you wish to send, any other services I can arrange for you . . ."

"I have everything I require, I think," André answered with a faint smile. "You said your name was Captain Master?"

"At your service, sir."

"How strange. Then I believe I had the pleasure of dining with your father and your sister, just recently." And seeing James's look of surprise, he remarked: "I did not guess then that I should have the honor of seeing you also. Perhaps you would like to hear how they are."

Fully ten minutes passed while André gave him an account of his father and sister. They were both in perfect health and good spirits, André assured him. No, he had to confess, he had only seen young Weston fleetingly, but he knew from Abigail that the boy was well and enjoying his time at school. Such news was welcome to James indeed. During the winter, communication with his family had been impossible, and he had only received news of them once in the last few months when he'd been able to see Susan. Having satisfied all his questions, and after a brief pause, André said quietly: "When I was down at Charleston with General Clinton, I also had the pleasure of coming to know an old friend of yours. Grey Albion."

"Grey Albion?" James stared at him, and almost remarked that he feared he might find it difficult to think of Albion as a friend any more. But he quickly recovered his manners and said politely that, indeed, he had fond memories of living in the Albions' London house.

"I learned in Charleston of Albion's deep attachment to your sister," André went on. "And it was charming to hear from her that his regard for her is returned."

"Ah," said James.

"Let us hope," said André, "that when this unfortunate war is concluded, in one manner or another, these two charming young people may be able to find the happiness together that they desire." He paused. "Perhaps I may witness it," he shrugged, "from above."

James said nothing. He looked down at the floor, thought for a moment and then, having formed his face into a pleasant mask, inquired: "If they do marry, was it your impression that Grey means to return to live in London?"

"Without a doubt. The family's situation there, I understand, is very agreeable."

"It is," said James, and rose to go.

"There is one thing you could do for me, my friend," said André now. "I have already made my request to the general, but if you have any influence with him, you might be kind enough to urge my case. A spy is hanged like a criminal. It would be a kindness if he would allow me to be shot like a gentleman."

❖

In October, her father told Abigail that he'd received a letter from Grey Albion, to say that the army was moving north. It seemed that Cornwallis thought he could roll all the way up the east coast. John Master was less sanguine.

"Clinton's worried. He says Cornwallis isn't a bad commander—he's vigorous, and always on the attack, but that's also his weakness. Unlike Washington, Cornwallis has never learned patience. After his recent victories, he's the hero of the hour, and with all his aristocratic connections, he deals directly with the ministry, and thinks he can do as he pleases. Clinton is now forced to send men to support him, but he's afraid Cornwallis will overreach himself."

He did not say so, but Abigail understood what her father was hinting. "You mean that Albion may be in more danger than he thinks, Papa."

"Oh, I dare say he'll be safe enough," her father answered.

Late in the year, Clinton was forced to send still more troops to help Cornwallis. He placed them under the competent command of his new recruit, the traitor Benedict Arnold.

··⊹··

James Master had not gone to André's execution. André's request for a firing squad had not been granted, but he'd been allowed to fit the noose around his own neck, and had done it skillfully, so that when the cart was pulled away and he dropped, his death was almost instant.

However, in the months that followed, James had brooded constantly on what André had told him about Abigail. Had he been able to visit his sister he would certainly have confronted her about the matter at once. But short of getting himself smuggled into the city—at the mere thought of which Washington would have been outraged—there was nothing he could do. He had started to compose a letter to his father, but had laid it aside for several reasons. It was clear, firstly, that Grey Albion was not in New York, and so the relationship was hardly likely to advance at present. Nor was it a subject he cared to trust to a letter, which might always fall into the wrong hands. But most of all, he felt a sense of hurt, both that Abigail should have acted against his wishes, and that neither she nor her father had seen fit to tell him about it. So he brooded.

And God knows, during the winter that followed, he had time to brood.

Washington made his main winter quarters at Morristown again. But this time he split his forces among several places, in the hope of getting them, and the horses also, more adequately fed. The winter had not been like the previous one, but it had been full of sorrow. The Continental

paper currency issued by the Congress was now virtually worthless—it
had depreciated by a factor of three thousand times. The troops were supposed to be paid by the province from which they'd come, and those from
Pennsylvania, in particular, had not been paid in three years. Discovering
that a large group were on the point of mutiny, General Clinton had sent
messengers to them offering full pay if they would switch sides, but angry
though they were, the Pennsylvania men had treated this bribe with contempt, and fortunately Pennsylvania had finally paid up. There had been
other protests also, but the Patriot forces had still come through the winter more or less intact.

All the same, it was clear that the Patriot cause was very close to collapse. Though Washington had sent the rugged Nathaniel Greene to rally
what was left of the Patriot army in the South, he knew how small the
forces down there were. Tower of strength though he was, he confided to
James: "If the French will not join us this summer for a mighty strike,
either in the North or in the South, then I do not know how we can continue." And if the Patriot cause collapsed, nobody cared to think of the
consequences.

Meanwhile, there was little to do. Through the long and miserable
months, therefore, James thought about Albion and his sister. If the world
around him was dismal and filled with awful threats, in his imagination,
also, he was assailed by phantoms. He felt deserted by his family, powerless, impotent. Memories of his own unhappy marriage came to haunt
him, thoughts of English arrogance, coldness and cruelty crowded into
his mind. Sometimes it seemed to him, however unfairly, that Albion and
Abigail were deliberately acting deviously, and then he suffered a blinding
rage. At the least, he decided, Albion was planning to steal his sister, break
up his family and take her away to a country he had come to hate. Why,
he even thought, if I should not survive this war, perhaps they and my
father will take little Weston to England too.

For behind all these imaginings, with which he tortured himself, there
lay one great assumption, a passionate feeling of identity that, before the
war, would not have occurred to him. Abigail and Weston, his precious
family, were not to be English. Never. He could not bear the thought of it.
They were not English, they were Americans.

In the spring, news filtered up from the South. The Patriots had
engaged Cornwallis and inflicted casualties. Even the fearsome Tarleton

had been badly beaten in a skirmish. But Cornwallis was pressing into Virginia with Benedict Arnold. Richmond had been taken. And now Arnold had set up a base on the coast.

It was typical of Washington that, though he did not know the cause, he should have noticed that James had something on his mind. One day, therefore, James found himself called into the general's presence.

"We can't let Cornwallis and Arnold range freely in Virginia," Washington told him. "So I'm sending three thousand men down there, to see what we can do. I'm giving the command to Lafayette, because I trust him. And I think I should like it, Master, if you went too."

❖

May passed, and June. The weather was warm, and New York was quiet for the moment. It was known that Lafayette had gone south, but most people still thought that if he could get enough support from the French, Washington must soon make a move in the North.

No one had heard from James, and so Abigail was not sure if he was still nearby or far away. But for some reason, at this time, she began to experience a feeling of dread that would not go away. Indeed, as the weeks passed, this sense of ill omen grew stronger. To share her fears, she felt sure, was to invite the fates to accomplish them. The only thing to do was keep them to herself.

"I've just been with Clinton," her father announced one afternoon. "He's convinced that Washington means to attack New York. He wants to bring Cornwallis's main force back up here, but London's all for Cornwallis's damned Virginia adventure and won't hear of it." He shrugged. "Cornwallis has engagements with Nathaniel Greene and wins them, but each time he does so, he loses men, and Greene regroups and comes at him again. Our commanders still expect a great Loyalist rising, but it never happens, and Patriot partisans make raids against every outpost. Cornwallis is digging himself into a hole. Clinton's told him to set up a naval base and send troops up here, but although Cornwallis says he's creating the base at Yorktown, he hasn't sent Clinton a single man."

In high summer, the news that Washington longed for and Clinton dreaded came. A new fleet, under Admiral de Grasse, was coming from France. Soon, it appeared on the horizon. By July, Rochambeau, with his five thousand veteran French troops, had moved out of Rhode Island and come to meet Washington just above the city at White Plains. Washington was deploying his forces closer and closer now. British scouts reported: "We've seen the Americans. They could be here in hours." Inside the city, the streets were full of drilling troops. The northern palisade was being strengthened. Young Weston was excited.

"Will there be a battle?" he asked.

"I don't suppose so," Abigail lied.

"Will my father come to protect us?"

"General Clinton has all the soldiers we need."

"I still wish Father would come," said Weston.

But strangely, nothing happened. The long days of August passed. The city was tense, but still the French and American allies made no move. They seemed to be waiting for something.

And then, late in the month, they suddenly went away. The French troops, the main body of Washington's forces, the big French fleet, they all went off together. Evidently, there had been a change of plan.

"Perhaps they have decided New York is too difficult to take," Abigail suggested. But her father shook his head.

"There's only one explanation," he said. "They think they can trap Cornwallis."

⁘

But the fate of the British Empire did not rest upon the army. It never had. It never would. It was the British Navy that controlled the oceans, supplied the soldiers, and saved them when in need.

At the end of August, a dozen ships arrived in New York harbor. Admiral Rodney, a first-rate leader, had command. "But he's only brought twelve ships," Master complained. "We need the whole fleet."

Learning of the threat to Cornwallis, and adding twelve New York warships to his own, Rodney set off at once for the Chesapeake. But it was not long before the sails appeared again in the bay, and his ships limped back into the harbor.

"There weren't enough of them, Abigail. De Grasse beat them off," her father said. "Rodney's ready to try again, but he'll have to refit."

Meanwhile, a squadron of French vessels from the French base at Newport had appeared, waiting to pounce, out in the bay.

The refitting of the British ships was slow. They'd suffered considerable damage.

"Clinton's heard from Cornwallis," Master reported. "It seems he's trapped all right, and he can't get out."

But still the shipwrights took their time, and it wasn't until mid-October that the fleet set out again.

··❖··

James Master stared toward Yorktown. It was just a small place, with modest docks, on the edge of the York River. Across the river lay a much smaller British encampment on Gloucester Point. The French and Patriot forces had Cornwallis enclosed in a large semicircle. If he had been stronger, he would have held four outlying redoubts that dominated his lines. But he had reckoned he couldn't hold them, and so these were already occupied by the allies.

And allies they certainly were. When the French general, Rochambeau, had first met with Washington, he had immediately, and courteously, placed himself under his command. Washington in turn had taken every decision with him jointly. The French in their smart white coats were on the left of the semicircle, Washington's Continentals wore blue coats, when they had them, and the militias were in rough clothing. Without reinforcements from the North, Cornwallis's Southern army of red-coated British and Prussian-blue Hessians now totaled six thousand men. The allies had over sixteen thousand.

The siege had started at the end of September, and it had been going on for two weeks now. Five days ago, firing the first gun himself, Washington had begun the bombardment. It had been steady and effective. The British were being slowly blown to bits, but the bombardment was still long-range. Now the time had come to move the lines forward and bring the bombardment closer. To do that, it would be necessary to storm the inner line of redoubts.

The plan that Washington had prepared was somewhat devious. All day the usual bombardment had continued, then, at half past six in the evening, a party of French was to make a diversionary move against one of the redoubts to the west. Soon after, the army was to begin what looked like a general attack on the Yorktown lines. Only when the enemy was thoroughly alarmed and confused was the real move to be made.

A pair of moves, actually. Two parties of men, each four hundred strong, were to rush redoubts numbers 9 and 10, which lay close to the river on the eastern side. Redoubt 9 would be attacked by the French; number 10 by the Patriots. The attack would be led by Alexander Hamilton, and with Lafayette's permission, James Master was to accompany him.

So now James was waiting, glad of the chance of action—indeed, he could scarcely remember when he'd been more excited. The attack would certainly be bloody. The men had their bayonets fixed, and a number were also carrying axes to break through the redoubt's defenses.

The evening was drawing closer, but there was still plenty of light. Across the lines, he saw the French diversion begin. He looked at the faces of the men. The wait might be a little fearful, but when the moment for the rush forward began, everything else would be forgotten. There were only minutes to wait now. He could feel the blood coursing in his veins.

He became aware of the lines of troops right across the battlefield beginning to maneuver. What a terrifying sight that must be, seen from the battered British lines. He waited for the signal. The minutes seemed eternal. In his hand he held his sword. He also had two loaded pistols. He waited. And then the signal came.

They were off. It wasn't far to the redoubt, only a hundred and fifty yards. How strange. They were charging yet it seemed as if everything was moving so slowly. The British defenders had seen them. Fire crackled out, and he heard a musket ball hiss by his head, yet scarcely noticed. The high earthwork walls of the redoubt were looking up before him now. They were rushing the outer defenses, the men hacking at the fencework with axes and bursting through. They got across a big ditch, started to clamber up the parapet. He saw a British helmet in front of him, pressed toward it, ready to strike the man down. But a trooper was just ahead of him, lunging with his bayonet.

As he came over the parapet, there seemed to be redcoats everywhere. They were falling back, trying to get off a volley. Speed was the thing. Without another thought he rushed forward, aware that there were three or four other fellows close by his side. A redcoat was just lifting his gun as James thrust his sword, as hard as he could, into the fellow's stomach just below the chest. He felt the steel burst through the thick material of the uniform, then strike into the backbone behind. Raising his foot against the body, he dragged the sword out before the redcoat fell.

The next few moments were so confused, he hardly knew what he was doing himself. The redoubt seemed to be a jostling mass of bodies, and the sheer weight of the attacking numbers seemed to be pushing the redcoats back. He found himself beside a tent, worked his way round it, found a redcoat in front of him with a bayonet which he parried aside, while another of his own men ran the redcoat through. Strangely, the tent seemed to act like a magic barrier in the middle of the hubbub. Coming to the tent flap, he found it open. A British officer, who must have just been wounded, had staggered in there and was lying on the ground. Blood was coming from his leg. His helmet was off, and James saw a tangled mass of hair. He took out his pistol, and the officer turned, clearly expecting death.

It was Grey Albion. He stared at James, astonished, but he didn't smile. This was battle after all.

"Well, James," he said evenly, "if someone's going to kill me, I'd rather it was you."

James paused. "If you surrender," he said coldly, "you're my prisoner. If not, I shoot. Those are the rules."

Albion glanced around. The fighting seemed to have moved beyond the tent as the British were falling back. There would be no help from that quarter. His sword was on the ground beside him, but his leg was wounded and James was armed. Unless James's pistol misfired, he had no options. He sighed.

And then James spoke again. "One other matter. You are to leave my sister alone. You are to cease from all correspondence with her and you are never to see her again. Do you understand?"

"I love her, James."

"Choose."

"If I refuse?"

"I shoot. No one will be any the wiser."

"Hardly the word of a gentleman."

"No." James pointed the pistol at his head. "Choose. I require your word."

Albion hesitated. "As you wish," he said at last. "You have my word."

❖

With the redoubts taken, Cornwallis's camp was open to close bombardment. Two days later, he tried to break out and get troops across the river, but stormy weather prevented him. Three days after that, on October 19, having no other option, he surrendered. As his troops marched out, they played the dance tune "Derry Down."

⁙

On November 19, 1781, a ship came into New York from Virginia. On board was no less a person than Lord Cornwallis himself. While his troops had been held in transports, the general had negotiated a release on parole, so that he could go to London to explain himself.

Awaiting a vessel to England, he retired to a house in the town where he busied himself with correspondence. He certainly hadn't come to New York to enjoy its society. Relations between himself and General Clinton were said to be strained. If Clinton thought Cornwallis had been rash, Cornwallis could point out that he had obeyed instructions from London, and considered that Clinton had not done enough to support him. In the wake of the disaster, both men were preparing their cases.

The same ship also carried a letter from James. It was affectionate and full of news. It seemed that Washington had considered following the victory of Yorktown with a strike against New York that might have ended the war there and then. But Admiral de Grasse was anxious to go and do more damage to the British in the Caribbean. "So I dare say," he wrote, "that I shall be spending some more weeks sitting outside the gates of New York, and thinking of my home and my dear family within as I do so." He seemed to believe, nonetheless, that the end of the war must now be in sight.

He then gave them some account of the events at Yorktown, and the attacks on the redoubts. The next part of his letter, her father handed to Abigail without a word.

And now I must give you sad news. As we stormed the redoubt, the British fought bravely, none more so than a British officer whom I only realized toward the end of the engagement, when he fell, to be Grey Albion. He was not killed, though badly wounded, and was carried by us back to our lines, along with the prisoners we took. There he was well looked after. But, sadly, his condition was such that he was not thought likely to recover. I have just returned to the camp to be told, to my great sorrow, that two days ago he died.

Abigail read it over twice, then hurried from the room.

✤

By the early days of 1782, New York had resumed its usual quiet. Corn-wallis was already in London. General Clinton wondered if a mass upris-ing of American militias might sweep into the city, but as winter turned to spring, the Patriots seemed to be sitting tight. Though whether James was right in supposing that the war would soon be over, or whether Lon-don would decide some new, bold initiative, nobody could guess.

"We shall just have to await the king's pleasure," said Master wearily. Or the king's displeasure, as it turned out.

In the last election, though King George had faced opposition from many Members of Parliament who were dissatisfied with the conduct of the war, he had still managed, by the usual means of patronage, promo-tion and honest bribery, to secure a solid majority in his favor. It had cost him a hundred thousand pounds.

But even in the best-organized legislatures, there comes a point where votes can no longer be bought. And when Parliament heard that York-town was lost and the whole of Cornwallis's army taken, the king's major-ity crumbled. Even Lord North, faithful to his royal brother though he was, threw in the towel. The ministry fell. The opposition were in. That spring the Patriots sent four clever men—Ben Franklin, John Jay, John Adams and Henry Laurens—to join the peace negotiations with the pow-ers of France, Spain, the Dutch and the British, whose commissioners were gathering, in Paris.

For Abigail, it remained a sad time. She thought often of Albion. It was lucky that she had Weston to occupy her—that was a blessing—and her father also tried to find ways of distracting her. General Clinton returned to London, but his replacement was a decent man, and the life of the British garrison continued more or less as before. There were young offi-cers, especially from the Navy, in the city, and her father told her it would be ill-mannered not to attend their occasional parties. But she could not take much pleasure in their company.

Occasionally, those she met aroused her curiosity. One of the king's sons, hardly more than a boy, was serving as a midshipman on one of the vessels stationed at New York. He was a pleasant, eager young fellow, and she observed him with some interest. But he was hardly much company for her. More to her liking was a fresh-faced naval officer, only a few years older than herself, yet already a captain, whose merits, as well as his family connections, promised him the chance of rapid promotion. Had she not been grieving for Albion, she might have been glad of the attention of Captain Horatio Nelson.

Master also encouraged her to be busy. As it happened, that summer, a new and interesting business opened up. For as more and more of the Tory merchants of New York concluded that they had no more future there, and prepared to ship out, whole households of goods came up for sale. Hardly a week went by when her father did not ask her to inspect a sale for him. She found china and glass, fine furniture, curtains, rugs to be had at knock-down prices. After advising her father on a few of these sales, he said to her: "I leave it all in your hands now, Abigail. Buy as you think best, and let me have an accounting." As the months went by, she had so much inventory that the only problem was where to store it. The prices were so low that she felt almost guilty.

By the fall season, quite a number of Patriots were returning to the city to claim their property. If they found soldiers living in their house, there were often some hard words spoken. But there was little violence. Winter passed quietly enough, and in spring came news that all hostilities between the British and the Patriots had ended. As more Patriots came into the city, and Loyalists prepared to leave, Abigail knew of a score of houses where angry Patriots had just walked in and taken over. Meanwhile, the Patriot Governor Clinton of New York was still eagerly dispossessing as many Loyalists as he could.

It was at this time that James appeared. He still had duties to perform with Washington, he explained, but he could stay with them two days. Weston was overjoyed, and the family passed some happy hours together. James and his father quickly agreed that Master should make over the house and other city property to him, so that they could not be confiscated as Loyalist possessions, and this was speedily done with a lawyer.

On the second afternoon, the family were walking together on Broadway when they encountered Charlie White. Their greeting was friendly enough, but they could see that Charlie was looking a little glum.

"Anything you need, Charlie?" Master inquired.

"Not unless you've got a house," said Charlie sadly. "Mine was burned down."

"Come round tomorrow," said Master quietly, "and we'll see if something can be arranged."

The next day Charlie owned a house in Maiden Lane. And Abigail saw to it that the house was well furnished, and had better china and glass in it than Charlie ever dreamed of.

⁘

If Abigail had silently grieved for Grey Albion for many months, the pain gradually began to subside. She had to reflect that many had lost fathers and husbands. It was a tiny incident that caused her to realize that her own wound was healing. It was occasioned that summer by another visit from James. He came, this time, with a friend.

"Allow me to present my comrade-in-arms from the French Army, the Count de Chablis."

The young Frenchman was a delightful person. He was as beautifully turned out as a new pin, and he seemed delighted with New York, and indeed, by all the world around him. His English was not good, but understandable. And by the end of the day, she had to confess, she was entirely charmed.

"Your friend is so agreeable, it's hard to imagine him fighting," she remarked to James, when they were alone.

"It's just his aristocratic manner," he replied. "Lafayette is rather the same. Chablis is actually brave as a lion."

They stayed two days and, by the end of that time, she found herself rather regretting that the count was soon to leave for France.

It was during that visit also, however, that she learned to appreciate the business shrewdness of her father. For after dinner on the first day, after the count had retired and they were sitting in the parlor together, James produced a piece of paper and handed it to her father. "I thought you might be interested in this," he said.

It was a letter from Washington, to the Patriot governor of New York.

I understand, my dear sir, that you have confiscated the estates of the Tory, John Master, of New York. I should be vastly obliged if you would convey those lands to Colonel James Master, who would otherwise have inherited them, and who has, from first to last, during these long years, done our cause the greatest service.

His father smiled. "You're made a colonel now, I see. My congratulations."

"Thank you, Father. I'm afraid Washington's letter didn't do me much good, though. The farms have already been sold and I shall have a devil of a job getting them back."

"In that case," said his father, "I have something to show you." And rising from the table, he returned a couple of minutes later with a pile of papers, which he handed to his son. James looked at them with surprise.

"This is Patriot money, Father."

"Promissory notes from your Congress, to be exact. To be redeemed at par—if Congress ever has the ability to pay, that is. Down the years, as you well know, your Congress's notes have been increasingly discounted. I started buying them soon after Yorktown—only paid pence for them. I believe you'll find, however, that Congress will now accept them, at full value, as payment for confiscated Loyalist land."

"There's a small fortune here," exclaimed James.

"I believe we shall end this war," said Master, with quiet satisfaction, "with considerably more land than we had when it began." Then he turned to Abigail. "You have been buying china and glass, Abby. I have been buying debt. It's all the same game. The risk was high, so the price was low. And of course, I had the money ready to do it."

If the merchant felt pleased with himself about these transactions, however, there was something else that pleased him also. It was the day after James and his friend had left that he spoke quietly to Abigail.

"I noticed, Abby, that the Count de Chablis was rather agreeable to you."

"Was it so plain, Papa? I hope I did not embarrass myself."

"Not at all. But a father notices these things, you know. And I was very glad, Abby."

"Why, Papa?"

"It will soon be two years since Albion died," he said gently. "You have mourned for him, as you should. But it is time, now, for you to begin your life again."

And she knew that it was true.

⁖

As the summer of 1783 turned to autumn, it was clear that the British must soon leave the city. But the British commander was firm. "We'll leave as soon as every Loyalist who wants to leave has safely departed."

They were leaving by their thousands. A few were New Yorkers, but most were Loyalists who were coming through New York from elsewhere. Some shipped to England, the majority to maritime Canada. The British government paid their passage.

And then there were the former slaves that the British had freed. They too were departing, though for a different reason—to escape their Patriot owners. Hardly a day went by when Abigail didn't hear of some Patriot arriving in the city and scouring the streets and waterfront for his former slaves.

"Washington's quite clear about it," Master remarked. "He says they've every right to reclaim their property, but the British say that's not fair. Anyway, the poor devils would sooner freeze up in Nova Scotia than be slaves again."

About one slave, however, there was no news. It had taken some time, but Master had finally been able to discover the fate of his missing French prize. "She's back in French service, down in the Caribbean. But what happened to Solomon, I can't discover. He isn't aboard her now, that's for certain." To Hudson he promised: "I am still searching for him. He may well have been sold, but we shouldn't give up hope." To Abigail he confessed: "If I find him, I'll buy him back for Hudson and give him his freedom immediately. But I fear that the chances of finding him are not good."

❖

It was at the start of October that the letter from Vanessa arrived. It was addressed to John Master, as usual. It informed him, in her bold hand, that she was leaving London, being obliged to go to France. She didn't say why. She expressed regret that she was unable to come to New York to see Weston, and her usual gratitude that he was in his grandfather's safe hands. But it was the postscript that caused Master to cry out in utter astonishment.

The news in London is that Grey Albion was last week married.

Abigail found her brother at West Point. Hudson took her there. She was directed up to the ramparts, where, as soon as she reached him, she handed him the letter.

As he read his wife's plans to leave London, and her words about their son, James's face remained grave, but impassive. As he read the postscript, Abigail watched him closely. He gave a start. Then he frowned, and read it again. But he did not look at her. Instead, he stared out from the ramparts, over the River Hudson far below, for a few moments.

"They told me he was dead," he said tonelessly.

"You did not ascertain?"

"There was so much going on. Washington sent me across the river to where the other British forces—Tarleton's men—had also surrendered, the very same day. By the time I returned, I heard that several prisoners had been buried. I assumed . . ." He shrugged.

"Surely you would have heard that he lived?"

"Not necessarily. I had little to do with the prisoners after that." He continued to stare out into space. "He must have recovered, then returned to London, perhaps on parole. That is possible." He frowned again. "His father said nothing in his letters?"

"No. That is another mystery."

James pursed his lips. "Under instruction from his son, perhaps. Who knows?"

"I find the business very strange," she said.

"So do I." James glanced at her, then looked away, apparently deep in thought. "All manner of strange things happen in war, Abby," he said slowly. "In war, as in matters of the heart, none of us can be sure how we'll behave. We do not know ourselves what we may do." He looked back at her gravely. "But whatever caused Grey Albion to leave without a word, let us hope that he has found happiness now." He paused. "So many unexpected things happened in this war, Abby, that I have learned that it is useless to question why they fell out as they did. It is destiny. That's all. I don't think," he added, "that we shall see him again."

"No," she said, "I don't suppose we shall."

⁜

On November 25, 1783, at the head of eight hundred Continental troops, General George Washington came peacefully down the old Indian trail from the village of Harlem, and entered the city of New York. Riding slowly down the Bowery and Queen Street, to the cheers of the crowd, he turned into Wall Street and crossed to Broadway, where he was greeted with a fulsome public address.

The Master household went to Wall Street to watch. James rode in Washington's company, only twenty feet behind him. Abigail noticed that her father seemed quite pleased with the whole affair.

"Washington has a most stately air," he remarked with approval.

But it was a tiny incident later that afternoon that gave him even more pleasure. The general was to be given a banquet at Fraunces Tavern, only a stone's throw from the Master house, where James came to dress beforehand. As James was departing, a clatter of hoofs in the street announced the arrival of Washington and a party of officers, on their way to the gathering. James greeted them in the street, while Abigail and her father stood at the open door, watching.

And it was then that, glancing across at them, the tall, grave-faced general bowed to Abigail courteously and, as he had once before, but with a nod of recognition this time, and even the ghost of a smile, gravely touched his hat to her father, who bowed low in turn.

At dinner with Abby and young Weston, a little while later, having told Hudson to break out a bottle of his best red wine, Master raised his glass in a toast.

"Well, Abby," he said with considerable cheerfulness, "and you too, Weston, my dear grandson, the world that I knew is turned upside down. So let's drink to the new one."

The Capital

J OHN MASTER GAZED at them all. The hot summer day made the air in the house close. Perhaps he'd had too much to drink. It was a pity that Abigail wasn't here—she could always keep him in order. But with her first child due any day now, she was staying at her house up in Dutchess County. So he stared at them all—at his son James, graduate of Oxford, his grandson Weston, about to go to Harvard, and at their distinguished visitor, whose outrageous statement James and Weston seemed content to accept without a protest.

"As far as I'm concerned," he said to Thomas Jefferson, "you can go to Hell."

Not that Thomas Jefferson believed in Hell, Master supposed, or Heaven for that matter.

Until now, John Master had found himself surprisingly content to be a citizen of the United States of America. For Washington himself he had a deep respect. At Washington's inauguration in the nation's capital of New York, he had stood in the crowd on Wall Street as the great man took the oath on the balcony of the Federal Hall, and he had taken pride in the fact that, when he walked down the street with James, the great men of the new state—Adams, Hamilton, Madison—would greet his son as a respected friend.

As for the new Constitution that the wise men of the nation had framed in Philadelphia, Master had been very impressed. It seemed to him that, with its admirable system of checks and balances, the document could hardly be bettered. When Madison and the Federalists had argued, against the Antifederalists, that the states must yield some of their independence, so that the republic could have a strong central government, he'd thought the Federalists were quite right.

"We should accept the Constitution as it is," he had argued. But here, his natural conservatism had come into conflict with his son.

"I follow Jefferson," James had declared. Jefferson was acting as the new state's representative in Paris at that time and, while approving of the Constitution, he had raised one objection.

"The Constitution still fails to protect the freedom of the individual. Unless an amendment is made, our republic will finish up just as tyrannical as the old monarchies like England." This was a gross exaggeration, his father had responded, but James had been insistent. Freedom of religion was not sufficiently guaranteed, he insisted, nor was freedom of the press. On the latter subject, he'd even started to give his father a lecture about the Zenger trial until Master had been forced to remind him: "I know about the Zenger trial, James. I was here at the time."

"Well then, Father, you surely were not against Zenger, were you?" Wryly remembering his unfortunate boyhood performance during the visit of his Boston cousins, John Master had contented himself with replying: "I listened to my cousin Eliot from Boston speaking for Zenger strongly—and a damn sight more elegantly than you," he had added, just to keep James in his place.

"Back in '77," James had continued, "Jefferson proposed a bill to guarantee religious freedom in Virginia. What we need is an amendment along those lines. New York won't ratify the Constitution without one, nor will Virginia." And when the First Amendment had appeared, James had treated the matter as though it were a personal victory for Jefferson.

No doubt it was his innate conservatism, but for all his respect for the new republic, Master could not feel entirely comfortable with what he now sensed was a profound, secular tolerance at its very heart.

Even Washington was guilty. Of course, the president always observed the proprieties. While Trinity was being rebuilt after the fire, the Masters had attended the handsome chapel of St. Paul's nearby, and it always gave John Master pleasure to see the president and his wife in their pew there—even if Washington did leave before communion. But there was not the least doubt, for Washington made it clear, that the president couldn't care less what religion his fellow citizens followed. Protestant or

Catholic, Jew or atheist, or even a follower of the prophet Mohamet—so long as they observed the new Constitution, Washington declared, it was all one to him.

Others, it seemed to Master, were more devious. Before he died that spring, old Ben Franklin had claimed to be a member of every Church, and prayed with each congregation in turn. The cunning old fox.

But Jefferson, this handsome, Southern patrician with his fine education and his fancy Parisian friends, who had returned to America to run the nation's foreign affairs—what was he? A *deist*, probably. One of those fellows who said that there must be a supreme being of some kind, but who didn't seem to think they needed to do a damn thing about it. A fine belief for a coxcomb.

And now here he is, thought Master, giving me, a vestryman of Trinity, lectures about New York's bad moral character and her unworthiness to be the capital of America. This from a man who's been happily living in the flesh-pots of Paris, if you please!

It was intolerable.

"You may like it or you may not," Master continued heatedly, "but New York, sir, is the capital of America, and it's going to stay that way."

It was certainly starting to look like a capital. Life hadn't been easy since America became a nation. Saddled with British and European trade restrictions, not to mention the war debt, many of the states were still struggling their way out of depression. But New York had been recovering more rapidly than most places. Entrepreneurial merchants found ways to trade. A constant stream of people flowed in.

True, there were still areas where the fires had left charred ruins. But the city was rebuilding. Theaters had opened. The tower and spire of a new Trinity Church rose splendidly over the skyline. And when Congress had decided that their city should be the capital of the new nation, New Yorkers had reacted instantly. City Hall on Wall Street—Federal Hall, they called it now—had been splendidly refurbished as a temporary home for the legislature, while down at the foot of Manhattan, the old fort had already been torn down and used as landfill, to make room for a magnificent new complex to house the Senate, the House of Representatives and the various government offices by the waterside. Where else would you get such action, except in New York?

James intervened now, trying to smooth things over.

"The fact is, Father, many people say the New Yorkers worship only money and love luxury too much."

"Doesn't seem to bother Washington," his father retorted. The president's magnificent cream-colored coach and six was the finest equipage in the city. George and Martha Washington had already moved into a splendid new mansion on Broadway where they entertained on a scale quite as lavish as any New York merchant prince. And anyway, where was the harm in that?

But if Master chose to curse Jefferson, that gentleman was quite capable of responding in kind. His finely chiseled face set hard, and he fixed the merchant with a steely gaze.

"What I find unseemly about New York, sir," he said coldly, "is that despite the fact that we fought a war of independence, this city is chiefly populated by Tories."

There he had a point. If the war had brought all sorts of Patriots and low fellows into prominence, it was quite remarkable how well the city's old guard—and many of them were indeed Tories—had managed to survive. When you looked at the people who had bought up the houses and lands of the great landowners who'd fled or been dispossessed, the names spoke for themselves: Beekman, Gouverneur, Roosevelt, Livingston—rich merchant gentlemen like himself.

But did that make the city unfit to be America's capital?

No, it was all jealousy, Master reckoned. Jealousy, pure and simple. It was one thing that Philadelphia was angling to be the capital—that he could understand. Every city looks for its own advantage—though now that Ben Franklin was dead, Master suspected that Philadelphia might be a less lively place. But the real pressure wasn't coming from Philadelphia.

It was coming from the South. They might call him a damn Yankee, but it seemed to Master that he'd heard enough from the Southern states. In his view, the South should be satisfied with the Constitution. If many Northern Patriots were becoming uncertain about the morality of owning slaves, they'd still agreed to guarantee the institution of slavery for another generation. And when the South had negotiated that every three slaves should count as two white people in calculating the population of each state, hadn't that neatly boosted the number of representatives the Southern states would be allotted in Congress?

Their latest complaint was typical.

Master liked young Alexander Hamilton. There he could agree with James, who'd served with him in Washington's army. Hamilton was a clever fellow, with a lot of go in him—born illegitimate, of course, though his father was a gentleman. But illegitimacy often spurred men to great deeds. And now that he was appointed Secretary to the Treasury, young Hamilton had made a perfectly sensible proposition. He wanted to take all the vast overhang of war debt—the worthless Continental paper—and bundle it all up into a new government debt, backed by tax revenues that would stabilize the nation's finances.

Of course, these arrangements were never entirely fair. Some Southern states had already paid off their debts. "So why should we pay taxes to bail out the others?" they demanded. But the real bone of contention, the thing that drove the South wild, was the role of New York.

For before Hamilton announced his plan, he'd had to consider one big question. By the end of the war, the promissory notes issued by Congress, and the individual states, had become almost worthless. So how much of the good new paper would you get for them? Ten pounds for every hundred of the old notes? Twenty? How generous should the government be?

Just as Master had done a few years before, some brave speculators had bought up quite a bit of the old debt at huge discounts, from men who needed the cash and were glad enough to get something for their worthless notes. Many of these sellers were from the South. Of course, if a speculator could have got inside information about what the conversion rate was going to be, he'd make a killing. Quite properly, until the public announcement, Hamilton hadn't breathed a word.

Not so his deputy. A New York man, of course. He told his friends.

And the word was—astoundingly that the debt would be redeemed at par. Full price. Any speculator who could get his hands on the paper cheap could make a fortune.

Among the lucky merchants of New York, therefore, a feeding frenzy had developed. Southern gentlemen, not privy to what was afoot, were glad to find eager takers for any paper they cared to sell. Until they discovered the truth. Then there was an outcry.

"You accursed New York Yankees—you're feasting upon the sorrows of the South."

"If you weren't short of cash, or understood the market, you wouldn't be in this mess," the New York insiders cruelly responded.

Such insider dealing might still be legal, but one thing was certain:

New York was hated. And not only by the South. Anyone who'd sold their paper cheap felt aggrieved. As for Jefferson, as a Virginia plantation owner himself, there was no doubt where his sympathies lay. He looked upon the New York profiteers with loathing.

❖

And John Master was just about to give Jefferson a few choice words about the shortcomings of improvident gentlemen from the South when, seeing James and Weston's embarrassed faces, he paused, and checked himself.

What was he thinking of? In a short while, his grandson would be departing for Harvard. James, too, would be departing, for God knows how many months, to England. Did he really want to incur James's anger, and leave young Weston with the memory of his grandfather making a scene with the great Thomas Jefferson?

James's journey was necessary. It was some years since Albion had retired from his business in London. Despite what he saw as Grey's poor behavior, John Master had continued to do business with the senior Albion, but on his retirement the Masters had selected another agent, who had proved to be unsatisfactory. James was going over to London to find another. In a way, Master wished that his son were not going just now.

"You're traveling to Europe at an interesting time," he had remarked to him. But a dangerous one also, in his estimation.

When the news of the revolution in France had reached New York in the fall of 1789, many people had rejoiced, including James. Before long, James had received a letter from his friend the Count de Chablis. "He says that Lafayette and his friends are all supporting it. They want a new republic. America is their model." Soon, even young Weston had been talking about the blessings of the new French freedoms—Liberty, Equality, Fraternity. It all sounded very fine. But not to John Master.

"It will end in a bloodbath," he warned them. "Lafayette may dream of America—I dare say he does—but this French business isn't the same at all. It'll turn into a civil war, and civil wars get ugly."

James did not agree. Chablis was confident, he told his father, that a compromise would be reached and that the French would soon be living with a limited monarchy, run by a parliament—something like England.

John Master, however, had reminded James and Weston bleakly: "You forget the power of the mob. When there was a civil war in England, they cut off the king's head."

"You're just a Tory, Grandfather," Weston had said with a laugh.

"Take care, all the same," Master had counseled James. "And stay away from Paris, whatever you do."

He did harbor one other hope for James's journey, though. No word had been heard from Vanessa for a long time. He supposed she was probably in London now. Though James had been having a discreet affair with a charming widow in New York for the last couple of years, Master hoped that his son might settle down with a new wife one day, but first his nonexistent marriage to Vanessa would have to be formally ended. Perhaps, he had gently suggested to James, this might be a useful business to attend to while he was over there.

So now, to restore peace and harmony, he bowed stiffly to Jefferson.

"I must apologize, sir, for my intemperate language," he said politely. "And you must forgive me if I rise to defend the city where I was born. I am like a loyal husband, who defends his wife against criticism, even if he knows she has her faults."

It was graciously said, and James looked relieved. Weston was glancing hopefully at Jefferson.

But Jefferson, who was not entirely without vanity, did not seem ready to reciprocate just yet. Tall, ramrod-straight, his finely hewn face still wore an expression of distaste. And it was while the brief silence persisted that Master, as much to reassure himself as anything, added one further thought.

"I am bound to say, sir, that whatever New York's shortcomings, when you consider its position, its great harbor and its natural advantages, I hardly think it likely that a better capital could be found."

And now a little gleam of triumph appeared in the great man's eye.

"I believe you will discover," he responded, "that the matter of America's capital will soon be settled. And not," he added firmly, "as you wish."

"How so?" Master frowned. "Is Congress so anxious to return to Philadelphia?"

"Philadelphia is a fine city, and I should sooner be there than here. But I believe we shall build a new capital, further south."

"Build a new capital?"

"Exactly."

"That will cost Congress a great deal of money," Master remarked drily. "I hope they can afford it. And may I ask where?"

"Down on the Potomac River."

"The Potomac?" Master looked astonished. "But it's all swamp down there."

"Frankly, I'd sooner a swamp than New York," said Jefferson, not without relish.

Could the Virginian be telling the truth? New York was to be abandoned in favor of a swamp? The idea seemed preposterous. Master glanced at his son. But James only nodded.

"That is the latest word, Father," he said. "I just heard of it today. Philadelphia will be the interim capital, then everything will move to the new place."

For a moment Master could scarcely believe them, as he looked from one to the other.

"Is this a joke?" he cried.

"No, Father," said James. Behind him, Jefferson gave a faint smile.

And then, his good intentions all forgotten, poor Master burst out in a rage.

"Then damn your Potomac swamp, sir," he shouted at Jefferson. "And damn you too!"

"I think," said Jefferson to James, in a dignified manner, "it is time that I left." And he turned. But Master would have the last word.

"You can do what you like, sir," he cried, "but I'll tell you this. New York is the true capital of America. Every New Yorker knows it, and by God, we always shall."

Niagara

T HE INDIAN GIRL watched the path. A number of men from
the boat had already taken the trail through the woods. She had
seen them emerge onto the big platform of grass and rock, and start at the
sudden roar of the water.

She was nine. She had come to the mighty waterfall with her family.
Soon they would continue into Buffalo.

✣

Frank walked beside his father. It was a bright October day. Above the
trees the sky was blue. They were alone, but he could tell from the
crushed red and yellow leaves on the trail that many people had been that
way.

"We're nearly there," said his father. Weston Master was wearing a
homespun coat, which he'd unbuttoned. The mist had made it damp, but
it was being warmed by the sun. He had tied a big handkerchief around
his neck. Today he'd fastened a wampum belt round his waist. It was an
old belt and Weston did not wear it often, so as to preserve it. He was carrying a stout walking stick and smoking a cigar. He smelled good.

Frank knew his father liked to have his family around him. "I don't
remember my mother at all," he would say. "As for my father, he was away
fighting when I was a boy. And after I went to Harvard, I never saw him
again." At home in the evening he'd sit in his wing chair by the fire, and
his wife and five children—the four girls and young Frank—would all

have to be there, and he'd play games or read to them. Weston would read amusing books, like Washington Irving's tale of Rip Van Winkle, or the funny history of New York, told by his invented Dutchman Diedrich Knickerbocker. "Why is he called Diedrich?" he would ask. "Because he Died Rich," the children would chorus.

Every summer, the whole family would spend two weeks with Aunt Abigail and her family in Westchester County, and another couple of weeks with their cousins up in Dutchess County. The more members of his family he had around him, the happier Weston Master seemed to be.

But last month, when the governor had invited him to come north for the opening of the big canal, Weston had said: "I'll just take Frank with me."

It wasn't the first time Frank had been up the Hudson River. Three years earlier, soon after his seventh birthday, there had been a bad outbreak of yellow fever in New York. There was often some fever in the port. "The ships bring it from the south," his father would say. "And we're always at risk. New York's as hot as Jamaica in the summer, you know." But when a lot of people in the city had started dying, Weston had taken his whole family upriver to Albany until it was over.

Frank had enjoyed that journey. On the way up, they'd gazed west at the Catskill Mountains, and his father had reminded them: "That's where Rip Van Winkle fell asleep." Frank had liked Albany. The busy town was the capital of New York State now. His father had said this was a good idea, since Manhattan was at the bottom end of the state, and had plenty of business anyway, but Albany was nearer the middle, and growing fast. One day, Weston had taken them all to the old fort at Ticonderoga, and told them how the Americans had taken it from the British. Frank wasn't very interested in history, but he'd enjoyed seeing the geometric lines of the old stone walls and the gun emplacements.

This time, after coming up the Hudson as far as Albany, Frank and his father had headed west. First they'd taken a coach along the old turnpike road across the northern lip of the Catskills to Syracuse, then along the top of the long, thin Finger Lakes, past Seneca and Geneva, and after that, all the way across to Batavia and finally Buffalo. It had taken many days.

Frank reckoned he knew why his father had brought him. Of course, he was the only boy in the family, but it wasn't only that. He liked to know how things worked. At home, he enjoyed it when his father took him onto the steamboats and let him inspect their furnaces and the pistons. "It's the same principle as the big steam-powered cotton gins they have in England," Weston had explained. "The plantations we finance in the South mostly produce raw cotton, which we ship across the ocean to those gins." Sometimes Frank would go down to the waterside to watch the men packing the cargoes of ice, so that it would stay frozen all the way down to the kitchens of the big houses in tropical Martinique. When the workmen had installed gas lighting in their house that spring, he'd watched every inch of piping as it went in.

So it was only natural, he supposed, that his father should have chosen him of all his children to accompany him now, to witness the opening of the huge engineering project in the North.

❖

Weston Master took a draw on his cigar. The path was like a tunnel, but a short way ahead there was an arch of bright sky, where the trees ended. He glanced down at his son and smiled to himself. He was glad to have Frank with him. It was good for a boy to spend time alone with his father. And besides, there were some particular things he wanted to share with his son on this journey.

More than thirty years had passed since the unexpected death of his own father in England. The letter, which had come from old Mr. Albion, who had gone to some trouble to discover all the details of the affair, explained that he had been set upon by ruffians in the city, probably intent only upon theft. James Master had put up such a fight, though, that one of the fellows had struck him a terrible blow with a cudgel, from which he had not recovered. The news had not only come as a great shock to Weston, it had also set the seal on a prejudice that remained with him for the rest of his life. All through his New York childhood, for reasons he never quite understood, England had seemed to claim the mother who was missing from his home. It was the war with England, also, which kept his father away, and made the other boys at school call his father a traitor. And these wounds had only partly healed when this news came that, like some ancient god who can never be satisfied, England had taken his father's life as well. Even though he was a rational young man at Harvard when it happened, it was not so surprising that a primitive sense of aversion to England and all things English had settled in his soul.

As time passed, the scope of this aversion grew wider. While he was at Harvard, at the time of the French Revolution, it had seemed to Weston that perhaps in that country, inspired by the example of America, a new European freedom might be dawning. But as the liberal constitution for which Lafayette and his friends had hoped gave way first to the bloodbath of the Terror, and then to Napoleon's empire, Weston had concluded that the freedoms of the New World might never be possible in the Old. Europe was too mired in ancient hatreds and rivalries between nations. The whole Continent, in Weston's imagination, was a dangerous place, and he wanted as little to do with it as possible.

He was in excellent company. Hadn't Washington, in his farewell address, warned the new American nation to avoid foreign entanglements? Jefferson, that standard-bearer of the European Enlightenment, and former resident of Paris, had likewise declared that America should stick to honest friendship with all nations, but entangling alliances with none. Madison agreed. Even John Quincy Adams, the great diplomat, who'd lived in countries from Russia to Portugal, said the same. Europe was trouble.

Proof of their wisdom had come a dozen years ago, when Britain and Napoleon's empire were locked in their great struggle and the United States, bound to France by a treaty of friendship, had found itself trapped between the conflicting powers. Weston had felt first irritation as Britain, unable to tolerate America's neutral trade with her enemy, had started to harass American shipping; then despair, as the disputes grew into a wider conflict; and then fury when, in 1812, America and Britain had once again found themselves at war.

His memories of that war were bitter. The British blockade of New York harbor had nearly ruined his trade. The fighting all along the eastern seaboard, and up in Canada, had cost tens of millions of dollars. The damn British had even burned down the president's mansion in Washington. When the wretched business finally drew to a close after three years, and Napoleon had left the stage of history, Weston's relief was matched by an iron determination.

Never again should America be in such a position. She must be strong, like a fortress. Strong enough to stand entirely alone. Recently, President Monroe had taken the idea even further. To make America really secure, he had declared, the whole of the western side of the Atlantic—North

America, the Caribbean, South America—should be an American sphere of influence. The other nations could squabble in Europe if they liked, but not in the Americas. It was a daring claim, but Weston was in total agreement with it.

For why should Americans need the Old World across the ocean, when they had their own, huge continent on their doorstep? Mighty river systems, rich valleys, endless forests, magnificent mountains, fertile plains— a land of endless opportunities, stretching westward beyond the sunset. The freedom and wealth of a continent, thousands of miles of it, was theirs for the taking.

And it was this great truth, this grand vision, that Weston wanted to impress upon his son on their journey west.

For New York at least, and for the Master family in particular, the great canal that had just been built was an integral part of this grand new equation. And before they had left the city, he'd tried to show Frank its importance. Spreading out a map of North America on the table in his library, he had pointed to some key features.

"See, Frank, here are the Appalachian Mountains, beginning way down in Georgia, and extending all the way up the eastern side of the country. In North Carolina they become the Smoky Mountains. Then they run right up through Virginia, Pennsylvania, New Jersey, and into New York, where they become the Catskills first, and then the Adirondacks. The old Thirteen Colonies were all on the east side of the Appalachians. But the other side is the future, Frank. The great American West." And he had grandly swept his hand across the map all the way to the Pacific.

The parts of the map that already belonged to the United States were colored. The territory in the far west, beyond the Rocky Mountains, was not. After the War of 1812, the Spanish had given up Florida, but their huge Mexican empire still swept all the way up the Pacific coast until it came to Oregon Country, the open territory which America and Britain controlled together. The vast swathe of territory east of the Rockies, however, from Canada all the way down to New Orleans, was colored. This was the Louisiana Purchase, as big as the old thirteen states put together, and which Jefferson had bought from Napoleon for a song. "Napoleon was a great general," Weston told Frank, "but a lousy businessman." Most of the Louisiana Purchase hadn't been organized into states yet, though

Weston believed that that would come in time. It was the nearer west, however, under the Great Lakes, to which he had directed his son's attention.

"Look at these new states, Frank," he said. "Ohio, Indiana, Illinois—with Michigan territory above them, and the states of Kentucky and Tennessee below. They're rich in everything, especially grain. The future breadbasket of the world. But New York doesn't benefit. All the grain, and the hogs and the other goods from the west are flowing south, down the Ohio River, then down the Mississippi"—he traced the line of the huge river systems with his finger—"until they finally come to New Orleans for shipment." He smiled. "So that, my boy, is why we have built the Erie Canal."

Geography had certainly been kind to the New York men. Up near Albany, on the western side of the River Hudson where the Mohawk River came to join it, the huge, broad gap between the Catskills and the Adirondack Mountains offered a viable terrain through which to lay a canal. From the Hudson, the canal ran westward all the way to the edge of the Great Lakes in the Midwest.

"Here," said Weston, "just below Lake Ontario and above Lake Erie, lies the town of Buffalo. All kinds of produce come in there. And the canal ends just below Buffalo."

"So now we can use the canal to ship goods east instead of south?"

"Exactly. Bringing loads overland is expensive, and slow. But barges filled with grain can get from Buffalo to New York in only six days. As for the cost . . . that drops from a hundred to only five dollars a ton. It'll change everything. The wealth of the West will flow through New York."

"Not so good for New Orleans, I guess."

"No . . . Well, that's their problem."

Yesterday, Weston and Frank had spent the day inspecting the final sections of the canal. Those had been happy hours. An engineer had shown them round. Frank had been doing what he liked best, and Weston had been proud to see that the engineer was impressed with the boy's questions.

But today there was something else he wanted to share with his son.

He had introduced the subject already, once or twice, during their journey. As they started up the Hudson, he had looked back, past the stately cliffs of the Palisades to where, in the distance, New York harbor was a haze of golden light, and remarked: "It's a fine sight, isn't it, Frank?"

But it had been hard to tell what the boy was thinking. As they came to West Point, and stared at the splendor of the Hudson Valley as it wound its way northward—a sight that always brought a thrill of romance to his own heart—Weston had again called the scene to his son's attention. "Mighty fine, Pa," Frank had said, but only, his father suspected, because he reckoned it was expected of him. As they'd taken the long road westward, passed lakes and mountains, seen magnificent panoramas and gorgeous sunsets, Weston had gently pointed them out, and let the boy take them in.

For as well as the continent's scope and wealth, it was America's spiritual lineaments he wanted to show his son. The vast splendor of the land, the magnificence of its freedom, the glory of nature and its testimony to the sublime. The Old World had nothing better than this—equally picturesque perhaps, but never so grand. Here in the beauty of the Hudson Valley, it stretched to the plains and deserts and soaring mountains of the west: nature, untrameled, under the hand of God. America, as seen by its native sons, for countless centuries before his own ancestors came. He wanted to share it with his son, and see its mighty wonder thrill the boy's heart.

That's why he had brought him here today. If the stupendous sight they were about to see didn't stir the boy, then he didn't know what would.

"Lake Ontario is higher than Lake Erie," he said quietly to Frank, as they came toward the end of the path, "so as the water flows through the channel that leads between them, it comes to a place where it has to drop. It's a pretty big drop, as you'll see."

Frank had enjoyed preparing for the journey. Back in the city, he'd been interested, when his father had demonstrated the purpose of the canal on the map. Frank liked maps. In his library, his father also had a big framed print of the commissioners' plan for New York City. It showed a long, perfect grid of streets. The city had already advanced several miles from its old limits under the British, but the plan was that one day the grid should run all the way up to Harlem. Frank loved the simple, harsh geometry of the plan, and the fact that it was about the future, not the past.

He'd enjoyed inspecting the canal yesterday, too. The Big Ditch, people called it, for a joke. But there was nothing to joke about really, because the canal was truly amazing. Frank knew every fact about it. The canal plowed its mighty furrow westward for a hundred and sixty miles up the Mohawk River Valley, and then another two hundred miles across to the channel near the town of Buffalo. In the course of its long journey, the level of the canal had to rise six hundred feet, by means of fifty locks, each with a twelve-foot drop. Irish laborers had dug the trench; imported German masons had built its walls.

Yesterday, he had been allowed to operate the sluices and help move the massive gates of one of the locks, and the engineer had told him how many gallons of water were displaced, and at what rate, and he'd measured the time it took with a stopwatch. And this had made him very happy.

Tomorrow at the official opening, Governor DeWitt Clinton was going to welcome them aboard a barge that would take them through all fifty locks and down the Hudson to New York. The governor was the nephew of the old Patriot Governor Clinton from the time of the War of Independence. He was taking two big buckets of water from Lake Erie, so he could pour them into New York harbor at the end of the journey.

Frank and his father were at the end of the path now. As they came out of the trees, Frank blinked in the bright light, and the roar of the waters hit him. People were scattered in groups on the broad ledge; some of them had climbed up onto some rocks for an even more dizzying view of the falls. He noticed a group of Indians, sitting twenty yards away on the right.

"Well, Frank, there it is," said his father. "Niagara Falls."

They gazed at the falls in silence. The stupendous curve of the great curtain of water was the biggest thing Frank had ever seen. The spray boomed up in billowing clouds from the river far below.

"Sublime," said his father quietly. "The hand of the divine, Frank. The voice of God."

Frank wanted to say something, but he did not know what. He waited a little. Then he thought he had an inspiration.

"How many gallons of water go over it in a minute?"

His father didn't answer at first. "I don't know, son," he said finally. His voice sounded disappointed. Frank lowered his head. Then he felt his father's hand on his shoulder. "Just listen to it, Frank," he said.

Frank listened. He'd been listening for a little while when he noticed the Indian girl. She was about his own age, he reckoned, and she was staring toward them. Perhaps she was looking at him. He wasn't sure.

Frank wasn't much interested in girls, but there was something about the Indian girl that made him glance at her again. She was small, but neatly made. He guessed she was pretty. And she was still staring in his direction, as if something interested her.

"Pa," said Frank, "that Indian girl is staring at us."

His father shrugged. "We could go down to the river, if you like," his father said, "and look up at the falls from below. There's a path. Takes a while, of course, but they say it's worth it."

"All right," said Frank.

Then Frank saw that the Indian girl was coming toward them. She moved with such a light step, she seemed almost to float over the ground. His father saw too and stopped to look at her.

Frank knew a bit about Indians. When the War of 1812 had come, a great leader called Tecumseh had persuaded a lot of them to fight for the British. Here in Mohawk Country, many of the local Indians had joined him, which had been a big mistake. Tecumseh had been killed, and they'd lost out badly. But there were still plenty of Mohawks around these parts. He supposed that's what she must be.

The other people on the ledge were watching the Indian girl and smiling. Nobody seemed to mind her coming up to them like that. She was such a pretty little thing.

Frank had thought the girl was looking at him, but as she came close, he realized with a shade of disappointment that her eyes were focused, not upon him, but his father. She went right up to him and pointed at his waist.

"It's my wampum belt she's interested in," his father said.

The girl seemed to want to touch it. Weston nodded, to let her know she could. She put her fingers on the wampum. Then she walked round his father, who obligingly lifted aside his coat so that she could see all of the belt. When she had done, she stood in front of his father, looking up at him.

She was wearing moccasins, but Frank could see that she had neat little feet. He also noticed that, although her skin was brown, her eyes were blue. His father noticed too.

"Look at her eyes, Frank. That means she's got some white blood in her somewhere. You see that occasionally." He addressed the girl. "Mohawk?"

She signed that she was not. "Lenape," she said quietly.

"You know who the Lenape are, Frank?" said his father. "That's what they call the Indians that used to live around Manhattan. You hardly see any now. What was left of them scattered, joined larger tribes, went west. There's quite a few in Ohio, I believe. But one group stayed together and settled at the far end of Lake Erie. The Turtle clan, they're called. There's not a lot of them, and they don't give trouble. Keep to themselves, mostly."

"So her people were around when our family first came to Manhattan?"

"Probably." He gazed down at her. "She's a pretty little thing, isn't she?"

Frank didn't answer, but then the girl turned and stared into his eyes, and he felt awkward, and looked away.

"She's all right, I guess," he said.

"You want my wampum belt, don't you?" his father said to the girl. He used a calm, friendly voice, the same as when he was talking to the dog at home. "Well, you can't have it."

"Can she understand you, Pa?" asked Frank.

"No idea," said his father. Then something caught his eye. "Hmm," he said. "What's that?" And he signed to the girl that he wanted to look at an object hanging round her neck. Frank could see that the girl didn't want him to, but since his father had let her look at his belt, she couldn't very well refuse.

Without making any sudden movement, his father reached forward.

It was so neatly made. Two tiny rings of wood glued together formed a little double-sided frame, with a cross of twine binding them together for extra security. A thin leather thong passing through the frame made a loop, so that the girl could hang it round her neck. The precious object in the little frame gleamed softly in the light as his father held it up and examined it.

"Well, I'm damned," he said. "Do you know what this is, Frank?"

"Looks like a new dollar."

"It is and it isn't. We've been minting US dollars one way or another for forty years now, but this is older. It's a Dutch dollar. A lion dollar, they used to call them."

"I never heard of that."

"People still used them when I was a boy, but they were so old and worn by then, we called them dog dollars. This one's never been in circulation, I'd swear. It must be a hundred and fifty years old—maybe more—but you can see it's still like new." He shook his head in wonderment, and handed it to Frank.

Frank looked at the coin. He could see there was a splendid lion depicted on the front and a knight of some sort on the back. He gave it back to his father.

His father looked at the girl, considering. "I wonder if she'd sell it to me," he said. He made a sign to the girl that he wanted to buy it. She looked alarmed, and shook her head. "Hmm," said his father. He thought for a moment. Then he pointed to the wampum belt. "Trade?"

Frank saw the girl hesitate, but only for a moment. Then she shook her head again, and put out her hand for the coin. She looked unhappy.

But his father wasn't a man to give up easily. He smiled at her and offered again, keeping the coin well out of her reach.

Again she shook her head and held out her hand.

His father looked over to where the Indians were sitting. They were watching impassively.

"That'll be her family, I should think," he said. "Maybe they'll tell her to sell it to me." He wound the leather thong round the coin, making a little package of it. "I reckon I'll speak to them," he said.

By now the girl was visibly distressed. She thrust out her hand again, urgently.

"Give it back to her, Pa," said Frank suddenly. "Leave her alone."

His father turned to him with a frown, surprised. "What's the matter, son?"

"It's hers, Pa. You should give it back to her."

His father paused a moment. "I thought maybe you might have liked it."

"No."

His father wasn't too pleased, but he handed the coin back to the girl with a shrug. She took it and, clasping it tightly, ran back across the grass to her family.

His father stared out irritably at the water.

"Well," he said, "I guess that's Niagara Falls."

After they had started back along the path, his father said: "Don't get emotional when you're trading, Frank."

"I won't, Pa."

"That girl. She may have got white blood, somewhere back, but she's still a savage, you know."

That evening, they ate with the governor in a big hall, and all the people who were coming on the boat tomorrow toasted the new canal and said how grand it would be. Frank was pretty excited at the thought of the trip ahead, and all the locks they would be going through.

Then after the meal, while the men were sitting at the table, drinking and smoking their cigars, Frank asked his father if he could go outside for a while.

"Course you can, son—only don't go too far. Then when you come back, we'll go to the lodgings and turn in. Get a good night's sleep before tomorrow."

Buffalo was quite small. People referred to it as a village, but Frank reckoned it was a small town really, and you could see the place was expanding. There was no one about, so it was quiet. It was clear overhead, but it wasn't cold.

He crossed over the canal and came to a short stretch of riverfront where there was an open area, with some rocks and a stand of pine trees, and he sat on one of the rocks and gazed at the water. He could feel a light breeze pressing softly on his cheek, and soon he reckoned that it was getting a little stronger because he could hear it, now, up in the trees.

And as he sat there, the image of the girl came into his mind, and he thought about her for a while. He was glad for what he had done, and he wondered where she was now, and if maybe she was thinking about him too. And he hoped she might be. So although he was getting a little cold, he stayed there some time, and thought of her some more, and listened to the voice of the wind, sighing in the trees.

After that, he went back.

Past Five Points

MARY O'DONNELL LEFT the store early. She was moving quickly. Instead of following her usual route past Fraunces Tavern, she ducked into Whitehall, glancing over her shoulder as she did so, just to make sure the devil wasn't there. Not a sign of him, thank God. She'd told him she wouldn't be leaving for another hour. If he came looking for her, he'd find her long gone. He wouldn't be pleased about that. Not pleased at all.

She didn't care. Just so long as he didn't know where she was.

The area had changed a lot in recent years. Two big fires—the first in 1835, when she was little more than a baby, the second four years ago—had gutted many of the handsome old blocks below Wall Street. The fine old houses, Dutch and Georgian, had gone. The southern tip of Manhattan was commercial rather than residential now. The store where she'd been working wasn't so bad, but she wanted to make a break, escape from where she was and start a new life. Away from the devil and all his works. And now, thanks to her guardian angel, she might have a chance.

Normally Mary's route took her up the East River, past the docks and the merchants' counting houses on South Street as far as Fulton. Then west for a block. Then northward, picking up the Bowery. She'd hurry past Five Points, then cross Canal by the Bull's Head Tavern with its bear-baiting pit. From there it was only four blocks more to Delancey Street, where she and her father lived.

But today, walking quickly up Whitehall, she turned with a sigh of relief into the great long thoroughfare of Broadway. The sidewalk was crowded. No sign of the devil.

Soon she was at Trinity Church. Some years ago, it had been rebuilt in High Gothic style. Its pointed arches and sturdy spire added a note of old-fashioned solemnity to the scene, as if to remind the passer-by that the Protestant money men of Wall Street, who frequented it, preserved a faith just as good as any piety from medieval times. Opposite its doors, however, Wall Street was more pagan than ever. Why, even the Federal Hall, where Washington had taken his presidential oath, was now replaced with a perfect Greek temple, whose stout columns contained the Custom House.

She gazed ahead. Back in the days of Washington, the houses on Broadway started to peter out into fields and farmsteads a half-mile or so above Wall Street. But now Manhattan was completely built up, from river to river, for another three miles. And each year, the great grid of New York extended further—as if some giant, with a mighty hand, was planting rows of houses every season. In front of her, Broadway's busy thoroughfare stretched in a wide, straight line for another two miles until it made a half-turn to the north-west, and continued on its way in a great diagonal, up the line of the old Bloomingdale road. Her destination was a good half-mile above that turn.

She came to the old Common. It was still a large triangle of open ground, but some while ago a huge new City Hall had been built there. Like some gaudy French or Italian palace faced with marble, it stared proudly southward down the broad avenue. If one looked across the back of City Hall, however, one noticed a curious thing. The north facade was not faced with marble like the front, but with plain brownstone. At the time it was built, most of the city, and all the best quarters, had lain to the south. There had been no need to spend money on the northern facade therefore, which would only be seen by poor folk. And behind the gaudy palace, in the big, central sink of the city, there were poor folk in abundance.

In Five Points.

Once upon a time, there had been a big old pond there, and the village of freed slaves, with swampy land beyond. The pond and the swamp had still been there in Washington's day, as the city started to extend northward around it. But then the city authorities had drained them, and lain a canal to draw away the water. And after that, they had built over the canal with streets of brick houses.

Five Points. It was a swamp now, all right. A moral swamp: an infected warren of streets and alleys, tenements and whorehouses. In the middle of it all, the old hulk of a former brewery, like a cathedral of vice, opened its doors to welcome all that was unholy. If you wanted to watch cocks fight, or dogs kill rats, or have your pocket picked, or find a whore and catch the pox, you went to Five Points, where someone would be sure to oblige you. If you wanted to see gangs of Protestant Bowery Boys fight gangs of Catholics, you could often see that too. Travelers said it was the most absolute slum in the world.

And who lived there? That was easy to tell. Immigrants.

There were plenty of them. George Washington had known a city of thirty or forty thousand souls. By the time the Erie Canal was completed, one could add another hundred thousand, a population which far surpassed any other city in America, even Philadelphia. During Mary's childhood, the increase had accelerated even faster. She'd heard the population was well past half a million now.

They were all sorts. Many were escaping from the Old World to take their chance in the New. Her own family had come from Ireland twenty years earlier. Others came from the upstate farmlands, from Connecticut, New Jersey or further off, looking for whatever the city might offer. In the last two years, however, a new and sudden tide had washed against America's shores, larger than any before, and sent there by the tragedy of the Irish Famine.

They came by the shipload. And though they weren't the poorest Irish—for at least they, or relations in America, had been able to pay the fare—once they had arrived, they usually had few resources. And for newcomers to the city, if all else failed and you'd nowhere to go, then the last resort was the filthy tenements of Five Points. God knows how many poor Irish were crowded in there now.

The area contained one noble building: a huge rectangle, the size of a castle, whose tall window frames and thick stone columns were splendidly sculpted in the Egyptian style—so that you might have thought the ancient pharaohs had deserted their pyramids and come to live in New York. Whether its inmates appreciated the architecture was doubtful, for this was the local prison, known as "The Tombs"—a blunt reminder that the New World, too, could be cold and hard as stone.

But as she glanced in the direction of Five Points, there was one thing Mary was sure of: every prisoner, every prostitute, every tavernkeeper, every poor Irish newcomer—every one of them knew the devil, and he knew them. Like as not, he was in there now. She quickened her pace, therefore, until she was well past.

Only once did she pause, for a moment or two, at Reade Street, to look into the handsome windows of A. T. Stewart's Dry Goods Store. She didn't go past it often, but who could resist peeping at the calicos and silks, the beautiful gloves and shawls set out there? Once, she'd even dared to go in and look at some of the ladies' underwear they kept in drawers behind the counter. Such lovely lacy things. Not that she could think of buying them, of course. But it gave her a thrill, just to look.

She paused not even a minute, and was turning to hurry on, when she felt a hand clamp upon her shoulder.

"Jesus, Mary and Joseph!" she cried.

"Going somewhere?" asked the devil.

"Mind your own business."

"You said you had to work late."

"The manager changed his mind."

"Don't lie to me, Mary. I always know when you're lying. I've been following you all the way from Fraunces Tavern," her brother Sean said.

"You're the devil all right," she said.

She couldn't remember when she'd first given Sean his nickname. A long time ago. The devil. It suited him. She could never be sure what he was up to, and often it was better not to know. He was only sixteen when he first killed a man—or so it was rumored. For when people were killed in Five Points, their bodies usually disappeared. Anyway, his reputation had helped him in his career.

Not that he was anything but a kind brother to her—she couldn't deny it—but he was always wanting to control her. And that she couldn't tolerate.

"So where are you going? You may as well tell me, since I'm sure to find out."

"Damn you to hell."

"You're too late for that, I should think," he said cheerfully.

"I'm looking for a position."

"I told you there's a job at Lord & Taylor," he reminded her. "It's a good store. Doing well."

But Lord & Taylor was in Catherine Street, which was too near to Five Points. She didn't want to go there. Anyway, she wanted something entirely different.

"I'm going into service," she said. "In a decent house."

"Does Father know?"

"No," she answered, "I haven't told him."

"Well," said Sean, "I can't blame you for that."

Their father, John O'Donnell, had been a good man, until 1842. That was the year his work on the big aqueduct had ended. Also the year his wife had died. After that, he'd changed. Not dramatically at first. He'd done his best to keep the family together. But then he'd started drinking a bit, and got into a fight or two. He'd been dismissed from his next job, and the one after that. By the time she was ten, although she was the youngest, Mary had been keeping house for him while her two elder sisters went their own ways. Her brother Sean had helped her then, and still helped her now. She had to give the devil his due.

But the last months had been impossible—since the death of Brian Boru.

Brian Boru had been her father's bull terrier, and he'd been prouder of that dog than anything. Whatever money he had was tied up in Brian Boru. "He's my investment," he'd say. You'd have thought he owned a bank. Brian Boru was a fighter—put him in the ring, and there weren't many dogs he couldn't tear apart.

John O'Donnell used to bet on Brian Boru. He called these bets investments. So far as Mary knew, apart from the money she brought home and anything Sean gave him, Brian Boru's winnings had been her father's only source of income for some years. As the owner of Brian Boru, even when he was the worse for drink, Mr. O'Donnell had carried himself with a certain style. But now Brian Boru was dead, and her father had nothing to live for. The drinking had got worse. If she gave him her wages, they'd be gone in a day. And it wasn't only the money. The lodgings they had on Delancey Street were no palace, but at least they were a good half-mile up the Bowery from Five Points. The way things were going, however, she was sure the landlord would soon tell her father to leave. Even Sean might have difficulty preventing that.

"I've got to get out, Sean," she cried.

"I know," said the devil. "I'll take care of Father."

"Don't kill him. Sean, promise me you won't kill him."

"Would I do such a thing?"

"Yes," she said, "you would."

"You've a terrible view of my character," said Sean with a smile. "Now would you guess where I was before I came looking for you?"

"With some woman, no doubt."

That was how she usually saw him, with a woman on his arm, two women sometimes, strolling down the Bowery dressed in his fancy coat. A poor man's dandy, with a smile on his face—and a knife in his pocket.

"No, Mary. I was at a bar mitzvah."

"A bar mitzvah? For the love of God why? Are you not a Christian any more?"

"We don't only look after the Irish, Mary. Christian, Jew or heathen: if they're in my ward, I'm their friend. I helped that family get naturalized when they arrived."

"I wouldn't feel comfortable in a Jewish house."

"The Jews are like the Irish, Mary. Do a Jew a favor, and he'll never forget." He grinned. "They quarrel with each other, too." He paused. "So where are you going?"

"Uptown."

"I'll walk with you."

That was the last thing she needed. Uptown, the streets became genteel again. Rich people lived up there. The place she was going wanted a quiet, respectable girl. What would they think if they caught sight of Sean, the Bowery boy in his loud coat, the devil from Five Points? She'd sooner they didn't even know she had a brother. For if they knew, they'd be sure to ask what he did, and what could she say?

What did Sean do? Organize the local ward? Yes. Help the poor? No doubt. Stuff ballot boxes? Certainly. Run errands for his friend Fernando Wood? Why not? Enforce his will, at point of knife? Better not ask.

Sean would do whatever it took to please the boys at Tammany Hall.

Tammany was a sort of Indian name. The Tammany men called themselves Braves, and their leaders were sachems, just like an Indian tribe. It was organized a bit like a tribe, too—a loose collection of groups and gangs who'd banded together for mutual assistance. They had a meeting place, though, which they called Tammany Hall, on the other side of the Common. And they were certainly effective. If you were a new immigrant, you went to Tammany Hall. They helped you find a place to live,

maybe helped with your rent, found you a job—especially if you were
Irish. You might become a fireman. Your wife and daughter might work
at home, stitching ready-to-wear clothes for Brooks Brothers. Then
Tammany Hall told you who to vote for. And made sure they were
elected, too.

If Tammany did favors, it expected favors in return. You kept on the
right side of Tammany, if you had any sense. And there were fellows like
Sean to persuade you of the wisdom of doing so, should you have any
doubts. Respectable people didn't like Tammany.

"I'm all right by myself," she said.

"I'll treat you to the train," he offered.

This might have been tempting. The coaches of the New York and
Harlem Railroad were so plush that even the rich Wall Street men rode in
them. Leaving from beside City Hall, they lumbered sedately northward
past Five Points, then trundled up the Bowery and picked up Fourth
Avenue. Until they reached the end of the residential neighborhoods,
where quiet was demanded, they were pulled by teams of heavy horses.
Above the residential area, the coaches were coupled to steam engines for
the long journey up to Harlem.

"I can't," she said. "I promised to meet Gretchen along the way."

"Oh God," he cried. "I might have guessed. The chocolate girl. Little
goody two-shoes."

Mary might have said, "She doesn't like you either." But she didn't.

"So it's Gretchen that's found you this position."

"It's a family she knows. I may not get it."

He shrugged. "Suit yourself."

They walked on together, past the hospital and the Masonic Hall. At
Canal Street, Broadway rose a little where it had once crossed over marshy
ground. A few minutes more and they came to Houston Street. Here the
planned, rectangular grid of the new city, obscured by the older, V-shaped
pattern at the southern end of the island, began to make itself plain. The
cross-streets began to have numbers instead of names. At Grace Church,
where Broadway made its turn, Mary said, "Gretchen's meeting me up the
road," and her brother said grumpily that she could go on alone. But as
they parted, he reminded her: "I shall find out all about this place, you
know."

Just so long as you don't come there, she thought to herself.

✢

Sure enough, at the corner of Union Square, there was Gretchen.

"Will I do, Gretchen?" Mary cried as she reached her. And she turned herself around to be inspected.

"You're perfect," her friend assured her.

"Not," said Mary, with a sigh, "compared to you." Small, proper, orderly, blue-eyed little Gretchen always had her face well scrubbed, and her golden hair pulled back and pinned. Not a hair out of place, not a speck of dust on her coat. She was as perfect as a china doll. But if Gretchen Keller was your friend, she never let you down.

The Kellers were German. They'd arrived in New York two years before Mary's mother had died. Mr. Keller and his wife kept a little chocolate store on the Bowery at Sixth Street. Mr. Keller's brother, Uncle Willy, kept a cigar store a few doors down, and Gretchen's cousin Hans worked for a piano-maker in the same quarter.

Though most of the Germans who'd come to America were farmers, quite a few were staying in New York. And unless they could afford better, they were settling in the quarter that stretched across from the Bowery to the East River and from Delancey Street in the south, where the O'Donnells lived, up to Fourteenth Street. A mixed quarter had therefore developed, German and Irish, but the two communities got along well enough, because they didn't tread on each other's toes. The Irish men in that quarter were mostly in the laboring and building trades, and the women in domestic service. The Germans worked as tailors, artisans and shopkeepers. So many had come in during the last decade that, despite all the Irish there, people were starting to call the quarter "Kleindeutschland."

So it wasn't surprising that the blonde German and the dark-haired Irish girl should have met and become friends. The Kellers might not approve of John O'Donnell, but they were kind to Mary, and Uncle Willy would still give her father a cigar, out of charity, from time to time. But the future was increasingly clear. South of Delancey Street, as you got closer to Five Points, the area became poorer. North of Delancey, the streets became more and more respectable. The Kellers would soon be moving northward. John O'Donnell looked to be heading south.

"I'm so frightened," Mary confessed, as they walked along Fourteenth Street and turned into Irving Place. "What'll they think of me?"

"The lady's been buying our chocolates for years," Gretchen reminded

her. "She's very nice. And it isn't as if we've come knocking on her door—
it was she who asked my mother if we knew of a girl who'd might like a
position."

"That's because she wants someone respectable like you."

"You're very respectable, Mary."

"What if they saw Sean?"

"They won't."

"What if they ask me what my father does? The last regular work he
had was laying bricks on the aqueduct. And that was years ago. As for
what he does now . . ."

"We'll say your father's a mason. It sounds better. Apart from that,
Mary, just be yourself and tell the truth. You've nothing to worry about."

"Thank God you're coming with me," said Mary, as they entered the
square at the end of Irving Place.

⊹

Gramercy Park was a gracious place. Its rows of big, wide, red-brick
houses, as spacious within as many city mansions, were arranged in a
broad rectangle around a pleasant central garden. It might have been one
of London's quieter, aristocratic squares. If some of the houses built in
New York recently were encumbered with opulence, those of Gramercy
Park kept a classical dignity and restraint. Fit for judges, senators, merchants with libraries. "We are new mansions," they seemed to say, "for old
money." Why, even the land under them had been purchased from one of
Peter Stuyvesant's descendants.

Frank Master had a modest library, but when he got home from his
counting house, he'd gone into the dining room, so that he could unroll
the maps he was carrying along the entire length of the table. It was a fine
room. The table, under a big chandelier, could seat more than twenty.
Over the fireplace hung a large painting, of the Hudson River school,
depicting Niagara Falls.

As he started to unroll the maps, he turned to his wife.

"This Irish girl," he said. "Before you engage her, I want to see her."

"Of course, dear," said his wife. "If you wish it." Her voice was gentle,
but he did not miss the slight edge in it. A danger signal. This was household business. He was trespassing on her territory.

Frank Master loved his wife. They'd been married six years now, and they had two children. If her body was a little fuller than when they'd married, he thought it suited her very well. And she was kind. Hetty Master's religion was simple, warm and practical. She tried to help people whenever she could. He suspected that she secretly felt that the Lord was directing her acts of charity, but rather than say that, she'd just remark that she felt the business in hand was fated. He'd also noticed that, from time to time, she was capable of giving fate a nudge.

When it came to running the household, however, Hetty was not quite so easy-going. A few months before their wedding, Frank's father Weston had died, and they'd begun their married life together with his mother, in the big family house. It had lasted four months. After that, Hetty had gently told him that she and his mother couldn't both run the household, and so they'd better be moving. That very day, as it happened, she'd heard about a house that was available. "I do believe," she'd said firmly, "that it's fated." So that was that. They'd moved to Gramercy Park.

If Frank was determined to interview this Irish girl, he didn't press the point at once. It was better, he'd learned, to play for time. So he changed the subject.

"Look at these maps, Hetty," he said, "and tell me what you think." The reason why he needed the whole table was that the maps covered a territory that ran all the way up the Hudson, from New York to Albany. "The Hudson River Railroad," he said with satisfaction. "The northern sections are all complete. Before long it'll reach us here."

Hetty obligingly gazed at the maps, and smiled. "That'll teach the damn Yankees," she remarked.

George Washington might have called John Master a Yankee, but in the last generation a distinction had grown up. One might speak of Connecticut Yankees, and Boston was certainly Yankee, but the New York men liked to think of themselves as different. Taking the name of the fictitious author of Washington Irving's delightful mock history of the city, they'd started calling themselves Knickerbockers. Of course, there were plenty of Connecticut Yankees, and Boston men too, among the merchants of New York, but the genial distinction was still made. And when it came to any rivalry between New York and Boston, then the Boston men, sure as hell, were damn Yankees.

It wasn't too often that the Boston Yankees got the better of New York. The Knickerbocker merchants had managed to bring most of the Southern cotton trade through their port; more of the swift China trade clippers left from New York than anywhere else, many of them built on the East River too. So maybe a touch of arrogance had blinded the Knicker-bockers to the fact that the Boston men, seeing all the trade coming across from the Midwest by the Erie Canal, had built a rail line across to Albany, to carry goods swiftly to Boston instead of down the Hudson to New York.

Well, that oversight was going to be remedied. When it was completed, the Hudson railway line should pull those goods back to New York again. But that wasn't the only reason why Frank Master wanted to look at the map today.

"So what is your plan, Frank?" his wife asked.

"To be as rich as John Jacob Astor," he said with a grin. Perhaps that was a little ambitious—yet not impossible. After all, the Masters were already rich, whereas everyone knew Astor's story. A poor German immigrant from the little town of Waldorf, Astor had come from his brother's London musical instrument workshop to seek his fortune in the New World, and somehow landed up in the good old fur trade. Before long he'd entered the China trade too.

The richest China trade, of course, was in drugs. British merchants, supported by their government, ran huge quantities of illegal opium into China. Recently, when the Chinese emperor had protested at what this was doing to his people, the righteous British government had sent war-ships to attack him, forced the Chinese to buy the drugs, and taken Hong Kong for themselves as well.

But Astor was no drug dealer. He'd sold the Chinese furs. Importing silks and spices in return, he'd multiplied his profits. And with those prof-its, he'd made the simplest investment in the world: he'd bought Manhat-tan land. He didn't develop it, usually—he just bought it, leased it, or sold it on. As the city was rapidly expanding, the land values shot up. He'd qui-etly continued the process, become a revered city elder, the patron of Audubon, of Edgar Allen Poe, and even founded the Astor library. Last year, he had died worth twenty million dollars, the richest man in America.

"You think the railroad business could be that big?" Hetty asked.

"I do," said Frank. "When I was a boy, my father took me to the open-ing of the Erie Canal. That canal alone transformed the shipping of grain and caused a huge expansion of places like Albany. Given time, the new railroads will far exceed what the canals accomplished—they'll change the whole continent. Unlike canals, they're easy to build, and the speed at which freight, and people, can travel is going to increase by leaps and bounds. Land prices are going to rise all the way along the new railway lines, if you can just figure out the right places. There'll be opportunities to invest in the railroads themselves, as well."

"Let's look at the maps, then," said his wife, with a smile.

She'd always been his partner, right from the start. Always supported him, whatever he wanted to do, joined in his interests and enthusiasms. Once, when someone had asked him when he'd first been sure he wanted to marry Hetty, to their great surprise they'd received the answer: "It was the Croton Aqueduct that did it." But it had been perfectly true.

If the old water supply of New York had been inadequate for decades, the city's eventual solution was magnificent. Forty miles to the north the River Croton, which ran into the Hudson, was dammed to make a huge reservoir. From there, water was carried south in a covered canal until it crossed by bridge over the Harlem River onto the north end of Manhattan. Passing over two more high aqueducts on the way, it flowed down through conduits into a thirty-five-acre receiving reservoir, which extended between Eighty-sixth and Seventy-ninth Streets on the city plan. Another five miles of conduits and pipes brought water from the receiver to Murray Hill, where the distributing reservoir, a splendid building just below Forty-second Street, and which looked like a fortress, held twenty million gallons.

The whole thing was a masterpiece of engineering, and it hadn't surprised Hetty in the least that, just before its completion in 1842, while they were still courting, Frank had said that he wanted to inspect every inch of it. What astonished him, and everyone else, was that she cheerfully announced: "I'm coming too."

And so she had. They'd taken the family carriage up Manhattan, right across Westchester County to the Croton dam, where an engineer had been delighted to show them the sluices and the start of the canals. They'd driven down, looked into the gatehouses at the Harlem River and walked across the bridge. They'd inspected the aqueducts, the reservoirs, the pipes. The whole expedition had taken four days, and many miles of walking.

And finally, right in front of that fortress-like reservoir at Forty-second Street, Frank Master had turned to this remarkable young woman, gone down on one knee and asked her to marry him—which, all in all, Hetty reckoned was worth the walk.

Now, therefore, with the maps spread out on the table, Frank Master and his wife spent a happy half-hour looking at the towns and territories up the new Hudson railroad that seemed most promising for future development. And they were still busily engaged in this manner when a maid announced that Miss Keller and the Irish girl had arrived.

"I want to see this Irish girl, Hetty," said Master, "because we need to be very careful."

"Most of the servants in this city are Irish, Frank," his wife pointed out.

"I know. But there's Irish, and Irish. There are plenty of respectable ones. The people to avoid are the Irish from Five Points—half of them are so weak that they're prone to disease."

"Someone's got to help them, Frank."

"Yes, but we've young children to consider. And the ones that aren't sick are criminals. Gangs of them. Look what happened at Astor Place the other day."

That had been an awful business—a riot of Irish from the Bowery, set off by the appearance of an aristocratic English actor, at the new Astor Opera House, no less. One could understand the Irish blaming England for the horrors of the Famine, but with revolutionary elements causing disruptions all over Europe that year, the New York authorities weren't taking any chances. The militia had been called in, and they'd fired on the crowd. A hundred and fifty wounded, and more than twenty dead.

"I don't want any Irish from the Bowery," Master said firmly.

"Gretchen says she's very quiet and respectable."

"She may be. But I want to know about her family—are they respectable people too? And there's another thing to watch out for."

"What's that, dear?"

"Tammany Hall." It was as obvious to Frank as it had been to his ancestors that the better sort, the solid men of property, should rule the city. The men that Tammany Hall elected in the city wards were just the kind to beware of. "I don't want any of those people insinuating themselves into this house," he declared.

"I'll be careful, Frank," said Hetty.

"I want to know about her family," Frank repeated. "No Five Points, no Bowery, no drinking or gambling, and no Tammany Hall."

✦

When they came from Irving Place into Gramercy Park and Mary saw the size of the house, she took a deep breath. They went to the trades entrance, but in no time a maid in a starched cap led them through the stately main hall, across the echoing marble floor, and into a sitting room with a thick Turkish carpet, where she told them they might sit on a padded sofa.

"Oh God, Gretchen," whispered Mary, "will you look at this place? I wouldn't know what to do in a house like this."

"You'll be fine," said Gretchen. "She's very nice."

As if to confirm this fact, Hetty Master appeared at the door, and sat down in an armchair opposite them.

"So you are Mary," she said pleasantly. "And Gretchen, of course, I know very well." She smiled. "You've been acquainted with each other a long time, I believe."

The lady of the house was wearing a pale brown silk gown. Her hair, which had a hint of red in it, was parted in the middle and neatly arranged in ringlets over her ears. She was still young, about thirty, Mary guessed. And she certainly seemed friendly. But even so, at this moment, all Mary could manage was a nervous, "Yes, ma'am."

Gretchen came to her aid.

"When I first came to New York, Mrs. Master, Mary and her family were very kind to me. Mrs. O'Donnell, God rest her soul, helped me to learn English." She turned to Mary with a smile. "There's been hardly a day since when one of us hasn't been in the other's house."

Mrs. Master nodded with approval, and Mary marveled at her friend's cunning. Gretchen wouldn't set foot in the O'Donnells' lodgings if she could help it. But since Mary was often at the Kellers', technically the statement was true.

"Yet you seem very different," Mrs. Master remarked.

More than you know, thought Mary. But amazingly, Gretchen contradicted her.

"I'm German and Mary's Irish," she said, "but we both come from big farming families—my father has cousins farming in Pennsylvania—so I suppose farming families all think the same way."

Mary knew about the Kellers' farming cousins. But the O'Donnells'? Sometimes, after a drink or two, her father would speak of the family land back in Ireland, though God knows whether that meant her ancestors had lived in a farmhouse or a hovel. But Gretchen made it sound so solid and respectable.

"And your two families live near each other in Germantown?"

"Yes," said Gretchen. She smiled. "Mr. O'Donnell goes to my uncle for his cigars."

"And what does your father do?" Mrs. Master asked Mary, looking straight at her.

"He's a mason," said Mary.

"I see. Can you tell me any of the places he has worked?"

"Well . . ." Mary hesitated. She didn't want to lie. "A mason's work takes him to different places. But I know," she added hopefully, "that for a long time he worked on the Croton Aqueduct."

"He did? The Croton Aqueduct?" For some reason, Mrs. Master looked delighted. "Did he work on the bridges and the reservoirs as well?"

"I think so, ma'am. I think he worked on all of it."

"I know every inch of that aqueduct," Mrs. Master said proudly.

What this meant Mary couldn't imagine, but she bowed her head respectfully.

"Perhaps you saw him there, Mrs. Master," ventured Gretchen.

"Well," said Mrs. Master, more pleased than ever, "perhaps I did." She seemed to catch herself for a moment. "Is your father connected in any way to Tammany Hall?"

"My father? Oh no. Not at all."

"Good. So tell me, Mary," she continued, "what experience have you of household duties?"

"Since my mother died, ma'am, I have kept house for my father," Mary answered. "I've had to do everything." She saw Gretchen nodding vigorously. It's lucky the lady can't see the place, she thought.

"You're not afraid of work, then?"

"Oh no," said Mary, "not at all." At least she didn't have to think about that.

"But"—Mrs. Master suddenly looked thoughtful—"if your father relies upon you to keep house for him now, Mary, would you not be deserting him, rather, if you came to live here?"

Mary stared at her. Then she and Gretchen looked at each other. They hadn't thought of that. The question was so logical, yet the truthful answer would demolish the entire edifice of respectability that Gretchen had just built up. Mary felt herself going pale. Whatever could she say? She couldn't think of anything.

But already Gretchen had turned to Mrs. Master. She was speaking quite calmly.

"I can't tell you this for certain, Mrs. Master," her friend was saying, "but"—she seemed to hesitate for just a second before continuing—"if perhaps there was a widow who was thinking of marrying Mr. O'Donnell, a lady used to running a house of her own . . ."

Mary's mouth opened. What in heaven's name was Gretchen talking about? A respectable lady marry John O'Donnell? Had she gone out of her mind?

But Gretchen was blithely ignoring her. She was talking to Mrs. Master as if she were imparting a secret that Mary mightn't want to discuss.

"If that was the case, and the lady had strong opinions of her own about how to run a house . . ."

And now Mary understood. She stared at Gretchen in wonderment. How was it possible that her neat little friend, with her angel face, could be making this up so easily as she went along? How could she tell such lies? Well, not technically a lie, she wasn't actually saying this widow existed—only asking: what if she did? But all the same . . . Mary knew she couldn't have done such a thing herself in a thousand years.

"It would be difficult for Mary, then, to live in that house," Gretchen explained. "It may seem foolish—"

But Mrs. Master interrupted her. "It does not," she said, very firmly, "seem foolish at all."

⸭

Frank Master was just looking at Saratoga on the map when Hetty appeared. She was alone.

"The girl was no good?" he asked.

Hetty smiled. "Actually, she's perfect. Very respectable. She and Gretchen live practically next door to each other. In Germantown."

"I see. Her family?"

"The father's a mason. A widower, about to marry again, I think. And guess where he worked for years?"

"Tell me."

"The Croton Aqueduct." There was a gleam in her eye. "Who knows, he may have seen you propose to me."

"Ah."

"I do feel, Frank," she said, "that this is fated."

Frank Master gazed affectionately at his wife. He wasn't a fool. He knew when he was beat.

"We'd better hire her, then," he said.

Crystal Palace

T HE EASIEST DECISION that Frank Master ever had to make in his business career occurred in the summer of 1853. He was standing in his counting house. It was a nice old brick building, with a warehouse behind, that looked out onto the South Street waterfront. The sun was shining brightly on the ships crowding the East River beyond. Two of those ships belonged to him—one a sailing ship, a rakish clipper bound for China, the other a side-wheel steam vessel about to depart for the isthmus of Panama. The cargo of clothes she carried would be taken overland across Panama, then carried by another steamer up to California. The people who'd been flocking to the gold-rush towns in the last few years might, or might not, find gold. But they needed the tough, durable clothes manufactured in New York, and Frank Master had made plenty of money shipping them.

Master was in cotton, tea, meat-packing, property speculation. But he wasn't getting into this deal.

"Gentlemen," he said, "I want no part of it. And if you take my advice you'll give it up before the commodore comes back. Because when he does, it's my belief, he'll skin you alive."

"Won't be much he can do," said one of them.

"He ain't so tough," said the other.

"Wrong," said Master, "on both counts."

There was always something Cornelius Vanderbilt could do.

Steam-powered vessels had been in use on the River Hudson for more than thirty years, yet the steamship had taken a surprising time to enter the Atlantic trade. A British rail company had started it off, but it was an enterprising Loyalist family named Cunard, who'd fled to Canada a couple of generations back, who'd first run steamships successfully across the ocean. The New York men aimed to catch up quickly, though. And none had been more daring than Vanderbilt.

He came from old New Yorkers, English and Dutch, but he'd started poor—even poorer than Astor. Hetty Master didn't like him. "That foulmouthed waterman," she called him. It was true that he'd started life rowing a boat, and his language was certainly colorful, but he had genius, he was ruthless, and his steamships had made him one of the richest men in the city. Crossing the commodore was a bad idea.

Frank Master never crossed Vanderbilt. He'd made friends with him. When Master had wanted to run steamships down to Panama for the California trade in which Vanderbilt was powerful, he'd gone to the commodore and asked him what he thought.

"How many ships?" the commodore had asked.

"A couple, maybe."

"All right." Vanderbilt had favored him with a curt nod.

"You asked his permission?" Hetty had said in disgust.

"Better than being run out of business."

Yet while the commodore was abroad, these two men, both employed by Vanderbilt, were planning to steal a piece of his empire.

You had to admire the audacity of the plan. Instead of running his goods across Panama, the commodore had opened up a cut-price route across Nicaragua, and taken a thousand sailing miles off the journey.

"But the government of Nicaragua ain't too strong," the two men told Master. "What if we could finance a revolution there? Put in our own man as president, who'll give us an exclusive contract to run goods across the place, and leave Vanderbilt out?"

"You really think it could be done?"

"Yes, and for no great outlay. Do you want in?"

"Gentlemen," said Master with a laugh, "I'm not afraid to topple the government of Nicaragua, but annoying Cornelius Vanderbilt? That frightens me. Please don't include me in your plans."

He was still chuckling about the two rogues an hour later, when he went uptown to meet his wife.

⁜

Hetty Master stood at the corner of Fifth Avenue and Fortieth, with the great fortress of the distribution reservoir behind her. Half the world was passing by the place that day, so you might have expected her to be taking some notice of them. Or you might have thought, at least, that she'd be looking out for her faithful husband who was coming to meet her.

But she wasn't. She was reading. Just standing there like a statue, under her parasol, and reading.

If she'd taken any notice of the scene around her, she might have reflected that close by, nearly eight decades ago, poor George Washington had beaten his troops with the flat of his sword, to try to stop them running away from the redcoats. Or she'd surely have recalled that this was where Frank proposed to her. But she didn't. She just read her book.

Of course, she'd always loved to read. Back in the days when she and Frank were courting, the great Charles Dickens had come over from London to begin his triumphal tour of America. People had turned out in thousands, and she'd dragged Frank to no less than three events to see her favorite author, and listen to him read. "I love his characters and stories," she'd told Frank, "and his plea for social justice is beyond all praise." Certainly, his tales of London's poor folk found a ready echo in New York. But it wasn't Charles Dickens that she was reading today.

It was something more dangerous.

Frank didn't see her at first. But then there were so many other things to catch the eye. The tallest was the Latting Observatory, a conical latticework of wood and iron that rose three hundred and fifty feet to a viewing platform high over Forty-second Street. You could go up the first two stages of the tower in a wonderful new machine they were calling an elevator. Master was eager to try that. But the Observatory was still a sideshow to the main event—which lay just behind the reservoir, its upper parts clearly visible as Frank approached.

The Crystal Palace.

Two years ago, when the British had staged their Great Exhibition in a huge crystal palace of glass and iron in the middle of London, six million people had come to see this world's fair of culture and industrial design. The palace in Hyde Park, like a vast greenhouse, was over six hundred yards long, and covered nearly seven acres. So New York had decided to have one of their own. And though the Crystal Palace at Fortieth Street might not match the vast scale to be found in the capital of the British Empire, it was still a mighty handsome building, with a splendid dome, a hundred and twenty-three feet high. It had just opened the day before, and Frank Master couldn't wait to see what was inside it.

Then he saw his wife. And inwardly groaned. She was reading that damn book again.

"Put the book aside now," he said gently, as he took her arm, "and let's see the exhibition."

The main entrance on Sixth was splendid. With its ornate classical portico and dome, it looked like a Venetian cathedral, made of glass. The French and British flags flew to left and right, and a huge Stars and Stripes over the center.

Frank knew most of the organizers, especially William Cullen Bryant and August Belmont. They had promised an exhibition of the industry of all nations, and it seemed to Frank they had done a pretty good job. As he conducted Hetty round, they saw scientific instruments and guns, water pumps and ice-cream makers, equipment for taking photographs and for sending telegrams—not to mention the huge statue of George Washington riding a horse. It was the machinery of the new industrial age, and he loved it.

"Look at this clock," he'd prompt Hetty. "We should have one of these." And she'd smile and nod. "Or what about this sewing machine?" he'd try. "Yes dear," she'd say.

But though they went round together for an hour, and she dutifully inspected everything, he knew that she wasn't really paying attention. "Let's go to the observation tower," he said.

The view from the top of the Observatory was very fine. Eastward, one could see over Queens, westward, across the Hudson to New Jersey, and northward, over the miles of rural Manhattan into which, like columns of infantry, the grid lines of avenues were gradually making their way. They both enjoyed the elevator which served the tower's lower platforms. But when they emerged, another exhibit nearby caught Frank's eye. Hetty wanted to sit down for a while, so he went in alone.

"It's the damnedest thing," he reported back. "Fellow by the name of Otis. He's designed an elevator like the one we just rode in, but he's added a system of safety catches so that if the cable breaks, it won't fall. I reckon you could install something like that in a big store, or even a house." He nodded. "He's setting up in business. Might make an interesting investment, I'd say."

"Yes, dear," said Hetty.

"Let's go home," he said at last, with a sigh.

He knew what she was going to talk about. She didn't start at once, but waited a whole block, then began at Thirty-ninth Street.

"Frank," she said, "something's got to be done. I want you to read this book."

"Goddammit, Hetty," he said, "I'm not going to." And then, to hide his irritation, he smiled. "No need to, when you've already told me all that's in it."

The author, Harriet Beecher Stowe, was no doubt a good and honest woman, but he wished to hell she might have found some other way to occupy her time than writing. For her *Uncle Tom's Cabin* had been like a plague in his house for nearly a week now. A plague to the whole country, as far as he could see.

A curse to the slave owners of the South, that was for sure.

The wretched thing had started quietly enough, as a serial in a little magazine that was only read by the abolitionist crowd anyway. But then, last year, some fool of a publisher had put it out as a book, and it had broken all records. Three hundred thousand copies sold in America already, and still going strong. He'd heard they'd sold another two hundred thousand in England as well. Though a friend just back from London had told him: "The English are delighting in it, not so much for the slavery issue, but because they say it shows what a bunch of savages we uppity Americans really are." There was no end to its run in America in sight, either. The publisher was putting out a deluxe edition now, with nearly a hundred and twenty illustrations, and the lady herself was publishing another work about how she came to write the book in the first place, called *A Key to Uncle Tom's Cabin*. No doubt that'd be a best-seller too.

And what was the thing about anyway? The story of a slave family and their trials and tribulations. Nothing new there. But it was written in the sentimental style, with a black mammy, and sweet pickaninny children, and a slave family broken up, and dear old Uncle Tom, the faithful, fatherly, suffering slave, dying at the end. No wonder all the women liked it.

"Our family had a slave like Uncle Tom," he remarked. "By name of Hudson. My grandfather knew him. He was happy enough, I believe. I certainly never heard he complained."

"He wasn't a slave, he was free," Hetty corrected him. "And he lost his only son, who was captured and probably sold into slavery in the South.

Your family tried to find the boy for years, but never could. Your father told me all about it."

"That may be," he allowed. "But the book's just a sentimental tale about an old slave who loves everybody. There are no Uncle Toms in real life."

"That just shows you haven't read it, dear," she said. "Uncle Tom's as real as you or me, and not at all sentimental. When it's necessary, he encourages slaves to run away. As for the rest, slaves are separated from their children, flogged and sold down the river. Are you saying these things don't happen?"

"I guess I'm not," said Frank.

"Everyone agrees it's a wonderful book."

"Not in the South, they don't. I heard that a man in Arkansas was run out of town for selling it. The South says the book's a criminal slander. They're furious."

"Well, they should be repentant."

"It's not surprising really," he continued mildly. "After all, the villain of the book is a typical Southern slave holder."

"Actually," said Hetty, "if you'd read the book you'd know he's a Yankee who moved south. The Southern gentleman in the book is a kindly man."

"Well, people in the South don't like it, anyhow."

"The point is not about any individual, Frank. It's about a system."

They had walked as far as Thirty-sixth Street. Seeing a cab, Master hailed it, hoping the business of getting in would break his wife's concentration. It didn't.

"The system, Frank," she continued, as soon as they were seated, "whereby one human being can own another as a chattel. This book"— she took it out, and clearly meant to give it to him—"is a Christian book, Frank. A challenge to all Christians. How can we countenance such an evil in our land?"

"And what," he asked wearily, "do you expect me to do about it?"

She paused. Evidently she had been thinking about it.

"I think, Frank," she said quietly, "that we ought to consider whether we do business with slave owners."

He almost cried, "Are you out of your mind?" But fortunately, he caught himself, and waited a few moments before he replied.

"Hard to be a New York merchant and have nothing to do with the cotton trade."

That was quite an understatement. Generations of New York men had assiduously courted the cotton planters—at first, buying the Southerners' raw cotton and shipping it to England (when, had they been a bit sharper, the Southern planters could have shipped direct and saved themselves New York's commissions), and thereafter making their grand, all-purpose trade so indispensable, and their finances so entangled with the South, that it was hard to imagine the one without the other. Frank Master shipped cotton; and he sold goods, and debt, to the South. It was a good percentage of his business.

She put her arm on his. "I know, Frank. I understand that it wouldn't be easy. But you are also a good Christian. I didn't marry you just for your money," she added with a smile.

And I didn't marry you, he thought to himself, to have you interfere with my making it. As the cab took them home, he said nothing more, but he sensed that his wife was determined about this business. In more than ten years of marriage, he and Hetty had never had a serious quarrel, and he wasn't sure what it would be like if they did.

※

At about the time when Frank and Hetty Master had ascended the Observatory, Mary O'Donnell had prepared to leave her friends. They had spent such a pleasant afternoon, the four of them: Mary and Gretchen, and Gretchen's little brother Theodore and cousin Hans.

Mary was fond of little Theodore. He was five years younger than Gretchen, and his blue eyes were darker than hers, and set very wide apart. If his sister was blonde, he'd inherited his father's curly brown hair. And from an early age, he'd possessed a remarkable sense of his own identity. When he was five, a lady in the shop, meaning only kindness, had asked him: "Do people call you Teddy?" Theodore had shaken his head. "Why not, dear?" she'd asked. "Because," he had answered solemnly, "I do not wish it." By the age of ten, he'd also announced that he wouldn't be following his father in the chocolate business. "What will you do, Theodore?" the family had asked him. "Something with no chocolate in it," he'd said. This had displeased his mother considerably, but his father had been more understanding. "Leave him be," he had said. "Anyway, this isn't such a good business." Gretchen and Mary usually took Theodore with them, even though he was so much younger.

But Hans was another matter. He'd been a distant figure when Mary was young, though Gretchen would speak of him, so Mary knew that he was serious and worked long hours for the piano-maker. Once or twice she'd caught sight of him, but there wasn't much reason for them to meet, and Gretchen certainly wasn't going to bring him to the O'Donnell household.

Mary had been out walking with Gretchen one day, after she'd been working for the Masters a couple of months, when her friend had said she wanted to call in at her cousin's place of work. They hadn't stayed long, but Mary had had a good chance to observe him. Hans was still in his early twenties, a tall, slim young man whose sandy hair was already receding, and who wore small, gold-rimmed spectacles. He was obviously busy, but friendly enough. Gretchen asked him to play something for them on one of the pianos. "He's very good," she said. "They ask him to show off the pianos for the customers." But Hans told them he couldn't just then, so they left. He was obviously very serious about his work. Mary liked that.

A week later, Mary just happened to be passing the piano store and decided to look in. At first Hans didn't remember who she was, but when she told him, he smiled, and showed her the piano he was working on. She asked a few questions, and he explained what wood was used, how it was molded and put together. Then, taking her to another piano that was finished, he showed her how it was tuned.

He talked very quietly, looking at her gravely from time to time through his gold-rimmed glasses. And maybe it was just to get rid of her politely, but at the end, he went over to the best piano in the store and, sitting down at it, began to play.

Mary didn't know much about music, though she liked to sing. She'd heard people play the piano in the theater, and in a saloon of course, but she'd never heard anything like this. He played a Beethoven sonata, and she listened entranced, by the beauty of the music and by its power. And she watched Hans with fascination, too. His skill was remarkable, and his hands beautiful, but even more intriguing was the transformation that came over his face. She saw concentration, absolute concentration, intelligence—and a sort of remove. For when he played, she realized, he entered another world. It wasn't a world she knew anything about, but she could see that Hans had just gone there, right in front of her, and she was enchanted. She hadn't realized how fine he was.

And suddenly a thought came into her mind. All her childhood, she'd heard the priests speak of angels, and she'd always thought of them like the ones she'd seen in paintings, with placid faces and unlikely wings. But seeing his face now, she thought, no—this must be what an angel is like, full of beauty, and spirit, intelligence and power.

"You should play for a living," she said to him, when he had finished and returned to earth.

"Oh no," he said, with a touch of sadness, "you should hear the real pianists." He smiled kindly. "I have to get back to work now, Mary."

Ten days later, she and Gretchen had taken a pleasure-boat trip into the harbor, and he had joined them. Whether it was his idea, or Gretchen's, she didn't know, but he'd been very easy and friendly, and they'd had a good time.

Some time after that, when Gretchen had casually asked her what she thought of her cousin, Mary had laughed and said, "I'd like to marry him." But she wished she hadn't, for Gretchen had frowned and looked at the ground, and Mary had realized the truth. What a fool I am, she'd thought, to be dreaming of such a thing, when I haven't a cent to my name. A clever young man like that needed a wife with some money.

The trouble was that whenever she met young men after this, they always seemed so crude and coarse by comparison.

And then there'd been the man that Sean proposed.

All in all, she had to say, Sean had behaved well since she joined the Masters. He'd found out all about them in no time—you could be sure of that. "But I'm very impressed, Mary," he told her. "You landed on your feet there." And he'd stayed away from their house. "Just so long as I know you're all right," he told her. "Of course," he'd added, with a reassuring smile, "I'll cut his throat if he harms you."

He'd been good about her father too. John O'Donnell had gone down-hill pretty fast after she left. Sean had stepped in to help, but it wasn't much use. She'd felt so guilty that she'd wondered whether to give up her job, to try and save him. But Sean had been adamant.

"I've seen a dozen like him, Mary," he told her. "He'll go the same road, whether you're there or not."

He'd sent a boy to her with a note when her father had died six months ago.

The funeral had been conducted with all due ceremony. There was a dusting of snow on the ground, but a surprising number of people turned up. At the burial, Sean had arrived with a small black box which, after a brief consultation with Father Declan the priest, he'd reverently placed on the coffin as it was lowered. Then they all went back to the lodgings, which she'd vigorously cleaned.

"What was the box you placed in the grave?" she'd asked him on the way back.

"The remains of the dog."

"Of Brian Boru?"

"I dug him up last night."

"Jaysus, Sean, have you no respect for the dead?" she cried. "It's probably sacrilege."

"It's what our father would have wished," he said blandly. "I asked Father Declan, and he quite agreed."

He'd seen to it that there was food, and a fiddler, and plenty to drink. They gave John O'Donnell a rousing old wake.

And that was where he'd introduced her to Paddy Nolan.

Surprisingly, she'd liked him. Surprising because she was naturally suspicious of anyone connected with her brother. Nolan was a quiet man, about thirty, with dark hair and a neatly clipped beard. He was very polite, almost formal toward her, calling her Miss Mary. He seemed to treat her with great respect, and she rather liked that. He evidently considered her brother a fellow of some importance. After a time, he asked if he might have the honor of calling upon her some day, and, not wishing to be rude, she said that he might.

"He's quite respectable, you know," Sean told her afterward. "And he has money. He owns a saloon, though he never drinks a drop himself."

"And you've known him a while?"

"We've done business together." He smiled. "He likes you, Mary. I could see that. And God knows, he could have his pick of women, with the establishment he has."

She went out with Nolan ten days later. He treated her to a meal, then they looked in at his saloon, which was down on Beekman Street.

A saloon wasn't a place where a woman would normally go. But seeing her in the company of the owner, the men in there gave her a polite nod. It was certainly a cut above the usual establishments of its kind, patronized by gentlemen who worked or wrote for the nearby newspapers and magazines, like the *New York Tribune* and *The Knickerbocker*.

"I get all kinds of literary gentlemen in here," Nolan told her with quiet pride. "Mr. Lewis Gaylord Clark, Mr. William Cullen Bryant,

Mr. Herman Melville." Over in one corner he showed her a table stacked with recent publications. "The newspaper gentlemen leave them here for others to read," he told her. Clearly he meant the place to have something of the tone of a club, and she had to admit she was impressed.

Afterward they took the train up Fourth Avenue, and he escorted her politely back to the door of the Masters' house.

She normally had Sundays off, and they went out several times. After a month, she let him kiss her. Once, they met some of his friends, who were very nice to her. The only moment when she felt awkward was when, discussing an acquaintance's marriage, he remarked: "Treat a woman right, I always say, and she'll do whatever you want." The men had laughed, and the women had glanced at her, but Nolan had given her a friendly smile and added: "A man should never take a woman for granted, Mary, don't you agree?"

The remark before had been harmless enough. But she still felt a little uneasy all the same, even if she wasn't sure exactly why.

The next time they were out, and walking by the waterfront, he said something about the cotton trade. Living in the Masters' house, and hearing the merchant's conversation, she'd picked up a bit of knowledge about that business. And hardly thinking, she told Nolan he was wrong. For just a moment, a cloud passed across his face. Then, without looking at her, he gave a tight-lipped smile. "Now don't you go contradicting me," he said quietly. And she could see he meant it.

She knew she shouldn't mind these things too much. Most men were the same. And you had to admit, Nolan had many things to recommend him. By late spring, it seemed to her that he would ask her to marry him.

She'd discussed Nolan with Gretchen, of course. For Gretchen had a fiancé of her own now. Her parents had made the arrangements. He was a German boy, a distant cousin with the same family name, whose father had a bakery and confectionery store, an only child who'd inherit the business. His name was Henry and Mary thought he was nice enough. He had a little mustache, and he liked to talk about confectionery.

Mary didn't quite understand her friend's engagement. Gretchen didn't seem to spend much time with her fiancé, but she seemed quite contented, as if she was glad that a matter which might otherwise have caused her trouble had been settled for her easily. "I don't even have to change my name," she remarked cheerfully. "I'll still be Gretchen Keller."

"Do you love him?" Mary had once asked her friend. "Oh yes, I like him," Gretchen had answered placidly, though she never seemed to bring him along when she and Mary went out together. Gretchen and Henry were due to be married at the end of the year.

When they discussed Nolan, Gretchen never asked if she loved him. But she asked if he was attentive, and kind, and if he had a good business. And as the weeks went by, and Mary had time to reflect on her situation, and she compared the Kellers' solid family household with the morbid chaos of Five Points, she concluded that Gretchen's attitude might be wise. At the end of May, when Gretchen had asked her whether, if Nolan proposed, she would accept him, she had answered, "I expect I might."

Nolan had made his move in June. At noon on a Sunday, he'd picked her up from the house in Gramercy Park. It was a warm summer day, not a cloud in the sky. He'd hired a nice little two-seated gig and, with a picnic basket and blanket behind, he drove her up Broadway and out onto the old Bloomingdale road. It wasn't long before the city streets gave way to empty lots and countryside. They'd gone about three miles, and she'd supposed they might be going to some pleasant spot overlooking the Hudson, but instead he turned right and continued a little way until they came to a large tract of wild ground, with small hills and rocky outcrops.

Drawing up, and tethering the horse, he took the basket and blanket and led her down a path.

"Where in the world are you taking me?" she asked.

"A place I discovered a while ago," he said. "You'll see." They passed a high outcrop of rock half concealed by trees and bushes. "Just a step," he said as, taking her hand, he guided her between the trees. "There."

She had to admit that it was a delightful spot. A little dell, where the sun fell gently onto an open bank of grasses which, most charmingly in that summer season, were sprinkled with wild strawberries.

"Perfect spot for a picnic," he said.

He'd brought a bottle of wine, fresh salmon, jellied chicken, bread that smelled as if it had just come out of the oven, sweetmeats, fresh fruit. She'd never had a more delightful meal. And during the course of it, he talked easily of this and that, and even told some funny jokes which, she had noticed, was not a thing he often did.

So when he kissed her, she had been expecting it, and had no objection. And when, lying beside her on the grass, he began to kiss her more passionately, she returned his passion. And when his hands began to caress her she gave a little gasp. But when he started to go further, and rolled on top of her, she found she did not wish it, and she resisted him, and asked him to stop.

He did so, but it was clear that he did not believe her, and suddenly he was at it again.

"No, Paddy," she said. "Please." She sat up and looked at him reprovingly. "I am not your wife."

He rolled on his back and looked up at the sky, and she wondered if he was going to ask her to marry him then. And indeed, she had the distinct impression that he was considering it. But instead, after a while, he sat up. He was looking a bit thoughtful.

He poured her a glass of wine, which she took, and he poured some for himself. Then he smiled.

"It's a beautiful day, Mary," he said. "Can't think what came over me."

He didn't say much more, but after a while he began to collect the remains of the food and put them in the basket. Then with a sigh he remarked that he wished he didn't have to do some work at the saloon. "But duty calls."

So he led her back to the two-seater, and drove her home.

After he'd gone, she sat in her room for a couple of hours, taking stock of the situation. What did it mean? Was he not serious about her at all, and only intending to seduce her? He wouldn't try to force himself on her, she was sure—he would know that Sean would put a knife in his back if ever he did that. And he surely wouldn't have spent all this time courting her when he could have plenty of easy women as a mistress, if that's what he wanted. No, from everything that had passed between them, she was sure he was thinking of her as a wife.

She wished she could talk it over with Gretchen, but Gretchen and her family had gone away that week to visit relations in New Jersey. Anyway, she told herself, she was perfectly capable of thinking it out for herself.

What was his game, then? Simple enough, she supposed: he wanted to sample the goods before he bought. She couldn't really blame him for that. Out in the country, it was thought decent enough so long as you married before the first child was born.

And she'd refused him. Why? A sense of her own reputation? God knows, the place he'd chosen was discreet enough. Had she wanted him? Perhaps not. Not just then. She hardly knew. Was that such a good reason to refuse? Was he disappointed? Was he angry? Had she lost him?

It was early evening when she left the house. It was still her day off. She walked down Irving Place to Fourteenth Street, across to Fourth Avenue, and took a train down to City Hall. It was only a short walk to Beekman Street from there.

She hadn't quite decided what she was going to say, or do, when she got to the saloon. But at the least, she would speak to him, let him know that she was sorry for disappointing him. More than that she hadn't decided. She'd see what reception she got, and take it from there.

She was halfway down the street when she saw him. He'd just come out of the saloon, and he was looking angry. It made her pause, nervously, and her first thought was that his bad temper was probably her fault. He turned along the street, with his back to her. There weren't many people about, but she didn't want to call out to him, so she started to walk quickly, to catch up with him.

She noticed that there was a ragged street urchin in his path, a little boy of seven or eight, by the look of him. He was standing there with his hand out for a coin. Nolan waved him out of the way, irritably, as he drew near. But the little fellow stood his ground, his hand still out. Nolan reached him, and paused. His hand seemed to go to his pocket. And then, silently, and with great deliberation, he smacked the urchin across the face so hard that the little boy was lifted clean off his feet and sent rolling in the gutter. People turned at the sound. The little boy lay in the street so shocked he didn't even scream. And Nolan walked on as though nothing had happened.

She stopped. She stared. Normally she'd have rushed to the boy, but others were doing that, and besides, for some reason she couldn't. She turned and started to hurry away. As she did so, a sudden feeling, not only of shock, but a kind of nausea, overcame her.

She turned up toward City Hall. A train was leaving and she quickly got on. It wasn't only that she wanted to sit down, but somehow to remove herself from the street. As the train slowly trundled up the Bowery, she tried to make sense of what had just happened.

She'd seen Nolan. Seen him when he had no idea she was there. Seen him, as it were, unclothed. Seen him angry. But no anger—even if she was the cause of it—gave him the right to do what he just did. It wasn't just the violence of the blow—you could see worse than that any day around Five Points. It was Nolan's cold, deliberate cruelty that had been exposed.

And this was the man who she'd been thinking of marrying, the man who'd kissed her, the man who, only hours before, had pressed his body into hers. And foolish though it might be, and though it was the boy he struck, and not herself, she felt a terrible, sickening sense, as though she had been violated.

When he called at Gramercy Park again the next week, she sent out word that she was unwell. A few days later, she asked Mrs. Master to help her. She gave few details, simply telling her that Nolan had been courting her, and that she had discovered something bad about him. And after a little gentle questioning, Mrs. Master told her she'd take care of it. The following Sunday, when Nolan called to know how Mary was, Hetty Master herself told him plainly that Mary did not wish to see him any more, and that he was not to call at the house again.

"He was not best pleased," she told Mary afterward, with some satisfaction.

The only thing Mary dreaded was that Nolan might complain to her brother, and that this might cause Sean to come to the house, but mercifully it didn't. The next Sunday, though, when she'd gone down to Gretchen's house, it didn't surprise her to see Sean waiting for her in the street.

"What've you done to Nolan?" he asked. "You've embarrassed me."

"I can't bear to be with the man any more," she said. And she told him plainly what she'd seen.

"All right, Mary," said Sean. And he hadn't mentioned Nolan since.

Today, however, she'd been able to put Nolan completely out of her mind. She'd met Gretchen at the shop, and they'd walked arm in arm with Theodore along the street.

"Where are we going?" she'd asked.

"Oh, just to pick up Hans," Gretchen had answered cheerfully.

Her heart had missed a beat, but she didn't think it showed.

"I haven't seen him for ages," she'd said.

So they'd picked him up at the piano store, and they'd walked along the East River all the way down to Battery Park. They had eaten ice cream beside the big entertainment hall, and stared out across the harbor to Staten Island. Someone had laid out a little bowling alley, so they'd played ninepins for a while, Hans being best at it. And she'd watched him all the time without his seeing it. After that they'd walked round the point and gazed up the Hudson. Once, when he'd taken her arm to point out a boat to her, she had almost lost her breath, but she'd kept quite still so he shouldn't notice.

On the way back, he'd mentioned that the next time they got together, there was a young lady that he'd like them all to meet. And Gretchen had whispered to her that she already knew that Hans and the girl were likely to get married. So after Mary had smiled and said she looked forward to it, and overcome the sudden cold sensation in her stomach, she'd told herself that she was glad, and happy for him.

She was just approaching the house in Gramercy Park when she noticed the man entering the front door. She only had time to get a glimpse of him, but she could have sworn it was her brother Sean.

But why in the world, she wondered anxiously, would Sean be seeing Mr. Master?

✣

After the distressing conversation with his wife about slavery, Frank Master had been glad to retire to the library. He sat down in a leather armchair with the latest copy of the *New York Tribune*, found a dispatch from the paper's new correspondent in London, a fellow called Karl Marx, and started to read it.

He was rather surprised when the butler brought in a card bearing the name Fernando Wood. And even more surprised when he heard that the gentleman was not Mr. Wood himself, of Tammany Hall, but his representative.

A visit from the enemy. He frowned. After a moment's hesitation, however, he judged it wise to discover the reason for the visit, so he told the butler to bring the stranger in. And shortly thereafter found himself gazing at Sean.

The Irishman was expensively dressed, his suit a little too snugly fitting for Master's taste, and his side whiskers just a bit too assertive; but at least his boots were polished to a shine that Master could approve of. He gestured the young man to a chair.

"You come from the chief sachem of Tammany Hall, I understand."

"From Mr. Fernando Wood, sir," Sean answered smoothly. "Indeed I do."

If Frank Master had been asked to name the biggest rogue in New York—and it was a competitive field—he wouldn't have paused a second before naming Fernando Wood. Born in Philadelphia, that place had been far too genteel for his talents. He'd come to New York, made a modest fortune, by one means or another, before he was thirty, and got himself in with Tammany Hall. Then he'd turned politician.

You couldn't deny the genius of Tammany Hall. Fifty years ago, that wretch Aaron Burr had built up Tammany as a political power to get himself elected vice president. And after Tammany had successfully backed Andrew Jackson for the presidency, its Democratic Party machine had become awesomely efficient.

Tammany had got Wood elected as a Democrat to Congress. Then they'd run him for mayor of New York and nearly pulled that off too. Soon the damn fellow was going to run again. In the meantime, with the help of his Tammany Hall friends, Wood had his finger in every pie in the city.

"Might I ask your own name, sir?"

"O'Donnell is my name, sir. But in anything I say, I am speaking for Mr. Wood."

"And what is the nature of your business with me?" Master inquired.

"You might say it is political, sir," the Irishman replied.

Surely, Master thought, his visitor couldn't imagine he'd support Wood for mayor.

"I suppose you know, Mr. O'Donnell," he said evenly, "that I'm not a great friend of Tammany Hall."

"I do, sir," the young man answered coolly, "yet I believe that you and Mr. Wood have an interest in common."

"And what might that be?"

"Parcel of lots on Thirty-fourth Street, west of Broadway."

Master looked at him in surprise. It had been six months since he'd bought four lots on that block for future development, and he was still deciding what to do with them.

"You're well informed," he remarked drily.

"Mr. Wood is also thinking of purchasing in that block," his emissary continued. "But there is a problem. It seems that a certain gentleman owning property there is desirous of starting a rendering plant."

"A rendering plant?"

"Yes, sir. Grinding up carcasses from the slaughterhouse. Dead horses, too. Amazing what you can get out of them. Good business, they tell me. But messy. Not good for other property owners."

"Not at all."

"Bad for you, sir. Bad for Mr. Wood."

"And what can we do?"

"Fight it, sir. We believe there's a legal remedy, though lawyers are expensive and courts take time. More efficiently, you might say, one or two of the aldermen might be persuaded to deny the permit."

"To vote it down?"

"We think the problem can be made to go away."

"I see," said Master reflectively. "But that would cost money."

"There, sir," said the emissary, "you come to the nub of the matter."

"And my contribution would be . . . ?"

"A thousand dollars."

Then Frank Master threw back his head and laughed.

"Cigar, Mr. O'Donnell?"

Frank Master didn't mind a bit of corruption. Give a man's son a job, and he'll do you a favor later. Give a theater manager a tip for a good investment, and he'll send you tickets for the opening of a new play. These were the kindnesses that made the world go round. Where did corruption become a vice? Hard to say. It was a question of degree.

He'd thought he knew most of the Tammany Hall tricks. Apart from the basics, like the small bribes for permits, or the larger bribes for contracts, the big stuff was to be found in the padded contracts. Supply the city with food, say, for the poor. Add a percentage to the true invoice. Split the difference with the man who gave you the contract. Continue it year after year. Hard to detect, harder to prove, almost impossible to prosecute—assuming anybody even wanted to. Over time, the money could be huge.

But this trick of O'Donnell's was new to him. As they lit up their cigars, he gazed at the young man benevolently.

"Nice try."

O'Donnell looked at him sharply, but said nothing.

"Thousand bucks is a pretty good shakedown," Master continued amiably.

"The threatened plant . . ."

"Doesn't exist, Mr. O'Donnell." Frank Master smiled. "I'm used to paying the city boys for this and that. But the threat of a non-existent rendering plant is a refinement I admire. Do many people fall for it?"

Sean O'Donnell was silent for a moment or two. Then he gave his host a charming smile.

"Between us, sir?"

"Yes."

"An amazing number."

"Well, my respects to Mr. Wood, but I'm not one of them."

O'Donnell considered the new position. "There's one problem, sir. I wouldn't like to return to Mr. Wood empty-handed. It's not a good idea."

"I suppose not. What'll he take?"

"Five hundred, minimum."

"Two fifty."

"Won't do, sir. You know he's quite likely to be mayor at the next election."

"And you'll be stuffing ballot boxes?"

"Of course," said Sean cheerfully.

"Two hundred for him, and the same for you."

"You're most understanding, sir."

Frank Master rose, left the room for a minute, and returned with a bundle of banknotes.

"Cash acceptable?"

"Certainly."

Master settled himself in his chair again, and puffed on his cigar.

"We have a girl by the name of O'Donnell who works here, Mary O'Donnell," he remarked easily.

"It's a common name," Sean answered.

Master continued to puff on his cigar.

"My sister," Sean said finally. "But she doesn't know I'm here. Doesn't approve of me, in fact."

"I think we treat her well."

"You do."

"She said there was a fellow bothering her. My wife told him not to come round any more."

"He won't be troubling her again."

"And you don't want me to tell Mary I met her brother?"

"I'd prefer not." Sean's gaze went round the richly appointed room. Master watched him.

"You know," Master said quietly, "you Tammany boys didn't invent the game. My ancestors were doing this kind of thing even before Stuyvesant was here. I reckon it's the way cities always have been. Always will be, I dare say." He nodded contentedly. "New crowd. Same game."

"So one day my grandson might be sitting in a place like this?"

"Maybe. You seem like a coming man."

"I'd like that," Sean said frankly. Then he grinned. "Perhaps even my sister would approve of me then." He paused. "You've treated me very well, sir. I shall remember it. Especially considering the great difference between us."

Master took a slow draw on his cigar, sighting the young man through half-closed eyes.

"Not so different, O'Donnell," he said softly, "just dealt a better hand."

Lincoln

W HEN HETTY HAD asked him to accompany her, Frank had
almost refused. And when he did decide to go, it wasn't really to
please her, but because he supposed he'd better take a look at this damn
fellow Lincoln, since he'd turned up in New York.

The first time Frank Master had heard of Abraham Lincoln was a couple of years earlier, when Lincoln had made a name for himself in Illinois
running for the Senate against Douglas, the Democratic incumbent.
When the two men had held a series of public debates, the newspapers
had covered them extensively, and since the principal subject of the Lincoln-Douglas debates had been the slavery question, Master had read the
accounts carefully. Though Lincoln hadn't taken the seat, it was clear to
Frank that the fellow was a skillful politician.

After that, however, Frank hadn't paid much attention to the Illinois
lawyer until this month when, as the election year opened, the influential
Chicago Tribune had suddenly, and rather surprisingly, endorsed him for
the presidency. So despite the fact that he shared none of his wife's enthusiasm, and it was a chilly, damp February evening, he nonetheless set out
with her to the Cooper Institute's Great Hall at Astor Place. Since the hall
was only a dozen blocks away down Third Avenue, they decided to walk.

As they left Gramercy Park, he offered his arm, and Hetty took it. Years
ago the gesture would have been the most natural thing in the world. God
knows, Frank thought, how many miles they had walked arm in arm back

in the early days of their marriage, when she was still the young woman who'd come with him to the Croton Aqueduct. But they seldom walked arm in arm nowadays, and as he glanced at her he wondered, when exactly had the coolness between them begun?

He supposed it all went back to when she'd read that infernal book. *Uncle Tom's Cabin* had been no help to his marriage, that was for sure. It was amazing to Frank that the issue of slavery could have come between him and his wife; yet perhaps, he considered, he shouldn't be so surprised when it had managed to divide the whole country. Nor was it only the rights and wrongs of the slavery question, but the profound difference in philosophy that the argument had revealed—a difference about which, at the end of the day, he could do nothing.

If Hetty believed that slavery was wrong, Frank didn't disagree with her. But to his mind, it wasn't as simple as that. "We have to deal with the world as it is, not as it should be," he would gently point out.

It wasn't as if the issue was new. Washington and Jefferson, both slave owners, had recognized the inconsistency of slave-owning with the principles of the Declaration of Independence. Both had hoped that slavery would slowly disappear, but they also realized how difficult that would be.

A few summers ago, Frank and Hetty had gone up the Hudson to the resort of Saratoga. At the hotel, they had got to know a charming family from Virginia who owned a small plantation. Frank had particularly liked the father, a tall, elegant, gray-haired old gentleman, who had been partial to sitting in his library reading a good book. They had enjoyed many hours of conversation, during which the Virginian had been very frank about the slave question.

"Some people say that slaves are like the family servants of their owners," he'd remarked. "Others say that slaves are treated worse than animals. In a way, both statements are true, because there are two kinds of slave plantation. In small plantations like mine, the slaves that work in the house are more like family retainers, I'd say. And I hope we treat the men in the fields kindly as well. But there's a reason why we should. Back in the last century, remember, most slaves were imported. Slave owners might be considerate, or they might not—usually the latter, I'm afraid. But once they'd got all they could out of a slave, they just bought another one. Early in this century, however, when Congress ended the slave-importation business, slaves had to be home-grown, and their owners had an incentive to treat them as valuable livestock, if you like, rather than chattels to be worked to death. So you might have thought that would improve the lot of the slave.

"Down in the Deep South, however, there's another kind of plantation entirely. Those are huge—like vast factories—and there a slave may still be worked to death." He'd nodded grimly. "The most similar conditions I can think of are in the industrial factories and coal mines in England, where the workers are hardly better off, though they are at least paid a pittance. The only difference is that—in theory at least—the English poor have some rights, whereas, in practice, the slaves have none. Those big plantations, sir, eat up slaves and need fresh ones all the time. And where do they get them? Mostly from further north. Sold down the river, as they say. Virginia ships huge numbers every year."

"Do you?"

"No. But I haven't so many slaves, and unlike some of my neighbors, I'm not in need of cash. Otherwise, the temptation would be enormous." He had sighed. "I'm not defending the system, Master. I'm just describing it. And the sad truth is that the big planters in the South need slaves, and many farmers in Virginia rely on the income they get from supplying them."

"Yet the plantation owners are a tiny minority," Frank had pointed out. "Most of the farmers in the South have few slaves or none at all. Do they have such an incentive to support the system?"

"A white man in the South may be poor, but at least he can look down on the black man. He also has two great fears. The first is that if ever the black slaves become free, they'll take a terrible revenge. The second is that free black men would steal jobs from him and compete for land. For better or worse, Master, the wealth of the South is all tied up in slaves, and so is its culture. Destroy slavery and the South believes it will be ruined. For the fact is that the South has always feared the dominance of the North. They don't want to be under the thumb of your ruthless New York money men, or your arrogant Yankee puritans." He had smiled. "Even such kindly ones as your wife."

When it came to anything mechanical, Frank Master had always been excited by whatever was new and daring. But in political matters, like his Loyalist great-grandfather, he was naturally conservative. If the South was wedded to slavery, then he'd rather look for compromise. After all, that's what Congress and the government had been doing for the last half-century. Every effort had been made to preserve the balance between the two cultures. As new slave states like Mississippi and Alabama had been created, they had been matched by new free states in the North. When Missouri had entered the Union as a slave state three decades ago, the free state of Maine had been created out of northern Massachusetts to keep the balance even. Conversely, free Hawaii had failed to become a state because of opposition from the South; though slave-holding Cuba had nearly been annexed as a new slave state several times.

As for the issue of slavery itself, wasn't it best to ignore it for a while? Even in the North, most states still reckoned the black man was inferior. Negroes in New York, Connecticut and Pennsylvania might be free, but they couldn't vote. In 1850, the Fugitive Act had made it a federal crime, even up in Rhode Island or Boston, if you didn't turn over an escaped slave when his Southern owner claimed him. Such awkward compromises might enrage the moralists and abolitionists, but in Frank Master's opinion, they were necessary.

And that was the difference between him and Hetty. Frank Master loved his wife for her intelligence and strength of character. She'd been his intellectual partner in everything. He understood that if she believed strongly in something, she couldn't remain silent, and he was not surprised when she joined the abolitionist cause. But if he could agree with her that the abolitionists were morally right, that did not make them wise.

At first, when she had argued with him, he had tried to smooth things over. But as time passed, she became more passionate. One day, returning from a meeting at which a powerful abolitionist minister had preached, she had even gone down on her knees to him and begged.

"Slavery is an evil, Frank. You know in your heart that it is so. Please join with me—others like you have done so. We cannot let this continue." For her, the issue was so profound, so much a question of personal morality, that it was impossible not to take a stand. But he could not, and would not.

Gradually, therefore, without desiring it, she had come to think less of her husband. And he, sensing that her respect for him was diminishing, drew somewhat apart. Sometimes they had arguments. It was true, for instance, that a number of merchants and bankers in the city, moved by the moral arguments of the preachers, had become abolitionists. But most had not. New York shipped the cotton, supplied the finance and sold all manner of goods to the slave-owning South. Was he supposed to tell his friends to ruin themselves? Frank asked. They should find other trade, she said.

"Or look at the English," he pointed out. "They are entirely against slavery, but the cotton mills of England aren't closing because the cotton's picked by slaves."

"Then they are despicable," she replied. And since these judgments, he supposed, must equally apply to him, Frank felt a mixture of hurt and impatience with his wife.

During the few years, as the relations between the North and South had grown worse, he had refused to be swayed by any of the rhetoric. And when the great dispute had arisen, not over the states, but the territories beyond them, he had insisted on analyzing the question as calmly as if it had been a practical problem of engineering.

"I love railroads," he'd remarked to Hetty one day, "but it's really the railroads that have caused all this trouble." Everyone had agreed that the Midwest needed railroads, and in 1854 the leading men of Chicago had reckoned it was time to build transcontinental lines across the huge, untamed tracts of Kansas and Nebraska. The only problem had been that none of the railroad companies would undertake the investment until Congress organized those wild western lands as proper territories. And it was surely a pity, Frank thought, that after a struggle, Congress had yielded to Southern pressure and granted that slavery should be allowed in these territories. "It's a foolish decision," he'd pointed out at the time. "There are hardly any slaves in those territories, and the majority of settlers don't even want them." But this was politics, and reality was not the point. In no time, the overheated politics of North and South had taken over.

"The Nebraska Territory reaches right up to the Canadian border," the North complained. "The Southern slavery men are trying to outflank us." And when the new, Northern Republican Party had been formed to keep slavery out of the territories, its leaders, including Abraham Lincoln, were soon wondering openly whether the South mightn't try to make slavery the law of the whole nation. "These Northerners would abolish slavery and make the poor white man no better than a Negro," the Democratic Party roared back from the South.

Some proposed that the territories should be able to decide for themselves whether they should be "free soil" territories or allow slavery.

Northern reformers sent free soil settlers into Kansas; the South sent in slave holders. Before long there was bloodshed. Even in Washington, a Southern representative beat a Northern senator over the head with his cane.

It was then, with horrible timing, that the Supreme Court gave the South an unexpected present. In its Dred Scott decision, the court announced that Congress hadn't the right to bar slavery from any territory, and that the Founding Fathers had never intended that black men should be citizens in the first place. Even Frank was shaken. Hetty was outraged.

Finally, to add fuel to the fire, John Brown had raided the armory at Harper's Ferry in Virginia, in the foolish hope of starting a slave uprising. The thing was doomed to failure from the start, and Brown had been hanged by the State of Virginia. But in no time Hetty had informed Frank: "John Brown was a hero."

"He was not a hero," Frank had protested. "He was a madman. His attack at Harper's Ferry was completely hare-brained. You also seem to forget that he and his sons had already murdered five men in cold blood, just for being pro-slavery."

"You just say that."

"Because it's true."

As 1860 began, relations between North and South had never been worse. And there was one other factor that, in Frank's estimation, made the situation even more unstable.

Frank Master had lived long enough to realize that the great transatlantic economic system, like the weather, had great cycles of its own. From boom to bust, it went round in a circle, always finishing up bigger than it had before, but subject to crisis every few years, and with each crisis, merchants were destroyed, but if one was prudent, the bust could be as profitable as the boom.

For a while now, the transatlantic system had been going through stormy economic weather. But not everyone had suffered—his own business had even managed to prosper. The people who had been entirely unaffected, however, were the big Southern planters. Boom or bust, the world seemed to need more and more cotton. The big planters had never done better.

"Cotton is king," they could say triumphantly. And so confident were they in the good fortune of the South that some voices could even be heard declaring: "If the Yankees elect a Republican to ruin us, then to hell with the Union. Let the South go it alone."

Few in the North took it seriously, of course. "Those Southern braggarts are absurd," Hetty remarked contemptuously. But Frank was not so sure.

The coming presidential election, in his opinion, could be a dangerous business. Whatever the *Chicago Tribune* might say, he thought it unlikely that Lincoln would be the Republican candidate. Others surely had stronger claims. But he was quite curious, nonetheless, to take a look at this Lincoln fellow, and see what he was like.

✢

The huge, dark red mass of the Cooper Institute occupied a triangular site between Third Avenue and Astor Place. Frank had always admired its founder, Peter Cooper, a self-taught industrialist who'd built America's first railroad steam engine before founding this splendid college to provide free night classes for working men and day classes for women. The most impressive part of the place, in Frank's opinion, was the Great Hall. It was only last year that he'd come there for the Cooper Institute's official opening, but already the Great Hall had become one of the most popular places for holding meetings in the city.

They arrived in good time, and it was as well that they did, for the hall was rapidly filling. Glancing about, Frank made a quick estimate, and remarked to Hetty: "Your man can certainly draw a crowd. There'll be fifteen hundred people here tonight."

The minutes passed, and Hetty seemed quite happy to look around at the crowd. Here and there she saw people she knew. Frank contented himself with calling to mind as many items as he could from the reports of the Lincoln-Douglas debates. After a while, he could not resist bringing up one of them.

"Your Mr. Lincoln believes in freedom and equality for the black man, doesn't he, Hetty?"

"He certainly does."

"Yet in the Illinois debates, I distinctly remember, he said that on no account would he give the black man the vote or allow him to serve on a jury. What do you think of that?"

Hetty looked at him steadily. "I think that's very simple, dear. If he said anything else, he could never get elected."

Frank was just about to point out that she seemed happy to make moral compromises if it suited her, when a movement at the side of the stage signaled that the proceedings were about to begin.

The gentleman who introduced the speaker did not take long about his business. Some brief, polite words about the distinguished speaker, the hope that they would accord him a good welcome, and find interest in what he was to say, and the introduction was done. He turned to bid the speaker come forward. And Abraham Lincoln appeared.

"Good God," muttered Frank, and stared.

He'd seen one or two pictures of the man in the newspapers, and assumed they were unflattering. But nothing had quite prepared him for the shock of seeing Lincoln for the first time in the flesh.

Across the stage, walking stiffly and somewhat stooped at the shoulders, came a very tall, thin, dark-haired man. Six foot four, at least, Frank guessed. His long frock coat was black. One gangling arm hung at his side, the other was bent, for in a huge hand, he carried a sheaf of foolscap papers. When he reached the rostrum in the center of the stage, he turned to the crowd. And Frank almost gasped.

The lines in Lincoln's clean-shaven face were so deep that they were like chasms. From under his shaggy eyebrows, his gray eyes surveyed the crowd gravely and, it seemed, without hope. Frank thought it was the saddest face he'd ever seen. Placing his hands behind his back, Lincoln continued to look at them for a moment or two longer. Then he began to speak.

And now Frank winced. He couldn't help it. From this tall, angular man came forth a sound so high, so harsh and so unpleasing that it grated upon the ear and made the hearer wish he'd stop. This was the man the Chicago newspaper said should be president? However, as there was nothing else to do, he listened. And after a short while, he noticed several things.

In the first place, Lincoln made no attempt at high-flown rhetoric, indulged in no emotion. Simply and plainly, in a careful, lawyer-like manner, he put his first argument to them. And it was this.

His opponents, boosted by the strange Dred Scott decision, had argued that the Founding Fathers who framed the Constitution had never intended that Congress should have the right to forbid or legislate at all on slavery in any territory. So Lincoln had researched the subject, and had found evidence for twenty-one of the thirty-nine Founding Fathers—and discovered that every one of them had, in fact, legislated on precisely that question. And Washington himself had signed measures forbidding slavery in territories into law. So either the founders were denying their own Constitution, or the Constitution did indeed give Congress the right to make such decisions.

Of course, Lincoln could have simply pointed this out as a statistical and legislative fact, and added some high-flown phrases, to make his point well enough. But his rhetorical genius lay in being painstaking. Slowly, deliberately, giving the date, naming the Founding Fathers concerned, and explaining the circumstances of the case, Lincoln picked apart each vote. Again and again he did it. And each time he did so, he drew the same conclusion in almost identical words: "that nothing in their understanding, no dividing local from Federal authority, nor anything else in the Constitution, forbade the Federal government to control as to slavery in Federal Territory." And as the words were repeated, not with a hammer blow, not triumphantly, but quietly and reasonably, as one man to another, the effect was devastating.

He made no other claim. He just showed, beyond all reasonable doubt, that the Congress had the right to decide the issue. By his appeal to their reason, he held his audience's attention completely. They were enraptured.

And as he warmed to his theme a strange transformation seemed to take place in the speaker too. Lincoln's face relaxed. He appeared to be inspired with an inner light. He would raise his right hand from time to time, as he became animated, even jabbing his long finger in the air to emphasize a point. Most remarkable of all, Frank suddenly realized that he no longer even noticed Lincoln's voice. All he knew was that the man before him possessed a remarkable authority.

Having dealt with the Republican stance on slavery in the territories, Lincoln had two other points to make. The first was that his party believed in the Constitution, and the South's threat of secession if a Republican president were elected was like putting a gun to the head of the Northern voters. But he also had words of caution for his own Republicans. They must do all they could, he told them, to reassure the South that Republicans might not like slavery, but they had no designs against the existing slave states. In order to reassure the South, they must support the runaway slave laws and return slaves to their Southern owners.

Having said these words of political caution, he ended with a brief summary of his party's moral position. Let slavery alone in the South, because it is already there and necessity demands it, but Republicans still stand by what they believe. And he rounded off with a brief but ringing peroration.

"Let us have faith that Right is Might, and in that faith, let us, to the end, dare to do our duty as we understand it."

He was given thunderous applause. And Frank was no less impressed than most of the audience. He had seen a brilliant speaker, a politician who was moral but also a realist. Behind Lincoln's words, he thought he sensed a certain puritan contempt for the South, but if so, that was hardly surprising.

As they started home Hetty turned to him and asked: "Well, Frank, tell me honestly, what did you think of him?"

"Impressive."

"I thought so too." She gave him a smile. "I'm glad we can agree on that."

"So am I," he responded kindly.

"I believe he will be president, Frank."

"Could be." He nodded, and offered her his arm as he had done before. As she took the arm, she gave it a little squeeze.

So he did not add what was really on his mind: that if Lincoln became president, he viewed the future with dread.

The Draft

I T WAS A lovely day in July. Not a cloud in the sky. Mary was so
excited that she hugged Gretchen, as they sat in Mrs. Master's handsome open carriage and were driven round the park.

"I have a surprise for you," said Gretchen.

"What?"

"Before we take the ferry. Wait and you'll see."

You'd hardly guess that the city was at war at all. Not a soldier in sight,
and the park looking so splendid and so green.

Two weeks earlier, it had been a different story. At the end of June,
when General Lee and his Confederates had crossed the Potomac River
and pushed into Pennsylvania, New York had been in a ferment. Every
regiment in the city had been sent southward to bolster the Union army.
"But if Lee defeats them, or gives them the slip," Master had pointed out,
"he could be here in days."

By the start of July, a big battle had begun down at Gettysburg. At first
no one knew who was winning. But on the fourth, last Saturday, news
came up the wires that the Union had gained a great victory. And by
Thursday, Mrs. Master had told her: "I think, Mary dear, that it's safe for
you to go on your holiday now."

Free at last. The holiday had been planned the month before.
Gretchen's husband had insisted that she needed a week of rest. He'd con-
tinue to mind the store, while their three children would stay nearby with
Gretchen's parents. It had also been agreed that Mary should go with her,

so that Gretchen could travel with safety and propriety, and the two friends keep each other company. A respectable hotel had been booked out on Long Island. Before they took the ferry that afternoon, Mrs. Master had kindly told them to use her carriage as they liked, and so they had begun with a whirl through Central Park.

What with Gretchen's children and a store to run, it wasn't possible for the two friends to see each other as they had in the old days—though they always kept in regular touch, and Mary was godmother to one of the children. They were both delighted, therefore, with this chance to spend a week away at the beach together, and already they were laughing like a pair of girls.

"Look at us fashionable ladies going round the park," cried Mary.

She loved Central Park. It was only a few years since the great, two-and-a-half-mile rectangle had been laid out to the inspired design of Olmstead and Vaux, to provide a much needed breathing space, the "lungs" in the middle of what would clearly, one day, be the city's completed grid. Swamps had been drained, a couple of ragged hamlets swept away, hills leveled. And already its lawns and ponds, woods and avenues provided landscapes quite as elegant as London's Hyde Park or the Bois de Boulogne beside Paris. Why, the contractors had even done their work without any graft. No one had ever seen anything like it.

And the two women were certainly well dressed. Gretchen could afford it, but Mary had some nice clothes too. Servants in New York made twice as much as a factory worker, with room and board besides, and most sent money back to their families. In the fourteen years she'd been with the Masters, without any family to support, Mary had saved a tidy sum.

Of course, if ever she'd needed money, Sean would have helped her. Her brother was becoming quite a wealthy man. Eight years ago, he'd taken over Nolan's saloon down on Beekman Street. When she'd asked him what had happened to Nolan, he'd been evasive.

"He wasn't getting along with some of the boys," he'd said vaguely. "He may have gone to California, I believe."

To tell the truth, she didn't care what had happened to Nolan. But one thing was certain: Sean was making a fortune out of the saloon. He'd married and had a family now, and was quite the respectable man.

"You don't have to work as a servant, you know," he told her. "I've a place for you any time you want."

But she preferred to keep her independence. And by now, in any case, the Masters' house had become her home. If little Sally Master was in any kind of trouble, it wouldn't be long before she was knocking on Mary's door. When young Tom Master returned from Harvard for the summer, Mary felt the same thrill of pleasure as if he'd been her own.

Did she still think of getting married? Perhaps. It wasn't too late, if the right man came along. But somehow he never seemed to. If Hans had asked her, she supposed she would have said yes. But Hans had been happily married for many years. Time had passed, and she never thought of him nowadays. Well, hardly ever.

"Down Fifth, James," Gretchen called to the coachman, and a minute later they passed out of the bottom corner of the park and onto the carriage thoroughfare.

"Where are we going?" said Mary. But her friend didn't answer.

If Broadway had dominated the social scene for generations, the upstart Fifth Avenue was bidding for prominence now. And though fashionable Central Park was still waiting for the city to reach it, isolated mansions on Fifth were already getting close.

The first house of note, seven streets down from the park, was a palatial mansion nearing completion on an empty site. "That's Madame Restell's," Gretchen remarked. "Doesn't she live fine?" Having made a fortune with her husband procuring abortions for the good people of the city, Madame Restell had recently decided to build herself a house on Fifth where she could enjoy her retirement in state. And if Mary looked at that house with some horror, it was only another block before she reverently crossed herself.

Fifth at Fiftieth. St. Patrick's Cathedral. A decade had passed since Cardinal Hughes had laid the cornerstone of the great church which the city's huge new population of Irish Catholics so obviously deserved. And there was no doubt about its message. If Trinity's claims on the Gothic style had seemed impressive for a while, the vast new Catholic cathedral rising on Fifth would put the Protestant Episcopalians in their place—and provide a mighty reminder that honor was due to the Irish Catholics too.

Mary was proud of St. Patrick's. Increasingly, as time went by, the Church had been a comfort to her. The religion of her childhood, and of her people. At least you knew that it would always be there. She went to Mass every Sunday, confessing her few, small sins to a priest who gave her kindly dispensation and renewal of life. She prayed in the chapel, where the shadows comprehended all human tears, the candles promised love, and the silence, she knew, was the stillness of the eternal Church. With this spiritual nourishment her life was, almost, complete.

They swept on down Fifth, past the orphanage for poor Negro children at Forty-third, past the fortress-like splendor of the reservoir, all the way down to Union Square, where they picked up the Bowery.

"Have you guessed where we're going?" asked Gretchen.

✢

Theodore Keller's photographic studio was well equipped, and divided into two sections. In the smaller section, there was a camera set in position opposite a single chair placed in front of a curtain. For like the other photographers on the Bowery, his bread-and-butter business in recent years had been taking quick portraits of young men standing proudly, or sheepishly, in their unaccustomed uniforms, before they went off to fight against the South. Quicker than the old daguerreotype to take, easy to reproduce on paper, he'd get thirty a day sometimes. It paid the rent. At first, these small "*carte-de-visite*"-size portraits had seemed jolly enough, like taking someone's picture at the seaside. Gradually, however, as the terrible casualties of the Civil War had mounted, he had realized that the dull little portraits he was taking were more like tombstones, last mementoes before some poor fellow vanished from his family forever. And if he tried to make each humble one as splendid as he could, he did not tell his customers the reason.

The larger section was a more elaborate affair. Here there was a sofa, rich velvet curtains, numerous backdrops and props for grander pictures. When not working, this was the part of the studio where he relaxed, and to the discerning eye, there were hints to suggest that he privately considered himself not only a professional, but an artist and even, perhaps, something of a bohemian. In one corner, in a case, there was a violin which he liked to play. On a small round table against the wall, he would often drop any books that he happened to be reading. Today, besides a well-thumbed edition of the tales of Edgar Allan Poe, there were two slim books of poetry. One of them, the *Fleurs du Mal* of Baudelaire, was safely in French. But the other poems were by an American, and if it hadn't been his own sister that was coming to visit, he'd have put those verses safely out of sight in a drawer.

As he prepared for Gretchen's arrival, he still hadn't decided which backdrop to use. If there was time, he liked to look at his subjects, decide the scenery and arrange them on the inspiration of the moment. He saw his sister and her family frequently, of course, but he hadn't seen Mary in quite a while. And besides, he wanted to see the two of them together, see how they looked and what they were wearing, before he decided on the best tableau.

His sister's idea of giving Mary a portrait of herself as a present had struck the young man as an admirable idea, and he'd offered to do it for nothing.

When the two women arrived at his studio, he welcomed them. Mary, he could see, was both pleased and a little self-conscious. The first thing he did, therefore, was to show her some of the better portraits he had done. She supposed that this was so that she might admire his work, but his real purpose was different; and it was not long before, by watching her expression and listening to her comments, he knew exactly how she would like to look herself.

For the art of the commercial photographer, he'd found, was surprisingly close to that of the painter. Your subject had to sit still, of course—depending on conditions the exposure might be more than thirty seconds. Then there was the color of the lights he used—often he found a blue light gave a better result—and also the direction of the light. By placing his lights well—that is to say, by letting his subject's face cast shadows—he could show the true volumes of the head, the structure and stress lines of the face, the character of the sitter. Sometimes he was able to do this; but usually, a revealing picture was the last thing people wanted. They were hoping for something quite different, something fashionable, something conventional, something entirely uninteresting. And he was used to obliging them, hoping that, with luck, the session might present enough of a technical challenge to amuse him.

Mary's hopes were simple. She just wanted to look like a lady, and a little younger than she was. And in twenty minutes he was able to make a portrait of her, sitting on an upholstered chair, before a velvet curtain and a table supporting a placid urn—a picture which, he was sure, would give her great joy, and be given to her family so that, one day long hence, someone could say: "See, that was how your Aunt Mary looked when she was young. Quite a handsome lady."

Gretchen's case was different—she already had the portraits she needed. In recent years, though, he had observed some subtle changes in his sister. Partly, of course, it was because she had listened to him talk about his work, and she had begun to understand the difference between the interesting and the humdrum. But there was something more than that. He'd detected it several times lately: a mischievous humor, a sense of adventure, even a trace of anarchy, perhaps, under her well-ordered exterior. Could it be that Gretchen had secret depths?

"It's time," she announced, "for our tableau."

He wasn't sure why, but Theodore knew what he wanted, now. It was a backdrop he hadn't used for some time. Most people would have felt it was out of date. He went to the back of the studio, found what he was looking for and hoisted it up.

It was a flowery, eighteenth-century garden scene, rococo and sensuous. It might have been painted by Watteau or Boucher, for the French court. In front of it he placed a swing with a wide seat. Deftly, he tied a few ribbons to the ropes of the swing, to match the spirit of the painted scene behind. Then he produced a pair of broad-rimmed straw hats and told the two of them to put them on.

"Mary, sit on the swing," he commanded. "Gretchen, stand behind."

It worked rather well. Humorous, yet charming. He told Gretchen to pretend she was in the act of pushing Mary on the swing. It took a minute or two to get the tableau right, but in the end it really did seem as if the swing was on the very point of motion and, telling the girls to hold their positions, he took his picture.

"One more," said Gretchen.

He didn't argue, set up the camera, went under the black cloth. And just as he did so, Gretchen reached forward and knocked off Mary's hat. Mary burst out laughing, shook her head back so that her dark hair fell loose. And with a flash of inspiration, Theodore took the picture.

As he emerged from under the cloth, he gazed at the two women, at his sister mischievously grinning, and at Mary with her loosened hair. And to himself he thought: How did I not see before how beautiful she is?

He offered them lemonade and seed cake. They chatted pleasantly about their families and the coming holiday. He made himself agreeable to Mary, while Gretchen glanced cheerfully round the studio. Suddenly her eyes alighted on the book of verse.

"What's this, Theodore?" she asked. And her brother smiled.

"It's a wicked book, Gretchen," he warned her.

"*Leaves of Grass*," she read. "Walt Whitman. Why have I heard of him?"

"He wrote a poem called 'Beat! Beat! Drums!' about the war, which got quite a bit of attention a couple of years ago. But this little book came before that, and caused something of a scandal. Interesting verse, though."

Theodore glanced at Mary, and saw to his surprise that she was blushing. Since Whitman's homoerotic verses had never, as far as he knew, been discussed much outside literary circles, he was rather curious as to how Mary would know about them. But he decided not to ask. Then the thought suddenly occurred to him that she might suppose that, reading such material, he harbored those tendencies himself.

"Whitman has genius, but I think Baudelaire's even better," he said. "Listen to this now." He smiled at the two young women. "Imagine you're on an island in the summer sun. Everything's quiet, just the sound of the little waves on the shore. The poem's called 'Invitation au Voyage.' "

"But it's in French," Mary, who had recovered herself now, objected.

"Just listen to the sound of it," he told her. And he began to read: "*Mon enfant, ma soeur, Songe à la douceur, D'aller là-bas vivre ensemble . . .*"

So Mary listened. She'd only been embarrassed for a moment when Theodore mentioned Walt Whitman. Not that she knew much about the man herself, but she did remember the name on account of a conversation she'd once overheard at the dinner table at the Masters' house. So she knew that Mr. Whitman was considered an indecent man, and she had some idea what that might mean, and then she'd suddenly been embarrassed in case Theodore might suppose that she knew all about those sorts of people, and that had made her blush. But she wasn't going to make a fool of herself again now, so she sat very still and listened.

Nobody had ever read a poem to her before, and certainly not one in French, but she had to admit that the poem's soft, sensuous sounds did seem rather like the waves of the sea, and she supposed that if she spoke French she might find the poem just as wonderful as Theodore evidently did.

"Thank you, Theodore," she said politely, when he had done.

And then Theodore suddenly said: "Let me show you some of my other work before you go." Mary didn't know what he meant, but while Theodore went over to a set of wide drawers and withdrew some folders, Gretchen explained.

"This means we're honored, Mary," she said. "Theodore takes portraits for a living, but he cares even more about his private work. He doesn't often talk about it."

When Theodore came back, he put the folders on the table in front of them and opened the covers. Soon Mary found herself looking at pictures which were entirely different from the portraits she'd seen. A few were pictures of individual people, one or two taken close up. Most were bigger, often in landscape format. There were scenes of the city streets and of the countryside. There were studies of alleys and courtyards where the light threw shadows across the image. There were pictures of ragamuffins and beggars. There were pictures of the busy docks, of the open harbor, of ships in the mist.

Mary wasn't sure what to make of some of them, where the images seemed to her to be random. But a glance at Gretchen and the way she was studying them carefully told her that there must be some special observation at work, some organization of image that she herself had not yet understood. It was strange to look at Theodore, too. He was still the same young fellow with the wide-set eyes that she had always known, but the self-absorbed seriousness that had seemed so funny and endearing in his childhood had turned into something else now that he was a young man. There was a concentration and intensity in his face that reminded her of the look on Hans's face when he had played the piano for her. And seeing the brother and sister together, sharing this art that she did not understand, she couldn't help wishing that she could share these things with them too.

One picture in particular struck her. It was taken on the West Side, where the line of railroad tracks ran up alongside the River Hudson. Above, there were heavy clouds, whose gleaming edges seemed to echo the dull gleam of the metal tracks below. The river was not gleaming, though, but lay like a huge, dark snake beside the tracks. And upon the tracks, some close by, others already far in the distance, walked the sad, scattered figures of Negroes, leaving town.

It was a common enough sight, she had no doubt. The underground railroad, as everyone called it, had always brought escaped slaves up to New York. But now, with the Civil War raging, that trickle had turned into a flood. And when this tide of Negroes reached New York, they mostly found neither jobs nor welcome, so that, on any day, you might see them setting off up another kind of railroad, hoping maybe to catch a ride on a passing train, or at least walk along the iron road that led to the far north, in the hope of a warmer reception somewhere there.

With its strange, eerie light, the hard gleam of the tracks and the black-ness of the river, the photograph captured perfectly the desolate poetry of the scene.

"You like it?" asked Theodore.

"Oh yes," she answered. "It's so sad. But . . ."

"Harsh?"

"I didn't realize that a rail track like that"—she hardly knew how to say it—"could also be so beautiful."

"Aha." Theodore looked at his sister with a pleased expression. "Mary has an eye."

They had to leave soon after that. But as the carriage took them south-ward toward the ferry, Mary turned to her friend and said: "I wish I understood photographs the way you do, Gretchen."

Gretchen smiled. "Theodore taught me a little, that's all. I can show you some things, if you want."

The ferry left from near Battery Point, and the journey took a couple of hours. It was delightful, on a sunny day, to pass across the upper corner of the great harbor where the ships entered the East River. From there they followed the huge curve of Brooklyn's shore until, reaching the nar-rows between Brooklyn and Staten Island, they sailed gradually out into the vast openness of the Lower Bay.

At one point, passing a small fort that lay just off the Brooklyn shore, one of their fellow passengers remarked: "That's Fort Lafayette. They've got a bunch of men from the South in there. President's holding them without charge and without trial." Though whether he approved or dis-approved of this violation of the Southern men's rights the gentleman didn't say.

Nor just then did Gretchen or Mary want to know about the fate of the prisoners. For as the salty Atlantic breeze caught their faces, and the ferry began to dip and roll excitingly in the choppy waters, they got their first glimpse, to the south-east, of the broad and sandy beaches of their desti-nation.

Concy Island.

✛

The quarrel between Frank Master and his wife the following afternoon went exactly as he planned. It was four o'clock when he got home and he found her in the parlor.

"Tom here?" he asked cheerfully. He was told their son was out. "Well, anyway," he said with a smile, "it's all fixed. He won't be drafted. Paid my three hundred dollars and got a receipt. Then I went uptown to see how the draft was going. Didn't appear to be any trouble."

Hetty greeted this information with silence.

In the·two years since the armed conflict between the Northern and Southern states of America had begun, all the Union regiments had been volunteers. Only recently had President Lincoln been obliged to order a draft. The names of all eligible males were put into a big lottery, and a selection made by a draw.

Unless you had money, of course. If you had money, you sent a poor person to fight in your place, or paid three hundred dollars to the authorities, who'd find someone for you.

To Frank Master it seemed reasonable enough. And it sure as hell seemed a good idea to young Tom, who had no desire to go down to the killing fields.

For if the upper classes of Europe were proud of their military prowess, the rich men of the Northern states of America had no such illusions. In England, aristocrats and gentlemen, especially younger sons, crowded into the fashionable regiments, paid money for their officers' commissions, and thought themselves fine fellows when they paraded in their uniforms. Were they not—in fact, or at least in theory—descendants of the barons and knights of medieval England? The aristocrat did not trade. He did not draw up your will, or cure you of sickness. God forbid. That was for the middle classes. The aristocrat lived on the land and led his men into battle. And in America, too, among the old landed families from Virginia southward, some echo of that tradition might still be found. But not in Boston, Connecticut or New York. To hell with that. Pay your money and let the poor fellow be killed.

The poor fellows knew it of course.

"It's a rich man's war and a poor man's fight," complained those who could not afford the fee. And the city authorities had been concerned that the draft might lead to some trouble.

Accordingly, that Saturday morning, they'd chosen to begin the selection at the Ninth District Headquarters, which was an isolated building set among some empty lots up at Third and Forty-seventh, well away from the main body of the city. Frank Master had gone up there to take a look, and found a large crowd watching the marshal draw names from a barrel. But they'd seemed quiet. And after a while, evidently relieved, the marshal had stopped, announcing that selection wouldn't resume until Monday.

"You don't look very pleased," Frank remarked to Hetty.

Still his wife said nothing.

"You actually want Tom to go and fight in this damn fool war? Because he doesn't want to, I can tell you."

"He must make his own choice."

"He did," said Master firmly, in a voice that clearly implied: "So you're on your own."

❖

If Frank and Hetty Master's marriage had been under strain at the time of the Cooper Institute speech, events since had not made things any easier between them. Lincoln had become the Republican candidate, and he'd run a shrewd campaign.

"Whatever your mother believes," Frank had explained to young Tom, "the truth is that people in the North are against slavery on principle, but they're not that excited about it. Lincoln can include the slavery issue on his platform, but he knows he can't win on it." As the elections of 1860 had drawn near, "Free Soil, Free Labor, Free Men" was the Republican motto. Hard-working Northerners, supported by the government, should take over the western lands, build railways and develop industries, while the men of the South, morally inferior through their support for slavery, would be left behind. "He's offering free land and government aid," Frank had remarked drily. "A pretty good inducement for doing right."

The election had been close, but Lincoln had squeaked in. Upstate New York had voted Republican. But not the people of Democratic New York City—they'd voted Lincoln down.

For whatever ticket Lincoln ran on, he was going to cause trouble with the South. And if the wealth of the merchants depended on the South, so did the jobs of every working man. Tammany Hall knew it. Mayor Fernando Wood knew it, and said so loudly. If Lincoln wanted to put the city's jobs at risk, he declared, to hell with him.

The working men of New York weren't too sure how they felt about the Republicans in general, either. Republican free farmers, with their notions of individual effort and self-help, were no friends to the working men's unions, whose only bargaining power lay in their numbers. Working men suspected something else too. "If Lincoln has his way, there'll be millions of free blacks—who'll work for pence—headed north to steal our jobs. No thank you."

Hetty Master was disgusted with this attitude. Frank thought it understandable. He was also proved right in his fears about the secession.

On December 20, 1860, South Carolina had left the Union. One after another, the states of the Deep South had followed. By February 1861, they were forming a Confederacy and had chosen a president of their own. Other Southern states were holding back from such a drastic step. But the secession states now saw an interesting opportunity. "If the Union's breaking up," they declared, "we can refuse to pay all the debts we owe to the rich boys in New York." Delegations of merchants, both Democrat and Republican, went down from New York to Washington, anxious to find a compromise. Lincoln passed through the city, but satisfied no one.

It was Mayor Fernando Wood, however, who issued New York's most striking threat. If Lincoln wanted war with the South, and the ruination of the city, then New York should consider another option.

"We should secede from the Union ourselves," he announced.

"New York City leave the United States? Is he mad?" cried Hetty.

"Not entirely," said Frank.

A free city; a duty-free port: the idea wasn't new. Great European cities like Hamburg and Frankfurt had operated like independent states since the Middle Ages. The merchants of New York spent several weeks considering its feasibility, and it was actually the Confederacy in the South which had brought discussions to an end, with the move they made in March: the Southern ports would drop their customs duties.

"They'll cut us out," Frank announced grimly to his family, "and trade with Britain direct."

There was nothing you could do after that. Reluctantly, New York City fell into line behind Lincoln. The next month, when Confederates fired upon Fort Sumter, the Civil War had officially begun. Either the South's insurrection must be put down, argued Lincoln, or the Union of states built by the Founding Fathers would be lost. The Union must be preserved.

Since good manners can preserve a marriage, and he still felt affection for her, Frank Master did his best to be polite, and tried to avoid saying things that would upset his wife. For Hetty, however, the issue was more difficult. She loved Frank, but what does a woman do when her husband looks every day at a great evil and, for all his politeness, doesn't seem to give a damn? Nor did it help that, when the war began, it proved that he had been right about the South seceding, and he could not help saying, "I told you so." By the time the Civil War was in its first year, though their personal union endured, Frank and Hetty no longer looked at maps together or discussed the future. And in the evenings, where once they had often liked to sit on a sofa side by side, they would quietly take an armchair each, and read. Manners covered, but could not put out, the slow fire of their anger.

And sometimes, even manners failed.

❖

Today, by throwing their son and the draft in her face, he'd deliberately annoyed her.

"You hate this war because you think only of profit," Hetty said coldly.

"Actually," he countered calmly, "this war has made me richer."

He and many others. Partly it was luck. For after a few terrible months in 1861, when trade with the South had collapsed, fate had handed New York an unexpected bonus. The British grain harvest had failed—just as the Midwest had enjoyed a bumper crop. Massive quantities of wheat had flowed through the city, bound for England. The Hudson railroad and the dear old Erie Canal had proved their value a hundred times over. The city's grain trade had been booming ever since, along with cattle, sugar and Pennsylvania oil for kerosene.

But, chiefly, Frank Master had discovered what his ancestors from the previous century could have told him: war was good for business. The army's needs were huge. The city's ironworks were at capacity, fitting warships and ironclads; Brooks Brothers were turning out uniforms by the thousand. And beyond that, wartime governments needed stupendous funds. Wall Street was making a fortune floating government bonds. Even the stock market was booming.

Hetty ignored his remark, and went on the attack again.

"Your slave-owning friends are going to lose."

Was she right? Probably. Even after the wavering states like Virginia had thrown in their lot with the South, the contest was hopelessly unequal. If you looked at the resources of the two sides, the manpower, industry, even the agricultural production of the North dwarfed that of the South. The strategy of the North was simple: blockade the South and throttle her.

Yet the South was not without hope. Her troops were brave and her generals splendid. Early in the war, at Bull Run, Stonewall Jackson had withstood the Union men and sent them scurrying back to Washington. General Robert Lee was a genius. Furthermore, while the Union troops were fighting to impose their will on their neighbors, the men of the South were fighting, on their own territory, for their heritage. If the South could hold out long enough, then perhaps the North would lose heart and leave them alone. True, Lee had been turned back, with terrible losses, up at Antietam last year, and General Grant had just smashed the Confederates at Gettysburg, but it wasn't over yet. Not by a long way.

"The North can win," Master acknowledged, "but is it worth the price? The Battle of Shiloh was a bloodbath. Tens of thousands of men are being slaughtered. The South is being ruined. And for what?"

"So that men can live in freedom, as God ordains."

"The slaves?" He shook his head. "I don't think so. Lincoln thinks slavery is wrong—that I don't deny—but he went to war to preserve the Union. He made that perfectly clear. He has even said, in public: 'If I could save the Union without freeing a single slave, I'd do it.' His words. Not mine." He paused. "What does Lincoln want for the slaves? Who knows? From what I hear, his main idea for liberated slaves is to find a free colony in Africa or Central America, and send them there. Do you know he actually told a delegation of black men, to their faces, that he doesn't want Negroes in the United States?"

Fairly chosen or not, the fact that every one of these statements had some basis served only, as Frank knew it would, to rile Hetty more.

"That's not what he means at all!" she cried. "What about the Proclamation?"

Master smiled. The Emancipation Proclamation. Lincoln's masterstroke. The abolitionists loved it, of course—just as Lincoln intended that they should. He'd announced it late last year, repeated it this spring. Told all the world that the slaves of the South would be freed.

Or had he?

"Have you studied, my dear, what our president actually said?" Frank inquired. "He threatens to emancipate the slaves in any state remaining in rebellion. It's a negotiating ploy. He's telling the Confederates: 'Quit now, because if you delay, I'll set free all your slaves.' Yet his Proclamation specifically exempts every slave county that has already fallen to the Union. God knows how many thousand slaves are now under Lincoln's control. But of those, he's not freeing a single one. Not one." He gazed at her in triumph. "So much for the abolitionists' hero."

"Wait until the war is over," she countered. "Then you'll see."

"Perhaps."

"You only hate him because he has morals."

Frank shrugged. "Morals? What morals? He's got men held without trial in Fort Lafayette. So he evidently cares nothing for habeas corpus. He's thrown men in jail for writing against him. Seems our lawyer president has never heard of the Zenger trial, either. I'll tell you what your friend Lincoln is. He's a cynical tyrant."

"Copperhead!"

A poisonous snake. It was Lincoln's term, for those who questioned the war effort.

"If you mean that I think this war might have been avoided," he said in a voice that was dangerously quiet, "and that I'd like to see a peace negotiated, you are absolutely right. And I'm not alone. You think that makes me evil? Think it." He paused before suddenly shouting: "But at least I'm not trying to send our son to a pointless death. And I guess you are." He turned on his heel.

"That is unfair," she cried.

"I'm going to the counting house," he roared back. "Don't wait up."

And moments later, he was striding out of Gramercy Park. Only when he was halfway down Irving Place did he slow his pace and allow himself half a smile.

It had gone just as he planned.

✥

Mary gazed out at the ocean. The breeze made a faint, rasping whisper on the tufts of seagrass behind her, and played with her hair. The low rolls of surf broke with a light hiss, as they sent their spume to lick the sand.

Miles away to the west, they could see the low rise of Staten Island's southern shore. Ahead, between the two outer arms of the Lower Bay, lay the vastness of the Atlantic Ocean.

"Let's go to the Point," said Gretchen.

It was Saturday morning. Most of the weekend visitors had yet to arrive, and there were only a few people on the long expanse of beach.

Since the 1820s, when a shell road had been made across the creek between Coney Island and the mainland, people had been making Sunday excursions to its long dunes and ocean beaches. But it was still a peaceful place.

In the middle of Coney Island, a hamlet of small clapboard hotels and inns catered to the respectable families who came to enjoy a week or two of ocean air and quiet. A few celebrities, like Herman Melville, Jenny Lind and Sam Houston, had come to visit, but otherwise the fashionable world had not taken it up and so the place retained its discreet charm. Once people did discover Coney Island, they usually returned. The half-dozen families staying in the inn that Gretchen and Mary occupied came there every year.

They'd eaten a hearty breakfast of eggs, pancakes and sausages out on the broad porch that ran along the front of the inn, before they set out for a walk.

The island's western point was the only place on Coney Island where vulgarity raised its head. Some years back, a pair of sharp-eyed men had come out and decided to open a small pleasure pavilion there, so that when people came off the ferry, they could find refreshments and amusements. By midsummer, nowadays, a collection of card sharps, tricksters and other undesirables had made the place their own. The people at the hotel pretended it wasn't there—and indeed, you could neither see nor hear it from the hamlet. But Gretchen and Mary were quite content to spend half an hour watching the men who sold candy or offered the three-card trick.

Next, they walked round the landward side of the island until they came to the shell road.

If you looked from Manhattan across the East River nowadays, you'd conclude that Brooklyn was a busy place. There were the shipyards on the waterfront, the warehouses and factories along the shore, and the residential city that had grown up on Brooklyn Heights. When the British redcoats had camped there in 1776, Brooklyn had less than two thousand inhabitants. Now there were more than a hundred thousand. Why, there was even talk of laying out a fine public space, to be called Prospect Park, up on the high ground. But once you got past the Heights, you came down to a great sweep of open countryside, extending half a dozen miles or more, and dotted with small towns and Dutch hamlets that had hardly changed since the eighteenth century.

As she looked back along the shell road, therefore, across the open breezy tracts of sand dune, marsh and farmland toward the invisible city, Mary couldn't help remarking, with a smile: "We might be in another world."

After that, they crossed again to the ocean side and walked eastward along the great stretches of Brighton Beach, drinking in the sea air, for upward of an hour. By the time they returned to the inn, it was past noon, and they were quite hungry.

"Don't eat too much now," said Gretchen, "or you'll fall asleep."

"I don't care if I do," said Mary. And she laughed, and helped herself to a second slice of apple pie, and made Gretchen take another slice too. There were cane chairs on the grass in front of the inn, so they sat in those for a while. The breeze had dropped, and they covered their faces with straw hats because of the hot sun.

And some time passed before Gretchen said to Mary, "I have another surprise for you," and Mary asked, "What's that?" and Gretchen said, "Come upstairs, and I'll show you."

Their bedroom was charming. It had two beds with pink covers, and a window that looked toward the sea. The walls were painted white, but there was a pretty picture of flowers hanging in a gold-painted frame above each bed, and a small picture of somebody's ancestor in a blue coat and a tall black hat over the fire, and a striking French clock on the mantel, and a nice rug on the floor. It was very genteel—so Mary had guessed at once that, although Gretchen said they were sharing the cost of the room equally, Gretchen's husband must really be paying the lion's share.

Gretchen had opened her suitcase. Now she took out two packages wrapped in paper, and handed one of them to Mary. "I've got mine. This one's yours." She smiled. "Aren't you going to look at it?"

As she unwrapped, Mary could see this was clothing of some kind. She took it out.

"I don't know what it is," she said.

Gretchen laughed. "It's a bathing dress, Mary."

"But what would I be doing with that?"

"You'll be putting it on, and bathing in the sea," said Gretchen, as she held up her own in triumph. "Look: we match."

Each bathing dress was in two parts. The lower half consisted of a pair of pantaloons, tied round the calf with ribbons. Over these fell a long-sleeved dress that came down to the knees. Everything was made of wool, to keep the body warm. Gretchen was obviously proud of her choice. The pantaloons had frilly bottoms, and the dresses lacy fringes. Hers was a pale and Mary's a darker blue, so that they matched like sisters.

As they left the inn and walked down the path to the beach, Mary was still doubtful. They were both wearing their beach dresses, as well as stockings and shoes to protect against the unseen dangers of the sea floor. They carried towels, and wore their straw hats against the sun.

⁘

Theodore Keller stepped off the ferry. He was dressed in a loose linen jacket and was wearing a wide-brimmed hat. In one hand he carried a small leather traveling case. After asking directions, he began to walk in the direction of the inn. He was looking cheerful. It was years since he'd been to Coney Island.

He'd only decided to make the journey when he woke up that morning. It was done entirely on a whim—the day was so fine, the ferry seemed to call him out of the city. And of course, there was the pleasant prospect of spending time with his sister. And Mary O'Donnell.

Why did men pursue women? Theodore supposed there must be many reasons. Lust, temptation, the desire for the sins of the flesh, of course, were strong. He possessed as much lust as any other young fellow, and was certainly no stranger to the flesh—indeed, he was rather sensual—but his constant pursuit of women was driven, above all, by curiosity. Women interested him. When Theodore met women he liked, he did not talk about himself, as some men do, but questioned them. He wanted to know about their lives, their opinions, their feelings. They found it flattering. He was interested in all sorts of women, from the fashionable ladies who came to his studio, to the poor servant girls he met in the street. He made no distinctions. He appreciated them as individuals. And once his interest began, he did not stop. He wanted to discover all their secrets, and possess them, every one.

Not that his seductions were without any calculation. His photographic studio provided wonderful opportunities. Once a fashionable lady was standing or sitting in position, his blue eyes would stare at them intently for a few moments, before he adjusted the position of a light and stared at them again. Then he might ask them to look this way or that, and give a little grunt of appreciation, as if he'd just made an interesting discovery. It was an unusual woman who did not become intrigued and ask him what he'd seen.

His technique was always the same. If the woman was not a particular beauty, he would say something like: "You have a very beautiful profile. Did you know?" If, on the other hand, it was clear to him that the lady in question was used to being considered handsome, he'd remark, "I've no doubt people tell you you're beautiful," as if it were not important, "but there's something," he'd pause a second as if he were trying to analyze it, "something about the way your eyes settle on objects that I find interesting. You don't draw or watercolor, do you?" They nearly always did. "Ah," he'd say, "that's probably what it is, then. You have an artist's eye. It's rare, you know."

By the time the session was over, they'd usually made an appointment to visit the studio again.

So what was his interest in Mary? He wasn't sure yet. He'd been quite surprised at the studio when he'd suddenly realized how beautiful she was. As that cascade of dark hair had fallen against the pale skin of her neck, he'd observed that she had a flawless complexion. How come he'd never noticed before? He'd imagined what she might look like unclothed. All kinds of possibilities had occurred to him. He'd been intrigued.

His sister's friend, the young woman he'd known since he was a boy, turned out to be a Celtic beauty. She always seemed so prim and proper, but looks could be deceptive. What did she really think?

Even if she gave him the chance to discover, there were difficulties. Apart from the usual risks, he wasn't sure how Gretchen would feel about it. Mary had a brother, too—quite a dangerous fellow, he believed. Theodore had taken his chances with angry husbands before, but all the same, he'd have to be careful.

In any case, there couldn't be any harm in his spending a pleasant day or two with his sister out on Coney Island. The business with Mary might, or might not, come to anything. He'd just wait and see what happened.

✢

"Lots of people have taken up bathing recently," said Gretchen.

"Doctors say salt water's bad for the skin," Mary objected.

"We won't go in for long," Gretchen promised.

There were some bathing huts on wheels by a sand dune, where people could change. They inspected one of them. It didn't smell very nice, and they were glad they'd left their clothes in the safety of the inn. Looking along the beach, Mary could see about a dozen people, some way off, standing stiffly in the surf, probably just as uncertain about this new-fangled enterprise as she was. She took a deep breath. Then, taking Gretchen's proffered hand, she allowed herself to be led down the beach and into the sea.

The water felt sharp and cold on her ankles. She gave a tiny intake of breath.

"Come on," said Gretchen. "It won't bite."

Mary took a few steps more. The water came up to her knees now. Just then, a little wave rose up, washing past her and covering the lower part of her thighs for several seconds, causing her to give out a little cry. Then she felt the bottom of her bathing dress, suddenly heavy with water, clamp down coldly above her knees, while the legs of her pantaloons clung wetly to her flesh. She gave a shiver.

"Walk with me," said Gretchen. "It won't feel cold in a moment."

"Yes it will," laughed Mary, but she did as Gretchen said, and pushed her legs through the heavy water, as it enveloped her waist. And soon she realized that Gretchen was right. The water didn't feel cold, once you got used to it, though she was aware that the bathing dress she was wearing was probably heavy enough to sink her now, if she lost her footing.

She was glad that on her left there was support at hand, if she needed it. From the shallows out into the deep water ran a line of stout posts, spaced about ten feet apart and linked by a thick rope, like a sort of break-water. Holding onto the rope, bathers could work their way slowly out into the sea without fear of missing their footing or being swept away. Further out, the line of posts ran parallel to the beach, enclosing the bathers in a large pen. Mary didn't quite see the point of this until, when the water was almost up to her chest, a larger wave came in from the ocean and carried her off her feet. Struggling to keep her head above water, she was surprised to find that the ebb carried her away from the beach, and she realized the barrier was there to prevent her being taken out to sea.

"Take my hand," said Gretchen, and pulled her back into shallower water. "I said we'd go bathing," she remarked with a smile, "not that we'd swim." And glancing along the shoreline, Mary could see that most of the other bathers were standing contentedly about in the shallows, where the water hardly reached their waists.

So that is what she and Gretchen did. It was quite agreeable, feeling the cool of the water on her legs, and the sun on her face, and the salty sea breeze. The only thing she didn't like was that the wet wool of her bathing dress felt heavy, and scratched her skin a little. Then they sat at the edge of the beach with their legs in the shallows, so that the little waves broke over them, and tiny shells jostled, and the ebbing sand made a funny feeling on her legs each time the wave receded, making her giggle.

And they were sitting like that when, to their great surprise, Theodore appeared.

Mary was so astonished that she gave a little gasp, and blushed.

"What are you doing here?" said Gretchen, which sounded almost unfriendly, though Mary was sure it must have been because Theodore had taken her unawares.

"They told me at the inn that I'd find you on the beach," said Theodore cheerfully. He took off his wide-brimmed hat. "It was such a beautiful day when I woke up that I thought I'd get out of the city and join you here."

He glanced at Mary and smiled. Mary was suddenly rather conscious that he was fully dressed while she was sitting there with her legs showing. It made her feel a little awkward, but he seemed quite relaxed. He gazed round at the other bathers on the beach. "Maybe I'll take a dip later," he said.

"We're going back to the inn now," said Gretchen. So Theodore walked back with them.

When they got to their room, Mary undressed with care. She'd done her best to get rid of the sand outside, and Gretchen had brushed her down, but you couldn't get rid of all the sand, and she didn't want to make a mess on the floor. Taking off her pantaloons and stockings slowly, she was able to keep most of the sand inside them, so that she could take them downstairs and hang them on a clothes line, and dust them off when they were dry.

Mary had always been rather modest. Though she had known Gretchen most of her life, she had stood behind her bed when she changed, and slipped her bathing dress on quickly. So she was just wondering how to take it off now, in a modest manner, when she saw Gretchen pull hers down easily and walk, quite naked, across the room to the washstand, where she poured some water from the jug into the big china bowl, and started to wash herself down, as if it was the most natural thing in the world.

She had never seen Gretchen without any clothes on. Her friend had a nice body, not plump, but compact. Apart from a couple of little stretch marks, you wouldn't know she'd had two children. Her yellow hair was still pinned up as she turned to Mary and smiled.

"Just as nature made me," she remarked. "You don't mind, do you? It's how my husband sees me, after all."

"He does?"

Gretchen laughed. "I know some wives always keep themselves covered—partly anyway. My mother did—she told me." She shrugged. "My husband can see as much of me as he likes."

"That was a surprise, Theodore coming," Mary said.

"Nothing my brother does surprises me," said Gretchen.

Since Gretchen had taken her bathing dress off, Mary thought she'd better do the same. What would Theodore think, she wondered, if he could see me like this? She washed the remaining sand off herself as quickly as she could, and dressed.

The inn served dinner at five o'clock. It was a family affair, with children present, under their parents' watchful eyes.

The food was excellent: a cold salad, freshly made bread and a superb fish stew. The innkeeper prided himself on obtaining the best seafood—mussels, crabs, clams, and the many fish to be had in the Long Island Sound—all washed down with a cool white wine. To follow, he offered the first watermelons they'd seen that season, together with jellies and fruit trifle.

Theodore was in a very relaxed mood. At the start of the meal Gretchen asked him: "When's the last ferry, Theodore? You don't want to miss it."

"No need to worry," he answered pleasantly. "I'm staying here. They had one room left at the inn. It's rather small, but it'll do."

"Oh," said Gretchen. Mary was rather pleased.

So Theodore talked, and told them funny stories. Mary wished she could engage him in conversation about the things that interested him, but she wasn't sure how, and in any case, he seemed quite content to make small talk. She laughed at his jokes, and he smiled at her, and she felt very comfortable in his presence.

"Aren't you pleased I stayed?" he said playfully to his sister, toward the end of the meal.

"I'm surprised you're not out with one of your lady friends," she replied tartly. "He has a lot of lady friends," she remarked to Mary.

"A gross exaggeration," said Theodore, smiling at Mary. "I am an artist and I live like a monk."

"I don't think I believe you, Mr. Keller," said Mary with a laugh. "But I hope you don't imagine I'm shocked." After all, when she remembered all the girls her brother Sean had been with, let alone what she might have seen any day of the week in Five Points, there was no need to be prim if young Theodore Keller was getting his share too.

"It's not you that's shocked at the idea, Mary," he said. "It's me." And then they both laughed.

"So what is it you look for in your lady friends?" Mary asked him boldly.

He didn't answer at once, but stared thoughtfully across the other tables.

"To tell you the truth," he said, "I don't run after women for the sake of it, as some men do. If I seek a woman's friendship, it's because I find her interesting."

After the meal, the children were allowed to run about. Some of the grown-ups went to walk along the beach again, while others preferred the card tables set out on the porch. Theodore lit a cigar, and went down to the water. Gretchen and Mary played cards for a while with a pleasant man from Westchester and his wife, then went to sit on some long chairs to look at the sea, as the slow summer sunset began.

"It must be nice, being married and having children," said Mary. "I suppose I envy you that."

"It's all right. Hard work," said Gretchen.

"I'm sure. But having a husband . . ."

Gretchen was silent for a minute. "They take you for granted before long," she said.

"But your husband is kind, isn't he?"

"Oh yes." Gretchen stared up at the sky. "I can't complain."

"And you love your children."

"Of course."

"I suppose I might have married Nolan, if I hadn't discovered what a brute he was."

"So you're glad you didn't."

"Oh yes, of course I am."

"Do you feel lonely?" Gretchen asked after a little while.

"Not much. Perhaps a little."

They were silent for a minute or so after that.

"I suppose my brother will settle down one day," Gretchen said with a sigh. Then she laughed. "When he's about fifty." She glanced across. "Stay away from my brother, Mary. He's dangerous, you know."

No doubt Gretchen was concerned for her welfare, but it seemed to Mary that her friend had no business telling her to stay away from her brother like that, and she couldn't help a small flash of resentment and rebellion.

"I'm old enough to look after myself, thank you," she said.

When Theodore came back, they all agreed that after all the fresh air and exercise of the day, they were ready to turn in.

The sky was still red as Mary and Gretchen undressed and got into their beds. Through the open window, Mary could hear the soft sound of the sea. She was just dozing off when she heard a rustle, and realized that Gretchen had got out of her bed. She raised her head to see what her friend was doing, and found that Gretchen was standing beside her. Her hair, undone, was hanging down to her shoulders. Then Gretchen leaned over so that her hair brushed her face, and kissed her on the forehead, before getting back into her bed. And Mary was glad to know that, even if she had been cross with Gretchen for a moment, she was still, always, her friend.

⁜

Sean O'Donnell got up at nine o'clock that morning. His wife and children were still at breakfast when he went downstairs into the saloon, and found Hudson already at work, cleaning up after the night before. He gave the black man a brief nod, went to the street door and looked out.

Sunday morning. The street was quiet, but he stayed there a little while, for he was a cautious man.

He turned. This time, he gave young Hudson a thoughtful look.

"Thinking of going out today?" he asked.

"I got to be at the church later this morning," said the black man.

The Shiloh Presbyterian Church. It wasn't far away.

"Tell me," said Sean, "before you go."

It was three years now since he'd encountered Hudson. Like most of the Negroes in the city, he'd arrived after a long and dangerous journey up the underground railway, whose terminus had been the Shiloh Church. A journalist, a friend of the Negro minister at Shiloh, had asked Sean if he could find a place for Hudson. To oblige a regular customer, Sean had agreed to see the young fellow.

Personally, Sean wasn't too keen on helping runaway slaves. Like most Irish Catholics in the city, he disliked the privileged Protestant evangelical ministers who preached abolition, and had no wish to antagonize the South. But there were quite a few Negroes doing the menial jobs in New York saloons, and nobody paid them much heed.

"New York ain't a very friendly place for a black man," he'd warned Hudson.

"My grandaddy told me we came from here," Hudson had replied. "I was figuring to stay."

So Sean had given him a try, and Hudson had proved to be a good worker.

"Is Hudson your family name?" Sean had asked.

"My father was Hudson, sir. And I'm Hudson Junior. But I don't have no other name."

"Well, you need a family name," said Sean. "And 'Hudson Hudson' sounds foolish, in my opinion." He'd considered. "Why don't you take the name of River? Then you'd be Hudson River. That sure as hell sounds like a New York name to me."

And soon the young man was registered as Hudson River, and before long this curious name had made him something of a mascot in the saloon.

"Hudson," said Sean O'Donnell now, "step over and help me close these shutters, will you?"

Together they closed the big green shutters that covered the two windows that gave onto the street. Then Sean went outside and began to push and pull on the shutters, which rattled quite a bit. Then he went back in, and asked Hudson if the latch for the shutters had seemed firm, and Hudson said no, not very.

"Do you reckon you could fix a bar across the shutters that'll hold them firm?" Sean asked, for Hudson was good at those things. And Hudson said yes. "I want you to do it today," said Sean.

"We expecting trouble?"

Sean O'Donnell could smell trouble. You didn't survive thirty-eight years in the streets around Five Points without developing an instinct for danger. From his youth, he could tell from the way a man walked whether he was carrying a knife. Sometimes he could sense trouble before it came round a corner—though he couldn't say how he knew.

Now that he was older, and had become a man of property, that same instinct had been transferred to his business affairs. His attitude to the financial community was characteristic.

"The way I see it," he'd told his sister, "since most of the men in Five Points will rob you if they get the chance, and since I know there isn't a single alderman in the city that can't be bought, why would the merchants on South Street or the bankers on Wall Street be any different? They're all criminals, I reckon." Part of the reason why nobody knew how much money he had was that he refused to entrust it to any financial institution. He lent money, certainly, to men he knew personally and reckoned a fair risk. He invested in numerous enterprises, which he could watch over himself. And he held government bonds. "The government's as crooked as anyone else, but they can print money." His hoard of cash, however, was kept in locked boxes, which he hid in safe places.

This expedient, primitive though it might be, had at least saved him worry. Half a dozen years ago, when the head of the great Ohio Insurance Company, having made all kinds of shaky loans, closed the company's doors and tried to abscond with the remaining funds, half the banks in New York, who'd lent to Ohio themselves, were unable to meet their obligations. Since all the financial institutions had lent to each other, without the least idea of what backed the loans, the panic of 1857 had soon spread halfway round the globe, and though it was brief, innumerable men on Wall Street had been wiped out before it was over. One clever fellow called Jerome, who came into the saloons quite often, had seen the crash coming just in time, and had bet heavily on the falling market. A few months later, he'd quietly informed Sean: "I made better'n a million dollars in that crash."

As for Sean, he'd just gone to his chest of dollar bills, bought up some property that was going cheap, and continued to serve drinks to anyone who still had the money to pay.

But last night, listening to the talk at the bar, it wasn't financial trouble he'd sensed. It was something much more visceral, belonging to Five Points rather than Wall Street. The crowd in the saloon on Saturday nights was different from the rest of the week. Hardly any journalists. Mostly local Irishmen.

And that's what he'd sensed as he'd listened to them: danger. Irish danger.

The Irish community respected Sean. If there were people in Five Points who still remembered his knife with fear, there were many more among the countless immigrants who had come in following the Famine who had reason to be grateful to him for finding them a place to live, or a job, and generally easing their transition into this dangerous new society.

He was still close to Mayor Fernando Wood. Wood's brother Benjamin, who'd owned a newspaper and written a book, would come into the saloon from time to time. And though Mayor Wood had fallen out with the other Tammany Hall men recently, Sean maintained good relations. One of them, known as Boss Tweed, had quietly told him: "You're loyal to Wood. We respect that. But you're still one of us, O'Donnell. Come to me when Wood's gone . . ." At elections, Sean could deliver a thousand votes on his own authority.

In his saloon, he was king. Young Hudson had witnessed this soon after he'd started working there. In the fall of 1860, no less a person than Queen Victoria's son, the Prince of Wales, had made a goodwill visit to Canada and the United States. After watching Blondin cross over Niagara Falls on a tightrope—and politely declining the funambulist's offer to take him across the same tightrope in a wheelbarrow—the nineteen-year-old prince had arrived in Manhattan. The city had given him a royal welcome, for the most part. But to Irish immigrants, who blamed England for the Famine, his visit could not be welcome. The 69th Irish Regiment, to a man, had refused to parade for him. And to be sure, nobody was planning to take him round Five Points.

Why some well-meaning people, conducting him round the newspaper quarter, had suddenly decided to show him a New York saloon, nobody ever discovered. No doubt they reckoned that, with its regular daily clientele of journalists, O'Donnell's would be a pretty safe bet. But whatever the reason, at one o'clock that day, a party of gentlemen, among whom the incognito prince was instantly recognizable, entered the saloon and politely asked for drinks at the bar.

Naturally, there were a score of writers and fellows from the print trade in the place at the time. But there must have been twenty Irishmen too.

And the saloon fell silent. The newspapermen looked curious, but the

Irishmen were giving the young man a terrible, cold stare. Even a pair of Irish policemen in one corner had a look on their faces that suggested they might, at any moment, fail to see or hear anything. The royal party got the message. They were glancing around anxiously, wondering what to do, when, cutting through the awful silence, came Sean's calm voice.

"Welcome to O'Donnell's saloon, gentlemen," and now his eyes moved round every man in the room, "where we show Irish hospitality to travelers who have lost their way."

That was it. A quiet hum resumed. The royal party were served and, soon afterward, gratefully made their escape.

But the talk last night had been of a very different nature. This had not been about the Famine, or Irish resentment of England. It had been about the Union and New York. If his instincts were right, it meant trouble. Big trouble. And neither his nor anyone else's moral authority would be of any help at all.

⁕

Every politician knows how the public mood can change. Sometimes the change is gradual. Sometimes, like water held back by a barrier, it will suddenly break through and rush down like a flood, sweeping all before it.

When Fernando Wood had suggested the city should secede from the Union, his words might have been intemperate, but they caught the mood of many New York Irish at that time. Yet only a few weeks later, when the Civil War began, both the mayor and his Irish supporters had changed their tune entirely. Why was that?

Well, the South had made the running—cutting out New York shippers, refusing to pay their debts, and firing on Fort Sumter. But even so, New York's show of loyalty had been astounding. In the first year, it had fielded more than sixty regiments of volunteers. Every immigrant community had taken part: Kleindeutschland's Germans, the Polish legion, the Italians' Garibaldi Guards. And none more so than the mighty Irish Brigades. God knows how many regiments of brave boys, blessed by Cardinal Hughes, had marched out proudly under their Irish banners. Their mothers and sweethearts and other family had lovingly sewn those banners—Mary O'Donnell had eagerly sewn one of them herself.

Of course, the boys were getting paid. Ninety days of fighting service, and a return home with cash in your pocket—it wasn't such a bad deal for a brave young fellow out of work. If you hated England, you reckoned that hurting the South would damage the English cotton trade, which couldn't be bad. And for those who dreamed of returning one day to avenge Ireland and drive the English out, this was useful military training, too.

Above all, though, it was Irish pride.

You might blame the English for the Famine, but once you arrived in the New World, there was no one to blame for anything. And even here, in the land of boundless opportunity, you might have to crowd your family into a tenement hovel; and when you went to look for work, find a sign on the door that said: "Irish Need Not Apply." Humiliation, for the proud princes of Ireland.

No wonder they loved Cardinal Hughes for building them a magnificent cathedral, and for championing Catholic schools. No wonder they flooded into the police and the fire brigade, which gave them authority and honor. No wonder they sought and gave protection in Tammany Hall. And now they had a chance to prove their American loyalty and valour in battle. No wonder they marched out proudly, under their Irish banners.

But that was two years ago.

They'd thought the war would be over soon. It wasn't. Nor had anyone foreseen the horror of it. Perhaps they should have done. The increasing mechanization of war, the introduction of the rifle with its terrible range and penetration, not to mention the incompetence of some of the commanders, had taken a terrible toll. It was butchery. Not only that, the butchery was being photographed. Images were there in the newspapers for all to see. Soon Bellevue hospital was full of maimed and wounded. So was the Sisters of Charity hospital on Central Park. You saw the disfigured hobbling in the streets. And those were the lucky ones.

For so many had not returned. The Garibaldi Guards were no more. The brave Irish Brigades had ceased to exist.

And for those families with husbands or sons still at the front, where was the promised soldiers' pay? Lincoln's government had not paid some of them in almost a year. In other cases, their own officers had stolen the pay. The recruiting tent by City Hall had long since been folded. These days, you couldn't get a single volunteer.

So Lincoln had started the draft.

That's what the Irish had been talking about in the saloon, on Saturday night.

❖

It took Sean an hour to check all the inventory. By that time, Hudson was ready to leave. The day barman would be arriving shortly, so Sean went upstairs to ask his wife to let the barman in. Then he set out with Hudson.

It was only a mile or so up to Prince Street, where the Shiloh Presbyterian Church was to be found. As they walked up Broadway, past City Hall, Sean glanced across to the spot where the recruiting tent had stood. He didn't say it to Hudson, of course, but it did strike him as ironic. Here were his fellow Irishmen in the saloon, complaining about the draft. Yet when the free black men in the city had started drilling, so they could volunteer to fight, Police Commissioner Kennedy had told them: "For your own safety, stop at once, or the working men of this city are going to stop you." Not that Sean had been surprised. If he'd heard it once in his saloon, he'd heard it a hundred times: "Never give a nigger a gun." Later, when no less than three black regiments had volunteered, the Governor of New York had refused to take them.

What did Hudson make of it all? Sean wondered. The men in the saloon treated him well enough. To them, Hudson was part of the furniture. He seemed to know his place, and gave no trouble. But he couldn't have failed to hear the things they said. Did he secretly seethe with rage and humiliation, just as Irishmen had done when they were treated with contempt? Maybe. Sean wasn't going to ask. No doubt Hudson found strength and comfort among the black congregation of the Shiloh Church.

"You know what the preachers tell them in those black churches?" an indignant longshoreman had told him once. "They don't teach them Christian humility and obedience at all. They tell 'em that in the afterlife, God is going to punish us, the white men, for our cruelty and wickedness." Who knows, O'Donnell thought wryly, the black preachers might turn out to be right.

The trouble was, tempers had been running higher against the city Negroes lately. There had been strikes down in the Brooklyn docks not long ago, and the companies had brought in cheap black labor to break them. Hardly the fault of the black men, who wouldn't have been welcome in the strikers' unions anyway. But of course they'd been blamed.

But that was nothing to the effect of Lincoln's Emancipation Proclamation.

"Free the damn niggers in the South, so they can come up here and steal our jobs?" the laboring men of New York protested. "Dammit, there's four million of them." The fact that Lincoln had not actually freed a single slave was overlooked. But then politics was seldom about reality. "Our boys are fighting and dying so that their own kith and kin can be destroyed? No more they ain't."

Lincoln's war had been anathema for many months now, in the Saturday-night saloon.

And now, the tall, gawky president and his Republicans, with their rich abolitionist friends, were going to force them to fight for these damn niggers, whether they liked it or not.

"We, the working men, will be the cannon fodder. But not the sons of the rich abolitionists. Oh no. They'll send a poor man to die for them, or pay a fee to stay home and play. That's Lincoln's deal."

Yesterday it had come to a head. More than a thousand names had been chosen in the lottery that day. During the process, it had been quiet enough, but by the evening, people had had a chance to compare names and take stock of the process. In the saloon last night, everyone seemed to know at least three or four of them.

"My nephew Conal," cried one man, in a fury, "that was due to be married next week . . . Shameful!"

"Little Michael Casey, that couldn't shoot a rabbit at five yards? He won't last a week," joined in his neighbor.

Some men were cursing, others were in a sullen rage. At the end of the evening, when he came upstairs to bed, Sean delivered his verdict to his wife.

"I could save the Prince of Wales," he said, "but I tell you, if Abraham Lincoln had come into the saloon tonight, I couldn't have done a thing. They'd have strung him up."

And tomorrow, Monday morning, the draft selection was to resume.

Broadway was quiet as he and Hudson walked along. The sun was bright. They crossed Canal Street. Still no sign of trouble. But Sean knew that didn't mean a thing. Having got Hudson safely to Prince Street, he said to him as they parted: "Come straight back to the saloon after church. And when you get home, fix the bar on those shutters."

From Prince Street, he kept walking north. After a little while, he went right for a block, then picked up the Bowery. He was watchful as he walked. Still not many people about. At East Fourteenth, he turned right, then up Irving Place, into Gramercy Park.

He hadn't been to the Masters' house for some time. It was quite a few years now since his relationship with Mary had ceased to be a secret, and he'd come to see her there once in a while. Everyone knew that he could well afford to look after her, but she was perfectly happy where she was. He'd have liked to see her married, but she'd told him not to interfere, and he reckoned she was old enough to know what she wanted.

He encountered Frank Master from time to time. He'd long since repaid Master's kindly treatment of him back in '53, with an offer to buy into some property the mayor was releasing at a sharply discounted price. And a year after that, chancing to meet him down on South Street, Master had done him another good turn.

"There's a fellow I know who's got room for one more investor in a small venture," he'd told Sean. "Profits might be high, if you don't mind a little risk." Sean had only hesitated a moment. Trust the man, was his credo.

"I'd be interested," he'd said.

Sean had taken quite a bit of cash out of his strongbox to make that investment. And returned three times that amount to the box, a few months later. Since then, he and Frank Master had done small favors for each other, from time to time. In fact, he'd done a discreet service for Master just the other day.

Sean went to the front door, not the tradesmen's entrance. He always made a point of doing that. A maid came to answer it. But in reply to his question, she told him that Mary wasn't there.

"She went to Coney Island with her friend. She'll be gone all this week."

He'd known about the plan, and that they'd delayed it for a while. He felt slightly annoyed that Mary hadn't told him before she left. On the other hand, he was glad that she was out of the city just now. And he was just turning to leave when Mrs. Master appeared behind the maid and, seeing him there, motioned him to come in. He stepped from the bright sunlight into the shadowy space of the hall.

"Good morning, Mr. O'Donnell," she said. "I'm afraid Mary's away."

"I knew they were going," he said, "but I didn't know they'd already left."

Mrs. Master wasn't the kind of woman he liked. A privileged evangeli-

cal, a fervent abolitionist, a damned Republican. When ninety-two society ladies had got up a committee to improve the city's sanitation, he
hadn't been surprised to learn that she was one of them. Perhaps they did
some good. He didn't much care.

But she'd been a good friend to Mary. And that was the only thing he
needed to know.

"I have the address where they're staying," she offered. "Is there anything I can do?"

"No, I don't believe so." He paused a moment. "The reason I called,
Mrs. Master, is that I think there's going to be trouble."

"Oh. What kind of trouble, Mr. O'Donnell?"

"Trouble in the streets. I hope I'm wrong, but I wanted to tell her to be
careful. You and Mr. Master, too," he added.

"Oh," she said again. His vision had adjusted to the shadow of the hall,
and now he noticed that she was looking unusually pale. Her eyes were
red, too, as if she'd been crying. "If you happen to see my husband," she
said, "please be sure to tell him. In fact . . ." she seemed to hesitate, and he
saw a little look of desperation in her eyes—"just so I know he's safe, you
might ask him to come home."

❖

The St. Nicholas Hotel was huge. Its white marble facade dominated the
whole block between Broome and Spring Street on Broadway's west side.
Six stories high, six hundred rooms. Luxury on a huge scale. Well-heeled
tourists crowded in there, and their New York friends were glad to meet
them in its paneled halls, where you could take tea under frescoed ceilings
and gaslight chandeliers.

So if a New York gentleman happened to visit one of the guests, no one
was likely to notice. And Frank Master had been in the St. Nicholas Hotel
since Saturday afternoon.

The guest he was visiting also resided in the city. Her name was Lily de
Chantal. At least, that was her name nowadays. When she was born
thirty-three years ago in Trenton, New Jersey, it had been Ethel Cook. But
the professional name she had chosen, when she'd still had hopes of being
a soloist, was so pleasing to her and all those who met her, that she never
bothered to use her old name at all now, if she could help it.

Some successful lady singers had big bodies to go with their big voices,
and maybe Lily's voice wasn't quite big enough to propel her into the first

rank of singers, but her body was certainly a very pretty package indeed. Her speaking voice was quiet, but she had trained herself to speak with an actor's precision; so that, if her accent wasn't French, you certainly wouldn't have guessed—except for moments of private laughter, or passion—that she came from Trenton. You really couldn't have said where she came from.

Lily de Chantal had only had five significant lovers in her life. She had chosen each of them in the hope that they might further her career. The first, and best, choice had been an impresario, the next a conductor, and the other three were rich men of business. Of those, the first two had been significant patrons of the opera. Frank Master went to the opera, but that was all, and perhaps her choice of him indicated that she had recognized the need to look for other insurance policies now.

But while she was yours, it had to be said, she gave you her entire attention, which was well worth having. Besides that, she was always amusing, often tender, and sometimes vulnerable. All her ex-lovers were her friends. If only her voice had been a little better, she'd have had everything she wanted.

Frank Master wasn't really her lover yet. Though he didn't quite know it, he was still on trial. She found him intelligent, kindly, somewhat ignorant of opera, but maybe improvable.

It wasn't surprising that Frank Master should have met Lily de Chantal at the opera. Ever since the city's opera had been set up as a going concern the century before—by Mozart's librettist, no less—it had been a big thing in New York. Operas had been performed in numerous theaters, and not only for the rich elite. When Jenny Lind had sung for a huge open-air crowd, she had been the toast of the city. The main venue for opera these days, however, was the Academy of Music, on Irving Place, only a stone's throw from Frank Master's house in Gramercy Park. It was a handsome theater, seating more than four and a half thousand, with boxes for the regular patrons. Frank Master was a regular patron.

As far as Frank could see, it was time he had an affair. During most of his marriage, though he'd noticed other women, of course, he'd only really wanted Hetty. But the years of tension between them had taken their toll. And the sense that in her heart she did not really respect him had caused Frank, in self-defense, to say to himself: "I'll show her, even if she doesn't know it."

Lily de Chantal had been singing in the chorus on the night he met her. On the pretext of talking about the opera house, he'd persuaded her to meet him for lunch at Delmonico's the following week, after which she had invited him to a small recital she was giving. He had gone, and watched her with a new interest. He had liked seeing her standing up there alone in front of an admiring audience. It had impressed, and challenged, him. She had graduated that day from a pretty woman to an object of desire. All the same, he'd been quite surprised, at the end of the evening, when she'd discreetly intimated that, if he'd care to take her out to dine after a matinee the following week, she'd be glad of his company.

She had a pleasant little house near Broadway on East Twelfth, convenient for the opera house. And there, after their dinner, his advances had not been discouraged, but not been fully satisfied either.

"You must go home now, or you will be missed," she had said. "And besides, I have to think of my good name."

"Where can we meet?" he'd asked.

"They say the St. Nicholas Hotel is pleasant," she'd answered.

They had met there ten days ago. The meeting had been very satisfactory. He had gone there two afternoons running, and stayed each time until early evening.

He'd quickly realized several things. Perhaps it was just because he had lived so many years of his life with Hetty, and that all the women he met socially were like her, but the fact that Lily de Chantal had to work for her living seemed novel and exciting to him. She had a mind of her own. She knew far more than he did about the arts. She could open new doors of intellect for him, make him a more interesting and important fellow. His wife also had a vigorous intelligence. And what she did for the sanitation committee and her other charities was real enough, and important. But Lily de Chantal lived in a different world and had chosen a different path. Bohemian yet respectable, intoxicating yet safe: it seemed like the perfect adventure.

Yet if, on the one hand, she was independent, on the other, she was vulnerable. She needed someone to promote her, or at least protect her. The idea of having a mistress who was a public figure in her own professional right, but also needed him, gave him a subtle new sense of power which was as flattering as it was thrilling.

They had arranged to meet again that weekend. This time, Frank was determined to stay the night. And his row with Hetty, he thought with some pride, had been very well managed indeed. Hetty might think he had stayed at his counting house, or angrily gone to a hotel. But she hadn't the least reason to think he was seeing another woman. Nor would she be able to find him, since the room had been booked by a third party, on whose discretion Master knew he could rely.

For the official occupant of the room was a certain Mr. Sean O'Donnell.

And now it was Sunday afternoon. Should he go home? He gazed at the lovely figure reclining before him.

No. He'd remain here, and go home on Monday evening. Let Hetty suppose that, out of anger, he'd left for two nights instead of one. It was, so to speak, the economic choice.

·⊥·

After breakfast on Sunday, Theodore said he wanted to read a newspaper. So Mary and Gretchen set off alone. This time, instead of walking to the Point, they went eastward along the open strand of Brighton Beach. Before long, they had the place entirely to themselves. They went on a couple of miles. There was still a light breeze, but it seemed a little hotter than the day before.

"I ought to be in church," Mary said. "I always go to Mass on Sunday."

"Never mind," said Gretchen with a smile. "You'll have to be pagan for a day."

Mary was carrying a light canvas bag slung over her shoulder, and when Gretchen asked her what was in it, she confessed. "It's a sketching pad."

"When did you take up drawing? You never used to."

"It's the first time," said Mary. She'd been wondering what items she should take on holiday when Mrs. Master had suggested a sketchbook. It had seemed a rather ladylike sort of thing to do, but then she'd thought, why not? And seeing the sketching pad in a store the next day, she'd bought it, along with two A.W. Faber artist's lead pencils.

"I wouldn't have brought it if Theodore had been with us this morning," she admitted. "His being an artist."

"Well then," said Gretchen, "I'm glad he stayed behind."

After a time they came to a place where two landscapes met. On one side, seagrass and beach and shallow water went out in a bright sheen to find the ocean horizon; on the other, over some low dunes, there was green pasture and mossy ground, and a small wood offered shade.

"Why don't you sketch here?" said Gretchen.

"Not if you watch me," said Mary. "I'd be embarrassed."

"I'll stare at the seagulls," said Gretchen, sitting down on a hummock, and gazing at the ocean as though Mary wasn't there at all.

But Mary wasn't ready yet. So instead of sketching the seascape, she wandered over the little dune, and made her way along the broad green path toward the wood. Glancing back, she was surprised that she couldn't even see the sea, though its invisible presence was there. And she'd only gone a short way further when, to her surprise, she caught sight of something else.

It was a deer. A doe.

She stopped and stood still. The doe hadn't heard her. Neither she nor the deer would have expected the other to be there.

Long ago, when only the local Indians lived by these shores, there were plenty of deer. But once the Dutch and English had come to settle there, the deer had little chance. Farmers do not care for deer, so they shoot them. Nowadays, along the whole hundred-mile length of Long Island, there were only a few sanctuaries from which the deer had not been driven out. Nor could the deer get away. They could not swim across Long Island Sound. But some, evidently, had come across the creek, or used the shell road, to find safety in the open wastes of Coney Island.

The deer was not far away, and seemed to be alone. A few yards in front of Mary there was a small fallen tree. Carefully, she moved forward and sat on it. Then, drawing up her legs, she rested the pad on them, slowly opened a page, took out a lead pencil and began to draw.

The doe seemed to be in no hurry to move. A couple of times she raised her head, ears alert. Once she stared straight at Mary, but evidently did not see her.

Mary had made little drawings now and then: a standard house, or cat, or horse. But she'd never tried to draw anything from life before, and she hardly knew how to begin. The first lines she put on paper seemed to bear no relation to the doe. She tried concentrating on just the head, and drawing smaller. Not knowing any rules, she just tried to reproduce on the paper the exact line as it came into her eye. At first these lines seemed clumsy and formless, but she tried a few times more, and by and by they did seem to make shapes that were recognizable. Then, to her great surprise, something else seemed to happen.

Not only the form of the deer's head, but the lines on the page seemed to develop a kind of magic of their own. She'd never thought of such a thing, certainly never experienced it before. After half an hour, she had two or three little sketches, very imperfect, but which seemed to capture something of the deer's head.

She was enjoying herself, but Gretchen had been waiting patiently for a while, so she got up. The doe started and stared, then sprang away and ran into the trees.

Retracing her steps, she found Gretchen sitting in the same place where she'd left her. But to her surprise, Theodore was also there. He'd taken off his jacket, and his shirt was open at the collar, so that she could see little curly hairs at the top of his chest. It gave her quite a start. He looked up with a smile.

"Show me."

"Why?"

It was such a silly thing to say. She'd wanted to say "No," but that would have been rude, and somehow "Why" had come out. Theodore laughed.

"What do you mean, 'Why'? I want to see."

"I'm embarrassed. I've never done a sketch before." But he wouldn't be denied, and took the sketch pad from her.

Opening the pad, he stared at the drawings. He stared at them quite intently.

"You really looked, didn't you?" he said.

"I suppose so."

"Look, Gretchen." He showed the drawings to his sister. "Look at what she did." Gretchen nodded. Mary could see they were both impressed. "They're good, Mary," he said. "You try to draw, not what you think you should see, but what you really see."

"I don't know," said Mary, pleased, but not sure what to do with this flattery.

"You have an artist's eye," he said. "It's rare, you know."

"Oh." Mary almost blushed.

Gretchen stood up.

"Come on," she said. "Let's walk back."

They ate a little in the middle of the day, and while they did so, Theodore spoke again of Mary's drawing of the doe. "She should sketch here every day," he said to his sister.

In the afternoon, Mary and Gretchen changed into their matching

swimming dresses again. This time, Theodore joined them. His swimming suit covered most of his body, but Mary could see his manly form.
He was in a playful mood. He splashed both the girls in the water, and
they laughed. Then Mary fell down when a wave hit her, and he helped
her up, and Mary felt his strong arm holding hers for a moment. It
seemed to Mary that Gretchen was looking a bit put out, so when they
came out of the sea, Mary sat down beside her and told Theodore: "Now
you leave us girls alone." So Theodore went for a walk along the beach,
and Mary put her arm round Gretchen's shoulder, and talked to her for a
while until Gretchen was in a better mood.

"Do you remember how you got me my job with the Masters?" she
said. "I never knew you could lie like that, Gretchen. I was quite
shocked."

"I didn't lie."

"Saying my father, God rest his soul, was going to get married to a
widow with a house of her own?"

"I only said 'If he got married.' I never said it was going to happen."

"You're a monster."

"I am," said Gretchen, and smiled.

When Theodore returned, they all went back to the inn. Gretchen
asked Theodore if he was going back to the city now, but he said no, he
thought he might stay another day.

After they'd changed and dressed, they went downstairs, and for a
while Gretchen and Mary played cards with some of the other guests.
Theodore was sitting in an armchair deep in a book. The weather was still
sultry, and the fall of the cards seemed slow. Two days of sea air and exercise had made Mary feel wonderfully relaxed. "I could just laze around
and do nothing all week," she said to Gretchen. And her friend smiled
and said, "Good. Because this week, nothing is all you're supposed to do."

The evening meal passed much as before; there was quiet talk and
laughter, and by the end of it, the food and wine and sea air left Mary
with such a delicious sense of ease that she whispered to Gretchen: "I
think I had too much to drink."

"We'd better walk along the beach then," said Gretchen. "Clear your
head."

So when people finally got up from the tables, Mary and Gretchen,
with Theodore between them, walked by the sea together, and they all
three linked arms, and Theodore began to hum a little march. It felt very

nice, Mary thought, having her arm linked in Theodore's, and she couldn't help thinking how wonderful it would be if they were all one family, and she were married to Theodore and Gretchen was her sister-in-law. She knew it was impossible, of course, but she'd had a bit too much to drink and sometimes, she thought, you can't help thinking of things.

The sun was still some way above the sea when they came back to the inn. A few people, tired like themselves, were starting to turn in; others were sitting on the porch, waiting to watch the sunset. But Mary was still a little light-headed, so she said she'd better turn in. Theodore said good-night, and Gretchen came up to the room with her.

The soft evening light was coming through the window as they changed into their nightdresses. Mary tumbled into bed and lay staring up at the ceiling, which seemed to be moving, ever so slightly. Gretchen came over and sat on her bed.

"You're drunk," she said.

"Only a little," said Mary.

After a little pause, Gretchen said, "I wish Theodore would go."

"Don't say that," said Mary.

"I love my brother, but I really came here to have a holiday with you."

"We're having a good time," Mary answered sleepily.

Gretchen didn't say anything for a little while, but she gently stroked Mary's hair.

"Have you ever been with a man, Mary?" she asked.

"What do you mean?"

"You know what I mean."

"I'm a respectable girl," Mary murmured. She didn't want to talk to Gretchen about that, so she closed her eyes and pretended she was falling asleep. Gretchen continued stroking her hair, and Mary heard her give a little sigh.

"I don't want you getting hurt," she said quietly. Mary knew that her friend was trying to warn her, but she went on pretending to fall asleep. And as she did so, she thought to herself that she was twenty-nine years old now and she'd never been with a man, and if it were to be anyone, excepting Hans of course, then better Theodore than any other. At least he'd know how to treat her right. He wouldn't be like Nolan. If it were to happen, she'd have to be careful, because of the risk, and she was a respectable girl.

But why was she respectable? She knew why she was respectable in

Gramercy Park, because she wanted to be like the Masters. And she knew why she'd wanted to be respectable when she was a girl, so as not to be like the people in Five Points. But she was neither one thing nor the other, really, if she came to think of it. Somehow, out here, with nothing but the ocean and the soft sound of the surf breaking on the beach, she hardly knew what she might be any more. And Gretchen was still gently stroking her hair when she fell asleep.

✛

Sean awoke early on Monday morning, and went straight down to the bar. Opening the outer door, he took a quick look out into the street. All quiet. He closed the door, bolted it again and started to check the bar. He'd only been working a few minutes when his wife appeared. She gave him a mug of tea.

"You were restless last night," she remarked.

"Sorry."

"Still worried?"

"I was remembering '57."

If the history of Five Points was a long disgrace, six years ago the place had surpassed itself. It had been just this time of the year as well. Two of its Catholic gangs, the Dead Rabbits and the Plug Uglies, had started a big fight with their traditional rivals, the Protestant Bowery Boys. Who knew what had set them off in such a rage, or why? Who cared? But this time the battle had got completely out of hand and raged over so many streets that Sean had thought it might even reach his bar. Mayor Wood's police could do nothing. Finally, the militia had to be called in, and by then, some of the streets had been reduced to ruins. God knows how many died—the gangs buried their own dead. Sean knew where many of the bodies were hidden, in the dark recesses of Five Points.

"You think it could happen again?"

"Why not? The gangs are all there." He sighed. "I s'pose I was just as stupid, years ago."

"No." His wife smiled. "You'd kill someone, but not in anger."

Sean drank his tea. "You know who came in the bar yesterday?" he said. "Chuck White." There were plenty of the White family around. They'd had a bit of money sixty years ago, but two or three generations of large families, and they were mostly back where they'd started. Chuck White drove a cab. But he was also a volunteer fireman. "He ain't too pleased about the draft. Says they're supposed to exempt the firemen, but they didn't." He shook his head. "Bad idea, annoying the firemen." He took another gulp of tea. "They like fires. That's why they're firemen."

"They'll refuse to put them out?"

"No. They'll start 'em."

At six thirty Hudson appeared and silently began to clean up. Sean gave him a nod, but said nothing.

At a little after seven, there was a knock at the street door. Sean went to it, and looked out cautiously. It was a tobacconist from nearby. Sean opened the door.

"There's a bunch of men over on the West Side. Big crowd and growing. I thought you'd want to know."

"Where are they headed?"

"Nowhere yet. But they're going to head uptown, to Central Park. And then across to the Draft Office, I reckon. It's only three hours and some till the damn lottery starts again."

Sean thanked him, then turned to Hudson.

"We'll close the shutters and bar them now," he announced.

"You think they'll come down here afterward?" his wife said.

"They might." Sean inspected the shutters, checked the door again, and turned to Hudson. "You're going down to the cellar. You'll stay there till I tell you it's safe to come up."

"What's the draft got to do with Hudson?" his wife asked, after the black man had gone down, rather unwillingly, to the cellar.

But Sean O'Donnell didn't answer.

❖

At nine o'clock, Frank Master knew he really ought to be going. He gazed across at Lily de Chantal. She was sitting up in bed, in a lacy gown, and she looked delicious. But before he left, there was a question or two that he needed to ask.

"Should you like to go up to Saratoga, one day?" he inquired.

He loved Saratoga, and journeys to the fashionable resort could be accomplished in considerable style. For those who could afford it, there was a sumptuous steamer, like a little floating hotel, that plied its way up the Hudson all the way past Albany. Then carriages took you to the great summer houses and hotels of the spa. That journey upriver still felt as much of an adventure to him now as it had when he was a boy.

And there was no doubt in his mind, after that weekend, that he wanted to share the journey with her. They'd have to be circumspect, of course. He couldn't very well carry out a public affair with her, even up in Saratoga, with New York society there. But these things could be managed discreetly. He knew other men who did so.

The question was, did Lily de Chantal wish to go?

"You love the Hudson River, don't you?" she said. "When's the first time you went up it?"

"When I was a boy. My father took us all, to escape the yellow fever when it was in the city. Then, a bit later, he took me all the way across to Niagara Falls, for the opening of the Erie Canal."

"I can imagine you as a little boy. What was your father like? Was he a good man?"

"He was." Frank smiled. "He tried to show me the majesty of Niagara Falls. He wanted to share it with me. Wanted to open my heart."

"Did he succeed?"

"Not then—I only saw the volume of falling water—but I remembered."

"You feel it now?"

"Yes, I believe I do."

She nodded thoughtfully. "I will come with you to Saratoga, Mr. Master. But wait a little while. Then, if your heart tells you to, ask me again."

"As you wish."

"It's what I wish."

Suddenly Frank laughed. "I just remembered. I was angry with him that day. At Niagara."

"Why?"

"Oh, to do with a little Indian girl. It's not important. The Falls were the main thing."

"I may stay here a few hours before I go home," she said. "I feel rather lazy. Do you mind?"

"Keep the room as long as you like."

"Thank you."

It was in the hotel lobby that he heard about the marches.

"First the West Side, then the East," a fellow guest told him. "They're going uptown to protest against the draft. Quite a few of the factories along the East River have closed in sympathy."

"What sort of crowd?"

"Union men. Irish, of course, but a lot of the German workers too. They mean to surround the Draft Office, I believe."

"Violent?"

"Not that I've heard."

"Hmm." Master considered whether to go home. The union men wouldn't be interested in Gramercy Park, though, and the Draft Office was more than twenty blocks further north. He decided to go to his counting house first.

The air felt thick and heavy when he stepped into the street. It was going to be one of those hot and humid July days. He started to walk down Broadway—it was only a mile to City Hall. Things seemed quiet enough. He continued down to Trinity Church and turned across Wall Street to the East River. A few minutes more and he was at his counting house. His clerk was there, working quietly as usual.

After ten minutes, a young merchant looked in.

"Looks like things are getting rough up the East Side," he reported. "They've been pulling down the telegraph lines. Broke into one store and took a load of broad axes. I wouldn't care to be running the draft lottery today."

Telling his clerk he'd be back later, but to lock up if there was any sign of danger, Master started to walk along the South Street waterfront. At Fulton Street, he found a cab and told the driver to head up the Bowery and across into Gramercy Park. Everything there seemed to be quiet. "Go up Third Avenue," he said to the driver. He had no desire to encounter his wife just yet.

At Fortieth Street, the driver refused to go any further.

The crowd was huge and blocking the avenue. Some had placards saying NO DRAFT. Others were beating copper pans like gongs. There seemed to be a few dozen policemen guarding the marshal's office where the draw for the draft was supposed to start again, but it was obvious that they wouldn't be able to do much if the crowd turned ugly. He saw a respectable-looking man like himself standing nearby and approached him.

"Why so few police?" he remarked.

"Mayor Opdyke. Typical Republican. Hasn't a clue. Hope you're not a Republican," the man added, apologetically.

"I'm not." Master smiled.

"Oh my God," said the man. "Look there."

The crowd saw too, and sent up a roar of approval, as, dressed in their full firefighting gear, the entire Black Joke Engine Company No. 33 came marching out of a side street and made straight toward the building.

"Do you know why they're here?" the man asked Master, who shook his head. "Their chief was drafted on Saturday."

"Unfortunate."

"I'll say."

"What'll they do?"

"Think about it," said his companion, cheerfully. "The draft records are still inside that building. To destroy the records, therefore . . ."

"They will burn it down."

"They are logical men."

The Black Joke firemen didn't waste time. Within moments, volleys of bricks and paving stones smashed through the windows. The police were swept aside. Then the firemen marched into the building, found the drum used for the lottery draw, poured turpentine over everything, set fire to the building and marched out. They were very professional. The crowd roared approval.

And from somewhere, a shot was fired.

"Better be going," said the man, and hurried away.

Frank Master did not hurry away. He found a covered stoop a couple of blocks distant, and watched from there. The crowd was thoroughly roused now, tearing up paving stones and hurling them at the burning building. After a while, a body of troops appeared, moving up the avenue. But when he saw them come close, Master almost winced.

It was the Invalid Corps, the wounded soldiers, still recovering from the hospital, poor devils. All the able-bodied men had been sent to Gettysburg two weeks earlier. The invalids came up bravely.

But the crowd cared nothing for the invalids' bravery, or their wounds. With a roar they rushed at them, throwing paving stones or anything else they could find. Hopelessly outnumbered, the invalids fell back.

Now the crowd had tasted blood. While the flames still rose from the Draft Office, they began to move across town, smashing house windows as they went. Frank followed them. He saw some women with crowbars, tearing up the streetcar lines. At Lexington Avenue, he heard a roar. They'd discovered the police chief. They beat his face to a pulp. People were pouring in from the tenements to join the crowd. A huge party headed for Fifth Avenue, and started moving south. Then, as he was wondering what to do next, he heard another cry.

"Guns, boys! Guns!" And then, a moment later: "The Armory!"

A large group separated from the rest and started across town. There was an armory on Second Avenue at Twenty-second. Only a block and a half from Gramercy Park.

Master turned, and started to run.

···

Young Tom had never seen his mother in such a state. An hour ago, he'd nearly gone down to his father's counting house, but then decided he'd better stay home. To hell with his father if he was skulking down there, he thought. His duty was to make sure his mother was safe.

Hetty Master had hardly slept for two nights. The first evening she had told Tom quietly that his father had to be away that night on business. The second, she'd admitted that they had quarreled. "No doubt he will return tomorrow," she had added calmly. Looking at his mother's pale, drawn face, Tom had to admire her dignity.

But this morning had been too much, even for her strong mind. First, they'd heard the commotion as the marchers streamed up the avenues, though they hadn't come through Gramercy Park. Tom had gone out to see what was going on and met a neighbor who'd just come up from South Street.

"They're going uptown to protest against the draft," he'd said, "but everything's quiet down by South Street. No trouble downtown at all, not even in Five Points." This news had reassured the household, and Tom had decided not to bother with his father.

Since the news of the riot at the Draft Office reached them, however, his mother had become agitated. She stood at the big window, staring out at the square and murmuring: "Where can he be?"

"I'll go down and find him," Tom now offered, but she begged him not to. "It's bad enough having your father out there," she said. And feeling that he should probably stay to protect her, he didn't press it.

So he went up to the top of the house. From the attic window, he could see the flames rising from the Draft Office, twenty-five blocks to the north. He watched them for some time before coming down.

Reaching the hall, he did not see any sign of his mother. He called her name. No answer. The parlormaid came out.

"Mrs. Master's gone," she told him. It seemed his mother had seen a cab draw up at the house next door, run out and taken it. "She said you were to stay and mind the house," the parlormaid reported.

Tom sighed. It was obvious where she'd gone. So he might as well stay put, as she asked.

⁜

When Frank Master arrived at Gramercy Park, it was about noon. Young Tom didn't give him a very friendly reception. Having explained that his mother had left the house only minutes before, he asked his father where he'd been, and when Frank said, "Away," Tom gave him furious looks. It seemed to Frank that there was little point in following Hetty down to the South Street counting house, which was obviously where she'd gone, because he'd probably just miss her as she came back. The best thing was to wait for her at home. Meanwhile, if his son was going to give him these angry looks, he'd rather get him out of the house.

"Tom, there's a big mob on its way down to the armory on Second. You'd better watch out for them. Don't get near, but see what they're up to, and let me know." He looked around. "I'm going to close all the shutters."

⁜

The South Street waterfront was quiet. Hetty wasn't sure how long she'd been waiting at the counting house, but at least she knew now from the old clerk that Frank hadn't disappeared. That was something. And the clerk had been clear that Frank had said he'd be back. She resolved to wait for him, therefore. There was only a hard wooden bench to sit on. Like most busy merchants, Frank didn't encourage visitors to stay too long. She didn't care. So long as she saw him. But an hour passed, and there was no sign of him.

From time to time, people came in and were quickly dealt with by the old clerk. Apart from that, there was only the sound of his steel-nibbed pen, scratching on ledgers. She considered going back, but she couldn't bring herself to the thought that she might miss him on the way. It was almost two o'clock when a young clerk from one of the other counting houses stuck his head round the door.

"It's getting rough out there. We're shutting up shop," he told the clerk.

"What's happening?" she asked.

"Well, ma'am, I'm afraid there's been trouble on the West Side now. They've been chasing niggers up there. I don't know if they've hanged any yet, but I reckon they're looking to."

"Why in the world would they harm black men because of the draft?" she cried.

"Because if Lincoln has his way, the city'll be full of niggers taking the Irishmen's jobs. Least, that's what they think," he replied. "That, and the fact they don't like 'em," he added by way of further explanation.

Hetty was so horrified she could barely speak. "What else?" she asked the young clerk.

"They've been coming down Fifth Avenue, destroying houses. They were at the mayor's too. But he ain't there now. He's called his people to the St. Nicholas Hotel. They're meeting there to figure out what to do. That's all I know."

"I am Mrs. Master," Hetty told him. "You know my husband, I'm sure?"

"Yes, ma'am. Fine gentleman."

"You haven't seen him, have you?"

"No, ma'am. But quite a few merchants and Wall Street men were going over to the St. Nicholas to find out what the mayor intends to do. I should think he might be there."

"If my husband should come by," she told the old clerk, "tell him that's where I've gone."

⁜

Sean O'Donnell didn't leave the saloon until two o'clock. Though he opened for his usual customers, he kept the shutters closed and barred. Several of the regular men asked where Hudson was.

"I sent him out to Coney Island with some things for my sister," he lied calmly. "He'll be gone a day or two." Meanwhile, his wife took food down to the cellar to feed the black man.

"He's not very happy down there," she told him.

"He'll be happy he's alive when this is over," he answered. And soon afterward he visited Hudson and said to him once again: "You stay here, and don't make a sound."

At two o'clock, however, he decided to walk over to the St. Nicholas Hotel himself, to find out what was going on.

⁘

There were lines of policemen in front of the hotel when Hetty arrived, but they let her through. The hotel lobby was crowded. The mayor was in a private room, she was told, with a number of gentlemen. The manager himself happened to be at the desk at that moment, and he obligingly went in to the mayor to ask if Frank Master was there with him.

"Your husband isn't with the mayor," he told her, "but I'll have a boy ask round the lobby for you. He could be here somewhere." Five minutes later, the boy returned and shook his head. "You're welcome to wait, ma'am," the manager said, and told the boy to find her a seat.

Despite the bustle of people, the boy found her a sofa in a sitting room. It was by a large window from which she could see people entering the hotel. Gratefully, she sat down.

She'd been there about five minutes when another lady entered the room. She was elegantly dressed, but she looked somewhat agitated. She glanced briefly past Hetty through the window, and seemed to be hesitating about whether to remain, or go back to the lobby. She evidently had not recognized Hetty. But Hetty recognized her. She rose with a smile.

"Miss de Chantal?" Hetty held out her hand. "We met once at the opera. I am Mrs. Master."

Lily de Chantal seemed to go somewhat pale.

"Oh, Mrs. Master."

"I am looking for my husband."

"Your husband?" The singer's voice was a little high.

"You haven't seen him?"

Lily de Chantal gazed at her uncertainly. "There are a lot of people in the lobby," she said, after a slight pause.

"I know."

As though remembering her part after almost missing a cue, Lily de Chantal seemed to recover herself.

"I am sorry, Mrs. Master, if I seem a little distracted. I came in here for refuge. They have just told me that I should not go outside."

Hetty looked out of the window, then back at Lily de Chantal.

"I hardly know what's going on," Hetty said.

And it was perhaps as well that, just then, Sean O'Donnell came into the room.

⁘

Talking to people in the lobby, it hadn't taken Sean more than a few minutes to discover all he needed to know. The mayor's tactic of sending small detachments of policemen to individual trouble spots had been a disaster. In every case they'd been overwhelmed. It was also clear that the attacks on black people were mounting swiftly, and that he'd been right to hide Hudson. He was only having a quick look round the public rooms, in case there was anyone of interest in them, before hurrying home.

But knowing what he did about Frank Master and Lily de Chantal, the last thing in the world he'd expected was to see Lily and Hetty together. Whatever could it mean?

"Mrs. Master." He bowed politely. "What brings you here on such a day?" He made a quick bow to Lily as well.

"I went to my husband's counting house, Mr. O'Donnell, but he was not there. They told me he might have come here to find out what the mayor is doing about these riots."

Sean glanced at Lily, saw the look of relief on her face, and nodded gravely.

"That's exactly why I'm here myself," he said. "Wherever your husband is, Mrs. Master, the wisest thing would be for you to go home. But on no account should you try to walk. Nor you, Miss de Chantal. I'll speak to the manager and have him find you a cab, Mrs. Master. But it may take some time—most of them are off the streets." And then, he could not resist it: "Miss de Chantal, I'm sure, will be glad to keep you company until a cab is found."

⁘

The old clerk at Master's counting house had had enough. He had his own family to think of, and if Mr. Master hadn't come back by now, he reckoned he wasn't coming this day, anyhow. The only question was, what to do about the message from Master's wife. Pin a note on the door? That, it seemed to the clerk, would look wrong, and beneath the dignity of the business. No, he'd write him a note and place it on his desk. Master had the key to the door. If he did come back, he'd be letting himself in, for sure.

⁜

By two thirty, Frank Master was starting to become agitated. Round the corner, at the Second Avenue armory, a huge crowd had surrounded the building. But there was quite a large body of defenders inside, and they were armed. From time to time, stones were hurled into the building, but so far the crowd hadn't tried to storm it. Meanwhile, there were mobs appearing in one street after another. All around.

And where the devil was Hetty? Was she trapped down at South Street? Was she trying to walk back on foot maybe? Had she been waylaid? Was she hurt? If there was only some way that he could guess which route she might take, he could go after her. He hardly wanted to admit it to himself, but a terrible feeling of guilt was overwhelming him. If only he hadn't gone away with Lily. If only he'd stayed to look after her. What agony of mind must Hetty be in, let alone physical danger? His wife's distraught face rose up in his imagination like a nightmare. He began to have visions of her being chased by rioters, knocked down, worse.

It was his fault. His alone.

"Pa." It was Tom. "We need to get the carriage out. We've got to look for Mother."

"Yes, I think so too. See to it, will you, Tom? Then I'll go downtown, and you guard the house."

"No, Pa. You better stay while I go. If she gets back here and you're gone, I don't know if I can stop her going out again."

"That's nonsense, Tom, I have to go."

"Pa, she ain't going to stay put until she sees you. I'm telling you, it's you she wants."

⁜

It was after half past three when the hotel manager came to see Hetty. She had made several applications to the front desk since Sean O'Donnell had left, but to no avail.

"You're the first in line," they had promised her, "but we can't get any cabs to go uptown." Lily de Chantal had twice had to restrain her from walking. "I can't have your blood on my hands," Lily had cried, the second time. Though why Miss de Chantal should be so concerned about her welfare, Hetty couldn't imagine.

"Mrs. Master," the manager said, "there is a lady with a carriage who is going uptown, and who would be prepared to take you." He looked a little awkward. "I must tell you, it's the only hope of transport I can offer."

"I see. A lady?"

"Her name is Madame Restell."

✥

The wickedest woman in New York sat comfortably back in the plush seat of her carriage and gazed at Hetty. She was large-bosomed and her face was strong. Her eyes, it seemed to Hetty, were those of a bird of prey.

So this was Madame Restell, the abortionist. Hetty was aware of her by sight, but she had never thought, or wished, to be so close. If Madame Restell guessed all this, which she undoubtedly did, it was quite clear she didn't give a damn.

"Well, I found out what I wanted," she remarked. "That mayor's a fool." She gave a decisive sniff. "Almost as big a fool as Lincoln."

"I'm sorry you think the president a fool," Hetty remarked stiffly. She might have accepted a ride, but she wasn't going to let herself be browbeaten by Madame Restell.

"He's caused too much trouble."

"You are not a Republican, I take it," Hetty said.

"I might be. They say that people should be free to do as they like. That's what I think. But if they start preaching at me, they can go to hell."

"I suppose it depends on what you mean by being free."

"I help women to be free. Free not to have a child if they don't want it."

"You arrange abortions."

"Not the way you suppose. Not often. Mostly I give 'em a powder that'll stop it."

It was evident that Madame Restell not only liked to do as she pleased, but to talk about it as well.

"Perhaps in France they do things differently, madame," Hetty said, politely but firmly.

This, however, was met with a loud laugh.

"You think I'm French because I call myself Madame Restell?"

"I supposed so."

"English, dear, and proud of it. I was born in Gloucester. Dear old

Gloucester. Poor as church mice, we were. Now I got a mansion on Fifth. And I still think Lincoln's a fool."

"I see." Hetty let a silence fall. They passed Grace Church.

"Do you know Lincoln's wife?" the abortionist suddenly asked.

"I haven't the honor."

"Well, I never saw a woman shop the way she does, I'll say that for her. I watched her at it once. She's like a madwoman when she gets to New York—which is quite often, as you know. No wonder the Congress complain about her."

"Mrs. Lincoln had to refurnish the White House," Hetty said defensively.

"I'll say."

"Well," said Hetty, with dignity, "I believe people should be free, too. I believe every person has a God-given freedom no matter what their race or color. And I think Mr. Lincoln's right."

"Oh, he may be right, dear. I expect he is. I've got nothing against the darkies. They're no better or worse than you or me, that's for sure. But there's an awful lot of people getting killed for it."

They had come to Union Square now, and were about to turn right onto Fourteenth when the coachman slowed up, and tapped on the window with his whip. Along the street, at the foot of Irving Place, a mob of a hundred or more was blocking the entrance.

"Go round," Madame Restell ordered.

They went cautiously round Union Square and tried up Fourth Avenue. There seemed to be threatening groups on every street. As they came level with the top of Gramercy Park, the crowds grew thicker, and you could see across to the huge mob laying siege to the armory. At that precise moment, a hail of paving stones hit the building, and someone hurled a barrel of burning pitch through one of the windows. There was a huge roar from the crowd.

"This is no good," said Madame Restell decisively. "Go over to Fifth," she called to the coachman.

"I must get out," cried Hetty. "This is my home."

"Don't be silly, dear," said Madame Restell. "You won't be able to get to it."

Hetty wanted to jump out, but she couldn't deny the truth of what Madame Restell said.

They turned up Fifth. You could see that some of the houses had been looted, but the rioters had evidently turned their attention elsewhere for the moment.

"You'd better come to my house," said Madame Restell. "I've got a serving boy who can worm his way through any crowd. Regular little Five Points rat. He'll run down to your place and tell 'em where you are."

It might be good sense, but Hetty didn't like it. The avenue ahead was clear, and the coachman whipped up the horses. They flew past Madison Square. The heat of the day and the dust from the horses' hoofs made the brownstone facades of the houses unclear. She felt queasy, as if she were being pulled against her will up some strange, hot river of dust. They were in the Thirties already. On her right she saw an empty lot containing a nursery garden. A brick church suddenly towered, like an affront, on her left.

And then she saw the great, fortress-like mass of the reservoir. The place where Frank had proposed. Solid, in all this heat and dust. Unshakable as a pyramid in the desert. The foundation of her marriage. She was letting herself be carried past it. I must be mad, she thought.

They'd passed Forty-second Street.

"Stop!" She pulled open the window and shouted to the coachman. "Stop at once!"

The carriage slowed.

"What are you doing?" cried Madame Restell. "Go on," she fairly bellowed at the coachman. But too late. Hetty had already opened the carriage door and, before the coach had even halted, tumbled out into the dusty street. "You stupid bitch!" Madame Restell called down to her as Hetty, on her knees, picked herself up from the dust at Forty-third. "Get back in."

But Hetty didn't care.

"Thanks for the ride," she called, and turned to walk down Fifth. She might have a bruise or two, but she felt better. At least she was doing something.

As the carriage pulled away up Fifth, she did pause for a moment, though, to straighten her clothes. The heat and humidity were oppressive. She glanced around. On the corner opposite was a large building. And when she saw it, she even smiled.

If the reservoir represented the massive solidity of the city's engineering, the orphanage for black children opposite her was a welcome reminder, even on this day of chaos, that the city did have a moral compass too. For it was the wealthy people of the city, people like herself, who had paid for the orphanage, and it wasn't just for show. Two hundred and thirty-seven black children, from infants up, were housed, clothed, fed—and, yes, educated—in that building on Fifth Avenue. Two hundred and thirty-seven children given the chance of a decent life.

If Madame Restell, or her husband, or anyone else wanted to know what Lincoln was fighting for, she thought, let them come to the orphanage on Fifth, and see the children there.

✧

She did not see the mob until it was upon her. They came from the side streets and swept down the avenue. Men and women alike, they were carrying bricks, clubs, knives, anything they had picked up along the way. As they continued to stream into the avenue, there seemed to be hundreds of them.

They did not pause to smash windows. They did not even look at her. A single object was their sole intent. They were making for the orphanage.

As they drew close, a loud voice cried out: "Kill the nigger children!" At which the whole crowd let out a mighty roar.

And Hetty, forgetting even her dear husband for a moment, watched in horror. She couldn't just leave. She had to do something.

✧

Frank Master stood beside his son in front of the big picture of Niagara Falls in the dining room. Then he turned and went to the window, and stared out.

"I don't know what to do," he said.

The truth was, he was beside himself. He had cursed himself until he was worn out, and the impotent frustration was almost more than he could bear. He just wanted to take action, fight somebody, anything.

Tom had been gone so long he'd thought something must have happened to him, too. But when he finally got back, he'd explained.

"The counting house was locked when I got there. The place was deserted. I criss-crossed every street I could think of on the way back, Pa. That's why I took so long. But there isn't a sign of her. Nothing."

He'd only been back a few minutes when a great roar from the direction of the armory had caused Frank to go out into the street. The crowd had finally begun their assault. The building was catching fire. He could see figures appearing in the upper windows and on the roof of the building. It looked as if they'd be burned. Not that there was a damn thing he could do about it. The heat from the building combined with the suffocating heat of the day was awful. He hurried back to the house.

The assault on the armory had one effect: it seemed to be drawing all the mobs in the area to the scene. Gramercy Park was temporarily deserted. Cautiously, he opened one of the dining-room window shutters. Ten more minutes passed. The flames rising from the armory were sending flashes into the sky.

But now, suddenly, a boy came running up the steps to the front door, and was hammering on the door. The parlormaid appeared to ask what to do. He told her not to open.

"It may be a trap." Some fellow with a brick or a firebrand might be lurking out there to hurl his missile in as soon as the door was open. He pulled the shutter closed and went into the hall.

"What if it's a message from Mother?" said Tom.

"I thought of that." Signaling Tom to stand behind him, he went to the door, picking up a walking stick with a head like a cudgel on the way, slipped the bolts, and opened the door an inch. "Well?"

"You Mr. Master?"

"What if I am?"

"Your wife's up on Fifth by the orphanage in a heap of trouble."

"Who are you?"

"Billie, mister. I work for Madame Restell. She brought me. She's in her carriage over on Lexington. Says she ain't coming any closer. You'd better come quick, mister."

What the devil the infamous Madame Restell would want with Hetty he couldn't imagine. But Frank didn't hesitate.

"Guard the house, Tom," he called, and with the stick in one hand, and the boy's arm in a vice-like grip in the other, he let the boy lead him quickly to Lexington Avenue. "If you're lying," he told the boy quietly, "I will beat you to a pulp."

✢

Hetty hadn't much experience of crowds. She did not know that, caught at the right moment, in the right mood, a crowd can be made to do anything, or will of its own accord.

The crowd wanted to kill the children, because they were colored black. It wanted to destroy the building, because it was a temple of the rich Protestant abolitionists. The rich white Protestants who were sending honest Catholic boys to die so that four million freed slaves could come north and steal their jobs. For the crowd was mostly Irish Catholic. Not all, but mostly.

And the crowd meant to loot the building because the black children in there had food, and beds, and blankets, and sheets that they themselves, often as not, did not possess in their crowded tenements.

They had started stoning the building, and now men were running forward to break down the door.

Hetty tried to push her way through the crowd.

"Stop this," she cried. "They are children. How can you?"

The crowd wasn't listening. She struggled forward, but the press of people was too great. She found herself wedged beside a huge red-headed Irishman, bellowing with rage like all the rest. She didn't care. She beat with her fists upon his back. "Let me through."

And at last he turned, and looked down at her.

"Tell them to stop," she cried. "Will you let them kill innocent children? Are you a Christian?" His blue eyes continued to stare at her, like those of a giant looking down at its supper. Well, let him do what he liked. "Will you tell your priest you murdered children?" she challenged. "Have you no humanity? Let me through and I will tell them to stop."

Then the big Irishman reached down and picked her up in his powerful arms, and she wondered if he was going to kill her there and then.

But to her astonishment, he started pushing his way through to the front of the crowd. And moments later, she found herself in open space.

In front of her was the orphanage. Behind her, as the giant put her down and she turned, was the crowd.

It was a terrifying sight. Its rage came at her like a roaring hot breath. It was staring, screaming, hurling missiles and breathing fire at the orphanage beside her. Now that she was here, how could she speak to this terrible monster? How would she even be heard?

Then, suddenly, some of its many eyes started to look in her direction. Arms were pointing past her. Something behind her was catching a part of the crowd's attention. She turned to look.

A little way down the street, a side door of the orphanage had opened. A woman's head was looking out. Hetty recognized her. The matron of the orphanage. The woman looked up the street with horror. But it seemed that she had decided there was no alternative, for now a small black child appeared beside her, then another, and another. The children of the orphanage were filing out. Not only that: to her astonishment, Hetty saw that they were obediently forming up into a line.

Dear God, they might have been going to church. A moment later, the superintendent came out as well. He was shepherding the children into a little column. And there was nobody there but the matron and the superintendent to help them. They just kept coming, as the matron urged them to hurry, and the superintendent made sure they lined up in good order.

They were going to take all two hundred and thirty-seven children out, into that furnace, because there was nothing else they could do. And they were keeping calm. For the children's sake, they were keeping very calm. And the children kept coming out obediently, and the superintendent kept them facing away from the crowd so that they should not see.

And the crowd did not like it. The crowd did not like it at all.

For now, as by some awful magic, the part of the crowd that could not see down the street seemed to understand from the eyes that could that the children were there. And the crowd began to tremble with rage at the thought that its prey was daring to escape. And the crowd nearest to her started inching forward, a foot at a time, like a snake testing the way with its tongue. And somebody shouted out again, "Kill the nigger children!" while others took up the cry.

And the children heard, and flinched.

Then Hetty realized that there was no one except herself and the big Irishman between the crowd and the children.

Strangely, she understood, the crowd did not really see her. She was in its field of vision, but its focus was on the children. They were nearly all out now. She glanced back. The matron was telling the children to start walking. Quickly, but not too fast. The crowd saw too. A woman's voice called out: "The niggers is gettin' away." At any instant, she could feel it, people would start to break ranks and spill past her.

"Stop!" she cried out. "Would you harm little children?" She raised her arms and held them wide, as if that could stop them. "They are little children."

The crowd saw her now and fixed its stare upon her. It saw her for what she was, a rich Republican. Protestant, their enemy. The huge Irishman beside her was silent, and it suddenly crossed her mind that perhaps he had brought her there so that the crowd would kill her.

Yet just for a moment, the crowd seemed to hesitate. Then the woman's voice rang out again.

"They're nigger children, lady. It don't matter killing them."

There was a roar of approval. The crowd was edging forward.

"You cannot! You cannot!" Hetty cried desperately.

And then, to her surprise, the Irish giant beside her let out a mighty cry.

"What are you thinking of? Have you no humanity? Has none of you any humanity?"

Hetty did not understand crowds. The crowd, despite the fact they hated her, had hesitated to attack her for one reason only: she was a lady. But the giant beside her was a man. One of their own. And now a traitor, siding with their enemy to rebuke them. With a scream of rage, two women rushed at him. The men were close behind. If they might not have the children, then they'd have him. He was fair game.

His size did him no good at all. A giant is nothing to a crowd. It had him down in no time.

Hetty had never seen a mob attack a man. She did not know its violence and its power. They started with his face, punching, and kicking with their heavy boots. She saw blood, heard splintering bone, then could see nothing at all, as they threw her across the street, and his body disappeared under a rabble of men, stamping with all their strength and weight, again and again and again.

When they broke off, the Irish giant had almost disappeared.

The crowd had entered the orphanage now. There was plenty there for everyone. Food, blankets, beds: the home was stripped bare. But the children, thanks be to God, had been left to walk quickly away.

So Hetty slowly got up, and looked down at the pulped mess that had once been a mighty body with a face, and dragged herself into Fifth Avenue. And there, scarcely knowing what was happening to her, she suddenly felt a pair of strong arms around her and saw her husband's face. Then she clung to him, as he helped her stagger down to the reservoir and eastward along Fortieth until, at the next avenue, he lifted her into the big carriage that had brought him.

"Thank God you came," she murmured, "I was looking for you all day."

"I was looking for you, too."

"Never leave me again, Frank. Please never leave me."

"Never again," he said, with tears in his eyes. "Never, as long as I live."

✦

When Sean O'Donnell looked around his saloon in the early evening, he knew he was right to make Hudson stay in the cellar. All over the West Side, the crowds had been attacking the black people, burning their houses, beating them up. There were rumors of lynchings. Over at St. Nicholas Hotel, the mayor had been joined by the military. Troops were being summoned. President Lincoln had been telegraphed. With the Confederates in retreat after Gettysburg, he must spare them some regiments before New York went up in flames. A body of gentlemen had armed themselves with muskets and gone to defend Gramercy Park. Sean was glad of that. Meanwhile, he'd seen fires coming from Five Points.

"It can't be long now," he warned his family. "We'll be next."

It was a quarter of an hour later that a vigorous figure with the face of an adventurer and long, drooping mustaches strode into the saloon. Sean smiled.

"Mr. Jerome. What'll you have?"

Sean liked Leonard Jerome. The daring financier might not have been born at Five Points, but he had the instincts and the courage of the street fighter. He mostly ran with the rich sporting crowd like August Belmont and William K. Vanderbilt. But Jerome liked newspapers and newspapermen too. The rumor was that he was invested in newspapers. And he'd come into the saloon once in a while.

Once Sean had asked him where his family came from.

"My father's name was Isaac Jerome, so Belmont says I must be Jewish." Jerome had laughed. "Of course, you have to remember that Belmont's name was Schoenberg, before he changed it. But the truth's less interesting. The Jeromes were French Protestants. Huguenots. Came over in the 1700s. Farmers and provincial lawyers mostly, ever since." He'd grinned. "My wife's family swears they've got Iroquois blood, though."

"You believe it?"

"A man should always believe his wife, sir."

In answer to Sean's question now, he answered: "Whiskey, Mr. O'Donnell. A large one. I've a busy night ahead."

"You expecting trouble?"

"I thought they'd burn my house—they haven't yet, but they're coming down here. On the way already. You'd better hide your nigger."

"I already did. Think they'll go for the saloon?"

"Probably not. It's the abolitionist newspapers they're after: the *Times*, and others." He downed his whiskey and gave Sean a puckish grin. "So wish me luck, Mr. O'Donnell. I'm off to defend the freedom of the press."

"How will you do that?" Sean asked, as Jerome began to stride out of the saloon.

Jerome turned. "I got me a Gatling gun," he answered. Then he was gone.

A Gatling gun. God knows how he'd got it. The newly patented gun was hardly even used by the army yet. With its swiftly rotating barrels, however, it could deliver a devastating, continuous fire that would mow down any crowd. You didn't want to mess with Jerome, thought Sean. He knows how to fight dirty.

Once again, now, he checked all the shutters, but he didn't close the saloon. If the rioters wanted a drink and couldn't get served, that would really annoy them.

He was glad his sister Mary was safely out at Coney Island.

❖

Monday had started well for Mary. She'd come down to breakfast to find Gretchen already at table, in conversation with another mother. As Mary sat down with them, Gretchen was just remarking that the woman's son seemed rather like her own boy, and in no time this led to a discussion of motherhood in general. The lady asked Mary if she had children, to which she replied: "Not until I'm married."

"Quite right," the lady said with a laugh.

Theodore appeared after that.

They bathed in the morning. This time, holding the rope, Mary worked her way out until the water was right up over her chest, and then she swam out almost to the barrier ropes at the end. And while she was swimming there, Theodore came past and dived down under the rope and went on swimming with strong strokes out into the sea. He was out there quite some time. She and Gretchen were sitting together on the beach when he came back and emerged dripping from the water.

"Most invigorating," he said with a laugh, and started drying himself with a towel.

At lunch, Theodore asked her if she was going to sketch that day, and she said she thought she might. So after the meal, she went to get her sketch pad. When she came down again, Gretchen and Theodore were talking together, and Gretchen said, "You go on, Mary, and I'll catch you up."

She'd only walked a short way along the sand, however, when reaching into her bag, she realized that she'd left her pencils up in the room, so she had to go back. Arriving at the inn, she didn't see Gretchen and Theodore, so she supposed Gretchen might have gone up to their room. But the room was empty, so she collected her pencils and went out again.

She was just setting off along the path when she saw them. They were a little way off, standing together at the end of the inn's white picket fence, under the shade of a small tree. They didn't see her, because they were too deep in their conversation, nor could she hear what they were saying, but you could see at once that they were having a quarrel. Gretchen's normally placid face was screwed up in fury. Mary had never seen her looking like that before. Theodore was looking irritated and impatient.

The only thing to do was hurry away and pretend she had not seen.

The sight of her friends quarreling had made an unwelcome interruption into the idyllic day, like a dark cloud suddenly appearing in a blue sky. Mary walked swiftly along the beach, therefore, to put a distance between herself and the two Kellers. She did not want anything to spoil that afternoon. And by the time she'd gone a mile or so, and encountered nothing except the unbroken line of the ocean and the warm sand, she felt restored. She realized that she was approaching the place where she had sketched the day before, and crossing over a little dune, she started to look out in case the deer might be there again. She didn't see it though.

However, she did notice a little wooden shelter some way off, which had obviously been abandoned, for its roof was off, and the small posts that had supported it were pointing jaggedly into the sky. Taken with a couple of trees nearby, it made a strange, rather haunting composition, not too difficult to draw, and so she sat down and began to sketch. After a while, when she had caught some of it to her satisfaction, she put the sketch pad down and got up to stretch her legs. She went over to the dune and looked back along the beach to see if Gretchen was coming, but it was quite deserted.

Returning to her sketch, she drew a little more, and then took off her straw hat and leaned back for a moment to enjoy the sun. Her face and arms were bare, and the warmth of the sun upon them gave her a delightful sensation. It was very quiet. She could hear the faint, gentle sound of the spreading surf on the sand. It felt so peaceful, as if out here she were in a separate world, a timeless place which had almost nothing to do with the city life she'd left behind. Perhaps, she thought dreamily, if she stayed there long enough, she'd turn into a different person. She remained like that for several minutes, as the hot sun beat down. This, she supposed, must be how lizards feel as they drink in the sun's rays on a rock.

When she heard the faint rustle in the seagrass to her right, she raised her head a little, and was just opening her mouth to say, "Hello, Gretchen," when another head appeared.

"Ah," said Theodore, "I thought I'd find you here."

"Where's Gretchen?" said Mary.

"Back at the inn. She wanted to rest."

"Oh."

"Mind if I sit down?"

She didn't answer, but he sat down beside her anyway. He picked up the sketchbook and looked at her drawing.

"It's not finished," she said.

"Looks promising," he remarked, glancing toward the little ruined shelter. He put the sketchbook down on the other side of him, so she couldn't reach it, and then lay down full-length. She felt a little awkward sitting up, and wondered if she should put her hat back on. "You should lie down," he said. "The sun's good for you. At least, a little sun. When I'm in the sun like this," he said contentedly, "I pretend I'm a lizard."

She laughed. "I was just thinking of lizards when you came."

"There you are then," he said. "Great minds think alike. Or perhaps lizards do."

She lay back. She was all alone, lying beside a man, but nobody could see.

So when he turned and gently kissed her, she didn't resist. She let him do it. And when he said, "You are so beautiful, Mary," she felt as if she was.

And soon he began to kiss her in a way she had never been kissed before, exploring her lips and her tongue, and she knew that this must be the beginning of what she should not do. But she let him all the same and soon she was responding, and she felt her heart beating faster and faster. "What if someone should see?" she gasped.

"There's no one within miles," he said. Then his kisses grew more passionate, and his hands began to rove, and she became so excited that although she knew she mustn't, she didn't want him to stop. And why not? she thought. For if not now, perhaps it would be never.

She could feel him, hard against her. He was beginning to loosen her dress. His breath was coming in little gasps.

Then Gretchen's voice. Gretchen's voice from the beach. Gretchen's voice coming nearer.

"Mary?"

Theodore cursed, and pulled away from her. For a second she lay there, feeling abandoned. Then, with a sudden surge of panic, she scrambled behind Theodore, seized her sketch pad, found her hat and crammed it on her head. So that a moment or two later, as Gretchen came over the sand dune, she saw Mary, perhaps a little untidy, but quietly sketching, and her brother, sitting a few yards away, staring at her as she came toward them, with the stony gaze of a serpent that is ready to strike.

"Hello, Gretchen," said Mary calmly. "Why don't you take Theodore for a walk while I finish my sketch?"

⁘

It was late in the afternoon before they got back to the inn. Nobody had talked much. But as they entered one of the guests in the hall told them there'd been trouble on Manhattan that morning. News had come with the afternoon ferry.

"What happened?" asked Theodore.

"The Draft Office up at Forty-seventh was attacked. Set on fire, I believe."

After supper, the landlord said that there had been some more trouble in the afternoon. He'd heard it from the hotel along the street. There had been several fires.

"The telegraph isn't working," he reported, "so we haven't any details. It's probably nothing much."

The day had been hot and humid. Out here, with the sea breeze wafting in from the Atlantic, the humidity had been of no consequence, but over in the streets of New York, it must have been unpleasant. And even out on the porch after supper, it began to feel rather oppressive.

After a short while, Gretchen went inside for a few minutes.

"I'm going for a walk to look at the sea," Theodore announced, taking out a cigar.

"I'll come too," said Mary.

It was quiet on the beach.

"I'm sorry Gretchen came," said Mary.

Theodore nodded. "Yes."

"Are you staying a few more days?"

"I'd like to," he said. "Though I have work at the studio."

"Oh," said Mary.

They stared out over the water. Banks of clouds were gathering now, promising rain, and relief.

"We'll see what tomorrow brings," said Theodore.

That night, Gretchen and Mary went to bed as usual. Gretchen didn't say anything about Theodore. Just after dark Mary thought she was going to cry. She was glad that, moments before, the rain had begun to fall outside the window, masking all sounds.

It was the middle of the night when she awoke, and realized that Gretchen wasn't there. She waited a while. Not a sound. Then she got out of bed and went to the window. The rain had stopped, and the stars were visible again. Looking out, she saw nothing at first. Then she made out a pale shape, moving about on the little patch of grass. It was Gretchen, in her nightdress, pacing up and down in front of a bank of reeds.

Mary did not want to call to her in case it woke the household. She stole quietly out of the room, down the stairs and outside.

"What are you doing?" Mary whispered. "You'll get soaked."

"I can't sleep," Gretchen said. "I'm worried."

"Why?"

"The children. Those fires in the city."

"They said it wasn't serious."

"They don't know. You can't even see the city from here."

Mary felt her heart sink, but she only paused a moment or two.

"Do you want to go back, just to make sure?"

"That's what I was wondering."

"We'll take the ferry in the morning," said Mary. "We can always come out again if everything's all right."

"Yes."

"Come back to bed now, or you'll catch a chill."

❖

The first ferry was not due until mid-morning, but they were all three at the Point waiting for it—Theodore had insisted on accompanying them. The ferry was late. They waited an hour. Then another. Then someone arrived and said the ferry wasn't coming, so they went back to the inn, to see if anyone there had any news.

"The ferry's been attacked, set on fire they think," the owner of the inn told them. "We just had a man here who rode over with the papers from Brooklyn. There's all kinds of trouble in the city. Fires everywhere. They've sent to President Lincoln for troops."

"Can we send a wire to the city?" Theodore asked.

" 'Fraid not. All the telegraph lines are down. Destroyed. You're safer here."

"I have to get to the city," said Gretchen. "My children are there."

"I can get a cart to take you to Brooklyn," said the owner of the inn, "though it may not do you any good."

He did a little better than that. Within half an hour they were in a swift two-wheeled pony trap. By mid-afternoon, they were crossing Brooklyn Heights, from where they saw the city, spread out before them.

There were fires everywhere. Smoke was rising from a dozen areas. Only the Financial District appeared to be unscathed, for a gunboat was lying in the East River exactly opposite the end of Wall Street. The rest of the city might enter the fires of Hell, but the men of Wall Street would make sure that the money houses were safe. When they got down to the ferry, the news was even worse.

"Half the black neighborhoods are burned down," the man in charge of the ferry told them. "God knows how many niggers are getting killed. There are barricades all over the East Side. They're after the rich folks too. None of the merchants dare walk in the street—even Brooks Brothers has been sacked."

"I want to go across," said Gretchen.

"If anyone's going, I'd better," said Theodore. "You two should stay here."

"I'm going to my children," Gretchen answered firmly.

"And I'm going with you," echoed Mary.

"Well, nobody's going to take you," the ferryman told them. "They've half destroyed the ferry ships already, and they're cutting off the railroads too. The rioters are armed. It's war over there."

They went up and down the waterfront. Nobody would take them. As evening approached, Mary said: "We'd better find a place to stay the night."

But Gretchen didn't seem to hear her.

They saw a great flare of fire arise from the direction of the Bowery, where Gretchen's children were. Gretchen gasped, and Theodore looked grave. Mary thought it best to say nothing.

The sun was coming grimly down over the harbor when an old man walked up to them.

"I got a boat. Wife's over there." He indicated the area by South Street. "Soon as it's dark, I'll be going over. I can take you if you want."

⁜

It was strange, being rowed across the East River in the dark. Ahead, the houses of the city were mostly shuttered, therefore dark. Many of the gas lamps in the street were also out—though leaking dangerous gas, no doubt. All over the city, the glow of fires could be seen, and the faint crackling sounds and the smell of their smoke drifted over the water.

But the South Street waterfront was quiet now, and they were able to tie up the boat and clamber out. Theodore gave the old man several dollars for his kindness. Though Gretchen protested, Theodore and Mary persuaded her to let him go to her house near the Bowery, while Mary took her to Sean's saloon, which was not far off. "If there's one place that will be safe down there, it'll be Sean's," Mary pointed out.

Sean was just locking up when they reached him, and he ushered them quickly inside, not best pleased to see them.

"I thought you were safe on Coney Island," he said. But he understood. "A mother goes to her children," he said to Gretchen with a shrug. "What can you do?"

Half an hour later, Theodore arrived. The children were at their grandparents' house. "I can get you there safely," he told his sister.

As they left, he turned to Mary.

"We'll be speaking again, Mary, when this is all over," he said softly.

"Perhaps," she said.

Not that he wouldn't go through with it. If she went round to his studio, she was sure he would. But things had been different, out on Coney Island, and she was back in the city now. Back in her usual world. Well, she'd see.

The immediate question was, where should she go now?

"You'd better stay here," Sean told her. When she said she wanted to go to Gramercy Park, he reiterated: "I don't know what's going on up there, but you're definitely safer with your own family here."

But the Masters were her family now really, though she didn't say it, and she told him she wanted to go uptown all the same. So with no good grace, Sean escorted her. The approach to Gramercy Park had to be cautious, and as they came to Irving Place it was obvious that there had been trouble there. Broken glass and debris littered the whole area. Sean had heard that Twenty-first Street, on the north side of the square, was barricaded. When they reached the quiet square from its western side, they found their way barred by a patrol, not of rioters, but of residents of Gramercy Park, well armed with pistols and muskets. These men didn't know Sean, but one of them did recognize Mary. And after insisting that she part from her brother at the patrol point, he personally took her to the door of the Masters' house and roused them. Sean waited until he knew she was safely in.

Mrs. Master herself came from her room at once. In the kitchen she made her drink some hot chocolate.

"Now you must go straight to bed, Mary," she insisted, "and you can tell me all about your adventures in the morning."

⁘

But Mary didn't tell her adventures in the morning. Whether it was the heat, the shock of what she'd just seen, or some other cause, during that night she began to feel feverish. The next morning, she was shivering and burning up. Mrs. Master herself nursed her, making her drink liquids and placing cool compresses on her head. "Don't talk now, Mary," she said, when Mary tried to thank her. "We're just glad you're safely home."

So Mary was not aware of the burnings and killings that continued all over the city that day. She did not know that Brooklyn, too, had erupted into violence on the waterfront where she'd been, or that there had been killings down most of the East River. Only after her fever had broken, and she awoke feeling hungry on Thursday morning, did she learn that the troops had arrived at last, that they were scattering the rioters with fusillades, and that Gramercy Park itself was now being protected with how-itzers.

The terrible Draft Riots of 1863 were ending.

It was noon when the parlormaid came into her room with a bowl of soup, and sat beside her bed and began to talk. Did she know what had taken place in her absence, the girl wanted to know, how Mr. Master had gone missing, and then Mrs. Master too, and how she'd tried to save the orphanage and nearly been killed, and been rescued by Mr. Master and Madame Restell the abortionist. This astonishing news, at least, made Mary sit up in bed.

"So did anything happen to you?" asked the parlormaid.

"Me?" said Mary. "Oh, no. Nothing much, I suppose."

Moonlight Sonata

I F T H E C A R E E R of Theodore Keller advanced considerably in the eight years after his visit to Coney Island, it was due mainly to two circumstances. The first was that, at the end of the summer of the terrible riots, he had decided to go down to cover the later stages of the Civil War. The second had been the patronage of Frank Master.

And yet now, on a warm afternoon in October, on the very brink of the most important exhibition of his life, in the splendid gallery near Astor Place that Master had hired for the occasion, he was about to lose his temper with his patron.

"You'll ruin everything!" he cried to Master in exasperation.

"I'm telling you," said Master firmly, "it's what you need to do."

They'd already had one disagreement. Theodore had made no objection when Master suggested that one of the portrait photographs he'd taken of Lily de Chantal be included. But when his patron had warned him not to include the picture of Madame Restell, Theodore had been furious.

"It's one of the best pictures I ever took," he'd protested.

The portrait of Madame Restell had been a masterpiece. He'd gone to her house, found a huge, ornate armchair, and placed her in it, like Cleopatra on her throne. With her great bull-like face, she'd stared belligerently at the camera, as terrifying as a minotaur. Placed beside even General Grant, her portrait would have knocked his off the wall.

"Theo," Frank Master had told him, "that woman is now so notorious, they can't even sell the plot next to her house—on Fifth Avenue, if you please! No one will live there. If you put her portrait up, you'll never get another commission." Even Hetty Master had reluctantly agreed. When Madame Restell discovered she wouldn't be in the show, she had been furious.

And there were other aspects of the exhibition that had worried Master: the political pieces.

"Be careful, Theo," he'd said. "I don't want you to do yourself harm." His counsel was possibly wise, but Theodore didn't give a damn, and he'd refused to budge.

"I'm telling the truth," he'd said. "That's what artists do."

In this he'd had one unexpected ally. Hetty Master. "He's quite right," she'd told her husband. "He should include any photographs he likes. Except Madame Restell, perhaps," she'd added, a little reluctantly.

But the sudden message from Master that day, when the whole exhibition had already been hung, had driven Theodore into a fury. Nor had the arrival of his patron at the gallery to argue his case made matters any better. Quite the contrary.

"Think of it," Frank cried enthusiastically. "Put the three together on one wall. Boss Tweed on the left, Thomas Nast on the right, and that shot you took of the city courthouse just below them. Or above, if you prefer," he added obligingly.

"But the work isn't interesting," Theodore expostulated. The three photographs, from the thousands in his collection, were perfectly adequate, but nothing more.

"Theodore," said Frank Master as patiently as if he were addressing a child, "Boss Tweed was arrested today."

❖

If Tammany Hall knew how to make money out of New York City, it had to be said that Boss Tweed had taken the gentle art of the padded contract to heights never dreamed of before. It wasn't that he did anything complicated. Together with Sweeny the Park Commissioner, Connolly the Controller and Mayor Oakey Hall, he formed a ring for the awarding of city contracts. But where in the past a contract worth ten thousand dollars might have had a thousand or two added, the ring, since they controlled everything, felt free to do much better. For more than a decade now, the amount on a contract might be multiplied five, ten, even a hundred times. The contractor was then paid, with a large bonus on top, and the huge remaining amount split between the ring.

His noblest enterprise had been the courthouse, behind City Hall. It had been under construction for ten years now, with no end in sight. When eventually it was completed, there was no doubt that it would be one of the noblest buildings in the city—a regular palace, in the best neo-classical style. But the ring was in no hurry to finish it, since this splendid architectural receptacle was also a trough of liquid gold. Everyone bene-fited—at least, all the ring's many friends. Modest craftsmen with con-tracts for work there had already emerged from it as rich men. No one knew how many millions had flowed into this one building, but this was certain: the courthouse had already cost more than the recent purchase of Alaska.

Yet it hadn't been until two years ago that the press had attacked the ring in any serious way. But when it did come, the attack was two-pronged: from the *New York Times*, in words; and from the brilliant car-toons of Thomas Nast, in *Harper's Weekly*.

It was Thomas Nast's cartoons that Boss Tweed feared the more. His constituents mightn't be able to read, he said, but they could understand the cartoons. He even tried to buy Nast off with half a million dollars. But it hadn't worked. And now, finally, Boss Tweed had been arrested.

✢

Theodore hadn't been particularly pleased with the portrait he'd done of Tweed a couple of years back. With his high domed forehead and beard, he might have passed for any corpulent politician, although the light falling aslant the studio had brought out some lines of aggression and greed in his face. He'd enjoyed the session with Nast far more. They were about the same age, and both from German families. The clever cartoon-ist had a surprisingly smooth, round face, upon which he sported a bushy mustache and a jaunty goatee beard. But Theodore thought he'd captured the young man's lively, quizzical character quite well.

As for the photograph of the courthouse, it showed the growing build-ing well enough, but it wasn't interesting.

"This is just to attract publicity," he complained to Master.

"Publicity is good for your business," Frank replied.

"I know that. But can't you see what will happen? People will notice the Tweed pictures just because he's in the news today, and they'll fail to pay attention to the important work."

"Get a name first," said his patron. "The rest will follow."

"I won't do it."

"Theodore, I am asking you to do this. All the other work you want is there. People will see it, I promise you." He paused. "It will mean a lot to me."

It was said kindly, but Theodore could not miss the threat within it. If he wanted Master's future support, the money he provided for the exhibition, the customers he could supply, then the three photographs had to go up. He sighed. This was the price. The question was, would he pay it?

"It's four o'clock now," said Master. "I'll be back at six, before the opening."

"I'll think about it," said Theodore.

"Please do."

For the next half-hour he considered what to do. He would have liked to go for a walk to mull it over, but he couldn't leave because he'd promised to be here to meet someone else. He hoped she'd come soon.

⁜

It didn't take Mary O'Donnell long to walk from Gramercy Park to the gallery. She could have gone that evening with the Masters—indeed, Mrs. Master had suggested it. But even though she knew Gretchen would be there, Mary didn't really feel comfortable in the middle of a fashionable crowd. She'd much prefer to let Theodore show her round the exhibits in private. She always felt comfortable with Theodore.

After all, they had been lovers.

Not for long. Following the Draft Riots that summer of '63, she'd quite decided that she wouldn't go to see him. She knew that when he'd seduced her on the beach on Coney Island, he hadn't meant anything serious by it. She didn't mind. And once back in the city, her old life in the Master houschold took over at once, and after a week she even supposed that he was fading from her mind.

So it was really only on a whim, she told herself, that one Saturday early in August, having a free day and no other engagements, she happened to look in on his studio in the Bowery.

He was just finishing a portrait of a young man when she came in.

Greeting her politely, as though she were his next customer, he asked her if she'd wait in the larger studio. She'd sat down on the sofa there, then got up to look at the books on the table. There were no poems on the table that day, just a newspaper and an old copy of Nathaniel Hawthorne's *Scarlet Letter*. She'd read the book, so she contented herself with reading the newspaper. She heard the young man leave, and Theodore busying himself about the studio.

Then he entered, and stood there smiling.

"I didn't think you'd come."

"I happened to be passing," she said. "I said I'd look in."

"That was my last customer for the day. Would you like to eat something?"

"If you like," she said, and stood up.

He came over to her.

"We can go out to eat in a little while," he said. Then he began to kiss her.

Their affair lasted through that month and the next. Of course, there were only certain times when she could meet him, but it was surprising how, with a little ingenuity, they could contrive to get together. And on her free days they went out walking, or he took her to concerts or the theater, or other things he thought she might like. Now and then he'd explain to her how he took his photographs, the way he tried to compose them or arrange the light, and she discovered that she had some natural understanding for such things, so that quite soon she could tell which was the best work and sometimes how it was achieved.

She knew he would not marry her. She was not sure she'd even wish it. But she knew that she interested him, and that he had affection for her.

They did not tell Gretchen.

It was in the middle of September that Sean came to see her. They walked round Gramercy Park together.

"So what's going on with Theodore Keller?" he asked.

"I don't know what you mean," she said.

"Yes you do. I know all about it, Mary."

"Are you following me, Sean? I'm almost thirty years old. Have you nothing better to do?"

"Never mind how I know. I'm not having my sister trifled with."

"My God, Sean, how many girls have you trifled with in your life?"

"They weren't my sister."

"Well, it's my business and not yours."

"I can have him taken care of, you know."

"Oh my God, Sean, don't even be thinking such a thing."

"Do you love him?"

"He's very good to me."

"If there's a child, he must marry you, Mary. I wouldn't allow anything else."

"Sean, I don't want you interfering in my life. This is my doing as much as his. If you're going to be this way, I don't want to see you any more. I mean it."

Sean was silent after that for a moment or two.

"If you're ever in trouble, Mary, I want you to come to me," he said gently. "You've always a place in my house." He paused. "Just one thing you're to promise me. You'll never give a child away. Never. I'll look after any child."

"You're not to touch Theodore—he's not to blame. You must promise me that."

"As you wish."

That October, when Theodore had decided he should go down to the battlefields, she had suffered a good deal. But she hadn't let him see. And she'd realized also that it was better he should go then, before she became so attached that the parting would be too painful to bear.

He'd been gone a week when she wondered if she might be with child. During the time of her uncertainty, she'd been so frightened that it was all she could do to concentrate on her work in the house. And Sean's words had come to her often then. But to her relief, that danger had passed.

Theodore had been gone many months, and after his return, though very tempted, she had been determined to keep him only as a friend. God knows, she thought, he's sure to take up with other women if he hasn't already.

And so they had remained friends. She hadn't taken another lover, so far, and she hadn't found a man she wanted to marry. But she'd kept her secret memory, and she was proud of it.

She'd even been able to be helpful to him. When he had told her he was looking for a patron, it was Mary who'd gone to Frank Master and asked him to look at his work. That had been five years ago, and Master had been a fine patron ever since—commissioning work, providing contacts—everything that an artist could hope for. And when he said he

needed to get journalists to come to the opening of the exhibition, she'd
even made Sean speak to some of the newspapermen he knew.

So now, finding Theodore pacing about in a rage, she got him to tell
her all about it. And after she had looked round all the work and admired
it very much, she remarked to him gently: "If you put Boss Tweed and
Nast over there"—she pointed to a wall that had some spare space—"it
wouldn't look so bad."

"I suppose you're right," he said grumpily.

"I wish you'd do it for me," she said.

⁘

There was a good crowd at the opening that evening. Of course, everyone
went to see the portraits of Tweed and Nast, but Frank Master proved to
be right, for having done that, they were circulating round the rest of the
show, and lingering over some of the best work too.

So after greeting his sister, and making polite conversation with all the
people to whom the Masters introduced him, Theodore could almost
relax. Almost, but not quite. For there was one person who had still to
arrive. One person who was very important indeed. If he showed up.

The reporter from the *New York Times*. It was Sean O'Donnell who
had promised that the fellow would come, but at seven o'clock there
was still no sign of him. Nor at ten minutes past the hour. It wasn't till
nearly seven thirty that Master came to his side and murmured, "I think
that's him."

Horace Slim was a quiet man in his thirties, with a thin mustache and
sad eyes. He greeted Theodore politely, but though he wasn't giving anything away, something in his manner suggested he was only there because
he'd been sent and that, as soon as he had enough material for a short
piece, he'd be gone.

And Theodore needed more than that. He made himself keep calm,
though. He knew it was no good pushing too hard; one could only hope
for the best. But he'd handled journalists before, and he was not without
cunning. So, giving the man a professional nod, he said quietly, "I'll take
you round, Mr. Slim."

The exhibition filled several rooms, and was arranged thematically.
He'd already decided to start with the portraits, but not to go straight to
Boss Tweed. He'd got some famous people, after all. Names that should
give the journalist some useful copy.

"Here's President Grant," he pointed out. "And General Sherman. And Fernando Wood." Slim duly noted them. There were some big city merchants, with imposing architectural details behind them, an opera diva, and Lily de Chantal, of course. Theodore paused by her.

He'd always had a pretty good idea why Frank Master had suggested he take the picture of Lily de Chantal, though he wasn't such a damn fool as to ask why. It was a suspicion reinforced when, ten minutes ago, he'd heard Hetty Master drily remark: "She looks a lot older than that in real life." The picture was excellent, with a theatrical backdrop.

"I took this after her recital last year. Did you go to it?"

"Can't say I did."

"It was a notable event—quite a society occasion. Maybe worth a mention."

Slim had a look at the other portraits, and took down a couple more names. They'd been carefully chosen to attract more clients. Then they came to Boss Tweed and Thomas Nast, and the courthouse.

"Good timing," said Mr. Slim, making a quick note.

"I suppose so," said Theodore. "People have been looking at them."

"It'll make a good opening for an article," said Slim.

"So long as it's not the only thing you mention."

"Any other sitters you'd like to tell me about?" the journalist asked quietly. "Anyone of interest?"

Theodore glanced at him. Were those sad eyes better informed than they let on? Did Horace Slim know about Madame Restell?

"All my sitters are interesting," said Theodore carefully. But he'd better give the fellow a story. "I'll tell you whose picture's missing," he offered. "Abraham Lincoln—at the Gettysburg address."

⁜

At the end of that summer of the Draft Riots, when he'd decided to leave New York for a while and follow the war out in the field, there'd been only one sensible way to do it. And that was to work for Mathew Brady. Brady had the government concession. He'd send you out, even provide you with a special carriage, converted into a movable darkroom. And so, in November 1863, along with several other photographers, Theodore had found himself down in Pennsylvania, at Gettysburg, where a new cemetery had just been prepared to receive the fallen heroes of the great battle that had taken place nearby only months before.

There had been little doubt, by then, about the significance of the Battle of Gettysburg. Before July 1863, after all, both sides might have been getting sick of the war, but the Confederacy was still on the offensive. Down on the Mississippi, General Grant had so far failed to take the Confederates' mighty fortification at Vicksburg. Bold General Lee and Stonewall Jackson had taken on a Union army twice their size on the Potomac River, and though Jackson had died, Lee and his Confederate army had swept through Maryland and into Pennsylvania, threatening both Baltimore and the capital.

But then, on the Fourth of July, had come the double victory for the Union. Vicksburg had fallen, at last, to Grant, and Lee's army, after a display of matchless courage, had been smashed and turned back at Gettysburg.

The North had the initiative. The South was open to massive attack.

Not that the war was won. By no means. The riots in New York, after all, had been only the most extreme expression of a widespread Union dislike of the war, by then. The will of the North might crack. The South might yet outlast them. The government in Washington knew it very well.

The dedication of the new cemetery at Gettysburg had been important, therefore. A ceremony was called for. A big story for the newspapers. A fine speech.

The speech had been entrusted to the president of Harvard, the greatest orator of the day. Only later, as a courtesy perhaps, did anyone think of asking Lincoln himself to attend. Indeed, Theodore remembered, he and the other photographers hadn't been too sure that Lincoln was coming at all.

⁜

"But come he did," he remarked to the journalist now. "There was a big crowd, you know, governors and local people and all the rest. Maybe fifteen thousand altogether. Lincoln rode up with the Secretary of State, I think, and Chase, the Treasury Secretary. Then he took his place with the others, just sat there quietly with his tall hat off, of course, so that we could hardly see him. I'd caught a glimpse of him when he came to make his address at the Cooper Institute, when he was still clean-shaven, but I hadn't seen him with his beard before. Anyway, there was some music, and a prayer, so far as I remember. And then the president of Harvard rose to speak.

"Well, that was quite a speech, I can tell you. He gave full measure—two and a half hours—and when he finally came to his grand peroration, the applause was like thunder. Then there was a psalm sung. Then Lincoln rose, and we could see him well enough.

"Now we knew he wouldn't be speaking for long—we'd had the big speech—so we got ourselves prepared, myself and the other photographers, pretty quick. But I dare say you know how that is done."

It had been no easy business getting a picture in the Civil War. The photographs were always taken in 3-D, which meant that two plates had to be inserted simultaneously into a double camera, one to the left, one to the right. The glass plates had to be quickly cleaned, coated with collodion, then, while still wet, dipped in silver nitrate before being put into the camera. The exposure time might only be a few seconds, but then one had to rush the plates, still wet, into the mobile darkroom. Quite apart from the difficulties of having people in motion during the seconds of exposure, the whole process was so cumbersome that taking pictures of battlefield action was almost impossible.

"Well, dammit, I'd heard the first words of his speech—'Fourscore and seven years ago'—and I was on it, preparing my wet plates. And I'd finished ahead of the other fellows, and slipped them into the camera, and was ready to go, when I heard him say, '. . . that government of the people, by the people, for the people, shall not perish from the earth.' Then just as I was getting him in my sights, he stopped. And there was silence. Then he looked down at one of the organizers and said something. Seemed as if he was apologizing—he looked kind of discouraged. And then he sat down. Everyone was so surprised that they hardly even got round to clapping. 'Was that it?' said the fellow next to me, who was still trying to get the plates into his camera. 'Guess so,' I said. 'Jeezus,' he said, 'that was fast.' Of course, that speech is pretty famous now, but the audience didn't think anything of it at the time, I can tell you."

"So you got no picture of the Gettysburg address?" said Horace Slim.

"Not a damn thing. Nor did anyone, so far as I know. Did you ever see a photograph of that famous day?"

"That's a good story," said the journalist.

"Let me show you the West," said Theodore.

It had been an excellent opportunity. A government commission, to go into the western wilderness with the surveyors and bring back photographs that would attract settlers to take up land there. He'd done a good job. Big, rich-looking landscapes; pictures of friendly Indians. The government men had been delighted. One charming picture of a little Indian girl had caught Frank Master's attention, and he'd paid Theodore a good price for a print of it.

But the journalist was bored. Theodore could tell. Swiftly he took him into the biggest room.

"So," he said cheerfully, "these are the pictures I've been told not to show."

For they were of the Civil War.

⁘

Nobody wanted to know about the Civil War now. While it was still being fought, everyone did. When the dour Scotsman, Alexander Gardner, had taken his picture, *Home of the Rebel Sharpshooter*, it had made him famous. Yet when his collection, a world classic, was published the year after war's end, it didn't sell.

Then there was Brady himself. People often imagined he took every picture of the Civil War. After all, his name was on so many of the pictures taken by the photographers he'd hired—a fact they sometimes resented. Yet to be fair, it was Brady who'd been the first in the field. At the start of the war, when the Confederates smashed the Union men at Bull Run, Brady had been there on the battlefield, lucky not to be a casualty.

It wasn't Brady's fault that his failing eyesight made it difficult for him to take the pictures himself. But he'd sent out those keen young men, set them up, provided them with movable darkrooms, all out of his own pocket. And what had he got from it all, when the war was over? Financial ruin.

"People don't want to be reminded of those horrors," said Theodore. "They wanted to forget them the moment the war was done." In the South, he'd heard, the agony of defeat was so terrible that quite a few photographers had even destroyed their own work.

"So why do you show this work?" asked Horace Slim.

"Same reason you write, I dare say," answered Theodore. "A photographer and a journalist both have a duty to record: to tell the truth, and not let people forget."

"The horrors of war, you mean—the killing?"

"Not really. That was important of course, Mr. Slim, but others had already covered it."

"Like Brady."

"Exactly. In '62, when the most terrible battles began, Brady had photographers with General Grant when he went into Tennessee. They recorded the carnage at Shiloh. Brady's boys were in Virginia that summer, when Stonewall Jackson and General Lee saved Richmond from destruction. They were there when the Confederates struck back at us in Kentucky, and they were up in Maryland that fall, when Lee was turned back at Antietam. Do you remember the great exhibition Brady organized after Antietam, when he showed the world what the battlefield looked like after that terrible slaughter? It was a wonder to me, sir, that those photographs did not stop war altogether." He shook his head. "Brady had photographers at the Battle of Gettysburg the next summer also, but I wasn't one of them, you see—I didn't become a Brady photographer until a couple of months after that. So maybe my task was different. Anyway," he gestured to the photographs on the walls, "this is what I did."

The journalist took his time, which was exactly what Theodore wanted. The first picture that seemed to interest him was entitled *Hudson River*. It showed a New York street, and had a grainy, dusty feel to it. A couple of blocks away the street ended and beyond was a great emptiness which was clearly the Hudson, although you couldn't actually see the water.

"Draft riots?"

"That's right. The third day. Wednesday."

"Why call it *Hudson River*? The river's hardly visible."

"Because that's the name of the man you see."

There was only one man in the picture. A blackened bundle hanging from a tree. Blackened because he had been burned after he was lynched. Burned almost to a cinder.

"He was called Hudson River?"

"Yes. He worked in a saloon, for Sean O'Donnell."

"I know him."

"O'Donnell had hidden him in the cellar. Didn't even know he'd got out. Reckons he could have been drinking down there, or maybe he just couldn't stand the boredom any more—he'd been down there three days. Whatever the reason, young Hudson River sneaked outside. Must have wandered round Battery Park and started up the West Side. That's where they caught him. They were catching a lot of black men that day. Strung him up on that tree and set fire to him."

Horace Slim said nothing, and moved on.

"That's a strange one," he remarked by another photograph. "What is it?"

"An experiment, technically," Theodore said. "I was with General Grant's army at the time. The camera is looking through a magnifying lens that has been placed in front of the object, and you can actually see the magnified image of the object."

"I see. But what is it?"

"It's a lead slug. A bullet. But I have cut the slug open, so that you can see its internal construction better. You'll notice that instead of being of a consistency throughout, the slug has a cavity at its base. Invention of a Frenchman named Minié originally—that's why they call it a Minié ball. As you'll know, the old smooth-bore musket was never accurate except at short range. But the rifle, with its spiral grooves inside the barrel, causes the bullet to spin, so that it becomes far more deadly over longer ranges."

"And the cavity in the slug?"

"Under the pressure of firing, the open bottom of the slug expands outward, pushes it against the walls of the barrel so that it takes the rifling. That little cavity has brought death to thousands."

"Ingenious. The photograph, I mean." He moved on. "And this pair of broken-down shoes?"

"General Grant himself showed them to me—in disgust. They came from New York, too. You'd think they were years old, to disintegrate like that, but they're not a week old."

"I see. Shoddy goods."

It had been one of the greatest scandals of the war. Profiteers, not a few of them from New York, had got contracts to supply the army and sent them shoddy goods—uniforms that fell apart and, worst of all, boots that seemed to be made of leather, but whose soles were actually compressed cardboard. At the first shower of rain they disintegrated.

"This may interest you," Theodore remarked, leading the journalist across to another picture, which consisted of two posters. "I picked 'em up, in different locations, then put them side by side on a wall." Each advertised the rates being offered for joining the Union army. "You'll recall the reluctance of our own state to accept any black men into the army at all. But, of course, the black regiments came to be some of the best in the Union by the end of the war."

The posters were quite straightforward. A white private was offered $13 a month, and a $3.50 clothing allowance. The black private was offered $10 and $3 for clothing.

"And what point are you making?" the journalist asked. "Are you aiming to shock?"

"No," said Theodore, "it's just a little irony. A reminder, if you like. I dare say plenty of white soldier boys reckoned that difference was fair—after all, the white man's family would need more, because they lived better."

"Not everybody's going to like you," said Slim.

"I know. That's why my good friends told me not to show this part of the work. But I told 'em—in a friendly way of course—to go to hell. The record is the record, Mr. Slim. It is for you, as a journalist. And it is for me. If we don't tell the truth as we see it, we have nothing." He smiled. "Let me show you a landscape."

It was the only landscape in the Civil War section—actually three landscapes pasted together to make a wide panorama. And under it, the title: *Marching Through Georgia.*

"In the fall of '64, I'd gone back to New York. Grant was stuck in Virginia at that time, and the war so unpopular again that most people reckoned Lincoln would lose the election that year, and the Democrats would make peace with the South so the Confederates could have pretty much declared a victory. But then Sherman took Atlanta, and everything changed. The Union cause was up again, Lincoln would be re-elected, and Sherman would make his great march from Atlanta to the sea. A fine photographer I knew, named George Barnard, went down to join General Sherman there, and I went with him. That's how this picture came to be taken."

"*Marching Through Georgia*," Horace Slim remarked. "Fine song."

"Yes. You know who hates it? Sherman himself. Can't bear the sound of it."

"They play it wherever he appears."

"I know." Theodore shook his head. "Think of the lyrics of that song, sir." He sang them softly: "'Hurrah, Hurrah, we bring the jubilee! Hurrah, Hurrah, the flag that makes you free!'" He looked at the journalist.

"It has a joyous ring, don't it? That's what makes it so contemptible, to those of us that were there."

"Well, the slaves were glad enough to see you, surely?"

"Yes—'How the darkies shouted when they heard the joyful sound,' as the words of the song go. The slaves greeted Sherman as a liberator, it's true. And though when he set out, he hadn't been that interested in them, he came to believe in their cause and did much for them. But consider the lines that follow—'How the turkeys gobbled which our commissary found; How the sweet potatoes even started from the ground.'"

"Poetic license."

"Hogwash, sir. We took every provision we could use from that fine land, most certainly. We raped it. But anything that was left after that, we destroyed. It was deliberate, it was cruel, and the scale of it had to be seen to be believed. That was Sherman's intent. He believed it was necessary. 'The hard way,' he called it. I don't say he was wrong. But there was no joy in that land, I assure you. We destroyed every farm, burned every field and orchard, so that the people of the South should starve." He paused. "Can you quote me the words of the song that describe it?"

"'So we made a thoroughfare for freedom and her train; Sixty miles of latitude, three hundred to the main.'"

"That's right. A great swathe of total desolation, a blackened wasteland. Utter ruination. Sixty miles wide, sir, and three hundred miles long. That's what we did to the South. I do not believe anything more terrible was ever done in the history of war." He paused. "And some damn contemptible fool has made it into a popular song." He pointed to the landscape. "That's what it looked like."

The landscape in the photograph was wide indeed. You could see for miles. And it stretched to a distant horizon. In the foreground were the charred remains of a farmstead. And everywhere else, as far as the eye could see, was an empty, blackened wasteland.

There was one more room to visit. It was the smallest, and it contained pictures that were not united by any theme. The first to catch the journalist's eye was Theodore's picture of the black men walking up the railway tracks beside the gleaming river.

"I like that," he said.

"Ah." Theodore was genuinely pleased. "It's an early one, but I'm still quite proud of it."

There were some small studies of family and friends, including a fine one of his cousin Hans, the piano-maker, sitting at the keyboard, the fine lines of his face caught by the soft light coming from an unseen window.

On one wall were three views of Niagara Falls, commissioned by Frank Master. They were wonderfully striking, the long exposure adding a complexity to the billowing sprays rising from the base, and a dazzling clear sky making the whole scene almost unearthly, like a painting.

"Hmm," said Horace Slim. "You'll do well with those."

Theodore grinned. "Pays the rent, Mr. Slim. They are technically excellent, by the way."

There were a few scenes of New York, including one of the reservoir on Fifth Avenue. Hetty Master had commissioned it.

And that pretty much seemed to wrap the exhibition up. Except for one small, rather dark picture in a corner. Horace Slim walked over and took a quick look at it. The photograph had a title: *Moonlight Sonata*.

It took a few seconds to decipher what was in there. The scene had required a very long exposure, because it was taken by the light of a full moon. You could make out a trench line, and a sentry standing near a field gun, whose long barrel shone softly in the moonlight. There were tents and a little stricken tree.

"Civil War?"

"Yes. But it didn't seem to go in the other room, somehow. It's more a personal photograph, I guess. I may take it down."

The journalist with the sad eyes nodded, folded up his notebook and put it in his pocket.

"Well, I guess I'm done, then."

"Thank you. You'll give me a notice?"

"Yes. Don't know how long—that'll depend on the editor—but I have all I need."

They began to walk out together.

"Just out of interest, not for the piece, what was the story of the little dark picture?"

Theodore paused.

"Well, it was the night before an engagement. In Virginia. Our Union boys were in their trenches, and the Confederates in theirs, not more than a couple of stone's throw away. It was quite silent. The moonlight, as you saw, was falling on the scene. There must've been all ages, I suppose, between those trenches. Men well into middle years. And plenty who were little more than boys. There were women in the camp, too, of course. Wives, and others.

"I supposed they would soon fall asleep. But then, over in the Confederate trenches, some fellow started singing 'Dixie.' And soon they were all joining in, right along the line. So they sang 'Dixie' at us for a while, then stopped.

"Well, sure enough, our boys weren't going to let it go at that. So a group of 'em started up 'John Brown's Body.' And in no time the whole of our trenches were giving them that. Fine voices too, I may say.

"And when they'd done, there was another silence. Then over in the Confederate trench, we heard a single voice. A young fellow by the sound of it. And he started singing a psalm. The twenty-third psalm it was. I'll never forget that.

"As you know, in the South, with the shape-note singing, every congregation is well practiced in the singing of psalms. So again, all along the line, they joined in. Kind of soft. Sweet and low. And maybe it was the moonlight, but I have to say it was the most beautiful sound I ever heard.

"But I'd forgotten that many of our boys were accustomed to singing the psalms too. When you consider the profanities you hear spoken every day in camp, you might forget that; but it is so. And to my surprise, our boys began to sing with them. And in a short while, all along the lines, those two armies sang together, free for a moment of their circumstances, as if they were a single congregation of brothers in the moonlight. And then they sang another psalm, and then the twenty-third again. And after that, there was silence, for the rest of the night.

"During which time, I took that photograph.

"The next morning there was a battle. And before noon, Mr. Slim, I regret to say, there was scarcely a man from either of those trenches left. They had killed each other. Dead, sir, almost every one."

And, caught unawares, Theodore Keller suddenly stopped speaking, and was not able to continue for a minute or two.

Snow

THREE OF THEM sat down at the table in Delmonico's. Frank Master was nervous. He hadn't wanted to come—indeed, he'd been most surprised when Sean O'Donnell had asked him to meet Gabriel Love.

"What the devil does he want with me?" he'd said. Gabriel Love might be a well-known figure, but he and Master moved in different circles and Frank had no desire to do business with such a man.

"Just come and meet him," Sean had asked. "As a kindness to me." So, since he owed O'Donnell quite a few favors, Frank had reluctantly agreed.

Delmonico's restaurant, at least, had been a good choice. It used to be further downtown, but now it was at Twenty-sixth and Fifth, looking across Madison Park to Leonard Jerome's old mansion. Frank liked Delmonico's.

But before he walked in the door, he turned to Sean and said firmly: "Remember, O'Donnell, anything illegal, and I'm leaving."

"It's all right," said Sean. "Trust me."

Sean O'Donnell, these days, was a very elegant man. His face was clean-shaven; his hair was still thick, but silver. He was wearing a perfectly cut pearl-gray suit. The knot of his silk bow tie was tied to perfection, and the studs down his shirt front were neatly set diamonds. His shoes were so highly polished, it was hard to imagine their owner had ever stepped near a gutter in his life. He looked like a banker. True, he still owned the saloon, and looked in there from time to time, but he hadn't lived there for almost twenty years. Since then he'd owned a house on lower Fifth Avenue—not a great mansion, but as big as Master's house in Gramercy Park. Sean O'Donnell was a rich man.

How had he done it? Master had a pretty good idea. While Fernando Wood had known how to extort money from New York City, and his successor, the great Boss Tweed of Tammany Hall, had turned the business into an art form, O'Donnell had managed to be close to both men in turn, and he'd benefited hugely. He'd been able to develop scores of properties in the ever growing city, renting and selling at huge profit. "I never had any of the padded contracts," Sean had told him. Tweed had fleeced the city of millions with those. "But he did let me invest $10,000 in his printing company." Tweed had then pushed all the city's printing through the company, at inflated prices. "I got a dividend of $75,000 a year from a $10,000 investment," Sean had confessed.

And when Tweed had been exposed, and his inner circle had been disgraced, O'Donnell had been one of many who, having profited discreetly in those years, had been able to cover their tracks and continue quietly with their business.

And then there had been the dealings with Wall Street.

That had been the province of men like Gabriel Love.

Gabriel Love was large. He sat opposite Frank Master, and his watery blue eyes rested mildly upon Frank's face, while his big white beard flowed like a benign waterfall onto the broad expanse of his stomach, which caressed the edge of the table.

Everyone knew Mr. Gabriel Love. He looked like Santa Claus, and his gifts to local charities were legendary. He loved attending church, where he sang the hymns in a high, almost falsetto tenor. His pockets were always full of candies for children. "Daddy Love," people often called him. Unless, of course, they had been the victim of one of his devastating financial operations. Then they called him "The Bear."

Gabriel Love greeted Master politely. When the waiters brought the food, he announced that he would say grace, which he did in a voice of great reverence. Then he let Sean provide most of the conversation until he had finished eating an entire chicken. Only then did he turn to Frank and inquire of him: "Are you a betting man, Mr. Master?"

"Once in a while," said Master, guardedly.

"The way I see it," said Gabriel Love, "a Wall Street man is a betting man. I've seen men bet all afternoon on which raindrop on a window is goin' to reach the bottom first." He nodded thoughtfully. "A Wall Street man is greedy, too. No harm in that. Without greed, I always say, there'd be no civilization. But the Wall Street man doesn't have the patience to till the soil or manufacture things. He's clever, but he's not deep. He invests in companies, but he doesn't much care what they are, or what they do. What he wants is to bet on them. Wall Street will always be full of young men, betting."

"Young men?" Sean said. "What about older men, Gabriel?"

"Ah. Well now, as a young man gets older, he raises a family, takes on responsibilities. And then he changes—it's only human nature. You see it on the street all the time. The man with responsibilities does not bet in the same way. His operations are different."

"How different?"

Gabriel Love gazed at them both, and suddenly his pale blue eyes seemed to grow harder.

"He stacks the odds," he said sharply.

He knew it. As Frank stared at the great, white, deceptive beard of Gabriel Love, every instinct told him it was time to leave.

Sean O'Donnell was one thing. Sean might kill you, but not if you were on his side. For some time, fate had linked them through Mary, and in other ways since. Sean he could trust. But Gabriel Love was another matter. Did he really want to get involved with him, at his time of life?

Master was nearly seventy-three years old. You wouldn't have thought it to look at him—most people took him to be ten years younger. His hair was thin, and his mustache was white, but he was still a strong, good-looking man, and rather proud of it. He went to his counting house every day. And if, now and then, he felt a slight twinge of pain, or sense of tightness in the chest, he shrugged it off. If he was getting old, he didn't want to know it.

But he enjoyed the respectability that his age and long career had earned him. His fortune was considerable, and he could easily augment it without taking unnecessary risks. He had his grandchildren to think of now. And Gabriel Love had just as good as told him that something dishonest was afoot. He started to rise.

"Gentlemen," he said, "I'm too old to go to jail."

But Sean O'Donnell's restraining hand was on his arm.

"Wait, Frank—for my sake—just hear what it is that Mr. Love proposes."

✥

It was a week later that Lily de Chantal set out in her carriage, from the distant north-western territory of the United States, to drive down to Gramercy Park.

Dakota Territory. Still not a state: a vast, wild wilderness. But when, a couple of years ago, Mr. Edward Clark the developer had built a huge, isolated apartment building on the west side of Central Park—all the way up at Seventy-second Street—he had decided to call it the Dakota. It seemed Mr. Clark had a fascination for Indian names. He'd already built another apartment house called the Wyoming, and had hoped to name one of the West Side boulevards Idaho Avenue. In its splendid isolation, with neighboring blocks empty except for a few small stores and shanties, the mighty Dakota might just as well have been in some remote territory, as far as the fashionable world was concerned.

"Nobody lives up there, for heaven's sake," they said. "And anyway, who lives in apartments?"

The answer to that question was simple. Until some years ago, only poor people lived in apartments—houses split up by floors—or in tenements, where even the floors were subdivided. Splendid apartments might be a feature of great European capitals like Vienna and Paris. But not New York. The people you knew lived in houses.

Yet there were signs of change. Other apartment buildings had appeared in the city, though none as grand as the Dakota. The building, a somewhat barn-like version of the French Renaissance, stared rather bleakly across Central Park and the pond where people skated in winter. But, it had to be confessed, it had its points.

Aside from the monumental Indian motifs with which Mr. Clark had decorated the building, the apartments were huge, with plenty of servants' quarters. With their soaring ceilings, the reception rooms in the largest apartments were quite as big as those in many mansions. And soon people noticed something else. These apartments were rather convenient. If you wanted to go to your country house for the summer months, for instance, you could safely lock your door without even leaving a housekeeper to mind the place. Before long people were even saying: "Oh, I know someone who lives there."

Lily de Chantal, now in her fifties, had decided to give the Dakota a try. Today, she declared, she wouldn't think of living anywhere else. She'd rented out the house she owned, invested her other savings, and was able to live quietly and pleasantly at the Dakota with a small staff. Her style of life was made all the more comfortable by the fact that Frank Master, discreetly, paid half the rent.

This afternoon, however, in answer to a note she'd received the day before, she was on her way to take tea, not with Frank, but with Hetty. And understandably, she was a little nervous.

She wondered what Hetty wanted.

March had only just started, but the day was surprisingly warm. As she passed along the south side of Central Park, she saw banks of daffodils. Only as she crossed the top of Sixth Avenue did she frown.

She had never reconciled herself to the long, ugly line of the raised railway that ran down Sixth these days. The El, they called it—the elevated railroads, whose puffing, sooty steam engines rushed their noisy carriages over the heads of ordinary mortals, twenty feet above the street. There were other lines on Second, Third and Ninth avenues, though the one on Ninth gave no trouble to the Dakota, she was glad to say. They were clearly necessary, since they carried over thirty million passengers a year. But for Lily, they represented the ugly side of the city's huge progress that she didn't want to see.

The sight of the El was soon past, and a long block later, at the corner of the park, she was turning into the pleasant environs of Fifth Avenue.

You had to say, Fifth was getting better and better. If the El was the necessary engine of New York's burgeoning wealth, Fifth Avenue was becoming the stately apex. The avenue of palaces, the valley of kings. She'd only gone a short way when she passed what had once been the solitary mansion of the wicked Madame Restell. Solitary no longer. That notorious lady herself was no more, and across the street, now, the Vanderbilts had built their mighty mansions.

She passed the Cathedral of St. Patrick, all complete now, and soaring in Irish Catholic triumph over even those Vanderbilt mansions.

But despite the pace of advance, she was glad that only St. Patrick's, and Trinity, Wall Street, and a handful of other church spires rose into the sky above the city. The great residential mansions were still only five stories high; indeed, the largest commercial structures, using cast-iron beams, were seldom more than ten.

Moreover, even the most lavish of the newer palaces, whose opulent decorations might have seemed overdone, vulgar, in fact, to the Federal generation, even these plutocratic treasure houses still relied upon the basic motifs of the classical world, as did their cast-iron counterparts. There was tradition, and craftsmanship, and humanity in them, every one.

The city might be vast, but it still retained its grace. And perhaps because she was getting older herself, this was important to her.

She passed the reservoir at Forty-second Street. In the Thirties came the mansions of the Astors. And then she was turning into Gramercy Park.

It was just the two of them, herself and Hetty Master. When she was ushered into the sitting room, Hetty welcomed her with a smile.

"I'm so glad you've come, Lily," she said, and indicated that she wished Lily to sit on the sofa beside her.

You had to say, Lily considered, Hetty Master had worn very well. Her hair was gray. But then so would mine be, Lily thought, if I let it. Her bosom was matronly, but she had by no means let herself go, and her face was still handsome. Any sensible man of seventy should be proud of having such a wife.

But then, what man of any age was sensible?

During the last two decades, she supposed they must have met several times every year, at the opera, or in other people's houses. And on these occasions, Hetty had always been polite and even friendly to her. Once, about fifteen years ago, after a recital she had given—which Frank had financed, of course—Hetty had actually asked her some quite intelligent questions about the music. They had been in a big house with a music room, so Lily had taken her to a piano, and shown her which parts were the most difficult to sing, and why. They'd had quite a long talk, and by the end of it, she could tell that, whatever else her feelings might be, Hetty had genuinely respected her professionally.

But had Hetty guessed that Frank was her lover? There had never been any indication that she did. Lily had no idea what Hetty might have done if she had known, and, as she had no wish to cause Hetty pain, Lily hoped she didn't. She and Frank had always been discreet, and Frank was forever telling her: "Hetty has no idea."

Now Hetty poured the tea. She waited until the maid had left the room, however, before she began.

"I asked you to come round, because I need your help," she said calmly.

"If I can," said Lily, a little uncertainly.

"I'm worried about Frank," Hetty continued. She gave Lily a quick look. "Aren't you?"

"I?"

"Yes," Hetty said, in a businesslike fashion. "I'm worried about this girl. Have you met her?"

Lily was silent for a moment. "I think you have the advantage of me," she said cautiously.

"Have I?" Hetty smiled. "I've known that you were Frank's mistress for a long time, you know."

"Oh," said Lily. She paused. "How long?"

"Twenty years."

Lily looked down at her hands. "I don't know what to say," she said.

"If it was going to be somebody," said Hetty, "I suppose I'd just as soon it was you."

Lily didn't reply.

"You were quite discreet," Hetty continued. "I was glad of that."

Lily still didn't reply.

"It was partly my fault, I can quite see that now. I drove him away, so he sought comfort elsewhere." Hetty sighed. "If I had my life again, I'd act differently. It's hard for a man if he thinks his wife doesn't respect him."

"You're very philosophical."

"One has to be at my age. Yours too, if you'll forgive my saying so. In any case, I'd rather be the wife than the mistress."

Lily nodded. "You still have your marriage."

"Yes. Marriage may not be a perfect state, but it is a protection, especially as we get older. And we are all getting older, my dear." She glanced at Lily before going on. "I still have my home, my children and grandchildren. And a husband, too. Frank may have strayed, but he is still my husband." She eyed Lily evenly. "In every way."

Lily bowed her head. What could she say?

"I was hurt when Frank took a mistress, I won't deny it, but I'd still rather be me than you. Especially now."

"Now?"

"This young woman. The one who's stolen him from you."

"Oh."

"What do you know about her?"

"Not a lot."

"Well, I know a great deal." She watched Lily for a moment. "Would you like to know?" And when Lily hesitated: "Miss Donna Clipp is a little witch. She's digging for gold. Not only that—she was prosecuted for theft, in Philadelphia. I have proof."

"I see."

"I've had a lawyer investigate her. Frank paid for the lawyer, of course, though he doesn't know it. He thought he was paying for curtains. She cares nothing for him. But she's after his money."

"I suppose you think that of me too," said Lily sadly.

"Not at all, my dear. I'm sure he's generous, but he can afford to be. Not that I think little Miss Clipp will succeed in getting much out of him. Frank's not a fool when it comes to money, but she might kill him while she's trying." She sighed. "We both know my husband's getting old. And he's vain, like most men. She's a young woman—she's only thirty, you know—and I'm sure he wants to prove himself."

"And you think it might be too much for his heart?"

"Don't you?"

"Perhaps," said Lily.

Hetty looked hard at her. "Do you love my husband?"

"I have grown very fond of him."

"Then you'll help me."

"To do what?"

"Why, to get rid of this young woman, my dear. We have to get rid of Donna Clipp."

❖

When Mary O'Donnell had heard that Lily de Chantal was coming to tea with Mrs. Master, she had been surprised. She knew that the two women were only vaguely acquainted; she supposed Mrs. Master might be wanting the singer to perform at one of her charity events. When she was told that Mrs. Master wanted to see her as well, she couldn't imagine why.

She found the two of them sitting quite easily together on a sofa.

"Now, Mary dear," Mrs. Master announced with a smile, "we need your help."

"Yes, Mrs. Master," said Mary. Whatever could she want?

"We've known each other many years, Mary," Mrs. Master continued, "and now I have to ask you to be very honest with me, and to keep a secret as well. Would you do that for me? Would you promise?"

After thirty-five years of kindness?

"Yes, Mrs. Master, I promise."

"Well, then. I am worried about my husband. And so is Miss de Chantal. Miss de Chantal is a dear friend of my husband." She smiled at Lily. "We are both worried about him, Mary, and we think that perhaps you can help."

Mary stared at her. What was she saying? How much did she know?

"Your brother Sean has had dealings with my husband for many years, as you know, Mary. And Miss de Chantal tells me that your brother knows her too. What we need to know is, has your brother ever talked about Miss de Chantal?"

"About Miss de Chantal?"

"Yes. As a friend of my husband?"

"Why . . ." And Mary, despite her promise, was about to tell a lie. Except that she blushed. And Mrs. Master saw it.

"It's all right, Mary," said Hetty Master. "I've known for twenty years. How long have you known?"

"Ten," said Mary, awkwardly.

"Sean told you?"

Mary nodded. He'd kept it to himself for a long time, you had to give him that, but in the end he'd told her.

"Good," said Mrs. Master, "that might be helpful. And has he told you about Miss Donna Clipp?"

"Miss Clipp?" Mary hesitated. "I don't know the name." This was true. Two weeks ago, Sean had muttered that Master was making a fool of himself, and that at his age he'd better be careful. But that was all he'd said.

"Well, that's her name. Now, Mary, we need your help. Mr. Master is not a young man, and we must protect him. When are you next seeing your brother?"

"I often go to see him on Saturdays," said Mary.

"That's tomorrow," said Hetty Master, with great satisfaction. "Could you see him then?"

"I could if you want."

"Then here's what we need you to do."

�֍

There was no doubt, Sean thought, that Gabriel Love's plan was a work of art. And part of the beauty of the thing was that it was not what you'd expect Daddy Love to do.

Daddy Love liked to sell short. If he sensed that the market was going down, or better yet, if he had private information that a stock was going to be in trouble, then he'd offer to sell you a parcel of shares, at a future date, for well under their present price. Like a fool, you'd suppose you had a bargain. And sure as fate, when the day arrived, the price of those shares would have dropped far further than you would have dreamed, and he'd buy them cheap himself, and you'd be obliged to take them off his hands at the higher price you'd agreed, leaving him with a handsome profit and yourself with a massive loss. And all he'd needed to do was make the bet— or, more precisely, stack the odds, since he'd certainly known something about those shares that you didn't.

Only this time, Gabriel Love was going to do the opposite.

In any game there are winners and losers. In this game, the loser would be one Cyrus MacDuff.

"Cyrus MacDuff hates me," Mr. Love had explained to Sean. "That's his problem. He's hated me for twenty years."

"Why's that?"

"Because I once cheated him out of a boatload of money. But that's no excuse. If Mr. MacDuff exercised Christian charity, if he knew how to forgive, then the awful fate that is about to befall him might be avoided. It will be his evil nature, I believe, that will blind him to reality, and which the Lord will punish."

"Sounds good to me," said Sean. "How is God's will to be done?"

"Through the Hudson Ohio Railroad," said Mr. Love.

There was only one thing, in the year 1888, that you could say with certainty about the railroad business. It was dirty.

With the opening of the great American West, the opportunity for carrying goods by rail was expanding hugely. Great fortunes were being made. And wherever there is money, there is competition. While the British developed their far-flung empire, and the powers of Europe rushed to colonize Africa, so the bold entrepreneurs of the East Coast scrambled to build railroads across the huge tracts of the American West.

Sometimes there would be a fight for control of a certain route, or of a company that already had a route sewn up. Two groups could be building railroads almost side by side to see who got there first. Trainloads of armed men from rival companies might even shoot it out—the West wasn't called wild for nothing. Sometimes, however, the battles were subtler.

The Niagara line had been quite a modest affair. A nice little railroad that would bring wealth to a western farming region as soon as it was linked to one of the bigger railroads carrying goods across to the Hudson. Mr. Love had bought control of the Niagara three years ago, and believed he had a deal to link to the Hudson Ohio.

"And then, sir, that evil man, Mr. Cyrus MacDuff, took control of the Hudson Ohio, and blocked my way. Just to spite me. He was happy to lose the extra profits our Niagara traffic would have brought, just to see me burned. I invested heavily in the Niagara, but if I can't join the Hudson Ohio line, then my Niagara shares are worthless. Is that," Gabriel Love asked, "a Christian thing to do?"

"It isn't," said Sean. "So what do you propose?"

"I am going to bring light where there is darkness," said Mr. Love, in a tone of reverence. "I shall buy control of the Hudson Ohio from under his nose, and join it to the Niagara."

"That's daring," said Sean. "The Hudson Ohio's a big line. Can you do it?"

"Maybe I can, and maybe I can't. But I am going to make MacDuff think that I can. And belief," said Gabriel Love, with the smile of an angel, "is a wonderful thing."

It was only as Mr. Love outlined the rest of his plan that Sean came to see the remarkable beauty of his soul.

He had patience, for a start. Two years ago, he'd started quietly buying shares in the Hudson Ohio Railroad. Just a little at a time, always through intermediary companies. He'd done it with such skill that even the sharp eyes of Mr. MacDuff had not detected what was happening.

"At this time," he told Sean, "I now have thirty-six percent of the company. MacDuff has forty percent. Another ten percent is owned by other railroads and investors who I know for a fact won't sell. A scattering of investors have four percent and the last ten percent is in the hands of your friend Frank Master."

"I didn't know he was so big."

"It's his largest holding. He's built it over time, and in doing so he has shown his good sense—it's an excellent investment." He smiled. "But if he sold it to me, I'd have control of the company. And since he's a friend of yours, I'd like you to introduce us."

"You want him to sell his ten percent to you?"

Gabriel Love smiled. "No. But I want MacDuff to believe that he might."

So Sean had set up the dinner at Delmonico's. By the end of it, his admiration for old Gabriel Love knew no bounds. The neatness, the symmetry of the thing was a work of art. And what did Frank Master have to do? Nothing—except go away for a few days.

They were to meet once more, at Delmonico's, next Friday, to ensure that everything was in place.

⁘

Sean was contemplating this business on Saturday afternoon, when his sister Mary arrived to see him.

They spent a pleasant hour, chatting about this and that, and after a while, their conversation turned to the Master family.

"You know you told me that Frank Master was making a fool of himself, and that he'd better be careful?" Mary remarked. "Well, am I right in thinking he's got a young lady?"

"What makes you think that?"

"I don't know. He looks pleased with himself, but also a bit tired. I just wondered."

"Well," Sean smiled, "you're right. Her name's Donna Clipp. Clipper—that's his pet name for her. And he ought to give it up." He glanced at her. "Why, do you think his wife guesses?"

"She's never given any sign she's known about Lily de Chantal, all these years," answered Mary. "If she's never known about her, then why would she know about this one?"

"Glad to hear it," said Sean. "She's a good woman, in her way, and I'd be sorry if she was hurt." He paused a moment. "Did you know Master's going upriver on business next Sunday? He'll be gone a few days, and he's taking the girl with him." He shrugged. "I just hope it's over soon."

"No fool like an old fool," said Mary.

"Keep that to yourself, though."

"Did you ever know me to talk?"

"No," said Sean, approvingly, "I can't say I did."

✛

An hour later, Mary informed Hetty Master: "He's taking her with him upriver on Sunday. And he calls her Clipper."

"Good," said Hetty. "That'll do nicely."

✛

Frank Master had hesitated, but finally, on the following Wednesday, he made up his mind. Leaving his house late in the morning, he went eastward along Fourteenth until he came to the station, climbed up the open staircase of the El, and came out onto the platform.

As he climbed the stairs, he felt a faint twinge of discomfort, but it seemed to pass, so he took a deep breath, puffed out his chest, congratulated himself that he was still pretty damn fit, and lit a cigar.

It being quite late in the morning, there weren't many people about on the platform. He walked along it and gazed down at the clusters of telegraph lines strung between their poles, and the slate roofs of the small houses across the street. The rooftops were grimy with the soot from the El trains that passed above them, and they usually looked sad and depressed at this time of the spring. But the weather this March was so warm that they seemed dirty but cheerful in the morning sun.

Frank didn't have to wait long before a series of puffs and rattles announced that the El train was nosing its way along the high rails toward him. All the same, as the train carried him downtown, Frank wished he wasn't on it. For two reasons. First, he was going to see his son. Second, that meant a trip into Wall Street.

It was a couple of weeks since he'd last seen Tom. He loved his son, of course, yet there was always a faint tension in the air when they met. Not that Tom ever said anything—that wasn't his way—but ever since that day at the start of the Draft Riots, he'd had the feeling that Tom didn't approve of him. Something in his look seemed to say: You deserted my mother, and we both know it. Well, maybe. But that had been a long while ago—long enough to forgive and forget. True, he'd been seeing Lily de Chantal for most of the intervening time, but he was pretty sure Tom didn't know that. So there was no excuse.

However, Tom had his uses. And it seemed to Frank, as the train carried him downtown, that he needed Tom just now.

He got out at Fulton and walked into Wall Street.

Why did he feel uncomfortable in Wall Street? He used to like it well enough. Trinity Church was still there, presiding over the street's western end, in all its solemn splendor—a comforting sight. Wasn't Trinity the very soul of Wall Street's tradition? Hadn't the Master family belonged to Trinity, members of the vestry more often than not, for generations? Wall Street should have felt like home. But it didn't.

The place was busy as usual. Fellows in dark coats, rushing in and out of the Exchange with orders stuck into the bands of their high hats. Clerks hastening to their high stools and their desks. Messenger boys, street vendors, cabs delivering merchant gentlemen like himself. It was the old New York, wasn't it?

No. Not really. Not any more.

He passed a stern and bulky building. Number 23. The House of Drexel, Morgan. And as he passed, it was all he could do not to bow the head. Yes he, one of the Masters, friends to Stuyvesants and Roosevelts, Astors and Vanderbilts, must experience a trembling of awe as he passed the offices of Morgan. That was the trouble. That was why he didn't belong here any more.

But his son Tom did. And a few moments later, he came to his door.

❖

"Father. An unexpected pleasure." Tom pushed his big chair back from his roll-top desk. His tailcoat was hanging on a stand. But his gray waist-coat was as spotless as his white shirt, his silk cravat and the pearl pin that held it in place. Everything about him told you: this man does not handle goods, he only handles money. Tom was not a mere merchant like his ancestors; he was a banker.

"Got a moment?" said his father.

"For you, of course." Tom didn't need to say he was busy. The gold watch chain across his waistcoat told you his time was valuable.

"I need some advice," said Frank.

"Glad to help," said Tom. But in his eye, like a clergyman whose parishioner asks to see him alone, was a faint suggestion of caution, and impending judgment.

That was the trouble with bankers, thought Master. A merchant wants to know about the deal. A banker wants the money just as much, but he has appointed himself the enforcing conscience of the tradesman, and therefore affects an air of superiority. His son Tom was in his forties now, silky smooth and stinking rich and pompous.

Oh well, he needed his advice, and at least he wouldn't be charged for it.

"I own ten percent of a railroad," said Frank.

Then he stared at his son in surprise. He hadn't said it to impress—he'd just stated a simple fact. Yet the transformation in Tom was remarkable.

"Ten percent of a railroad?" Tom was all attention. "How big a railroad?"

"Middling sized."

"I see. Might I ask which one?" There was a politeness in Tom's voice that his father had never heard before.

"That's confidential for the moment."

"As you wish."

There was no question—he could see it in Tom's eyes: he was being treated with a new respect. Even his moral status seemed to have improved. It was as if the clergyman had been faced not with a vulgar tradesman, but a serious donor. Seeing his new situation, Frank did not fail to improve upon it.

"My ten percent," he said quietly, "gives me the balance of control."

Tom leaned back in his chair and gazed at his father with love. It was as if, Frank thought, all his sins had suddenly been remitted, and he was entering Heaven through the Pearly Gates.

"Why, Father," said his son, "this is exactly what we do here." His face broke into a smile. "Welcome to Wall Street."

᛭

It was the Civil War that had really changed Wall Street. The Civil War and the American West. Massive flows of capital were needed to finance the one, and to develop the other. And where was capital to be found? In one place only, the money center of the whole world: London.

It was London that had bankrolled America. Just as the century before, the economy of America had grown on the great triangle of London, New York and the West Indies sugar trade—and later on the Southern cotton trade—now a new, less visible, but equally powerful engine was making the running: the flow of credit and of stocks between London and New York.

That's where the House of Morgan had arisen. Junius Morgan, a respectable Connecticut gentleman whose Welsh ancestors had taken ship from Bristol to America two centuries before, had returned across the ocean and set up as a banker in London. He was liked, he was trusted, he was in the right place at the right time, and he had the intelligence to see it. He arranged loans from London to America, and those loans grew huge. In the course of this steady, respectable business, he'd become a very rich man.

But it was his son, John Pierpont Morgan, who was at the helm now. Over six feet tall, big-chested, with a great nose that would flare up like a swelling volcano when he was agitated, and commanding eyes like the headlights of an oncoming train, Mr. J. P. Morgan was becoming a legend in his own time. It was J. P. Morgan and a few men like him who were the kings of Wall Street now, and because of them, even a substantial merchant like Frank Master no longer felt comfortable there. For the bankers' deals and industrial combinations were growing so large, the sums of money involved so vast, that fellows like Master weren't of much account any more. The bankers didn't buy and sell goods; they bought and sold businesses. They didn't finance voyages; they financed wars, industries, even small countries.

Oh, Morgan might serve on the same vestry; Frank might meet him socially in the same New York houses. But Morgan's game was too big for him, and they both knew it. Frank found the fact humbling. And no man cares to be humbled.

But bankers were interested in railroads. Railroads were big enough.

Mr. Morgan himself was active in railroads—he'd placed huge quantities of the best railroad stock with London investors.

But now, Mr. Morgan had decided that it was time to sort out the chaos. Like a monarch faced with a land of barbarian warlords, he had called the railroad men to his house to try to end the warfare and bring order to the competing lines. And he was beginning to make progress. There was still time, however, for the unruly railroad barons to make some spectacular raids.

✦

"I've reason to believe that there's going to be a fight for control of the railroad," Master explained. "If there is, one of the parties is going to try to buy more shares. But unless I sell, there won't be enough out there in the market for him to buy. And that shortage will drive the price of my shares up."

"Sounds good to me," said his son.

"I'm intending to do nothing. Let the price rise. But if it gets high enough, I may sell—at least some of them."

"You don't care who controls the railroad?"

"I don't give a damn. Question is, am I breaking any laws?"

Tom Master considered. "From what you've told me, I'd say it's fine. Is there anything else I need to know?"

"One of the parties wants me to hold off selling, to drive the market up. He wants the other fellow to buy him out, but for a high price."

"Hmm. Is he paying you?"

"No."

"Then I'd say it depends what else he does, and what else you know. There are rules in the game these days." Tom smiled. "We bankers are trying to bring some order to the market."

We bankers: Tom was so proud of being a banker. He worshipped Morgan—even had a roll-top desk like his hero. But you couldn't blame him. And if the bankers were taking the moral high ground and telling everyone how to behave, you couldn't deny that they had a point.

The fact was, Frank thought, when you looked back over the last few decades, for most of his own lifetime really, the New York Stock Exchange had hardly been a respectable place. If the railroad show had been a big attraction, the stock market had been the fairground. You could get away with almost anything.

The easiest ploy was to control a company. Men like Jay Gould would cheerfully issue new stock without even telling existing shareholders, taking new money from new shareholders while diluting the stock values of the old ones. Watering the stock, they called it. You could set up new companies to buy the old ones until nobody knew what the hell they had. You could buy politicians to vote for concessions that would favor your business, and give them shares for doing it. Above all, you could manipulate the price of the stock of your own company, and then speculate in its shares.

But solid men like Morgan were insisting on new rules, now. The market was being cleaned up—slowly.

"The thing that's most frowned upon at the moment," said Tom, "is companies manipulating their own stock. For instance, a company offers to sell you a parcel of its stock at a discounted price. Then, by whatever manipulations, the company deliberately makes its own stock seem worthless. So it can satisfy your order by buying its own stock at a rock-bottom price. A week later, the artificial panic's over, and the company's made an extra profit. Some companies have done that sort of thing again and again. And of course, when brokers start placing bets on stock-price movements, they can get badly burned by these games. Gabriel Love is one of the great offenders. Do you know him?"

"Know the name," said Frank Master, cautiously.

"He belongs in jail," said Tom firmly. "But your railroad operation doesn't sound like that. Effectively, you'd have cornered the market in the shares, and you may profit accordingly. So long as there's nothing else going on."

"So you think it's all right?"

"I'd be happy to handle the business for you, if you like."

"That's kind of you, Tom, but I think I can take care of it."

"As you wish. If you get wind of anything that might be improper, you've a very simple option, you know. Just hold on to your shares. Don't sell them, or at least wait a while, till the whole thing's blown over. The stock may stay at the higher price, and you could lighten your holding then, and take some profit. That'd be all right."

"Thank you, Tom."

"My pleasure. You don't want to tell me what this railroad is?"

"Not just now."

"Well, good luck. Just remember one thing. Stay away from Gabriel Love."

"Thanks," said Frank. "I'll remember that."

⁜

The second dinner at Delmonico's took place that Friday. It was just the three of them again: Frank, Sean O'Donnell and Gabriel Love. As before, Gabriel Love lowered his great frame slowly into his chair, and gazed benignly over his white beard at them both. And Sean smiled at Frank reassuringly, as if to say: "Ain't he a character?"

Master had prepared himself carefully for this meeting. So, as soon as they'd ordered drinks, he came straight to the point.

"Mr. Love," he said, "I'd like you to go over the precise details of this transaction one more time." He smiled. "Just so that I know what I'm getting myself into."

As they had before, the pale blue eyes gazed out of their watery domain. But did Frank detect, in their benevolence, a hint of impatience?

"The business, my friends," said Mr. Love, in a voice of great gentleness, "is simplicity itself. And your role in it requires only that you should absent yourself from the city for a day or two—that you should take a small rest, away from the cares of business, in a place where you cannot be reached by the telegraph. Nothing more." He smiled in a kindly way. "In short, a vacation, free from all care." He turned to Sean. "Isn't that right?"

"That's it," said Sean. "Upriver."

"Tomorrow is Saturday," Gabriel Love continued. "The markets are open in the morning, before closing for the rest of the weekend. And tomorrow morning, just before the market closes, I am going to purchase, in the name of several third parties, some blocks of shares totaling one half of one percent of the Hudson Ohio Railroad. I know that I can secure them, because they are already in the hands of my agents, who will obligingly sell them to me. Those transactions won't cause any stir, but the activity will be noted by the market.

"Mr. Cyrus MacDuff is in Boston. He is attending his granddaughter's wedding tomorrow. In the unlikely event that his agent informs him of the share activity by telegraph, it is possible that he might try to send a cable to you. If he does, you will not respond. More likely, however, he will know nothing of this activity.

"On Sunday evening, a certain judge of my acquaintance is dining with Mr. MacDuff. He will inform MacDuff that he has heard I have secretly purchased over thirty-six percent of his railroad, and that my agents are rumored to have purchased some more on Saturday morning. Meanwhile, I shall see to it that the rumor is circulated widely in New York." He nodded sagely. "And that, my friends, is where the evil nature of Cyrus MacDuff will get the better of him. The devil will have that man in his grip.

"He will attempt to make contact with you, so that you can assure him you are not selling your ten percent. Or that you will sell it to him, and not to me. He will first try to cable you. He may even try to take a train to New York, if he can find one so late. But he will be unable to reach you, because you will have departed. All attempts to reach you will fail. He will not know if you are holding or selling. He will be in a state of great anxiety. And why? All because he hates me, and does not want me to have any part in his railroad. There will be wailing, gentlemen, and gnashing of teeth.

"On Monday morning, Cyrus MacDuff or his agents will be trying to buy shares in the Hudson Ohio Railroad. They will be urgent. They'll bid up the price of the shares. But there will be scarcely any shares to be bought.

"In fact, my agents will sell them a few of my own shares, to keep things lively. But not nearly as many as they will need. The market will see. The market will become excited. And then the market will remember something else. It will remember because my agents will be pointing it out. 'If Gabriel Love gets control of the Hudson Ohio,' they'll say, 'then he'll join the Niagara to it, and the value of the Niagara Railroad will multiply many times.' While MacDuff's men are scouring the market for Hudson Ohio shares, the share price of Niagara will go up like a rocket. It's a good bet, after all. And during that time, I shall sell my Niagara shares. By day's end, I expect to be out of it."

"And during this time, you want me to do nothing?" said Master.

"You will not be here, you will know nothing. But following our previous meeting, you have already left secret instructions with your broker."

"If the price of Hudson Ohio ever passes one twenty, he's to sell half of them for the best price he can get."

"Reasonable instructions, such as any investor might leave. And I think they'll go much higher. By that time the whole market will be after those shares. Nobody's going to know what's going on. I shall be selling my own shares too. We'll both have a handsome profit, Mr. Master. Very handsome indeed."

"It's beautiful," said Sean.

"Its beauty," said Mr. Love benevolently, "is that everybody gets what he wants. I shall be out of the market with a big profit. Mr. Master here will have a profit too, with no risk. Even the people who bought Niagara will do well. Because once he discovers I'm out of it, Mr. MacDuff will have no reason not to do the obvious thing, and join the Niagara to the Hudson Ohio, giving value to their shares. Even MacDuff will have what he wants, because he will surely end the day with an absolute controlling interest in the Hudson Ohio." And here Mr. Love's watery blue eyes not only grew hard, but seemed miraculously to narrow, until his whole face, instead of resembling Santa Claus, reminded you of a large, white rat. "But," he whispered, "he will have paid me through the nose to get it."

A brief silence followed. Then three waiters appeared, bearing three plates of lobster Newburg. Delmonico's was famous for it.

"I shall say grace," said Gabriel Love. And putting his fingers together, he gently prayed: "Oh Lord, we thank Thee for this Thy gift of lobster Newburg. And grant us also, if it be Thy will, control of the Hudson Ohio Railroad."

"But we ain't wanting control of the Hudson Ohio," Sean softly objected.

"True," said Gabriel Love, "but the Almighty doesn't need to know that yet."

Was it all right? It seemed to be. Frank glanced at Sean for reassurance. Sean smiled at him.

"What I like," said Sean, "is that it's all perfectly legal. You buy shares, MacDuff panics, the market gets excited, you and Master sell at a profit. Nothing wrong with any of that. And it'll work. So long as MacDuff doesn't smell a rat."

"That's why I waited until he was away," said Gabriel Love. "If he could walk into Master's office and confront him face to face, if he could even reach him by telegraph, my plan falls to the ground. But if he can't, then he must be uncertain, and uncertainty breeds fear. He will be off balance as well. It's his favorite granddaughter that's getting married and MacDuff is an emotional man." He sighed. "Human nature, gentlemen. It is original sin that leads men to misfortune, every time." He gazed at them both, serenely. "I am a speculator in the market, gentlemen, and that is part of God's plan. Men only learn through suffering. So I punish human weakness, and God rewards me."

"Amen," said Sean O'Donnell with a grin.

They had finished their lobster. Charlotte russe was proposed, and accepted, to be followed by brandied pears. The conversation turned to the theater, and from there to horse racing. A French dessert wine was served. Frank felt a little unwell; his brow was clammy. He decided he was eating too much, and held back when an extra portion of the charlotte russe was offered.

"So," Sean was saying to Gabriel Love, "after this trick, what are you going to do next?"

"Next?" Mr. Love surveyed the table placidly. "Nothing, Mr. O'Donnell. I shall do nothing."

"That's not like you," said Sean.

"I am retiring," announced Gabriel Love. "I am devoting myself wholly to good works."

"Lost your taste for the market?"

"Too many regulations, Mr. O'Donnell. Too many bankers like Morgan. They're too mighty for me. And besides," he shook his head sadly, "they are taking the life, and sweetness, out of the business."

There was a pause, while the two men contemplated the former sweetness of life.

"The sixties," said Sean O'Donnell. "Those were the days."

"True," said Gabriel Love.

"You had things wrapped up," said Sean. "You and Boss Tweed."

"Our system, back then," said Love, "approached perfection."

Frank listened. Of course, everyone knew about the years after the Civil War. If the railroad men of today were like feudal barons, the Wall Street of the late sixties had been like the Dark Ages—when New York City corruption had come to the markets. To hear the story told by one of the operators was an opportunity not to be missed.

"I always said that your friend Fernando Wood could have done even better for himself," said Gabriel Love to Sean, "if he'd stayed closer to Tammany Hall."

"Probably right," acknowledged O'Donnell.

"Tammany Hall is the answer to everything in this city, and Boss Tweed understood that. You can make money in a small way without politics. But to make the big money, you need to buy the legislature. Can't be done otherwise."

"City contracts," said O'Donnell, with affection.

"City contracts, certainly," Love echoed. "By all means, there's fortunes in city contracts. But that's only a beginning for a man with vision. And Boss Tweed had vision. You want your railroad to go a certain way, and the city or the state has to grant you the permission? Then you need to pay the legislators. Put some of them on your board. Your company is being sued? Then you need to buy a judge. Tammany arranged all that. Boss Tweed was your man." He closed his eyes for a moment, savoring the memory. "The police were all good Tammany boys. The judges, the legislators, even the governor of New York State, he'd bribed them. On Wall Street, we made hay. You could water stock, short-sell your shareholders, anything was possible. And if a judge ruled against you, why, he'd get another one to give you a counter-judgment that would keep the game in play for years.

"Those were the days for men of vision. Jay Gould—and he, in my opinion, was the greatest speculator of them all—he almost persuaded the

President of the United States, Ulysses Grant himself, to hold back the bullion reserves so that Gould could corner the gold market. For Ulysses Grant, great man though he was, did not understand such high matters. Yes, sir, he made use of the president himself. And if some interfering villain hadn't told Grant what Mr. Gould was up to, he would have pulled it off. That would have been sweet." He sighed. "But the Stock Exchange, and the damn Bar Association, and Mr. Morgan and his like, they're closing all that down." He shook his head at the folly of the thing. "The joy is leaving the market, gentlemen. The odds cannot be properly stacked. And Gabriel Love is leaving too."

"But the game's not over," said Sean. "There's plenty that can still be done on Wall Street—look at what you're doing now."

For just an instant, so quick you hardly saw it, Mr. Love shot O'Donnell a warning glance.

"Why, even Mr. Morgan could do what we're doing," he said reprovingly. Then he sighed again. "I've retired, O'Donnell," he said. "For me, the game is over."

During all this conversation, Frank had been listening with a horrified fascination. Not that a bit of corruption had ever worried him—that was part of city life. But to hear these two men, with whom he was doing business, describe the whole vast machine of fraud and corruption so lovingly, and with such familiarity, was making him nervous. This deal seemed legitimate, but was there something about it he didn't know? If Jay Gould would cheerfully use the President of the United States as his stooge, he thought, then is Gabriel Love making a fool of me? And the words of his son Tom came back to him with a terrible urgency: "Stay away from Gabriel Love."

The clammy feeling on his brow returned.

"Are you absolutely sure this business is legal?" he suddenly blurted out.

"It's fine," said Sean with a smile. "Trust me."

But Gabriel Love wasn't smiling. He was giving him a very strange look, one that Master didn't like at all.

"You're not going to let me down, are you?" he asked.

"No," said Frank, unwillingly.

"Don't ever let me down," said old Gabriel Love.

"He won't let you down," said Sean, quickly.

Gabriel gave Sean a look. Then his face broke into a smile.

The brandied pears arrived.

❖

The next morning, Frank Master ate his breakfast quickly. Then he went into the yard behind the house. The weather was still surprisingly warm, well into the fifties. An article in the newspaper had mentioned a storm afflicting the Midwest, but the forecast for the weekend was warm weather, turning cloudy with a few showers. At present the sky was blue. The little clumps of crocuses in the garden had all opened out days ago into a pleasing array of mauve and white and yellow.

After pacing about in the garden for a little while, Frank decided to go down to Wall Street.

This time, he took a cab—a mistake, as it happened. For as they reached the Lower East Side, they encountered a great fleet of laden wagons entering the city. The Barnum, Bailey and Hutchinson circus was arriving in town. He should have remembered. He must make sure he and Hetty took the grandchildren before it left. But the circus was blocking the streets, and it was some time before the cab could get through.

Saturday mornings were usually quiet on Wall Street. But the market didn't close until the middle of the day, and there were plenty of people about. Master walked into the Stock Exchange. A quick look at the floor told him that shares were trading moderately. He went up to a broker.

"Anything happening?" he inquired.

"Not much. Some Hudson Ohio stock was just bought. Nothing dramatic though."

"It's a good stock," said Master with a shrug.

So Gabriel Love had made his trades. The trap was set. Master waited about for a while. The market seemed ready to end the week without excitement.

What should he do? He'd been thinking about it ever since he awoke. His son's advice had undoubtedly been sound: If in doubt, do nothing. He just needed to give his broker a different instruction before he left. Tell him not to sell at any price. Simple as that.

On the other hand, if Gabriel Love's deal was legal, the profit on his stock would be substantial. At one twenty, he'd have doubled his money. And it might easily go higher. It was tempting, no question.

Was there really any reason to worry? Had he let his imagination run away with him at the dinner last night? For another twenty minutes, he hung around, unable to make up his mind. Then he cursed himself for a coward and a fool. The hell with it, he told himself. Be a man.

He was going upriver tomorrow with Donna Clipp. No one was going to know where he was, and he was going to have a good time. And if Gabriel Love stirred up the market while he was gone, so much the better. His broker would sell, and he'd arrive back in the city a damn sight richer. Why the hell not?

This was Wall Street. This was New York. And he was a Master, for God's sake. He was big enough to play the game. With a feeling of manly triumph, he walked out of the New York Stock Exchange.

He'd gone a hundred yards when he saw J. P. Morgan.

The banker was standing on a street corner. With his tall top hat and his tailcoat, his unsmiling face and his barrel chest, he made you think of a cross between a Roman emperor and a prizefighter. He wasn't fifty-two years old, but already he seemed to belong to the immortals. If J. P. Morgan wanted a cab, he didn't hail one. He just stood in the street and, like a lighthouse, turned his eyes upon the traffic.

And the great banker was directly in his path. He walked toward him. As he drew close, Morgan turned.

"Mr. Morgan." He bowed politely.

He thought Morgan would acknowledge him—it would have been rude not to—but you couldn't expect much, for Morgan was a man of notoriously few words.

The banker gave him a nod. It was hard to be sure, but under his bushy mustache there might even have been a faint smile.

Then, just for a moment, Frank Master had a foolish impulse. If only he could reveal the plan to J. P. Morgan. If only he could step into a saloon with the great man for a moment or two, sit down, tell him fair and square about it and say: "Mr. Morgan, without presuming upon our acquaintance, sir, how do you think I should handle this affair?" Of course, he couldn't do it. Unthinkable. He passed by respectfully.

J. P. Morgan stepped into a cab, and was gone.

And no sooner was he gone than, with a terrible sense of horror, Master realized the profound stupidity of the impulse. Who, Morgan would have asked, was proposing the deal? Gabriel Love, he would have had to answer. He'd have had to tell J. P. Morgan that he was in business with Daddy Love.

However great his ill-gotten wealth, however venerable his white beard, however much he gave to charity, Mr. Gabriel Love would never cross the threshold of the House of Morgan. Mr. Morgan did not speak to a man like Gabriel Love; wouldn't even look up from his desk at him. Some might call it Morgan's proudness. Some might call it snobbery. But the fact was, Morgan was right.

He was doing business with a dreadful old criminal, and he could only pray it turned out all right. Swiftly, Frank Master walked out of Wall Street and made his way home.

❖

It was already dusk when Mary left the house in Gramercy Park. The afternoon had passed quietly enough. Frank Master had seemed a little depressed when he returned from Wall Street, but after a nap he had brightened up again and busied himself with preparations for the trip he was making upriver to Albany the following day.

From Gramercy Park, Mary took a cab, which soon brought her down Fifth Avenue to her brother's house. After spending some time with his family, she asked to see him alone.

"I need a favor, Sean," she said.

"Tell me."

She took out a letter. It was just a small note, in a sealed envelope. On the front was written the name of Donna Clipp, and her address. She handed it to her brother, and he looked at it.

"That's Frank Master's hand," he remarked.

Mary smiled. In fact, the envelope, and the brief note inside, had been carefully written a few days ago by Hetty Master, who had plenty of examples of Frank's writing to copy. But Sean didn't need to know that.

"It has to be delivered tomorrow, about the middle of the morning, into the lady's hand. I have to know for definite that she has it. Could you arrange that?"

"I've got a boy that can deliver it, certainly."

"If he's asked, the boy must say you gave it to him."

"All right."

"And most of all—I didn't give it to you, Sean. You never got this until tomorrow morning. A gentleman you assumed to be Frank Master left it in a hurry with a servant at your door, with urgent instructions that it be delivered at once."

"This is the favor?"

"That's it. Just remember that it wasn't me that gave it to you."

Sean nodded. "Why?"

"You don't want to know."

"If you say so."

"I'll tell you this," she said. "It's for his own good."

He slipped the letter into his breast pocket. "Consider it done."

As Mary returned home later that evening, the cab driver told her: "There was a big circus parade downtown this evening. You'd think summer was starting already."

❖

The ferry was due to leave at four o'clock on Sunday afternoon. By five, it was still at the pier. The problem was the engine. The captain of the vessel apologized for the delay, but assured his passengers that it would be dealt with shortly.

Small comfort to Frank Master.

Where the devil was Donna Clipp? Not a sign of her. She was supposed to be there by three. Twenty minutes after that hour, he'd gone himself in a cab to her house. But she wasn't there, and her landlady said she'd gone out more than an hour before, telling her she wouldn't be back for a few days. He'd hurried back to the pier, but the ticket taker and the steward both assured him that no lady of her description had appeared while he was gone. It was almost four by then, so he'd gone aboard.

Had she had an accident? Possibly. But the alternative, he supposed, was more likely. She'd gone off elsewhere, left him in the lurch, and looking like a fool. Gone off, it could only be, with another man. A younger man, no doubt. He'd experienced a sickening feeling that he hadn't known since he was a young man, before he'd met Hetty.

He'd gone into the saloon on the boat and had a brandy. He was feeling foolish, and lonely. Every so often he'd go to the door and look along the pier, in case she'd turned up. But there was no sign of her. Just the empty jetty, and a couple of men in oilskins, and an unlit lamp, swinging in the wind.

And the rain.

The rain made everything worse. Much worse. It had started quite early that morning, and despite the weather forecast, it had not cleared at all. A steady downpour churned the Hudson's waters and drummed gloomily above the saloon, while from time to time men would appear from the engine room, report to the captain, and then disappear again.

"It might be an hour or two," the captain told him, at six o'clock.

Frank had already, twice, asked him what was wrong. An oil leak, he was told, the first time. Then, a problem with the cylinder. The explanations made no sense. Normally, he'd have gone down there to see for himself—he was certainly as competent as the vessel's engineer. But he was feeling too old and depressed, so he sat quietly and nursed his brandy. Most of the other passengers had retired to their cabins. Three or four sat together, chatting in the bar. But he didn't feel like talking, and remained alone.

At seven o'clock, he wondered whether to give up and go home. If he'd just been waiting for Donna Clipp, he'd have done so. But there was the matter of Gabriel Love and the railroad. He still had to absent himself from town. So he tried to think only of the profit he was going to make on the Hudson Ohio Railroad, refilled his brandy glass, and stared grimly into it for another hour. At this very moment, he reminded himself, up in Boston, Cyrus MacDuff was being told about Gabriel Love's raid on his railroad. At least, he thought, someone out there is having a worse evening than me. Very soon, he supposed, MacDuff would be trying to send him a wire. And he wouldn't be able to find him. This damned boat was his hiding place for this adventure. He might be lonely, but he was invisible. That thought cheered him up a little.

At eight o'clock, the captain announced that they'd be leaving soon. Frank Master took one more, foolish look down the pier, then sat at a table and demanded a meat pie and a plate of vegetables. This, at least, was brought promptly.

At nine o'clock, the captain whispered to him that the problem was fixed, and that they just needed to test the engine. Rather rudely, Frank said, "Tell me when it's done," and waved him away. He heard the engine start, then stop. Just before ten, it started again. This time it did not stop. A few minutes later, the vessel nosed out into the river, and was swallowed by the great, dark downpour.

✛

Donna Clipp had had enough. She would have left already, if it hadn't been for the rain. As far as she was concerned that bastard Frank Master could go to hell in a handcart. It was past ten o'clock at night.

His note had been clear enough.

Dear Clipper,

There has been a change of plan. Wait for me at Henry's Hotel in Brooklyn.

I'll be there as soon as I can after three o'clock. We're going to Long Island.

I can't wait to see you.

F.M.

Typical, she thought. He can't wait to see me, but he ain't coming. Men were all the same—and she ought to know. She'd known a lot of men.

Some of them had had money. The older ones anyway—not much point in being with an older man, if they hadn't got money. The question was, would they spend it?

And that was what she found so contemptible about most of them, really. They had plenty of money. They weren't going to live that long. There was no way they could go through the money they already had, yet they still saved it. Habit, she supposed. Skinflints.

Oh, they'd spend a bit. Buy you a bottle of champagne, a fur coat, maybe. Presents, to keep you happy—or so they thought. Even pay your rent, if you were lucky. But give you what you really needed? They seemed to think that if you were poor, you must be stupid.

She'd heard of women who'd been set up for life by older men. Heard of it, but never met one. Not girls like her, anyway. And why? Because men didn't care. They didn't respect you. They took what they wanted, but if you asked for anything in return they called you a gold-digger, or worse.

That was rich people for you, in Donna Clipp's opinion. Scum, really, when you thought about it. They might look good, but underneath, they were just scum. Worse than she was.

It was ten at night, pitch black and pouring with rain, and she was sitting in this stupid hotel on the wrong side of the Brooklyn Bridge, and not a smell of her so-called lover, the old fool.

Donna Clipp was a nice girl. She had thick blonde hair—natural blonde, too—and blue eyes that could laugh or give you a smoldering look, just as she pleased. She'd never walked the streets. Always had respectable jobs. She'd made dresses, and she'd sold them. She had an eye for fashion. She had some talent for acting and had tried to get theatrical jobs, but they usually told her she wasn't tall enough. Her short, rather full figure certainly hadn't been a problem in encounters of a closer kind, and she'd been kept, more or less, by various men. When she came to New York, she found respectable lodgings in Greenwich Village. Within a month, she'd met Frank Master. But though she'd been seeing him for some time now, she hadn't much to show for it.

So she'd been wondering, for the last three weeks, what to do with him.

There was one other matter that had been weighing on her mind lately. A letter she'd received a couple of weeks ago, from a friend with whom she'd shared lodgings in Philadelphia. The letter had been cautiously worded, but she'd understood very well the message it contained.

Someone had been round asking questions about her. Her friend didn't seem to know if it was the police, or possibly some person with a grudge. But it looked as if someone was on the trail of certain missing articles of value. The gold bracelet she was wearing, for instance.

She might claim that it had been given her as a gift. But was it really likely that a rich man would steal his own wife's jewelry to give to his mistress? Would a jury believe that? She didn't think so.

If he hadn't brought her on a pretext into the house, and if she hadn't seen all the lovely things his wife had, it wouldn't have happened. She blamed him, in a way. But that wasn't going to do her any good. If they were on to her in Philadelphia, would they find her in New York? They might. Not at once, but one day. She wasn't sure what to do about that.

The simplest thing would be to get rid of the offending items—you couldn't prove anything then. But they were valuable. She really needed Frank Master to come up with something before she did that.

So when he'd suggested the trip up the Hudson, in all the comfort of the finest steamer too, she'd thought that things might be looking up after all. She'd prepared herself carefully. And she'd been rather disappointed when his note, announcing the change of plan, had come on the very day of their departure. But the only thing to do was go along with it, and see what was on offer.

She'd put her bags in a cab, therefore, and set off from Greenwich Village to Brooklyn.

It was a pity that it had been raining. When the Brooklyn Bridge, with its mighty suspended span, had opened five years ago, it was counted as one of the wonders of the New World. Over a mile long, soaring a hundred and forty feet over the entrance to the East River, its two stupendous supporting towers with their pointed arches, and the great, graceful arc of its steel cables combined to evoke all the power and beauty of this new industrial, Gothic age.

Down its center went two sets of tracks for railcars. On each side, with views up or downstream, lay roadways for horses and carriages. And over the rail tracks, for pedestrians, stretched a seemingly endless walkway, suspended in the air, in an elegant rising curve, between the firmaments of the river below and heaven above.

If you took the outside lane in a cab, the view over the river was magnificent.

But not today. With the rain coming relentlessly down, she could see neither the water below, nor even the tower ahead. Instead, it was as if she'd entered the rain cloud itself, humid, insistent, depressing, sealing her off from every hope.

As the rest of the afternoon had passed, she'd assumed that Master had just been delayed. Early in the evening, she had wondered if something might have happened to him. By eight she'd concluded that the weather was so bad he'd called the whole thing off; but he might at least have sent a message to her, and a cab to take her home. She'd asked the waiter to bring her a pot of tea, and continued to wait, just in case he turned up. At nine, she'd ordered some hot soup. Now it was after ten, and she'd had enough. She didn't care what had happened to him, she was going home. She asked the hotel porter to find her a cab.

But an hour passed, and there was no cab to be found.

✢

It was gone midnight before Lily de Chantal decided to turn in for bed. She'd been rehearsing for her part the next day. Not that the role was difficult, but she wanted to be sure she performed it perfectly. And truth to tell, she was savoring it as well.

Revenge, even for someone with her kindly nature, was sweet.

Nine in the morning would be about right, she thought. If little Miss Clipp wasn't back from the wild goose chase she'd been sent on already, she would be by then. Catch her first thing, before she had time to collect her wits.

"I can't do it myself, my dear," Hetty had said, "because if Frank ever found out, he'd hold it against me. But you could do it. A man can forgive his mistress more easily than his wife. Besides," she'd added with a smile, "you owe me a favor, I think."

So the tasks had been assigned. Hetty had written the note, Mary had arranged the delivery, and now she, Lily de Chantal, was going to send the little bitch packing.

. Hetty had given her everything she needed, and Lily had rehearsed her speech precisely.

"I am afraid, Miss Clipp, that I have proof—absolute proof—that you stole jewelry from Mrs. Linford of Philadelphia. I even have witnesses who can perfectly describe seeing you wearing the items after the theft. You will go to jail, Miss Clipp. Unless, of course, you'd like to leave New York, today—and to leave without saying a word to Mr. Master. And if you make any attempt to contact him in the future, then we shall take all this evidence to the police."

Donna Clipp would go fast enough after that. She'd have to.

The neatness of the plan had been summarized by Hetty, days before.

"I want Frank to think she's jilted him. Failed to turn up for the ride upriver, then left before he comes back. That'll hurt his pride, I'm afraid, but it'll bring him back to his senses. He'll be looking for comfort; he'll be looking to us."

"Us?"

"To you, to me, to the way things were. I think we're too old to quibble about those details now, aren't we?"

"You," said Lily de Chantal, "are a remarkable woman, and he's lucky to have you."

"Thank you, my dear," said Hetty. "I quite agree."

Yes, thought Lily now, she'd be glad to dispatch little Miss Clipp on her way, for both of them.

So she was greatly astonished, twenty minutes later, when the doorman knocked upon the apartment door to ask if she wished to receive a visitor. And still more so to see behind him, soaked to the skin, the figure of Frank Master.

✛

At one in the morning, at Henry's Hotel, Brooklyn, there was a battle of wills. To the great annoyance of the manager, Donna Clipp had demanded a bedroom and refused to pay for it, on the grounds that it was the hotel's fault that they hadn't found her a cab.

"I could put you out of doors," he had said.

"Try it," she'd replied. "You never heard me scream."

He did step out of doors, with a view to ejecting her, all the same. But when he got outside, he discovered something strange. The rain was turning to snow. And the temperature, so warm all week, was dropping like a stone. He was just turning to go back indoors again, when he heard a great growl and a moan from the direction of the river. And a second later, a howling gust of wind rushed down the street, slamming shutters, bending small trees, and almost rolling the manager off his feet as it smacked him with its icy blast. Holding onto the side of a doorway, he pulled himself back into the entrance and slammed the door behind him.

"Here." He gave her a key. "Nobody can go out in this weather." He pointed to the stairs. "Up there. Second on the left."

But he didn't offer to help the bitch with her bags.

❖

Looking out of her window across Central Park, while Frank sat in a hot bathtub, Lily de Chantal watched the wind whip tornadoes of snowflakes across the empty spaces. In Gramercy Park, for some time, Hetty had gazed in puzzlement at the strange telegram that had come for Frank earlier in the evening, from Boston, asking him if he was selling a railroad. But now, hearing the strange howl and whistle of the wind, she pulled back the curtains and looked out in astonishment to see a maelstrom of snow, and hoped poor Frank was safe, out on the cold waters of the Hudson, on such a terrible night.

Where on earth, she wondered, could such a blizzard have come from?

❖

It had come from the west. A great snowstorm with freezing wind, carried all the way across the continent from the Pacific on an icy airstream, at six hundred miles a day. But it took two to make this storm. Up from Georgia had come a huge, moist, warm front. Near the mouth of the Delaware River, some hundred and twenty miles below New York, the two had collided.

The temperature had fallen, pressure had plummeted, and suddenly the sea and the river had been whipped into a fury. Then, up the coast, had come a mighty blizzard. Soon after midnight, New York's rain turned to snow, the temperature dived below freezing, and the wind began to gust at eighty miles an hour.

It went on all night. When dawn came—or should have come—the blizzard ignored it, smothered it, blotted it out. As the hours of morning passed, the whole north-eastern seaboard and every creature on it was swallowed up in the great, white hurricane.

❖

There was nothing they wouldn't do for you at the Dakota. But this went so far beyond the call of duty that Lily de Chantal was almost embarrassed. The porter's boy didn't mind, though; he seemed to relish the challenge, and the porter assured her: "This boy of mine could find his way to the North Pole and back, Miss de Chantal. Don't worry about him."

So she gave young Skip the note, and told him to be careful.

It was ten o'clock on Monday morning when Skip left the building. He was fourteen years old, small for his age, but wiry. He was wearing stout boots with a heavy tread, and his leggings were tied tightly with string around his ankles. He wore three sweaters and a short coat, which made it easier to move. He had a thick wool cap over his head, earmuffs, and a scarf wound round his face. Skip was happy.

As he left the safety of the big entrance yard, he'd already decided what to do. There was no point in trying to cross the park, which was like an arctic landscape, with the blizzard blowing as hard as ever. He didn't even try to go down beside it. Instead, he walked west half a block and turned down Ninth Avenue. A few blocks south, and he'd be able to pick up the great diagonal of Broadway.

It wasn't easy even to walk. The icy gusts almost blew him off his feet, the wind was so strong that the snow couldn't settle in any normal pattern. In some places, it had driven the snow into drifts that were already above his head. In other places, where the wind had almost brushed it clean, he could see the ground.

The avenue was almost empty. People had tried to get to work—this was New York, after all—but most had been forced to give up. The El above him was silent, its tracks so solid with ice that, even had an engine tried to set out, its wheels would not have had enough grip to move.

After struggling down two blocks, however, Skip saw a welcome sight. A single carriage drawn by two patient horses had just turned into the avenue and was plowing its way slowly along. Skip didn't hesitate for a moment. As the carriage passed, he nipped up beside the coachman. That individual was about to knock him off his cheeky perch and let him fall down into the roadway when a gruff voice from inside the carriage called out: "Let him be."

"You're lucky," said the driver.

"Where've you come from?" asked Skip.

"Yonkers, Westchester County," answered the coachman.

"That's a long way," said Skip.

"Been going since six this morning. I thought the horses would've died, but they kept at it. Big hearts."

"Why not stay at home?"

"My gentleman in there has business in the city today. Says a blizzard ain't goin' to keep him from that."

"It ain't keeping me from mine either," said Skip happily. That was the spirit of New York, the boy thought. He wouldn't care to live anywhere else.

"No trains from Westchester?" he inquired.

"We crossed a bridge and saw one stuck fast in the snow. I reckon they all are, most likely."

At Sixty-fifth Street, they picked up Broadway. When they reached the south-west corner of Central Park, the carriage started south down Eighth, and Skip jumped off. He wanted to follow the line of Broadway.

People had been shoveling for a while already, doing their best to keep a path open along one of the sidewalks. It was more like a trench. Skip noticed that the untidy masses of telegraph lines were all frozen. Soon he came to a point where they had been brought down entirely, into a great tangle of wire and ice that went on for several blocks. At Fifty-fifth Street he slipped and fell, but he was so bundled up that he wasn't hurt. He laughed, and looked about to see if he could find another ride. There was nothing. No cabs, no carriages, hardly anyone even trying to walk. Some of the stores and offices seemed to be open, but no one was going out or coming in. He slipped and slid another two blocks and came to a saloon. He went inside. Here, there were a few men, wrapped up like himself, standing at the bar. He unwound his scarf.

"Drink, son?" offered the barman.

"No money," said Skip, though it wasn't true.

One of the men at the bar put a few coins down and motioned him to approach. There was a smell of whiskey and hot rum at the bar.

"On me, boy," said the man. "Give him a car driver's," he instructed the barman, who nodded. "It's just ale and red pepper," he told Skip. "It's what the coachmen take. It'll keep you warm for a bit."

Skip drank it slowly. He could feel the warmth in his stomach. After a while, he thanked his benefactor, and headed out into the street again, wrapping his scarf tightly round his face at the doorway. And it was as well that he did, for as soon as he stepped into Broadway, the snow whipped round his face as if it meant personally to attack him and rip his scarf away again. But steadying himself against a railing, he put his head down and staggered on.

And then, a few blocks further down, he got lucky again. For what should he see, but a brewer's wagon. Behind his scarf, his mouth drew into a grin. Nothing ever stopped the brewers. When the supply of beer in New York came to a stop, you'd know the world had come to an end.

The wagon was big, and loaded with kegs of ale. It was lumbering slowly along like a great ship through an iceflow. It was pulled by no less than ten massive Normandy horses. Unseen by the driver, he hopped in the back. And was thus conveyed, in ponderous but cheerful style, all the way down to Twenty-eighth Street. From there, clinging onto railings or whatever support he could, he made his way through the blizzard to Gramercy Park.

⁂

Hetty Master was most astonished when Skip arrived with a note from Lily de Chantal, but she read it eagerly. The note wasn't long. Frank's boat had been forced to turn back the night before, she said. He'd arrived soaked, and seemed to have taken a chill. "But I have him safely tucked up in a bed, and I give him a little hot whiskey every hour. He doesn't want anyone to know he's in the city, though he won't say why." Hetty couldn't help smiling; at least Frank was safe, and Lily would look after him. There was also a postscript.

> It's clear that our little friend never turned up at the boat. I wonder if she's trapped in Brooklyn!
> I'll make sure to see her, as we agreed, before I let Frank out on the street again.

Hetty almost laughed. She hoped little Miss Clipp was freezing her toes off, wherever she was. In its curious way, the plan was still working.

❖

In fact, at that moment, Donna Clipp was standing by the entrance to the Brooklyn Bridge. And she was getting angry.

She could have stayed at the hotel, of course, but they were getting pretty insistent that she pay. And anyway, she was bored. Donna Clipp didn't like doing nothing. One of the other guests had offered to lend her a book. But Donna could never see the point of reading. That was boring too.

So she'd decided to go home. She'd taken the few valuables she had and stuffed them into her handbag. Then she'd demanded a length of rope and tied her suitcase with it in a series of intricate knots that it would have broken your fingernails to tackle. Then she'd made the manager give her a written receipt for it, and told him she'd collect it herself in a few days, and that if it wasn't there, she'd fetch the police. Then she'd announced she was leaving. There was no transport of any kind. The whole of Brooklyn was staying indoors. But the manager did not try to stop her. He hoped the blizzard would freeze her to death, just as soon as she was well away from his hotel.

Donna Clipp had made her way to the Brooklyn Bridge, which wasn't far. And though she looked like a walking snowman by the time she got there, she was still very much alive. There were railcars across the bridge, and once she was over, she'd manage to find a way across to her lodgings, somehow or other. At the bridge, however, she encountered a check.

"The bridge is closed," the policeman told her.

The mighty structure was, indeed, totally deserted. Its huge span rose into the blizzard and disappeared in the whiteness. There were barriers across the roadway, and the railcars were sitting by their platforms, frozen solid. The policeman had wisely occupied the tollbooth, where pedestrians paid their penny to cross. He had a lamp in there to keep himself warm, and was unwilling even to open the little window to speak to her.

"Whaddaya mean, it's closed?" she cried. "It's a goddam bridge."

"It's closed. Too dangerous, lady," he shouted back.

"I gotta get to Manhattan," she protested.

"You can't. There's no ferry, and the bridge is closed. There's no way to get there."

"Then I'll walk across."

"Are you crazy, lady?" he exploded. "I just told you the bridge is closed.

Especially to pedestrians." He pointed to the path that led into the howling blizzard. "You'd never get across."

"So how much is the toll? It says a penny. I'm not paying more than a
penny."

"You ain't paying a penny," the policeman bawled, "because I told you
three times, the bridge is closed."

"So you say."

"I do say. Get out of here, lady."

"I'll stand here as long as I like. I ain't breaking any law."

"Jeezus," cried the policeman. "Freeze to death where you are, then.
But you ain't crossing this bridge."

Five minutes later, she was still there. In exasperation, the policeman
turned his back to her. He stayed that way for a minute or two. When he
turned round, she'd gone, thank God. He sighed, glanced up at the
bridge, and shouted with fury.

She was up there on the walkway, a couple of hundred yards already,
and about to disappear into the snowstorm. How the devil did she get
past the booth? He opened the door, and the freezing storm smacked him
in the face. He started after her, with a volley of oaths.

And then he stopped. Any minute now, he reckoned, the wind would
like as not lift her up and blow her over the railings, then either drop her
onto the tracks or, better yet, deposit her in the freezing waters of the
East River below. He went back into the booth. "I never saw her," he
muttered.

Let the bitch die, if that's what she wanted.

Donna Clipp moved steadily forward. The tollbooth was long out of
sight, and she knew she must be reaching the apex of the long suspended
walkway now. The wind was moaning. Every now and then, the moan
turned to a howl, as though some vast, angry leviathan were thrashing
about in the harbor and the East River below, some huge sea serpent
intent upon claiming her as its prey. The snow had already stung her face
until it was numb. She had forgotten that, in that high, empty exposure
over the water, the cold would be worse, far worse, and she knew that
if she didn't find some shelter soon, she'd get frostbite. Perhaps she
could die.

Donna Clipp didn't want to die. That wasn't in her plans at all, for a
long time yet.

So there was nothing to do, but make her way through this terrible white tunnel in the sky, and get down the other side.

Progress was painfully slow. If she let go of the rail for even a moment, she could be blown off her feet and hurled down into the abyss. All she could do was keep a tight hold on the rail, and pull herself across, step by step. She knew she mustn't stop. If she could just get to the other side. If she could just keep going.

She managed to reach the halfway point. From there, it was a long descent. She managed another hundred yards. Then another. Then, just ahead of her, she saw something that gave her a shock.

And she stopped.

❖

The blizzard continued all that day. Some people called it the White Hurricane. But soon they had another name for it. Given the snowbound wastes that, rightly or wrongly, were associated with the territory, they called it the Dakota Blizzard.

If the city was impassable that day, a few strongholds tried at least to make a showing. Macy's department store opened for a bit, but no customers came, and the poor lady clerks had to be sheltered there until the Dakota Blizzard was done, since they could not get home. Some banks tried to open, but decided to extend all their loans a few days, since nobody could reach them. The New York Stock Exchange opened, and even traded a few shares that Monday morning. But there were only a handful of men there, and soon after midday, they sensibly gave up.

Of the few shares traded, none concerned the Hudson Ohio Railroad. For Mr. Cyrus MacDuff was quite unable to give orders for any trades since the telegraph lines between Boston and New York were all down. Nor could that furious gentleman come to save his railroad in person, since every road was feet-deep in snow, the rail lines were all blocked, and the sea was so wild with the storm that ships along that coastline were sinking by the score.

As the Dakota Blizzard raged outside, inside the great apartment building of that name, Lily de Chantal continued to nurse Frank Master, who became a little feverish in the evening.

By Tuesday morning, he seemed to be a little better. But the city was cut off from the outside world, and the Dakota Blizzard was still raging.

During the afternoon, however, human ingenuity made one small but useful discovery. Some sharp fellows in Boston realized that there was a way to make telegraph contact with New York after all. They used the international cable and sent their messages, on a triangular route, via London.

⁜

On Wednesday morning, the storm began to diminish. The city remained at a standstill, but people were beginning to dig out. As the wind dropped, the freezing temperature rose, a little.

All the same, Hetty Master was most surprised when, at eleven o'clock that morning, her son Tom and another gentleman she did not know arrived at the house to see Frank.

"He's away," she said.

"I have to reach him, Mother," said Tom. "It's urgent. Can you please tell me where he is?"

"I don't believe I can," she answered, a little awkwardly. "Can't it wait a day or two?"

"No," said her son, "it can't."

"Could I speak to you alone?" she said.

⁜

It was quite a shock to Lily de Chantal when Tom Master and another gentleman arrived at the Dakota at noon. How they came to know that Frank was there, or what possible explanation they could have been given for his presence, she had no idea. They certainly didn't seem to have the least interest in discussing such a matter. But they did, most emphatically, want to see Frank.

"He's not very well," she said. "He's had a fever."

"Sorry to hear it," said Tom.

"I'll ask if he will see you," said Lily.

⁜

Frank Master, propped up in bed, gazed at his visitors. He couldn't imagine how they'd found him, but there wasn't much he could do about that now. Tom's companion was a quiet, well-dressed man in his mid-thirties, who looked like a banker.

"This is Mr. Gorham Grey," said Tom. "Of Drexel, Morgan."

"Oh," said Frank.

"Thank you for seeing me, Mr. Master," said Gorham Grey politely. "I should make clear that I am Mr. J. P. Morgan's personal representative, and he has asked me to come to see you."

"Oh," said Frank, again.

"Knowing your son, I went to see him first, to ask him to make the introduction," said Gorham Grey.

"Quite right," said Tom.

"What's it about?" asked Frank, nervously gripping the edge of the bed sheet.

"Mr. Morgan is desirous of buying a parcel of shares from you," said Gorham Grey. "In the Hudson Ohio Railroad. You own ten percent of the outstanding stock, I believe."

"Oh," said Frank.

"I should explain very openly," continued Gorham Grey, "that Mr. Morgan yesterday received an urgent telegraph from Mr. Cyrus MacDuff, who is presently in Boston and who, as you'll be aware, is the largest shareholder in the Hudson Ohio. Mr. MacDuff was unable to reach you himself, as he is cut off in Boston. So he thought it wisest to entrust the whole business to Mr. Morgan, to handle as he sees fit."

"Quite right," said Tom.

"Put simply," said Gorham Grey, "Mr. MacDuff believes that Mr. Gabriel Love is trying to steal his company away from him. Do you know Mr. Love?"

"Hardly at all," said Frank, weakly.

"After a brief investigation, it appeared to us that the underlying issue is that Mr. Love owns shares in the Niagara line, and that MacDuff has been blocking Niagara's access to the Hudson Ohio."

"Really?" said Frank.

"The solution, therefore, seems to Mr. Morgan to be simple. He has informed Mr. MacDuff that he will only act in this matter if he, Mr. Morgan, is able to secure Mr. Love's shares in the Niagara at a reasonable price, and if Mr. MacDuff gives him, Mr. Morgan, an assurance that the Niagara will be joined to the Hudson Ohio. To this, Mr. MacDuff has agreed, on condition that he, Mr. MacDuff, is able to secure an absolute majority shareholding of the Hudson Ohio. This means, sir, that we should like to purchase half of your ten percent from you."

"Oh," said Frank. "What about Gabriel Love?"

"I purchased his Niagara shares three hours ago," said Gorham Grey.

"He hoped, I think, to make more of a killing. But once I made clear that Mr. Morgan will not be buying anything unless he is satisfied as to all the arrangements, and that Mr. MacDuff will buy nothing without Mr. Morgan's recommendation, we were able to reach an agreement. Mr. Love has sold at a good profit, so he's better off than he was."

"What'll you pay for my shares?" asked Frank.

"The current market price for Hudson Ohio is sixty. Shall we say seventy?"

"I was hoping for one twenty," said Frank.

"Love's plan is busted," said Mr. Gorham Grey, quietly.

"Ah," said Frank.

There was a brief silence.

"Mr. Morgan thinks that the future Hudson-Ohio-Niagara will be a logical amalgamation, and profitable to all parties," continued Gorham Grey. "Your remaining Hudson Ohio shares will undoubtedly increase in value. And though he has paid well over the present market price, Mr. Morgan expects in due course to see a fair profit from the Niagara shares he has bought. In short, everyone gets something. So long"— he gave Master a severe look—"as people are not too greedy."

"I'll sell," said Frank, not without relief.

"Quite right," said Tom.

The weather continued to improve for the rest of that day. On Thursday morning, Frank returned to the house on Gramercy Park, to be welcomed by Hetty as though nothing had happened at all.

⁜

It was three days later that Lily de Chantal came to see her. When they were alone, Lily gave her a strange look.

"I have news for you," she said. "About Miss Clipp."

"Oh?"

"I went to her lodgings, but she wasn't there."

"Still in Brooklyn?"

"I went to the hotel. She left on Monday morning. They still have her suitcase."

"You don't mean . . . ?"

"They've been digging up quite a few bodies around the city, as you know. People caught in the blizzard, who froze to death."

"I heard it's close to fifty."

"They found one up on the walkway of the Brooklyn Bridge. Had her bag. A notebook with her name in it, and other things. Nobody's come forward looking for her, and the city authorities are busy enough as it is. They'll bury most of the bodies tomorrow, I believe."

"Should we do anything? I mean, we sent her to Brooklyn. It's our fault."

"Are you sure you want to?"

"No. But I feel terrible."

"Really?" Lily smiled. "Ah, Hetty, you are too good for us all."

⋅⁛⋅

So ended the great Dakota Blizzard. By the following week the trains were all running again, and New York was returning to normal.

On the following Wednesday, as a train was leaving that was bound all the way to Chicago, no one took particular notice when a neatly dressed lady, with dark hair and a new suitcase containing a new set of clothes, quietly boarded. Inside the car, she sat alone, with a book open on her lap. Her name was Prudence Grace.

When the train began to move, she gazed out of the window as the city slowly receded. And if anyone in the car had happened to glance in her direction as the last view of the city disappeared, they would have noticed her whisper something that might well have been a little prayer.

Then Donna Clipp sighed with satisfaction.

It had been a moment of inspiration when she'd found that body up on the Brooklyn Bridge. Dead as a doornail. Frostbitten and frozen to a block already. The woman hadn't looked especially like her, but roughly the same age, brown hair, not too tall. Well worth a chance. It had only taken a moment or two to leave her bag with the dead woman and enough identification to give the body her name.

Then she'd forced herself on, down that long, terrible walkway, almost dead herself, but with a new and urgent reason for staying alive.

If the police ever caught up with her now, they'd find she was dead. She had a new name, a new identity. Now it was time to move on to a new city, far away. And a new life.

She was free, and it amused her. That's why, as New York was lost to sight, she'd thought one last and final time of Frank Master and whispered: "Good-bye, you old fart."

Old England

O N A W A R M June evening, in the year 1896, Mary O'Donnell, looking very grand in a long white evening dress and long white gloves, walked up the steps of her brother Sean's house on Fifth Avenue. As the butler opened the door, she smiled at him.

But her smile masked the terrible fear that was gnawing within her.

At the foot of the sweeping staircase stood her brother, looking very elegant in white tie and tails.

"Are they here?" she asked quietly.

"They're in the drawing room," he said, using the English term.

"How did I let you get me into this, you devil?" She tried to make it sound lighthearted.

"We're just having dinner."

"With a lord, for God's sake."

"Plenty of those where he came from."

Mary took a deep breath. Personally, she didn't give a damn about any English lord. But that wasn't the point. She knew why the English lord was there, and what her family expected of her. Normally, she coped well enough with social occasions, but this would be different. Questions might be asked, questions that she dreaded.

"Jesus, Mary and Joseph," she murmured.

"Chin up," said Sean.

It was five years now since Mary had finally given in to her brother and left the employment of the Masters. And she'd only done that because she knew it was what the younger generation wanted.

By chance, a house had become vacant on the side street a few doors down from Sean's mansion on Fifth Avenue, and Sean had bought it. "I don't want to rent it out," he told her, "so you'd be doing me a favor if you'd live in it for me." Compared with his own place, the house was quite modest, but it was still far bigger than she needed. When his children and grandchildren had begged her to live there, however, she had taken the hint. Apart from her own bedroom, which was very simply furnished with some things she liked, she had let them decorate the house as they wished. Hardly a week went by without one of the younger generation calling in there with friends, to have tea with their Aunt Mary. And she'd entertain them in just the style they would have encountered in the Masters' house in Gramercy Park. That wasn't difficult; after all, she'd been watching Hetty do it for forty years. In this way, she was able to complete the picture of the family's new wealth and respectability to everyone's satisfaction. She didn't mind doing so, if it made them happy.

But this evening was different. His Lordship might ask probing questions. Like: What had she been doing for the last forty years of her life?

If the truth were told, when she first came to live in her grand house, she'd rather missed her little room at the Masters'. But then events had brought about a new arrangement.

She'd been in her house a year when Frank Master had fallen sick and died. Hetty Master had only been widowed a couple of months when she asked Mary to call, and told her: "I get a little lonely, Mary. There's always a room for you here, any time you'd like to stay and keep me company." And when Mary had proposed spending two or three nights a week in Gramercy Park, Hetty had suggested: "I thought you might like to use the blue bedroom."

Her old room had been up on the servants' floor. The blue bedroom was on the same floor as Hetty's. Mary had accepted. Everyone understood. The servants called her "Miss O'Donnell" now. They knew she was rich.

So Mary divided her time between Fifth Avenue and Gramercy Park, and she was quite happy. Her new regime left her with time on her hands, but she found many agreeable ways to fill it. She liked to draw, and she went to art classes. She and Hetty became frequenters of exhibitions and lectures. Her taste in music remained quite simple, but when the brilliant

operettas of Gilbert and Sullivan came from London to New York, she
always went. She'd seen *The Mikado* and *The Yeoman of the Guard* three or
four times.

She had her family and a few friends, especially Gretchen. Theodore
had been married a long time now, and had children, but she still saw him
from time to time. She'd asked herself many times down the years if she
shouldn't have tried harder to get married, but somehow or other she'd
never met Mr. Right. The truth was, she realized, that she'd always wanted
someone like Hans or Theodore, and they weren't so easy to find. Perhaps
if she'd taken up Sean's offer long ago and stopped working for the Masters, she'd have had a chance. Well, it was no good worrying about that
now. And taken all together, she considered, it wasn't such a bad retirement for a girl who'd been raised within sight of Five Points.

Five Points. What if His Lordship asked her where she'd been born and
raised? What was she supposed to say? "Down Fourth Avenue," Sean had
told her. But the thought of those days, and the memories that came with
them, had filled her with an awful, cold horror. She'd blush, she'd say
something foolish, she'd expose the sordid truth about the family and let
them all down. "Don't worry," Sean had said. "Leave it all to me."

It wasn't so bad for Sean. He already knew these people. After losing his
wife three years ago, he'd taken up travel, and he'd made a trip to London
the previous year with his son Daniel and his family. That's when Daniel's
daughter Clarissa had met young Gerald Rivers. She was a well-brought-
up young lady, a good horsewoman, and she'd been hunting when she'd
met him. He had just returned from a visit to America himself, and was
soon captivated by her lively American ways. His parents must have taken
note of her obvious fortune too. But Gerald and Clarissa were both
young, and it had been agreed by all the parties that they should wait
some months before any negotiations were entered into about an engagement.

When Sean had first told Mary about the business, she hadn't been that
surprised. Everyone knew about the British aristocracy's new interest in
American heiresses; Sean himself had described it very well.

"They're just trying to get some of their money back from the place it
went to," he'd said. For since the canals and railroads had opened up the
American Midwest, the cheap imports of American grain and meat to
England had undercut all the local producers. The value of England's
mighty, historic harvests had plummeted, and the lordly incomes which

had supported the aristocracy's huge houses were only a fraction of what they had been. You could hardly blame them, then, if they looked across the Atlantic where there was now a plentiful supply of heiresses whose mothers were eager to trade them. And the heiresses usually had more education and were livelier company than the English country girls.

"But what's in it for the Americans?" Mary had asked her brother.

He'd shrugged. "When a man's made a fortune, and bought all the things he wants in America, he looks around for other worlds to conquer. So what's left? He turns to Europe and sees things that can't be had in America. Centuries of art, ancient manners, titles. So he buys them. It's something to do. And of course, for the mothers, it becomes a social competition."

Mary wondered whether the girls themselves were always happy. She remembered reading about the marriage of Consuelo Vanderbilt to the Duke of Marlborough. It had been a great society event, a triumph for Consuelo's mother. And the bridegroom had received some Vanderbilt millions, so that he could keep his great palace up. But she remembered hearing the other side of the story from Hetty Master.

"Poor Consuelo's entirely in love with Winthrop Rutherfurd, you know. He's from fine old American stock, but her mother was just determined to have a title in the family—she actually locked the poor girl up, and forced her to marry the duke. Consuelo was weeping during the wedding ceremony. It was really shameful."

Clarissa wasn't in love with anybody else, anyway. Indeed, she'd taken a great liking to Lord Riverdale's second son. He was a handsome young fellow, an officer in a good regiment, who liked the outdoor life. Not a bad prospect, if he had some money to go with it. Sean, who had three granddaughters, seemed to find it amusing.

"But she's Catholic," Mary had pointed out, "and he's sure to be Church of England."

"That's up to Clarissa," said Sean. "Her father says he don't care."

"And her mother?"

"Her mother," Sean said quietly, "would like her to marry the son of a lord."

It had come as rather a surprise when Lord and Lady Rivers had announced their intention to visit America themselves. But Sean had quickly made arrangements that suited them admirably. A few days in

New York, followed by a steamer up the Hudson, some days in Saratoga, and then across to Boston, which they had expressed a wish to see.

While Lord Rivers was in New York, Sean intended to play his part, which was to make the O'Donnells look respectable. Of course, the British usually assumed—quite incorrectly—that all American money must be new. Nevertheless, the presence of Clarissa's rich old grandfather and his entirely respectable sister would do much to ease Clarissa's way into her new life.

So when Sean had remarked the day before, "We'll put our best foot forward here, sis, if you know what I mean," Mary had felt a little sinking of the heart.

"I can't lie, Sean," she'd said. "I'm never any good at it."

"Of course not," he'd said.

"What is it you want me to do?"

"Just be yourself."

"And what are you going to do?"

"Nothing much." He smiled. "I may let them think we've had money a little longer than we have, if you know what I mean."

"Oh, I'm sure to put my foot in it. Leave me out of it, Sean. Tell them I'm sick."

"Nonsense," he said, "you'll be fine."

With a sinking heart, therefore, she now went in to meet the Riverdales.

⁘

Well, they were certainly very friendly, she'd say that for them. Young Gerald Rivers was only twenty-five or so, and obviously quite determined to like his fiancée's family. Lord and Lady Riverdale were both tall, dark-haired and elegant; and whatever their private thoughts and intentions might be, a lifetime of practiced perfect manners protected their hosts and themselves from any awkwardness. Daniel and his wife seemed quite at ease, and Clarissa was looking radiant. So after some greetings all round, it only remained for Mary to make small talk with the new arrivals, ask them about their voyage on the White Star Line, and whether their hotel was comfortable. Lady Rivers asked a question or two about the city's museums and galleries, and was obviously quite impressed that Mary could tell her all about the best exhibitions to see.

"We shall be glad of your guidance," she remarked, "for my husband

and I have come here, I'm quite sure, with all the ignorance of Mark Twain's travelers in *The Innocents Abroad.*"

All in all, the conversation passed very pleasantly until dinner was announced.

Sean's dining room was impressive. They often seated twenty in there, and his dinner service was magnificent. Mary could see that the Riverdales were favorably impressed. Since they were eight, they dined at a round table. "It's so awkward seating eight, isn't it?" she remarked to Lady Rivers as they were about to take their seats, thanking heaven that she knew from Hetty Master the perils of correct "*placement*" at dinner. Starting very properly, speaking to the person on one side of her, then switching sides with each course, she could go through all the correct motions of the dinner party to perfection. But with an intimate party like this at a round table, some general conversation might also be permitted. Lord Rivers inquired where she lived and was duly informed that she had a house just round the corner from her brother, and that perhaps, if Lady Rivers had time, she might like to come to tea there. His Lordship then remarked that he'd heard the Vanderbilts had built some huge mansions further up Fifth Avenue; and she was just wondering how to respond, when a little phrase that Hetty used about Gramercy Park suddenly came into her mind.

"We like the fact that it's a little quieter down here," she said. It was the sort of thing old money said, and His Lordship inclined his head.

"Quite, Miss O'Donnell," he acknowledged, understandingly.

So far so good.

It was soon clear that the Riverdales were anxious to stress every American connection that they could think of.

"We've met a charming compatriot of yours, several times," Lord Rivers remarked to Mary. "Mr. Henry James, the author. He's been living in London for years, and is quite a fixture at dinner parties there, you know."

"A very distinguished man," said Mary. "Though I'm afraid I don't always read his books."

"Ah," said His Lordship, with a smile, "nor do I."

Lord Rivers then spoke to her about his family a little, and in doing so, let fall some rather interesting information.

"The Rivers family, you know, were in the navy mostly, for generations. Two admirals, I may say. It was only when a quite distant cousin died that the title and estate came across to my father. And there's an American connection too. Our branch descends from a Captain Rivers, who had plantations in Carolina, until he lost them soon after 1776." He smiled. "He was a Loyalist, I'm afraid."

"We shall have to forgive him," said Mary. "What happened to the plantations?"

"They were taken over by friends of his, a New York family called Master. But I don't know anything more than that."

"Master?" Mary was so surprised that she let her voice rise a bit. As she said it, she saw her brother, her nephew and young Clarissa all look at her nervously.

"I believe they're still people of some consequence in New York," His Lordship said, "Do you know them?"

The abyss had opened before her, and her family were staring into it. Her decades as a servant in the Masters' house. Mary caught her breath, then smiled a perfect smile.

"Hetty Master is one of my closest friends," she said firmly. "Why, I've known her nearly fifty years." It was true, every word of it.

"Well," said Lord Rivers, quite delighted, "it's a small world, isn't it?"

"It certainly is," said Mary.

By the time the fish course arrived, she and His Lordship were getting along famously, but now it was time to give her attention to young Gerald. As she knew nothing of hunting, shooting, fishing or the army, Mary wasn't sure what to talk to him about, but after a quick pass at the theater, she discovered that he loved Gilbert and Sullivan, and so that kept them going quite agreeably for a while. But it was clear to her from the way he glanced boyishly at Clarissa, and then round the table, that Gerald Rivers, who'd had a glass or two to drink, felt he'd like to make a bit of an impression on his future wife's family; and Mary wondered what form this would take.

The young man's chance came during the main course when Lord Rivers asked her if she knew a charming New Yorker who lived in England now. "A Mr. Croker. He has an estate in Surrey," he said. Rather astonished, she answered softly: "Everyone in New York knows Mr. Croker."

And now, Gerald decided to cut in.

"When I was in America visiting the New York Yacht Club last year, Father," he said a little too loudly, "they told me he was mixed up with Tammany Hall, and he skipped across the Atlantic to stay out of jail."

Though he was perhaps a little tactless, young Gerald Rivers was perfectly right. If Boss Tweed had embezzled on a huge scale, his successor Croker had continued the good work, until the complaints became so loud that he'd decided to go overseas for a while. The idea of his living in England as a respectable country gentleman was amusing indeed.

"Is it true?" Lady Rivers asked Sean. But Sean was far too close to Tammany himself to start throwing stones in that glass house.

"Tammany Hall is a complex affair," he said carefully. "It's a very important political machine, and has to be handled with caution."

"Ah," said Lord Rivers knowingly. Aristocrats evidently respected politics. But young Gerald Rivers wasn't finished yet.

"I met a splendid fellow called Teddy Roosevelt in New York," he said. "He has great plans for cleaning up the New York Police—they're completely corrupt as well, I heard."

"They're not perfect," Sean allowed. He gave Lord Rivers a wise look. "Young Mr. Roosevelt has a lot of energy, but he may find the task harder than he thinks."

"But you wouldn't deny that New York City is corrupt?" Gerald pursued.

And now Sean looked across the table at the young aristocrat with an even gaze.

"I wouldn't deny it. And I'm afraid it has been so for two hundred and thirty years." He paused just a moment. "Ever since the British took it over from the Dutch."

"Oh, well done," cried Lord Rivers. He and his wife were obviously very pleased with this bit of repartee. And you had to admire Sean, thought Mary. He'd made his assessment of these English aristocrats, and knew exactly how to handle them.

"Now the American I should like to have met in London," Sean continued, looking around the table with a twinkle in his eye, "is the lovely Jennie Jerome, as she used to be. Lady Randolph Churchill, now. I remember her as a girl."

The two Riverdales looked at each other.

"Beautiful," said His Lordship, cryptically.

"Not good?" Mary asked.

"There's a particular set around the Prince of Wales, Miss O'Donnell," said Lady Rivers quietly. "We do not belong to it. They are what we call 'fast.' Lady Randolph Churchill is part of it."

"Oh," said Mary. "In New York, men quite often have mistresses."

"Well," said Lady Rivers, "the fast set believes in perfect equality between the sexes, in that regard."

"A remarkable woman, Jennie Churchill, all the same," said His Lordship. He paused a moment. "Tell me, as you would know, there was a rumor that the father was"—he dropped his voice a bit—"Jewish."

"Sounds it, but isn't," Sean assured him. "The name Jerome is French. They were Huguenots." He chuckled. "There may be some Indian blood there, but that's on his wife's side."

"Does Jennie have children?" asked Mary.

"Two boys," Lady Rivers answered. "We saw the eldest, Winston, not long ago."

"Not everybody likes him," Gerald interrupted, and earned a bleak look from his father.

"Why's that?" asked Sean.

"People say," replied Gerald, "he's too pushy."

"I'll tell you a story, then," said his host. And he recounted how Leonard Jerome had come to him during the Draft Riots. True, he omitted to say that he was keeping a saloon at the time—O'Donnell's Saloon became his office—but the rest was unchanged. "So he came by my office and told me: 'I'm off to defend my property from the mob.' 'How will you do that, Jerome?' I asked him. 'I've got a Gatling gun,' he cried. How or where he got such a thing I don't know, but that was Jerome for you. The man was a street fighter. So if young Winston Churchill's pushy, now you know how he comes by it." He laughed. "Young Winston Churchill sounds like a true, cigar-chomping New Yorker to me!"

They loved it; Sean had them eating out of his hand. Mary relaxed. She'd hardly touched her wine during the meal, but now she drained her glass. Everything was all right. She gazed at them, contentedly, and only gave half her attention to the conversation until she heard Lord Riverdale say:

"When Gerald came back from New York, he brought me a photograph of the city. Taken from the harbor at sunset, I think, with the

Brooklyn Bridge in the background. It really is the most beautiful thing. Made me want to get in a ship and go there at once." He gave his son a smile. "Very good of him."

"A wonderful photographer," said Gerald Rivers. "You might have heard of him. Theodore Keller."

And Mary beamed. She beamed at them all. Then she glanced at her brother. If he could play this game so well, why, so could she.

"I not only know him," she said, "it was I who persuaded Frank Master to sponsor his first important exhibition. I have several of his photographs myself."

"You know him well?" asked Gerald, delighted.

"I know his sister better," she answered without a blink. She smiled at Sean. "Actually," she said, "my father used to get his cigars at their uncle's store." It was perfectly true, in a sense.

"And what did your father do?" said Gerald.

"My father?" She'd been so pleased with herself that she hadn't anticipated any further questions. "My father?" She could feel herself starting to go pale. The awful horror of their lodgings' squalor, of Five Points, of everything she must not speak of, suddenly filled her with a terrible, cold fear. Her family's eyes were all on her. What on earth was she supposed to say?

"Ah," said Sean, loudly. "Now there was a character."

Their eyes were on him at once.

"My father," said Sean, "was an investor. Mind you, like many investors, he had his good days and his bad ones, so we were never sure if we were facing riches or ruin. But," he smiled genially, "we're still here."

After her near drowning, Mary was coming up for air again. She watched her brother, fascinated. He hadn't exactly lied—their father certainly liked to call his bets investments, and he had good days and his bad days all right. The fact that somehow Sean had implied that the old man was on Wall Street, without quite saying it, she could only admire, as she would the dexterity of a pianist. As for saying "We're still here," it was a masterstroke. Of course they were still here, or they wouldn't be sitting at this table. But it could mean, and surely would be taken to mean, that the family fortune had never been lost, and only improved upon. Her brother hadn't finished, though.

"But above all, like Jerome and Belmont and so many others, my father was a sporting man. Loved the races. Loved to bet." He glanced across the table and looked Mary straight in the eye. "He had his own racehorse, his greatest pride and joy, called Brian Boru."

It was all she could do not to choke. She looked down at the table. That terrible old fighting dog, kept in their stinking lodgings, had been transformed, as only a true Irishman can transform things, into a race-horse, swift and sleek.

"And when he died," Sean continued, "the remains of that horse were buried with him."

"Really?" Lord Rivers was most appreciative; English aristocrats liked sportsmen and eccentrics. "What a splendid fellow. I'd like to have met him."

Sean still wasn't done yet. "Not only that, but the family priest it was who buried them both." And he sat back in his chair and gazed benevolently at them all.

"Magnificent," cried His Lordship and his son together. Style, eccentricity, a high-born disregard for the respectable, and a churchman who knew better than to make a nuisance of himself: this Mr. O'Donnell was clearly a natural toff, a man after their own hearts.

"Did the priest really bury them both?" Lady Rivers asked Mary.

"I was there, and it's true, the priest buried my father with Brian Boru."

There wasn't a word of a lie in it.

✛

Later, after the Rivers family had left, Mary and Sean went into the drawing room together, and sat down to review the evening.

"I need a drink," said Mary.

He fetched it. She nursed the brandy for a while.

"What are you thinking, Mary?" he asked.

"That you are the devil himself," she answered.

"Not true."

"Brian Boru."

And then she laughed, and laughed. And laughed, until she cried.

Ellis Island

SALVATORE CARUSO WAS five years old when he came to Ellis Island. It was New Year's Day, 1901. The day was icy cold but clear, and over the snowy landscape all around the wide waters of the harbor, the sky was crystal blue.

The Caruso family had been fortunate. From Naples they'd taken the *Hohenzollern*—the German ships were best, his father said—and they'd crossed the Atlantic in less than ten days. It had been crowded, down in steerage. The smell of the latrines almost made him throw up, and the throbbing of the engines, his mother said, was a punishment sent by God. But there had been no storms during the crossing, and they were allowed up on deck to get the fresh air for an hour every day. His mother had brought food—ham and salami, olives, dried fruit, even bread, tightly wrapped in napkins—that had lasted through the voyage. Each evening Uncle Luigi had led the singing of Neapolitan songs, like "Finiculi, Finicula," in his soft tenor voice.

There were eight of them altogether: his parents, his mother's brother, Uncle Luigi, and the five children. Giuseppe was the eldest, fifteen years old, strongly built like his father, a good worker. All the children looked up to Giuseppe, but being so much older, he was somewhat apart. Two other little boys had not been so strong, and died in infancy. So the next in line was Anna. She was nine. Then came Paolo, Salvatore, and little Maria, who was just three.

As the ship passed through the narrows into the waters of New York harbor, the deck was crowded. Everyone was excited. And little Salvatore would have been happy too, if he hadn't discovered a terrible secret.

His mother was holding little Maria by the hand. Until Maria came along, Salvatore had been the baby of the family. But now he had someone to look up to him, and it was his job to protect her. He liked to play with his baby sister and to show her things.

His mother was wearing a black coat against the cold. Most of the women had their heads covered with a white shawl, but despite the winter weather, his mother had put on her best hat. It was black also, with a tattered little veil and a limp artificial flower on the brim. Salvatore had heard that once there had been two flowers, but this was before he was born. He understood that she was wearing her hat now so that the Americans should see that the family were people of some standing.

Concetta Caruso was short and dark and fiercely proud. She knew that the people of her village were superior to the people of the neighboring villages, and that the Italian south, the Mezzogiorno, was finer than all the other lands of the world, whatever they might be. She did not know what people of other nations ate, and did not care. For Italian food was best.

She knew also that, whichever of the saints she asked to help her, God saw all the sins of the world, and that He would decide whether any mercy was to be shown.

That was fate. It was inescapable, as certain as the blue dome of the sky over the Earth. Going to America wasn't going to change that.

"Why are we going to America?" Salvatore had asked, as they sat in the cart, on their way from the family's little farm into Naples.

"Because there is money in America, Toto," his father had answered. "A heap of dollars to send to your grandmother and your aunts, so they can keep the farm."

"We can't get dollars in Naples?"

"In Naples? No." His father had smiled. "You will like America. Your Uncle Francesco is there, and all your cousins that you have never met, and all waiting to greet you."

"Is it true," Salvatore had asked, "that everyone in America is happy, and you can do whatever you want?"

But before his father could reply, his mother had cut in.

"It is not for you to think of being happy, Salvatore," she said firmly. "God will decide if you deserve to be happy. Be grateful that you are alive."

"Yes, Concetta, of course," his father began. He was not so religious. But Concetta was implacable.

"Only bandits do what they want, Salvatore. *Camorristi*. And God will punish them. Obey your parents, work hard, look after your family. It is enough."

"There are still choices," Uncle Luigi had said gently.

"No," Concetta had flared up, "there is no choice." She'd gazed down at her little son. "You are a good boy, Salvatore," she said in a softer voice, "but you must not hope for too much, or God will punish you. Always remember that."

"Yes, Mama," he'd said.

Next to his mother, holding little Maria's other hand, was Uncle Luigi.

Uncle Luigi was small. He had a round head, and the strands of hair he plastered across it could not conceal the fact that he was bald. He was not powerful like Salvatore's father, who only tolerated him. He had worked in a store; he could also read and write, and liked to go to church with his sister, neither of which impressed the other men in the family. "Reading and writing is a waste of time," Salvatore's father would say. "And the priests are all rogues." Uncle Luigi was a little strange. Sometimes he would hum to himself, and gaze out into space, as though in a dream. But the children all loved him, and Concetta protected him.

Salvatore had been put between Anna and Paolo. Anna was slim and serious. Though she was only nine, she was the eldest daughter, and she helped her mother in all things. She and Paolo didn't always get along, but Salvatore liked Anna, because she used to take him out for walks into the woods when he was little, and give him chocolate.

As for Paolo, he wasn't even two years older than Salvatore. Paolo was his best friend; they did everything together. During the voyage, Paolo had been sick, and he kept coughing, but he seemed better now, and Uncle Luigi said the fresh air would put him right.

Salvatore loved his family. He could not imagine life without them. And now they had all crossed the ocean safely, and Ellis Island lay just ahead of them. There, he knew, they would all be inspected before being allowed into America.

And that was the terrible secret he had heard his father tell his mother, not an hour before. One of the family wasn't going to make it.

✢

Rose Vandyck Master stared at the picture. It was a charming watercolor of her cottage at Newport, and she had been so pleased with it that she had hung it on the wall in her boudoir, over the little French bureau where she liked to write letters. Her husband William was at work, and the children were out, so she could concentrate in peace. She had just put on her pearl choker. For some reason, she always seemed to think best when she was wearing her pearls. And she needed to think clearly, for she was facing one of the most difficult decisions of her life.

The life of Rose Master was privileged, and she knew it. She was a loyal wife and a loving mother, and she ran her houses to perfection. But she hadn't come by all this good fortune without hard work and calculation. And having got so far, it was hardly surprising that she meant to go further. If her husband was working to increase the family fortune, then her task, as she saw it—and most women she knew would have agreed—was to raise their social position. Indeed, for a married woman of her class and time, blessed, or cursed, with ambition, there wasn't much else one could do.

The question before her was by no means simple. There were many things to calculate, opportunities to seize, social pitfalls to avoid. And the further up the social scale one went, the more one's freedom of choice was restricted.

Where was the family going to live?

Not in the summer, of course; that was settled long ago. They'd always be at the cottage.

Every family needed a cottage. By "cottage," of course, one meant a summer house on the coast. It might be modest or it might be a mansion, but that's where mothers and children spent the summer months, and one's husband, assuming he had work to do in the city, came for weekends. And the truly fashionable had cottages in Newport, Rhode Island.

Newport had been chosen for good reason. As the British and French had discovered in centuries past, its harbor was deep, sheltered and magnificent. The New York Yacht Club, which now trounced Britain's elite Royal Yacht Squadron in the America's Cup every year, had its home there. Newport's many miles of unspoiled shoreline provided space for all the cottages that society might need—indeed, more than enough, for Newport society was exclusive. Once one belonged in Newport society, one had reached the top.

Naturally, presence was required. A couple of years ago, when her husband had taken her to London for the season, she had still insisted that she be back in Newport by the second week in July. Of course, with dozens of American heiresses already married into the English aristocracy, and a regular American colony now enjoying the British capital, some fashionable folk—the "steamer set"—preferred to winter in New York and summer in London. But Rose liked to be seen in Newport. "Otherwise," she informed her husband, "people might think we've fallen off the end of the Earth."

Newport was perfect for the summer. The problem was New York.

The family was well represented in the city. William's grandmother, old Hetty Master, was still in isolated splendor at Gramercy Park. His father Tom had recently bought the late Mr. Sean O'Donnell's splendid house on Lower Fifth, after he died on a return voyage from England. And for the last few years, William and Rose had been renting a fine place, further up the avenue. But now the owner wanted it back, and it was time to buy a place of their own.

"You'd better decide where we go, Rose," William had genially remarked. "Brooklyn or Queens, Manhattan or the Bronx. Staten Island if you like. So long as it's in the city."

Technically, of course, all the outlandish places he mentioned were part of the city now. Just before the new century began, these surrounding areas—Brooklyn and Queens County on Long Island, part of the old Dutch Bronx estate above Manhattan to the north, and rural Staten Island across the harbor to the south—had all been incorporated within the expanded City of New York. Brooklyn, proudly independent, had only just been persuaded to join. But the resulting Five Boroughs of New York made the metropolis, after London, the most populous city in the world.

And there were splendid houses, and pleasant parks, and delightful open country in any one of those five boroughs. But Rose Master wasn't free to choose them. The family could only live in Manhattan, and not in many places there.

Lower Manhattan was out. The area of the old city was all commercial now. Even the pleasant areas around Greenwich Village or Chelsea, a little to the north and west, had been overrun with immigrants, and turned into tenements mostly. Respectable New York had moved gradually north, and kept on moving. The fine old Broadway stores, like Tiffany's the jewelers, had moved uptown with their customers. Lord & Taylor, and Brooks Brothers, both fashionable now, were already in the Twenties.

Then there was the question of noise. After the terrible blizzard of 1888 had brought the city to a standstill, everyone had agreed that the telegraph wires should be buried underground. This was easy to do, and it had improved the look of the place. Many people also argued for underground transport, which would be out of sight, and impervious to weather. But this was taking much longer. So for the time being, the El trains, with their noise and smoke, and tracks running past everyone's windows, were still puffing and clattering up the avenues on the East Side of the island, and up parts of the West Side too.

As fashionable New York advanced northward, therefore, it avoided the smoke and noise, and hugged the quieter center. Fifth and Madison avenues, and the streets close to them, were the best residential quarters.

"What about Park Avenue?" William had suggested.

"Park?" she had cried, before she'd realized he was teasing her. "Nobody lives on Park."

The trouble with Park Avenue went back thirty years, to when old Commodore Vanderbilt had erected a big railroad shed on Fourth Avenue at Forty-second Street, to act as a kind of terminal. Fourth had changed its name to Park Avenue these days, which sounded well enough. But the terminal was a mess, and the railroad yards spread in a hideous swathe for a dozen blocks to the north of it. Even above Fifty-sixth Street, where the tracks narrowed and were covered over, the noise and smoke rising from the center of the avenue indicated that the infernal regions were only just below.

"What about the West Side then?" he'd said. "It's better value there."

She knew he was gently teasing her. Not that the West Side was to be despised; gone already were the days when the Dakota was in the wilderness. The West Side was quieter and land prices were lower; the big family houses in the side streets were often larger than their equivalents on the East Side, and some real mansions were arising there too.

But who lived there? That was the point. What was the tone of the place? Would a West Side address sound as perfect as the cottage in Newport?

No, it had to be somewhere close to Fifth and Madison. The question was, how far up?

Almost twenty years had passed since the Vanderbilts built their mighty mansions on Fifth, in the Fifties. Since then, people had been building further north. Palaces in all kinds of styles, designed by architects like Carrère & Hastings, Richard Morris Hunt, and Kimball & Thompson, had arisen in the Sixties and Seventies, on Madison and Fifth. French chateaux, Renaissance palaces, the greatest styles from the architectural menu of Old Europe were being splendidly plundered and copied so that their owners could gaze over Central Park like the merchant princes they were.

The Masters couldn't afford a palace like that. They could live near one, though. But should they?

J. P. Morgan didn't live up there. Pierpont Morgan's mansion was on the east side of Madison, down at Thirty-sixth Street. Mr. Morgan had openly stated his opinion that some of the mansions going up on Fifth were vulgar monstrosities. And one couldn't deny that he had a point. Most of those mansions were being built by new money. Very new money indeed. Morgan's great fortune might only derive from his father Junius, but it had come from banking in London, in the grandest manner. The Morgans, besides, had been well-to-do in Connecticut since the seventeenth century. Compared to all but the oldest Dutch families, they were old money.

And that was the point.

Rose was always grateful to her father-in-law for the names he had chosen for his son. The fact that it had come about by chance, that for some reason Tom's wife had taken a fancy to the name of Vernon and that Tom had disliked it and suggested the old family name of Vandyck instead, didn't matter. What mattered was that Rose could, quite properly, call herself Mrs. William Vandyck Master—and in doing so, proclaim that her husband came not only from Anglo-Saxon Protestant money, but from Dutch ancestors who went all the way back to the days of Stuyvesant and before.

The Masters were only modestly rich, but their money was old. As long as a family could afford to stay in society, that counted for something.

So this was the delicate balance she needed to think about this afternoon. How close could she—should she—live to those ostentatious palaces which, secretly, her heart desired? Or how far should she maintain a staid and distant attitude? If she could play her cards right, she would achieve the perfect result: the new princes would invite her to their palaces, and wonder if she'd come.

William had given her the pearl choker for their third wedding anniversary. It was just like the one that Alexandra, the Princess of Wales, always wore in the society photographs from London, and it meant more to Rose than any other piece of jewelry she possessed. She let her fingers play over it now, as in her mind she went up and down Fifth and Madison, street by street, thinking about who lived on each block and whether, should she find the perfect social territory, there might be a house, or a building lot for sale there.

⁘

"There it is, Toto." Anna was pointing. The bridge of the ship had obscured the great monument from view, but now the passengers were all pressing toward the port side to get a better look as it approached. "The Statue of Liberty."

There was hardly any need to move to the rail. The mighty statue towered over them. Its upraised arm, torch in hand, seemed to scrape the sky. Salvatore gazed up in silence. So this was America.

Salvatore didn't know much about America. He knew it was big, and that the people there spoke English, of which Uncle Luigi spoke a few words, and that when you worked, they gave you dollars to send home. He had never heard of the Anglo-Saxon Puritans or the Dutch settlers, or the God-fearing farmers of New England. His family had never spoken of the Boston Tea Party, or Ben Franklin, or even George Washington. Nor, gazing at the Statue of Liberty, could he have derived any clue as to the existence of such a Christian or democratic tradition.

Yet instinctively, as the Mediterranean boy looked up, he understood what he saw.

Power. The colossal, pale green, pagan god rose alone on its huge pedestal above the waters. Hundreds of feet up, under its mighty diadem, the blank, heroic face stared with Olympian indifference across the clear blue sky, while its upraised arm signaled: Victory. If the statue bade him any welcome at all, the little boy sensed, it was to an empire like that of his ancestors. Only one thing puzzled him.

"Is it a man," he whispered to Anna, "or a woman?"

She also gazed, uncertain. The huge face seemed to belong to a male god, yet the massive drapery that fell over the statue's body might have suggested a stately Roman matron. Anna tugged at Uncle Luigi's arm, to ask him.

"She is a woman," said Uncle Luigi. "The French gave her to the Americans."

Had Uncle Luigi known it, he could have added that the sculptor came from Alsace, on the Franco-German border, had studied in Egypt as well, and that therefore it was not so surprising if this monument to Liberty, timeless as the pyramids, should also echo that modern version of the classical spirit, the French Second Empire—with a hint, perhaps, of German power as well.

They sailed straight past Ellis Island. The first- and second-class passengers, the people with cabins, did not have to pass though that ordeal. They had already been given a brief and courteous inspection on board before the ship entered the harbor, and were free to disembark at their leisure.

On the starboard side, the ship passed Governor's Island, then the tip of Manhattan with its little fort and park. Beyond, in the East River, both the funnels of steamships and the huge masts of sailing ships graced the waters. On the port side, Salvatore saw the high cliffs of the Palisades up the Hudson. Then, moments later, the ship began to make its slow turn toward the Hoboken piers on the New Jersey side, where the German liners docked.

Across the river, New York stretched for miles. Street after street of brick and brownstone houses; here and there, clumps of office buildings, several stories higher. Nearby, the dark spire of Trinity, Wall Street, and further off, the Gothic towers of the Brooklyn Bridge rose into the sky. Even more dramatically, nearly a dozen tall skyscrapers, each over three hundred feet high, soared into the heavens above them all. But while everyone gazed eagerly at the city, Salvatore started thinking of something else.

It had been at the turn of the metal stairs going up to the deck. That's where he'd heard his father say it. The other children didn't hear, because they'd already turned the corner above.

His parents had been arguing about Uncle Luigi just before. His father was complaining about something Uncle Luigi had done, and his mother was defending him, which wasn't unusual. Salvatore hadn't really been listening. But then his father had turned to his mother and announced:

"You know what's going to happen at Ellis Island? They are going to send your brother back."

"Do not say such a thing, Giovanni." His mother had sounded shocked.

"But it's true—I know what happens, I spoke with a man who has been there. It's not only your chest and eyes they inspect—they have special doctors there to spot the ones who are crazy. They chalk a cross on their chest and they make them sit on a bench, and then they talk to them. And in a minute . . ." he made a gesture—"it's over. They can always tell. They are specialists, from the finest lunatic asylums in America. So they will understand at once that your brother is crazy, and they will send him back to Italy. *Ecco*. You will see."

"Do not say it, Giovanni. I will not listen," his mother had cried.

But Salvatore had listened. And when they got up on deck, he had tugged at his father's sleeve and whispered: "Is it true, Papa, that they will send Uncle Luigi home because he is crazy?"

His father had looked down, with a serious expression.

"Shh," his father had said, "it's a secret. You mustn't tell anybody. Promise me."

"I promise, Papa," Salvatore had said. But it was a terrible secret to keep.

It took an hour before they were let off the ship. His father, Giuseppe and Uncle Luigi each carried a heavy suitcase. Uncle Luigi's case was made of rattan, and it looked as if it might burst open at any moment. There was also a wooden trunk which was taken across on a trolley. The steerage passengers were led straight along the wharf to where a barge was waiting. His father made them hurry, to be near the front. He had talked to men who'd come back to Italy from America, so he knew exactly how things were done.

"They sometimes keep you waiting for a whole day on the barge, before they let you off at Ellis Island," he'd been told. "So in this weather, it's better to be inside than on deck."

Once they were all on board the barge, it only took a few minutes to get to the island. And though they had to wait a while, within another hour they had joined the slow line making its way toward the big doorway.

The main facility on Ellis Island was a large, handsome red-brick building, with four stout towers at its corners, protecting the roofline of the huge central hall. The line of people moved slowly but steadily toward the entrance. When they got there, a man was shouting, and porters were taking people's bags away. His mother didn't want to give up her bag, because she was sure it would be stolen, but they made her all the same. Then they entered the vestibule, and he noticed that the floor was covered with small white tiles. There were military surgeons standing here in dark uniforms with high boots, and attendants in white who could speak Italian and tell people what they had to do. Soon Salvatore had several labels pinned on him. He kept close to his mother and Anna.

Then the men were told to go one way, and the women and children another. So his father and Giuseppe and Uncle Luigi had to leave them. That made Salvatore sad, because he knew his uncle wasn't coming back, and he called out, "Good-bye, Uncle Luigi," but his uncle didn't seem to hear him.

In front of him, a young doctor was checking everyone's eyes. Salvatore saw him mark one child with the letter T. When he finally came to the Caruso family, he started with little Maria, probing her eye gently with his forefinger. Then he did the same to Salvatore. And Salvatore was relieved, because his father had told him that they might lift his eyelid with a little buttonhook and that it would hurt and that he must be brave. The doctor carefully inspected Paolo, Anna and his mother, and waved them on.

There was a broad, square staircase next. His father had warned them all about this. "It is a trap," he told them. "And you have to be very careful, because they are watching you. Whatever you do, don't look tired or out of breath."

And sure enough, Salvatore saw that there were the men in uniform quietly watching them from the hallway below and from the stairway above. One of the men in uniform was standing at one corner of the stairs, saying a word to people as they passed.

The family in front of them was large, and the doctors seemed to be taking a long time with them. While this was done, the line was held up, and Salvatore started to get quite bored. But at last the line began to move again. When Salvatore reached the man in uniform, he was asked his name, in Neapolitan so that he should understand, and Salvatore said it loudly, so that the man smiled. But when he asked Paolo his name, Paolo coughed before he gave it. The man didn't say anything, but he made a mark in blue chalk on Paolo's chest. And a few moments later one of the men took Paolo away. His mother became very agitated.

"What are you doing?" she cried. "Where are you taking my son?"

"To the doctor's pen," they told her, "but don't worry."

Then one of the men told Salvatore to take a deep breath, and he puffed his chest out, and after a moment the man nodded and smiled. After that, another man inspected his scalp and his legs. It took a while until they had all been checked, but at last his mother was told they could all proceed.

"I will wait here until you return my son," she said. But they told her: "You have to wait for him in the Registry Room." And there was nothing else she could do.

They entered the Registry Room through a big double door. To Salvatore, it looked like a church—and indeed, the huge space, with its red-tiled floor, its side aisles, its soaring walls and high, barrel-vaulted ceiling, exactly copied the Roman basilica churches to be found all over Italy. About twenty feet above their heads, an iron balcony ran round the walls, and there were officials observing them from up there too. At the far end there was a row of fourteen desks, in front of which there were long lines of people snaking back and forth between dividing rails, but there was also quite a crowd of people waiting to join the lines.

They looked around, but there was no sign of Paolo. Nobody said anything.

Nearby they saw a man they had spoken to on the ship. He was a schoolmaster, a man of education. Seeing them, he smiled and came over, and Concetta told him what had happened to Paolo.

"It's just a cough that he has," she said. "It's nothing. Why have they taken him?"

"Do not worry, Signora Caruso," replied the schoolmaster. "They have a hospital here."

"A hospital?" His mother looked horrified. Like most of the women in their village, she believed that once you went into hospital, you never came out.

"It's different in America," said the schoolmaster. "They cure people. They let you out after a week or two."

Concetta was still doubtful. She shook her head. "If Paolo is sent back," she began, "he cannot go alone . . ."

Salvatore was thinking that it wouldn't be much fun in America without Paolo. "If Paolo has to go home, can I go with him?" he said.

His mother let out a cry, and clasped her breast. "Now my youngest son wants to desert his family?" she screamed. "Has he no love for his own mother?"

"No, no, signora." The schoolmaster was soothing. "He is a little boy." But his mother had turned her face away from Salvatore.

"Look!" cried Anna.

It was Paolo, with Giuseppe and their father.

"We waited for him," Giovanni Caruso explained to his wife.

Paolo was looking pleased with himself. "I had three doctors," he said proudly. "They made me breathe in, and cough, and they looked down my throat. And two of them listened to my chest and another to my back."

"You are safe, then?" cried his mother. "They have not taken you away?" She clasped him to her bosom, held him close, then released him and crossed herself. "Where is Luigi?" she asked.

Giovanni Caruso shrugged. "I don't know. He got separated from us."

Salvatore knew what had happened. The doctors from the madhouse were questioning Uncle Luigi. But he didn't say anything.

The family joined the line in front of the desks. It took a long time before they reached the head of the line, and there was still no sign of Uncle Luigi, but finally they were approaching the big desks where the officials were waiting, some seated, others standing close behind.

"The men behind are the interpreters," his father whispered. "They can speak all the languages of the world."

When they reached the desk, the man addressed Giovanni Caruso in Neapolitan, which anyone from the Mezzogiorno could understand.

Checking their names against the manifest, he smiled. "Caruso. At least the ship's purser could get your name right. Sometimes they mangle them terribly." He grinned. "We have to follow what's on the ship's manifest, you know. Are you all here?"

"Except my brother-in-law. I don't know where he is."

"He's not named Caruso?"

"No."

"I'm only interested in Caruso." The man asked a few questions, and seemed satisfied with the answers. Had they paid for their own passage? Yes. "And have you a job in America?"

"No," Salvatore heard his father answer firmly.

Salvatore knew about this. Giovanni Caruso had warned his whole family. Although their Uncle Francesco had found work for him, none of them must say that he had a job, or the men at Ellis Island would send him back. There were two reasons for this strange rule, he explained. The first was that the United States wanted men who were anxious to take any job they could find. The second was to discourage an illicit trade. For there were *padroni* who promised jobs, paid people's passage, and even traveled with the immigrants on the ship—though the *padrone* was in first or second class, of course. Foolish people trusted the *padrone* because he was a fellow Italian. He'd be waiting for them in the park near the docks, and take them to lodgings. And before long the new arrivals were in his power, trapped like slaves, and fleeced of all they had.

Satisfied with his inquiries, the man at the desk was waving them through.

"Welcome to America, Signor Caruso." He smiled. "Good luck."

They passed through a turnstile, down a flight of stairs, and then into the baggage room. Here they were given a box lunch and a bag of fresh fruit. They found their suitcases and the big wooden trunk. Nothing had been stolen. Salvatore watched as his father and Giuseppe started to put the trunk and cases on a trolley. They were told that they could have them delivered free to any address in the city, but Concetta was so relieved that they hadn't already been stolen that she wouldn't let them out of her sight again.

She was still looking about anxiously for Uncle Luigi, but since Salvatore knew he wouldn't be coming, he didn't bother.

Then, suddenly, his mother started crying out.

"Luigi! Luigi! We're here. Over here." She was waving excitedly. And sure enough, at the far end of the room, Salvatore saw his uncle coming toward them. He was smiling.

"Uncle Luigi!" Salvatore started running toward him. His uncle was carrying his suitcase. He scooped Salvatore up in his free arm and carried him back to his sister.

"Where were you?" she asked. "We couldn't see you."

Uncle Luigi put Salvatore down. "I came through before you. I've been waiting here ten minutes."

"Thanks be to God," she cried.

But Salvatore was even more excited. "They let you into America, Uncle Luigi. They let you in after all."

"Certainly they let me in. Why shouldn't they let me in?"

"Because you're crazy. They send all the lunatics back."

"What's this? You're calling me a lunatic?" His uncle slapped Salvatore's face. "Is this a way to talk to your uncle?" He turned to Concetta. "Is this how you bring your children up?"

"Salvatore!" cried his mother. "What are you saying?"

Hot tears came to Salvatore's eyes. "It's true. They put a cross on the lunatics, and the doctors from the madhouse question them, and send them home," he protested.

Uncle Luigi raised his hand again.

"Enough," said his mother, while Salvatore buried his face in her skirt. "Luigi, help Giovanni with the suitcases. As if we hadn't enough troubles in the world. *Poverino*, he doesn't know what he is saying."

Minutes later, when Salvatore was beside his father, he whimpered, "Uncle Luigi hit me."

But his father gave him no comfort.

"It's your own fault," he said. "That will teach you to keep a secret."

۞1907۞

It was just before noon on October 17 when the telephone rang. The butler answered. Then he came to inform Rose that her husband needed to speak to her.

"Tell him I'll be down in a minute," she said. She was fastening her pearl choker. It looked elegant with her gray silk dress.

Much as she loved William, she'd rather that he hadn't called just then. He ought to have remembered she'd be busy. For this was the day of the month when she took his grandmother out for a drive.

Taking old Hetty Master out once a month might be a duty, but Rose also found it a pleasure. Hetty was almost ninety now, but her mind was still sharp as a razor. She sometimes went out in her own carriage, but she liked to be taken out too, and there was never any shortage of things to talk about. She read the newspapers every day, and once Rose had brought her up to date with the latest doings of the children, Hetty would be sure to ask her sharp questions about the relative views of the Pulitzer newspapers or those of Mr. Hearst, which Rose often had some trouble in answering.

It was also very agreeable for the family—and her ambitions for them—to have such a splendid figure in the background.

Sometimes, on the pretext that it might entertain the old lady, she would bring society friends with her on these monthly expeditions. Then the friends, having seen inside the fine old house on Gramercy Park, could not only marvel at how sharp Mrs. Master was—which reminded them that Rose's own children inherited good brains from every side— but also, at Rose's gentle prompting, hear the old lady reminisce about the days when the opera was still just down the street on Irving Place and the Master family had one of the few boxes there. Newer money hadn't been able to get those boxes, despite the huge sums it was ready to pay. Vanderbilts, Jay Gould, even J. P. Morgan himself, had all been unsuccessful— which had caused them to set up the new Metropolitan Opera House where everyone went now. But the Masters had always had a box at Irving Place. That told you everything.

"And didn't your husband leave the Union Club?" Rose would prompt.

"I always liked the Union Club," Hetty would say. "I don't know why people left it."

"They said it was letting in too many of the wrong sort," Rose would remind her. "That's when they set up the Knickerbocker Club," she'd explain to her guests, "where my father-in-law's a member now."

"There was nothing wrong," old Mrs. Master would repeat, "with the Union."

Anyway, it was time to put on her coat and go out. Rose hoped her husband wasn't going to delay her. Downstairs, the butler handed her the telephone.

"What is it, dear?" she said.

"Just thought I'd call. Things are a little rough down here, Rose."

"In what way, dear?"

"I don't exactly know yet. I don't like the look of the market."

"I'm sure it will be all right, William. Remember what happened in March."

There had been some anxious days that spring. After a period of easy credit, it had suddenly emerged that several significant companies were in trouble. Then an earthquake had hit California, there had been panic selling in the market, and credit had become tight. The trouble had subsided, but all through the summer while she and the children were at Newport, rumbles had come up from the city as the market went up and down uncertainly.

She knew William took risks—plenty of people did—and this was not the first time her husband had suffered an attack of nerves; she didn't suppose it would be the last, either.

"We'll talk about it tonight," she said. "I have to take your grandmother out now."

She was wearing a hat with an ostrich feather round the brim, and a coat trimmed with fox fur as she stepped out of the house on Fifty-fourth Street. She had done very well in finding that house. It stood between Fifth and Madison, a little closer to the latter, just a few blocks below Central Park therefore, and close to the great mansions of the Vanderbilts on Fifth. But as it happened, the side streets here were even better than the avenue.

She'd sensed it at the time she was looking. The character of Fifth was about to change—not further up along the park, but here, at the great fashionable intersection of thoroughfares. And sure enough, within a few brief years of their purchase, the change had come.

Hotels. The St. Regis and the Gotham. Splendid hotels, to be sure, but hotels all the same, on Fifth at Fifty-fifth. Now a commercial building was going up on the block above. Rumor said that Cartier, the Paris jewelry firm, intended to be there. Nothing could be more elegant, but it was not a private house. The side streets were another matter, though; they would remain as residences.

A few doors down lived the Moore family. He was a rich lawyer, and they had a fine, five-story limestone townhouse, three classical windows wide, with a central entrance between railings and lamps, and a carved stone balcony at the *piano nobile* floor. The Master house was one of several big brownstones in the same block, with steps coming down over the stoop. Not so handsome, certainly, but impressive enough.

Rose kept a careful eye on the Moore household, using it as a yardstick. The Moores had nine servants in the house. William and Rose had six— a Scottish butler, an English nanny, the rest of the domestic staff being Irish. Twice a week, the children went across Central Park to Durland's Riding Academy on West Sixty-sixth. It was with a sense of general satisfaction, therefore, that she started down the steps to the street.

If she had only known what old Mrs. Hetty Master had in store for her that day, she would have gone straight back into her house.

Instead of which, she smiled. For in front of her now, gleaming like the

chariot of Apollo, was a new possession that marked the family out from
even the richest in New York. As the chauffeur held the door for her, she
stepped in.

"This is nothing to do with me," she would exclaim with a laugh. "It's
my husband's little madness." His insane extravagance, certainly.

To say that William Master was a fanatic for the motor car would have
been an understatement. The last twenty years had seen huge changes in
the city: the quieter cable-car lines up Third and Broadway, the recent
electrification of the El trains. Why, even the horse-drawn cabs were being
replaced with motorized cabs with taxi meters now. Private motor cars,
however, were for the rich.

Even so, there were quite a few makers to choose between, from the
Oldsmobile curved dash, the first mass-produced car, to the more expensive Cadillac, named after the aristocratic French founder of Detroit, and
the many models of Ford. William Master knew them all. He could discourse on the benefits of Ford's top-of-the-line Model K, which would set
you back an astonishing $2,800, over eight times the price of an Oldsmo-
bile, to the European rivalry of Mercedes and Benz on the racing circuits.
That spring, he had become highly excited about the news coming from
Britain.

"The new Rolls-Royce is out—Claude Johnson's been testing it up in
Scotland, and the results are astonishing. *Autocar* says it's the best car in
the world. And it's so silent, Johnson's called his own car the Silver Ghost.
There's only a handful been produced so far, but everyone's going to want
one. Well," he'd smiled, "those that can afford it."

"What does it cost?"

"Well, Rolls-Royce sells you the chassis and engine. I guess that's
around a thousand British pounds. Then you order your own custom
bodywork from the coachbuilder—that's another hundred or so. There
are other things besides. Maybe twelve hundred pounds."

"How many dollars to the pound, William?"

"A pound is four dollars and eighty-six cents."

"That's six thousand dollars! Nobody's going to pay that," she cried.

William had said nothing. Last week it had arrived at the docks.

"I had mine done like Johnson's: silver paint, silver-plated fittings.
Johnson had green leather seats, but I went for red. I'm calling mine the
Silver Ghost, too. Isn't she handsome?"

She was indeed. For the rest of that week, William and the chauffeur drove the car together. Yesterday was the first day the chauffeur had been allowed to drive it alone. And today Rose sat in it, feeling like a duchess, as she was driven down Fifth to Gramercy Park.

When she got to the house, Hetty Master was waiting. She inspected the car with interest, asked what it cost, and said, "I don't approve." But she got in happily enough. Sometimes she liked to include her friend Mary O'Donnell on these outings, but today she was alone.

Few people could enjoy getting old, but insofar as it was possible, Hetty Master did so.

She was a rich old woman in the full possession of her faculties. Her family loved her and lived nearby. She said and did what she liked. She could indulge a few mannerisms which, when she was younger, it had been wiser to keep in check. She could even, to amuse herself, cultivate some new ones.

Though Hetty had never been so interested in the social world herself, and she was certainly less conservative than Rose, she understood the younger woman's ambition and respected her. She was also not above teasing Rose, once in a while.

"Where shall we drive to?" Rose inquired.

"I'll tell you as we go," the intrepid old lady answered. "First we'll pick up Lily."

Rose knew better than to ask too many questions, and as they went back up Fifth, it was Hetty who led the conversation. From Twentieth to Thirtieth, she wanted to know all about the children. At Thirtieth, she remarked that the car was certainly very comfortable, but much too expensive, and that she'd have to tell young William that he was too extravagant. Only when they reached Thirty-fourth did Rose interrupt her. And when she did, it was to groan.

"Even after ten years," she now declared, waving her gloved hand toward a sumptuous building, "when I think of the scandal, and my poor, dear Mrs. Astor, I can't bear to look at it. Can you?"

For they were passing the Waldorf-Astoria Hotel.

❖

There were several Astor wives of course, but throughout Rose's child-hood and youth, by common consent, and whatever her official title might have been, it was Caroline Schermerhorn Astor who had been *the* Mrs. Astor. The divine Mrs. Astor. Rose's heroine, mentor and friend.

She was very rich indeed. That went without saying. She and her husband had occupied one of two huge Astor mansions on the site. But if the Astor family had become rich and established enough to assume New York's social leadership, Caroline, through her Dutch Schermerhorn ancestors who went back to the founding of the city, could claim it as a birthright. And with all this power at her disposal, Mrs. Astor had undertaken a labor worthy of Hercules. She was going to polish New York's upper class.

By chance she had a helper, who encouraged her to do it. Mr. Ward McAllister, a Southern gentleman who'd married money and toured Europe to observe its aristocratic manners, devoted his life to these things. He declared Mrs. Astor, who was short, swarthy and somewhat plump, to be his inspiration, and together they set about giving New York a higher social tone.

Not that America was a stranger to class. Boston, Philadelphia and other fine cities, including New York, were trying to establish a more permanent order by compiling Social Registers. In New York, the ancient Dutch landowners and old English merchants with their boxes at the Academy of Music had known how to be snobbish. When Mr. A. T. Stewart, the store owner, had made his fortune and built a mansion on Fifth, they didn't think he was a gentleman, and ignored him so cruelly that he left in despair.

But New York had a particular problem: it had become the big attraction.

With its banks, and its transatlantic connections, it was so much the money center of the continent that every big interest needed to have an office there. Copper and silver magnates, railroad owners, oilmen like Rockefeller from Pittsburgh, steel magnates like Carnegie, and coal barons like Frick, from the Midwest and the South and even California, they were all flocking to New York. Their fortunes were staggering, and they could do anything they wanted.

Yet surely, Mrs. Astor and her mentor argued, money alone was not enough. Old New York had always been about money, but it was not without grace. Money had to be directed, tamed, civilized. And who was to do that, if not the old guard? At the apex of society, therefore, there needed to be a cadre of the best people, the old money crowd, who would let in the new-money families slowly, one by one, after a period of exclusion during which they must show themselves worthy. McAllister set the opening barrier at three generations. In short, it was what the English House of Lords had been doing for centuries.

Exceptions could be made. The Vanderbilts were new, and the old Commodore, who had a fouler mouth than a bargee, never gave a damn about society. But the next generation was very rich, and very determined, and even before they'd got a duke in the family, they'd been let in. One had to be practical.

Yet who was to select this inner circle? Ward McAllister already led a committee of the region's greatest gentlemen that decided who was eligible to attend the yearly Patriarchs' Ball. Once he had Mrs. Astor beside him, she became the queen of the event and gave the list her regal stamp. And how many guests should there be? It varied, but not more than four hundred. That, McAllister declared, was the total number of people in the great metropolis who would not feel or look awkward in a ballroom. If one considered the thousands of people in New York who were well accustomed to dances, and who had probably been to as many grand resorts as McAllister, this last claim might have seemed a little specialized. But it pleased Mr. McAllister, and so four hundred it was.

It had to be said that Mrs. Astor's lists were quite remarkable for their consistency. There were the newer families of massive wealth, of course, from the Astors themselves to the most recent Vanderbilts. There were the solid old-money families of Otis, Havemeyer and Morgan, and eighteenth-century gentry like Rutherfurd and Jay. But sprinkled all over the list were great names, still rich, and going back to the region's seventeenth-century beginnings: Van Rensselaer, Stuyvesant, Winthrop, Livingston, Beekman, Roosevelt. If Mrs. Astor wanted to keep the quiet wealth of old New York as the example of how things should be done, then you'd have to acknowledge she'd pulled it off.

When Rose met her future husband William, the first thing she had discovered, even before his heaven-sent second name, was that the old-money Masters were on Mrs. Astor's list. And when after her marriage, old Mrs. Astor had taken her up, Rose became a willing acolyte. Many an afternoon she had sat at her feet, to learn the finer points of social etiquette.

Only one of these rules had caused her any difficulty.

"Mrs. Astor says," she'd told William, "that one should always arrive at the opera after the performance has started, and leave before it ends."

It was an interesting idea, imported from Old Europe, where the best people went to the opera to be seen. Presumably, if the artists ever had the good fortune to perform for an audience composed entirely of aristocrats, there would be a mass exodus just before the end, leaving them to conclude their opera to a silent and empty house—and thus, most conveniently, obviate the tiresome need for curtain calls and flowers.

"I'll be damned if I'm going to miss the overture and the finale when I've paid good money for it," her husband had quite reasonably replied. He might have added that it was an insult to the music, the artists and the rest of the audience. But he had wit enough to know that this was part of the point. Aristocrats were supposed to be above the music, and care not a bean for the feelings of the artists or the audience. "You can go," he'd told her, "but I'm staying."

And indeed, Rose might have hesitated to observe this convention herself if she hadn't felt a loyalty to Mrs. Astor.

She and William found a compromise, however. Rose would leave just before the end of the opera and wait in the carriage a few yards down the street so that, as soon as William came to join her, they could get away quickly from the vehicles of the less instructed.

❖

"When I think," she now remarked to Hetty Master, "of the way Mrs. Astor was treated, by her own family, it just makes my blood boil."

It was Mrs. Astor's young nephew who was the culprit. He'd lived in the house next door. And because his father had died, and he could claim, technically, that he was the head of the family, he had demanded that it was his wife who should now be called Mrs. Astor, and that Caroline must revert to the less senior appellation of Mrs. William Astor.

"Of course," Rose said, "he was never a gentleman. He even wrote historical novels."

Anyway, Mrs. Astor had quite rightly refused. Age and reputation should be given their due. So in a huff, young Astor had left for England, and not returned. He'd even become a British citizen, like the turncoat he was. For a man to let his daughter marry an English aristocrat was one thing, in Rose's opinion, but to become an Englishman himself was quite another.

"They tell me he lives in a castle now," Hetty Master remarked. It was quite true. He'd bought Hever Castle, in Kent, the childhood home of Anne Boleyn. "Perhaps he'll write another novel there," she added.

But he'd taken his revenge on his aunt all the same. He'd turned his former New York house into a hotel, thirteen stories high. It towered over hers, destroying all her privacy. He called it the Waldorf.

Four years later she'd admitted defeat and moved uptown. The Astor family rebuilt her house as a second hotel, the Astoria, and soon the two had been joined, by the gorgeous Peacock Alley, into a single establishment. Rose still refused to set foot in it.

"Mrs. Astor deserves a statue in her honor," Rose stated with finality.

There was a pause.

"They say," said Hetty, "that she's entirely demented nowadays."

"She's not well," Rose conceded.

"Well, I hear she's demented," said Hetty, inexorably.

The Rolls-Royce passed into the Forties. The old reservoir was no longer in use now, and they were building a magnificent new public library on the site. Everyone in the family knew that this was where Frank had proposed to Hetty, and Rose maintained a reverent silence while Hetty gazed at it as they passed. Soon St. Patrick's loomed ahead on their right. As they reached the Fifties, and the new hotels rose into the sky by the Vanderbilt mansions, Hetty observed that everything in the city seemed to be getting very tall. "I'm surprised you like living up here with all these hotels," she said.

"We're in a side street," said Rose.

"I know," said Hetty. "All the same . . ." At her request, they went west across Fifty-seventh Street. This took them past the fine concert hall that Mr. Carnegie, the steel magnate, had financed. The new millionaires might not always be elegant, but they certainly knew how to support the arts. "I was at the opening gala," Hetty reminded her. "Tchaikovsky himself conducted."

Soon after that, they were bowling up Central Park West. It was looking increasingly handsome these days. The Dakota had company: its sleeker sister, the Langham, was now on the next block up. Other splendid buildings also stared across the park.

At the Dakota, Lily de Chantal was already waiting downstairs. The years had been good to her; she still looked handsome. The two women embraced, and sat in the back seat together, while Rose moved to the front beside the chauffeur.

"We'll go to Riverside Drive first," said Hetty.

The Upper West Side might not be so fashionable, but it had many fine streets. On West End Avenue, there were houses with wide reception halls, splendid curving staircases, and music rooms or libraries. Some of the apartment buildings were truly magnificent—in one place, an exquisite facade that might have come from gothic Flanders, only stacked twice as high; in another, a huge, rusticated, red-brick block, big as a castle, and crowned with the bulbous mansards of France's belle époque. The people who lived there—doctors, professors, owners of middle-sized businesses—paid a lot less than the people across the park, and lived very well indeed. But it was as they came to the high and magnificent sweep of Riverside Drive above the Hudson, that Hetty exclaimed: "There. That's what I wanted to see."

The sight before them, it had to be said, was quite extraordinary. The house had only just been completed. Its magnificent grounds occupied an entire block, and overlooked the Hudson far below.

It was a French Renaissance chateau, built in limestone, with turrets, and it contained seventy-five rooms. Even the biggest mansions of Fifth, because of their cramped sites, looked bourgeois by comparison. Its owner, Mr. Charles Schwab, having the boldness and intelligence to realize that the city's greatest asset was the magnificent view over the Hudson River, and ignoring timid fashion entirely, had, like a true prince, built his mansion where he liked. They might not know it, but he had left them—Astors, Vanderbilts, everyone, save maybe Pierpont Morgan—far behind. His former boss and partner, Andrew Carnegie, said it all. "Have you seen Charlie's place? Makes mine look like a shack."

They stopped the Rolls for several minutes in front of the gateway to admire the place. Rose had to confess that, West Side or not, it was something to talk about.

"Now," Hetty announced, "we'll go up to Columbia University." She smiled. "We're going to pay a call on young Mr. Keller."

"Mr. Keller?" Rose's face fell.

"Why yes, dear. My friend Theodore Keller's son. He's expecting us."

"Oh," said Rose. And she looked thoughtful. She did not want to see Mr. Keller, of Columbia. She did not want to see him at all.

The journey up Riverside Drive was beautiful. They passed several people on bicycles. For it was all the rage these days to ride up to the great mausoleum over the Hudson where Ulysses Grant and his wife were now entombed.

"I wish I could do that," Hetty remarked.

Before getting that far, they turned east, passed by the site where the mighty Anglican cathedral of St. John the Divine was arising, and came to the campus.

Columbia University was already a college of some antiquity. Having begun its life downtown in the mid-eighteenth century, as the mainly Anglican King's College, it had later changed its name, relocated to mid-town, and only a decade ago moved once more, to the splendid site at 115th and Broadway. The campus was already handsome; indeed, the broad dome of the Low Library that presided over it could have graced Harvard or Yale.

It was now, as they pulled up, that Rose tried the only ploy she could think of.

"I'll wait for you in the car," she declared, and indicated to the chauffeur that he should escort the two old ladies in. But it was no use.

"Oh you can't do that, dear," said Hetty. "He knows you're bringing us. That would seem awfully rude."

So a few minutes later, she found herself in the pleasant office of an athletic man in his late twenties, with dark brown hair and bright blue eyes, who had placed three armchairs before his desk, and was clearly delighted to see them.

"Welcome to my lair," said Mr. Edmund Keller with a pleasant smile. There were bookshelves round the walls, a print of the *Mona Lisa*, and a photograph of Niagara Falls, taken by his father. A glance at the books revealed that he was a classical scholar and historian. Rose allowed herself to be introduced, then tactfully kept silent.

"Lily and I saw your father only the other day," Hetty declared. "He stopped round at my house for tea."

Rose let them chatter. She remembered that Theodore Keller lived on East Nineteenth Street, only a stone's throw from Gramercy Park, and she knew of course that old Frank Master had been the photographer's patron. And that was all well and good. But his son was another matter entirely. She'd heard what kind of character young Mr. Edmund Keller was, and she'd heard it from an unimpeachable source. To be exact, from no less a person than the president of Columbia University himself.

Nicholas Murray Butler was a very impressive man. He was a distinguished academic, internationalist and political figure. President Theodore Roosevelt called him a friend, and his views were as sound as they were conservative. Everybody said he was doing great things with Columbia. So if he had suspicions about young Mr. Keller, you could be sure it was for a very good reason.

She'd met Mr. Butler at a gala, and they'd chatted quite a while. She always took care to keep informed about everything that was going on in the city, so she'd listened carefully as he told her about the improvements he was making up at the university. They'd got along rather well. When she asked him if he was satisfied with the students applying, he'd answered yes, before adding in a low voice: "Perhaps too many Jews, though."

Rose hadn't anything against Jews herself. Some of the most notable men in New York—people like the great banker Schiff, whom even Morgan held in high regard—were Jewish and one met them socially. The old German Jewish families that lived on the Upper West Side, or in the pleasant suburb of Harlem now, were often highly respectable.

Of course, the masses of poor Jews who had flooded into the Lower East Side during the last quarter-century were quite another matter. One felt sorry for them, naturally—they'd been fleeing those terrible pogroms in Russia and places like that. But such people. She'd seen them, of course, in that noisy, bustling quarter, and she couldn't imagine that they would provide the genteel young men that Mr. Nicholas Murray Butler would want.

"Don't misunderstand me," he'd continued. "I have distinguished Jewish professors, and we take in plenty of Jewish boys. But I have to limit the numbers, or they'll swamp the place."

It was then, trying to think of something else to say, and remembering she'd heard that Theodore Keller's son was teaching at Columbia, that she'd mentioned his name. And she'd been quite surprised when Butler's brow had darkened.

"You know him?" he'd asked.

"Not personally."

"Hmm." He'd hesitated. "He is entitled to his opinions, of course, but I may have some political differences with him."

"Oh? Serious ones?"

Again he'd paused. "Well, I go only by things he has said in public, but I have the impression—no, I must say that I believe—that Edmund Keller's views are socialistic."

Rose Master did not know a great deal about socialists. One heard about them, of course, in places like Russia, and even in more familiar European countries, too. Socialists, communists, anarchists, revolutionaries. People who had no respect for private property. People without roots, or morals. She remembered something a British politician had told her at a dinner party, when she and William had made their visit to London. "These people would take away every individual freedom we have. They call us capitalists, whatever that may mean, and say our capitalism is evil. That is their excuse for destroying everything we cherish. If they had their way we'd become servants of an all-embracing state, like the oriental empire of Genghis Khan. Moreover, because they believe they are right, they will do anything—they will create strikes, they will kill, and they will lie, they will always lie—to achieve their ends."

"A socialist. That's terrible," she'd said to Mr. Nicholas Murray Butler.

"I hope I'm mistaken," he'd said, "but I believe his opinions tend that way."

"What will you do?"

"Columbia is a university, Mrs. Master. I'm not a policeman. But I keep an eye on him."

So now, as Hetty and Lily chatted to the seemingly pleasant young man, Rose watched him also, as carefully as one might watch an alligator or a snake.

By and by, Hetty remarked that Rose had brought them in a Rolls-Royce. Rose observed Keller intently now; the thought of such a capitalist luxury would surely bring a glint of rage to his eye.

"Rolls-Royce?" He was looking straight at her. His eyes were very blue, intense. "Which model?"

"My husband calls it a Silver Ghost," she answered reluctantly, watching him more closely than ever.

But his face lit up with joy.

"The Silver Ghost? That's just been tested? Side valve? Six cylinders, three and three? A trembler coil with a magneto as well?" He had almost jumped up from his desk. "A masterpiece. However did you get it so soon? Oh, I should love to see that. May I see it?"

"You can see it when you escort us down," said Hetty pleasantly.

"Well," added Lily, "it seems we've made your day."

"You have," he answered, with charming frankness.

But Rose wasn't fooled. She remembered what she'd been told. They lie. They always lie.

Ten minutes later, they were down in the street. To the great amusement of the two old ladies, Mr. Keller even had the chauffeur open the hood so he could inspect the engine. Once he had finished, he beamed at them all, before saying farewell.

"Now, the next time you come to see your father, you must promise to look in to see me, too," Hetty told him. "It's only up the street."

"Certainly I will," he replied.

"Now, dear," the old lady turned to Rose, "you'd better give Mr. Keller your card so that he can call upon you too. I'm sure William would be delighted to take him out in the car. They can talk about the engine."

"That's very kind," said Keller. "I'd enjoy that."

Rose's face turned to stone. No doubt you would, she thought. But if Edmund Keller with his socialist ideas supposed he was going to insinuate himself into her house, he was mistaken.

"I haven't a card with me," she heroically lied. "But I will send one," she added, without enthusiasm.

"Don't worry," said Hetty. From her small handbag, she took one of her own cards, together with a little silver pencil, and wrote Rose's address on the back. "It's easy to find. Just around the corner from the Gotham Hotel."

"Thank you. I'll call," said Keller, as they drove off.

"Well," said Hetty, "wasn't that nice?"

⁂

Early that evening, when William got home, Rose told him all about it. He listened and nodded, but seemed preoccupied. Then he told the butler to bring him a large whiskey.

"It's been a pretty bad day on the markets," he said.

"I'm sorry, dear." She smiled understandingly. "I'm sure it'll get better . . ."

"Maybe." He frowned, drank his whiskey, and went upstairs to see the children. At dinner, she brought the subject of Keller up again, and he said, "I could just take him out in the car, and get it over with." But that wasn't what she wanted. She was determined that Mr. Keller should never darken her door. At the end of dinner, William said he was tired and went off to bed.

So she could only sigh. She'd have to try and deal with Keller herself.

✧

On Friday afternoon, William Vandyck Master entered Trinity Church, Wall Street. He sat down in one of the pews near the back. Then he started to pray.

Trinity was a fine church. Thanks to its land endowments back in the seventeenth century, the church still owned much of the area. It was rich, and it had used its money wisely and well. It had founded numerous other churches in the growing city, while the Trinity vestry had been the first to provide education for the city's Negro population at a time when many other congregations disapproved. And for all its wealth, the interior of the church retained a pleasant simplicity. There was a single stained-glass window at the east end; all the other windows were plain, and bathed the interior in a soft light. The walls were wood-paneled. It almost reminded William of a library, or a club—but if so, a club of which the kindly Deity was certainly a member.

William wasn't very religious. He went to church; he supported the vicar. It was what you did. He didn't pray much—just in church on Sundays, really. But although it was only Friday, he was trying to pray today. For he was very much afraid.

He was about to lose everything he had.

When you thought about it, William considered, there were only two ways to make a lot of money on Wall Street. The first was the more conservative. You persuaded people to pay you to manage their money, or even just to move it, from one place to another. That was the banker's way. If the sums were large enough—if you could persuade a government, for instance, to put its funds in your hands—then the fee, or the tiny percentage on the transaction you took, could amount to a fortune.

The second way was to gamble.

Of course, gambling with only your own money was unlikely to get you very far. You needed to borrow huge sums. Borrow a million, make ten percent, return it with a little interest, and you'd just made nearly a hundred thousand. And all the transactions that you might undertake, the complex bets that you placed on the future price of this or that, the hedging of positions, the science and the art still came down to this one and only fundamental: you were placing bets with someone else's money.

In the process, naturally, you might lose their money from time to time. And so long as they didn't know you'd lost their money, you should be able to string them along, and borrow some more, and recoup it. But at some point—perhaps far off, or if there was a panic, horribly soon— you would have to pay them back.

William Vandyck Master couldn't pay. He'd done the numbers. His obligations exceeded his assets. And now that a panic had started, every- one wanted their money. He was wiped out.

He hadn't told Rose. There wasn't much point. Anyway, he couldn't. So there was just himself and God, now, to discuss the position. And he was wondering whether, by any chance, God would care to bail him out.

If only he'd done what his father wanted. William knew he'd disap- pointed him. Tom Master's dream had always been that his son would be a banker. A real banker. And when Tom Master said a real banker, William knew that his father had only one man in mind.

J. P. Morgan. The mighty Pierpont. His father's hero. Since the days when he'd started reorganizing the railroads, the great banker had moved into shipping, mining, all kinds of industrial production. When he put together the great combination that was U.S. Steel, it became the mighti- est industrial corporation ever known to man. The power of the House of Morgan was huge, and through its board directorships, it controlled industries worth far over a billion dollars.

Morgan's reach was global. He ruled, and lived, like a king. And was feared like a king as well. Perhaps more than a king. Perhaps a god. Jupiter, the men on Wall Street called him.

When William was still at Harvard, Tom Master had managed to get him an interview with the great man. Morgan's reputation was fearsome and William had been pretty terrified, but Morgan had sent word that he should come to his house on Thirty-sixth Street in the evening, and when he'd been ushered into the great man's presence, he'd found the banker in a gentle mood.

Morgan was sitting at a long table. The curtains were drawn, the lamps lit. His tall frame, leonine head and bulbous nose were just as William had expected. The angry stare of his eyes was legendary, yet alone in his home, his eyes seemed almost soft. One end of the table was piled with ancient books. At the other end, still in its wrapping, a marble classical head, and, and, on a dark cloth, a collection of gemstones—sapphires, rubies and opals—that glowed softly in the lamplight. Open in the middle of the table was an illuminated medieval manuscript that the great man had just been inspecting.

What did Morgan look like, William wondered: an ogre in his den? A pirate surrounded by his treasure? A Renaissance prince, a Medici? Or something more Celtic, rich and strange: Merlin the magician, perhaps?

"Look at this," he invited young William.

William looked down at the illuminated page. The colors were rich. The gold leaf shone mystically.

"It's beautiful, sir." He'd heard that Morgan spent a good part of the bank's huge profits buying such things.

"It is," Morgan murmured, then turned his attention away from the treasure to his guest. "We'll sit down." He motioned William toward a pair of leather armchairs by the fire. As soon as they were seated he began. "Your father tells me you like machines."

"Yes, sir."

"Study engineering?"

"It's a hobby."

"Mathematics?" The eyes, like shuttered coal furnaces now, were resting on him.

"I like machines more than numbers."

"What else do you like?"

William hesitated. He wasn't sure. Morgan was watching him, not unkindly.

"If you've something specific, you can come to see me again," he said. And then he got up. The interview was over.

"Thank you, sir," said William, as he left the room.

"How did it go?" his father asked eagerly, on his return.

"He said I could come to see him again."

"He did? That's splendid, William. Splendid."

And in truth, William realized, the great man had been perfectly fair to him. It had taken Morgan rather less than half of one minute to see, with absolute clarity, that this young man had no idea what he wanted, no burning ambition, no particular talent, no achievement—in short, nothing whatsoever that could be useful to the Morgan bank. So he hadn't wasted any time. Come back, he had said, when you've something to offer. And he was right.

But to his father's chagrin, William had never gone back.

Several of his friends had been going into brokerage houses, others into trusts. "If Morgan takes you, he'll work you to death," they warned him. And in any case, he'd known in his heart that Morgan wouldn't take him. There was no reason why he should.

Months had passed, and he'd quietly let the matter slide. His father had been disappointed, but had said nothing.

And in the years that followed, he hadn't done so badly. He was a partner in a brokerage, nowadays. He speculated a little, but the biggest money he'd made came from his partnership in a trust.

Trusts were a way to make a lot of money. Originally, they were set up to take care of the funds for old-money families like the Masters. When grandfather made a will, with a nice big trust, the money would be managed for the family until it was all paid out. Depending on the terms of the trust, that could be many years. So trust companies were sound, conservative—trustworthy, in other words. At least, that was the idea.

But then some bright young fellows discovered that there was a legal loophole in these arrangements. The trust companies could also take in money, and invest it as they liked. Behaving like a bank, but without any of the rules that restrained a proper bank, they would pay high interest rates to attract the extra funds, and then undertake the wildest speculations. In short, despite their respectable-sounding names, most of them were pirates. Proper bankers, men like his father, were suspicious of the trusts.

"What sort of cash balances do you fellows keep?" Tom Master had once asked him.

"Oh, quite enough," he'd said, which of course meant next to none.

"I met Pierpont Morgan at a reception the other day," his father had continued. "I asked him what advice he'd give to a young man in a trust. You know what he said? 'Get out.'"

Well, Pierpont Morgan was semiretired now. He spent a good deal of time supporting the Episcopal Church and its liturgy. He'd built a magnificent library next to his house to keep his fabulous collection of books and gems. Every year he went on his travels to Europe and returned with priceless treasures—old masters, Greek and Egyptian antiquities, medieval gold. Often as not, he just gave it straight to the Metropolitan Museum. His son Jack Morgan, a first-rate banker, but not so terrifying, was running the bank day to day.

The great man might despise him, but at least, William had been able to reflect, he had managed to prosper pretty well in recent years. The market had mostly been rising. The trust had made a fortune; the brokerage house, too. If you were making money, then you must be doing something right. They took in ever more money, pledged against the value of the stocks they held, and speculated some more with that. The higher you could build the house of cards, the better you did. Obviously.

He'd still been riding high when he read about the new Rolls-Royce. But even then, the cracks in the system had begun to appear. That spring, when the market had been shaken and credit had been tight, a number of the biggest men in American industry had come together to discuss the situation. Coal was represented by Frick, railroads by Harriman, oil by Rockefeller, banking by Schiff and the Morgans. They'd wanted to form a consortium to support the market. Jack Morgan had agreed, but old Pierpont had not, and the proposal had come to nothing.

All through the summer, William had watched as the market dithered, hoping it would strengthen, or at least send him a sign. Wasn't the market supposed to be wise? So people said, but William wasn't so sure. Sometimes, it seemed to him, the market was nothing more than an aggregate of individuals, like a great school of fish, feeding upon small hopes until some fright causes them all to swerve together. Amid all this doubt, the thought of the Rolls-Royce on its way to him had kept his spirits up. And when it was delivered, the solid magnificence of the thing seemed to say: No man who owns a Rolls-Royce can be in trouble.

How ironic then that the rotten timber that was about to bring the whole market crashing down should be the one with the most splendid name.

The Knickerbocker Trust. By the sound of its name, you'd have thought it was as solid as a rock. Knickerbocker meant tradition, his father's club, old money, old values. Well, by noon today, the word on the street was that the Knickerbocker was in trouble.

At three o'clock, the partners of William's trust had reached a terrible conclusion.

"If the Knickerbocker goes, it'll start a panic. Everyone'll want their money. The trusts will start going down like ninepins. Ours included." And that would only be the start of things.

After the meeting, he'd gone into his office and closed the door. He'd taken a piece of paper and tried to figure things out. What did he owe? He really wasn't sure, but more than he had. And what was he going to do about it? Nothing he could do.

Pray.

✣

That weekend, on Saturday, William Master took his wife and children out in the Rolls. They drove up into Westchester County. It was quite warm, and with the fall leaves turning to red and gold, it was a beautiful drive. They went up to Bedford, and had a picnic there. A perfect day.

On Sunday, of course, they all went to church. The service was all right. A bit insipid. The vicar was away, down at a liturgical conference in Virginia with the great men of the Episcopal Church, including J. P. Morgan. The curate gave a sermon on Hope.

That evening, he read to his children. For no particular reason, he chose the tale of Rip Van Winkle. As they came to the place where the ghostly Dutchmen play ninepins in the mountains over the Hudson, he could not help thinking of the terrible crash of financial ninepins that was probably coming on Wall Street, but his face gave nothing away. Let his family remember one last, happy weekend.

And that night, when Rose remarked that two of the wives she'd met at church had whispered that there was likely to be big trouble ahead in the market that week, he smiled and said: "I dare say it'll get sorted out."

Not much point in saying anything else.

✣

Sometimes William wondered if all things in the world were connected. But he hadn't thought about Alaska. He was in the brokerage house the next morning when he saw the message on the wires. It looked innocent enough. The Guggenheims, the mighty German Jewish mining family, were going to develop huge copper reserves in Alaska. A good thing, one might think. But when William saw it, he cried out: "It's all over."

It was some time since a small group of speculators had decided to corner the copper market. He knew the men. The copper supply was limited, and the price was soaring. There hadn't been a word about these damned Alaska mines. To buy the copper, they'd borrowed a fortune from the Knickerbocker Trust; but with huge new supplies from the Guggenheims in prospect, copper prices would fall through the floor. The corner, and the speculators, were surely bust.

It took just two hours for the price of copper to collapse. William went over to the trust offices. He'd no sooner walked through the door when one of the directors whispered to him, "Knickerbocker just asked for a loan, and was refused." This was it, then. Knickerbocker's credit was gone.

The market groaned. The market swooned. All afternoon stocks fell. William felt sure that the Knickerbocker Trust must fail now. And after that . . .

It was mid-afternoon when one of his partners came in with unexpected news.

"Morgan's going to try to save the trusts."

"Jack Morgan's away in London," William pointed out. "Hard to see what he can do from there."

"Not Jack. Old Pierpont. He took a private train up from Virginia. He's been here since last night."

"But he hates the trusts. Despises us all."

"Yes, but there's so much money tied up in them, he reckons there's no choice. If they fail, everything goes."

Was it a ray of hope? William doubted it. Even Jupiter with his thunderbolts could hardly remove this massive mountain of bad debt.

But it was the only hope on the horizon. That evening, when Rose asked him anxiously what was happening, he smiled bravely and told her: "Morgan's going to sort it out." No point in starting a panic in his own home. Anyway, he couldn't face it.

❖

On Tuesday morning, a crowd formed outside the offices of the Knickerbocker Trust. Soon they had to be formed into an orderly line by a policeman. They wanted news. They wanted reassurance. They wanted their money. Inside, Morgan's men were going through the books.

At lunchtime, William went for a walk down Broadway. As he came to Bowling Green, he passed the offices of the two great shipping lines, Cunard and the White Star. Continuing down to the waterside he stared across the harbor at Ellis Island.

How long would it be before he was as penniless as the poor devils who came in there every day? he wondered.

As poor as an Italian peasant? Well, not in absolute terms. His wife and children would be looked after by his parents, no doubt. Perhaps his grandmother would do something for them, too. But it wouldn't be easy. Most of her money was in a trust that went to Tom. Tom's two sisters were expecting their share of any inheritance, too. The Rolls-Royce would be gone. His wife's pearls. God knows what sort of address they'd be living at.

He wondered how Rose would take it. She loved him, in her way. But she'd married into a certain kind of life. That was the deal. Old money, with money. Take away the money and what sort of marriage would they have? He honestly didn't know. At least the Jewish refugees and the Italian peasants arriving at Ellis Island had been poor when they married each other. They had nowhere to go but up. In a way, they were free.

It was almost funny really, when you thought about it. All his life, he'd been rich. But he'd been living in a prison cell—in the great jail, called Expectation. And he couldn't get out of it.

Well, there was one way out. Maybe, when he'd tidied up his affairs as best he could, he'd go to the White Star Line and buy a passage to London. Say he was going on business. It needn't even be a first-class ticket. No one would know. Then, somewhere out in the Atlantic, when it was dark, he'd quietly jump off the ship. Not such a bad way to go. Wouldn't give anyone any trouble.

What sort of a life would he be leaving? Had he been happy? Not really. Did he like his house? Not so much. He loved his new Rolls-Royce—he was sure of that. But what did he love about it? The fact that it was expensive, the silver body, the red leather seats, the admiration and envy it evoked? No. It was the engine. That's what excited him. The way it worked, the beauty of it. He'd have been just as happy if he was a poor mechanic.

The man who built that Rolls-Royce was the lucky fellow, William considered. A fellow doing something he loved, and doing it supremely well.

Do I love what I do? he asked himself. Not much. Do I do it well? He was mediocre, at best. And right now, he had failed, completely and utterly. How did he feel? Ashamed, humiliated, probably unloved. And very, very afraid.

By the time he got back to Wall Street, the news was out. Morgan's men had concluded that the trust was past praying for. The Knickerbocker Trust had failed. Lines were already forming outside the other trusts, including his own. People were withdrawing their money.

The partners had already decided what to do if this happened. Pay out as slowly as possible. When he walked into his office, it was already under way. They would probably get through the afternoon, but after that? He had no idea. He watched the line. It was moving slowly but inexorably, like a river. Not even Pierpont Morgan could stop a river.

That evening at home, he smiled cheerfully through dinner with his family. Yes, there had been a little panic on Wall Street, he confessed to the children. They'd see it in the papers, and hear about it, but it would soon pass.

"The fundamentals of the market are good," he assured them all. "Indeed, this is probably an excellent time to buy."

✛

The next day, people were camping outside the trust offices by dawn, hoping to get their money out before the rest. Meanwhile, the trust partners were looking for cash. The moment they opened for business, they went to the brokers, calling in all their loans. When he walked into his brokerage house, his partners there told him: "We'll be lucky to get through the day. By tomorrow we'll be gone."

William went outside. There was nothing more to be done. He gazed sadly up at the sky. It was hard, and terrible. He turned, to walk to Bowling Green again, wanting to be alone.

But he had only gone a short way when one of the clerks from the trust caught up with him. The man was looking excited.

"Come quickly," he cried. "Oh, sir, rescue is at hand."

✛

President Theodore Roosevelt had reason to be suspicious of New York City. A decade ago, he'd labored to reform its corrupt police. He'd also witnessed the mighty industrial combinations that J. P. Morgan was building up—and he didn't like what he saw. Too much economic power was in too few hands, he believed. Elected governor of New York State, then chosen as vice president, the assassination of President McKinley had unexpectedly brought him, at the age of only forty-two, to the White House, where he had continued to speak against the might of Wall Street. For Pierpont Morgan himself, however, Roosevelt had a high regard.

In the early hours of that Wednesday, therefore, a remarkable thing had occurred. The government of the United States put the huge sum of twenty-five million dollars into the hands of Pierpont Morgan, with only one request:

"Do whatever you think best. But save us."

And now Jupiter, greatest of all the gods, began to fling his thunderbolts.

⁜

When William Master looked back on those days, it was like remembering a great battle: periods of waiting; moments of sudden excitement and confusion; and a few haunting images that would never leave his mind again. Using the government money, and raising even greater private sums by the sheer force of his personality, old Pierpont Morgan went to work. On that Wednesday, he began saving trusts. The next day he saved the brokerage houses on the New York Stock Exchange. On Friday, when Europe started withdrawing funds, and credit became so tight that Wall Street came to a halt, Morgan strode in person up to the Clearing House and had it issue its own scrip currency, so that money could flow. Yet perhaps the truest measure of his authority was seen that evening, when he summoned the clergy of New York to his house and told them: "You'll be preaching on Sunday. Here's what you have to say."

It took two weeks for Morgan to rescue the financial system. Along the way, when New York City declared it was also going broke, he rescued that too. In his final act, he called all the biggest bankers and trust men of Wall Street to meet him in his princely library, locked the doors, and refused to let them out until they did what was needed.

But the abiding image that remained in the mind of William Master came from Wall Street itself. It was on that first Friday. He was walking westward as he came to the street's main intersection. On his left, on the corner, number 23, the House of Morgan. Across from it, the splendid facade of the New York Stock Exchange. On his right, Federal Hall and, a short way up Nassau Street, the Clearing House. Ahead, only a hundred yards or so, was Broadway and Trinity Church. Here was the very center of American finance. This week, at least, it was the cockpit of the world.

And just at that moment the doors of number 23 opened, and out strode Morgan. The street was crowded. Millionaires and managers, clerks and messenger boys, they were all there milling about between the Stock Exchange and Federal Hall. There were brokers, whom Morgan considered too vulgar to mix with, but who had cheered his name to the roof of the Exchange when he saved them. There were trust men, whom he despised, but who camped outside his door to beg for favors. All manner of Wall Street fellows filled the narrow financial forum as the tall, burly banker in his high top hat strode out of his temple.

Jupiter looked neither right nor left. His eyes glowered as though lit by volcanic fires. His swollen, bulbous nose bulged from his face like a mountain from which his mustaches spread down like silver lava flows. Did Vulcan fashion his thunderbolts in there? Quite likely.

As he strode rapidly down the street, the crowds parted in front of him, as mortals before a deity. And so they should, thought William. Morgan might support his church, and like to sit with bishops, but when he descended into Wall Street from banking's Mount Olympus, he was above mortal men. Then, truly, Morgan was Jupiter, king of all the gods.

⁂

But alas, he was still a man. In the months that followed, one question was often asked: "Morgan will not always be with us. What'll we do then?"

Some argued that more regulation was needed, to stop the abuses that had led to the crisis. But William Master was sure this was a bad idea.

"Things got a little out of hand," he agreed. "But we don't need socialism. The banks can regulate themselves, as they do in London."

It would take six years before a Federal Reserve system with limited powers was instituted.

For William, however, life soon returned to normal. When his wife asked him, "Did we nearly lose everything?" he reassured her.

"I suppose if all the trusts had failed, Rose, then we should have failed too. But we were never really in trouble." It seemed to comfort her so much that, after a while, he almost believed it himself.

The first weekend in November, he took the Rolls-Royce out alone, for a fifty-mile drive. He thought of taking young Keller, too, but decided not to. If Rose had found out, it would only have annoyed her.

⁂

If the panic of 1907 was to change the life of young Salvatore Caruso, it was a small event the month before that he always remembered.

He had already dressed up. He was wearing the suit with long trousers that his older brother had worn before him. His white shirt was spotless.

He might be going to his first communion. But to everyone, except his mother, at least, the meeting today was more important even than that. So he was anxious to complete the errand as quickly as possible.

It had been his mother's idea to send him to the priest's house. Not their own parish priest, but the silver-haired old man who'd come to say Mass in their church the week before. And where did he live? In the Jewish quarter, of all places.

It wasn't far. You only had to cross the Bowery and you were in it—the Lower East Side's tenth and thirteenth wards, which ran across to the river just below the old German quarter. Its poor streets—around Division and Hester streets, through Delancey, and all the way up to Houston—housed small factories, varnish shops, ironworks and tenements which, for a generation now, had been filled to overflowing with the Jews of Eastern Europe. On Rivington Street, however, near the river, was a Catholic church.

Salvatore hadn't enjoyed the old man's sermon. It had been about Christ's temptation in the desert, when Christ had gone up to a mountain and the devil had told him to jump off, so that God could save him. But rightly, the priest reminded them, Jesus had refused.

"Why didn't he jump?" Salvatore had whispered to Anna. After all, if Jesus could walk on water, why not fly? It seemed a grand idea. But not to the old priest.

"Tempt not the Lord thy God!" he had cried, looking straight at Salvatore. God is all-powerful, he had explained, but He does not have to prove Himself. It is sacrilege—again he looked at Salvatore sternly—to challenge God to do anything. He does only what is necessary for His plan, which we do not understand. If He gives us poverty, if He gives us sickness, if He takes a loved one from us, that is part of His plan. We may ask for His help, but we must accept our fate. "Do not ask Him for more than you deserve. If God wanted man to fly, he would have given him wings. So do not try," he told them firmly. "For that is the temptation of the devil."

Concetta Caruso had liked the sermon very much, and she had thanked the old priest afterward. They had talked. She had discovered that his mother came from the same village as her own. And that he had a liking for sugar-coated almonds.

But why had she chosen that day of all days to send Salvatore to his house with a bag of sugared almonds? Who knew? It must have been fate.

Salvatore hurried through the Jewish quarter as quickly as he could. Not that he was afraid, but he always felt uncomfortable over there. The men with their black coats and hats, their beards and their strange language seemed so different from everyone else. The boys were mostly so pale, and as for the ones with ringlets, he tried not to look at them. But they didn't give him any trouble. He'd never had to fight them. Making his way through the crowded mass of pushcarts and stalls, he soon came to Rivington Street, and saw the Catholic church ahead.

That was another strange thing about the Jews. They didn't seem to have parish churches like the Christians. Even the larger synagogues were squat little buildings, squashed between tenements, without a churchyard or a priest's house. Some were just announced by narrow doorways leading to single rooms; you might see three or four in a block. His mother did not approve of the Jews. She said they were heretics, and that God would punish them. But his father only shrugged.

"Haven't they been punished enough before they came here? There are no pogroms in America, Concetta, thank God. *Basta*. It is enough. Leave them be."

The priest seemed delighted with his mother's gift, and told Salvatore to thank her.

Salvatore was so anxious not to be late that he ran all the way back. Crossing the Bowery into the Italian quarter, he went three blocks before turning left into Mulberry Street, where his family lived. They were waiting in the street already, dressed up for the great occasion. His parents and Giuseppe, his brother Paolo, his face scrubbed. His older sister Anna was still doing little Maria's hair.

"At last," said his father, as Salvatore arrived, "we can go."

"But where is Angelo?" cried his mother, while his father made a sign of impatience. "Anna, where is Angelo?" As the eldest daughter, expected to help her mother, Anna was in charge of Angelo most of the time.

"Mama, I'm doing Maria's hair," said Anna plaintively.

"Salvatore will find him," said his mother. "Quickly, Toto, get your brother Angelo."

"We did not know it," his father liked to say, "but when we arrived at Ellis Island, Angelo was already one of the family." He'd been born eight months later. Angelo was six now, though still the baby of the family. They all loved the little boy, but his father couldn't help being impatient with him sometimes. He was small for his age and rather frail. And he was so dreamy. "He's like his Uncle Luigi," Giovanni Caruso would sigh. Anna used to defend Angelo. "He is sensitive and clever," she would declare. But it didn't impress anyone much.

Salvatore ran into the house. It was a typical tenement house of the Lower East Side. Originally it had been a five-story row house with steps up to the door. But long ago, the owner had realized that he could double the small rents he received by a simple expedient. Building out as cheaply as possible into the small yard behind, he had been able, for no great outlay, to double his rentable space. And since both the owners of the house next door and of the house in the next street that backed onto his had done the same thing, the only ventilation for the back part of the house now came from two sources: a narrow air shaft between this house and the one beside it, and the tiny yard remaining at the very back, where a pair of latrines served the needs of all the tenant families.

When their cousins had first shown them the place, the day after they'd come through Ellis Island, Giovanni and Concetta Caruso had been disgusted. Soon they discovered they were lucky. They had three rooms on the top floor, at the front. True, you had to climb up the stinking stairwell to get there, but there was fresh air from the street, and you could go onto the roof above, where the washing was hung out to dry.

Angelo was standing in the back room when Salvatore burst in. He had his shirt on, but he had not tucked it in. And he was looking down at his feet miserably.

"You're six years old and you still can't tie up your bootlaces?" Salvatore cried impatiently.

"I was trying."

"Keep still." He'd have dragged his little brother down the stairs as he was, but Angelo would have been sure to trip. Hurriedly, he started to tie them for him. "You know who we're going to see?" he asked.

"No, I've forgotten."

"Idiot! We're going to see the greatest Italian in the world."

He did not say the greatest Italian who ever lived. That was Columbus. After him, for northern Italians, came Garibaldi, the Patriot, the unifier of Italy, who'd only died a quarter-century ago. But for the southern Italians of New York, there was only one great hero, a living hero too, who had come to dwell among them.

"Caruso," Salvatore cried. "The great Caruso, who shares our own name. We are going to see Caruso! How can you forget?"

To their father, Enrico Caruso was a god. In America, the opera might be the preserve of the rich, but the Italian community followed the career of the great tenor and his performances as closely as they would have followed that of a great general and his battles.

"He has sung all over the world," their father would say. "Naples, Milan, London, St. Petersburg, Buenos Aires, San Francisco . . . He has sung with Melba. Now he sings with Geraldine Farrar. Toscanini conducts him. And what did the great Puccini himself say, when he first heard Caruso sing? 'Who sent you to me? God Himself?'" Not just Italian, but born in Naples, and he even shared their name. "We are related," his father declared, though when Salvatore asked him to explain the relationship, his father had only shrugged, as if the question were foolish, and answered: "Who could know such a thing?"

And they were going to meet him today.

It was thanks to Uncle Luigi. He had found work in a restaurant nearby. Not a grand one—this, after all, was the poor Italian quarter. The richer, northern Italians, the doctors, the businessmen, the men of education who looked down upon their fellow countrymen from the south—regarded them as animals almost—they lived in other parts of town—Greenwich Village was favored—and they had fine restaurants over there.

But Caruso never forgot the poor home in Naples he came from. He liked to eat down in Little Italy, and recently, he'd come to dine in the restaurant where Uncle Luigi worked, and Uncle Luigi had asked him if he might present his family the next time Caruso came, and the great man had said certainly, because that was his noble character. He was having his midday meal there today.

Salvatore had just got Angelo downstairs when his brother said he had to go pee-pee. With a cry of frustration, Salvatore took him to the door of the backyard, so that he could go out to the latrines. "Hurry," he told him, while he waited irritably by the door. After a few moments, Angelo came out. "Hurry," he cried again.

Then he'd cried out once more. Too late.

Despite the fact that the communal latrines were there, the people above the yard continually threw their refuse out of the window to be cleaned up later. The journey to and from the latrines was always perilous, therefore. Everybody knew to look up when they moved through the yard. Everybody except Angelo.

The sheet of dirty water from above came from a pail someone had used while mopping the floor. It was black. Little Angelo looked up just in time to get the contents full in the face. He fell down. His shirt was soaked and filthy. For a moment he sat in a black puddle, too shocked to speak. Then he began to wail.

"*Stupido!* Idiot!" screamed Salvatore. "Look at your shirt. You disgrace us." He seized his little brother by the hair and dragged him weeping along the corridor and out into the street, where the family greeted him with cries of vexation.

His father threw up his hands, and started to blame Salvatore. But Salvatore started shouting that it wasn't fair. Was it his fault his brother couldn't tie up his shoes or look out for himself when he went to the latrines? His father made an impatient gesture, but he didn't disagree. Meanwhile, his mother had taken Angelo inside.

"Let him stay at home," Salvatore complained, "instead of disgracing us." But in a few minutes, looking contrite, his little brother was back again, his head scrubbed and wearing a shirt that was clean, though much older than the first. Then they all set off up Mulberry Street.

The Italian streets were almost as crowded as the nearby Jewish quarter, but there were differences. Small trees gave shade along some of them. Here and there, a handsome Catholic church, sometimes with a walled churchyard, would break up the line of houses. Each street, moreover, had its particular character. People from the Neapolitan region mostly lived on Mulberry, the Calabrians on Mott, the Sicilians on Elizabeth, with each major town taking a particular section. They re-created their homeland as best they could.

Not that Concetta ever felt at home. How could she, when all the life she'd known before had been in the warm Italian south? They might have been poor, but they had their land, their village, the ancient beauty of the Mediterranean shore and the mountains. All she had here was the roar and clatter of narrow streets, set on the edge of an endless, untamed wilderness. This place called itself a city, yet where were the piazzas, the places to sit and talk, and be seen? Where was its center?

True, at the bottom of Mulberry Street, where the city authorities had finally pulled down a group of tenements so foul that they rivaled the neighboring Five Points, there was now a small park, overlooked by the Church of the Transfiguration. People went there, yes, but it didn't feel like a proper Italian space.

"Everything here is ugliness," she would sigh.

As for the crowded house, with its narrow staircase, its flickering gaslight, peeling wallpaper and stink, her spirits sank every time she entered it. Whenever she could, she would go up on the roof, where the women from the nearby houses liked to meet and gossip. Sometimes she'd sit and darn clothes, or make tomato paste. In summer, she slept up there with the smaller children, while Giuseppe and Anna slept out on the fire escape. Anything to escape the airless little tenement rooms.

But if America was terrible, it gave you money. A generation ago, strong Irish newcomers had labored on the building sites, dug the canals, built railways and cleaned the streets. But many of those Irish families had moved on. They were policemen, firemen, even professional men now. It was the turn of the new Italian arrivals to take on the heavy work now. It was not well paid—only black people were paid less—but Giovanni Caruso and his son Giuseppe were strong and worked hard. And with Anna taking in piecework too, the family was still able, like most Italian families, to save something. Every month, Giovanni Caruso went to the Stabile Bank on the corner of Mulberry and Grand streets and sent dollars back to his sisters in Italy. He was also able to put away a little for himself. In a few years, he hoped to have enough saved to open a small business, or buy a house, maybe. That was a dream that would make the long years of hardship worthwhile. Meanwhile, to please his wife, he had even kept Paolo and Salvatore in school—although thirteen-year-old Paolo was quite old enough, he reminded her, to be earning his living.

Another few years. Especially with the help of Signor Rossi.

Like everyone else in Little Italy, Signor Rossi had come there because he had to. But he was a *prominente*, a man of distinction. "My father was a lawyer," he would say with a shrug, "and but for his untimely death before my education was completed, I'd be living in a fine house in Naples." Nonetheless, Signor Rossi was a kindly man with knowledge. Above all, he spoke good English.

Even after six years in New York, Giovanni Caruso spoke only the most broken English. Concetta spoke none at all. Most of their neighbors, their friends, even their cousins who had come to America long before them, were in the same situation. They had re-created Italy, as best they could, in their own quarter; but the great American world outside was still strange to them. So if help was needed in negotiating with the city authorities, or understanding the meaning of a contract, Signor Rossi could explain things like a notary. He was always dressed in a well-tailored suit; he had a quiet presence that reassured doubtful Americans, and he was glad to speak to people on your behalf. For these services he would never take any payment. But if he came into any little grocery, or needed work done in his house, the money he offered was always refused with a smile. His business, however, was to help you look after your savings.

"Money in the bank is good, my friend," he would explain, "but money that grows is better. The Americans make their money grow, so why shouldn't we share in their good fortune?" Over the years, Signor Rossi had become quite a successful *banchista*. He knew how to invest, and dozens of families had been grateful to put their savings in his hands. Each month, Giovanni Caruso would add a little more to the savings he had placed with Signor Rossi, and each month Rossi would give him a brief account of how his little fortune was growing. "Be patient," he would counsel. "If you invest wisely in this country, you will prosper."

The family walked proudly up the street. Giovanni with his grown-up son, then Concetta with little Angelo, Anna with Maria, while Salvatore and Paolo brought up the rear, talking and laughing as usual.

The little restaurant was not yet crowded. In the middle, Uncle Luigi, with a napkin over his arm, was serving beside a large table at which a single man was sitting. He was a thickset, Neapolitan fellow, not unlike their father, but in his eyes there was a special gleam. As they entered, and Uncle Luigi gestured for them to approach, the man at the table beamed at them and, opening his arms expansively, invited them to sit at table with him.

"Welcome," he cried, "the family of Caruso."

Salvatore would never forget that meal. He had never seen so much food in his life.

Not that the food in the Italian quarter was bad. Even his mother would grudgingly admit that, in America, you ate more meat than you did in the Mezzogiorno, and pasta too. No thick peasant bread, either. In America, you ate light white bread, like the rich.

But of course, the great tenor, who was paid thousands of dollars a week, could have all the food he wanted, and soon the table was groaning with Italian pasta, American *bistecca*, a huge bowl of salad, jugs of olive oil, piles of olives, bottles of Chianti—and Lacryma Christi also, from the base of Vesuvius, in honor of the Naples region—baskets of breads, plates of salami and cheeses . . . And over it all, a wonderful, rich smell of tomato, pepper and oil. "*Mangia*, eat," he urged, as he pushed the food toward them, and he insisted that a *bistecca* be placed in front of every child. It seemed to Salvatore that he was in heaven.

From the great Caruso, also, there exuded an aura of warmth and generosity that seemed to fill the whole room. "Italy in America," he remarked to Giovanni Caruso with a grin, "it's even better than Italy in Italy." He patted his growing stomach. "This is where we Italians come to grow fat." For indeed, even in the stinking tenements of the Lower East Side, the thin immigrants from the Mezzogiorno would nearly always put on weight after a year or two.

To Concetta Caruso, he was charming. He knew her village, even one of her relations. Soon, she was beaming. As for Giovanni Caruso, who knew very well the tenor's legendary generosity, he was anxious to make sure that Caruso should not think they had come there looking for charity.

"We do well," he told him. "Already I have savings. A few years more and I shall buy my own house."

"Bravo," said Caruso. "Let us drink to the land of opportunity."

"But you, Signor Caruso," his father added respectfully, "have brought honor to our name. You have raised us all."

Like a tribal chief, Caruso acknowledged this tribute. "Let us raise our glasses, my friends, to the name of Caruso."

During the meal, he spoke to each of the family in turn. He congratulated Giuseppe on helping his father, and Concetta on raising such a fine family. Anna, he saw at once, was the family's second mother. Paolo admitted that he wanted to be a fireman, and when it came to Salvatore's turn, he asked him about his school.

The Church of the Transfiguration stood between Mott and Mulberry streets, on the small rise overlooking the little park. When the Carusos had first arrived there, an Irish priest ministered to an Irish congregation in the main church, while an Italian priest conducted a service for the Italian congregation, in their own language, down in the crypt below. But since then, the Italians and their priest had moved upstairs, a signal that it was they who had taken charge of the area now. Beside the church was the school which the Caruso children attended.

"You must learn all you can," the great man told Salvatore. "Too many of our southern Italians despise education. They say, 'Why should a son know more than his father?' But they are wrong. Work hard at school and you will get ahead in America. You understand?"

Salvatore had no love of school, so he was not pleased to hear this, but he bowed his head respectfully.

"And this young man," Caruso turned to little Angelo, "do you learn things at school?"

Angelo might be dreamy, but he did well at school. In fact, he could already read better than his elder brothers. He also had a talent for drawing. He was too shy to say anything, so his mother informed the great man of these facts, while Salvatore, who couldn't see that Angelo's talents did him any good, made a conspiratorial face at Paolo. So he was a bit taken aback by the next question.

"And your brother Salvatore, is he kind to you?"

There was a pregnant silence. Then Angelo burst into life.

"No," he cried loudly, "my brother is not kind to me."

Paolo thought this was funny, but Caruso did not, and he rounded upon Salvatore.

"Shame on you."

"Anna looks after Angelo," his mother interceded, not wanting the great man to think that her youngest child was neglected. But though he nodded, Caruso's attention remained on Salvatore.

"Your brother is a dreamer, Salvatore. He is not so strong as you. But who knows, he may be a thinker, a priest, a great artist. You are his big brother. You should protect him. Promise me you will be kind to your brother."

At that moment, Salvatore was ready to give Angelo a beating, but all the same he felt himself go very red, and promise, "Yes, Signor Caruso."

"Good." From nowhere, the great man produced a chocolate and gave it to Salvatore. "This is for you only, Salvatore, so that you remember you have promised me to be kind to your brother." He held out his hand, so that Salvatore had to shake it. "*Ecco*. He has promised." He looked at them all, just as seriously as if he had signed a legal contract.

And Salvatore looked at little Angelo, whose eyes were now very round, and at the tenor, and at his family, and secretly cursed his fate. Now what was he going to do?

✢

It did not take long for the news to travel. Within a day, the whole of Little Italy seemed to know that the Carusos had had a family meal with the great tenor. Giovanni Caruso was wise, though. When people said to him,

"So the great Caruso is your relation?" he only laughed and said: "There are many Carusos. We are a tribe, not a family." In this way, people were soon saying: "Giovanni Caruso does not admit that they are related, yet Caruso himself treats him like a brother. No smoke without fire." By half denying the relationship, therefore, he made people suspect it existed. Even their landlord, seeing him in the street one day, stopped Giovanni with a smile and asked him to be sure to let him know if there was any little favor he could do him.

As for Salvatore, he felt obliged to be kind to little Angelo. To Paolo, of course, this was an opportunity for harmless fun. Hardly a day went by that he didn't persecute Angelo by taking an apple away from him, or stealing one of his boots, and gleefully telling the little boy: "Don't worry, your brother Salvatore will get it back for you." Angelo had to fight him several times.

He was scarcely aware of the financial panic on Wall Street the following month. Such things had nothing to do with the poor folk on the Lower East Side. Then Uncle Luigi came by and said that one of the *banchiste* who dined frequently at the restaurant had lost a lot of money, his own and his clients'. "I hope your Signor Rossi is all right," he had said. "Signor Rossi is far too clever to make any mistakes," Giovanni Caruso had answered. But later that day Salvatore had seen his father looking worried.

Two days later, his father went out to see the *banchista*. When he returned, his face was ashen. He went up on the roof to talk alone to Concetta, and Salvatore heard his mother scream. When the family was all together in the little apartment that evening, Giovanni broke it to them.

"Signor Rossi has lost everything. All his clients' money. It is very complicated, and many others are in the same situation, but our savings are gone. We must start again."

"It's a lie," cried their mother. "Money can't disappear like that. He has stolen it."

"No, Concetta, I assure you. Rossi has lost most of his own money as well. He told me, he hardly knows how he will eat."

"You believe him? Don't you see, Giovanni, what he is doing? He will wait a while, then he will disappear with all the money. He is laughing at you, Giovanni, behind your back."

"You do not understand these things, Concetta. Signor Rossi is a man of honor."

"Honor? You men are fools. Any woman can see what he is doing."

Salvatore had never heard his mother speak to his father with such disrespect. He wondered what would happen. But his father chose to ignore it, the business was too terrible already to worry about anything else.

"Paolo and Salvatore must go to work now," their father said quietly. "It is time for them to help us, as Anna does. There is plenty of work. Maria and Angelo will stay in school for the present. In a few years, we shall recover, and there will be better times."

For Salvatore, the change of circumstances was a distinct improvement. He didn't have to go to school, and he was exempt, therefore, from the great Caruso's instruction that he should study. And he and Paolo were so busy out in the streets that it was easy enough to be nice to little Angelo when he saw him. They found plenty of ways to earn money in the streets, but mostly he and Paolo plied their trade as bootblacks. They would go across to Greenwich Village and shine the shoes of Italian men who were lunching there. They found an Italian enterprise where they were allowed to enter the office and shine the boots of the men who worked there. Working together, they would take turns to put on polish and shine, although even Paolo had to admit that Salvatore could get a better shine on any shoe than he could. "It must be something in your spit that I didn't inherit," he would say regretfully.

For his mother, the loss of their savings meant a change of regime. A sewing machine was installed in the best lit of their three small rooms, close to the window. There, she and Anna would take turns to do piecework by the hour. It paid poorly, but they could remain in the house, look after the smallest children and feed the family while they also worked. After her original outburst over Signor Rossi, Concetta had never said anything more about it, but Salvatore knew she could not be happy. One evening he heard his parents talking quietly up on the roof. His father's voice was gentle, persuasive, though Salvatore could not hear exactly what he was saying. But he heard his mother's words.

"No more children, Giovanni. Not like this. I beg you."

He understood what his mother meant.

It was toward the end of the year, and he was walking down Mulberry Street with his father, when Uncle Luigi suddenly came running out of his restaurant after them. They must come at once, he told them. The great Caruso was eating inside and wanted to speak to them.

Caruso greeted them warmly, and he asked after all the family. "You'll give my respects to your wife," he told Giovanni, who promised he would. Were they doing well? he asked.

"*Assolutamente*," Giovanni assured him. "Everything goes well."

"*Bene. Bene*," said Caruso. "And are you being kind to your brother?" he demanded, turning to Salvatore.

"Yes," Salvatore promised, he was.

"And you are studying hard at school?"

"He studies as never before," his father cut in, before Salvatore could reply. Salvatore saw his Uncle Luigi stare in surprise, but Caruso was not looking that way, so he did not observe it. Instead, he drew an envelope from his pocket and handed it to Giovanni.

"Two tickets to the opera, for you and your wife." He beamed. "You will come?"

"Of course." Giovanni Caruso stumbled to convey his thanks.

They had walked a little way down the street after this interview when his father turned to Salvatore.

"I could not tell him about our misfortune, Toto," he said awkwardly. "I could not let him know you were no longer in school."

"I know, Papa," said Salvatore.

"I am a Caruso too. I could not make a *brutta figura*." A loss of face. Italian pride. Salvatore understood. He even dared to squeeze his father's hand.

"You were right, Papa," he said.

On the day that she was to go to the opera, however, his mother said she did not feel well.

"Take one of the children with you," she told her husband. "Anna can go." But his father, after thinking for a minute, said that since Salvatore was with him when Caruso gave the tickets, it was he who should go.

How proudly Salvatore walked beside his father as they approached the opera house on Broadway that evening. The big square-faced building that took up the whole block between Thirty-ninth and Fortieth Streets looked to Salvatore like a department store. But there was no doubt about the elegance of the people in evening dress who were entering it. He even noticed a silver Rolls-Royce gliding to rest near its entrance.

Salvatore hadn't been to this part of town before. He knew the busy streets of the Financial District and the waterfront, but he seldom had any reason to go north of Greenwich Village. At the bottom of Fifth Avenue, he had seen elegant ladies go in and out of their houses, but the sight of such crowds of people in evening dress was new to him.

As they went inside, Salvatore gasped. The vast auditorium with its mighty chandelier was like a celestial palace. A massive curtain of gold damask hung across the stage, and on the huge curved proscenium, he saw the names of great composers. Beethoven he'd heard of, Wagner he hadn't. But there, for all to see, was the name to make every Italian swell with pride: Verdi. And it was Verdi's *Aida* that was being performed tonight.

He soon realized that Caruso, sensibly, had not given them expensive seats, where everyone would be in evening dress. They were both in suits and clean shirts, of course—his father had even put on a tie—but as they made their way through the throng, Salvatore couldn't help noticing that the patrons of the opera were looking at them strangely. When he blacked the boots of the rich businessmen by day, they were friendly enough. But now that he was invading their home territory, several of the men gave him and his father cold glances. A woman quickly pulled her gown away, lest it be contaminated by their touch, while her husband muttered, "Damn Italian wops."

"They like our opera, Toto, just not us," his father remarked sadly.

When they found their seats, they could see that their neighbors were simple Italians like themselves, perhaps also the recipients of Caruso's generosity. His father began to chat to them, but Salvatore was thinking about the way the rich people had looked at them. And he continued to brood about it until the curtain went up.

The plot of *Aida* was easy to follow, especially, he thought to himself wryly, if you were Italian and could understand the words. The Princess Aida, a captured slave in Egypt; her lover, the hero Radames. The love triangle completed by the daughter of the Egyptian pharaoh. But with what grandeur Verdi handled the simple theme! What majestic marches, what haunting scenes. With his magnificent voice, thrilling as any tenor, rich as any baritone, Caruso the hero had the audience enthralled. As for the production, the Metropolitan Opera had provided a new staging that season, of unrivaled magnificence. As Salvatore responded to the music and drank in the scene, he sensed that all the splendor of his native Mediterranean, from Italy to Africa, was here. He felt profoundly stirred.

But perhaps the most moving moment for the boy came at the end, when the hero, condemned to death, is walled up in a huge tomb. The dark walls, dimly lit by stage lights, towered above him, hard and immutable, closed as fate. And then, suddenly, he discovers that his lover Aida, whom he thought had betrayed him, has hidden in there, choosing to share his fate. It was then, as the two lovers began their final, haunting duet in the darkness, that Salvatore glanced at his father.

Giovanni Caruso's face was tilted up. It was quite an ordinary face— broad and dark, the face of a working man from the Mezzogiorno. Yet seen in profile, it seemed to the boy that it was as fine as that of any Roman noble. And in the faint light, Salvatore could see that his father's face, though perfectly still, was wet with tears.

He would have been most astonished to know that, in her box, a fashionable lady named Rose Vandyck Master had already risen to retire, before the opera's end.

⁂

It was the following spring that Salvatore had his only quarrel with his brother Paolo. It happened when they were on their usual rounds in a crowded office, shining shoes.

It was amazing how fast people seemed to forget the financial panic of the previous fall. Business had been good. The men in the office were obviously making money, and if they were in a good mood, they might even give the boys a dollar tip before they left. On this occasion, after they'd finished half a dozen shoes and been paid, one of the men, who was busy on the telephone, stretched out his hand and gave Salvatore a dollar just as they were going out of the door. They had just reached the elevator when Salvatore looked at it and realized that it wasn't a dollar. It was five. He showed it to Paolo.

It was surely a mistake, and quite an easy one to make. The dollar bill had a bald eagle and portraits of Lincoln and Grant on its face; the five-dollar bill had a running deer. But they were the same size, and the man had been busy on the telephone.

"I guess we'd better tell him," said Salvatore.

"Are you crazy?" Paolo stared down at him contemptuously.

Paolo had only been a little taller than Salvatore until recently. But in the last year he had suddenly started to grow so fast that he was already nearly as tall as their father. "Giuseppe never grew like that," their mother declared. "Maybe it's America makes him grow so big." She didn't seem to be pleased about Paolo's sudden new height. And maybe Paolo wasn't either, because his mood appeared to change. He and Salvatore were companions in everything they did, but he didn't seem to joke the way he always had before. And sometimes, when they walked down the street together, Salvatore would look up and realize that he had no idea what his brother was thinking.

Salvatore didn't think it was so crazy. Five dollars was a huge sum of money. The man had surely made a mistake. Taking his money seemed dishonest.

"He made a mistake. It feels like stealing."

"That's his problem. How were we to know he didn't mean to give us five?"

"He'll be mad when he realizes," Salvatore countered, "and then he'll hate us. Anyway, he's always been good to us. If we show him the five dollars, maybe he'll be pleased, and let us keep it."

"You don't understand anything, do you?" Paolo hissed. He was starting to look really angry. At that moment the elevator arrived, and he pushed Salvatore inside and made a sign to him to keep silent. Only when they had left the building and were on the sidewalk outside did he turn on him.

"Do you know what he'll think if we show him the five dollars? He'll despise us. This is New York, Toto, not a convent. You take everything you can get." Seeing that Salvatore wasn't convinced, he took him by the shoulder and shook him. "What do you think those men do in that office all day? They trade. They buy and sell. If you make a mistake, you pay. If you win, you get rich. Those are the rules. You won't take the money? You look like a loser."

"Papa says it's important that people trust you," Salvatore said obstinately.

"Papa? What does he know? Papa trusted Signor Rossi, who took all our money. Our father's an idiot. A loser. Don't you know that?"

Salvatore stared at his brother in amazement. He had never heard anyone speak about their father in such a way. Paolo's face had contorted into a scowl. It made him look ugly.

"Don't say such a thing," he cried.

When they got back that evening, they placed all their money on the table for their mother, as usual. Paolo had changed the five-dollar bill into singles, but she was still surprised at the amount. "You earned this? You did not steal?" she asked suspiciously.

"I would never steal," said Salvatore, which satisfied her.

But in the months that followed, though some of Paolo's good humor returned, it seemed to Salvatore that a secret rift had opened between himself and his brother. They never spoke of it.

It was his sister Anna to whom he drew closer. If she'd seemed bossy to him before, now that he was older and working, the age difference between them seemed less. He could see how much she did with their mother in the house, too, and he tried to help her. During part of the day, the two youngest children were at school, but when they came home it was Anna who usually looked after them and prepared the evening meal while her mother worked. In particular, she would try to keep Angelo away from his father, who couldn't help being irritated by his youngest son's dreamy ways. Little Maria was easier to deal with. Round faced and bright-eyed, she had become the family pet.

Most of the day, his mother sat at a small table by the window in the front bedroom, on which there stood a Singer sewing machine, bought on the installment plan. There she would do piecework for the garment trade by the hour. Sitting in a little armchair nearby, Anna would do the hand-stitching. It was not so bad in summer, but on long winter evenings, it was another story. The tenement only had gaslight to work by. Even with a kerosene lamp to help them, Salvatore would see the two women peering anxiously at their work, and sometimes his mother would shake her head and say to Anna: "Your eyes are younger. Tell me if this is straight."

He knew that all over the Lower East Side, Jewish and Italian women were huddled in small rooms, in the same way. Some families set up little sweatshops in their lodgings, hiring girls even poorer than they were to work in shifts round the clock. That was the way the garment industry worked. Anna would arrive from a garment-maker carrying a great pile of unfinished items piled on her head. When the pieces were finished, Salvatore would sometimes offer to take them back for her.

He was on this errand one evening in June when he happened to pass a building from which a crowd of young women were emerging. Most of the girls were Jewish, but they didn't seem to mind when the curious Italian boy asked them what sort of work they did. They answered his questions cheerfully before going on their way. All the way home, Salvatore thought about what he had learned. At the evening meal, he told his family.

"There's a factory where they make garments. There are lots of girls there of Anna's age. They work in a big room with high ceilings and electric light, and rows of sewing machines. The pay isn't too bad, and they have fixed hours. Maybe Anna could work there too."

Any such decision would have to be made by his father. And Giovanni Caruso shook his head at the idea of Anna being out of the house; his wife, though, was prepared to consider it.

"Anna is ruining her eyes at home," she said. "She'll be blind before she finds a husband. Let me look at this place, Giovanni, just to see what it is like."

She and Anna went there the next day. A week later, Anna Caruso began work at the Triangle Factory.

✧

Salvatore's day now took on a new routine. He would shine boots with Paolo until early evening, when he would take Angelo to meet Anna.

The Triangle Factory was in a cobbled street just east of Washington Square Park, at the foot of Fifth Avenue. In the park, standing on a granite plinth, there was a fine statue of Garibaldi. A north Italian, admittedly, but at least an Italian. The great hero had even lived on Staten Island briefly during his years of exile, and it made Salvatore proud that Garibaldi should be so honored in the middle of the city now. Every evening, he and Angelo would wait beside the statue for Anna to appear. Sometimes she'd be told she had to work late; and if she didn't appear, he'd take Angelo back. But usually she arrived, and then they would all walk home together, once in a while stopping for an ice or a cookie on the way.

Anna was happy. The Triangle Shirtwaist Company, as it was called, occupied the top three of the ten floors of the big square building. The factory mostly made the ankle-length skirts and the white, narrow-waisted, Gibson Girl blouses, called "shirtwaists," that were fashionable for working girls and women. Most of the work was arranged at long tables where rows of sewing machines were driven by a single electric engine. It was a lot more efficient than the pedal machine their mother used at home. Many of the employees were men, some of them employed in teams under a subcontractor, though there were plenty of girls too. Most of the workers were Jews, maybe a third related in some way or other to the owners, Mr. Blanck and Mr. Harris, but there were some Italian girls too. Everyone complained about the pay and the hours.

"But at least there's plenty of air and light," Anna would say, "and the girls are friendly." Salvatore guessed that she was glad to get out of the house, too.

Another effect of the new regime was to bring Salvatore closer to his little brother.

Angelo was still a dreamer. At school, he learned his lessons erratically, but the one thing he loved was to draw. He would carry a little pencil in his pocket, and use any piece of paper he could get his hands on. When he and Salvatore were on their way to meet Anna, they would often pick different routes. Nearly every time he'd find something that interested him, and he'd start to sketch it, until Salvatore had to drag him away. Often he would notice some fine bit of carved stonework over a doorway, or high up on the entablatures and cornices of the tall office buildings. No one in the family thought much of his efforts, except Uncle Luigi.

"Of course he likes the carvings," he declared. "Who do you think did those carvings? Italian stonemasons. All over the city. Look at the Americans' houses—copied from ancient Rome. Now they make tall office buildings—great cages of steel—but they clothe the cages with brick and stone, and add Roman cornices round the top so that they look like so many Italian *palazzi*. New York is turning into an Italian city," he cried enthusiastically. "Our young Angelo will be a great architect, a man of honor. That is why he draws."

This ambitious design was so obviously impossible that nobody paid any attention. But his father did say grudgingly: "Perhaps he could be a stonemason."

As for Angelo himself, he went upon his dreamy way. Once Anna confided to Salvatore, "You and I will have to watch out for Angelo all his life."

For over a year, Anna worked at the Triangle Factory without incident.

✢

The year 1910 began on a Saturday. In New York, there was a light dusting of snow. But on Sunday morning, when Rose Master got into the Rolls-Royce and set off downtown, the sky was clear and blue.

There was still an hour to go before she was due to join old Hetty for lunch, but she was leaving extra time to make sure that the arrangements she had made were all in place. As she stepped into the car, she told the chauffeur that she'd be picking up some people on the way. When they started off, she gave him the address. It was at this point that the astonished chauffeur glanced in his mirror and asked her if there wasn't some mistake.

"None at all," she said. "Drive on."

The last thing Rose wanted to do—the last thing she'd ever thought she'd have to do—was get in a fight with old Hetty Master. She'd talked to William about it. "Am I wrong?" she'd asked. "No," he'd said, "but you can't stop her." She'd reasoned with his grandmother, gently pointing out why this luncheon might be a bad idea. But Hetty had been obdurate. And the trouble was, people were already talking about it. Hetty's name was being mentioned everywhere, and Rose feared, with good reason, that there could be some reference to the old lady in the newspapers. Something had to be done.

So Rose had made her plans. They were subtle, and devious. She had even employed a journalist she knew, a sound man she could rely upon, to draft a story which would have the desired result. With luck, it might be possible to turn the whole business to some good account without personally offending Hetty too much. But whatever the outcome, she was determined about one thing: the Master family name must not be sullied.

✥

Edmund Keller walked briskly down Fifth Avenue. He liked to walk, and the cold air on his face felt good. He'd spent the first part of the morning with his Aunt Gretchen's family, up on Eighty-sixth Street. Like so many of the inhabitants of the old *Kleindeutschland*, they'd long ago moved to the Yorkville area on the Upper East Side, where Eighty-sixth Street was called the German Broadway now. Gretchen had died a couple of years ago, but he was still close to her children and their families.

It was only sixty-five blocks or so down to Gramercy Park. He could walk that comfortably on a bright cold day like this. A dozen blocks every ten minutes, going north to south. Walking across town, the blocks were longer, but he only had to get from Fifth across to Lexington.

He'd been invited to lunch by Hetty Master. The old lady must be over ninety now, he thought, so he didn't want to disappoint her. The last time they'd met had been at his father's, a week ago. The discussion had been all about the extraordinary goings-on with these girls in the garment industry. Perhaps she wanted to talk about that. He really didn't care. When he'd satisfied the old lady, he was going to walk round to his father's and stay for dinner.

Fifth Avenue was sedate on Sundays. He passed the red-brick facade of the Metropolitan Museum, and continued down the long strand where the palaces of the millionaires gazed at Central Park. In the Fifties, he crossed to the west side of the street to avoid a crowd of people coming out of St. Patrick's Cathedral. At Forty-second, he noted that the new library with its magnificent classical facade was almost complete. But it was not until he got all the way down to Twenty-third, where Broadway made its great diagonal cut across Fifth, that Edmund Keller smiled with pleasure.

There it was: the Flatiron Building.

There were some tall buildings uptown these days, but it was only when you got to the Flatiron Building that you entered the realm of the real skyscrapers. The Flatiron Building, however, was one of a kind. Over twenty floors high, on a triangular groundplan at the intersection of the two great boulevards, and looking at Madison Square, it was one of the most elegant landmarks in the city. The narrow corner offices were especially prized.

Edmund Keller liked skyscrapers. He supposed it was natural that commercial and financial men in the crowded world of Wall Street should try to get the maximum use out of the sites their offices occupied, which meant building up. In the last twenty years, the development of iron girder construction had meant that the weight of buildings no longer had to be carried by their walls, but could be cheaply and effectively carried by huge networks of steel. Back in the Middle Ages, medieval builders had been able to raise soaring buildings using pillars of stone and complex frameworks of wood, but these structures were massively expensive. Steel construction, by contrast, was simple and cheap.

Yet it was also in the spirit of the age, he thought, that the mighty business titans of America should send their buildings soaring into the sky, so that they could look out, like eagles, upon the vast new continent. And if the summits of the buildings were like mountain tops, he foresaw that the avenues between them would soon be great canyons, down which the daylight would come striding, bold as a giant.

From the Flatiron Building to Gramercy Park was a short walk, not even five blocks. As the butler opened the door, the buzz of voices told

Keller that he was to join quite a large company. He did not see that, behind him, a silver Rolls-Royce was drawing up by the curb.

⚜

As Rose caught sight of Edmund Keller, she nodded to herself. She'd managed to keep him at a distance quite effectively so far. Once, he'd come round to call at the house during the afternoon, and she'd told the butler to say she was "Not at home." It was standard social procedure, and he'd gone on his way. A while later he had written a brief letter to say that he hoped to call, and she had sent an equally polite reply to say that as one of the children had measles, this would be a bad idea. He hadn't troubled her after that. Seeing him entering Hetty's house now, she thought: Well, if socialist Mr. Keller was coming, that just proved how right she was to intervene. And if he wanted war, he was going to get it.

"This is where we get out," she said to the two young people who accompanied her. And a few moments later she was sweeping them past the astonished butler.

She was smiling brightly, though as she saw the other guests gathered in the house, she couldn't help feeling glad that dear Mrs. Astor had died eighteen months ago. Thank God, she thought, that the poor lady wasn't alive to see this.

⚜

The whole, wretched business had begun in the fall. Some of the garment workers in the downtown factories had started to complain about their working conditions. Perhaps they had a case. Rose didn't know. But in no time, agitators—socialists and revolutionaries from Russia mostly, she'd heard—were whipping them up. The garment workers were threatening to strike, and the factory owners were outraged.

But not Mr. Blanck and Mr. Harris, the owners of the Triangle Factory. They had provided an in-house union for their employees, but they told them firmly that anyone who joined the militant outside union would be dismissed.

Soon the whole garment district was in an uproar, with the workers calling a general strike, and the braver employers, headed by Triangle, locking them out and hiring others instead. Some employers paid thugs to beat up the leading strikers. Tammany Hall, which controlled the police, was on the side of the employers, and there were arrests. But the union used women on the picket lines, and when they were jailed and sent to hard labor, there was some public sympathy. Even the *New York Times*, which usually supported the employers, began to waver.

Rose didn't condone the bad treatment or the violence, but these things had to be kept in proportion, they mustn't get out of hand. And things wouldn't have got out of hand, if it hadn't been for a certain group of women. The women in this room.

You had to give it to old Hetty, Rose thought grimly, she'd assembled quite a crowd. There were half a dozen Vassar girls—they should have known better, for a start. Rose was never sure what she felt about women going to college. Vassar and Barnard in the state of New York, Bryn Mawr down in Philadelphia, and the four colleges up in Massachusetts—the Seven Sisters as they were called, like a sort of female Ivy League. All respectable enough, no doubt; but did one really want girls from the old families getting a lot of foolish ideas put in their heads? Rose didn't think so.

Just look at the results. Vassar girls had been parading round the city with billboards supporting the strike. They'd been living down on the Lower East Side with the poor. All for what? To show they were enlightened? Well, at least they had the excuse of being young. And that certainly could not be said for the next figure to greet her eye.

Alva Vanderbilt—at least that was her name in the days when she'd forced her daughter Consuelo to marry the Duke of Marlborough. Alva always got her way. After she'd divorced Vanderbilt for a pile of money, married August Belmont's son and built a huge mansion up in Newport, Rose suspected Alva had got bored. So next she'd decided to make herself look important by demanding votes for women. One might argue about the rights and wrongs of female suffrage, but not about Alva's unquenchable thirst for publicity. And it was wholly typical of Alva, seeing the strike in the garment district, to decide to hitch these unfortunate women to her own bandwagon and proclaim that their dispute was about women's rights.

To the astonishment of the factory women, she'd started turning up in the courts to pay their fines. She'd organized monster rallies. She'd even shipped in Mrs. Pankhurst, the British suffragist leader, to make an appearance. She certainly had a genius for publicity, and the Hearst and Pulitzer papers were trumpeting the cause. But her shrewdest move had been to go to the woman who was approaching Rose and her two young charges now.

"Hello, Rose. Didn't expect to see you here." Elizabeth Marbury was wearing a dark coat and skirt, with a small black hat on her head. She always filled any room she was in. It wasn't just that she was broad in the beam; it was her presence. Literary agent to Oscar Wilde, George Bernard Shaw and many others, she went where she pleased. Having taken up the cause of the women strikers, she'd brought support from the acting profession, and money from the wealthy Shubert family. She'd even hosted a lunch for a group of the strikers within the sacred portals of the ladies' Colony Club.

At least she hadn't brought her friend. She and Elsie de Wolfe, the designer, had been living together for years. Women lovers. The fashionable worlds of New York, Paris and London accepted them, but Rose didn't approve. Elizabeth Marbury eyed Rose calmly.

"Who are your young friends?" she asked.

Rose smiled, but shepherded them past her without explaining. The other people in the room were mostly society ladies, and a few old friends of Hetty's. Lily de Chantal was in bed with the flu, but Mary O'Donnell was there, faithful as ever, and Rose went to greet her.

"Are you going to Carnegie Hall tonight?" Mary asked. "I feel I ought to go with Hetty—she's quite determined to be there. But if you or William took her," she added hopefully, "I could stay at home."

For this was what the luncheon was all about. A gathering, a social rally, before the huge event.

Tonight's meeting at Carnegie Hall was going to be the climax of the last two months. It could even be the start of a general strike. It was actually a union meeting, but if anyone thought that was going to keep people like Alva out, then they didn't know the rich and powerful women of New York. On behalf of her Votes for Women League, she had a private box.

"I'm sorry, Mary," Rose said, and Mary looked disappointed.

"We're only waiting for one more person now," Mary said. Then, glancing toward the door, she added: "And here she is."

Even as Rose turned to look, she had an instinct who it would be. Alva Belmont and Marbury were bad enough, but if there was one woman in New York whom she truly hated, one woman she couldn't forgive . . . well, she was walking into the room now.

Anne Morgan. She was wearing a wide-brimmed hat and a fur stole and, thought Rose, looking pleased with herself as usual. Rose had never liked her, but since she'd taken up with Marbury and de Wolfe, she'd become impossible. They'd all gone to live together in France for a time—in a villa in Versailles. Who did they think they were? Royalty? As for the nature of the relationship, Rose didn't know, and didn't want to know. And now Anne Morgan was busy donating huge sums to the garment workers' cause, funding Russians and socialists, and making a nuisance of herself. God knows what her father thought of it all.

Who would ever have believed that the great Pierpont, J. P. Morgan himself, could have such a daughter? She was only carrying on like this because he gave her twenty thousand dollars a year. Rose couldn't understand it. Why didn't he just stop her allowance?

For this was Rose's complaint. If she believed for one moment that these women really cared about the working conditions of people like the two young persons she'd brought with her, she mightn't have minded; but for their own purposes, their own sense of power—their own vanity, in her opinion—these rich women, from old families, the very people who were supposed to take the lead in society and set a good example, were funding strikers and whipping up public support for a cause behind which, she was quite sure, were socialists, anarchists, people whose mission was to destroy the very society which gave them their wealth. These women were traitors, fools perhaps, but destroyers. She hated them.

And she could just see the articles in the newspapers. "Mrs. Master Hosts Luncheon for Mrs. Belmont and Miss Morgan before Carnegie Hall Meeting." Or even worse: "Master Family Backs the Strike."

Well, it just confirmed how right she'd been to bring these two young people here today.

❖

As they all sat down to luncheon in the big dining room, old Hetty Master couldn't help feeling pretty pleased with herself. She'd worked hard for this, and the timing had been perfect.

She'd taken an interest in the garment workers right from the start. She and Mary had toured the area, and attended some of the meetings. She'd talked to Alva Belmont and some of the others. And one way and another, it had been agreed that there would be a rendezvous at her house on the day of the Carnegie Hall meeting.

For a ninety-year-old woman to host an event like this was quite a social coup. It wasn't too often these days that she had a chance to be in the thick of things, and who knew if such a chance would occur again?

She might be ninety, but Hetty believed in moving with the times. She'd seen so much change. She'd seen canals come, then railroads, gaslights, then electricity, steamboats and now the motor car. She'd seen the old crowd at the Academy of Music yield to the rich crowd at the Metropolitan Opera, and families you'd never heard of, like the Vanderbilts, get into Mrs. Astor's Four Hundred. If Rose wanted life to be a bit more decorous, Hetty in the last years of her life wished she had a bit more excitement. In fact, just for once, she thought she'd like to be in the forefront of fashion.

And the garment strike was the fashion just now. She had every sympathy with those poor girls in the factories, though she wasn't going to pretend that she knew all the issues. But today's lunch would be remembered. However small, Hetty Master was going to see if she couldn't get herself in as a footnote in New York's history.

So she surveyed the guests at her table with great satisfaction.

Inviting Edmund Keller had been an afterthought. She'd seen him at his father's the week before, and asked him to come along, as it was always nice to have a man around. As for Rose, she really hadn't meant to invite her at all. Indeed, she'd been surprised when her grandson's wife had got wind of the event and said she wanted to come. "There's no need, dear," she'd told her. But Rose had been so insistent, it would have been awkward to refuse. And now she'd turned up with two young people from the Lower East Side, and insisted they sit with her. Had she suddenly been converted to the cause?

The conversation was all about the meeting that evening. Important union people would be there. Samuel Gompers, the labor leader, and his lieutenants were moderate; they wanted better pay and conditions, if they could get them. Others, with a political agenda, might be more strident. Nobody knew what was going to happen. It was all very exciting. She'd almost forgotten about her granddaughter-in-law and her young people when suddenly, just as the main course was being served, Rose stood up and announced that there was a young woman from the garment district whom she'd like them all to hear, and turning to the young woman at her side, she said: "You can stand up now, dear."

⁘

Anna Caruso glanced down at Salvatore. She'd only agreed to come if her brother was there to protect her. "Just tell your story simply, the way you told it to me," Rose had said. But faced with all these people, in this big house, and the fact that she knew her English still wasn't so good, she couldn't help being nervous.

She'd been surprised when Mr. Harris at the factory had called her over last week. "This lady," he'd explained, "wants to talk to one of our loyal workers, and I've told her you're a sensible girl." It was pretty clear that she'd better do what he said. So she'd told the lady what she wanted to know. Then the lady had said she'd like to come back to her house and see her family. So at the end of the day, she'd collected Salvatore and Angelo from the park, and the lady had driven them all back to Mulberry Street in her car. The sight of the Rolls-Royce stopping outside their house had caused quite a stir. When the lady had said she wanted to take her next Sunday to tell her friends about the factory, her father had been dubious, but when Mrs. Master had given him her visiting card and address, and offered twenty dollars for the inconvenience, it was agreed that she should go, as long as she was accompanied.

"My name is Anna," she began, "and my family lives in Mulberry Street." She told them how they had arrived in America from Italy when she was a little girl, how her father had lost their years of savings in the panic of 1907, how her brothers had had to leave school, and how they were all working to get back on their feet again. She could tell that they liked her story. There had been murmurs of sympathy about the loss in the panic, and of approval for the way they were all working so hard. She explained how difficult it was for her mother, working at home, and how she had gone to the Triangle Factory, where the conditions were better.

And now the lady started asking her questions.

"Is there a union at the factory?" Rose asked.

"There is a friendly union inside the factory."

"It was the outside union, the Women's Trade Union, that the owners did not like. Did you want to join it?"

"No."

"So when the owners locked out the workers, what happened to you?"

"My parents wished me to continue working. Our priest also said I should work. So I went to Mr. Harris at the factory."

"And he gave you back your job?"

"Yes."

"Did he employ new girls to work at the factory?"

"Yes."

"Are they mostly Italian, Catholic, respectable girls, like you?"

"Yes."

"The girls who lost their jobs, who have joined the WTU, are they mostly Jews?"

"Yes."

"Thank you, dear. You can sit down." Rose turned to the assembled ladies. "I think everyone here can see that this is an honest young woman," she declared. "And I'm sure there are grievances at some of the factories which need to be addressed. But I think we need to be careful. What is it the Jewish girls want that Anna here does not? Are they really striking for better conditions, or is their object political? How many of these Russians are socialists?" She gazed round in triumph. "I believe it's a question we need to ask."

Rose enjoyed the silence that followed. In the first place, she'd brought a little common sense to the place. The people in the room would have been even more surprised had they seen the little press story that gave an account of how, at a luncheon at old Mrs. Master's house, members of the Master family who were well acquainted with the true conditions of the workers, not all of whom were on strike, had questioned the motives of some of the socialist agitators behind it. Old Hetty could still have her moment of glory—her luncheon would be remembered—just not in quite the way she had planned. And the family's reputation would be saved. The story would be printed in several papers that evening.

In the silence that followed, Hetty stared. She couldn't believe it. Her own grandson's wife had come here to ruin her party, in this act of public disloyalty. Her reaction was instant and natural. No doubt Rose knew the trust funds would flow down to William anyway, but if she thought that anything from this house was coming to her, she could forget it.

Hetty looked round for someone to save the day. Her eye alighted on Edmund Keller. It was worth a chance.

"Well, Mr. Keller," she asked, "will you be our knight in shining armor?"

Edmund Keller paused. He liked old Hetty Master, and he would be glad to oblige her. But even more important for him was the cause of truth. And truth was more complex than Rose was making it out to be.

He understood the city well enough to know that the Russian immigrants, having suffered political and religious persecution, were determined to fight anything that looked like oppression in their new home. The Italians, on the other hand, were only fleeing poverty. They sent money back to Italy; many of them didn't even plan to stay in America—sometimes at the docks there were more Italians returning home than arriving. They had less reason to cause trouble, or to enter the political process, therefore. And they might put up with bad treatment when they shouldn't. But even having said that, the situation wasn't straightforward. And if there was one thing, as an academic, that Edmund Keller hated, it was people who simplified evidence until it was misleading.

"Are there picket lines outside the Triangle Factory?" he asked Anna.

"Yes, sir."

"Are there Jewish girls in the picket lines?"

"Yes, sir."

"Are there also Italian girls in the picket lines?"

"Yes, sir."

"Are, I don't know, maybe a quarter of the picketing girls Italian?"

"I think so."

"Why do you not stand in the picket line?"

Anna hesitated. She remembered the day the woman from the WTU had accosted her as she went into work, demanding to know why she was betraying all the other girls. She had felt so guilty. But when she had talked to her parents about it that night, her father had ordered her never to raise the subject again.

"My family does not wish it, sir."

There was a murmur round the room. Keller turned to Rose Master.

"I think we need to be careful here," he said. "The factory owners would no doubt like us to think that this is entirely a Jewish strike, a socialist strike perhaps. But they may be misleading us." He didn't mean to be rude. He just wanted to be accurate.

Old Hetty was beaming. Rose's face was a mask.

But it was then that Edmund Keller made a great mistake.

He wasn't a fool, but he wasn't worldly. He was still an academic. He did not entirely grasp that for the powerful ladies of New York—or London or Paris for that matter—politics was a social game, to demonstrate who had the most influence. He supposed that, behind all these activities, there was actually a search for truth. So he didn't realize that in setting the record straight, he was humiliating Rose.

"Of course," he continued casually, "one can see why this girl's family wouldn't want her to join the WTU. But in fairness, European history shows that factory workers were nearly always exploited until a powerful union or a government intervened."

If the ladies had been holding a historical seminar, a balancing argument like this might have been a point to raise. But they weren't. And he had just given Rose her opening to strike back.

"European history? You'd know all about that, Mr. Keller, I'm sure. And isn't it true Europe is full of socialists? And don't you know that when innocent Italian girls are bullied or deceived into supporting the unions, they're being used by Russian socialists? But you know all about socialists, Mr. Keller, from what I hear. Since you, Mr. Keller, I have it upon good authority, are a socialist."

Keller hadn't particularly studied the socialist question. Nor had he the least idea that the president of Columbia, disliking his somewhat liberal views, had told Rose that he was a socialist. He stared at her in great surprise, therefore, which she, naturally, took to be guilt.

"Aha," she said, triumphantly.

"Well," said Hetty, seeing that things weren't going at all as they should, "this is all very interesting, I must say." Which even Edmund Keller realized was a signal, in these circles, that the discussion should end at once.

✣

Anna was very nervous. "I hope she'll take us away now," she whispered to Salvatore when the meal ended. But Rose Master was busy talking, and so they were left standing alone.

Had she said the wrong thing about the Italian girls on the picket line? Would the lady tell Mr. Harris at the factory, and get her into trouble?

They had been standing together for a minute or two when the old lady who owned the house came across. She was with another lady, not quite so old.

"I'm Mrs. Master," the old lady said. "I just wanted to thank you for coming." She was very polite. "This is my friend Miss O'Donnell," she added.

You could see the other old lady was very rich, but she seemed kindly, and asked where they lived.

"I used to live not far from you, just the other side of the Bowery," she said. Anna looked at her in disbelief. She couldn't imagine the rich lady had ever lived anywhere near the Lower East Side in her life, but she didn't like to say so. The old lady saw the look on her face and smiled. "I used to have to walk past Five Points every day."

"You mean you lived in a tenement like us?" Anna finally ventured.

"I did." Mary O'Donnell paused, as if remembering. Then she glanced at Hetty Master and smiled. "Actually, my father was drunk most of the time, and didn't even work. As for our lodgings . . ." She shook her head at the memory. "I had to walk out in the end." She turned back to Anna and Salvatore. "Your father sounds a good man. Whatever you do, keep your family together. That's the most important thing in the world."

Just then, Rose appeared. Fortunately, she seemed quite pleased about everything, and she took them away. So Anna never found out how the rich lady got out of the Lower East Side.

❖

At Hetty's request, Mary O'Donnell remained after everyone else had gone. Mary knew it was nice to have someone to discuss a party with, when it was over.

"It went well," she told Hetty. "Everyone will remember it. And the conversations certainly made everybody think."

"I am not pleased with Rose," said Hetty.

"Mr. Keller did quite well."

"He meant well. Rose," Hetty continued, "was very disloyal."

"I suppose we must forgive," said Mary.

"I may forgive," Hetty replied, "but I'll be damned if I forget."

"The Italian girl was sweet," said Mary.

"That reminds me," said Hetty. "Why did you tell her that your father was a drunk who didn't work? Your father was a perfectly respectable man. He was a friend of the Kellers. I remember very well the day that Gretchen told me all about you."

Mary paused, and looked at Hetty a bit sheepishly.

"When I saw that girl and her brother," she confessed, "and heard about how they were living, it all suddenly came back to me. I don't know what made me blurt it out, though."

Hetty eyed her. "Are you telling me, Mary O'Donnell, after all these years, that you came to work here under false pretenses? That you weren't from a respectable family at all?"

"I don't think I could have done it. But Gretchen could. She was my friend." Mary smiled, affectionately. "I'm afraid she told you the most dreadful lies."

Hetty considered. "Well," she said finally, "I'm very glad that she did."

⁘

Edmund Keller spent a pleasant evening with his father. It wasn't until the next morning that he heard what had happened at the meeting at Carnegie Hall.

And what a night it had been. The radicals had produced a splendid speaker, Morris Hillquit the socialist. With soaring oratory, he told the packed hall that the factory owners and the magistrates who had fined them were nothing more than the mailed fists of oppression. "Sisters," he cried, "your cause is just, and you will be victorious." Not only that, he assured them, the garment women's strike was the beginning of something altogether more wonderful. Through the union, they could lead the great socialist cause of a class struggle that would soon transform not only the factories of the Lower East Side, but the entire city, and even the whole of America. It was a thrilling speech, and they cheered him to the rafters.

True, he was followed by a moderate lawyer who counseled restraint and a legal battle instead. But his speech was so boring that the crowd grew restless. And when Leonora O'Reilly of the WTU spoke next, and chided the lawyer, and told the women that their strike had done more for the union movement than all the preaching of the last ten years, they cheered her too. No wonder they were in high spirits.

But not everyone was happy. Tammany Hall liked political power, not revolution. The conservative leaders of America's big unions, men like Sam Gompers, didn't think that preaching revolution was a good strategy either. From that evening, support in the smoke-filled rooms of the labor movement began to fade. And something else began to ebb away rapidly. Money.

Had Rose's intervention at old Hetty's lunch made an impression? Who knew? But one thing was certain. When Anne Morgan attended the Carnegie Hall meeting, she didn't like what she heard. The very next day she let everyone know that she'd support the garment women's rights, but not socialism. She wasn't giving money to start a revolution. Other wealthy donors followed her lead.

It wasn't until early February that the strike wound down. The women got a shorter working week, down to only fifty-two hours; they were even allowed to join a union. But the Triangle and the other factories could employ whomever they liked, union member or not.

Edmund Keller supposed that Rose must be pleased about that. He'd been puzzled that she thought he was a socialist, but since he wasn't, he'd shrugged the accusation off as made in the excitement of the moment.

He did not quite understand that because she believed him to be a socialist, and because she thought he'd tried to make a fool of her in public, Rose Master was now, in fact, his enemy.

꧁

The year 1910 was a happy one for Salvatore. He was fourteen years old now, and starting to feel himself a young man. It was also the year that he and Anna decided they were going to make little Angelo stronger. Anna's method was to give him more food. Each day when they went home together from the Triangle Factory, they would stop at the restaurant where Uncle Luigi worked, and the owner would give them a little bag of leftovers. "For the sickly one," he'd say.

Salvatore's method was more robust. He made some little weights, and forced his nine-year-old brother to work with them in front of him each day. "I'm building up his muscles," he told everybody. In the summer, he started taking him to the East River where, although it was illegal, the boys of the area used to swim. When Anna found out, she had a fit. "The water's filthy. You'll make him sick," she cried. As the months passed, however, Angelo did seem to become sturdier. He stayed just as dreamy, though.

As for Anna, at eighteen she had filled out into a young woman, but she was still almost as slim as she had been when she was a young girl. Men turned to look after her in the street; she had no young man though, and said she wasn't interested. Salvatore was sure of one thing. "If any young man comes calling for you, he won't just have to get past Father," he told her, "he'll have to be inspected by *me*." Only the best would do for his sister.

"And if you don't approve of him?" she teased.

"I'll throw him in the East River," he said. He meant it.

At the start of December it was Anna's birthday, and on the fifth, Uncle Luigi took the whole family out to the theater. They went to the American Music Hall on Forty-second Street, to see a show called *The Wow Wows* given by a British troupe on tour from London. The star was a talented young English actor named Charles Chaplin. They had a wonderful time. The next week, Anna told them that she'd got a raise at work. She was already making $12 a week; now she'd get an extra dollar. So the year ended well.

Except for one thing.

It was one bright morning in October when Paolo suddenly told Salvatore that he should go on alone because he had some other business to attend to. "I'll meet you on Broadway and Fulton at four o'clock," he said, and before Salvatore could ask him anything, he was gone.

That afternoon, he told Salvatore that he mustn't speak of his absence. "There's a man I'm doing some work for," he said. "That's all." He produced some money, about what he'd have made shining shoes, but Salvatore had a feeling that his brother had more in his pocket.

One day the next week, the same thing happened. Soon it became a regular occurrence. At Christmas, he gave presents to all the members of the family. He said he'd secretly been saving up to do so. Everyone was pleased. Salvatore got a pocket watch; Anna a lovely shawl. But Concetta looked worried. Just before the new year she questioned Salvatore about his brother's movements. Salvatore lied as Paolo had told him to, but he could see that his mother didn't believe him.

"He is working for some *camorrista*," she said. By that she meant any sort of bad person. "Or maybe worse. Maybe the *Mano Nero*." The Black Hand. It wasn't really an organization. Any gang wanting to extort money—usually from the richer Italians in their own community—would seek to increase their victim's fear by using the dreaded symbol of the Black Hand.

"No," said Salvatore.

"It's the fault of the police," said his mother. "Why do they do nothing?"

Of the thirty thousand policemen in the city, many of them Irish fellow Catholics, hardly any could speak Italian. True, the NYPD had started an Italian squad. But its chief had been killed on a visit to Sicily by a gangster named Don Vito, and the squad had become insignificant after that. So long as Italian crime remained within the Italian quarter, the New York police didn't interfere too much.

That evening, she accosted Paolo and accused him of being a criminal. But he denied it all, and became very angry; and in the end their father said the matter was not to be spoken of again.

✢

The young man appeared in March 1911. Salvatore, Angelo and Anna had called in at the restaurant where Uncle Luigi worked one evening. They'd been made to wait a few moments, during which time Salvatore had noticed a good-looking young man watching them with interest. But he'd soon forgotten about it. The next day, however, as he was walking up the street, he'd met Uncle Luigi, who was eager to speak.

It seemed that the young man had already noticed Anna several times. His name was Pasquale, and he was very respectable, with a good job as a clerk. He wanted to meet her, but he was a little shy.

"If you already *knew* him," Uncle Luigi suggested with a wink, "then it would be natural for him to meet Anna one day."

"And if I don't like him, then Anna doesn't get to meet him?" Salvatore asked, pointedly.

"*Si, si*, of course."

Salvatore agreed, and the next day he came by the restaurant where Pasquale was having coffee and a *dolce*. To Uncle Luigi's great pleasure, Salvatore liked the young man. He was serious, clearly a good worker. His family were not rich, but they had more money than the Carusos. By the end of the conversation it was agreed that he would come by the restaurant as usual, after Anna finished work the following Saturday. If he saw Pasquale there, he would introduce him to Anna, and Uncle Luigi would give them all a *dolce*.

Salvatore was rather pleased with his new role. He looked forward to Saturday with some anticipation. He wondered how much to tell Anna.

✢

On Saturday, March 25, 1911, Anna went to work as usual. It was a fine day. Saturday was the shortest working day at the Triangle Factory. Work began at nine in the morning and finished at 4:45 p.m., with a forty-five-minute break for lunch. By the time she arrived, there was a crowd outside waiting to go in.

Although it was the Jewish Sabbath, and both the owners and most of the workers were Jewish, only a handful of the people at the Triangle Factory observed the Shabbat, and there would be nearly five hundred people working there today.

There were two entrances to the building, one on Washington Place, the other round the corner on Greene Street. She went in at the Washington Place entrance and took the stairs. The elevator was for the management and visitors.

The Triangle Factory occupied the three top floors of the building, the eighth, ninth and tenth. On the stairs, she met Yetta, a Jewish girl who worked on the eighth floor, and she went onto that floor to finish their conversation. As well as the lines of work tables and sewing machines, the eighth floor contained the cutting tables, under which there were big boxes that would soon fill with discarded scraps of cotton as the cutters toiled. Beside one of the tables, Yetta showed Anna the steps of a new dance called the turkey trot. They both liked to dance, but a stern look from one of the foremen soon put a stop to that, and Anna made her way up to the ninth floor, where she worked.

The morning passed uneventfully. Not long ago the ninth floor had been refurbished with better washrooms and a nice wooden floor that caught the sunlight. At lunchtime, she went outside and walked about in Washington Square Park. She thought of the dance steps her friend had shown her. She wondered if Pasquale liked to dance.

It hadn't taken her long to find out about Pasquale. As soon as Salvatore casually mentioned that they might be meeting a friend of his at the restaurant, she'd guessed he was up to something. As for Salvatore's pathetic attempts to deny it, she'd soon dealt with that. When he confessed, she pretended to be angry. What she didn't tell her brother was that she'd already noticed the young man looking at her, and she didn't mind meeting him at all. But she told Salvatore that she didn't know if she'd come with him or not, just to give him grief. She was smiling to herself as she went back into the building at the start of the afternoon.

Saturday afternoons were always a little hectic. At the end of the week's work, the shipping clerks would be running around trying to get all the final orders completed. As finishing time approached, the pay packets were given out. You couldn't go before the final bell, of course, but some of the girls who had young men waiting for them were getting ready to make a speedy exit. As the bell went, and the power to the machines was cut off, everybody rose. But Anna wasn't in a hurry. She took a little mirror out of her bag. Might as well make herself look nice before meeting the mystery man. She attended to this while the girls started moving toward the door. She was still sitting there when she heard something strange. Someone was shouting.

⁜

From the statue of Garibaldi, there was a good view across to Washington Place. In summer, the leaves on the trees obscured it. But as Salvatore looked now, he could see the higher floors of the building clearly, and the sign—a triangle in a circle—that hung from the corner. He glanced at the watch Paolo had given him for Christmas.

"It's time," he remarked to Angelo.

"Will Uncle Luigi give me a hot chocolate?"

"Sure." Salvatore looked across at the building. Any moment now, the first girls would start coming out of the door. A young man strolled by, paused for a moment, to look in the same direction.

And just then, a curious thing happened. There was a little popping sound. Nothing much, just a pop, from one of the windows up on the eighth floor. An instant later, a little puff of smoke came out of the window, and a tiny tinkle of glass could be heard from the street below. A horse standing there suddenly bolted with its cart. From above, smoke began to drift out of the broken window. A man ran across the street.

The fellow who'd paused beside the statue set off quickly toward the scene, leaving Salvatore and Angelo standing there. Moments later, whistles sounded from a fire station. Then a cop on horseback clattered down the street and ran into the building. People were spilling out onto the sidewalks, and from the far side of the park, a fire wagon came clanging into view.

"Stay here," Salvatore told Angelo. "If Anna comes, wait for me."

When he reached the building, he checked first the front doorway, then the one around the corner on Greene Street. There was no sign of Anna. Moments later, a group of girls came out of the front entrance. He spoke to one of them and learned that they'd come down from the eighth floor in the elevator. "The fire's caught the boxes of cotton," she told him. "They went up like they were kerosene."

"What about the girls on the other floors?" he asked. But she didn't know.

More and more fire wagons were arriving. You had to say, the speed of their response was impressive. Firemen—they seemed to be mostly Irish—were running hoses from the fire hydrants in the street, and taking them into the building.

They weren't letting anyone go in. All Salvatore could do was rush from one entrance to another, trying to get whatever information he could from the girls coming out, or chance words he heard from the firemen.

The building's own water hoses weren't working, he'd heard, but the pressure in the hydrants was good. The fire had started on the eighth floor, which was now engulfed in flames, and the firemen couldn't get past it. Somebody said there was a fire escape that went down the well in the center of the block. But it had collapsed. Some girls had managed to reach lower floors that way, but others were on it when it fell. Smoke and flames were pouring out of the upper windows now, on the Greene Street side.

Salvatore saw people pointing up at the roof, and he ran back a little way so that he could see. A crowd of workers were standing on the roof, and people from the adjoining New York University building, which was a little higher, had let down ladders so they could escape. Had the girls from the ninth floor got up there? It was impossible to know.

He went back to the statue of Garibaldi.

"Where's Anna?" Angelo was wide-eyed.

"She'll come."

"Where is she?"

"Maybe she's coming down in the elevator, though some of the girls are going by the roof. She'll find us if we wait here."

"Is it dangerous?"

"No." Salvatore tried to smile. "Look at all the fire wagons and the firemen, and all the people coming out."

Angelo nodded. But he looked frightened all the same.

Then Salvatore saw her.

Anna was standing by one of the ninth-floor windows. Girls were appearing at the other windows on that floor too. They seemed indistinct, and then he realized that there must be smoke in the room behind them. One of the girls opened a window, and some smoke came out. There was a faint flickering of light in the cavernous space behind them. The flames must have reached that floor.

Why were the girls by the windows? Couldn't they get out? It must be getting hot in there. Very hot.

The girl stepped out onto the window ledge. Above the ninth floor, a heavy cornice ran round the building, jutting out a foot or two. The girl looked up at it. Perhaps she was wondering if she could get up there and work her way round to safety. Perhaps she didn't know that the fire was already on the tenth floor above. But the floors of the building were twelve feet high; there was no way she could get up there anyway.

Other windows were opening now, and other girls edging out onto the ledges. A young man stepped out, too. They were looking down; the street was a hundred feet below. You could see the flames behind them now. Obviously they couldn't stand the heat inside any more.

The firemen saw them and trained one of the hoses up there. The arc of water shot skyward, but by the time it got to a hundred feet high, it broke into a sprinkle. They started to run a fire wagon ladder up the side of the building, but that was no good—it couldn't reach within thirty feet. The ladder rested there, tempting but useless. They were opening nets now, above the sidewalk. The people on the ledges were looking down at them. Would the nets hold if they jumped? It was an awfully long way down. The firemen didn't seem to be telling them to jump. They hesitated.

Then Salvatore saw that Anna was looking toward them. She could see the statue of Garibaldi from up there, for sure, and she must be trying to find him and Angelo. With the water from the hoses and the smoke from the floor below, though, it mightn't be so easy to make them out. He waved. Beside him, little Angelo waved too. But Anna didn't wave back.

"Are we waving at Anna?" Angelo asked. "Can you see her?"

Salvatore didn't answer. One of the girls had jumped. The young man jumped after her. Then Anna jumped.

Angelo didn't see.

"Wait here," Salvatore cried, and ran toward the building.

The nets were useless, of course. The firemen had only put them there as a last resort. By the time Salvatore got there, the fire chief was already telling his men to take them down again.

The young man who jumped had gone straight through the net. Anna and the other girls who'd followed her had hardly been slowed at all before they hit the sidewalk. Amazingly, Anna's face was quite preserved, though the back of her head was entirely crushed. He didn't need the fireman to tell him she was dead.

"That's my sister," he told the fireman, and gave him his name. "I have to take my little brother home, then I'll be back." He was amazed how composed he was.

He got back to the statue.

"Did Anna jump?" Angelo asked.

"Yes. She's all right, but she's hurt her leg, so they may take her to the hospital. She told me to take you home, and tell Mama. Then we'll all go to see her later."

"I want to see her now."

"No, she told us to go straight home."

"Are you sure she's all right?"

"She's fine."

✦

On May 23, 1911, no less a person than the President of the United States was in the City of New York for an important ceremony. On the site of the old fortress-like reservoir, the big library on Fifth Avenue was finally opening for business.

The collection, based on the amalgamation of the Astor and Lenox libraries, was huge. Backed with bequests from Watts and Tilden, the splendid new beaux arts building, designed by Carrère & Hastings, stretched across the two blocks from Fortieth Street to Forty-second. It might have taken an inordinate time to build, but it was worth it. The marbled facade and broad steps, flanked by two lions, could hardly be more magnificent, yet the place was also welcoming. Thanks to a huge donation from Andrew Carnegie, the New York Public Library system was among the most generous free institutions in the world.

Though the building would not be open to the general public until the following day, there was quite a crowd of the city's richest and most important folk looking round after President Taft had done the honors.

Old Hetty Master moved rather slowly.

"I'm so glad," she said to Mary O'Donnell, "that I've got you to go round with me."

The last year had seen rather a decline in Hetty, which was only to be expected at her age. As they moved through the great marble entrance hall, however, she insisted on walking up the stairs.

"It's two floors up," Mary warned her. And the floors were terribly high.

"I can walk," the old lady insisted. "And I want to see this Reading Room they keep talking about." The Reading Room on the third floor spanned the entire length of the building, almost a hundred yards. "I remember coming here when they had the Crystal Palace just behind it," she remarked.

"I know," said Mary.

It took time, but they got to the Reading Room, and when they did, they were impressed. It stretched away like one of the vast corridors in the Vatican.

"Well," said Hetty, "it's certainly large."

"It is," said Mary.

"I hope," said Hetty, as she gazed at the rows of tables, "that they can find that many people who want to read. I always fall asleep in libraries, don't you?"

"I hardly use them," Mary confessed.

"Plenty of room to sleep in here," said Hetty. "Let's go down."

It was a bright day outside as they came slowly down the steps onto Fifth Avenue.

"I'm pleased I saw it," said Hetty, "but I'll be glad to go home. I feel a little tired." She paused while Mary looked out for a cab. "Did I tell you," she said, "that my husband proposed to me right here, when they'd just built the reservoir?"

"Yes," said Mary, with a smile.

"That was a wonderful day," said Hetty.

"It must have been," said Mary.

Then Hetty suddenly said, "Oh."

"What is it?" said Mary.

But Hetty didn't say anything. She staggered, as if she'd suddenly been struck.

"Are you all right?" said Mary. But before she finished the question, Hetty started to fall. Mary tried to hold her, but she couldn't, and Hetty crashed to the ground.

It was quite a piece of luck that a shoeshine boy should have been passing right beside them just then. He put down his things and helped them right away. He propped Hetty up, and while Mary held her, he hailed a taxi, and then, since Hetty seemed to be unconscious, he helped Mary get her into the taxi and asked if he should come with her to the house.

"Oh," said Mary, "that would be so kind."

So the boy put his things on the floor of the taxi, and Mary told the taxi to go down Fifth, and in no time they were on their way. Hetty's mouth had fallen open; she seemed to shudder. The boy leaned forward and propped her up, awkwardly, in the corner of the seat.

"Gramercy Park," said the boy to the driver.

"How do you know that?" asked Mary.

"Been to the house," said the boy.

Then Mary realized she had seen him before.

"Why, you're the brother of the Italian girl who came to lunch a few months back," she said. "Your sister works at the Triangle Factory."

The boy said nothing. And Mary remembered the terrible tragedy that had happened there in March. That awful fire. It was a huge scandal—one hundred and forty people had died, mostly the Jewish girls who worked there.

"I hope your sister was all right," she said anxiously.

For a moment, Salvatore Caruso did not reply. He was looking at the older woman. He realized, which Mary still did not, that Hetty Master had just died. That would be enough for this nice lady to worry about today.

"She's fine," he said.

Empire State

OR OVER A century, the United States of America had avoided the tragic quarrels and follies of the Old World. Three years ago, when the countries of Europe, trapped in their complex tangle of rivalries and alliances, had begun the Great War, William and Rose Master, like most thinking Americans, had hoped their country could stay out of the futile quarrel. And for a while it had seemed that this would be accomplished.

Was there a strategic necessity to become engaged? Not really. Was there an emotional reason? Although most Americans assumed that their country was predominantly English, there were in fact more Americans of German descent than either English or Irish. Nor, in the year 1917, were the British too popular. For Britain's cruel crushing of the Easter Rising had enraged Irish Americans, at least; and the British naval blockade had harassed countless American vessels. President Woodrow Wilson, who still liked the British, sent them food. But that was about it. If the Europeans wanted to tear themselves apart again, most people said, that was their problem. Avoid foreign entanglements.

In the end, it was Germany that brought America into the war. Up until recently Wilson, trying to keep his country neutral, had managed to handle the Germans. When their submarines sank the *Lusitania* with Americans on board, he'd protested, and the German high command had stopped the submarine war. Now, however, everything had changed. The Germans had behaved abominably: seeing Russia collapsing into chaos, and the British nearly starving, they had concluded that they could win the war with a final push. Suddenly, German submarines had gone into action again. "Since your ships carry food to the British," Germany told President Wilson, "we'll torpedo any American vessel on the seas." In an astounding insult to the United States, German representatives even told Mexico: "Attack America, and we'll help you take back Texas, New Mexico and Arizona."

It had to be war after that. The massive American mobilization now in progress would soon teach the Germans what it meant to tangle with the free nation across the Atlantic. Only last week, William and Rose had gone down Fifth to Washington Square Park to see the big bonfire where some enterprising young people were burning an effigy of the German Kaiser.

To date, the faraway European conflict had not affected the Master family very much. Indeed, William Master had been surprised to find that he had done quite well out of it. For a few months in 1914, the Stock Exchange had been closed, but a busy market in war bonds had developed, and soon there had been huge business to be done supplying the warring nations of Europe. American manufacturing was still forging ahead; Henry Ford was mass-producing cars on his new assembly lines.

In fact, the greatest immediate worry confronting Rose and William was their son Charlie.

He had not had to register for the draft, at least. That was something. The Draft Registration of May 1917 applied only to men aged twenty-one to thirty-one. But Charlie had given his parents plenty of other reasons to be apprehensive.

Rose had been concerned when Charlie had insisted on going to Columbia University instead of Harvard. "He likes being in New York," her husband pointed out. "I know," she'd answered. "That's what worries me." Quite apart from the fact that Harvard was Harvard, she'd also reckoned that Charlie would get into less trouble in Boston. "I'm just afraid that he'll make undesirable friends."

He had. Before he'd even gone to Columbia, Charlie had shown a precocious interest in the nightlife of the great city. He'd disappear into the theater district or Greenwich Village, and nobody would know where he was. More than once he'd come home drunk.

"And yet, underneath," his mother quite correctly pointed out, "he's still a child."

As for his opinions, now that he was at university, one never knew what he was going to say next. He'd already told her that the Bolsheviks in Russia had a good cause; the other day he'd said he was thinking of joining an anti-war protest. His ideas and enthusiasms seemed to alter every week.

Her husband William might find it all amusing, but she was well aware that Nicholas Murray Butler at Columbia was determined that his university should be seen as patriotic and politically sound at this critical time. He'd warned the faculty and undergraduates that if they started any public protest against the war, they'd be dismissed, and recently Charlie had confessed that two of his friends had been expelled. She lived in terror that any day he might come home and tell her that the same thing had happened to him.

"I'm sure," William said cheerfully, "that if Charlie gets in trouble, you'll be able to smooth things over with Butler. Just ask him to one of your parties."

It was true that Rose Master was quite a force to be reckoned with, these days. After the death of old Hetty Master, a good deal of money had flowed down to William's parents. And when, a couple of years ago, William's mother had died, and Tom Master had followed her not a year later, the trust funds had left William and Rose in possession of a considerable fortune, to do with as they pleased.

Recently they'd moved up to a considerably larger townhouse just off Fifth Avenue in the Sixties, only a couple of blocks from the magnificent new palace of Henry Frick. The house had a fine classical facade and a further, special feature, copied from Mr. Scribner the publisher's house, which stood nearby. Most people with motor cars kept them in converted stables nearby, but in the Masters' new house, the entrance was through a double gateway, leading into a little courtyard, where the car descended into a basement garage by a private elevator. William had also bought a new Rolls-Royce, the Sedanca de Ville model, which resided there.

If Rose, over the last decade, had built up a reputation as a hostess who entertained delightfully, but with a well-judged, old-money restraint, she was now able to do the same thing on a considerably grander scale. And through her entertaining, it was perfectly true, she could wield surprising influence.

But she was well aware of her limitations.

"If Charlie annoys Nicholas Murray Butler," she said, "I don't think I could save him."

And now, she very much feared, Charlie was about to commit a dangerous error.

✤

So it was in no uncertain terms that she told Charlie, one November evening: "No, Charles, I will not have that man in my house."

"But, Mother," he protested, "I already invited him."

Why, of all the people lecturing at Columbia University, Charlie had singled out Edmund Keller as a hero she had no idea. As far as Rose was concerned, the relationship between their two families had died with old Hetty. But earlier that fall, when Charlie had met the popular lecturer and Keller had expressed his warm remembrance of the Master family's role in his own father's career, Charlie had been delighted.

"I realized we still have some of his father's photographs," he told his mother. "He even asked me if I meant to be a patron of the arts."

"He's trying to flatter you."

"It's not like that," Charlie said, with a frown. "You don't understand. Keller's a pretty important person at Columbia; he doesn't need us."

It was true that, with commendable restraint in her opinion, Butler had allowed Mr. Keller to continue his career as a university teacher, and that Keller had done quite well. But in her mind, two facts remained. Firstly, Edmund Keller had been, and no doubt still was, a socialist. Secondly, her son was far too impressionable.

And now Charlie, in an act of childish idiocy, had asked the man to one of her select parties. But looking at Charlie's fair-haired, blue-eyed face, it now occurred to her that it might be wiser if she used a little subtlety. Keller must be dealt with, but in a way that wouldn't antagonize her son.

"He really wouldn't like the party, Charlie," she said. "But let's do something even better. Ask him to come to dinner with us, just a family dinner, where we can get to know him better, and talk."

A week later, Edmund Keller, suitably attired in a dinner jacket and black tie, came to call at the house. When Charlie had first suggested he come to a party at his parents' house, he'd been a little uncertain. He remembered that Rose had once referred to his views as socialistic at a luncheon—though it had been said during an argument, and was years ago anyway—so he'd assumed that she didn't much care for him. But the pressing invitation he now received to a family dinner seemed to indicate that there were no bad feelings at all.

He wasn't a fool, but the world in which Edmund lived operated in a slightly different manner from Rose's. It had not occurred to him that if Rose Master invited him to a family dinner, it was not a compliment at all, or an expression of friendship, but a signal that she didn't wish him to meet her friends. He walked quite contentedly, therefore, unaware that he was an undesirable.

The first thing that happened was that he met Charlie and his father in the courtyard. They were dressed for dinner, but William was about to put the car away. They spent a most agreeable few minutes discussing the Rolls-Royce, and then William asked him if he'd like to come out for a quick spin. Keller politely wondered if they'd be keeping his hostess waiting. Knowing that, for all his wife cared, Keller could have driven to Maine, William assured him it was all right. So they drove all the way down Fifth to Washington Square, then circled round, came up Sixth, back along Central Park South, past the Plaza Hotel, to Fifth. William clearly enjoyed driving his car, and he gave Keller a lively explanation of its technical merits. They got back, descended in the elevator to the garage, and then, cheeks flushed from the night air, joined Rose in the drawing room. Moments later, dinner was announced.

They ate in the dining room. All the leaves of the dining table had been removed, so although the dinner was formally served, they were quite intimate. He sat between William and Rose, with young Charlie opposite him.

The conversation was easy. He told Rose how much he admired the car, then Charlie introduced the subject of Theodore Keller and his photography, and the splendid photograph of Niagara Falls that William's grandfather had commissioned. Theodore Keller was in his late seventies now, and when the old man finally departed, Edmund explained, he would be the custodian of all his father's work. "It's quite an archive," he remarked. This led to a discourse on the Civil War, and then the conversation turned to the present war with Germany.

William and Edmund discussed whether the convoys would be able to get past the enemy submarines in the Atlantic, and they all wondered how long the war would last. Then Keller remarked that, as well as its terrible cost in human lives, the war was also a cultural tragedy.

For no sooner had the United States entered the war against Germany than an ugly anti-German hysteria had begun. Anything that sounded German was now suspect. German-language journals were being closed, while in Britain, Keller pointed out, even the Lord Chancellor had been forced out of office because, in an unguarded moment, he'd remarked that he still loved German music and philosophy.

"What about me?" he said. "My family were German, and I'm certainly not going to stop listening to Beethoven or reading Goethe and Schiller because of the war. That would be absurd. Why, I even speak German."

"Really?" said William.

"Yes. My father could hardly speak a word, but a few years ago I got interested in German literature and wanted to read it in the original, so I started taking lessons. I speak it almost fluently now."

From there the conversation turned to the temperance movement, which had been becoming increasingly strident recently.

"I hate those people," Charlie declared with passion. His father smiled and remarked that this was hardly surprising. Keller then politely inquired what Rose thought about it.

"We belong to the Episcopal Church," she answered, quietly. Surely Keller must know that people like herself had nothing to do with these growing calls—which had even reached Congress now—for Prohibition. The whole thing was driven by Methodists, Baptists, Congregationalists and other churches that mostly catered to a different class of person.

"The irony," William said, "is that if Prohibition does get passed, we shall probably have the war to thank for it. The Episcopal and Catholic Churches may not support the idea, but the most effective lobbying against it has always come from the brewing interests, which are mostly owned by families with German names. And as you rightly say, Keller, everything German's so unpopular now that nobody wants to listen to them. It's really absurd."

And what did his hostess think of votes for women? Keller asked.

"Votes for women?" Rose paused. Alva Belmont's cause had been making some headway, though the suffragists were quieter now, with the war claiming everyone's attention. Rose hated to be on the same side as Alva Belmont, but she admitted grudgingly: "I think it will come. It should."

Rose could see that, although William understood her reservations about Keller, her husband still found the historian interesting. What was Keller's opinion of the situation in Russia? he wanted to know. Rather to her surprise, Edmund Keller seemed pessimistic.

"It's impossible to predict," he said, "but if history is anything to go by, then I am fearful. The French Revolution might have been splendid, but it still introduced a reign of terror."

"The tragedy to my mind," William Master remarked, "is that despite all Russia's problems, the economy was growing rapidly until this war began. Russia might have developed into a prosperous and contented nation."

Here, however, Keller could not agree. "I just don't think that the tsar's autocracy could be sustained," he said. "As a historian, I may foresee bloodshed, but it's hard to blame the Russians for wanting a change of government."

"Even by socialists?" Rose asked.

Keller considered. He wanted to be fair. "I dare say if I were a Russian I'd think so."

Rose said nothing more. It was a clever answer, but it did nothing to change her view of Edmund Keller's politics. Charlie, however, was eager to explore this dangerous territory further.

"Don't you think capitalism oppresses the workers?" he wanted to know. "I think it does."

Keller hesitated. "I suppose," he said pleasantly, "that any system that gives power to a particular class will tempt that class to exploit the powerless. It seems to be human nature."

"The capitalist system is a tyranny," Charlie announced, "based on greed."

His mother turned her eyes to the sky. His father smiled and murmured: "Remind me to stop your allowance." But Keller, as teacher, could not help giving every proposition its due consideration.

"You could argue," he said, "that any strong belief can blind people to other realities. Belief in profit at the expense of other things can be a cruel master. Look at that wretched business at the Triangle Factory, for instance."

Rose stared at him. Did he really mean to bring up the Triangle strike now? To remind her how he'd tried to embarrass her, at Hetty's luncheon, seven years ago? To start that argument over the factory girls again, when he was a guest in her own house? Was he being supremely tactless, or outrightly aggressive?

"Those striking girls," she said very firmly, "were being used by socialists and revolutionaries. And the meeting at Carnegie Hall proved it very clearly."

Keller looked puzzled for a moment. "Oh," he said, "I'm sorry, I didn't mean the strike, I meant the fire."

For it was the aftermath of the Triangle fire that most people remembered. It had been a huge scandal when Blanck and Harris, the factory owners, had been taken to court and sued. It had turned out that the exit from the ninth floor, where so many girls had died, had been locked, and the fire precautions totally inadequate. Even after that, it had only been union pressure that had improved the standard of worker safety in the city.

"My point," he went on, "is that the factory owners were so blinded to their workers' safety by their pursuit of profit that they actually lost some of their own relations in the fire, and could have perished themselves."

"The fire? Oh. I see."

"It was sad about the girl, wasn't it?"

"The girl?"

"The Italian girl you brought to that lunch. Anna Caruso. I noted her name at the time."

"What about her?"

"She died in the Triangle fire. I noticed her name when the newspapers published the lists."

"I wasn't aware."

"Mother!" Charlie was looking at her, in disbelief. Rose felt herself blush.

"How should I know such a thing?" she said irritably.

"I'm embarrassed," said Charlie to his tutor.

Rose stared at Edmund Keller. So he'd made her look a fool again. In front of her own son, this time. For all she knew, Charlie was going to start respecting him more than he did his own mother very soon. If she'd disliked the socialistic Mr. Keller before, she felt a positive aversion for him now. But she did not show it.

"Tell me, Mr. Keller, about your work at the university," she said very sweetly. "Are you writing a book?"

❖

The burgundy was excellent. By the time they were halfway through the main course, the butler had refilled Edmund's glass more than once, and he felt quite at home as he talked about his researches for a book on Greece and Rome. Young Charlie was looking happy, his father had shown himself to be friendly and interesting, and even his hostess, about whose feelings he was a little uncertain, was listening with every show of interest. It seemed to Keller that he was among friends. After a slight pause, he decided it would be pleasant to share a confidence with them.

"Between ourselves," he told them, "there's a chance I might be going to England next year. To Oxford."

"Oh," said Charlie, looking rather disappointed.

"I heard things were awfully quiet there," said William Master.

"That's just the point," Keller said. "So many of the Oxford under-graduates and faculty are away fighting in the war that the place is half empty. I could live in one of the colleges as a visiting fellow for a year, do a little teaching, and work on my book. I'd also have the chance to make myself known there. I might even get a permanent fellowship."

"How did this arise?" William asked.

"Through Elihu Pusey," said Keller. "Perhaps you know him?" They didn't. "Well, he's a rich old gentleman here in New York, and a notable scholar. I met him through some research I'm doing. He has connections with two Oxford colleges, Trinity and Merton, and he's going to put in a good word with them both on my account."

"How fortunate," Rose murmured.

"The only thing that would hold me back is my father. He's getting so frail that I don't like to leave him. But he insists I should go, and he's offered to finance the whole thing."

"Selfishly, I hope you stay here," said Charlie.

"Don't repeat what I've told you, please," said Keller.

"Of course not," said Rose.

The thought of Edmund Keller being removed from Columbia for the rest of Charlie's time there was certainly most attractive to Rose. But with all her social connections she couldn't quite see what she could do to make it come about. If Elihu Pusey meant to recommend him to people he knew, well and good, but she had no means of influencing an Oxford college.

She'd almost put the business out of her mind, therefore, when just a week later, at a gathering to support the New York Public Library, she saw that Mr. Pusey was also one of the guests, and asked to be introduced to him.

He was a distinguished-looking old gentleman. It didn't take her long to steer the conversation to Columbia University, to mention that her son was there, and that she knew Mr. Nicholas Murray Butler.

"I know Butler, of course," he said politely, though she didn't detect any great warmth in the statement.

"There's a lecturer my son likes very much named Edmund Keller. I wonder if you have ever met him."

"Edmund Keller?" Now Elihu Pusey brightened visibly. "I certainly know him. A historian of great promise. In fact . . ." He seemed to be about to say something, and then to have changed his mind.

"He was at my house for dinner the other day," she said, pausing for a reaction. "He and my husband share an enthusiasm for Rolls-Royce motor cars," she continued gently. "Mr. Keller is quite an Anglophile."

"Ah." Elihu Pusey looked at her sharply. He paused a moment. "Do you know him well?"

"Not especially well, but I know a lot about him. My husband's grandparents, Frank and Hetty Master, were great supporters of his father, the photographer, in his early days."

"I see. Master." She could see him calling to mind what he knew about the name. "Then you are the Mrs. Master who lives just off Fifth Avenue? I have heard of your dinner parties."

"I'm so glad. Could I persuade you to come to one of them?"

"Most certainly." He brightened again. Whether it was the prospect of dinner, or more probably that he knew of her reputation for sound, conservative opinions, Elihu Pusey seemed to be ready to divulge more of whatever was on his mind. "Perhaps," he said quietly, "you could give me your opinion on a rather sensitive matter. In confidence, that is."

"People in my position know the value of discretion, Mr. Pusey."

"Quite. The fact is that I was going to write a letter for young Keller, a recommendation."

"I see."

"But before doing so, I thought I should make one or two further inquiries. His family is German, I understand. German-speaking, even. And I wondered whether, in the present circumstances . . ."

She could guess exactly what Elihu Pusey must be wondering, and she could sympathize. He's imagining those Oxford colleges, she thought, and what it will do to his reputation if Keller arrives there on his recommendation, and starts making pro-German statements.

"I remember hearing that Edmund Keller had to study German in connection with his reading at one time," Rose said blandly. "I believe he speaks several languages. But I can tell you for a fact that his father Theodore doesn't speak a word of German. The family is as American as, I don't know, Astor or Hoover, or Studebaker."

"Ah." Elihu Pusey hesitated. "There is another matter, perhaps more serious. I spoke to Nicholas Murray Butler, and he did express to me a slight concern. He feared that some of Mr. Keller's views might be . . ." the old man hardly liked even to pronounce the word, "somewhat socialistic."

If there was ever a time to dissemble, this was it. For just a moment, Rose looked completely astonished.

"Socialistic?"

"Yes."

She smiled. "You know Mr. Butler well, I am sure, Mr. Pusey, and he is a man who has prejudices."

"True."

"Well, I know from my son that Mr. Keller in his lectures, for instance, is always scrupulous to present both sides of a case. And I can imagine Mr. Butler, if he does not care for somebody, accusing them of," she shrugged, "I don't know what. But I can assure you of one thing: if Mr. Keller was any kind of a socialist, he'd never have set foot in *my* house."

"Butler can be unreasonably prejudiced," Pusey agreed. "But are you sure about Keller's private views?"

"I am for this reason, Mr. Pusey. Just a few years ago, when there was all that trouble about those garment workers striking, I was at a private luncheon. And I heard Mr. Keller speak out—very strongly—against the strikers. He warned everyone there, in the plainest terms, that the strikers were being whipped up by socialists and Russians and anarchists, and that we should give them no consideration at all. He spoke with great passion. I remember it well. And how right he turned out to be." And having delivered herself of this monstrous, bare-faced lie, she gave old Mr. Pusey a meaningful nod. "So much," she said drily, "for Nicholas Murray Butler."

"Ah." Elihu Pusey looked immensely gratified. "That is most helpful, Mrs. Master. Really most helpful."

❖

It was a couple of months later when Charlie informed her that Edmund Keller would be going away to Oxford.

"I know it's what he wanted," she said with a smile. Three thousand miles away from her impressionable son—everything that she could wish for, but that would remain her little secret.

"And Keller says that you put in a good word for him with the man who was recommending him. You never told me you did that. Keller's so grateful to you."

"It was nothing. I just happened to meet Mr. Pusey at a party, that's all."

"I know you used not to like Keller too much. I guess you must have changed your mind, after he came to dinner."

"Evidently."

"I'm so impressed that you could do that. Change your mind, I mean."

"Well, thank you."

"I can tell you one thing."

"What's that, Charlie?"

"Edmund Keller," he said, beaming at her, "is now your friend for life."

❧ 1925 ❧

Strangely, it was not the death of Anna, nor the war, nor even the bizarre new law—inexplicable to anyone from a wine-producing country —that forbade Americans to consume alcoholic drinks, nor the increasing estrangement of Paolo from his parents that changed the life of Salvatore Caruso's family. It was his eldest brother Giuseppe and the Long Island Rail Road.

The LIRR was a wonderful thing. A huge and complex amalgamation of railways and trolley lines, some going back nearly a century, the mighty system ran from Pennsylvania, across Manhattan to Long Island. Through Penn Station in Manhattan, and the great junction at Jamaica, Long Island, millions of commuters now flowed. Naturally, the railroad did everything it could to persuade the world of the merits of Long Island as a place to live, from which you could easily get into the big city. And the expanding island railway lines were chiefly built by Italians.

As a result, Italian communities had been settling at numerous places along Long Island's pleasant south shore.

When America first entered the war, before any conscription lists had been started, Giuseppe Caruso had decided to enlist. His father was not sure it was a good idea, but Giuseppe had told him: "We're Italians, Papa. Still outsiders. We have to show that Italians are good Americans, like anyone else. And as I'm the oldest son, it should be me."

Salvatore always remembered the day that his big brother had come back safely, and walked down Mulberry Street in his uniform, getting smiles and congratulations from their neighbors, and even a friendly nod from an Irish policeman who happened to be passing. And perhaps that was the moment when Salvatore truly became American, as he proudly watched his brother who, by his service, had already led the way.

It was soon after his return that Giuseppe had decided to join a group of his comrades-in-arms who were going to work on the Long Island Rail Road. And it was not a year before one of his workmates introduced him to a nice young Italian girl. Her family lived on Long Island, out near Valley Stream, but what really impressed the Carusos was that Giuseppe told them: "Her family have land."

Not much, to be sure, but you didn't need a huge farm to grow vegetables. Plenty of other Italians were setting up as small Long Island farmers now. One enterprising family named Broccoli, who grew the vegetable of that name, had contracts to supply some of the finest restaurants in New York.

The girl's family made a modest living. Better yet, as she had no brothers, Giuseppe and she would take over the farm one day from her parents, in the old-fashioned way. And the Caruso family would be back where it belonged, farming the land.

The wedding was a traditional affair, just like a village wedding back home. Within a year, Giovanni and Concetta Caruso had moved out to Long Island. They couldn't afford to retire, but Giuseppe had found some easier work for both of them. For the first time in the twenty and more years since she'd come to America, Concetta Caruso looked contented. Maria went with them to Long Island, and soon found work in a local store.

So that just left Salvatore, Angelo and Uncle Luigi in the city.

And Paolo, of course. Not that you ever saw him. A few months after Anna's death, he'd given up shining boots. He told the family he was working for a man who owned property in Greenwich Village. Salvatore went to the place once, and found an office where several Italian men were keeping books. When he said he was looking for his brother Paolo, they told him Paolo was out, and didn't encourage him to wait. That was all Salvatore ever discovered. Each week Paolo would put money on the kitchen table for their mother, but she only took it reluctantly; if he offered her presents, she always refused them. As time went on, Paolo and she hardly spoke, and in the end he announced that he'd found another place to live.

Every few months, however—usually when Salvatore was alone somewhere—Paolo would suddenly appear. He was always sharply dressed. He'd smile and embrace Salvatore, and they'd chat and maybe eat something together. But there seemed to be a hardness about Paolo now; Salvatore could imagine him becoming cold, and threatening. Their old comradeship was gone. Before departing, Paolo always left money with Salvatore for their parents.

Salvatore and Angelo had discussed going out to live on Long Island, but they soon agreed that neither of them wanted to. So they rearranged the family lodgings so that Uncle Luigi could move in with them too, and with three men working hard and splitting the rent, they could all put a little money aside each week. Uncle Luigi, who pocketed his tips and consumed almost nothing beyond the leftovers he ate in the restaurant, must have accumulated quite a lot of savings, Salvatore suspected, though his uncle's finances were always a mystery. Once, when he asked Uncle Luigi what he did with his money, his uncle told him: "I invest it." And when Salvatore asked him how he decided what to invest in, Uncle Luigi answered: "I pray to St. Anthony." Salvatore never knew if he was serious about this or not.

Salvatore never forgot what Anna had said. He always looked out for Angelo, and he really didn't mind. He loved his little brother. After Anna's death, he'd started showing him the world. When the Carusos first arrived in New York, the subway system would take them up as far as Harlem; but in the two decades that followed, it was extended up into the Bronx, across to Brooklyn and far into Queens. The fare was only five cents, no matter where one went. Sometimes he and Angelo would ride out into the growing suburbs just to say they'd been there.

Salvatore would also take Angelo to a ball game. With Babe Ruth playing for the Yankees, baseball in New York was exciting. Thanks to Paolo, who'd somehow got them tickets, they'd also gone up to the Polo Grounds to see Jack Dempsey fight Luis Firpo, El Toro Salvaje de las Pampas. That had been an event to remember, with Dempsey knocked clean out of the ring before he came back to win.

But Angelo's favorite outing was going to the movies. The movies weren't expensive. They'd watch the Keystone Kops, and Charlie Chaplin, who'd settled in America and switched from stage to screen. They'd see D. W. Griffith's great stories over and over. From the moment that the organist started to play, Angelo's face would become rapt. He also had an amazing memory, and he could name every movie his favorite stars had performed in, and facts about their performances and lives in the way that other kids could remember baseball scores. He followed the careers of Mary Pickford and Lillian Gish with special devotion.

These stars, however, seemed to be the only women in Angelo's life. Salvatore liked going out with girls, and one day he wanted to marry, but not until he'd saved up some money. In the meantime, once a week, he'd make a visit to the old Tenderloin District, around Broadway in the Thirties. There were plenty of prostitutes in Little Italy, but he preferred to keep this part of his life private. Uncle Luigi knew what he did, and always cautioned him to be careful. "Do you know," he told him, "they made it so difficult for our troops to get rubbers in the war that nearly three-quarters of our boys caught something?" He even told him where he could buy the rarer latex ones. Salvatore took precautions. As he told his uncle, with a shrug: "Whores cost money, but it's better than going crazy."

Salvatore wasn't sure why Angelo had so little contact with women. Perhaps he was too shy. Salvatore wondered if he ought to do something about it, but Uncle Luigi advised him to leave well alone.

What worried Uncle Luigi was not Angelo's leisure, but his work. When Salvatore had become a bricklayer, Angelo had quietly joined him, and whether or not it was thanks to the weights he still worked out with, he had grown into quite a wiry young man, so he could handle the physical labor without difficulty.

"But he shouldn't be laying bricks," Uncle Luigi would protest. "He has talent." Uncle Luigi might have abandoned his foolish dream that Angelo should be an architect, but there were other things the young man could be: a house painter, a decorator, something at least where he could use the gifts God gave him. It seemed, though, that Angelo preferred to work with his brother. Yet he'd never stopped drawing. Salvatore might go out to a bar after supper, but Angelo would stay at the kitchen table, occasionally reading a book, but usually drawing. And at these times, his young face would take on a look of concentrated intensity. Sometimes, coming home early, Salvatore had entered the room and stood for several minutes beside Angelo while he was drawing before Angelo even noticed that he was there. Uncle Luigi had taken some of the drawings, framed them and sold them to customers at the restaurant. But his attempts to persuade Angelo to take orders for pictures from customers had so far gotten nowhere. "I get paid for laying bricks," he told his uncle with a smile, "and then I can draw what I like."

At least there was no shortage of work. Maybe the war had made America nervous about aliens, Salvatore wasn't sure, but the government had put quotas on immigration. Apart from a lot of black people who came up from the South, the flood of new immigrants into New York had turned to a trickle. Meanwhile, the city was booming. Wages were good, and rising.

The years had passed. By 1925, Salvatore's cache of savings had grown enough for him to wonder whether, maybe, he could think about looking for a wife.

⁂

He was walking down Sixth Avenue on a cold day in December when he met Paolo. His brother was looking sharp, in a double-breasted overcoat and a derby hat. He might have been taken for a banker. Or a gangster. He was evidently surprised to see Salvatore, but he grinned.

"You chose the right place to meet, kid," he said. "Come in and eat." The Fronton occupied a basement a block to the west of Washington Square, by Sixth Avenue. Run by young Jack Kriendler and Charlie Berns, it was one of the best speakeasies in town. Salvatore noticed that as soon as Paolo's face appeared at the entrance, where visitors made themselves known through a peephole, the door was instantly opened, and Paolo was greeted by name.

The Fronton was a spacious cellar. The floor was mostly taken up by tables with white tablecloths. There was a bar along one side of the room, and pictures of the Wild West on the walls. The place was already filling up with the lunchtime crowd, and Salvatore noticed one or two well-known faces. But Paolo was given a table at once. They each ordered a steak, and in the meantime, they were served Irish whiskey. Salvatore remarked that Paolo looked well, and Paolo smiled, raising his glass.

"Let's drink to Prohibition, brother. It's been good to me."

When the temperance movement had triumphed, and the Eighteenth Amendment to the Constitution banning the sale of "intoxicating liquors" went into effect in 1920, the face of America might have changed. But it sure as hell hadn't stopped people drinking. The law was the law, but millions of people didn't believe in it. Respectable restaurants would adopt subterfuges—a bowl of soup, for instance, might turn out to be liquor. And in cities like New York, there were the speakeasies—subject to police raids, but ever-present. And of course, as with every law that denies people something they are determined to have, Prohibition had created a huge and profitable market, where illicit supply could name its price. Bootlegger operators like Rothstein, Waxy Gordon, Frank Costello, Big Bill Dwyer and Lucky Luciano were making fortunes. Salvatore had wondered for a long time if his brother was involved in bootlegging. Now Paolo had as good as told him.

They chatted about the family. Paolo asked Salvatore about his love life, and then told him: "I can get you a real high-class girl, I mean one of the best. For free." He grinned. "She owes us a debt. You want to try her?"

"I'll think about it," Salvatore said, but he had no desire to get mixed up with Paolo's friends, and they both knew it. "Maybe I'll find a nice girl and get married," he added.

"*Bene. Bene.*" Paolo looked pleased. "You'll invite me to your wedding?"

"Of course. How could my brother not be at my wedding?"

They talked about Angelo next, and how Uncle Luigi still wanted him to make more of his life.

"Maybe Uncle Luigi's right, though," said Paolo. "The kid could go to painting school or something. If you need money . . ."

Salvatore gazed at his brother, and felt a wave of affection. Behind the gangster—for that's what his brother was—the old Paolo was still there. He wanted to do right by his family. He was trying to show his love, maybe receive love too. Salvatore reached over and squeezed his brother's arm.

"You're a good brother," he said softly. "I'll tell you if Angelo needs anything."

They finished their steaks. Paolo ordered coffee.

"Can I ask you something?" Salvatore said.

"Sure."

"Does it worry you, being on the wrong side of the law?"

Paolo paused before replying.

"Do you remember 1907, when Rossi lost all our father's savings?"

"Of course I do."

"And do you remember 1911, when Anna got killed in the factory?"

"How could I forget?"

"I remember too, Salvatore." Paolo nodded, and suddenly a suppressed passion came into his voice. "I remember with anger. With bitterness. Because my family was poor, because they were ignorant, because they were losers, people dared to steal from them, to let them fry in fire traps." He shrugged, furiously. "Why not? We were only Italians. Wops. Dagos. So I said to myself, I will not be a loser. I will do whatever it takes, but I will win." He paused again, seemed to collect himself, then smiled. "Maybe I'll get rich and marry and buy a big farm for us all. How about that, little brother?"

So then Salvatore understood his brother's dream.

A party of four was just being seated at the table next to theirs. Salvatore glanced across. They were uptown people. There was a young man in his twenties, somewhat carelessly dressed, and a young woman, a typical flapper, he thought. By the look of it, the middle-aged couple with them were the parents of the young man. The father seemed like a Yankee Wall Street type, handsome and blue-eyed. The mother was wearing a pearl choker and a fur. She looked about nervously. Salvatore thought he'd seen her before. He tried to remember where.

"I just hope, Charles," she said, "that there isn't going to be a police raid. It would be so embarrassing."

The young man laughed and told her not to worry, but she didn't look too happy.

Then, to Salvatore's surprise, Paolo leaned over toward their table.

"Forgive me, ma'am," he said smoothly, in a voice Salvatore had never heard before, "but I think I can put your mind at rest."

Salvatore observed with amazement. He had never seen his brother like this before. The Paolo he had known since his childhood, who still spoke with the hint of an Italian accent, had suddenly disappeared. In his place was an elegant man who sounded like an uptown lawyer.

"Oh," said the lady, looking pleased, "I'd be so glad if you would."

"Well," Paolo smiled, "there are two reasons. The first is that, if the police were going to raid this establishment, I would already know about it. The second is that, two tables behind you, is the mayor of New York."

Her husband looked at the table in question, gave a huge grin to Paolo and burst out laughing. For there indeed was none other than James J. Walker, the charming Irish mayor of New York, who did as he pleased in all matters, including wine, women and song.

With a smile to the lady, and a respectful nod toward the mayor, Paolo rose to leave.

"Would you really know if the place was going to be raided?" Salvatore asked as they came out onto the sidewalk.

"Course I would, kid. The cops are all taken care of—Lucky Luciano pays the police over $10,000 a week." He chuckled. "That lady had some nice pearls, whoever she was."

"Actually," said Salvatore, "I just realized. I know her."

⁘

"Well," said Rose to Charlie, "when you take us out to lunch, it's always an adventure." This wasn't a compliment. And because he knew that, Charlie laughed.

The last time he'd taken his parents out, it was to the Algonquin Hotel. They had quite enjoyed that. After all, it was not even a block from Fifth Avenue, on West Forty-fourth Street. The Harvard Club was just a few doors down, and, better yet, the New York Yacht Club, that nexus of his mother's summer at Newport, had its magnificent city clubhouse almost beside it. "Why," as his mother declared, "I must have been within yards of this hotel a hundred times, and never thought to look inside."

The great feature of the Algonquin was the big table at which, every day, the literary luminaries of the city met together. He'd pointed out the writers Benchley and Sherwood, the critic Dorothy Parker, and Ross, who'd just started his *New Yorker* magazine that year. Rose was especially pleased about seeing Ross. People were starting to talk about the *New Yorker*.

As Charlie glanced around the speakeasy, he wondered if there was anyone, apart from the mayor, that he could point out to his mother. "That's Edna St. Vincent Millay, the poetess," he said, indicating a strikingly beautiful woman sitting in one corner. "She won a Pulitzer Prize." He was tempted, but decided not to add that she liked to sleep with interesting people of either sex. He had enough trouble with his mother as it was.

Rose Master didn't approve of Charlie's desire to be a writer. He understood. "You can buy pictures, but people like us don't paint them, dear," she'd once told him when he was a boy, and it was almost the same with writing. A professor could write history of course; a gentleman of leisure might write a memoir. During the war, one of the distinguished Washburn family had even been a war correspondent for *The Times* of London. That was different. But to live in lodgings in Greenwich Village, make undesirable friends, and hang about Tin Pan Alley, trying to write plays and songs, was a shocking waste of a life for a young man with everything to live for. When he confessed that he'd like to write like Eugene O'Neill, she'd been appalled. "But he's a drunk," she protested. "And his friends are communists."

Charlie also suspected that his mother's fear was not only that he'd permanently adopt a bohemian lifestyle, but that he wouldn't be able to make a decent living.

Strangely enough, his father had been his secret ally. William had given him a job in his office, but the work was very light, and as long as he turned up for a few hours each day, his father didn't seem to mind.

"Making money's quite boring, really," William had said. "I have more fun with my car."

Though this was probably true, Charlie reckoned that his father must be making a fortune, on top of the fortune he'd inherited.

Most people they knew seemed to be doing well. For although, at the Great War's end, there had been the usual post-war recession, it hadn't lasted long. And once it was past, in New York at least, the Roaring Twenties had begun.

It was an amazing time to be a New Yorker. Europe, devastated by the war, was still on its knees. The British Empire was severely weakened. London was still a great financial center, but New York was now richer and more powerful. All over America, helped by anti-trust legislation and other safeguards, modest enterprises had blossomed. American industries and cities were booming. But New York was the financial center through which this new wealth flowed. Wall Street men bought into the newly created wealth, traded its stocks and prices soared. Brokers get rich when stocks are traded. Speculators get richer still. William Master speculated, but his main business was the brokerage house, which he pretty much owned these days.

If his father was so accommodating toward his literary ambitions, Charlie shrewdly guessed that behind this lay two calculations. First, that William reckoned it was wiser to keep a genial eye on his son than provoke a quarrel. Second, that the family now had so much money that it didn't matter anyway.

And Charlie was happy. He loved the Village, with its intimate atmosphere, its theaters, its writers and artists. He took the modest salary his father paid him, and never asked for anything more. He showed up at the house for social gatherings if his mother wanted, and when he did, he was charming to her guests, who found him witty and amusing. If he'd written some songs for the music publishers in Tin Pan Alley, they thought it was delightful. They promised to come to his play, when it was performed. "Young people are leading such exciting lives, these days," they said.

Which brought him to Peaches. His parents hadn't met Peaches before, and his mother was eyeing her, cautiously.

"What a very pretty ring, my dear," she said, at last.

Peaches was wearing a short dress and a smart coat with a fur-trimmed shawl collar, which she'd opened when she sat down. Her hair was bobbed, under a cloche hat. Her lips were dark red. While the waiter was getting their drinks, she'd taken out a cigarette holder, put a cigarette in it, and taken a long draw, blowing the smoke politely over Rose's head. The ring was an elegant little art deco piece, a pair of garnets set in white-gold filigree. The garnets matched her lips.

"It was made by a friend," she said. "He's the bee's knees."

Rose didn't like the flappers. She thought their haircuts made them look like boys, and their dresses were much too short. Before the war, the Gibson Girl look, the trim blouses and skirts that places like the Triangle Factory had catered to, had suggested a new female freedom. And the end of the war had brought them a very real freedom: the right to vote. But to Rose, freedom meant responsibility, yet the flappers seemed to think they could be free with their morals as well. They smoked and danced the charleston; many of them quite certainly made free love. And they seemed to be everywhere you looked.

She wasn't surprised that Charlie had taken up with a flapper, but, as usual, she was disappointed in him.

"Where do you come from?" she asked the girl. A simple enough question.

"London." She looked bored. Charlie for some reason seemed to think this very funny. "Paris too," she added. "Then Washington."

"Did you like Washington?" Rose asked coldly.

"It was dull."

"And where did you meet Charles?"

"In a speakeasy. He was half cut."

"I was plastered," said Charlie with a grin.

"But I could see he was no kluck," Peaches added, obligingly.

"I'm just a flypaper," Charlie said.

"Stick around."

How Rose hated the way these young people talked. She'd heard it all before, of course. They thought they were so clever. It had also dawned on her that Peaches had not lived in either London or Paris, or even Washington probably, and that this was just her way of letting them know she had no intention of answering any questions if she didn't feel like it.

"You work in the city?" Rose asked.

"In the music business."

William Master stepped in now. He liked Broadway musicals. He'd been at the opening of Kaufman's *The Cocoanuts* just the week before— the Marx Brothers were the stars. He asked Peaches if she'd seen it, and was favored with a smile. "It's good," she acknowledged.

"Think it'll run?"

"Yes. Then it'll tour. The Gershwins have a premiere later this month, too."

"I know. *Tip-Toes*. We have seats. Do you and Charlie want to join us?" This provoked another smile.

"We'll come," said Charlie. "When Father went to the *Rhapsody in Blue* concert last year," he told Peaches, "he said it was the most beautiful piece of music he'd ever heard."

"That's good." She turned to William. "I could use another drink."

"You like to drink?" remarked Rose.

"She always carries some hooch with her," said Charlie cheerfully.

Rose glanced at the little handbag Peaches had been carrying. It was too small to hold more than some lipstick and powder. Peaches laughed.

"Not there," she said. She stood, and pulled up her short skirt.

Halfway up her thigh was a garter. And above that, tucked into the top of her stocking, a silver hip flask. "Here," she said.

Rose stared. She noticed that her husband was also gazing at the girl's thigh, without disapproval.

"Well, dear, I'm glad it's somewhere convenient."

Only when they were on their way home afterward did Rose express her true feelings to her husband. "It's time," she said firmly, "that you gave Charlie some work to do."

⁘

It was at the start of the following June that Salvatore took Angelo to Coney Island. Anyone who'd last visited the place half a century earlier, when it was a seaside village, would have been astonished to see it now. First came a carousel, next a roller coaster, then vaudeville houses and amusement parks. By the end of the nineteenth century, more than a hundred thousand visitors might go there on a summer day. You could even take the subway to Coney Island now.

The day was warm. Angelo was enchanted with the place. They strolled along the boardwalk past the Brighton Beach Hotel, then along Oriental Boulevard. They had sundaes at an ice-cream parlor. Salvatore encouraged Angelo to look at the pretty girls bathing in the sea.

They were standing near the garish lights of the Luna Amusement Park when he noticed the two young women. They looked as if they might be Italian, but he wasn't sure. One of them was too tall for his taste, but the other caught his attention. The light sunburn on her face suggested she might come from a farm. She was wearing a cotton dress. Her breasts were not large, but full, and her legs were nice, a little plump. He liked that. Her brown hair was swept back in a bun, and her eyes were kind.

He walked over casually with Angelo, and paused beside them, as if wondering whether to go in. The girl glanced at him and smiled, but not in a flirtatious way. She turned back to her companion.

"Well," she said in Italian, "if you won't go on the roller coaster, do you want to go in here?"

Salvatore smiled. Then he addressed her in Italian.

"My brother's afraid of the roller coaster," he lied.

"My cousin's the same."

"Maybe if we all four go together, that will give them courage."

The girl gave him a quick look, decided he was respectable, and turned to her cousin, who shrugged.

"*Andiamo*," said the girl. "My name is Teresa," she added.

"Salvatore. You're Italian?"

"Almost." She laughed. "Albanian. From Inwood."

For a moment, Salvatore was surprised. Inwood, at the top of Manhattan, was a mainly Irish and Jewish neighborhood. But then he remembered. Here on Long Island there was another Inwood, on the eastern side of Jamaica Bay. He knew that Albanians had often been forced to flee their native land down the centuries. In southern Italy there were whole populations who spoke a part Albanian dialect called Tosca. And there was a large Albanian-Italian community out at Inwood, Long Island.

So Teresa and Salvatore and her cousin and Angelo all went on the roller coaster together. Then they went on the bumper cars, and out to the small racetrack, and came back and had hot dogs at Nathan's, and visited a dance hall.

At the end of the day, he asked Teresa if he might see her again, and she said that she and another cousin were coming into the city the following Sunday. So it was agreed that they would meet at Uncle Luigi's restaurant for an ice, and then go out on the town.

"You can bring your cousin," he said, "and I'll bring Angelo." At this suggestion of extra company, he thought she might have looked a little disappointed. He was pleased about that, but he wanted to proceed carefully and do everything with propriety.

⁕

Uncle Luigi liked Teresa. He thought she was a nice, sensible girl. Albanian, he said, was almost as good as Italian. And Teresa seemed to like Uncle Luigi too. After they'd had their ices she said she wanted to walk in Central Park, and then visit the stores. Salvatore soon understood that though she loved her family, who all lived together on Long Island, Teresa's greatest joy was to come into the city.

Two weeks later, he went out to meet her at the racetrack by Coney Island. Teresa was with a young male cousin, but Salvatore came alone. They all enjoyed the races, and as they walked to the subway, she linked her arm in his in a friendly way. Her cousin left them for a few moments, and Salvatore kissed her on the cheek. Teresa laughed, but she didn't seem to mind. Then she told him she'd be coming into the city again in two weeks, and they agreed to meet.

This time he had Angelo with him, with orders that if Teresa came with her cousin, he was to stay, but that if she came alone, he was to make himself scarce. Angelo didn't seem to mind. Rather to Salvatore's disappointment, she was accompanied. But they went to a dance hall, and all danced together, and had a good time, and agreed to do the same thing in another two weeks.

In the weeks that followed, Salvatore considered his moves carefully. He had not felt a sudden rush of passion for Teresa, yet from the moment they met, he had felt certain that she was the one. In confidence, he talked to Uncle Luigi about it. Uncle Luigi was humble. "What do I know? I have never been married," he declared.

"I trust your judgment all the same."

"Then I think it is important that your wife should be your friend."

It would have been easier if Teresa lived in the city so that he could see her often. But each time they did meet, he felt a growing sense of friendship and of tenderness for her, and though she was careful not to show him too much, he was sure that she had feelings for him too. She would walk arm in arm with him, and let him kiss her on the cheek. By late summer, he was planning to push the relationship further. And he was wondering what move he should make when she took the matter in hand herself.

At the end of August a terrible event occurred. It shocked all Italians, and most of the women in the Western world. Rudolph Valentino, the Latin lover, the most adored male star of the silent screen, died suddenly, after an operation in New York. He was only thirty-one. As the news broke, a hundred thousand people converged on the hospital.

His latest movie, *The Son of the Sheik*, was just being released, and there were long lines to get in. A few days afterward, Salvatore took Teresa to see it, along with her cousin and Angelo. As they came out Teresa told him that there would be a big lunch party at her family's house the next Sunday, and casually suggested that he and Angelo should come.

So, she wanted him to meet her family.

The following Saturday the two brothers went out to see their parents at their brother Giuseppe's on Long Island. Sunday was a fine day. It only took them an hour to walk from Giuseppe's to Inwood.

Teresa's family lived in a big clapboard house. It stood on a half-acre plot, had a wide porch, and a Victorian turret at one corner. In the back-yard stood a small secondary dwelling. Teresa was looking out for them when they arrived, and immediately took them inside, introducing them to people as they went.

Within moments they had encountered three brothers—two of whom were married—a married sister and two others. One of the married brothers and his wife lived in the little house just behind. And though Teresa's married sister and her other married brother had their own places nearby, this house was obviously the center of the family operations.

Everyone was friendly, and the place was buzzing. There were half a dozen children running around. Teresa's brothers and sisters spoke to Salvatore in Italian, though their children seemed to speak English. "My parents speak a little English," Teresa said with a smile, "but they usually speak to each other in Tosca."

She led them through to the kitchen. "This is Salvatore and Angelo," she said to a strong-faced woman, who gave them a quick, sharp look. "My mother," Teresa explained. "And this"—she turned toward a tall man with a graying beard who had just entered the room—"is my father."

Teresa's father moved with an unhurried dignity. There could be no doubt who was the head of this extensive family. He looked like the pictures of Garibaldi. He greeted the two young men politely, but said nothing more.

Salvatore soon realized that, outside the family, he and Angelo were the only guests. Before the time even came to sit down for the meal, he had discovered that as well as owning some fields, Teresa's father ran a fruit and vegetable store with one of his sons. His son-in-law was in the local shellfish business, and his two other sons ran a local trucking business.

The table was arranged in a large T, so that the fourteen adults and half-dozen children could all be seated in the biggest room. Teresa was seated in between Salvatore and Angelo. Her brother-in-law, a thickset, rather earnest man of thirty, sat opposite Salvatore. Her father, at the head of the table, was just a few places away where he could keep an eye on them all. At the start of the meal, out of politeness, he addressed a few questions to Salvatore, asking about his family and where they came from.

Salvatore answered that he was Italian and lived in the city, but that the rest of the family were out on Long Island now, and that his elder brother would inherit a farm. Teresa's father nodded at this, and remarked that he hoped Salvatore and his brother would soon be able to leave the city themselves.

"My father thinks the city is unhealthy," Teresa explained with a laugh.

Teresa's father did not trouble him further, and the meal proceeded in a friendly fashion. Teresa was quite lively, and told him funny stories about her relations. As Salvatore looked around, it seemed to him that this was how the Caruso family might also have been, if they had been richer.

Teresa was talking to Angelo during the dessert course when her brother-in-law quietly engaged Salvatore in conversation. He asked him about his work, and hearing that he was a bricklayer, he shook his head.

"Manual work is not so bad when you're young, but one must think ahead. Are you able to save?" When Salvatore nodded, he continued earnestly. "That's good. One needs money to start a business. What will you do?" Salvatore had never thought of this. To him, his savings were to have something put by for clothes, or periods of sickness, or any of the other things one might need, especially if you got married. Seeing his uncertainty, the fellow carried on. "The old man"—he indicated Teresa's father—"will want his daughter to marry a man with a business of some kind. Or at least some assets." He helped himself to a piece of pie. "Very important to him."

Salvatore said nothing. After the meal, the young men all went for a walk while the women cleaned up. Since Teresa had guests, she was allowed to walk out with the boys. They went down to the water where the fishermen brought in the oysters and clams. Teresa told him that she'd like to come into the city to see a movie. "My father doesn't like the city, but I do," she said. So they arranged to meet again in two weeks.

On his departure, he thanked Teresa's parents for their hospitality, and though they were polite to him, they did not express a hope that he should return. And he might have felt a little awkward, if Angelo hadn't suddenly appeared with a piece of paper.

"A gift from me and my brother," he said with a smile, handing it to Teresa's mother, who frowned slightly as she took it. But then, as she saw what it was, she beamed and showed it to her husband. It was a drawing of their house, an excellent likeness to which he had cleverly added some seabirds circling overhead. Their parting was much warmer after that.

All the same, when he got back to the city, Salvatore pondered. He had no doubt that Teresa's brother-in-law had spoken the truth. Was there really any chance that Teresa's family would accept him? When it came to it, would she be happy with a poor fellow like himself? He wasn't sure. And he wasn't sure what he should do about it.

✤

Charlie Master often went to Harlem. He went there for the jazz. Sometimes he met Edmund Keller up on 142nd Street, at the Cotton Club. The audience at the club was strictly "Whites Only"—though a few black celebrities and their friends might be found in there sometimes.

But then Harlem itself, in the mixing of races, was still a frontier area.

Until the terrible attacks on them back in the Draft Riots of 1863, most of the city's Southern blacks had lived downtown. After that, there was a move to the Tenderloin area on Midtown's West Side. Soon, their cabarets and theaters were so successful that the area became known as "Black Bohemia." By late in the century, immigrants from Virginia and the Carolinas, fleeing the Jim Crow laws, had swelled the population, and once again, tension with the Irish community was rising. But it was only during Charlie's own childhood that the big move of African Americans into the mainly Jewish and Italian streets of Harlem had begun. They weren't made very welcome—they were usually charged higher rent—but they came all the same. Now they were making the area their own.

The Cotton Club was quite a scene. From the street, with its big corner site on Lenox Avenue, and brightly lit entrance, one would have thought it was a movie theater. Only the patrons in evening dress getting out of their expensive cars gave a clue as to what it was really like inside.

The club was big and elegant. The clientele sat at small round tables, each with a single candle in the center of a spotless white linen tablecloth. There was room for dancing, but the key to the place was the show. The proscenium stage was large and lit with footlights on each side. This evening, the front of the stage had a mirrored floor, so that the reflection of the chorus girls exploded into the space above. The back of the stage was filled by the Fletcher Henderson Band.

Charlie had been planning to bring Peaches here tonight, but Peaches wasn't coming. Peaches was out with another man. Charlie was pretty upset about that. But it was no good getting upset, he reminded himself, when it came to Peaches. He'd known that when it started. He knew it now it was finished.

He'd called Edmund Keller and asked him if he'd like to meet at the club, and fortunately Keller had been free. They'd ordered their meal and listened to the music. "God, Henderson is good," said Keller. Charlie nodded.

They finished their food and ordered another drink. Charlie glanced around the room.

"See anyone?" asked Keller.

One never knew who would be at the Cotton Club. The mayor, of course—it was his kind of place. Music people like Irving Berlin and George Gershwin, singers like Al Jolson and Jimmy Durante. Anyone from the fashionable New York crowd. Charlie had recently started to write a novel. He liked taking note of any scenes he might be able to use some day, and he always made a point of talking to people—both because they interested him, and because they might give him useful dialogue.

"I wondered if Madden was here," Charlie said.

Did it worry any of these good people that the place was owned by Owney Madden, the bootlegger, who had bought the club while he was still in Sing Sing, doing time for murder? It never seemed to. Madden might kill people who crossed him, but why worry about a few murders when he ran the best jazz club in town? Madden had friends, too. The police hadn't raided the club in a long time now.

Charlie had talked to Madden once or twice. Despite his Irish name, Madden was born and raised in northern England, and proud of it. The bootlegger and jazz club owner's accent was broad Yorkshire.

Charlie was just finishing his survey of the room when he noticed the table just behind them. Three men had been sitting there, talking quietly, but he hadn't paid particular attention to them. Now two of them were leaving. The third man remained, with his back to him, but then he turned to look at the stage.

The face was familiar, but it took Charlie a few moments to place it. Then, seeing an opportunity to talk, he glanced at the man again, gave him a brief nod, and smiled. The man stared blankly.

"You won't remember," said Charlie easily, "but I saw you in the Fronton one time. You were nice to my mother. Told her not to worry about the police."

The man frowned, then slowly remembered. "Right. There was a girl, too."

"Not any more."

"Sorry."

"Don't be." He held out his hand. "Charlie Master."

"Paul Caruso." The man was smooth, but watchful. Charlie knew enough to tread carefully. His uptown, cheerful manner usually disarmed people.

"Interesting name. Any relation to the great Caruso?"

"We've met," said the Italian cautiously. "My family's eaten with him."

"Great man. Big heart," said Charlie. Something in the Italian's manner suggested that he wasn't anxious to have a conversation about his family. Charlie decided to say no more. So he was surprised when Edmund Keller suddenly joined the conversation.

"I once met a girl of that name, years ago. Anna Caruso. She worked at the Triangle Factory." He turned to Charlie. "Your mother brought her to old Mrs. Master's house, I told you once. I'm afraid she was killed in that terrible fire, though."

Charlie watched the Italian. Paolo Caruso's face was perfectly still, but he glanced down at the table before replying: "It's a common Italian name."

"It's been good talking to you, Mr. Caruso," said Charlie. "I'm afraid we have to go now." He smiled. "Until the next speakeasy." He held out his hand.

Paolo Caruso took his hand briefly and nodded. He didn't smile.

"That was awkward," Charlie remarked to Keller when they got outside.

"Why?"

"I think the girl was his family."

"He said she wasn't."

"That's not quite what he said. I think he didn't want to talk about it." Charlie shrugged. "Maybe I'm just being a novelist." Novelists liked to imagine the interconnectedness of things—as though all the people in the big city were part of some great organism, their lives intertwined. He thought of the poet's saying that the preachers liked to quote: "No man is an island." Or the other: "Do not ask for whom the bell tolls, it tolls for thee." Foolish, sentimental tricks of the mind, probably. Reality was fragmented. "Forget it," he said. "What the hell do I know?"

⁜

Paolo Caruso remained where he sat. He did not think about Anna at first. There were other things he had to consider.

Briefly, he thought about the two men. When Charlie had first addressed him he'd wondered for a moment if these men could be spies, sent to track him down. But they were certainly uptown, no part of his world. Besides, he did remember the incident with Charlie's mother in the speakeasy. He put the idea aside as foolish.

He'd come to the club with a couple of business associates. Men he trusted. But he'd also been hoping to see Owney Madden. He'd done a small service for Madden a couple of years back, and he trusted the man's judgment. Maybe the owner of the Cotton Club could help him out. But Madden wasn't around, and no one could tell him whether he'd be in that evening or not.

He decided to wait a while. At least he was safe. No one was going to start trouble inside a swank place like the Cotton Club. Maybe Madden would show up.

If only he had left that business last week alone. It hadn't been part of his regular employment. His bosses didn't know about it yet, and they wouldn't be too pleased when they did. He'd have to be careful how he explained the thing to Madden, too. Madden had risen through the Gopher gang when he was young. He had his own bootlegging operation now, in Hell's Kitchen on the West Side waterfront, and he mightn't be too sympathetic to a man who'd gone off on his own without permission. But he had interests in so many businesses. Maybe he could find something for him out of the city and protect him. It was a long shot but worth a try.

It wasn't the first contract Paolo had taken on. There were always gangland killings, but when you were asked in from outside to do something special, the money was tempting. He'd taken one before this—done the job just the day after he'd had lunch with Salvatore in the Fronton speakeasy. That had gone off well. No doubt that's why he'd been offered this other job.

But last week had gone terribly awry. There was nothing wrong with the plan, but even the best plan can be thrown off course by an unexpected event. It was dark. The wind was strong and gusting, perfect for dispersing the sound of the shots. The street had been deserted. He'd stepped out from the doorway just in front of his man, with his hat pulled down to shield his face, and taken aim. Do it at point-blank range. Do it so swiftly that his victim would hardly have time to register surprise.

Who could have imagined that a slate blown from a roof above would crash at his feet, at that precise moment, causing him to jerk his head up?

The other fellow had thought quicker than he had, then. Instead of running away, he'd barged straight into him, knocking him over and kicking the gun out of his hand. Then he'd run fast up the street, dived round the corner, loosed off a couple of rounds that had only just missed. Paolo had his gun by then. He'd returned fire, and given chase. But his victim had vanished. And he'd seen Paolo's face.

So now there were some very angry people in Brooklyn.

The question was, what to do? Probably best to leave town. But where should he go? Maybe Madden could suggest something.

The orchestra was playing "Gin House Blues." A Henderson composition. A couple of years back, the Henderson sound had been enriched by a young trumpet player named Louis Armstrong. He'd departed for Chicago, unfortunately, but maybe he'd be back. Paolo knew that Madden also had his eye on another up-and-coming band leader, Duke Ellington, who played over at the Kentucky Club. That was what was so impressive about Madden. He was always looking for something new.

Paolo glanced at his watch. It was nearly two in the morning. He doubted Madden would show up now, but he decided to wait a little longer.

His thoughts turned to the conversation with Charlie and his friend. How strange that the friend should have met Anna. He remembered those terrible days after her death. He recalled his anger, his sense of rage and impotence. That was what had set him on his path, really. This rocky, dangerous path, to this high, dark place, from which he now feared to fall. He had loved Anna. Loved all his family, really. If only, he told himself, they weren't such losers. He shrugged. Maybe he was going to be a loser too, pretty soon.

He signaled for the check and paid it. No use waiting any longer.

As he stepped onto the sidewalk outside, he buttoned his coat tightly. The temperature had fallen, and it had begun to snow. There was half an inch on the street already. He looked around carefully; he could only see a few black people. It was white men he had to beware of. He pulled his hat down over his eyes, partly to hide his face, but mostly against the snow that the wind was whipping along the street. He started to walk.

As a precaution, he'd moved lodgings three days ago, to a place off

Eighth Avenue where he wasn't known. He'd walk to the subway, make sure he wasn't being followed, and take a circuitous route home. He turned down Lenox Avenue.

Hell, it was cold.

⁙

Salvatore didn't see Teresa during the month of October. There wasn't a telephone at his lodgings, but there was a payphone nearby, and Teresa's family had one in their house. He waited ten days before calling and asking to speak to her. He listened carefully to the tone of her voice. She sounded pleased to hear from him.

"My parents say thank you again for the picture," she said. "Will you tell Angelo?"

"Sure."

"I won't be coming into the city for a little while."

"Is that because of your parents?"

"My parents say I have to go with my cousin and she's not free right now," she said. It sounded like an excuse. "But I'd like to see you," she added.

"I'll call again," he promised.

Was there some hope? He had a long talk with Uncle Luigi about his finances. "You may not have much," Uncle Luigi advised, "but at least increase what you have. Put your savings in the stock market. You can't lose. It's going up all the time. The whole country's getting richer every day." He grinned. "Let your little boat rise with the tide." It seemed to make sense. But the childhood memory of his father's savings and Signor Rossi still weighed on Salvatore's mind, and for a while he hesitated.

It wasn't only a question of money, either.

"Her family may want a man with a business," he told his uncle, "but even if I had the money, what would I do?" True, the work he did was hard, physical labor, but his body was strong, and he liked being out in the open, even when the weather was cold. There was a freedom to it, too. You went to work, you did the work, you were paid, and then you were free. There were plenty of jobs for a skilled laborer like himself too. He had no worries. But if he had a business of his own to run, he knew very well that he would always have worries. He'd have to sit in an office or a store, instead of working as a real man should, in the open air.

He thought about this for a week or two. In the end he decided that if this was the price of getting Teresa, then it was worth it. Whether he could do anything that would satisfy her family, though, was another matter.

In late October, Angelo fell sick. Nobody knew what the sickness was. It began like the flu, but although his fever left him after ten days, he remained very weak, and coughed continually. Uncle Luigi nursed him by day, Salvatore in the evenings. By late November, Salvatore sent for their mother, who decided at once that Angelo should come out to Long Island.

A few days later he telephoned Teresa's house to tell her what had happened.

"Maybe I could go and visit him," she suggested, "if you think he'd like company. It's not far to bicycle." She paused. "If you came out at the same time, I could see you too."

He grinned. She'd found a perfect excuse to see him. He promised he'd be out there before Christmas.

✜

It was a cold December evening when the two Irish cops came to the door. There had been snow the night before and it was still lying by the roadways. Uncle Luigi was out at the restaurant. He knew he'd done nothing wrong, so he wasn't alarmed when they asked for him by name. Then they told him why they'd come.

The morgue they took him to was up in Harlem. There was a big bare room in the basement. Maybe it was so cold because of the snow outside, or maybe they always kept it cold. There were quite a few pallets in the room, each covered with a sheet. They led him to one near the middle and pulled back the sheet.

The gray corpse lying there was in evening clothes. His jaw had been bandaged to hold it up, and the face looked quite handsome. The white dress shirt he wore, however, was covered with great blackened bloodstains.

"Five bullets," one of the cops said. "Must've killed him right away." He looked questioningly at Salvatore.

"Yes," said Salvatore. "That's my brother Paolo."

✜

The family gathered in the city for the funeral. Neighbors and friends came too. The priests tactfully spoke of Paolo as a much loved son and kindly brother, the victim of unknown hoodlums up in Harlem. Everybody knew the truth, but nobody said it.

At Christmas, the family gathered out on Long Island. Salvatore had spoken to Teresa to tell her about the death, but he didn't suggest a visit.

Angelo was looking pale. His mother wouldn't let him go out of the house during the cold weather, and he spent part of the day resting, but he didn't seem in bad spirits. "Mostly," he told Salvatore, "I feel bored." He had managed to get hold of all kinds of newspapers and journals, some of them a little out of date, but he waved toward a great pile of these and said he'd read them all.

Uncle Luigi decided that this was a good opportunity to work his financial magic, and had a long talk with Angelo about investing his savings. Rather surprisingly, Angelo said: "Maybe you're right. I should do that." And he listened to his uncle most carefully for more than an hour, nodding his head gravely from time to time. "I only have a little to invest," he said, but when his uncle asked how much, he just smiled gently and answered: "A little."

"He is like me," Uncle Luigi cried delightedly. "Never tell anyone how much you have. Keep them guessing."

As for Uncle Luigi's help in making any transactions, Angelo said that his uncle could put him in touch with a trustworthy person to buy any shares for him, but that he'd make the decisions himself. He said this in such a quiet way that Salvatore was impressed. His little brother seemed to be growing up.

Giuseppe and his wife had persuaded Angelo to take a small commission. They wanted him to make them a nice sign with the name of her family's farm on it. Although he disliked working to order, Angelo had agreed, and on Christmas Day he presented it to them. He had taken the piece of wood they had given him, painted it white, and put the name, Clearwater Farm, in blue letters, together with a little picture of a farmstead, floating like Noah's Ark, on a blue sea. It was so ingenious and memorable that they were quite overjoyed. And Salvatore could see that Angelo was flattered and pleased by the attention his effort received.

Two days after Christmas, however, Angelo said he felt unwell, and he rested during the remaining days that Salvatore was there.

❖

In the third week of January, when Salvatore next went out to see his parents, Teresa came over, she and her cousin arriving on bicycles. The visit was a big success. Teresa was polite and respectful to his parents. "You can see that she comes from good people," his mother declared. Salvatore also noticed with pleasure how kind and gentle she was with Angelo. She sat quietly with Angelo and told him stories to make him laugh.

Angelo was looking a little better and his cough was almost gone. But he was still very pale, and spent most of his day indoors, sitting in a big chair. He had obviously been active, though. On the table beside him, Salvatore saw a number of cuttings from the newspapers' financial pages, some of them ringed in red pencil. There were also designs for a storefront for the local bakery. This was a commission that their father had arranged. They were only paying a little money, but Angelo seemed glad to have something to keep him occupied. When Teresa made a suggestion for an improvement to one of the designs, Angelo looked at the design very intently for a few moments and then said quietly, "No. That is not what I want," and for a moment Teresa looked a little offended. But then she smiled and lightly remarked: "The patient knows what he wants."

After that, Angelo said he would make two drawings, one of her and one of her cousin, which he would give them to keep. This pleased both girls, and while this work was in progress, Salvatore went over to see Giuseppe. Then he and Teresa went for a walk to the seashore and back, while her cousin remained, keeping Angelo company. As they were walking together, Teresa told him she'd be coming into the city again soon.

After the girls had gone, he found Angelo looking thoughtful.

"Do you think I shall ever get married?" Angelo asked.

"Of course you will," said Salvatore.

"Maybe." Angelo looked uncertain. "I think you should marry Teresa, Salvatore," he said suddenly. "As soon as you can."

"She'd have to agree first. And her parents." Then he laughed. "Maybe you should marry her cousin." But to his surprise, Angelo looked quite serious. "They are a good family," he said quietly.

A few minutes later, his mother said: "Don't let Teresa get away, Toto. That's the one for you."

"Maybe, Mama," he said. But he still wondered what he could do to satisfy her family.

✦

It was two weeks later, on a Friday, that he returned from work to find a tall, thin man waiting for him. The fellow was in his fifties. His black coat was buttoned tightly up to his throat. He handed Salvatore his card.

"I am a lawyer," he explained. "I represent your late brother, Paolo Caruso. My firm is the executor of his estate. May we go inside?" When they were upstairs in his lodgings, the lawyer asked: "Were you familiar with your brother's affairs?"

"I didn't even know where he'd been living," Salvatore confessed with a shrug.

"He'd moved," said the lawyer. "We have his clothes, by the way. I still have to issue probate, but he has left the residue of his estate to you."

"To me? What about the rest of the family?"

"His will is very clear. I will let you know as soon as everything is completed. Then you will need to come to my office so that we can complete the formalities." He paused. "There is more than ten thousand dollars."

"Ten thousand? For me?"

The lawyer gave him a faint smile. "In his will you are called 'Salvatore Caruso, my brother and best friend.' He wished you to have it all."

❖

That Sunday, out at his parents' house, Salvatore decided to say nothing. Perhaps it was superstition, but until he had the money in his hands, he did not wish to tempt the fates by speaking of it.

He had already decided what to do with the money. Giuseppe was already set up. Their parents were looked after, and if anything more were needed, he could supply it. His sister Maria was married and not in need. Uncle Luigi had everything he wanted, and God knows what his investments were worth. So that just left Angelo. The money would help him look after his brother.

The rightness of his decision was confirmed that very day.

Teresa and her cousin had arrived again, and while her cousin sat with Angelo, Salvatore and she strolled over to spend time with Giuseppe and his family. They chatted about family matters, and then the talk turned to Angelo. Salvatore noticed that at the mention of his name, his brother's two children looked at each other and cried "Uncle Angelo." Then they laughed. Giuseppe's wife explained.

"Angelo's been helping them with their lessons. He draws pictures for them at the same time."

"That's good," said Salvatore. "He likes to be occupied."

"Actually," said Giuseppe, "Angelo can be quite useful. I had to write some business letters about the farm, and he did them for me. Better than I could have done."

"I hope you're paying him something for all this work," said Salvatore. But Giuseppe only shrugged.

"He's my own brother. Let him be useful to the family."

"He doesn't ask for anything," his wife concurred.

This did not please Salvatore. It seemed to him that the family were taking advantage of Angelo's good nature a little too easily, but he did not say anything. He couldn't help thinking, however, that if anything happened to himself and Uncle Luigi, Angelo would only be valued by them to the extent that he was useful. Then it occurred to him that it might be a good idea to test Teresa on this subject, too. On the way back to his parents' house, therefore, he said: "I worry about Angelo, you know. Before my sister died in the Triangle fire, she told me that I'd always have to look after him. And I think she was right." He paused. "So whatever I do, even if I have a wife and family some day, my house has to be a place where Angelo can live if he needs to. Does that seem crazy to you?" He watched her carefully as he put this proposition.

"Of course not." She gave him a warm smile. "How could I like you if you'd said anything different?" She considered for a moment. "People may not appreciate Angelo, but he is talented, and he is kind."

"He approves of you too," Salvatore assured her. Then he laughed. "He says one day he'd like to marry someone from a family like yours."

"He does? What a compliment. We'll have to find him someone like me, then." She looked at him playfully. "But this will be difficult I hope you don't think that people like my family grow on trees."

"I don't. There is only one of you."

"I'm glad you think so."

It seemed to him that the conversation was going very well, so he decided to take the subject a little further. "Perhaps," he went on cautiously, "if I can get the money, I'll set up some kind of business. Maybe in the city, maybe here, near my family. Only I don't know what."

She did not answer for a moment or two, but when she did, he had the impression that she had already thought about the subject.

"Don't do anything you don't want to, Salvatore," she said. "I can't imagine you working indoors. Maybe you could grow things out here, or get into the fishing business, like my brothers. But you must do what makes you happy. This is what I wish for you."

She said it so earnestly, and with such kindness, that he almost told her about his good fortune there and then. But he made himself hold back. Instead, he took her in his arms and kissed her. And she kissed him back, before pulling away and laughing. "It's lucky my parents didn't see that," she said. But he could tell she was happy.

⁘

The lawyer summoned him late in February. The inheritance was as promised. That same day, Salvatore deposited just over ten thousand dollars at the Stabile Bank on Mulberry Street and Grand.

On Sunday, he was due to go out to Long Island and meet Teresa at his parents' house again, but a cold prevented him. When he telephoned Teresa to tell her he couldn't come, she asked if Angelo would be disappointed. Certainly, he replied.

"Do you want me to visit him?" she said. "So he won't be lonely? I know you worry about him."

"You would do that?"

"For you? Of course." It was said so sweetly.

"Go," he told her. "Next time I come, I shall have some exciting news to tell you."

⁘

The proposal took place in the living room of his parents' small house, on the third Sunday in March. The afternoon was rather gray, but there was a fire in the grate, whose soft light seemed to reflect the kindness in her face.

First he told her that he had ten thousand dollars. Then he told her that he would be happy to live in the city or out on Long Island, or anywhere else for that matter, but that there was only one thing that could bring him happiness. Then he told her he loved her and asked if she would marry him.

He was rather surprised by her reaction. She did not answer at once, but looked down, as if she were considering.

"May I have a little time?" she said at last.

"Time? Certainly." He frowned. "Is something wrong?"

"No." She seemed to hesitate, and looked troubled.

"Perhaps you do not like me."

"Salvatore, you are the best man I have ever met. I am honored by your proposal. I did not say no."

"It's your parents, isn't it? I will speak to your father."

"No." She smiled. "Not yet. Give me a little time, Salvatore, and I will give you my answer."

That was all she would say. Somewhat confused, he returned to New York.

❖

A week passed before he spoke to her again. When he called the house she answered the telephone herself. She sounded very friendly. But when he said he was thinking of going out to Long Island on Sunday, she said her parents required her to be at home that day, so he decided not to go.

It was on the following Thursday that Uncle Luigi came in excitedly. He had received a telephone call at the restaurant from Long Island. The Carusos had received visitors.

"Teresa and her parents," he told Salvatore. "She brought them over so that Angelo could make a drawing of her father—they paid him for it, too. Her father and mother spent time with your parents, and it seems they got on famously. They are friends already."

And hearing this, Salvatore was lost in admiration for the girl he loved. Clearly, he'd been right; there *had* been objections raised about his family. Now, on a simple pretext, she had got her parents to his family's house, and let them discover that they liked the Carusos. She was paving the way for their marriage.

He waited eagerly for her next move.

❖

The weather grew warmer in April, and Angelo grew stronger. At the end of the second week, he returned to the city and announced he was ready to work. He certainly looked well.

The building site where Salvatore was working stood on the corner of Fifth Avenue and Forty-fifth. Mr. French was the developer and had decided that the building was to bear his name—with good reason, for it was going to be one of the loveliest skyscrapers ever built.

To prevent New York from becoming a great grid of dark canyons, the city had insisted that skyscrapers could not arise vertically from the boundaries of their sites, but that at specified heights there must be set-backs to let the light in. At its crudest, this sometimes caused builders to raise skyscrapers that looked like upturned telescopes. But architects had soon seen that this was an opportunity to create complex patterns with elegant steps, shelves and cutaways. The French building was nearing completion, and with its carved bronze entrance, inspired by the Ishtar Gate, and its high terraces like hanging gardens, it might have come from ancient Babylon. Passing through its rich art deco lobbies was like entering a temple. But most lovely to Salvatore was the soaring facade of warm orange brick, trimmed with deep red and black at the edges. There was no other brickwork like that in New York.

For the next two weeks, the brothers worked together on the splendid building, and Angelo seemed glad to be there. Then Teresa came into the city.

Had she come to give him her decision? It was hard to tell. She came with her cousin as usual, and suggested that all four of them go to a movie. After the movie, she asked if Uncle Luigi would be at the restaurant, because she had not seen him in a while. Certainly, Salvatore told her.

So they went to the restaurant, and Salvatore treated them to a meal, and Uncle Luigi waited on them. It was a lively meal. Salvatore told some good jokes, and everyone was laughing. Uncle Luigi, who always followed the news avidly, was full of the latest about the daring aviators.

"Any day now," he told them, "someone's going to win the big prize."

Mr. Orteig, the French-born owner of the Lafayette Hotel in the city, had for years been offering a prize of $25,000 to the first aviator to fly non-stop either way between New York and Paris. Just recently, two brave American airmen had been killed in the attempt, taking off from Langley. But Uncle Luigi had heard that two French airmen would shortly take up the challenge from Paris.

"Now you have money," said Angelo with a smile to Salvatore, "here's your chance to make even more!"

"The top of a skyscraper is high enough for me," he said.

It was toward the end of the meal that Teresa asked Uncle Luigi if she could speak with him privately for a few minutes. She did not explain herself further, but the two of them sat together at another table, deep in conversation for nearly a quarter of an hour. At the end of it, she got up and kissed Uncle Luigi.

"It's nice to have a real talk with your uncle," she said as she sat down again. "He is very wise."

After the meal, Teresa said that she must go home. Uncle Luigi wanted Angelo to run an errand for him, so Salvatore escorted the two girls to the station. When he kissed Teresa good-bye, he gave her a little questioning look, but she only returned a gentle smile.

"I'll be coming back soon," she promised.

❖

On Wednesday, Uncle Luigi had the evening off, and it was agreed they'd go out to eat together. It was a fine day, and Salvatore was enjoying working up in the clear blue sky. At the top of the building, on the flat roof, a large water tank would be screened by outside walls with gorgeous colored panels. The big tiles arrived that morning, and the foreman obligingly showed the designs to the brothers. Two panels depicted the god Mercury, but the most dramatic was the huge green rectangle, in the center of which a bright red rising sun was flanked by two griffins with golden wings. Angelo was quite enraptured by this.

When they got home, however, Angelo complained of feeling tired. Salvatore looked at him with concern, but his brother assured him he'd be fine.

"We'll go out," said Uncle Luigi. "Let him rest. We won't be late."

They found a little steakhouse near Greenwich Village. It wasn't too crowded. They both ordered sirloin and Uncle Luigi chose a red wine. While they ate their steaks, Uncle Luigi discussed the latest news from the aviators.

"The Frenchmen took off from Paris on Sunday. They were seen heading out over the Atlantic from Ireland. Then nothing."

"They must have gone down over the ocean."

"Brave men," said Uncle Luigi, then he glanced at Salvatore thoughtfully. "Are you brave, Salvatore?"

"I don't know," said Salvatore.

"I suppose we never know until we are tested."

They ordered crème caramel. When it had been served, Uncle Luigi looked at Salvatore thoughtfully again.

"Tell me, Salvatore," he asked, "do you love Teresa?"

"Yes," said Salvatore.

"And do you think she loves you?"

"I'm not sure. I think so."

"Well, she does. She loves you, Salvatore. She has told me so."

"That's good."

"Yes. But I have bad news. It may not be possible for her to marry you. That is why she spoke to me. She is very distressed, and she does not know what to do."

"Is it her parents still?"

"No."

"Is she sick? I would look after her."

"No. You must be brave, Salvatore. She has fallen in love." Uncle Luigi paused. "It is very difficult for her. This was a love she did not seek, and it has taken her by surprise. She has fought against it, but now she believes she cannot marry you with a good heart." The older man sighed. "She is an honest woman, Salvatore, who does not want to cause you pain. I admire her."

Salvatore was silent for a while. "That explains everything," he said quietly. He gazed at the table. "Who is the lucky man?" he asked at last.

"Your brother. Angelo."

❖

Salvatore was stunned by how quickly everything happened after that. At first, for some hours, he had been stupefied. After that, rage had set in. It wasn't only that he'd been hurt. It wasn't only that the woman he loved had preferred his little brother. But his own kid brother, with the connivance of his uncle, had made a fool of him.

For it didn't take long for the rest of the truth to come out. Uncle Luigi had told Angelo about Teresa's feelings while Salvatore was taking her to the station. So for three days Angelo had worked beside him and never said a word. He'd been betrayed.

"You must understand," Uncle Luigi had explained, "that Teresa confessed her feelings to me, but not to Angelo. It was I who had to talk to him, to discover whether her love might be returned. I discovered that it would be. He loved her, absolutely, but in his mind, she belonged to you. He was distraught. He was lost. He didn't know what to do. It was I who told him to say nothing, until I had talked to you."

Salvatore listened to these explanations, but they did not alter the fact. Angelo had stolen his bride, and he had lied. For days, he could hardly bear the sight of his brother. At work, they joined different gangs so that they could avoid each other. They spent as little time in their lodgings as possible, and when they were both there, Salvatore did not speak to Angelo. After a few days Angelo asked him: "Do you want me to leave?" But Salvatore only shrugged.

"What's the point? You'll be going soon."

The next weekend, Angelo disappeared. It was obvious that he'd gone to Long Island. Salvatore stayed in the city. When Angelo returned, he said nothing, but the next day Uncle Luigi gave Salvatore a letter from Teresa, which Angelo must have brought. The letter was full of expressions of affection. She hoped he could forgive her, that he would understand, that they might remain friends. He almost tore it up, but finally put it in a drawer with feelings of disgust.

"Maybe I'll go to California," he told Uncle Luigi, who remarked sadly: "I'll be lonely."

His uncle did tell him one other thing, in the hope that it might be of some comfort.

"Understand, Salvatore, that nobody except myself and the parties concerned even know that it was you who were courting Teresa. Nothing was ever said. Nothing happened. All anybody knows is that Teresa became friendly with two brothers and that she is marrying one of them. You haven't made a *brutta figura.*"

At the time this seemed small comfort. But as the weeks went by, at least it was something.

What also astonished him was how quickly Teresa's family seemed to take Angelo over. It was decided that he would move out to Long Island straight away. They would set him up with a little house-painting business. But as well as this, he was to design signs for the local businesses and undertake other decorative work. One thing was certain: with the family's local connections, there would be plenty of commissions to start him off.

"I thought he didn't like taking commissions," he remarked to Uncle Luigi.

"Ah, but now he is to get married," said his uncle. "He told me that when he was sick, he started to realize that he couldn't rely on bricklaying to make a living. And he enjoyed those commissions he did more than he thought he would." Uncle Luigi made a gesture with his hands. "It is necessary to adjust. A man has to accept responsibilities."

But perhaps the thing that amazed Salvatore the most was the way that Angelo seemed to be taking charge of his bride. He had been living on

Long Island only two weeks when he came back to the lodgings to fetch some things. On this occasion, Salvatore brought himself to speak to his brother. But when he remarked that Teresa might want to live in the city one day, Angelo just smiled and shook his head.

"No," he said calmly, "she deceives herself about that. I'll make her stay on Long Island."

Salvatore could hardly believe it was his little brother speaking.

It took more time, but gradually after that he began to realize, even if it was hard to accept, that however humiliating it was, Teresa, her parents and Uncle Luigi had all been right.

It was his brother who had the talent. It was his brother who would be content to work with his head, and not with his hands. It was Angelo who would sit in an office, write letters, look after the accounts, while he, Salvatore, lived in the open air. Despite even the ten thousand dollars he now possessed, it was not he but Angelo who would become the businessman. Fate was cruel, but it was fate.

⁘

The wedding took place on the second Sunday in June, on Long Island. Understandably, Salvatore did not want to be best man, so Uncle Luigi had tactfully arranged for Giuseppe to perform that role. It was certainly a big affair. The Carusos had invited a few friends from the city, but Teresa's family had summoned half the people in the area—an impressive display of their importance in the community.

The ceremony could not be without pain for Salvatore. When he saw Teresa, and how lovely she looked, his heart missed a beat. And as he gazed at her, suddenly smitten by an anguish of love, he asked himself: How could this have happened?

As for his little brother, when he first saw him, just for a moment, he didn't recognize him. Angelo's hair had been cut short, and he'd grown a mustache. His face, thinner than those of his brothers, no longer looked delicate but fine, manly and strikingly handsome. When he came to greet Salvatore, he seemed to move with the grace and confidence of a dancer.

And once again, with force, but with awful justice, it struck him that Teresa and her family had shown their wisdom. They had picked the one person in the family who was out of the ordinary, the one who had the capacity to grow. And, in their own humble way, they were going to help him succeed. He felt jealous, but he recognized the truth for what it was.

"I am so proud of you," he whispered to Angelo as he embraced him. And he meant it.

Following the wedding Mass, they all walked back to Teresa's family's house. This being an Italian wedding, the best man was waiting at the door of the house, with a huge tray of drinks, so that everyone could toast the bride and groom. After that, they walked past the table where their mothers were sitting just behind the women helpers who were recording the presents people brought.

Of course, the family had already given gifts to the couple. Teresa's extended family had showered them with gifts, and although Angelo's family could not quite keep up with this, their honor was preserved by Uncle Luigi's fine set of china, and the gift, together with a big signed photograph, sent by the great Caruso himself. These were displayed for all to see. Salvatore had thought long and hard about what present he should give, and a beautiful crystal vase from him stood beside Uncle Luigi's china.

During the dancing, the bride would also wear a silk purse into which the men would stuff money.

But the table was something different. Here, the guests who had obligations toward the family would present their gifts for all to see, and the helpers would write them down with a note of their value. Woe betide the guest who failed in his obligations. Everyone would know they were cheap—they'd have made a *brutta figura* indeed.

Since he was one of the family, they were not expecting him to pause at the table. When he reached it, however, he stopped and gave the helpers his name.

"I wish to add a further present to the one I have given," he said quietly. "This is for my brother Angelo, that I love, on his wedding day." And drawing from his pocket a slip of paper, he laid it on the table in front of the helpers, who gasped. It was a check, made out for five thousand dollars.

⁜

On the second Monday of June 1927, a great event took place in New York City. In the first half of May, searches had been made for the two gallant French aviators who had vanished in their plane after setting out across the Atlantic. No one had seen them again, but rumors that an aircraft engine had been heard over Newfoundland and Maine had raised hopes. Nothing had been found, however, and whatever had become of them, they certainly hadn't reached New York.

On May 20, however, a young American that few people had ever heard of managed to take off from Roosevelt Field, Long Island, in a single-seater, single-engine monoplane that he called the *Spirit of St. Louis*. By the night of the next day, after flying through rain, wind and fog, sometimes above the clouds and sometimes only feet above the Atlantic waves, the young fellow arrived at Paris's Le Bourget airport, where a night-time crowd of 150,000 had gathered to meet him. From that moment young Charles Lindbergh became an international sensation. Despite losing two of their own national heroes that month, the French took the young American to their hearts. Breaking all protocol, the Foreign Ministry at the Quai d'Orsay flew the Stars and Stripes from its flagpole. The President of France gave Lindbergh the Légion d'honneur.

Now Lindbergh was back in America, and it was not an opportunity that sporting Mayor Walker of New York was going to miss. On Monday, June 13, Charles A. Lindbergh was honored with a ticker-tape parade.

Salvatore and Uncle Luigi watched it together, as it passed down Fifth Avenue. As the ticker tape rained down like confetti, the huge crowds roared. Uncle Luigi was especially excited.

"Do you know when the first ticker-tape parade was given?" he shouted to Salvatore.

"No," said Salvatore, "but I'm sure you're going to tell me."

"In 1886, to celebrate the dedication of the Statue of Liberty. You see? The statue was a gift from France, Lindbergh makes the first flight to Paris, we give him the same honor."

"I get it. *Vive la France.*"

"*Esattamente.*"

As they walked back home together afterward, Salvatore looked at his uncle with affection. Uncle Luigi was in his sixties now, yet he had just the same curiosity and enthusiasm about the world as he had in his thirties. Live forever, Salvatore thought, I should be lonely without you.

"That was a fine thing you did for Angelo," Uncle Luigi remarked. "I do not think I could have done it."

"Not really," said Salvatore. And in truth, it hadn't been so difficult.

Partly, it had to be said, it had raised his own status within his family. It had certainly impressed everyone at the wedding. He was sure, also, that Paolo had intended him to share the money with Angelo. And one other thought had also been in his mind.

"It was what Anna would have wanted," Salvatore said.

In a way, it made him free.

⊰1 9 2 9⊱

It was halfway through September when Uncle Luigi went to see his broker. He enjoyed these visits, usually. It was twenty years earlier that he'd overheard someone in the restaurant talking about the firm. He always tried to listen, if Wall Street men came into the restaurant—and as its reputation for first-rate Italian family cooking spread, they sometimes did. By doing so he'd learned a lot of things. The brokerage house in question, he'd heard, was very grand, and patronized by important men on the street, but they took small accounts as well, and treated all their customers with nearly equal courtesy.

He liked going in through the handsome doorway, and seeing all the clerks at their desks, and sitting down in the big leather chair in the paneled room where, once a year, a senior clerk would politely review his account with him.

"I'm wondering," Uncle Luigi told him, "whether to sell my holdings."

"Why would you want to do that?" The clerk was a small, dapper man, in his forties.

"The market's down a bit."

"There's been some profit-taking, but that doesn't surprise us."

"Nothing goes up forever," Uncle Luigi pointed out. "Look at real estate."

It was true that since 1925, despite the astonishing boom in the stock market, the overall price of houses in America had actually been going down. But the clerk only shrugged.

"Real estate's one thing, the market's another. The fact is that in the last six years, the market has gone up by five times. On the third of this month, the Dow was at three hundred and eighty-one. That's the highest in its history, you know."

"But that's partly what worries me," Uncle Luigi said. "On average, the prices of stocks are now over thirty-two times their earnings."

The clerk smiled, to show that he was impressed that this little Italian should know all this.

"We would agree that future gains may not be so steep, but we don't see any reason for the market to come down. We think it's moved to a higher plateau. And I can assure you, the investment is still coming in."

Uncle Luigi nodded thoughtfully. What the broker said was true. People were still piling money into the market, but they were being encouraged to do so. A year ago, this dapper man had politely informed him: "We have been dealing with you for many years now, sir, and your investments are excellent collateral. We should be glad to lend you extra funds if you'd like to increase the size of your portfolio." Luigi had declined the offer, but he wondered how much of the money now invested in the stock market was borrowed. The greater the borrowing, the more like a bubble the thing must become.

"So you advise me to hold on to my stocks?" he asked the broker, after a pause.

"We expect the market to rise soon. I'd hate to see you miss out." The clerk smiled. "I'm buying myself, I assure you."

⁘

Rose Master made a very big decision that night. It wasn't easy, and she'd been thinking about it for some time. It might, she reckoned, affect the family's future happiness and position more than they imagined. For clever though her husband and her son were in their different ways, she believed she had more foresight.

It concerned the cottage in Newport.

Charlie came to dinner that evening. She'd been rather hurt by her son that summer. During the whole time, he had come to Newport just once, and his father had undoubtedly dragged him there on that occasion, telling him, "At least come once, to please your mother." Of course when he did come, he'd been absolutely charming to everyone. But that didn't really make her feel any better.

She was getting seriously worried about him nowadays. He was nearly thirty and still living in Greenwich Village, on Downing Street—though why anyone would want to live there she couldn't imagine. He was pretending to work for his father and the last she heard he was writing a play. She didn't know what kind of women he was seeing, and didn't want to. He probably wasn't getting enough exercise of that sort or any other, to judge by his waistline, and he was drinking too much. It was time her son took a pull at himself. And it was time for him to get married too. After all, what was the point in doing all you could for the family if there was no future generation to carry it on?

All in all, she was distressed, and she felt she should speak her mind. But William had cautioned her.

"I know he's hurt you, but don't quarrel with him," he warned. "You might drive him away."

So when Charlie turned up for dinner that evening, she had gently suggested that he should take more care of his health, but said little more on the subject.

They talked of all sorts of things. Charlie told her anecdotes about some of his playwriting friends, and she pretended to be amused. She told him that she was thinking of redecorating the Newport house, and he pretended to care. They all discussed the stock market. Rose knew that some people were saying it was too high, and she remembered the terrible scare back in 1907. But her husband didn't seem to be concerned. Conditions were quite different now, he assured her.

"By the way," Charlie remarked to his father, "do you know we've got a new competitor to the brokerage, in the street right across from our offices?" He grinned. "Guess who it is. The boot boy."

"The boot boy?" cried his mother.

"I swear to God. He was cleaning my shoes, and he started offering me stock tips. He has his own portfolio. Good news, by the way: he told me the market was going up again."

"Do we have his account?" his father said with a smile.

"I don't believe so."

"Well, bring him in then. Earn some commission, boy."

"You're not serious, are you?" Rose said.

But William shrugged. "Everyone's in the market now, Rose," he said.

"I have another piece of news," Charlie told them. "Edmund Keller's bringing out a new book. It's the story of the great days of Rome, but written for the general market. He's hoping it'll be a big seller." Keller had been working on the project ever since he'd returned from three very happy years in Oxford.

"Splendid," said William. "We'll buy a copy or two."

"Any chance you'll put on a party for him?" Charlie inquired. "You know how he feels about you."

Rose saw her opportunity.

"If you promise to take some exercise and work on your waistline. And that has to be a promise."

"All right. I guess that's a deal," her son ruefully agreed.

When Charlie had left, William kissed his wife.

"That was nice of you," he said. "And clever," he added. "Charlie was really grateful, you know."

"Well, I'm glad," she said.

The time had come. Everything that had been said at the dinner just strengthened her resolve all the more.

"William, my dear," she said gently, "I need you to do something for me."

"Anything."

"I want to do some work on the Newport cottage. I want to make it really special."

"You have a decorator in mind?"

"Actually, dear, I'm going to need an architect. And I'm going to need some money. Could I have some money?"

"I don't see why not. How much do you need?"

"Half a million dollars."

❖

In early October, after drifting down for almost a month, the stock market started to rise again. It wouldn't be long, people were saying, before it was back at its peak again. On Thursday, October 17, Mrs. Master threw a party to celebrate the publication of Edmund Keller's *Mighty Rome*. The word was that the book was very good.

Rose left no stone unturned. She invited everybody: people who gave parties, people who gave presents, people who owned bookstores, donors to the New York Public Library—sadly old Elihu Pusey had died—and a slew of journalists, magazine and literary editors drummed up by Charlie. The cream of the social, business and literary world was there. Even Nicholas Murray Butler put in an appearance. An event like this, after all, was quite useful for the university. Keller was put at a table and made to sign copies of his book. They cleared two hundred, and Rose bought another fifty to give away to friends who'd spread the word.

Edmund Keller was overwhelmed by her kindness. And he gave back in return. For the highlight of the evening was the charming speech of thanks that he gave. His years of lecturing had made him a quite delightful and polished performer. He made them all laugh, closing to loud applause; but what gratified Rose most of all were the words he spoke about the Master family.

"This event is a particular pleasure and honor for me. More than sixty years ago my father, the photographer Theodore Keller, had the good fortune to come to the notice of one of this city's oldest leading families, when Mr. and Mrs. Frank Master became his patrons and started him on his successful and, if I may say, eminent career. I was glad some years ago, at Columbia, to have the pleasure of teaching their great-grandson Charles Master, whom I nowadays call my friend. And if he could see us now—I hope he can—I know how delighted my father would be to see his son also honored by the kindness and support of the Master family today."

Sixty years of patronage, one of the city's oldest leading families. Old money. Rose beamed at him. This party had really turned out better than she could have expected.

⁕

It wasn't very often that Uncle Luigi went to church, but on Sunday he did, and to keep him company, Salvatore went too.

The last two weeks had been very difficult for Uncle Luigi. As the clerk at the brokers had predicted, the market had been going up, clawing its way back toward the peak of early September. Yet Uncle Luigi could not help being troubled. His savings had really accumulated in a remarkable way. He didn't want to stop working yet, but if he did stop, he had enough to live quite a pleasant life of retirement. He'd never told him, but he'd already stated in his will that Salvatore should inherit his money. It seemed only right. So from a personal point of view, and for his nephew's sake, he had a duty to safeguard those savings.

Several times he'd almost sold up. Each time, though, the voice of the broker's clerk had echoed in his head: "I'd hate you to miss out."

No one wants to look like a fool. No one wants to be left behind.

Finally, in the hope that a visit to church might give him inspiration, or at least clear his mind, he gave religion a try.

The Church of the Transfiguration was quite well attended that morning. But the priest did not fail to notice that Luigi, whom he knew perfectly well, had put in a rare appearance. Since he hadn't been to confession either, Uncle Luigi decided not to take the wafer—he didn't want to come even closer under the priest's eye. He listened to the sermon, though.

It was a sermon about Christ's temptation in the desert. It surprised Uncle Luigi that the subject should be chosen now, since it normally belonged in Lent, but he paid close attention. The priest reminded the congregation how Our Lord had gone up to a high place, and the devil had urged him to jump out into the void, since the angels would surely save him. "Thou shalt not tempt the Lord thy God," Christ had replied. We must accept God's will, the priest explained. We must not overreach, or make bets that God will help us. This, and much more, the priest said, and Uncle Luigi listened carefully.

Salvatore had not been so enthralled. He'd fidgeted irritably.

"I'm sure I heard a sermon like that when I was a child," he remarked to his uncle when they got outside.

"And what did you think of it the second time?"

"Not much," he said.

Uncle Luigi *was* thinking about the sermon, though. He was thinking about it a lot.

❖

Wednesday, October 23, was a windy day. As usual, William Master was driven to his office in his Rolls-Royce.

There were quite a few Rolls-Royces in New York, these days. A decade earlier, the company had set up an American factory in Springfield, Massachusetts. But only the richest people had them. The sight of Mr. Master arriving at his brokerage house in the Rolls each morning had become quite a tradition. It was reassuring. It was good for business.

William had had this model for five years. The grand old Silver Ghost had given way to the Phantom now. William's Phantom, its bodywork by Brewster, who operated out in Queensboro, Long Island, was also painted silver. The next model, the Phantom II, had just come out, and if he got that next year, he'd have that body painted silver too.

After being dropped at the office, he'd told Joe, the chauffeur, that he wouldn't be needing him any more that day, so Joe was to take Rose out shopping. Joe was a good man, came from the Midwest somewhere, said he had an Indian grandmother. Always friendly, but only talked if you asked him to.

But then he'd been called to a meeting up on Forty-second Street, to which he'd taken a taxi. And after the meeting was over, he walked along the street toward Lexington to get a little exercise. As he did so, he glanced up at the soaring skyscraper on the corner. Then he stopped and stared. Then his mouth fell open.

"My God," said William Master.

You had to hand it to Walter Chrysler. He had style. When the automobile man had taken over the building project that now bore his name, he had insisted on daring art deco designs that incorporated images of wheels, radiator caps and much else besides. The top of the building, which was under construction now, consisted of a beautiful series of arches rising to a capstone, all to be covered in stainless steel. Supremely elegant, there would be nothing like it in the world when it was done.

And then there was the question of height. The tallest building in the world, of course, was the Eiffel Tower in Paris. But the daring men of New York were getting close. A financier named Ohrstrom was building a soaring tower down at 40 Wall Street to compete with Chrysler, and word was that Ohrstrom's building, if not quite so elegant, would be the taller of the two, rising above any other skyscraper in the city. A third building down at Thirty-fourth might also challenge for the crown, but work hadn't started on that yet.

Far above, at the top of the Chrysler Building, the pyramid of arches, still unclad, rose as a network of girders into the sky.

But now, as William Master watched, something extraordinary was happening. Suddenly, from the center of the building's peak, a metal framework tower began to push its way out. Foot by foot it was rising, like the section of a slender telescope. Ten feet, twenty, thirty. It must have been concealed inside the main structure, and now, by some mechanism, it was being raised. Forty feet, fifty now, it was pushing its way up toward the clouds. There was a Stars and Stripes attached to the tip, streaming out in the high wind. William had never seen anything like it. Stranger still, as he glanced around the busy street, no one else seemed to have noticed.

How much higher could it be going? He couldn't imagine. The clouds were racing across the sky above it—God knows what the wind must be up there—but the great spike kept on rising. A hundred feet, a hundred and twenty, a hundred and fifty, higher and higher.

When it stopped at last, he reckoned it must have added nearly two hundred feet to the building. And now riveters were swarming like ants around its base, fixing the huge spike in place.

Finally, he saw a single, tiny figure climbing up the narrow framework. He just kept going until he was right up there with the streaming flag, halfway to heaven. What was he doing? He was letting down a plumb line, checking that the skyscraper was standing straight. After a little time, satisfied that the thing was as it should be, he came down.

Master continued to observe, fascinated. Only when he tried to glance at his watch, and found he had such a crick in his neck that he could hardly look down, did he realize he'd been staring up for nearly an hour and a half.

He didn't mind. He'd just witnessed a piece of history. Cunning Chrysler, by this brilliant ploy, must have added the best part of two hundred feet to the height of his building, taking his rivals completely by surprise and vanquishing them. Master wasn't certain, but he was pretty sure the Chrysler Building had just surpassed the Eiffel Tower itself.

How fitting that it should be so. New York was the center of the world. The market was soaring. The skyscrapers were soaring. It was the spirit of the age.

Late as hell, but not caring at all, he hailed a cab and went cheerfully downtown to his office.

As he approached the door, he passed a little old fellow who was leaving. Maybe in his sixties, Italian by the look of him. He'd encouraged his people not to despise these small investors. "Don't forget," he'd tell them, "they are the future of America." So when he got inside he asked the senior clerk who the fellow was.

"An Italian man, sir. Had an account with us for years. Remarkable really. He works in Little Italy as a waiter, but he has quite a respectable account."

"What's he good for?"

"About seventy thousand dollars. Unfortunately he's just sold all his stock. We gave him the funds today."

"Sold everything?"

"I tried to persuade him not to, but he came in on Monday and said he'd decided not to tempt fate." The clerk smiled. "Said he'd had a sign from St. Anthony."

"Really? Well, I think he was mistaken." He grinned. "But I guess he didn't know: God only talks to the Morgans."

"Yes, sir. Though actually, sir, while you've been out, the market's been falling quite a bit."

÷

The start of the great crash of 1929 is usually given as Black Thursday, October 24. This is incorrect. It began on Wednesday, the very day that the Chrysler Building became the tallest structure in the world, when stocks abruptly tumbled 4.6 percent. Strangely, few people had yet noticed the clever trick that Walter Chrysler had played. But everybody noticed Wednesday's stock market collapse.

On Thursday morning, William Master went into the Stock Exchange as it opened its doors. The atmosphere was tense. Glancing up at the visitors' gallery, he saw a face he thought looked familiar. "That's Winston Churchill, the British politician," one of the traders remarked. "He's chosen a hell of a day to call."

He certainly had. As trading began, Master was aghast. The market wasn't just falling, it was in headlong panic. By the end of the first hour, there were cries of pain, then howls. Men with margin calls were being wiped out. A couple of times, sellers were shouting out prices and finding not a single buyer in the market. As noon approached, he reckoned the market would soon have fallen nearly ten percent. The anguished hubbub from the floor was so loud that, unable to bear it any longer, he walked outside.

In the street, the scene was extraordinary. A crowd of men had gathered on the steps of Federal Hall. They seemed to be in shock. He saw a fellow come out of the Exchange and burst into tears. An old broker he knew passed him and remarked, with a shake of the head: "Ain't seen anything like this since the crash of 1907."

But in 1907, old Pierpont Morgan had been there to save the day. Maybe his son Jack could do something? But Jack Morgan was on the other side of the Atlantic in England, for the shooting season. The courtly senior Morgan partner Thomas Lamont was in charge.

As if on cue, at that moment, a group of men went up the steps of 23 Wall Street, the House of Morgan. He recognized at once the heads of the greatest banks. Could they stop the rot?

It seemed they could. At one thirty that day, Richard Whitney, the president of the Stock Exchange and a broker for Morgan, walked calmly out of 23 Wall Street, went straight to the floor of the Exchange, and started buying. Big money, big stocks, at well above the asking price. The banks had given him $240 million to use if he needed, but he only had to use a fraction. With a great sigh of relief, the market began to calm down.

The godlike spirit of Pierpont Morgan had descended from Olympus to rule the street once more.

That night William attended a big meeting of brokers. Everyone agreed the panic was unnecessary. On Friday, and on Saturday morning, the market suffered no further crisis.

He spent the rest of the weekend quietly. On Sunday, Charlie came by for lunch. "Technically," William told them, "this sell-off has left the market in better condition than it's been in for months." After that, asking Charlie to keep his mother company, he went for a walk in Central Park.

The truth was, he needed some time alone, to think.

What had really happened? The underlying problem, he reckoned, was that for the last few years, there had been too much cash in the stock market. Funnily enough, it wasn't that everything was booming. Farming and commodity prices had been weak, so instead of investing in those traditional staples, people had been looking for gains in stocks. Cash flowed in; brokers, banks and other finance houses mushroomed. Even in the huge American economy, there weren't really enough productive stocks for all this cash, so prices rose. And then, of course, giddy greed set in.

Small investors, who should have been putting some savings in solid stocks, were buying wildly. Out of the total population of a hundred and twenty million, two, maybe three million were in the market now. That was a hell of a lot. And more than half a million of these little guys were even buying on a ten percent margin—putting down only a hundred dollars for every thousand they invested, with finance houses lending them the rest. Respectable brokerage houses like his own were lending clients two-thirds of the funds to purchase stocks. Money pushed stock prices ever higher. You couldn't lose. And not only stocks. William knew damn well that some of the banks were parceling up their worst Latin American debt and selling it to suckers as valuable bonds. So long as everything went up, nobody noticed.

And not just the man in the street—the brokers and traders were not much better. Seduced by their own success, most of them had never seen a bear market in their lives.

William walked right across the park, until he was opposite the Dakota. Then, deep in thought, he walked slowly back.

Maybe this market shock was a good thing. Maybe it was time for a shock to the system. Not only to the market, but to the whole city as well.

The fact was, the whole of New York seemed to have forgotten its morals. What had happened to responsible investing? To hard work and saving? What had happened to the old puritan ethic in the world of speakeasies, and bootleggers, and gangland killings, and loose women? Life was too easy; they'd all gone soft. He himself was just as guilty as any of them. Look at Charlie. Charming, and all that, but at bottom, a spoiled rich kid. And it's my fault as much as his, he thought. I let him get this way.

So what was to be done? He was damned if he knew. But if this little crisis reminded people about the fundamentals of life, then maybe it was worth whatever it had cost him.

Truth to tell, he wasn't quite sure how much that was right now. The brokerage must have taken a hell of a hit, but they weren't wiped out. He'd have to go over the books with his clerk in the morning.

✛

Charlie Master was in the office with his father all the time that week. Maybe it was something his mother had said, or perhaps an instinct for drama had drawn him there. If so, his instincts were rewarded. For Wall Street's Black Monday and Black Tuesday were events never to be forgotten.

During the weekend, the public had read the newspapers, pondered the reassuring statements of the bankers, and come to their own conclusion. It consisted of a single word. Sell.

On Monday, Charlie watched as the market collapsed. That day the Dow fell over twelve percent. Yet Tuesday was even more dramatic. The percentage fall was almost the same, but it was the volume of shares that was so astounding. Over sixteen million shares changed hands. No one had ever seen anything like it. The number of transactions was so huge that the ticker-tape machines were two and a half hours behind. As he watched his father anxiously, he wondered if any brokerage house could withstand such carnage.

Perhaps it was as well that William Master knew his son was watching him. It helped him get through. Courage under fire, grace under pressure: call it what you will, he did his best to set his son an example. As the market lost a quarter of its value in two days, his face never once broke into even a grimace. He was grave, but he was calm. On Wednesday morning, Joe drove him to his office as normal, in the silver Rolls-Royce. When he got out, he summoned all his people and told them: "Be vigilant, gentlemen. Very soon, perhaps even today, there will be a great buying opportunity."

And lo and behold, there was.

On Wednesday, October 30, the market went back up by a staggering twelve and a half percent. A little before noon, William confided to Charlie: "I'm buying." The next day, the market closed at lunchtime, up another five percent. As they left the office, he told Charlie: "I just sold again."

"Already?" said Charlie.

"Profit-taking. I lost a bit of money last week, but I just made half of it back again."

The following week, however, the market slumped again. Five percent on Monday; nine percent on Wednesday. And it just kept sliding, day by day. By November 13, the Dow was at 198, only just over half its September high.

Investors, small and large, with big margin calls were being wiped out. Brokerage houses that'd lent money that couldn't be repaid were failing. "Plenty of the weaker banks may fail, too," William told Charlie. But each morning the street witnessed William Master arriving at his office in his silver Rolls-Royce, as he calmly carried on with business as usual. "We've taken losses," he told people, "but the firm is sound. And so is this country's economy," he liked to add. He said the same thing to his wife and son.

His confidence was rewarded: after reaching its November low, the market stabilized; and as 1930 began, it started to rise. "There's plenty of credit, at low rates," William pointed out. "And if people are borrowing more carefully, that's no bad thing."

Meanwhile, Charlie became aware that his father was trading vigorously on his own account. He didn't see the trades, but he knew they were large. "Are you buying on margin?" he asked. "Somewhat," was the reply. Late in March, however, when a clerk checked one of these deals with him instead of his father, Charlie saw that William was borrowing nine dollars for every one he put down himself—just like the ten percent margin boys before the crash. When he asked his father about it, William took him into his office and closed the door.

"Fact is, Charlie, last November I had to put my own money into the brokerage to hold things together. Don't tell your mother. Or anyone else. Confidence is everything in this game. But I'm making my money back pretty fast."

"You're sure the market's going up?"

"Look, 198 was the bottom, Charlie. I don't say we'll get back to 381, but we'll see 300. I'm sure of it."

And from that day, this message became the daily litany of the Master brokerage. "We'll see 300," they told each other. "We'll see 300," they told their customers. "Mr. Master says so." And before long, it looked as if Master was right. On April 30, the Dow hit 294.

✢

It was a hot morning in August and Salvatore Caruso was high in the sky. He was setting bricks rapidly and with precision. But he was hardly paying attention to his work. Every few minutes he found himself glancing down, searching the street far below, looking for signs of news.

Not that he was unhappy in his work. He'd been on several sites in the last eighteen months, but this one was easily the most exciting. The job was on Fifth Avenue, down at Thirty-fourth Street. At the start of the year it had still been magnificently occupied by the Waldorf-Astoria Hotel. By March there had been nothing but a huge hole, forty feet deep, down to the solid bedrock below. Now, arising from that bedrock with astonishing speed, was the skyscraper to surpass all the skyscrapers that had gone before.

The Empire State.

Everything about the project was larger than life. The entrepreneur, Raskob, had risen from poverty to be the right-hand man of the mighty du Pont family, and chairman of the General Motors finance committee. The frontman, Al Smith, was still poor, but he'd been New York's Democratic governor, and might have been elected President of the USA if he hadn't been a Catholic. Both men were flamboyant. Both hated the hypocrisy of Prohibition. Both loved a challenge.

And if Walter Chrysler thought that his clever, stainless-steel spike was going to leave him king of the New York skyline, then he'd better watch out. The Empire State Building was going to top it, and soon.

Salvatore had been working with the same team of bricklayers for the last couple of years. They went from site to site together, and were known as a good gang. They all got along, but sometimes, for all that had happened between them, he missed the days when he and Angelo were working side by side.

His eyes searched the street again. He was waiting for news of Angelo now.

The site was organized to perfection. In order not to disturb the residents of Fifth Avenue, the roadway was always kept clear. Every morning, on a strict schedule, the trucks swung into the site from one street and left by the other, while their loads were hastily raised to the floor where they were needed.

The materials came from so many places. The big T girders from Pittsburgh, limestone from Indiana, timber from the Pacific coast, marble from Italy and France, and when those suppliers couldn't keep up, the contractors had bought a whole quarry in Germany.

Most dramatic of all was the speed of the work. As the vast steel framework climbed steadily into the sky, the bricklayers and stonemasons followed right behind it. The Empire State Building was going up almost a floor per day.

Just then, a few floors up and to the left, a large iron girder swung silently into view. Sitting astride it were a couple of men.

"There go the Injuns," one of the gang remarked.

There were scores of Mohawk Indians on the site. Whole families of them had learned their ironworking skills on Canada's bridges half a century before. Now they had come down from their reservation to work on the skyscrapers of New York. Salvatore liked to watch the Mohawks sitting calmly on the girders as they were swung up to dizzying heights in the sky. There, they guided them into the building's mighty frame, where the riveters, working in teams of four, went about their deafening work. The Mohawks and the riveters were some of the most highly paid men on the site.

Salvatore's own pay as a bricklayer was excellent: more than fifteen dollars a day. Most important of all, he was employed. For there were plenty of good men who couldn't find work, these days.

It was a strange irony. Just as the Empire State Building had started to go up, America itself had begun to stagger. The country wasn't hit by another stock market crash—there was no sudden crisis—but like a boxer who has taken a series of heavy blows, and starts to lose his legs, the mighty American economy had finally begun to sag.

From its April high, the stock market had given up its new year rally. Each day, as the Empire State Building went up another floor, the market went a little lower. Not a lot, just a little. But day after day, week after week, the market kept on falling. Its defenses were down; it had given up the fight; it no longer saw any reason to rise. By summer, credit was getting tight. Companies were laying people off; companies were failing. Quietly, steadily, it just went on and on.

Of course, many people declared that things would soon get better, that the market was now undervalued, and the economy still sound. Like seconds in the corner, they were shouting at their man to keep his gloves up. But their man was giving ground, and he seemed to have lost his heart. Wherever jobs were to be had, there were long lines waiting for them.

At eleven o'clock, Salvatore noticed a silver Rolls-Royce passing down Fifth Avenue. He remembered the lady with the silver Rolls who'd once taken him and Anna to Gramercy Park, and wondered if it was the same person.

⁜

As it happened, it was. Far below, Rose had just remarked to a friend: "When I think of my poor Mrs. Astor—and I mean *the* Mrs. Astor, of course—and that hotel they put on her house . . . Well, that was bad enough, but now they're building this huge, dreadful *thing* . . ." She turned her head away from the site. "I won't look at it," she declared.

⁜

When lunchtime came, most of the men went down to the base of the building, where an excellent cafeteria had been provided. Only the Italian workers stayed away. They knew that only Italian food, prepared by Italian hands, was edible. They brought their own lunches.

Salvatore had just put some ham and mozzarella on a piece of bread when he looked out over the edge of the building again. A few floors above, the stone setters were at work on the outer face of the building, on a duckwalk suspended from above. Just below him was another line of suspended scaffolding, to catch anything that fell, and about fifteen floors below that, a second line of netting. There had been very few injuries on the huge site so far. Nobody had fallen off the outside.

He was gazing down at the netting far below when he caught sight of

Uncle Luigi. He was standing, perilously, in the middle of Fifth Avenue while the traffic went past him. He was waving his arms like a lunatic.

The news had come. It didn't take Salvatore long to reach his uncle, who embraced him and kissed him on both cheeks.

"The child is born, Salvatore. All is well."

"*Bene*. Another girl?" Angelo and Teresa had produced a baby girl within a year of their marriage. They had called her Anna.

"No, Salvatore. It's a boy. A boy for the Caruso family."

"*Perfetto*. We shall drink to him tonight."

"You'd better." Uncle Luigi beamed. "He will be called Salvatore. They want you to be his godfather."

❖

William Master didn't go straight home that evening. Walking up Fifth, he paused by St. Patrick's Cathedral. At the moment, the city appeared to be quite untidy—there seemed to be building sites wherever you looked. Down on Thirty-fourth, the Empire State Building was the tallest edifice going up, but the biggest construction site was surely the huge complex that ran for three blocks all the way from Fifth Avenue to Sixth, which John D. Rockefeller, Jr., was developing single-handed. Master had no doubt the finished article would be wonderfully elegant, but it was going to take years to complete, and until it was done, the area opposite St. Patrick's was going to be a big mess.

On Fifty-second Street, he turned west and walked a few yards to a doorway on the north side of the street. He needed a drink.

The 21 Club had only been there since the start of the year, but to those in the know, it was already the place to be seen. Charlie had taken him there soon after it opened, for its owners were the two young men who'd run the Fronton speakeasy down in the Village. Having moved uptown, they'd finally settled at number 21 West Fifty-second Street, a much tonier address than where they'd started.

In the big downstairs room, you could sit at one of the booths round the walls and have a drink in peace. If the 21 Club was ever raided, the police might have some difficulty locating the liquor—it was behind a concealed, two-and-a-half-ton metal door, in the basement of the house next door.

William sat quietly and nursed his drink. He was glad to be alone.

Charlie was coming round to dinner that evening, and he'd be glad of his company. But there were still things he hadn't told his son. Things he hadn't told anybody.

Damn it, the market couldn't keep going down forever. But if it didn't pick up soon, he didn't know what the hell he was going to do.

When he got home, Charlie was already there. He kissed his wife, and she gave him a friendly smile. He was glad of that.

He'd been sleeping badly for a month now. Sometimes he'd been so restless that he'd retired to the couch in his dressing room, to let Rose get some sleep. It had been some time since he'd made love to his wife. Partly he'd just been too tired; but more than once lately he'd tried, and been unable. She was very nice about it, but these failures hadn't helped his morale.

Their supper passed pleasantly enough. They talked of this and that, but nobody mentioned the markets. They had fruit for dessert, and as Rose was cutting an apple, she casually remarked: "I'm going to need another hundred thousand dollars for Newport. You don't mind, do you?"

William stared at her. He hadn't even seen the damned house at Newport this summer. Rose had been up there, but she told him it wasn't habitable with all the workmen. He hardly knew what she was doing to the place, though she assured him it would be spectacular when it was done. Meanwhile, she talked about her plans to all her friends.

Strangely enough, her activities had been quite helpful to the brokerage. "If Master's spending all that money on his Newport house," people said, "the brokerage must be in good shape." At a time when so many others were going under, it had raised his prestige on the street.

Even so, another hundred thousand?

"God, Mother," exclaimed Charlie, "do you have to?"

His mother ignored him.

"What's it for, Rose?" William gently inquired.

"Marble, dear. From Italy. The hall's going to be all marble. Nancy de Rivers has a marble hall," she added, with a hint of reproach.

"Ah," said William.

"You're obsessed," said Charlie.

"Can you finish the house if I give you another hundred thousand?" asked William.

"Yes," said Rose.

"All right then," he said.

He'd just have to find the money, somewhere.

✢

By Friday, September 19, the great steel cage of the Empire State Building was nearly complete. It was almost two weeks ahead of schedule. The bricklayers had been keeping pace, and they only had about ten floors to go. Eighty-five floors in six months from the start of construction. A staggering achievement.

The foreman was in a friendly mood when Salvatore approached him with his request. Could his brother Angelo spend the day with him? "He's an artist," Salvatore explained. "He wants to make drawings of us, working on the building."

The foreman considered. The site was by no means closed. Boys went up selling water to the construction workers all the time. Photographers had taken pictures of the steelworkers perched on their girders in the sky. The promoters liked that sort of thing. "Will he be safe?" he said.

"He used to be a bricklayer," Salvatore told him. "He won't do anything stupid." He grinned. "In fact, he just made a sketch of you a few minutes ago." He gave the foreman a small drawing Angelo had dashed off.

"Well, blow me down, that's me all right," said the delighted foreman. And he waved them through.

As they went up in the service elevator, he glanced at his brother. Angelo was wearing a suit and a small homburg hat. He looked as handsome and contented as on his wedding day. The only change was that his face was a little fuller, and he had an air of modest success about him too. There was enough painting work to keep him busy, evidently. He'd also designed the logos and paint jobs for the trucks of several Long Island businesses. There was no question, Angelo had found his feet.

The new Otis elevators that would soon carry the occupants to their offices had been specially designed to travel up at almost double the speed of any elevator before, but even the works elevators moved at a rapid clip. Salvatore was proud of the building, and described its wonders as they went.

"Any day now," he said, "they'll start to build the mast on the top."

The Empire State Building's top office floor was higher than the tip of the Chrysler Building by two feet. But whereas Chrysler had beaten out the opposition with his cheeky, but useless spike, the Empire State would be topped by a huge mast, containing observation platforms, at the top of which there would be a dock at which huge dirigibles could be moored and their passengers disembark. "The whole place will be ready to open by Easter next year," Salvatore said.

They came out at the seventy-second floor, and Salvatore went over to the outer wall where he was working.

The construction of the Empire State Building had proceeded rapidly because its design was so simple. First came the network of huge steel girders which carried the building's entire weight. Some of the vertical steel columns would support a weight of ten million pounds, but they could have taken far more. The building was massively over-engineered. Between the girders were curtain walls, whose only structural function was to keep the weather out.

But here the architects had shown their genius. The outer edges of the vertical girders were given a chrome-nickel trim that rendered them a soft gray. Apart from that, the entire working facade of the mighty tower contained only these principal elements: first, pairs of rectangular, metal window frames; second, above and below each frame, a single aluminum panel, called a spandrel; third, between each pair of windows, large slabs of pale limestone. Thus the facade soared up in pure stone and metal vertical lines. Only at the very top of each high column of stonework or window was there an elegant art deco carving with a vertical direction to satisfy and uplift the eye. Essentially, therefore, the men working on the facade just moved up behind the girder riveters and, as it were, clipped the frames, spandrels and blocks of limestone into place.

And then there were the bricklayers.

"We work from inside, you see," Salvatore explained. "Two courses of brick, eight inches thick." The brick went in behind the limestone and the spandrels, supporting and insulating them. But the brick had another important function. "The brick protects the girders," Salvatore pointed out. Being fired when they were made, the bricks were flame-resistant. In high heat, even steel girders are vulnerable. The brick would clothe and protect them. "The building is strong as a fortress, but it would be almost impossible to burn it down as well."

While Salvatore and his gang went to work, Angelo sat on a pile of bricks with his sketchbook, and began to draw. High above, the deafening noise of the riveters at work would have made conversation difficult. Some days the racket went on from seven in the morning until nine at night, echoing down to the street below. The local residents just had to put up with it.

As well as sketching the bricklayers, Angelo's attention was caught by a stack of the aluminum spandrels that had been stashed near the elevator. Shreve, Lamb & Harmon, the architects of the building, had been trained at Cornell and Columbia mainly, though Lamb had also been to the École des Beaux-Arts in Paris. But they really came from New York's Carrère & Hastings stable, and were dedicated to the French art deco style.

The spandrels were a perfect example of this elegance. Repeated hundreds of times on the building's facade, each panel carried the same simple design—stylized, art deco lightning bolts to left and right, a gap in the center between them. Like electric ice tracks on the metal they soared, vertically, into the blue.

Angelo stared at the design intently, and began to draw it.

As his brother drew, Salvatore noticed that, just for a moment, as he started, Angelo's face took on the same dreamy look it so often had when he was a child, but that as he became engrossed in his drawing, there was an intense, purposeful concentration in his eyes that was even a little frightening.

Uncle Luigi had been right. Angelo was an artist. He belonged in the company of the men who had designed this building, not among the bricklayers.

And so they continued, Angelo sketching all kinds of things that caught his eye, Salvatore laying bricks with his gang, until the noontime whistle blew for the lunch break.

Salvatore had brought enough food for both of them. He gave bread to his brother and cut the salami. When they had eaten, Angelo said that what he'd really like would be to go up to the top of the building and look out from there.

The riveters had stopped for the time being. A strange, unwonted peace pervaded the huge terrace of open girders, where the only sound was the small hiss of the wind that rose, now and then, to a little moan in the branches of the narrow cranes.

High across the sky stretched a veil of gray and silver cloud through which, like a voice offstage, the sun sent an echo of light. Ahead, beyond the cluster of pinnacles on Manhattan's tip, the wide waters of New York harbor wore a dull gleam.

As he looked around, however, Salvatore noticed something else. Smaller clouds, closer to the skyscraper tops, were moving in contrary directions. To the right, across the Hudson, they seemed to be hesitating over New Jersey before turning north; to the left, over Queens, they were already scurrying south. Was the breeze changing? Or had the wind decided to circle the city, with the great tower at the center of its turning world?

A sudden gust of wind slapped his cheek, reminding him that up here on these high places one could never predict the air's sudden eddies and flows.

Meanwhile, Angelo had gone over to the southern edge of the platform, the Thirty-fourth Street side. Over there, Salvatore knew, it was a sheer drop for nine stories to the stonemasons' duckwalk, then another seventy-five down to the street below. A couple of the Mohawk Indians were sitting quietly on a girder which made a temporary parapet there. They glanced at Angelo briefly, but seemed to take no further interest. Angelo sat down a few feet to their right, and he took out his sketch pad. He was leaning over the edge, looking down; something there had caught his attention. Perhaps it was the duckwalk. After a few moments, he started to draw. Salvatore moved over to one of the upright girders a few yards away and leaned against it, protected from the breeze.

There was certainly a wonderful view. It was as if, from that high place, all the riches of the world were laid out below them: the teeming city, the distant suburbs, busy Wall Street, the mighty harbor, the vast ocean beyond. If anywhere on earth could make the claim, the Empire State Building, surely, was the center of the universe today. This was it, the pinnacle of the temple of Man. And he, Salvatore Caruso, was here as a witness, and his brother was recording it in a drawing which—who knew—might be looked at for generations to come. He saw the paper on his brother's sketchbook flutter.

Angelo seemed to have forgotten him, but from where he was resting, Salvatore could observe his brother's face—keenly observant, intense and fine.

And quite suddenly at that moment, taking him entirely by surprise, the terrible pain, the sense of betrayal and jealousy he'd felt when he'd first discovered about his brother and Teresa, burst upon him. It hit him like a wave. Coming from nowhere, it seized him, possessed him, filled him with a cold horror and rage. Why had Angelo married the woman that he himself loved? Why had he given Angelo half his money? Why had Angelo accepted it? Why should it be Angelo who was talented, and handsome, and fine? Why was his little brother something that he himself was not, and never could be?

All these years he had protected him. He'd done what he thought was right, and what Anna would have wanted. He'd given Angelo everything. And what was his reward? To be surpassed, left standing like an onlooker, a fool.

Caught unawares by this realization, as it seemed to be, Salvatore could not help himself. He stared at his brother with hatred. Had they been alone in the desert, he would have struck him dead.

For a long minute, as the wind hissed, he gazed at Angelo with murder in his heart.

⁙

He sensed the danger just before it struck.

The wind does not break against a skyscraper. It wraps itself around it like a serpent. It breathes up and down; it strikes its head in suddenly through openings and rushes through to the other side. It squeezes and it twists. It is dangerous and unpredictable. Just before you feel it, you may hear the sudden bang of a heavy gust as it rushes across the open floor at you.

On the high girders of the Empire State, a gust could sweep a man off his feet.

As the gust came at Salvatore, he automatically caught the edge of the girder and braced himself. But it had been some time since his brother had worked on a high building, and besides, he was not paying attention.

The gust reached Angelo. It smacked into the sketching pad and tore it from his hands, carrying it thirty feet out from the building, where counter-winds buffeted it about like a kite. Instinctively, Angelo reached after his drawing as it flew from him. He was stretching out into space, grasping at empty air. He was tilting.

He was losing his balance.

Salvatore saw it even before Angelo knew it was happening, and he threw himself toward his brother. He was aware that the two Mohawks on

Angelo's left were moving also, but his attention was wholly on his objective. If he could just grab his brother's jacket.

Angelo was going over the edge. He did not have time to right himself. His slim body twisted back, his hands searching for something to hold on to. But it was too late.

Then suddenly, just as Salvatore's outstretched arms were thrown forward, just as he might have touched him, Angelo's body shifted, abruptly, to the left.

The Mohawks had him. They were dragging him toward them, and holding him fast, thank God.

Had Salvatore not swiveled to look at the Mohawks, he might have kept his balance. But as he crashed to the edge, he slipped, tripped over the girder, and went headlong into empty space.

Salvatore Caruso knew he was going to die. As he felt himself go over the edge, he was able to think fast, and clearly. I am going to die like my sister Anna, he thought. He wanted to tell Angelo that he loved him, and did not hate him at all. But then he realized that Angelo had no idea of the shameful thoughts that had passed through his mind in the moments before. So that was all right.

Nine floors below hung the duckwalk. The duckwalk had a hard roof to protect the stone setters from any falling debris. If he hit that roof the impact would surely kill him, but wouldn't stop his fall. He'd bounce off the roof, and then fall like a stone all the way down to the street. He must try to miss the duckwalk, and cry out as he fell, to warn the people on the sidewalk far below.

He heard a voice above cry out his name, "Salvatore." It was Angelo.

There was only one thing he had not thought of. He realized it a moment later.

He was not falling as fast as he should.

When the wind strikes a tall building, its current is checked. It searches for somewhere to go. Often, it will go up. Just as the wind will rush up a cliff and blow you back if you look over, great up-currents of air chase the soaring facade of a skyscraper.

Now, as he fell, Salvatore suddenly noticed that Angelo's sketchbook, which should have been below him, was rising, flapping like a bird, some way over his head. While the sudden gust from the west side had ripped the book from Angelo's hand, great eddies in the changing wind had also caused a column of air to funnel up the eastern facade.

And now, like an angel's hand, it took Salvatore as he fell and held him, then pressed him back against the framework of the building, so that he crashed with a thud onto an open parapet, three floors below.

The landing knocked him unconscious, and broke his leg.

❖

It was a spring morning in 1931, a Monday, and William Master was dressing. He did not know why he should have opened that particular drawer—he hadn't done so for months. It contained some old ties and a couple of waistcoats he never wore. Then he noticed the belt.

He pulled it out. The thing had been handed down in the family since God knows when. His father had told him: "Better keep it. It's wampum. Supposed to be lucky."

William shrugged. He could sure as hell use some luck today. On an impulse, he decided to put it on. Under his shirt of course—he didn't want to look like a damn fool. Then he dressed as usual, every inch the successful man. If he was going down, he'd go down in style.

Anyway, you should never give up hope.

He went downstairs, kissed Rose good-bye, as if this were any other day, and walked out the door.

Joe was waiting there smartly, beside the Rolls.

"Good morning, sir." Joe opened the door for him.

"Morning, Joe. Fine morning." Comforted for a moment, he got in. Joe was a good man. He wondered if he'd be employing him much longer. Probably not.

As they went down Fifth, he gazed out at the park. A sprinkling of daffodils and crocuses had appeared on the grass.

He'd told Charlie he wouldn't be needed in the office today. He didn't want to see anyone except the chief clerk. That trusted man had been going over the books all through the weekend.

For today was the day of reckoning. It couldn't be put off any longer. There was a bunch of calls due today that would bring everything to a close. Of course, if the market suddenly had a huge rally, that might make a difference. But the market wasn't going to rally. In April last year he'd said the Dow would get to 300. It never had. It was only a little more than half that now.

While the chief clerk went over the brokerage accounts that weekend, he'd done the same for his own affairs. Alone in his study, he'd reviewed his remaining assets. He shouldn't have tried to save the brokerage, of course. Shouldn't have used his own money to prop it up. Easy to see that now, but at the time, there had always seemed to be hope round the corner. He'd deluded himself that something would turn up. Fact was, he just couldn't bear the loss of face, couldn't admit his failure. Couldn't let go. Too late for that now.

The house would have to go. Hard to say what it would fetch in this market, but it was a hell of a house. A good asset. The Newport house was another matter. Three weeks ago he'd casually asked Rose if she had any of the $600,000 he'd given her left.

"Not a cent, William," she'd answered with a sweet smile. "Actually, I might need just a little more."

"The work's not finished?"

"Not by some way. You know these designers. Well, the builders, too . . ."

An unfinished palace in Newport. God knows how you'd sell that in the present market. Nobody was buying fancy houses that he knew of. He'd marked its value down severely.

So, absent a miracle, he'd find out in the next few hours whether his net worth was positive, zero, or negative. He preferred to do that alone. Then, when it was over, he'd have to go home and tell Rose that they were broke.

She had no idea.

"Pick me up at four o'clock, Joe," he said, as he got out.

❖

The sun was still shining quite brightly when Joe opened the door for him again that afternoon. He settled comfortably into the back seat, and looked out at the street.

"Take me for a drive, Joe," he said. "We'll go up the West Side." He smiled. "Take me to Riverside Drive."

It was a while since he'd driven up the Hudson. As they got into the Seventies, he looked out at its broad waters. They were pretty much the same, he supposed, as they would have been when the first Masters and Van Dycks had come to the city. That's what they would have seen. The Indians before them, too.

That reminded him. The wampum belt. He still had the damn thing on. He'd forgotten about it during the day. Well, it hadn't brought him much luck. So far as he could tell, when the brokerage was closed, the houses sold, and all debts paid, he had maybe fifty thousand dollars left in the world. Better than bankruptcy.

Three hundred years of accumulated family fortune, gone. Lost in its entirety. Lost by me, he thought. He'd been the one, the only one in all those generations, to achieve that. He continued to smile out of the window, as he took a deep breath, but it was no good. His body gave a sudden start. The shame of it made him squirm in his seat. He wasn't sure he could bear it.

Had Joe noticed his sudden movement from the driver's seat? There was no sign that he had. A good man, Joe. Never asked questions. He'd be all right.

William sat silently and stared out at the river. He tried not to cry. After a while, they passed Grant's Tomb.

Ahead of them now was a magnificent sight. The mighty American economy might be sinking, Wall Street might be in collapse, yet everywhere you looked in Manhattan these days, you saw these huge construction projects rising into the sky.

The suspension bridge nearing completion across the Hudson River was not just large, it was stupendous. Even the Brooklyn Bridge looked modest by comparison.

"You never married, Joe, did you?" he remarked to the chauffeur.

"No, sir."

"Any family? Parents?"

"Both dead, sir. I have a brother in New Jersey."

"That's a fine bridge, Joe."

"Yes, sir."

"Pull over when we get to it. I'm going to take a look."

At the entrance to the bridge, Master put on his hat and got out, then strode toward the bridge. The suspension cables were all in place. There was a walkway running across, and they were already laying the road. He passed some workmen, then a fellow who looked like a foreman came out to meet him. Master gave him a friendly smile.

"You boys are doing a great job."

"Thank you, sir."

"We were talking about you the other day." He could see the foreman wondering who exactly "we" might be. "You're well ahead of schedule."

"We are, sir. You're . . . ?"

"I'm Mr. Master," William said firmly. "Like to take me out there? I'd be glad to have a look."

The foreman hesitated just a moment, looked at the rich gentleman and, glancing toward the Rolls-Royce, evidently decided he'd better not take the chance of annoying him.

"This way, sir," he said. "You have to be careful, though."

As he stood on the walkway, William glanced northward. How mighty the river was, yet how unperturbed, as it quietly came down from the far-off states. How noble the stony cliffs of the Palisades looked. Yet how hard and immovable. Looking south, he gazed at the long line of Manhattan, at the distant towers of the Financial District and the open space of the harbor beyond.

So the family was back to the beginning now. Just him and the river.

William looked down at the water. If he was going to jump, now would be the time. Years ago, a fellow had jumped from the Brooklyn Bridge on a bet. He hadn't lived. Jumping off here would be a piece of cake, and not a bad way to go. With luck, the big river would swallow him up in its silence, and he'd never know anything more. Just walk out from his Rolls-Royce, as a gentleman should, and into oblivion. The family would manage all right. Better without him.

Or would they? Charlie would go on being Charlie. He'd be poor, but the way he lived, that would hardly make a difference. What about Rose, though? Rose with her foolish obsession with the Newport house, her dreams of marble halls and God knows what. How was she going to cope with the winding up of his affairs? Not well, evidently. He shook his head.

It took less courage to jump than it did to go home. But home he must go. He turned. The foreman, seeing him do so, came quickly over to accompany him back.

"You'll be here for the opening, Mr. Master?" he asked politely.

"Oh, I expect so."

⁜

He didn't tell Rose until late that night. She was looking very handsome that evening, in a silk gown. She was wearing the pearl choker that she loved. He wished he had happy news to tell.

He said nothing at dinner, with the servants there. Nor did he tell her while they sat by the fire in the library afterward, in case she should become distraught and make a scene. He waited until they had retired and were completely alone.

Rose had a small boudoir just off their bedroom. She'd told her lady's maid she wouldn't need her, and she was sitting there alone, taking off her earrings. He stood beside her.

"I've bad news, Rose," he said.

"I'm sorry, dear."

"It's very bad news. You have to prepare yourself."

"I'm ready, dear. Have we lost all our money?"

"Yes."

"Do we have anything left?"

"Maybe. Fifty thousand dollars. Something like that. The brokerage is finished. The houses have to go. This one included." He needed to stop for a moment. She glanced up at him, and took his hand.

"It isn't a surprise, you know. I've been expecting it."

"You have?"

"I guessed you were in trouble. So many people are."

"I don't know what to say."

"What do you want to say?"

"I'm . . . I'm just so sorry." He almost broke down, but he held himself together. "What'll you do?"

"What'll I do? Live with you, of course. However you like, wherever you like. That's all I want."

"But after all this . . ."

"We've had a wonderful life. Now we'll have another wonderful life. Just different."

"What'll Charlie do?"

"Work," she said, firmly.

"I just—" he began, but she stopped him.

"I want you to get into bed now," she said.

It was a minute or two before she came from her boudoir. To his surprise, she wasn't wearing a nightdress. She was quite naked, except for the pearl choker he'd given her. She was a middle-aged woman, but she'd kept her figure. The effect was wonderfully erotic. He gave a little gasp.

She stood by the bed, reached back and slowly unfastened the choker. Then she handed it to him.

"This should fetch quite a bit." She smiled.

He took it unwillingly. "I never want you to part with this," he muttered.

"You're all I need," she said simply. "That's what matters." And as she got in beside him, she pulled him to her.

"I don't think I can," he said sadly.

"Shh," she whispered, and pulled his head onto her breast. "I think you should weep, now. It's time."

✛

It was several hours later, long after they had made love and her husband had fallen asleep, that Rose Vandyck Master lay very still and stared at the ceiling.

She was glad it was over, really. Eighteen months had passed since she'd first guessed her husband was in trouble, and it hadn't been easy seeing him suffer. But there'd been nothing she could do except watch and wait.

She'd remembered how it had been, back in 1907. He'd nearly gone under during the panic then, and hadn't been able to tell her. So when things started to get bad in the markets this time, she'd reckoned it would be the same. Month after month she'd waited. It was so obvious he was distressed—she knew him so well—but he couldn't bring himself to tell her.

This time, anyway, she'd taken precautions. She couldn't do much, but at least it was something. And he hadn't suspected a thing.

The only question was, when should she tell him?

Not yet. Better wait until the dust had settled and the debts were paid. Strictly speaking, of course, if she concealed money from his creditors, it would be illegal. But she'd take that fence when she came to it. With luck he'd come out with something left. The main thing was, she'd been able to remove a chunk of money from him before he could lose it all in the brokerage.

Six hundred thousand dollars, to be precise. She had it safely stashed away, in five different bank accounts, in her own name. Not a cent of it spent.

It was fortunate really that he wasn't that passionate about Newport. If he'd insisted on going up there, he'd have discovered at once that, apart from a few tarpaulins carefully pulled over bits of the house, there was nothing going on there at all. No architects, no builders, no marble.

Nothing. She'd had workmen come from time to time, to give the appearance that something was going on, and the place was well screened by hedges. That, and a lot of talking, had been all that was needed.

Six hundred thousand. They'd be able to rent quite a decent apartment on Park Avenue. They had some beautiful things. They had friends, social debts to call in. While plenty of people with huge losses were vanishing from the social scene entirely, their own case would be different.

After all, they might be poor, but they were still old money.

Brooklyn

THE FIRST THING one noticed about Sarah Adler was the pair of big tortoiseshell glasses on her narrow face. Charlie had also noticed, when she leaned forward, the little Jewish star pendant on a necklace that rested between the tops of her breasts. But now as he looked into those glasses, he saw that her eyes were not only intense, but a magical brown and flecked with wondrous lights.

Sarah Adler was twenty-four. And right now, as those brown eyes stared at Charlie Master across the table in the elegant St. Regis, she was wondering: How old is he? Fifty maybe? Twice her age, anyway. But he looked in pretty good shape.

And you had to admit, older men were much more interesting.

The St. Regis, on Fifth at Fifty-fifth, was not just a hotel. It was a palace. He'd taken her for a drink, first to the paneled bar, where Maxfield Parrish's huge, luminous mural, *Old King Cole*, gave a rich glow to the whole room. She'd liked that. And then they had gone into the pillared dining room. Mr. Charles Master certainly knew how to treat a girl. And he talked well, too.

It was only three weeks since she'd taken the job at the gallery, even if it did pay peanuts. So when Mr. Master had walked in this morning with his incredible collection of photographs, and the gallery owner had told her to take care of it, she couldn't believe her luck. And now they were sitting in the St. Regis, and she was enjoying one of the most interesting conversations she'd ever had in her life.

This man seemed to know everybody. He'd been friends with Eugene O'Neill and all the theater crowd back in the twenties, and he'd written plays himself. He'd heard the jazz greats in Harlem before they were famous, remembered Charlie Chaplin when he was still performing onstage. And now he'd just told her something even more amazing.

"You know Ernest Hemingway?" She worshipped Hemingway. "Where did you meet him? In Paris?"

"In Spain."

"You mean you were in the Spanish Civil War?"

Sarah had only been seven years old when the Spanish Civil War began, but she had learned about it at school—and at home. At the Adler house in Brooklyn, the discussions had been endless. Of course, none of them supported the side that finally won. General Franco the fascist, with his authoritarian Catholics and monarchists, was everything the Adler family hated. "He's no better than Hitler," her father used to say. As for her mother, Esther Adler, who came from a family of liberals and trade unionists, she was ready to join the International Brigade and go to fight herself! Everyone was for the left.

Except for Uncle Herman. Her father's brother was a thickset man who used to pride himself on his knowledge of European affairs. And whatever the subject, he always knew best. "Listen," he'd declare, "Franco is an old-fashioned authoritarian. He's a son of a bitch, okay? But he's not a Nazi."

Then her mother would berate him.

"And those Catholic monarchists of his? You know what the Spanish Inquisition did to the Jews?"

And soon there would be a furious argument.

"You think the people fighting Franco are American liberals, like you? Let me tell you, Esther, half these people are Trotskyists and anarchists. Okay? They want to turn the place into Stalin's Russia. You really think that's a good idea? No!" Uncle Herman would suddenly shout when his brother tried to interrupt him. "I want to know if she really thinks that's such a great idea."

"Your uncle just likes to argue," her mother would tell Sarah, afterward. "He doesn't know what he's talking about."

But when he was alone with Sarah, Uncle Herman would give her candy and tell her stories in the gentlest voice, so she knew he was good and kind. It was just that he liked to argue.

Sadly, those were the only memories Sarah had of her Uncle Herman.

The Spanish Civil War was still in progress when he'd gone away to Europe—though not to fight in Spain. Maybe his fate would have been different if he had gone there.

For Uncle Herman had never returned. It was a subject her father couldn't bear to speak about. So the family never mentioned the poor man now.

"I was a journalist," said Charlie. "For the Hearst newspapers. I drank with Hemingway a few times, that's all."

Sarah laughed out loud.

"You're mocking me," he said.

"No. I'm impressed. What was Hemingway like?"

"Good company. I liked him better than Dos Passos or George Orwell."

"Dos Passos? Orwell? Oh my God, that must have been amazing."

"True. But civil wars are ugly. Bloody."

"Hemingway was wounded."

"So was I, actually."

"Really? How?"

"There was a man down, quite near where I was reporting. You could hear him screaming. They had a stretcher, but only one bearer." He shrugged. "I helped out. Took some shrapnel on the way back." He grinned. "There's a piece still in my leg, which speaks to me sometimes."

"You have a scar?"

"Of course."

"But you saved a man."

"He didn't make it."

Charlie Master had a mustache. It was flecked with gray. She couldn't decide if it reminded her more of Hemingway or Tennessee Williams. It looked good, anyway. He'd mentioned he had a son. Did he have a wife?

"So what did you do in the Second War?" she asked. "Did you fight in Europe?"

"Newport."

"Newport, Rhode Island?"

"Has one of the finest deep-water harbors in the country. The British used it during the War of Independence. There was a lot of activity there, especially in '43 and '44. Coastal defenses, naval schools, you name it. I was in the Coast Guard." He smiled. "A return to childhood for me, really. We used to have a cottage there."

"Like, one of those palaces, you mean?"

"No, but it was pretty spacious. After my father lost all his money in the crash, the Newport and city houses were both sold. My parents had to move to an apartment on Park Avenue."

She'd already figured that Charlie Master was some kind of blue blood. He had that soft way of speaking. But to move to Park Avenue because you were poor? This was another world.

"You really knew hardship in the Depression," she laughed, then regretted her sarcasm.

He gave her a wry look.

"It sounds kind of foolish, doesn't it? But believe me," he continued more seriously, "at the start of the Depression, it was only a step from considerable wealth to total poverty. There were lines around the block for every job. Wall Street brokers, I mean people you knew, were selling apples on the street. I remember walking with my father once, and he looked at one of those fellows, and he said, 'A couple of percentage points, Charlie, and that would have been me.'"

"You believe that?"

"Oh, absolutely. When my father's brokerage failed, we could have been bankrupt, completely finished. Did you ever see Central Park during the early years of the Depression? People put up shacks there, little shanty towns, because they had nowhere to live. One day, my father found one of his friends there. He brought him home, and he lived with us for months. I remember him sleeping on a couch. So, we were lucky but, believe me, we knew it." He nodded thoughtfully. "What about your family? How did you get by?"

"My crazy family? In my father's family, one of the children always got an education. So that was my father. He became a dentist. Even in the Depression, people needed to get their teeth fixed. We got by."

"That was good."

"Not so good. My father didn't want to be a dentist. He wanted to be a concert pianist. He still keeps a piano in his waiting room, and he practices while he's waiting for his patients."

"Is he a fine pianist?"

"Yes. But he's a terrible dentist—my mother would never let him fix our teeth."

Sarah didn't really want to talk about her family, though. She wanted to hear more about his life. So they talked about the thirties for some time. It was just so interesting. And she found she could make him laugh.

Finally, she had to go back to the gallery. Their next meeting was arranged for the following month, so she supposed she wouldn't see him until then. But just as they were parting, he remarked: "There's a new show at the Betty Parsons Gallery next week. Do you go to openings?"

"Yes," she said, taken by surprise.

"Oh, well, maybe I'll see you there."

"Could be."

I'll be there, all right, she thought. Though she still hadn't found out if he was married. But then, there were things he didn't know about her, either.

✛

On Saturday, Charlie took the ferry to Staten Island. It was a fine October day, so he quite enjoyed the ride. He took it every other weekend, usually, to collect little Gorham.

It hadn't been his idea to give his son the name. Julie had wanted him named after her grandfather, and his own mother had approved. "I think it's nice to carry the name of an ancestor who signed the Constitution," she had declared. Old money, and all that.

Julie was old money. And she had some money, too. She was blonde and blue-eyed and bland, and her family were Social Register, like the Masters. Mrs. Astor's famous Four Hundred might be a thing of the past, but the registers, those broader guides to the good old families of America, were very much around. Indeed, it was perfectly possible, Charlie supposed, to lead a fulfilling social life without stirring outside their pages. His mother had been delighted when, at the end of the war, he'd married Julie.

And not too pleased last year, when they'd divorced.

He'd supposed it was his fault. Julie had grown tired of his ever-shifting employment. Not that he didn't earn any money. In the thirties, though money had been tight, he'd always got by with a variety of freelance activities. And even during the Depression you could make money in the entertainment industry. He'd collaborated on plays and movies; by the time he married, he'd even had a small share of a Broadway musical. And after Julie bought the apartment, he'd always been able to pay the maintenance and that sort of thing. When their son was born, he'd hoped it would draw them closer.

Little Gorham. Most of the people one knew had nicknames. If you were John, you became Jack. Henry was Harry, Augustus was Gus, Howard was Howie, Winthrop was Win, Prescott was Pres. That's what people called you, people you knew, that is. But young Gorham, for some reason, had just stayed Gorham.

Then Julie had told him she wanted a divorce so she could marry a doctor, from Staten Island, for God's sake. Not that he had anything against Staten Island. The island borough of Richmond, as it officially was, had not been connected to any other borough by a bridge yet, so it still retained the rural, almost eighteenth-century character that Manhattan Island had entirely lost. The views across the water were pleasant, but it was inconvenient to go all the way out there to collect his son for the weekend.

Julie and Gorham were waiting for him at the terminal. Julie was wearing a new coat and a small felt hat. She looked good. He hadn't fought any of her demands for money when they divorced. It wasn't worth the hassle. She'd sold the apartment and, as the doctor she married had a handsome house already, she had plenty to spend on herself.

On the way back, he put his arm around his son and pointed things out to him. Gorham was five. He was fair-haired and blue-eyed like both of his parents. Children resemble various relatives at different ages, but for the moment at least, Gorham looked like his father. Charlie knew his son needed him, and he did his best for the boy.

"Are we going to a show tonight?" Gorham asked.

"Yes. We're going to *South Pacific*."

"We are? Really?"

"I promised."

A huge smile appeared on the little boy's face. "*South Pacific*," he murmured.

He was awfully young for it, but for some reason he'd set his heart on seeing the show, so what could you do? Some years back, when Charlie had first heard that James Michener's book was being adapted into a musical by Rodgers and Hammerstein, he had wondered how it would work. Well, half a dozen smash hit songs and nearly two thousand performances later, he had his answer. Even now, he'd had to pay double price to a scalper for the seats he wanted tonight. He hoped after all this effort that the little boy would enjoy it.

While his son contemplated the treat ahead, Charlie's mind wandered back to the meeting he'd had with the girl.

The photography collection was important to him. He'd been very fond of Edmund Keller. During the Depression Keller had not only been a good friend, but he'd even got him some lecturing assignments at Columbia that had provided some extra income. It had come as a hell of a shock when Keller told him a couple of years ago that he had cancer.

"Charlie, I want you to be the guardian of my father's photographs. There's no one in the family who'd know how to deal with this. If you make any money out of it, then you should take a fee and pass on the rest to my estate. Would you do that for me?"

The collection was magnificent. A small apartment in a building up on Riverside Drive, near Columbia, served as an office and storage space, and Charlie often liked to work up there. He'd made an approach to the gallery a little while ago, and the owner had come to see the collection and agreed on a show. Charlie would arrange the publicity.

He'd been decidedly frustrated when the owner had suddenly handed over all the arrangements to some girl who'd only just started there. Reluctantly, he'd given her the portfolio he'd brought with him, and let her take a look at it.

But instead of looking through it and making the usual polite noises, the girl had gone through the photographs, staring so intently through her glasses at each one that, for a few minutes, he wondered if she'd forgotten him.

"These ones," she pulled out half a dozen of the later photographs, "these could be early Stieglitz."

She was right. New York's legendary photographer and art entrepreneur had produced some beautiful work, around the turn of the century, after his return to New York from Germany, that was close to Theodore Keller's. "Did they meet?" she asked.

"Yes. Several times. I have Keller's diaries."

"We should mention that." She pulled out an earlier shot, of men walking up the railroad beside the Hudson River. "Great choice," she said. "Amazing composition."

They started to talk about Keller's technique. They kept talking. After an hour he'd said, "I have to be in Midtown after this. Shall we go to the St. Regis?"

He wondered if she'd turn up at the opening of the show at the Betty Parsons next week.

At the Manhattan ferry terminal, he found a taxi. Soon they were going up the East River Drive, and crossing to First Avenue. As they passed Forty-second Street, he pointed out the big new United Nations building on the right, overlooking the water. He liked its clean, modern lines. Gorham stared at it, but it was impossible to know what the boy was thinking.

"The River House is just up from here," Charlie remarked. "Your grandmother has a lot of friends in that building." Maybe the grandest apartment building in the city. But of course, little Gorham had no idea what that meant.

Charlie had always supposed that his son would live in the same world. Assumed it really. Until Julie went off to Staten Island. Could you breathe the spirit of the great, daring city out on Staten Island? Maybe. It was one of the Five Boroughs, after all. But would his son really understand? Would he know which were the best buildings on the Upper East Side? Would he know all the restaurants and clubs? And the intimate sights and smells of Greenwich Village, the grainy texture of Soho? Moments like this made Charlie realize how much he loved Manhattan. And it gave him a terrible pain, and sense of loss, to think that he might not be able to share the city with his son.

They turned left on Forty-seventh Street. As they crossed Lexington, Charlie pointed south. "Grand Central Station's just down there," he said. Gorham was silent. They reached Park Avenue and turned north. "When I was a boy," said Charlie, "there were railway yards here. Park Avenue wasn't so nice then. But the railway lines are all under the ground now, and Park Avenue looks pretty neat, don't you think?"

"Yes, Dad," said the little boy.

There was something else, he realized, that he wanted to convey to the boy. Something deep and important. Beyond the magnificent houses and apartments, the teeming life of the streets, the newspapers, theaters, galleries—the huge business of the place. What he needed Gorham to understand—what his son was heir to—the thing that really mattered—was the New Yorkers' indomitable spirit.

Even the Depression hadn't really brought the city down. Three giants had saved it. FDR, the president of course—and the good old Dutch name of Roosevelt was as New York as could be. It took the guts and daring of a New Yorker, Charlie reckoned, to push the New Deal through. Second, from the early thirties, right through to '45, New York's tiny, feisty Mayor La Guardia—a Republican technically, but a New Dealer all the way—had run the most honest administration the city had ever seen, and championed the poor through all those painful years. Third, and no less dramatic in his own way, that brutal giant Robert Moses.

No one had ever seen public works on the scale Commissioner Moses undertook. Those massive bridges—the Triborough, from Long Island to Manhattan; the beautiful Whitestone, from Long Island to the Bronx. A slew of public parks. Above all, the huge roadways that swept the ever growing traffic round New York's boroughs. With these titanic projects, Moses had brought countless millions of federal dollars into the city, employing thousands.

Some people said there was a cruelty about Moses and his methods. They said his big Long Island expressways avoided the great estates of the rich, but devastated the homes of the poor; that he only cared about the flow of motor cars, and ignored public transport. They even said the new highways created barriers, physically separating black neighborhoods from the public parks.

Charlie wasn't sure. New York's public transport was pretty good, he reckoned, and in this new age of the motor car, the city would have come to a standstill without the new roads. The criticism about the parks and the black neighborhoods might be true, but the layout of the roads was magnificent. When he drove up the West Side's Henry Hudson Parkway, which swept one gloriously along the great river all the way past the George Washington Bridge, Charlie could forgive Moses almost anything.

The question was, he thought, as they pulled up at his mother's building on Park, how was he going to explain all that to his son?

The white-gloved doorman took them to the elevator, and Rose was waiting for them at her apartment door. She might be over eighty, but she could have passed for sixty-five. She welcomed them warmly and they all went into the living room.

It was a nice apartment. According to the way they counted these things in the city, it had six rooms. Living room, dining room, kitchen, two bedrooms and a maid's room off the kitchen. The three bathrooms weren't counted. Respectable enough for a widowed lady, but not quite what a family like his should have. Charlie would have preferred an eight—that gave you another bedroom or library and a second maid's room. The rooms got bigger too, with an eight. When they'd been married, Charlie and Julie had had an eight, though not on Park.

Of course, if he'd gone into Wall Street, if he'd made money like some of his friends, Charlie might have got one of the big apartments on Park or Fifth by now. Ten rooms, fifteen. They were huge, really like mansions, with four or five maids' rooms for your staff.

Charlie had an apartment on Seventy-eighth and Third these days. Not far away from his mother. Seventy-eighth was a good street, and the apartments had big living rooms like artists' studios, so it was quite interesting for a single man. It didn't have a doorman, though. One really should have a doorman.

Rose was good with children. She showed little Gorham photographs of his grandfather and great-grandfather. The boy liked that. There were pictures of the Newport house as well. Things to remind the little fellow where he really belonged.

At noon, they went out and took a taxi across to the Plaza Hotel. In the Palm Court, they were ushered to a table. He could see that Gorham was impressed with the Palm Court.

"Sometimes I walk over to the Carlyle," said Rose. "But I like coming here. It's nice being near the park."

She picked at a salad while her grandson, having dutifully eaten a fish-cake, tucked into a chocolate eclair. They talked about the school he'd started at.

"When you're older," Rose said, "you'll go to Groton."

Julie hadn't given any trouble about that. They'd all agreed. To be precise, Charlie recalled, his mother and his ex-wife had agreed. He just had to pay the bills. He'd have liked Gorham to go to one of the day schools in the city, but you couldn't do that easily from Staten Island, and having the boy live with him, or his grandmother, assuming she was alive by then, seemed a bit difficult.

"Did you go to Groton, Dad?" the little boy asked.

"No," said Rose, "but he probably should have."

It was a fine place of course. The Massachusetts boarding school was closely modeled on Cheltenham College in England, and its Latin motto said it all: "Serve God and Rule" Charlie translated it. Muscular Chris-

tianity. Episcopal, of course. Good, sound education, nothing too intellectual. Plenty of sport. Cold showers. Like the rulers of Britain's empire,
the owners of America's great fortunes mustn't get soft.

"He'll meet the right sort of people there," Charlie said cheerfully.
Roosevelt, Auchincloss, Morgan, Whitney, du Pont, Adams, Harriman,
Grew . . . People with names like that went to Groton.

"Wasn't there somebody called Peabody there?" asked Gorham.

"Yes, Gorham." Charlie smiled. "He founded it. He was headmaster
there for fifty years. Well done."

"It's not Peabody, dear," said Rose. "It's pronounced Pee-bdy."

"Oh, Mother," said Charlie with a shrug. "At his age . . ."

"Pee-bdy," said his mother firmly.

It amused Charlie how old money in America had somewhat adopted
the English custom of leaving verbal traps for the socially unwary. Old
money pronounced certain names in ways that discreetly separated them
from the rest. There were other words, too. The modern custom of referring to a man's casual evening dress as a "tuxedo," or even worse a "tux,"
was definitely considered vulgar. Middle-class America said "tuxedo." Old
money said "dinner jacket."

"Mind you," said his mother quietly, "I hear Groton let in a black boy."

"They did," said Charlie. "A couple of years ago. Good thing."

"Oh well," his mother murmured, "at least it wasn't a Jew."

Charlie shook his head. There were times when you just had to ignore
his mother.

When they came out afterward, Gorham saw one of the pretty little
horse-drawn hansom cabs standing by the corner, and asked if they could
go for a ride. Charlie glanced at his mother, who nodded.

"Why not?" said Charlie.

It was a pleasant ride. First, they went down Fifth Avenue. His mother
was her usual self. As they passed Bergdorf's elegant department store, she
explained to Gorham: "That used to be the Vanderbilt mansion." A couple of minutes later, as they approached the High Gothic front of St.
Patrick's Cathedral, she said sadly: "This used to be all private houses.
Now it's just churches and stores."

Yet in fact, Charlie realized, they were actually coming to the true, spiritual center of Midtown. And it wasn't the cathedral, important though
that was. No, Manhattan's spiritual center lay opposite the cathedral,
right across the street.

How well he remembered those long years, all through the thirties and beyond, when one looked across Manhattan to see the huge tower of the Empire State Building, the great symbol, dominating the sky. But the symbol of what? Failure. Eighty-eight floors of offices—which couldn't be let. People did rent them eventually, but right through the Depression years, it was known as the Empty State Building. And you'd have thought others would hesitate to build more office blocks at such a time.

But not if you knew New York, or the Rockefeller family.

Just before the crash of '29, John D. Rockefeller, Jr., had leased twenty-two acres on the west side of Fifth Avenue to build a complex of art deco office buildings and an opera house. After the crash, the opera house had to be abandoned. But that didn't stop Rockefeller executing the rest of the project. Single-handed, the richest family in the world developed not one but fourteen office towers, with roof gardens and a central plaza, creating the most elegant street space in the city. Its delightful central court doubled as an open restaurant in summer and small ice rink in winter. Toward the end of a decade of building, some of the construction workers, one December, decided to put a Christmas tree in the plaza.

Rockefeller Center was a triumph. It was big, it was elegant, it was rich. It was created by New Yorkers who refused to take no for an answer. Even the Depression couldn't keep them down. That was it, Charlie thought. That was the point of New York. Immigrants came here penniless, but they made it all the same. God knows, the first Astor had come with almost nothing. It was the tradition, going right back to those hard, salty East Coast sea captains and settlers from whom he and his son descended. Rockefeller was a titan, like Pierpont Morgan, or President Roosevelt—princes of the world, and with the New York spirit, every one.

"That's Rockefeller Center," he said to his son. "They kept on building it right through the Depression because Rockefeller had money and guts. Isn't it fine?"

"Yes," said Gorham.

"A New Yorker can never be beat, Gorham, because he gets right back up again. Remember that."

"Okay, Dad," said the little boy.

The cab took them round, up Sixth and back through Central Park. It was really very pleasant. But as they came back to where they'd started, Charlie couldn't help reflecting upon one, inescapable truth. They'd just taken a horse-drawn hansom, like tourists. Tonight he'd take Gorham to a show, somewhat like a tourist. And tomorrow he'd have to take him back to Staten Island.

And then his son spoke.

"Dad."

"Yes, Gorham."

"When I grow up, I'm going to live here."

"Well, I hope you will."

The little boy frowned, and looked up at his father solemnly, as if he had not quite been understood.

"No, Dad," he said quietly, "it's what I'm going to do."

⁂

Charlie arrived at the gallery quite early, but Sarah Adler was already there.

The Betty Parsons Gallery was on Fifty-fifth Street. It had only opened in 1946, but it was already famous. Partly, no doubt, it was Betty's character. Born into old money, she'd followed the prescribed path, married young and respectably. But then she'd rebelled. She'd gone to Paris, and set up house with another woman. In the thirties she'd lived in Hollywood, and been a friend of Greta Garbo. Finally, an artist herself, she'd set up her gallery in New York.

And in the 1950s, if you were interested in modern art, New York was the place to be.

There had been American schools of art before: the Hudson River School in the nineteenth century, with its magnificent landscapes of the Hudson Valley, Niagara and the West; the American Impressionists, who'd often gathered in France, around Monet's place in Giverny, before returning home. But good though they were, you couldn't say they'd invented any new kind of painting. And indeed, the huge movements of modern abstract art, from cubism onward, had all been European.

Until now. Suddenly, a crowd of artists with huge, bold abstract work, unlike anything seen before, had burst upon the New York scene. Jackson Pollock, Hedda Sterne, Barnett Newman, Motherwell, de Kooning, Rothko—"the Irascibles," people often called them. The name of their school: Abstract Expressionism.

Modern America had an art that was all its own. And at the center of it all was a small, indefatigable lady, born into the world of New York private schools, and summers in Newport, but who preferred the company

of the most daring artists of her time: Betty Parsons. And her gallery, of
course.

It was a group show. Motherwell was there, and Helen Frankenthaler
and Jackson Pollock too. Charlie brought Sarah over to meet Pollock.
Then he and Sarah looked at the work.

The show was magnificent. One Pollock they particularly liked—a
dense riot of browns, whites and grays. "It looks like he rode around the
canvas on a bicycle," Sarah whispered.

"Perhaps he did," said Charlie, with a grin. Yet it seemed to him that,
as usual, in that apparently random, swirling mass of abstract color, you
could find subliminal repetitions and complex rhythms, which gave the
work amazing power. "Some people think he's a fraud," he said, "but I
think he's a genius."

There was a fine Motherwell, one of his *Elegy to the Spanish Republic*
series, with great black glyphs and vertical bars on a white canvas. "It feels
as if it's resonating," Sarah said. "Like an oriental mantra. Does that make
sense to you?"

"Yes," said Charlie, "it does." It was funny, he thought, it hardly mattered whether someone was older than you or half your age, when there
was a real meeting of minds. He smiled to himself. Money and power
were supposed to be the biggest aphrodisiacs, but shared imagination was
just as strong, it seemed to him, and lasted longer.

They both saw people they knew, and drifted apart to talk to them. He
said a few words to Betty Parsons.

He liked Betty. When he looked down at her neat New England face,
with its small square jaw and broad brow, and brave spirit, he almost
wanted to kiss her—though she probably wouldn't have welcomed that.

An hour had passed when, glancing across the room, he saw that Sarah
was deep in conversation with some young people of her own age, and
with an inward sigh, he decided he'd better slip away. He went over
though, to say good-bye to her first.

"You're going home?" She looked disappointed.

"Unless you'd like to eat? But you should stay with your friends."

"I'd like to eat," she said. "Are you ready?"

⁜

They decided on Sardi's. It was still early, long before the after-theater
crowd would fill the place. They didn't even have to wait for a table. Char-

lie always liked the theatrical decor of the place, with its cartoons of actors all round the walls. Out-of-town people might go to Sardi's because it was so famous, but it was still a lot of fun.

They ordered steaks and red wine, and soon needed a second bottle. They didn't talk about the show. Charlie told her about his outing with his son, and then they discussed the city in the thirties. He told her his feeling about Rockefeller and Roosevelt, and the ancestral New York spirit.

"But don't forget Mayor La Guardia," she reminded him. "He saved New York too."

"That is absolutely true." Charlie grinned. "Thank God for the Italians."

"La Guardia wasn't Italian."

"I'm sorry—since when?"

"His father was Italian, but his mother was Jewish. That makes him Jewish. Ask my family."

"Okay. How do they feel about Robert Moses? Both his parents are Jewish."

"We hate him."

"He's done a lot for the city."

"That's true. But my Aunt Ruth lives in the Bronx, and he's just destroyed the value of her property." The great Cross Bronx Expressway that Moses was carving across that borough was the most difficult project the masterbuilder had ever undertaken. A lot of people were being displaced, seeing their property values go down, and they didn't like it. "She says she hopes he breaks his neck." She grinned. "My family's close. We support her. Moses will eventually be destroyed."

"You have a big family?"

"A sister, two brothers. My mother's family all moved out of New York. Aunt Ruth is my father's sister." She paused. "My father had a brother, Herman, who used to live in New York. But he went to Europe before the war and then . . ." She hesitated.

"He didn't come back?"

"We don't talk about him."

"I'm sorry."

She shrugged, then changed the subject.

"So, your son lives on Staten Island. Does he have a mother?"

"Yes. My ex-wife."

"Oh. I guess it's not my business."

"That's okay. She and I get along." He smiled. "You know, when the gallery said you were going to organize Keller's show, I wasn't too certain about it."

"What changed your mind?"

"What you said about Keller's work and Stieglitz. Of course," he added, "I still have to discover if you're competent."

"I am. And I'm a big fan of Alfred Stieglitz, by the way. Not just his own photography, but all the other shows he arranged. Did you know he organized one of the first exhibitions of Ansel Adams in New York?"

The show of Adams's astounding photographs of the huge American landscape had been the highlight of Charlie's year, back in '36, shortly before he went to the Spanish Civil War.

"I was there," he said.

"I also admire his personal life. A man whom Georgia O'Keeffe marries must be pretty special."

In Charlie's view, the affair and marriage of the photographer and the great painter had been one of the most significant partnerships in the twentieth-century art world, though it had been quite stormy.

"He wasn't faithful," he said.

"He was Stieglitz." She shrugged. "You've got to hand it to him, though. He was nearly fifty-five when he started living with O'Keeffe. And he was sixty-four when he took up with that other girl."

"Dorothy Norman. I knew her, actually."

"And she was only twenty-two."

"Hell of an age difference."

She looked at him. "You're only as old as you feel."

⁘

On Friday afternoon, Sarah Adler took the subway to Brooklyn. She had a new book to read. *The Bridges at Toko-Ri* was a short, fast-paced novel by James Michener about the recent Korean War. She hardly noticed the stations go by until she got to Flatbush.

Sarah loved Brooklyn. If you came from Brooklyn, you belonged there always. Partly, perhaps, it was the basic geography of the place. Ninety square miles of territory, two hundred miles of waterfront—no wonder the Dutch had liked it. There was something about the light in Brooklyn, it was so clear. The English might have come and called it Kings County. Huge bridges might link it to Manhattan—in addition to the Brooklyn Bridge, there were the Williamsburg and Manhattan bridges now—along with the subway. Seventy years of growth might have covered much of its quiet, rural space with housing—though huge parks and leafy streets remained. Yet on a quiet weekend morning, walking along a street of brownstone houses with their Dutch stoops, you could still almost think, in that limpid Brooklyn light, that you were in a painting by Vermeer.

It was still light as she made her way from the station. The whole of Flatbush was so full of childhood landmarks, from the modest pleasures of the soda fountain where you had egg creams, the kosher delicatessen and the restaurant on Pitkin Avenue where you went for a treat, to Ebbets Field itself, that cramped but sacred holy ground where the Brooklyn Dodgers played. She went by the candy store where all the children used to hang out, then entered the street where they used to play stoop ball.

The Adlers lived in a brownstone. When Sarah was very young, her father had rented his surgery under the stoop. Wanting to secure good tenants during the Depression, the landlord had soon offered her parents the two floors above, with three months rent-free. It was an excellent accommodation and they'd lived there ever since.

When she arrived, her mother met her at the door.

"Michael's ready, and your father and Nathan will be down in a moment. Rachel was coming tomorrow, but she says they all have colds."

Sarah wasn't too dismayed about her sister. Rachel was two years older. She'd married at eighteen and couldn't understand why Sarah hadn't wanted to do the same. Sarah went to kiss her brother Michael. He was eighteen now, and getting to be rather handsome. Then she went up and knocked at Nathan's door. His room was just the same as ever, the walls covered with photographs of baseball heroes and Dodgers' pennants. Nathan was fourteen and a good student, who studied hard at yeshiva. But the Dodgers were still the biggest thing in his life. "I'm ready, I'm ready," he cried. He hated people coming into his room. Then she felt her father's hand on her shoulder.

Dr. Daniel Adler was short and round. His head was nearly bald on top, and he wore a small, dark mustache. If he regretted that he was a dentist and not a concert pianist, his comfort lay in his family and his religion. He loved them both—indeed, for him, they were one and the same.

Sarah was always grateful for that. It was why on Friday afternoons, whenever she conveniently could, she came home to Flatbush for Shabbat.

They gathered in the living room. The two candles were ready. While the family stood quietly, Sarah's mother lit them, and then, with her hands covering her eyes, she recited the blessing.

"Baruch atah Adonai, Eloheinu melech ha-olam . . ."

It was the duty of the mother to perform this *mitzvah*. Only then, to complete the *mitzvah*, did she uncover her eyes and look at the light.

Sarah appreciated the ritual, the whole idea of Shabbat: God's gift of a day of rest to His chosen people. The family gathering at sundown, the sense of intimate joy—she might not be a very religious person herself, but she loved coming home for it.

After the lighting of the candles, they walked in the dusk to the synagogue.

Sarah liked her family's religion. People who didn't understand these things sometimes imagined that the nearly million Jews in Brooklyn all worshipped the same way. Nothing could be further from the case, of course. Over in the Brownsville area, which was overwhelmingly Jewish, and where the streets were pretty rough, people were mostly secular. Plenty of Jews there never went to services at all. In Borough Park, there were a lot of Zionists. Williamsburg was very Orthodox, and in the last few years a number of Hasidim from Hungary had arrived there, and in Crown Heights. With their old-fashioned dress and their rigorous adherence to Jewish laws, the Hasidim really lived in a world apart.

Coming mostly from Germany and Eastern Europe, the Jews of Brooklyn had been Ashkenazim at the start. But in the twenties, a large group of Syrian Jews had moved into Bensonhurst. That Sephardic community was completely unlike the others.

As for Flatbush, it varied. There were Orthodox, Conservative and Reform Jews all living on the same street. A few of the Hungarian Hasidim had come into the area too. Everybody seemed to get along, though, so long as you supported the Dodgers.

The Adlers were Conservative. "To be Orthodox is good, if that's what you want," her father would say to his family. "But for me, it's too much. Yeshiva is good, but so is other education. So, I am Conservative, but not Orthodox."

A few doors down the street was a family who went to a Reform temple. Daniel Adler fixed their teeth, and Sarah had played with their children as a little girl. But even then, she understood there was a difference. "The Reform Jews go too far the other way," her father had explained. "They say the Torah is not divine, and they question everything. They call this being enlightened and liberal. But if you keep going down that road, then one day you have nothing left."

Most of Sarah's friends in the city were Liberal, or secular. They were her company during the week. Then she'd come home for the weekend. So far, she liked living in two worlds.

After the brief Friday service, they all walked back. At home, they gathered round the table, her parents blessed their children, her father recited *kiddush* over the wine, the prayer was recited over the two loaves of challah, and then they started their meal.

All through her childhood, Sarah had known what food she would eat. Friday was chicken. Wednesday lamb chops. That was the meat. Tuesdays meant fish, and Thursdays egg salad and potato latkes. Only Monday was unpredictable.

The rest of Shabbat passed quietly. The Saturday-morning service was always long, from nine to twelve. She used to find it burdensome, but strangely she didn't any more. Then the pleasant, leisurely family lunch. After that, her father read to them for a while, then went to take a nap, while she and Michael played checkers. Sarah and her brother always enjoyed each other's company. Michael was musical, and on Sunday afternoon, he and his father were going to a concert at the Brooklyn Museum. There was no television allowed until the end of Shabbat, but on Saturday evening, her father asked her if she'd like to listen to a record he'd just acquired. It was an RCA recording of Bernstein conducting his own First Symphony. So she sat on the sofa beside him, and watched affectionately as her father's round face relaxed into an expression of perfect happiness. They turned in early after that. It had been a perfect day.

On Sunday morning, however, when Sarah came into the kitchen, things weren't so good. Her mother was alone, making French toast. Downstairs, she could hear the sound of her father practicing on the piano, but when she started to go down to say good morning to him, her mother called her back.

"Your father had a bad night." She shook her head. "He was thinking about your Uncle Herman."

Sarah sighed. In the year before the Second World War began, Uncle

Herman had been based in London. But he spoke French well, and he'd been spending time in France, where he had a small exporting business.

If they didn't hear from Uncle Herman for a year, they weren't surprised. "He never writes letters. He just shows up," her father used to complain. But late in 1939 they did get a letter. It came from London, and said he would be going to France. That had worried her father. "I don't know how you get in there," he'd said, "or how you get out." Months had passed. No further word had come. They hoped he was in London. When the Blitz came, her father said: "Maybe I should hope he's in France."

The silence continued.

It was more than four years before they finally learned the truth. It was the only time Sarah had seen her father truly outraged, and inconsolable. It was the first time, also, that she had understood the power of grief. And seeing her father's suffering, young though she was, she had wanted so much to protect him.

Then the Adlers did what a Jewish family does when it loses a loved one: they sat shiva.

It is a kindly custom. For seven days, unless one observes a less strict practice, family and friends come to the house bringing food and comfort. After saying the traditional Hebrew words of condolence as they enter, the visitors talk softly to the bereaved, who sit on low boxes or stools.

Sarah's mother had covered every mirror in the house with cloth. The children all wore a black ribbon, pinned on their front, but their father ripped his shirt and sat in a corner. Many friends came by; everyone understood Daniel Adler's grief and sought to console him. Sarah never forgot it.

"The days we sat shiva for your Uncle Herman were the worst in my life," her mother said. "Worse even than the day I got fired."

The day her mother got fired had always been part of family lore. It had been long before Sarah was born, before her mother married. She'd gone to work in Midtown, and got a job as a secretary in a bank. Her father had warned her not to do it, but something had prompted her to prove him wrong. With the reddish hair she had then and her blue eyes, people didn't usually think she was Jewish. "And my name's Susan Miller," she said. "It was Millstein, once," her father said. He could also have added that Miller was the third most common Jewish name in America.

But the bank had employed her without awkward questions, and for six months she'd worked there and been quite happy. True, it had meant that she didn't observe Shabbat, but her family weren't religious, so they didn't mind too much.

It was a chance remark that had let her down. One Friday, she was talking to another girl who she was quite friendly with. They were talking about one of the tellers, a bad-tempered fellow who had been complaining about her friend. "Don't mind him," she'd told the girl, "he's always *kvetching* about something." She'd said the Yiddish word quite without thinking, hardly even realized she'd said it, though she did notice the girl looking at her oddly.

"And do you know, I can't prove it, but I believe that girl followed me home to Brooklyn. Because the next Monday morning, I saw her talking to the manager, and at noon that day he fired me. For being Jewish."

The incident had changed her mother's life. "After that," she'd declare, "I said to myself, enough of the *goyim*. And I went back to my religion." A year later, she'd married Daniel Adler.

These memories were soon interrupted, however, by Michael and Nathan arriving for their breakfast. Sarah helped her mother dish up, while her father continued his piano playing downstairs.

After her brothers went out, Sarah and her mother tidied up the kitchen for a while.

"So," her mother said, when they had put everything away, "you're still happy in the apartment you have?"

Her mother had not been too pleased about her move to the city, but the apartment had been a stroke of luck. The brother of one of her father's patients owned the apartment in Greenwich Village. He was going to California for a year or two, he wasn't sure for how long. On condition that she would vacate at once if he needed it back, he'd been glad to rent it for a very modest amount to a family his brother assured him he could trust. So Sarah had a nice little one-bedroom place where she could live, even on the tiny salary the gallery paid her.

"It's fine," she said, "and I love my job."

"Will you be coming home next weekend?"

"I think so. Why?"

"You remember I told you about Adele Cohen's grandson. The boy who went to Harvard? The one that's a doctor now?"

"The one who went to Philadelphia?"

"Yes, but he has a position in New York now. He's just moving there.

And he's coming out to see his grandmother next weekend. I believe he's very nice."

"You've never met him."

"If he's Adele's grandson, I'm sure he's very nice."

"How old is he?"

"Adele says he'll be thirty next year. And he's very interested in art. He bought a painting."

"You know this?"

"Adele told me. She thinks he's bought several."

"What sort of paintings?"

"How should I know? They're paintings."

"We should marry."

"You could meet him."

"Does he have money?"

"He's a doctor." Her mother paused as if to indicate that this should be enough. "When his father married Adele's daughter, he was an accountant. But he didn't like accounting, so he set up a business selling heaters for houses. He sells air conditioning too. All over New Jersey. Adele says he's done very well."

So, Adele's grandson had money. Sarah smiled. She could imagine her mother and Adele arranging all this. And why should she complain? Perhaps he would be perfect.

"I'll meet him," she promised.

✣

As she returned from Brooklyn late that afternoon, however, it was not the doctor who occupied her thoughts in the subway. It was Charlie Master.

She'd flirted with him at Sardi's, of course. She'd gently challenged him about his age. And he'd been interested, she was sure of it. But he'd been cautious, too, and she thought she knew the reason.

He wasn't going to do anything that, if it went wrong, might jeopardize the exhibition of Theodore Keller's photographs. He really cared about the work, and she respected that. So, half of him was attracted to her, and the other half wanted to keep the relationship professional. That challenge made the business of seducing him all the more interesting.

Sarah Adler liked her work. She loved her family. She respected her religion. But now and then, she also liked to break the rules.

Sarah Adler was not a virgin. Her parents did not need to know this.

Charlie Master was an interesting older man, and she was curious to know more about him. She wanted to learn what he knew. And, of course, he wasn't Jewish.

So he was forbidden.

It was certainly something to think about.

The next day, she began to prepare a potential layout of the Keller show. As she thought about the balance and flow, it seemed to her that it could be improved if they had more examples of certain periods of Keller's work. She made a note of these, and she also did a rough of the catalogue. Charlie Master was going to provide the text, but she outlined half a dozen points that she thought should be included.

The gallery had a good mailing list, but it occurred to her that if they had a list of collectors and institutions who'd acquired Stieglitz or Ansel Adams, then that would be useful. She made a note of this as well, asking if Charlie had any suggestions for how she could get this information. Then, having shown all the material to the gallery owner, she sent it to Charlie.

Whether I seduce you or not, Mr. Master, she thought, this is going to be one hell of an exhibition. Then she waited.

⁂

He did not fall in love with her at once. Ten days after he got the material, they met up at the little office near Columbia and spent a couple of hours going through the collection. Together they selected five more photographs for inclusion, and decided to leave out one of the previous selection.

She was wonderfully efficient. But she was also humble. He liked that.

"This is the first show I've organized for the gallery," she told him, "and I have so much to learn. I'm really afraid of making mistakes."

"You're doing fine," he assured her.

The following week they met at the gallery, and using a detailed diagram, she showed him how the show was going to look.

"We won't be certain until we start to hang the work," he said, "but so far I think it's looking good. Very good." When she was out of earshot, he complimented the owner. "She seems to have a real talent," he said.

"She was here until ten the other night, going over mailing lists," the owner told him. "You have to respect that."

A few days later, Charlie asked her to lunch, to meet a collector he knew. The collector was impressed.

"She seems very good," he remarked afterward. "And behind those glasses . . ." He grinned. "I see burning fires."

"You think so?" said Charlie.

"You haven't tried?"

"Hmm," said Charlie, "not yet."

Perhaps, he supposed, he could be her mentor.

✛

When it happened, it was by chance. He was walking back from a meeting one evening and realized he was close to the gallery. On impulse, seeing the lights on, he looked in. Sarah was there alone. She looked pleased when she saw him.

"I was about to close up."

"I just happened to be passing. Thought I'd look at the space again."

"Go right ahead."

There were two rooms. He went into the second one, and stood there, looking around the walls.

"You want more light?" she called.

"No. Thanks. I'll be getting home now. What are you doing this evening?"

"Actually, I have a friend who's in a little theater group. They're putting something on this evening—I don't even know what it is—but I promised I'd go."

"That sounds interesting."

"Maybe. Want to come?"

He paused, hesitant. "It's been a while since I went to a theater group." He smiled. "Why not?"

The theater was in the West Village. To be precise, it was a basement in a brownstone. There were two or three young people on the sidewalk. One of them had a mug of coffee. The door of the basement, however, was closed. There was a piece of paper pinned on it which said: "No performance tonight."

"Great," said Sarah.

"Maybe they didn't have an audience," said Charlie.

"That doesn't stop them," said the man with the mug of coffee. "Julian was sick."

"What about Mark?" said Sarah.

"He had a quarrel with Helga."

"Oh."

"Maybe tomorrow," said the man, helpfully.

"I'm so sorry," said Sarah to Charlie. "I shouldn't have suggested it."

"The situation is familiar to me," said Charlie easily. "Shall we get something to eat?"

They walked through the Village, looking at cafés and restaurants. They found a small Italian trattoria, ordered Chianti and bowls of pasta. Charlie grinned.

"I feel as if I were in my twenties again."

"Nothing wrong with that," she said.

While they ate, they talked about music. He told her where the best places were to hear jazz in the city. She told him about her luck in getting the apartment in the Village. After the pasta they had a crème caramel dessert.

"Do you ever walk about in the Village?" she asked, when they were done.

"Yes. Why?"

"I feel like walking."

"All right."

The little streets were quite busy; the restaurants weren't short of custom. Charlie wasn't sure where the evening was going, or where he wanted it to go. He felt a little awkward. They passed a little place where the tables were set for playing chess. Several men were sitting there, looking very solemn. The waiters brought them drinks from time to time.

"Want a game of chess?" Sarah asked.

"Okay. Sure, why not?" They sat down, and each ordered a small cognac. They played quietly for half an hour, then Charlie looked at her suspiciously. "Are you letting me win?"

"No."

"Are you sure about that?"

"Would I lie to you?"

"Yes."

"Trust me."

"Hmm. Checkmate."

"There." She laughed. "I never saw it coming."

When they left, they went up the street. At the corner, there was a candy store still open. Telling him to wait, Sarah went inside, and emerged with two little bags of fudge. She gave him one. "A present for you," she said.

"Thank you."

"Do you want coffee? My apartment's just around the corner, on Jane Street."

He hesitated a moment.

"You don't have to," she said.

"Coffee sounds good," said Charlie.

❖

All through that midwinter and early spring they would meet, two or three times a week usually, sometimes spending the night at his apartment uptown, sometimes at hers in the Village. In part, for both of them, it was an adventure. Charlie knew she was hungry to possess the knowledge and experience he had to offer. And for his part, he enjoyed sharing the things he loved with such an intelligent mind, and watching her grow and develop. But that was only the half of it.

By January, her slim, pale body had become an obsession with him. Often in the afternoons, while Sarah was busy at the gallery, he'd sit in the little office near Columbia, or in his apartment, and dream away an hour at a time thinking about her. Standing beside him, she only had to move her body sinuously close to his, and he would be overcome with a desire to possess her.

Each time, before their lovemaking, she would slip off the little pendant that she wore around her neck, and for him this little gesture, which she did quite unself-consciously, became a moment of excitement and great tenderness. In their lovemaking, she could drive him wild with passion. But she was more than a young mistress; there was something else that he could not describe exactly, something ancient, something belonging to the East, he supposed. He'd discovered that first night that her narrow breasts were larger, fuller than he'd expected. When they made love, and when she lay beside him afterward, it seemed to him that Sarah was not just a girl, however interesting, but a timeless woman, full of richness and mystery.

He spent so much time thinking about her that sometimes he cursed himself for not having enough to do.

Every other weekend, he would see little Gorham as usual. He almost wanted to introduce the boy to her. But even if he just said she was a friend, Julie would soon get to hear of it, and guess the truth, and then there would have to be explanations, and trouble. Besides, on these occasions, Sarah was always home with her family.

That was a small difficulty. He'd have liked to spend all his free weekends with her, but usually she insisted that she had to see her family.

"They'd get very suspicious if I missed too many weekends," she told him with a laugh.

Some weekends she could get away, though. Late in January, he took her skiing in Vermont. She fell down quite a few times, with good humor, looked at her bruises ruefully, and agreed she'd give it another try, but maybe not for a while. Then, in February, he treated her to a weekend at a country hotel in Connecticut.

It was a cold Friday afternoon when they drove out of New York. The roads were clear, though there was still snow on the banks beside them. Charlie owned a 1950 De Soto Custom Sportsman of which he was very proud.

He'd booked the room in advance, in a charming place he knew, only an hour's drive out of town. In the name of Mr. and Mrs. Charles Master. Hotels didn't usually inquire too closely, so long as you signed in that way. It was dusk when they arrived. They had a couple of suitcases which he carried himself to the door of the white clapboard house. There was a log fire in the lobby, and while the manager greeted Charlie and led him to the little counter to sign in, Sarah went over to it. After a moment or two she took off her coat and sat on the low ottoman in front of the cheerful blaze. She was wearing a white shirt and a cardigan. Charlie glanced over toward her and smiled; the fire was already giving her face a charming glow. Just then, an ember fell out of the fire. She reached forward for the tongs, in order to replace it, and as she did so the little Jewish star on its chain swung out from her neck, catching the firelight. Having put the glowing ember back on the fire, she got up and came toward the desk.

The manager of the place had just been starting to tell him about the room when Charlie noticed him look sharply across at Sarah as she leaned down by the fire. Now, as she came over, the man was staring at her neck.

"Nice fire," she remarked.

"Excuse me," said the manager, and went into the little office behind the desk. A minute or so passed before he came back.

"I am so sorry, sir," he said to Charlie, "but there seems to be a problem with the booking. When you came in, I mistook you for another guest. We don't seem to have a reservation for Master at all."

"But I telephoned. The reservation was definitely made."

"I cannot tell you how it happened, sir, and I do apologize. But I'm afraid we're entirely full. I just went to make sure. All our weekend guests are already here."

"There must be a room."

"No, sir. There's absolutely nothing. I don't know what to say."

"But I've just driven out from the city."

"Yes, sir. There's another hotel a couple of miles away I could direct you to. They may have space."

"Damn the other hotel. I booked here. I demand my room."

"I'm very sorry."

"Charlie." It was Sarah, at his side. "Come over by the fire, Charlie," she said softly. "I want to tell you something." With an irritated shrug, Charlie did as she asked.

"What is it?" he said.

"Charlie, I don't want to stay here. I'll explain in the car." Charlie started to protest, but she put her hand on his arm. "Please, Charlie."

Thoroughly angry, and mystified, Charlie took the bags and went out to the car with her. When they were sitting inside, she turned to him.

"It's me, Charlie. He didn't have a room when he saw me."

"You mean he saw you didn't have a wedding ring? I hardly think—"

"No, Charlie. It was my pendant he saw."

"Your pendant?"

"The Star of David. He realized I'm Jewish."

"That's absurd."

"They don't have Jewish people in this hotel, Charlie. This is Connecticut—how many miles are we from Darien?"

It was said that a Jewish person couldn't even buy a house in nearby Darien. Charlie didn't know if it was true; more likely just an ugly rumor. And anyway, the horrors of the thirties and the war had changed all that sort of thing. People weren't anti-Semitic now. You couldn't be.

"I don't believe it."

"If you go out with me, Charlie, you have to accept these things are going to happen. You think a Jew can get into most country clubs? My mother was fired by a bank for being Jewish. Are you telling me that people you know, like your own family, don't make anti-Semitic remarks?"

Charlie thought for a moment, then shrugged. "Okay. Maybe sometimes. But it's just a sort of Episcopal, old-money thing. People like my mother look down on anyone who isn't one of them. Jewish, Irish, Italian, you know. It's ridiculous, but they don't really mean anything by it. I mean, they'd never—"

"You're right, Charlie. I'm sorry. So how does it feel, being thrown out of a hotel?"

"I'm going to make him give us that room."

"Just take me back, Charlie. It was very nice of you to bring me out here, but can we eat in the city, please?"

And as the weeks went by Charlie realized that she was right. Of course, being involved with the theater and the arts, he'd always had plenty of Jewish friends. He had friends of all sorts, for that matter. When he was with them, they might refer to their Jewishness sometimes, or tease him a little for being an Episcopalian blue blood. But these things never came up very much. And when he was with his own crowd, people he'd known at school, that sort of thing, there might be things said about all kinds of races that you wouldn't say in other company. Harmless prejudices, little jokes. They hardly seemed to matter when it was someone else you were talking about. But now he began to observe with different eyes.

✢

He'd often told Sarah about his family. Just small stories about their life in the old days, and how his mother remained, in most of her attitudes, a splendid relic of those times.

"I'd love you to meet her," he once said.

"That might not be such a good idea," Sarah had remarked.

He'd continued to think about it, however, and one afternoon in early March, when they'd been visiting a gallery on Fifty-seventh, he suddenly said to her, "Let's go up Park and see my mother."

"I don't know, Charlie," Sarah said. "How are you going to explain me?"

"That's easy. You're the person who's organizing the Theodore Keller show. I told you, our family were his first patrons."

"I suppose so," she responded, doubtfully.

But in fact, the visit went very well. His mother seemed delighted to see them. She told Sarah how she'd given the big party for the publication of Edmund Keller's book, back in the old days. And she promised to bring people to the gallery opening.

"I want you to give me at least thirty invitations I can send out, my dear. I'll write a letter, and telephone. I know a lot of people who I'm sure would buy."

"That would be wonderful, Mrs. Master," Sarah said.

They were leaving the building when the tiny incident happened. George the doorman had hailed a taxi. Charlie disliked the usual business of people sliding across the seat, so he'd walked round the taxi while George on the sidewalk held the door open for Sarah. And just as Sarah got into the taxi, he saw the doorman staring down at her head with a look of disgust.

"Is there a problem, George?" he said sharply.

"No, Mr. Master."

"I hope not," said Charlie, threateningly. He'd be inheriting that apartment one day, so George had better watch out. He got in beside Sarah, frowning.

"So," she remarked as they started down Park, "what was that about?"

"Nothing."

"He looked at me like that when I arrived, too. But you didn't notice."

"I'll have him fired."

Sarah stared out of the window for a moment, then changed the subject. "Your mother's great," she said. "She could be really helpful with those invitations, you know."

It was a week later when he was having dinner at his mother's that she brought up the subject of Sarah.

"Your girlfriend seems nice."

"What do you mean?"

"The girl you brought round."

"Sarah Adler. She's doing a good job with the show, I think."

"I'm sure she is, dear; she seems very competent. She's also your mistress." Rose looked him in the eye. "I can tell, you know."

"Oh."

"She's very young. Can you manage?"

"Yes."

"That's nice. Is it difficult, her being Jewish?"

"Should it be?"

"Don't be silly, dear. This isn't exactly a Jewish building, you know."

"The damn doorman was impertinent."

"What do you expect? It's never arisen, as far as I know, but I don't imagine the co-op board would let a Jew buy into the building."

It was one of the features of apartment life in the city that Charlie had always found amusing. Most of the apartment buildings on Park were cooperatives now. His mother no longer rented the apartment, but was a shareholder of the building. And the shareholders elected a board which had the right to vet anyone trying to buy in. So if you wanted to sell your apartment to someone whom the other people in the building thought undesirable, the board could refuse to let you complete the sale. They might give reasons. They might not. But the unspoken rules were generally understood.

"It's absurd," he said. "We're in the 1950s, for God's sake."

"There are plenty of buildings that do. On the West Side, anyway." She gave him a thoughtful look. "You're not planning to marry her, are you?"

"No." He was quite taken aback by the idea.

"They'd take you out of the Social Register, you know."

"I hadn't thought about it."

"Well, I believe they would. They don't mind people being poor," said Rose, "but they care about who you marry."

"Damn the register."

"Anyway," she said, matter-of-factly, "you really can't afford another family, can you?"

✦

Another effect of the relationship was Charlie's realization that he didn't actually know much about Judaism. He had Jewish friends; he might go to a wedding or a funeral. The Jewish wedding service, apart from the chuppah and the breaking of the glass, didn't seem so different from a Christian wedding, as far as Charlie could see. The familiar Christian blessings were clearly taken straight from the Hebrew tradition.

But beyond that he knew very little. Sometimes he'd ask Sarah about her family life, and about Jewish customs. He became quite curious.

It was late in March when Sarah suddenly asked him:

"Do you want to come to a Passover Seder?"

"A Seder? Where?"

"In Brooklyn. With my family."

"You mean, meet your parents?" He was well aware that Sarah's parents had no idea of their relationship. Apart from anything, she had explained, they still imagined, or at least hoped, she was a virgin. The thought of meeting them intrigued Charlie, but also made him nervous. "You really think that's a good idea?" he said.

"They'd be so honored. Remember, they've heard of you as the owner of the Keller collection. My first really important client. They know you're a big deal to me."

When the day arrived, Charlie drove over the Williamsburg Bridge, and down through Brooklyn. He didn't know the borough that well. There were the huge acres of docks all along the waterfront, the endless collections of small factories, warehouses and plants that still made it one of the major places of production in the nation. You knew that, of course, but you didn't really get to see it in Charlie's world. He had a friend, a professor, who lived in a large and handsome brownstone on the Heights near Prospect Park; he'd been there a few times. It reminded him of the spacious houses on the West Side, and walking in the huge spaces of Prospect Park itself was delightful. A few miles further east, he knew, was Brownsville. He'd heard there were a lot of Jews there, but the thing he really knew was that it was a dangerous slum area where the gangland killing agency of Murder Inc. had been born. From Prospect Park, however, Flatbush Avenue ran south, so he supposed Flatbush itself might be quite a decent sort of place.

Needless to say, Sarah had made him a perfect map and directions, so he found her parents' house with no difficulty. She met him at the door, and brought him in.

They were all there. Her parents, her brothers, her sister Rachel and her family. Even her Aunt Ruth from the Bronx, who hated Robert Moses, had come. He felt a little out of place as the only Gentile in the house, but the Adler family didn't seem to mind at all. As Sarah had told him, he was the honored guest. "We shall explain the Seder to you as we go," her sister Rachel assured him. The idea seemed to please the whole family.

Dr. Adler turned out to be everything Charlie expected. As the father of the family, this was a very important day for him, and his face was beaming with pleasure. It only took Charlie a few moments to engage him in conversation about the composers he most liked to play, and the pianists Charlie had seen at Carnegie Hall.

The family also wanted to hear about the exhibition of Theodore

Keller's photographs which Sarah was working so hard at. So he told them about his family's relationship with the Kellers down the generations, and how close a friend he'd been to Edmund Keller, and how honored he'd felt when Edmund had laid this duty upon him.

"For me," he explained, "looking after and showing the collection is an obligation to the Keller family. But it's more than that. I have a duty of respect toward the work itself." He turned to Dr. Adler. "Imagine how you'd feel if the family of a composer you admired gave you all his papers, and you found dozens of compositions, even whole symphonies, that had never been played or published."

This was greeted with much respect.

"That's a big obligation," said Dr. Adler.

"Well," said Charlie, seeing his chance, "I am just so grateful to your daughter for doing such a wonderful job at the gallery. This is very important to me."

Dr. Adler beamed. The whole family looked delighted. If they were being friendly and welcoming before, there was a new warmth in their manner toward him now.

Only one false note interposed itself. Charlie was talking to Rachel when he overheard it. Sarah was speaking to her mother, a few feet away.

"So," he heard Mrs. Adler say, "you still didn't tell me. When are you seeing Adele's grandson again?"

"I don't know. Soon, I expect."

"Adele says he took you out to dinner in the city."

"Is nothing private?"

"She says he likes you very much."

"She knows this?"

"Yes, he told her so. He's a very good doctor."

"I believe it."

"Well, I won't interfere."

"That's good to know."

Charlie had been listening so carefully that he almost lost the thread of the conversation he was having with Rachel about her children. What doctor? When did Sarah have dinner with him?

Then it was time to begin. The table was laid magnificently. Every bit of silverware had been polished until it gleamed. As the meal took its slow, ceremonial course, Rachel or her mother would explain what was happening, with one of Sarah's brothers occasionally chiming in.

"The *mitzvah* of Passover is to teach the next generation about our bondage and deliverance out of Egypt," Rachel told him. "So, the ceremony is in two parts. The first is to remind us of our slavery in Egypt; the second is to remember our freedom."

"And that's the *matzo*, the unleavened bread," said Charlie, looking at a plate at one end of the table.

"Right. Three *matzos*. Also, on the Seder plate, we have bitter herbs, to remind us of the bitterness of slavery. And *charoset*—that's like a paste— for the mortar the Jewish slaves used when we built the storehouses of Egypt; for a vegetable, we have parsley. This we shall dip in salt water, to remind us of our tears. Also, as symbols, we have roasted egg, and roasted lamb-shank bone. During the meal we shall also drink four cups of wine—grape juice for the little ones—to remind us of the four promises God made to us."

Dr. Adler commenced the Seder with a blessing, which was followed by the washing of hands. The vegetable was dipped in salt water, the middle *matzo* broken in two, and then the telling of the first Passover began.

As the evening slowly progressed, Charlie watched with admiration. He'd never realized how beautiful it was. When the invitation to the Seder was recited, not in Hebrew but in Aramaic, it struck him with great force that, of course, these were exactly the proceedings that Jesus must have followed at the Last Supper. And as he considered the crisp New England Episcopalians he knew so well, he wondered how many of them truly understood the rich Middle Eastern texture to which their own religion belonged.

Then came the time for the youngest of Rachel's children to ask the Four Questions, beginning with: "Why is this night different from all other nights?"

How moving it was. Charlie thought of Thanksgiving, the most rooted family celebration in the American tradition, and the joyful sharing of food. Thanksgiving was real. It was important, and it was already over three centuries old. Christmas, of course, was an ancient festival. But modern Christmas celebrations, the dinner and the Christmas tree, and even Santa Claus—the things which made Christmas for everyone now— these customs weren't nearly as old as Thanksgiving, if the truth were told. Yet here in Jewish households was a tradition going back not for centuries, but millennia.

And all the time, the children were being instructed. The Telling of the

Passover, the Four Questions, the meaning of the Seder—the children had to participate actively in these. At some length, Dr. Adler spoke to them about the significance of the affliction and the delivery out of Egypt, and they enumerated the Ten Plagues. Then came the second cup of wine, another hand-washing, and blessings before the meal.

As the ritual of the Seder went on through the evening, Charlie was not only moved but impressed. Dr. Adler's face, so warm and fatherly, might have been that of any man sharing a meal with his grandchildren. Yet under it all was a passion, an intensity that Charlie could only admire. These people had respect: for tradition, for education, for the things of the spirit.

Were such things to be found among the Gentiles? Certainly, in the families of professors, schoolteachers and the clergy, but not with this intensity. Sarah's family belonged to a community which was conscious of roots going back three thousand years and believing, at least, that they had received the divine fire from the hand of God Himself.

Late that night, as he left to drive back to Manhattan, he parted from Sarah and her family, moved with a new respect and admiration.

⁜

Of course, he asked Sarah about the doctor pretty soon.

"Adele Cohen's grandson? He's a very nice person, just not my type. But I let my family think I might be interested. It keeps them happy." She gave him an amused look. "I suppose I'd have to marry him if he was my type. He's everything a nice Jewish girl could want."

Charlie wasn't sure what he thought about that. Thinking about it afterward, and feeling a pang of jealousy, he told himself not to be foolish. At some point, this girl would have to settle down with a proper young man of her own kind. But not yet. Not for a long time yet. Until then, he wanted her, very much, for his own.

The aftermath of the Seder had some other consequences as well. He began to ask Sarah questions. Some were quite simple. "Why do you say synagogue, but most Jews I know say temple?"

"It pretty much depends what kind of Jew you are," she explained. "The real Temple, the Temple in Jerusalem, was destroyed nearly two thousand years ago. Orthodox and Conservative Jews believe that one day it will be rebuilt. This will be the Third Temple. But the Reform movement says that we should not be waiting for the Temple to be rebuilt, and so they call their synagogues temples. So there are all kinds of names for synagogues in the diaspora. Orthodox Jews often call it '*shul*,' which is a Yiddish word. My family usually says synagogue. The Reform Jews usually say temple."

Other questions were more searching. What did Sarah feel about her duties as a Jew? How did she want to live? Did she truly believe in God? He discovered that she was surprisingly torn.

"God? Who can know about God, Charlie? No one can be sure. As for the rest, I break a lot of rules. Look what I'm doing with you." She shrugged. "I suppose the truth is, I'm secular during the week, and I go home to my tradition at the weekend. I have no idea how that's going to work out in the long run."

Once, she found him reading a book about Judaism.

"You're going to know more than I do," she laughed.

But it wasn't only Judaism that Charlie had become curious about. The encounter with her family had made him think about all the other communities he'd taken for granted in the big city. The Irish, the Italians, the people coming in from other places. What did he really know about his neighbors? Next to nothing, if the truth were told.

❖

The exhibition opened in April. It was a big success. Rose Master surpassed herself. Collectors, people on museum boards, people from the social worlds, she had managed to bring them all. The catalogue and the little historical notes that Sarah had put together were perfect. Charlie had brought journalists and literary people; the gallery had done the rest.

Before he died, Theodore Keller had produced thousands of signed prints, and even during the evening, a large quantity were sold. Not only that, a publisher approached Charlie to suggest they do a book on his work.

There were several Kellers there, the descendants of Theodore and his sister Gretchen. Sarah's family had come, modestly staying in the background, but clearly proud of her success. Charlie had a moment of panic when he realized that several of his friends knew about his affair with her, but a quick word with a couple of them ensured that no one said anything about the relationship to her family.

And Charlie made a charming speech about both Theodore and

Edmund Keller, and graciously thanked the gallery and Sarah in particular for the show which, he assured them, was everything that the artist himself could have wished.

Often at the end of an opening, the gallery would take the artist and a few friends out to supper. Obviously that wouldn't be the case here, but Charlie had wondered what he should do. The gallery owner and Sarah and her family were going out together, and he would have liked to join them. But his mother was tired, and after all she'd done, he felt he ought to take her home.

But as he said goodnight to Sarah and her family, he felt so proud of her, and yet, at the same time, so protective; and he experienced a sudden sense of desolation at being parted from her.

If only they could be together openly, he thought. But as what?

·‡·

One aspect of their relationship that amused Charlie was watching Sarah in his apartment. Since his divorce, he had reverted to his former bachelor ways. He wasn't untidy—indeed, his white-walled apartment was simply and precisely arranged. "It's almost like an art gallery," she'd remarked, the first time she saw it. But it was spartan. There was hardly any food in the kitchen, because he usually ate out. She bought him pots and pans and implements which he didn't suppose he'd ever use, and new white towels for his bathroom. She did it cleverly, however, and never in a way that was intrusive. And she seemed so pleased with the results, and so relaxed when she was there, that Charlie reckoned their tastes were very compatible. It hadn't occurred to him before that he might have difficulty living with a woman who wanted to change his household or started putting up floral curtains when he wanted plain venetian blinds, but he realized now that he really didn't want to go back to the conventional domesticity in which he'd lived when he was married to Julie.

"It's funny, but I don't seem to mind having you in the apartment," he once remarked.

"Well, thank you for the big compliment," she laughed.

"You know what I mean," he said.

The only time he ever experienced a flash of irritation, and a moment of fear, it was over almost at once. He had come into his bedroom early one evening and found her going through his drawers.

"Are you looking for something?" he asked in a sharp voice.

She turned. "Caught in the act," she said with a sheepish smile. "I need to see your ties."

In Charlie's experience, women never managed to give him ties he liked, and he was wondering whether to discourage her from attempting such an impossible task, when she frowned, and pulled something out from the back of the drawer.

"What's this?" she asked.

It had been a while since he'd looked at the wampum belt. He took it from her and gazed at it thoughtfully.

"Any guesses?"

"It looks Indian."

"It is." He ran his fingers over the tiny decorated beadwork, which was rough to the touch. "It's wampum," he explained. "You see all these tiny white beads? They're seashells. The dark beads make a pattern, as you see, and that's actually a kind of writing. This wampum belt probably has a message."

"Where did it come from?"

"It's been in the family for a long time. Maybe hundreds of years. I don't know how we first got it, but it's supposed to be lucky. Like a charm."

"Has it ever brought you any luck?"

"My father was wearing it the day he lost all his money—after the crash. He told me he had it on when he decided to jump off the GWB. But then he didn't jump, or I guess we wouldn't still have the belt. So that was lucky, you could say."

"May I look at it?"

He handed it back to her. She took it over to the small table by the window and studied it. As she was doing so, Charlie thought about the belt and the process of making it. How long had it taken? Was it a labor of love, or perhaps just a tedious duty? He liked to think the former, but there was no way of knowing.

"Whatever it means, this is an amazing abstract design," Sarah suddenly said. "Very simple, but strong."

"You like it?"

"I love it. That's a wonderful thing to have in the family."

"I suppose it is."

"It's a work of art," she said.

Ten days later, she had given him a tie. Needless to say, her choice was perfect—a rough silk with a dark red background and a faint paisley pattern. Discreet but elegant.

"Is it all right?" she asked.

"It's more than all right," he said.

"You'll wear it?"

"Absolutely."

She smiled with pleasure. "I have something else for you," she said.

"Another present?"

"Just something I saw. But I can take it back if you don't like it."

She handed him a rectangular package wrapped in plain paper. It looked like a book, but felt too light. He opened it carefully. Then stared, amazed.

It was a drawing by Robert Motherwell.

"I thought it might go over there," she said, and pointed to a space on the living-room wall. "If you like it, that is," she added.

"Like it?" He was still staring at the drawing, almost unable to speak. It was a simple abstract, black on white, which reminded him of a piece of Chinese calligraphy. And so beautiful.

"Don't move," she said, and taking the drawing from him, she went over to the place on the wall she had indicated, and held the drawing up there. "What do you think?"

It was more than perfect. It transformed the entire room.

"You're a genius," he said.

"Really?"

She looked so pleased.

What had it cost her? He didn't like to think. No doubt Betty Parsons would have given her terms, let her buy it over time. But Sarah, on her modest salary, would probably be paying for this drawing for months if not years.

And she was prepared to do this for him? He was both astonished and moved.

For days after that, he wondered what he could possibly give her in return. What would be appropriate? It had to be something that would give her pleasure. But more than that. An expensive coat or a piece of jewelry, something she couldn't normally afford, might give her pleasure, but it wasn't enough. He needed to find a present that showed he had gone to particular trouble. Something of significance. Something of emotional value. He racked his brains for what it could be.

And then, at last, the idea came to him.

It was a Sunday, on a clear, crisp day, just before noon, when he arrived at her apartment. She'd been out to see her parents in Brooklyn, but come back that morning to spend the day with him. He took the present carefully out of the taxi. It was awkward to carry, and he had to proceed slowly up the stairs to her door.

Inside, he laid his parcel down on the floor of her living room.

"For you," he said with a smile. "From me."

"Whatever can this be?" The package was certainly strange, about four inches wide and six feet long. It took her a minute or two to get the wrapping off.

"It's a little awkward," he said. But she was managing fine.

"Oh, Charlie." She was staring open-mouthed. "You can't give me this."

"I can."

"But this is an heirloom, Charlie. You have to give this to Gorham, for your children's children. It belongs in your family."

"He isn't expecting it. He doesn't even know about it. I think you'd appreciate it more than anyone I know. The framers did a good job, don't you think?"

They certainly had. The wampum belt had been laid flat and mounted on a long, thin, cloth-covered board with simple lip mounts, so that it could be easily removed. The board slid into a long white box with a glass front, and this display case could then be hung or fixed to a wall for display.

"Nice piece of abstract art," Charlie said with a grin.

"I can't believe you're giving me this, Charlie," she said. "Are you really sure?"

"I thought about it a lot, Sarah. I know you're the right person to have it."

"I'm touched, Charlie," she said. "I'm really touched."

"In that case," he said happily, "I guess it was a good present."

⁂

It was from that weekend that he began to wonder if they could be man and wife.

He thought about it every day. Of course, you couldn't deny the difficulties—there were plenty of those. But then again, what were they, if you really came to think about it?

He was older, yes. But not so old as all that. He knew of other couples where a man had married a much younger woman, and they seemed to get along. He made her pretty happy, he was certain of that.

What would they do about religion? he wondered. Her family would have wanted Sarah to marry the Jewish doctor no doubt. On the other hand, when all was said and done, marrying him would be quite a step up in the world for her. He wondered what sort of wedding ceremony they'd have. The simple Episcopalian ceremony was so close to the Jewish service anyway.

And when they were married, she'd be under his protection. If his mother's doorman dared even blink at his wife, he could say good-bye to his job. His friends would all welcome her—and if they didn't, then they weren't his friends. Were the old-money crowd so wonderful anyway? Did he really have that much in common with them? What if he just went his own way completely? He'd known other people, old-money people like his own family, who'd married appropriately the first time, been unhappy, married completely inappropriately the second time round, and been happy for the rest of their lives.

There was the question of finances to be considered. Being young, Sarah would probably want a child or two. Could he afford a new household, private schools and all that? If he really put his mind to it, Charlie reckoned he could make a hell of a lot more money than he did now. Being married to Sarah would inspire him. The Keller show had been so successful, and the book contract might bring in quite a bit of money. He'd be passing some of that on to the remaining Kellers, of course—that went without saying—but he wasn't actually obliged to give them any particular percentage. It had been left to his discretion, and God knows he'd done all the work. There was a bit of cash coming right there.

And besides, if he was really going to step out of the club, so to speak, then maybe he'd go even further. Little Gorham was going to be all right, with the private education he was providing, and his mother's money. Sarah's expectations for her children would be quite different. What if they moved out to some place like Greenwich, where the town had schools that were just as good as the private schools? You could do that. As he thought about all this, Charlie felt as if his life was flooded with a bright new light. He felt a sense of freedom.

In short, he was a middle-aged man in love with a younger woman.

✦

The day was pleasantly warm. It was May, almost June. They had just been to look at a collection of prints in the New York Public Library, and they had come out onto its broad steps.

"There's a bit of a family tradition associated with this place," Charlie said to Sarah.

"There is?"

"Dates back to the time when it used to be a reservoir. It's where my great-grandfather proposed to my great-grandmother. In the street somewhere, I suppose, though that would be a bit dangerous nowadays."

"Lethal. Were they happy?"

"Yes. It was a very successful marriage, as far as I know."

"That's nice."

Suddenly Charlie went down on one knee.

"Sarah, will you marry me?"

She laughed. "I get it. That must have been very romantic."

But Charlie didn't get up.

"Sarah Adler, will you marry me?"

A couple of people were coming up the steps. They looked at Charlie curiously. Then they started to whisper to each other.

"Are you serious, Charlie?"

"Never more so in my life. I love you, Sarah. I want to spend the rest of my life with you."

"Charlie, I didn't imagine . . ." She paused. "Can I think about this a little while?"

"Whatever time you need."

"Charlie, I really . . . You caught me by surprise. I'm so flattered. Are you sure about this?" She smiled. "I think you'd better get up now, you're collecting a crowd." It was true. There were half a dozen people watching them now, some of them laughing. As he got up, she kissed him. "I'm really going to have to think about this."

✦

Rose Master was most surprised, two days later, when George the doorman called up to inform her, in a voice that suggested he was keeping the visitor outside on the sidewalk, that there was a person called Miss Adler who desired to see her.

"Send her up," said Rose. She met Sarah at the door herself, and once they were in the living room, she was even more surprised when Sarah asked her if she might speak to her in confidence. "Of course you may," she said guardedly, "if that is what you wish."

"Has Charlie spoken to you about me?" the girl said.

"No." He hadn't.

"He wants to marry me."

"Oh. I see."

"So I came to ask what you think about it."

"You came to ask me?"

"That's why I'm here."

Rose stared at her. Then she nodded thoughtfully. "Well, dear, that's very nice of you." She paused. "You're very clever." She was sitting in an upright chair; Sarah was on the sofa. She glanced toward the window where the early-evening light from Park Avenue was casting a gentle glow.

"I'm sure you want me to be truthful."

"Please."

"Well, I don't think it's a good idea, though I can quite understand his being in love with you."

"A Jewish girl with glasses?"

"Oh yes. You're intelligent and attractive—I dare say he should have married someone like you in the first place. Of course, I'd have been horrified." She shrugged. "Well, you said you wanted me to be truthful."

"I do."

"I just think it's too late now. Do you like him?"

"Yes. I've been thinking really hard. I love him."

"Lucky Charlie. What do you like about him?"

"A lot of things. I think he's the most interesting man I've ever met."

"That's only because he's older, dear. Older men seem interesting, because they know things. But they may not be so interesting really."

"Don't you think he's interesting? You're his mother."

Rose sighed. "I love my son, my dear, and I want the best for him. But I'm too old to hide from reality. Do you know the trouble with Charlie? He's intelligent, he may even have talent, but he's old money. Not that he has any, you understand. But he belongs to it. That's my fault, I'm afraid." She sighed again. "I mean, it always seemed so important."

"It isn't important now?"

"I'm getting old. It's strange how your view of life changes when you get older. Things . . ." she made a gesture with her hands, "fall away."

"I never met old money before Charlie, Mrs. Master. I love Charlie's manners, and he's so charming."

"He is charming. He always was. But let me tell you the trouble with people like us, my dear. We have no ambition." She paused. "Well, sometimes people of our class have ambition. Look at the two Roosevelts. Two presidents from one family—*very* different branches of the family, of course, but still . . ." She stared out of the window again. "Charlie's not like that. He knows all kinds of things, he's interesting to talk to, he's thoughtful, he's very kind to me—but he's never *done* anything. And even with you beside him, dear, I'm afraid he never will. It isn't in his nature."

"You think it takes pushy Jewish people to get things done?"

"I don't know about Jewish. But pushy? Definitely." She looked at Sarah seriously. "If my son marries you, dear, I don't know how he'll be able to afford another family. But even if he finds the money, he will still be old a long time before you are. And as time passes, I'm afraid you will become impatient with him. You deserve something better. That's all I can tell you."

"I wasn't expecting to hear you talk like this."

"Then you wouldn't have learned anything, would you?"

"No," said Sarah, "I guess not."

⁘

On Friday Sarah went home as usual. It was good to be back with her family, and to hear about the daily lives of her brothers. The Shabbat meal passed quietly. During the morning service, she listened to the rabbi and tried not to think about anything else. In the afternoon, though, her brother Michael won three games of checkers against her so easily that he couldn't believe it. After that, she sat quietly with her thoughts.

What did she feel about Charlie? She really hadn't expected him to propose to her like that. She hadn't been prepared at all. Did she love him?

She realized one thing. Whenever he wasn't there, she missed him. If she saw a picture she liked, or heard a piece of music, or even a joke, she wanted to share it with him. The other day an objectionable client had come into the gallery, and she automatically found herself thinking: I wish Charlie were here, he would hate this man so much.

She liked to dress him the way she thought he ought to look. She'd bought him a blue scarf that he looked very nice in. But he had this terrible old hat, and he absolutely refused to stop wearing it. She didn't really mind—it just became a challenge to figure out how long it would take to get him to give it up. In fact, she liked the challenge. If he'd given it up without a fight, she'd have been disappointed.

So how would she feel if Charlie were her husband? Pretty good, actually. As for having a little boy that was like Charlie, or a little girl he could dote on—why, that seemed the most wonderful thing in the world.

But what about religion? Would the Master family insist that she or the children be Christians? That she couldn't agree to. However, Charlie hadn't raised the question, so he couldn't care about it that much, she supposed. She'd expected that old Mrs. Master would be the one really to object, but unless Rose was bluffing, Sarah's Jewishness no longer bothered her that much. If Christians used the term, Sarah thought, the Episcopalian Masters appeared to be secular rather than observant.

As for herself, though she loved her tradition, Sarah reckoned that she could probably live in Manhattan without too much difficulty as a secular Jew, and even bring her children up that way—so long as they could experience their heritage whenever they visited her parents. If Charlie would make that compromise, then she could cope. She knew it could be done. She had friends in the city with mixed marriages who seemed to be happy enough.

But that still left the big problem. Her parents. Her father especially. Everyone knew the views of Daniel Adler.

Might it help that her father liked Charlie? "I was worried about you going into the city," he had told her. "But the gallery is serious, this I can see. And your client Mr. Master—that is a distinguished man, a fine man." There was no question, her father had liked Charlie a lot. Perhaps that would count for something.

Besides, she could remind her father, his grandchildren would still be Jewish. They'd have a Jewish mother. Maybe Daniel Adler could reconcile himself to having secular grandchildren, so long as they came to Seder at his house where he could educate them. "After all," she could hear herself telling him, "this way, they still have the choice as they grow older. There's nothing to stop a child of mine becoming a rabbi even, if he wants to."

These were the hopes, the calculations, the little scenarios Sarah invented for herself as she sat in her home and thought about the man she loved.

Maybe it could all work out. She didn't know. Perhaps by the end of the weekend, she'd have a clearer picture. For the time being, she decided it would be better not to speak to anybody about it.

She was caught completely off guard, therefore, when her mother suddenly turned to her in the kitchen that evening before they went to bed, and said: "I hear this man, Mr. Master, is falling in love with you."

Fortunately, Sarah was so taken by surprise that she just stared at her.

"What do you mean?" she managed to say.

"Ach," Esther Adler threw up her hands, "you know nothing."

"Who would think such a thing? And why?"

"Your sister. She told me two days ago. She noticed it when he was here. She was talking to him when I asked you about Adele Cohen's grandson, and he overheard. He was listening so hard, Rachel said, that he didn't even answer her questions."

"And this means he's in love with me?"

"Why not?"

"You want everyone to be in love with me, Mother. Besides, he's not Jewish."

"I said he was in love with you, not that he could marry you."

"What does that mean?"

"It means be careful."

"I will be careful, Mother. Is this all?"

"If you need to talk to me, Sarah, you can talk to me. Just don't talk to your father. Do you understand?"

"No, I don't understand. Can I go to bed now?"

Her mother shrugged. "You can always talk to me."

Let's hope so, thought Sarah. For the moment, though, she was glad to escape upstairs.

╌╬╌

Sunday morning was peaceful. Sarah and her mother made French toast for the boys. Her father went downstairs to practice the piano. After a few scales, he began to play Chopin. He was playing well.

How happy she felt—how glad that she had a home like this. Charlie would be happy in this setting, she thought. He'd be quite content to read the Sunday paper while her father played the piano below. For him, with his views and his intellect, this wouldn't be such a terrible transition.

Should she speak to her mother about it, after all? Should she tell her the truth after breakfast, when they were alone? She wasn't sure.

The boys were still eating when they heard a ring at the doorbell. Her mother was at the stove, and there was no chance of the boys stirring from their food, so she went to answer it. For a foolish moment, and though she knew very well he was in the city with his son, she hoped it might be Charlie.

She opened the door.

There were two people standing on the top step. The woman was fair, in her fifties, a complete stranger. The man was burly, wearing a black coat and a homburg hat. She stared at them.

"I'm sorry it's so early," said the woman. She looked awkward. Her accent was British.

"Well," said the man, "aren't you going to ask your Uncle Herman in?"

❖

They were standing in the kitchen. Downstairs, her father was still playing the piano, oblivious to their presence.

"I told you he plays well," Uncle Herman said to his wife.

"You shouldn't have come," said Sarah's mother. "You should have written. You should have telephoned, at least."

"I did say to him . . ." said Uncle Herman's wife, but nobody paid attention to her.

"And be told to stay away?" said Uncle Herman. "So I'm here." He looked at Michael. "You I remember." He looked at Nathan. "You I don't know. I'm your Uncle Herman."

Esther Adler glanced at Herman's wife, then addressed her brother-in-law.

"I don't want to say what happened."

"She knows," he boomed. "She knows." He turned to his wife. "I told you. They sat shiva for me when I married you, because you're not Jewish. I'm dead to them. You understand? They treated me like a dead person. They called all their friends to come and mourn for me, and they never spoke of me again. This is what we do, in families like ours. We're very particular."

"I never heard of such a thing before," his wife said to them apologetically. "I didn't know."

"You don't have to worry," said Uncle Herman. "It's only me that's dead. Not you."

"You have to go, Herman," said Mrs. Adler. "I'll tell him you came. Maybe he'll see you. I don't know."

"This is stupid," said Uncle Herman.

Sarah said nothing. She slipped from the room.

Her father did not even hear her come into the waiting room where he was playing, but when he saw her, he smiled. His face seemed so contented, and as she looked at him, she felt such love. She stood beside him.

"Father," she said gently, "something's happened. I have to tell you something."

He paused in his playing.

"What is it, Sarah?"

"You have to be prepared for a shock."

He stopped and half turned. His face looked anxious.

"It's all right. Nobody's hurt. Nobody's sick." She took a deep breath. "Uncle Herman is here. With his wife." She paused. "The wife is quite nice. Uncle Herman doesn't listen to her." She smiled. "He's just like I remember him. But Mother's sending them away. Is that what you want?"

For a long moment, her father said nothing.

"Herman is here?"

"Yes. He just showed up. On the doorstep."

"With this woman he married? He comes without warning, and he brings this woman to my house?"

"He wants to see you. I think he wants to be reconciled. Maybe he'll apologize." She hesitated. "It has been a long time," she added gently.

"A long time. I commit an offense. I wait a few years. Does this make the offense go away? Does this make it right?"

"No, Father. But maybe if you talk to him . . ."

Her father was leaning forward now, staring down at the piano's ivory keys. He shook his head. Then he rocked his body back and forth.

"I cannot see him," he said softly.

"Maybe if—"

"You don't understand. I cannot see him. I cannot bear . . ."

And suddenly Sarah understood. Her father wasn't angry, he was in terrible pain.

"This is how it begins," he said. "Always it is the same. In Germany, the Jews thought they were Germans, and they intermarried. But then, even if you had a Jewish grandmother or great-grandmother . . . they killed you. You think the Jews will be accepted? It is an illusion."

"That was Hitler—"

"And before that it was the Poles, it was the Russians, it was the Spanish Inquisition . . . Many countries have accepted the Jews, Sarah, and always they have turned against them in the end. The Jews will only survive if they are strong. This is the lesson of history." He looked up at her. "We were commanded to keep our faith, Sarah. So let me tell you: every time a Jew marries out, we are weakened. Marry out, and in two, three generations, your family will not be Jewish. Maybe they will be safe, maybe not. But in the end, either way, all that we have will be lost."

"You feel this?"

"I know this." He shook his head. "I sat shiva for my brother. He is dead to me. Go up and tell him so."

Sarah hesitated, then turned toward the stairs. But before she got to see Uncle Herman, his voice came booming down from above.

"Daniel, I'm here. You won't speak to your brother?"

Sarah glanced at her father. He was still staring down at the keyboard. Uncle Herman's voice came again.

"Time has passed, Daniel." There was a pause. "I won't come here again." Another pause, then, in a voice of fury, "If that's what you want, it's finished."

A moment later, the front door slammed. Then there was silence.

Sarah sat on the stairs. She didn't want to intrude upon her father, but she didn't want to leave him. She waited a little while. Then she saw his shoulders were moving and, although there was no sound, she realized he was weeping.

She couldn't help herself, she had to go to him. She came back down the stairs, and stood by the piano, and put her arms around him and held him.

"You think I don't love my brother?" he managed to say, after a little while.

"I know you love your brother."

He nodded slowly. "I love my brother. What should I do? What can I do?"

"I don't know, Father."

He half turned his face to look at her. The tears were streaming down his cheeks to his mustache.

"Promise me, Sarah, promise me you will never do such a thing as Herman has done."

"You want me to promise?"

"I could not bear it."

She paused, but only for a moment. "I promise."

Perhaps it was for the best.

Verrazano Narrows

Everyone agreed that Gorham Master was going to be successful. He was sure of it himself. He knew exactly what he wanted, he had it all mapped out, and he wasn't going to take no for an answer.

At Groton he'd been impressive, and now he was a sophomore at Harvard. If his studies at the university were important to him, so was baseball, and he'd shown himself to possess the true outfielder's instinct for reacting to a ball as soon as it's been hit. Men liked Gorham and so did women. Blue bloods liked him because he was a blue blood; and everyone else did because he was friendly, and polite, and a good sportsman. Employers, in a few years' time, were going to hire him because he was intelligent and hard-working, and knew how to fit in.

His closest friends would have known two other things about him. The first was that, though not lacking in bravery, he had within him a decided streak of conservatism and caution. The second, which was related to the first, was that he was determined to be as unlike his father as he could.

But it was because of his father that he'd returned to New York from Harvard this chilly February weekend.

✢

His mother's message on Wednesday had been clear. Come sooner rather than later. And when he'd arrived at her Staten Island house on Saturday evening, Julie had been direct.

"You know I hadn't seen your father for a couple of years when he called me the other night. He wanted to see me to say good-bye. So I went, and I'm glad I did."

"Is it really so bad?"

"Yes. The doctor told him he has cancer. The prognosis is that it won't take long, and I hope for his sake that the end will come soon. Naturally I told you to come at once."

"I can't quite take it in."

"Well, you've got until the morning. And Gorham," she added firmly, "be nice."

"I always am."

She gave him a look. "Just don't get into a fight."

·!·

On Sunday morning, as the ferry started across the broad waters of the harbor, there was a cold wind coming in from the east. How many times, Gorham wondered, had he taken this ferry with his father when he was a child? Two hundred? Three hundred? He didn't know. But one thing was certain: every time he had taken that ferry, and stared across at the approaching shoreline of Manhattan, he had vowed that he was going to live there. And now, here it was again, looking somewhat bleak on a gray February morning, but no less inviting to his eyes.

Of course, the place had changed quite a bit since he was a child. The waterfront, for instance, had completely altered. When he was a young boy, the docks of lower Manhattan had still been crowded with working men unloading cargo vessels. Some of that cargo handling was skilled work, too. But then the big containers had started to take the place of the old cargoes, and there was less and less work for the men on the docks, even across on the Brooklyn wharfs. The new facilities with their giant hoists were at Newark and Elizabeth ports now, over in New Jersey. The passenger liners still came on the Hudson to the West Side piers, but splendid though it was to see the liners, the waterfront now was a genteel echo of what it had been once.

The city, it seemed to Gorham, was being tidied up and streamlined. The mighty hand of Robert Moses had continued to lay down highways for the motor car, and for the huge trucks which now delivered to, and frequently blocked, the Midtown streets. Moses wanted to sweep away the slums as well, and in numerous places along the East River, high-rise blocks, for better or worse, were springing up in their place. Urban renewal, it was called. The masses of small manufacturers and factories that had crowded the poorer districts, especially in Brooklyn and the New York waterfront areas—those dirty, grainy, humble powerhouses of the city's wealth—had also been melting away.

But if Manhattan was changing its character, if services were replacing manufacture, if Ellis Island was long since closed, and New York's huge floods of immigrants regulated into a less visible seepage through the nation's borders, the great city of New York still contained in its five boroughs vibrant communities from all the ends of the Earth.

Some of his friends at Harvard thought he was crazy to want to live in New York. For the city had been having big problems in the last few years. Its budget was in crisis, taxes had been going up. There was racial tension; crime was rising. There were almost three murders a day in the city now. Major corporations, which had been drawn to New York since the turn of the century, had been moving their headquarters to other cities. But to Gorham Master, New York was still the center of the world. As soon as he graduated, Manhattan was where he was going. Somebody might offer him a wonderful job, with a big salary, in some other city, but he'd turn it down for any decent job in New York. The only thing he hadn't reckoned on was that his father wouldn't be there.

He had to admit that, whatever his father's faults, life with Charlie Master was never dull. During the last two decades, the world around them had been changing fast. The certainties of the fifties had been challenged, restrictions been torn down. New freedoms had come, and new dangers.

Yet strangely enough, Gorham realized, he had learned the most about each change not from his own contemporaries, but from his father. While he'd been at high school, it had been Charlie who had joined the civil rights marches, and who had made him listen to tape recordings of Martin Luther King. Neither of them thought the Vietnam War was a good cause, but while Gorham was just hoping that the draft might be ended by the time he was due to graduate from Harvard, his father had made enemies by writing newspaper articles against the war.

At least Gorham could respect his father for his political views. But some of Charlie's other activities were a different matter. It was his father, not he, who knew all the bands, Charlie who explained psychedelic experiences to him, and who started smoking dope. "I don't mind Dad being young at heart," Gorham had complained to his mother Julie, "but does he have to go on getting younger and younger?" And during the last couple of years, his father's lifestyle had caused some friction between them. Gorham wasn't shocked by his father, he just thought that Charlie was turning into a middle-aged adolescent.

And yet, adolescent or not, in the last few years of his life, Charlie had had a big success. Having spent years trying to write plays for the stage, he'd become fascinated by television and earned some useful money as a comedy writer. Then, without telling Gorham, he had published his novel.

The ferry was well out into the harbor now. Looking back, Gorham stared at the huge span of the Verrazano Bridge, and shook his head with amusement. Whatever Charlie's faults, it amused his son to realize that for the rest of his life, whenever he looked at that huge New York landmark, he'd be forced to remember his father.

Verrazano Narrows had been a good choice of title. Not many people remembered that the first European to arrive in New York harbor, way back in the early sixteenth century, had been the Italian Verrazano. Everybody knew Hudson, though he'd actually got there more than eighty years later, but Verrazano was forgotten; and for years the leaders of the Italian community had been lobbying for recognition of the great navigator. When a vast bridge was finally constructed across the entrance to New York harbor, the Italians wanted it named after him. Robert Moses had opposed the name, but the Italians lobbied Governor Nelson Rockefeller, and finally got their way. And it was fitting that the great suspension bridge, joining Staten Island to Brooklyn, should bear an Italian name. For it was one of the most elegant bridges ever built.

Verrazano Narrows, by Charles Master, came out in 1964 in the same month that the bridge was opened. It was a novel, but it almost read like a poem. People compared it to a great book from the forties, *By Grand Central Station I Sat Down and Wept*. *Verrazano Narrows* was a love story about a man who lives with his son on Staten Island, and has a passionate affair with a woman in Brooklyn. The *Narrows* in the title also suggested the narrow prejudices the couple had had to overcome. Gorham had supposed that the story might be somewhat autobiographical, but if so, his father had never indicated the identity of the woman to him or to anybody else. Anyway, it had been a huge literary success. They'd made a movie out of it too. Charlie had toured the country, made friends with a bunch of people out in San Francisco, stayed on the West Coast for a while, and learned to smoke dope.

When he reached the ferry terminal, Gorham took the subway. There weren't many people about. At the far end of his car, a couple of blacks were standing, and they glanced toward him. He cursed inwardly. They were probably harmless, but one had to be careful these days, he thought. People in the city developed antennae that sent warning signals whenever trouble came near. As it happened, he was carrying quite a bit of cash with him today. He really shouldn't have entered a deserted subway car like this.

Was it reasonable to suspect two guys just because they were black? Was it right for someone who knew parts of Martin Luther King's speeches by heart to do so? No, it wasn't. But people did. The two blacks carried on their quiet conversation, and ignored him for several stations. Then other people got in, and the two men left.

Gorham came out of the subway on Lexington Avenue. There was only a block to walk across to Park. He reached the top of the subway stair, turned. And cursed. Then he stepped off the sidewalk into the street.

Garbage. Piles of black garbage bags all over the sidewalk. Garbage as far as the eye could see.

New York: city of strikes. Two years ago it had been a transit strike. That hadn't shut the city down, because New Yorkers walked to work. But it had done nothing for the city's reputation. Now it was the sanitation workers who were on strike. The mayor, John Lindsay, was a decent man and an honest one, but whether he'd be able to control the turbulent city and meet its financial problems remained to be seen. Meanwhile, the garbage bags were piling up on the sidewalks in ever increasing heaps. There was only one blessing. It was February. What the stench would be like if it were August did not bear thinking about.

So Charlie Master was dying while the garbage piled up in the streets. Somehow, irrationally, Gorham felt as if his father was being insulted by the city he loved.

Yet when he got to Park Avenue, he found his father in better spirits than he expected.

After Rose had died at the start of the decade, Charlie had taken over her apartment. For a while, he had kept his old place on Seventy-eighth, and used it as a gallery for his pictures. Then he'd given it up, and used the second bedroom on Park as a temporary store. He'd been talking about renting a small studio downtown this year, but Gorham supposed that wouldn't be happening now.

Mabel, his grandmother's housekeeper, was looking after Charlie, and a nurse came in a couple of times a day. If possible, Charlie wanted to stay where he was, right to the end.

When he entered the living room, Gorham found his father dressed and sitting in an armchair. He looked thin and pale, but he smiled cheerfully.

"It's good to see you, Gorham. How did you come?"

"I took the train."

"You didn't fly? Everyone seems to fly these days. The airports are doing great business." It was true. All three airports, Newark, JFK and La Guardia, were getting busier every year. The city had become a huge national and international hub. "Makes you wonder where they all go."

"Maybe I'll fly next time."

"You should. You just here for the weekend?"

Gorham nodded. Then he suddenly felt a wave of guilt. What was he thinking of? This was his father, who was dying.

"I could stay . . ."

Charlie shook his head. "I'd rather you kept studying. I'll call you when I need you." He smiled again. "I'm really pleased to see you."

"Is there anything I can get you?"

"I don't suppose you've got any grass?"

Gorham was about to say, "Oh for God's sake," but he bit the words back. Instead he just sighed. "Sorry, Dad. I haven't."

It was one of the causes of friction between them. Gorham had smoked marijuana only once in his life. That had been the weekend after he graduated high school, back in '66. He remembered his hesitation, how his friends had told him that Bob Dylan had introduced the Beatles to grass in '64, right here in New York, and that their best work had begun from then. Was all that stuff really true? He had no idea.

But Gorham had never done it again. Maybe he hadn't particularly liked it the first time. Perhaps his innate conservatism and caution had set in. He had friends who were getting into LSD, with terrible results, and in his mind he associated hard drugs with soft. Whatever the reasons, he ran with a group of friends who, for the most part, didn't do drugs, and it embarrassed him that his father did.

"It looks like a big mess outside. Garbage bags everywhere."

"It is."

"Nothing dims our affection for the city, though."

"Right."

"I guess you still want to come and be a banker here?"

"Family tradition. Except for you, that is." Had he allowed a hint of rebuke to creep into his voice? If so, his father had chosen to ignore it.

"Do you remember your grandmother giving you a Morgan silver dollar when you were a boy? It's nothing to do with the Morgan bank, you know. It's the name of the designer."

"Remember? I keep it with me every day. It's my talisman, the badge of my destiny." Gorham grinned a little sheepishly. "That's rather childish, I guess." In fact, the dollar had a more critical significance than that. It was the reminder of the family's past as bankers and merchants, in the days when they still had wealth—the wealth that his aberrant father had never even attempted to get back.

But rather to Gorham's surprise, his father looked delighted.

"That's good, Gorham. Your grandmother would be so pleased—she wanted to give you something you'd value. So you'll try to get a job with a bank as soon as you graduate?"

"That's right."

"It's a pity my father isn't here, he could have helped you. I know some bankers I could ask."

"It's okay."

"Bankers like people like you."

"I hope so."

"Do you worry about the draft?"

"Not right now, but I could be eligible when I graduate. Maybe I'll go to divinity school or something. That's what some people are doing to get out of it."

"Martin Luther King is saying that the war is immoral. But I guess you don't want to protest about it."

"I'll keep a low profile."

"You should go to business school later. Get an MBA."

"My plan is to work for a few years, and then go to Columbia."

"Then you'll marry, after the MBA?"

"When I make vice president. Maybe assistant vice president. AVP would do, if I find the right person."

"A good corporate spouse?"

"I think so."

Charlie nodded. "Your mother would have been a good corporate spouse. An excellent one." He paused. "Things don't always work out quite the way we plan, Gorham."

"I know."

"I should keep this place, if I were you. The monthly maintenance isn't too bad—I'll leave enough to cover that. And being in a good building will save you a lot of trouble."

"I don't want to think about that, Dad."

"You don't have to think about it. That's just the way it'll be. This place will suit you much better than me. I should have moved down to Soho." He sighed. "My mistake."

Soho: South of Houston Street. It was a quiet, bare area of former warehouses and cobbled streets, where artists could get a studio or a loft for very little money. A short walk northward and one was in Greenwich Village. Gorham could see that his father would have been happy there. And he was just wondering how to respond when Charlie suddenly said: "You know what I want? I want to see the Guggenheim. Will you take me there?"

They took a taxi. Charlie looked a little frail, but by the time they got out on the corner of Fifth and Eighty-ninth, he seemed to have gained energy.

Frank Lloyd Wright's great masterpiece might not be to everyone's taste, but Gorham could see why his father liked it. The museum's white walls, and its cylindrical stack, like the top of an inverted spiral cone, was in open contrast to and rebellion against so much of the recent public architecture of the city. The huge glass tower blocks that had been rising since the late fifties enraged Charlie Master. The setback laws that had forced architects to make creative designs for the higher, narrower floors of the previous generation of skyscrapers had been relaxed. Huge, flat-topped glass and metal stumps were soaring up forty floors and more, blocking out the sky. In compensation, they had to provide open plaza-like spaces for the public at ground level. But in practice, the spaces were frequently cold, and soulless, and not much used. As for the glass towers themselves: "They are ugly, and boring," Charlie would cry. He was particularly incensed about a group of Midtown bank towers on Park which he seemed to consider a personal affront to the avenue where he lived.

The strange, curved shape of the Guggenheim, however, was organic, like a mystical plant. Charlie loved it. He seemed quite content to look at the building from the outside. When he'd done, he told Gorham he'd like to walk down Fifth a little way.

If the volume of vehicles using the city streets had been going up for the last two decades, one relief had been granted. Most of the great avenues were one-way now. Park, with its broad arrangement of double lanes, carried traffic in both directions, but to the west of it, Madison carried the traffic uptown, and Fifth Avenue carried it down. Walking down Fifth on a Sunday morning, therefore, especially in February, was a quiet business. To avoid the garbage, they walked beside the park.

The Museum Mile, as people called it, was one of the most delightful walks in the city. Having left the Guggenheim, they passed opposite delightful apartment buildings. Then they went by the long, neoclassical facade of the Metropolitan Museum, and down another ten blocks or so toward the Frick. Charlie was walking a little slowly, but he seemed quite determined to continue, and from time to time, he would stare into Central Park, admiring the wintry scene, Gorham supposed. When they came level with the Frick, he sighed.

"I'm a little tired now, Gorham," he said. "I think we'd better get a taxi back." It seemed a rather short ride to Gorham, but he wasn't going to argue, and it was only a few moments before a yellow cab came by. When they were in the cab, Charlie gave him a wry smile. "Couldn't find what I wanted," he said.

"Which was?"

"A guy in a red baseball hat. He's usually in the park around there. He has good stuff."

"Oh." So the expedition had been about buying marijuana. Gorham felt a flash of annoyance. His father saw it.

"You don't understand, Gorham," he said quietly. "It helps with the pain."

When they got back into the apartment, Mabel had made them soup and a light lunch. They talked as they ate, mostly about things they'd done together when Gorham was a child. When lunch was over, Charlie said: "There's something I'm going to ask you to do for me, Gorham, when this is all over."

"Sure."

"There's a piece of paper with a list of names and addresses on it by the bureau. Would you bring it over?" Gorham brought the list. He could see about a dozen names on it. "Most of these are just friends of one kind or another. You'll see my doctor's there, and one of the Keller family, and some others. I've left them little mementoes in my will, nothing much, but it'd be awfully nice if you'd deliver them and say I asked you to do it. It's just that I'd prefer them to receive the presents from your hand, rather than from my lawyer in the mail. Would you do that?"

"I already said I would." Gorham ran his eye down the list. The doctor he knew, and several of the others. Others were unfamiliar. "Sarah Adler?"

"A gallery owner. I had some paintings from there. She might give you something if she likes you. You'll do them all?"

"Of course."

"I'm feeling a little tired now, Gorham. I'm going to sleep a while. I think you should get back to school now."

"I'll come back next weekend."

"Make it two weeks. I've got some things going on next weekend, and it's a long way for you to come. Two weeks will be fine."

Gorham could see that his father was getting tired, so he didn't argue. After parting from Charlie, he quietly told Mabel that he'd be telephoning to check up on him in the coming days.

Once he was outside, he realized that he had more than an hour to kill before the next Boston train. So he decided to walk a bit to get some fresh air. Crossing Madison and Fifth, he entered Central Park.

The trees were bare and there was snow on the ground, but the cold air was dry and bracing. As he went over the day in his mind, he decided that it could have been a lot worse. He hadn't criticized his father or lost his temper, even once. Their meeting had been loving and harmonious. Thank God for that.

He wondered how long his father had got. Surely some months, at least. He'd visit him plenty more times, and make his final days as gentle a passing as he could.

He'd been walking about ten minutes when he saw the guy with the red baseball hat standing by a tree.

He was a black man, over six feet tall, wearing a long black coat and a black scarf he'd wrapped around his neck many times. His narrow shoulders were hunched. As Gorham came near, the man looked at him, but obviously without much hope. As he passed, the automatic "Smoke? Grass?" came without conviction. Out of habit, equally, Gorham walked sternly by, trying to ignore him.

He'd gone a little way before his father's words came back to him. "It helps with the pain." He'd read about that, people with cancer taking marijuana. Why not? After all, they took other drugs to ease the pain. Maybe his doctor could give him dope on prescription. Could he do that? Gorham had no idea. Presumably not, or Charlie wouldn't be trying to buy it in the park.

He looked at his watch. Wasn't it time to be getting along to his train? Not really.

What was the law, exactly? The guy with the red baseball hat could be arrested, certainly, for selling the stuff. But what about if you bought some? In possession of an illegal substance—they arrested people for that, he was sure. What was it going to do to his chances of getting into a bank if he got arrested in Central Park? Not a good idea. He walked on.

So he was going to let his father suffer? His poor father who, in his own crazy way, had been good to him all his life? His father who had nothing in common with him, but treated him with all the kindness he might have reserved for a soulmate? The father who quietly ignored the little moments of irritation that he himself had been unable to conceal entirely even in the company of a dying man?

He turned round. The guy with the red baseball hat was still there. He looked about. Unless there was somebody hiding behind a tree, this section of the park was empty. He walked toward the dealer.

The guy looked at him questioningly. He had a thin face and a small, straggly beard.

"How much?"

"An eighth?"

The man said something, but Gorham hardly heard the price. He was looking around nervously.

"I'll take half an ounce," he said quickly. If the man was surprised, he gave no sign. He reached into his pocket and started pulling out little plastic bags. Gorham supposed he'd been given half an ounce, which he knew was plenty, but he had no idea what he was doing. He took the little bags and thrust them into a pocket of his pants, underneath his overcoat. He started to move away.

"You haven't paid, man," said the guy.

"Oh. Right." Gorham pulled out some bills. "Is that enough?" He was starting to panic now.

"That's enough," said the dealer. It must have been too much, but right now Gorham didn't care. He just wanted to get away. He hastened along the path, glancing back only once, hoping the dealer had vanished. But he was still standing there. Gorham followed the path until it led to another, and then made an eastward turn toward an exit onto Fifth. Thank God the guy was well out of sight by now.

He had just got to the sidewalk on Fifth when he saw the cop. He knew what he ought to do. He ought to look casual. After all, he was a respectable, conservative young man from Harvard who was going to be a banker, not a young guy with half an ounce of grass in his pocket. But he couldn't help it. He froze. He probably looked as if he'd just killed someone in there.

The cop was watching him. He came toward him.

"Good afternoon, officer," said Gorham. Somehow it sounded absurd.

"In the park?" said the cop.

"Yes." Gorham was beginning to get control of himself now. "I needed a little walk." The cop was still watching him. Gorham smiled sadly. "Do I look pale?"

"You might say that."

"I guess I'd better get a coffee before I go back then." He nodded grimly. "Not a good day. My father has cancer." And then, because it was true, he felt the tears come to his eyes.

The cop saw.

"I'm sorry to hear that," he said. "There's a place where you can get coffee if you follow this street to Lexington."

"Thank you." He crossed Fifth and kept going all the way to Lexington. Then he turned north, went up a few blocks and came back to Park Avenue.

His father was still up when Mabel let him into the apartment. He was sitting in the chair, but he was slumped over on one arm, and his face was drawn. Obviously the effort of that day had taken a lot out of him.

"I found the guy with the red baseball hat," Gorham said quickly, and he disgorged the contents of his pocket. He grinned. "I nearly got arrested."

It took Charlie a few moments to summon his energy. But when he did, he looked up at Gorham with a gratitude that was touching.

"You did that for me?"

"Yes," said Gorham. And kissed him.

After Dark

BY THE EVENING of Wednesday, July 13, the atmosphere, which had been hot and humid all day, was getting oppressively close. It felt as if a thunderstorm could break. Apart from this circumstance, Gorham had no other expectations for the evening ahead—except the pleasure of seeing his good friend Juan, of course.

Gorham had armed himself with a large umbrella as he walked swiftly northward from his apartment on Park. He only saw Juan every six months or so, but it was always an interesting occasion. Opposites in every way, they'd been friends since they were at Columbia together. And although Gorham took pride in the fact that he had a large network of friends from every walk of life, he'd always felt that Juan was special. "I'm sorry that my father isn't here," he'd told Juan once. "He would have liked you." This, from Gorham, was high praise.

By the year 1977, Gorham Master could reasonably claim that, so far at least, his life had gone according to plan. After his father's death, he'd let the Park Avenue apartment during the rest of his time at Harvard, staying at his mother's Staten Island house when he visited the city. He'd been fortunate to get a low number in the lottery and avoided the draft. Then he'd managed to impress Columbia Business School so much that they took him into the MBA program without previous work experience. Gorham didn't want to hang around; he wanted to get started. Columbia had been a wonderful experience, all the same. The business school had provided him with a sound intellectual framework for organizing the rest of his life, and a number of interesting friends as well, including Juan Campos. Emerging with his MBA, he'd found himself, still in his early twenties, in the enviable position of being the owner of a six-room apartment on Park Avenue, without a mortgage, and with enough cash to pay the maintenance for years to come—all this before he started his first job.

This might not be riches by the standards of his class, but if he had been a different character, the possession of so much money at the start of his life might have destroyed Gorham, by taking away his incentive to work. Luckily for him, however, he had such a strong ambition to restore his family to its former status in the city that, in his mind, it represented only the accomplishment of the first step—namely, that the present representative of the family should be seen to start his career from a position of privilege. The next step was to get a job in a major bank. After that, he intended to do whatever it took to get to the top. His father might not have been a conventional success, but Gorham was going to be. That was his mission.

But he missed Charlie, even more than he'd thought he would.

Charlie had died too soon; the very year of his death seemed to proclaim the fact. With all its tragedy, 1968 had been an extraordinary year. There had been the failure of the Tet Offensive, and the huge demonstrations in New York against the Vietnam War. April had seen the terrible assassination of Martin Luther King, and June of Robert Kennedy. There had been the memorable candidacies of Richard Nixon, Hubert Humphrey and George Wallace for the presidency. In Europe, the student revolution in Paris, and the Russian crushing of the Prague Spring in Czechoslovakia had changed the history of the Western world. Andy Warhol had been shot and wounded, Jackie Kennedy had married Aristotle Onassis. So many iconic events in modern history had taken place that year, and Charlie Master had not been there to witness and comment upon them. It seemed so unnatural, so wrong.

Yet in some ways, Gorham was almost glad that his father had not lived to see the last few years. For that depressing garbage strike at the start of '68 had not been the culmination, but only the beginning of New York's troubles. Year after year the great city his father loved had deteriorated. Huge efforts had been made to market New York to the world as an exciting place. Taking a little-known slang term for a large city that dated back to the twenties, the marketing men called it the Big Apple, and invented a logo to go with the name. Central Park was filled with concerts, plays, every kind of activity. But behind all the razzmatazz, the city was falling apart. The park was turning into a dust bowl, where it was unsafe to walk after dark. Street crime continued to rise. As for the poor neighborhoods like Harlem and the South Bronx, they seemed to be falling into terminal neglect.

Finally, in 1975, the Big Apple confessed it was bankrupt. For years, it seemed, the accounts had been falsified. The city had borrowed money against revenues it did not have. Nobody wanted to buy New York debt, and President Ford refused to bail the city out unless it reformed itself. "FORD TO CITY: DROP DEAD" the *Daily News* headline had memorably put it. Emergency help from union funds had saved actual collapse, but the Big Apple was still in a state of ongoing crisis.

Charlie would have hated New York's humiliation. But Gorham still wished that he had his father to talk to. They might disagree, but Charlie was never passive, always informed, and usually had an opinion. Since his passing, Gorham was left to make sense of the world by himself, and when he was alone in the apartment sometimes, he would feel quite sad.

He had performed all his obligations toward his father, of course. He had delivered the little presents to his father's friends, and heard their words of love and praise for Charlie. That had been a pleasant mission. All, that is, except one. Sarah Adler had been out of town at the time, on a trip to Europe. The present to her had been a drawing, carefully wrapped, so Gorham did not know what it was. He'd meant to deliver it several times, but somehow he'd always had something else to do, and after a year had passed, he had felt rather embarrassed to have waited so long. The gift was still sitting, fully wrapped, in a closet in the apartment. One day, he promised himself, he'd get round to dealing with it. God knows, he meant to.

His banking career had started well. The first choice had been what kind of bank he wanted to go into. Gorham knew that ever since the Glass-Steagall Act of 1933 had regulated the banking industry after the great crash, one had to choose between two kinds of banking career: the commercial, high street banks that took ordinary people's deposits, and the investment banks—the merchants banks, as they were called in London—where the financiers made their deals.

In a commercial bank, people told him, there was less risk, less frenetic hours, and probably a job for life; in an investment bank there were more risks, though maybe higher rewards. On the whole, he felt more attracted to the massive corporate respectability and power of the great commercial banks; he liked the solidity they represented. He'd been offered a position with a major bank, and he'd been very happy.

The life suited him. He did well in the bank's training program, and he was assigned to the automotive group. He spent long hours preparing the numbers for credit documents, but he worked fast, had an eye for detail, and when he got the chance to study the loan documents, he discovered that he had a natural understanding of contracts and their implications. And unlike some blue bloods, he didn't only do the work, but he asked for more.

"I see you're not afraid of hard work," his boss remarked to him after a long session.

"It's the way to go up the learning curve," Gorham replied cheerfully.

And when his boss took him to meet clients, they liked him. Client meetings in the automotive industry were a leisurely business, conducted on the golf course. Charlie had never had a country club, but Gorham had learned to play golf at Groton, and he'd kept up his game ever since. On these occasions, he did well, and his boss took notice. Client relationships were important in banking.

Two years ago, Gorham had made assistant vice president. He was on his way. All he needed now to complete the picture was the perfect corporate wife. He'd had several girlfriends, but none that seemed quite right to be Mrs. Gorham Master. He wasn't worried about that, however. There was plenty of time.

✢

At seven thirty, Maggie O'Donnell walked out of the Croydon rental building on Eighty-sixth Street, turned up Madison, walked a few blocks, past the Jackson Hole where she got her burgers, up to the tiny, enterprising restaurant where they served a very reasonable prix fixe menu with minimal choice, which changed every night. The Carnegie Hill area, lying as it did at the very top of the Upper East Side, contained a lot of young professionals who were glad of a chance to get an inexpensive meal in amusing surroundings, and the little restaurant's half-dozen tables were seldom empty.

She was going to meet her brother Martin. If he turned up.

To be fair to Martin, he had been quite specific. The bookstore where he worked had an author reading that evening. If he was needed, he'd have to take a rain check. If not, he'd see her at the restaurant.

Maggie had organized her time efficiently. She'd scheduled her doctor's appointment, for a check-up, at five thirty. That was on Park in the Eighties. It gave her time to return home afterward, do the laundry she hadn't been able to do the previous weekend, then go out to the restaurant. After she'd eaten, she'd take a taxi back to her Midtown office, and work until maybe midnight or one o'clock on a contract she was preparing. Maggie was a lawyer. She worked for Branch & Cabell. And like all the young associates at the big Manhattan law firms, she worked very hard. The lawyers at Branch & Cabell were almost immortals. They did not need to pause for rest or sleep. They worked in their wood paneled skyscraper, advising the powerful, and sent out their mighty bills for the midnight hours.

Maggie was happy with her life. She'd been born in the city, but when she was eight years old, her parents had moved out. Her father Patrick, whom she sometimes suspected was more interested in baseball than he was in being an insurance broker, always liked to say that after the Giants had departed the city for San Francisco, and the Dodgers for Los Angeles, he couldn't think of a damn reason to stay there. But the truth was that her parents had been just one of hundreds of thousands of white, middle-class families who, in the fifties and sixties, had deserted the increasingly troubled streets of Manhattan for the peaceful suburbs.

It had worried her parents that her brother had gone to live in the city back in 1969. When she had started working for Branch & Cabell they had been even more concerned. They'd insisted on seeing her apartment before she rented it, and when she told them that she intended to jog around the reservoir in Central Park, which was only minutes from her door, they had made her promise never to do so alone or after dark.

"I'll only jog when everyone else does," she told them. And indeed, in the summer months when she went out at seven in the morning, there were dozens of people doing the same thing. "Jackie Onassis jogs round the reservoir, too," she told her mother. Not that she'd ever seen Jackie Onassis, but she'd heard it was true, and she hoped it would help to reassure her.

This summer, there was another threat to worry them.

"I just wish the police would catch this terrible man," her mother would say, whenever she telephoned. Maggie couldn't blame her. The Son of Sam, as he called himself, had scared a lot of people in recent months, shooting young women, and sending strange letters to the police and a journalist, stating that he would strike again. His attacks had been in Queens and the Bronx so far, but reminding her mother of this fact, had done no good. "How do you know he won't strike in Manhattan next?" she had said, and of course Maggie hadn't got an answer.

It had been stiflingly hot and close all day. It felt like the start of a serious heatwave. She had changed into a light cotton skirt and blouse, and she was looking forward to a long, cold drink.

❖

Juan Campos stood on the sidewalk and stared across the great divide. He too had noticed the hot and muggy weather, and right now, he sensed a heavy, electric feel in the air. He expected the rumble of thunder at any time.

He looked toward Central Park. His girlfriend Janet lived on the West Side, on Eighty-sixth near Amsterdam. She was walking across the park to meet him.

An ambulance, siren moaning and horn blaring, came round the corner from Third Avenue and raced along the north side of the street toward Madison. This was nothing out of the ordinary. There were always ambulances making a noise on East Ninety-sixth Street, because the hospital was so nearby.

Juan was standing at the intersection of Ninety-sixth and Park. The apartment he'd recently moved into was the other side of Lexington Avenue, on the north side. He had a sublet for a year, and he had no idea whether he'd be there for longer. Nothing in his life so far had ever been certain, so he didn't suppose it would be now. But at least one thing was consistent: he was still living on the north side of the great divide.

His street. Ninety-sixth Street. It was a cross street of course, like Eighty-sixth, and Seventy-second, Fifty-seventh, Forty-second, Thirty-fourth and Twenty-third. The traffic moved both ways. If each of these great streets had their particular characters, Ninety-sixth Street, in the year 1977, was something entirely different. It was the border between two worlds. Below Ninety-sixth Street lay the Upper East and Upper West sides. Above it was Harlem, where people like his friend Gorham Master didn't go. But if most people from outside the city assumed that

Harlem was nowadays all black, they would have been quite wrong. There were numerous other communities in Harlem, but the largest of these, by far, lay in the southern portion, above Ninety-sixth and east of Fifth.

El Barrio, Spanish Harlem. The home of the Puerto Ricans.

Juan Campos was Puerto Rican, and he'd lived in El Barrio all his life. When he was seven his father had died and his mother Maria had struggled hard, taking cleaning jobs mostly, to support her only child.

Life in El Barrio was tough, but the spirit of Maria Campos was strong. She was proud of her heritage. She loved to cook the rich, spicy mixture of Spanish, Taino and African dishes that was the Puerto Rican cuisine. Black bean soup, *pollo con arroz*, stews, *mofongo* and deep fries, coconut and plantain, okra and passion fruit—these were the staples of Juan's diet. Sometimes Maria would go out, and dance to the beating drums of the *bomba*, or the lively *guaracha*. These were the few times that Juan ever saw his mother truly happy.

Above all, however, Maria Campos was possessed of a burning ambition. She knew that her own life was unlikely to change, but she could dream for her son, and her dreams were grand.

"Remember the great José Celso Barbosa," she would tell him. Barbosa had been a poor Puerto Rican, with imperfect sight, who'd worked his way out of poverty, become the first Puerto Rican to gain an American medical degree, and ended his life as a hero and benefactor of his fellow countrymen. "You could be like him, Juan," she'd told the little boy. Barbosa had been dead a long time, and Juan would have been the living hero, like Roberto Clemente the baseball star. But since he was small and short-sighted, Juan knew he couldn't hope for that destiny. All the same, he did his best to follow his mother's precepts—except in one respect.

"Stay away from your cousin Carlos," she always told him. But Juan had soon figured out that if he wanted to survive on the mean streets of El Barrio, then the person he needed more than anyone else was his tall and handsome cousin Carlos.

Every street has its gang, and every gang its leader. Among the kids where Juan lived, Carlos's word was law. If a boy wanted to rob a store, or sell drugs, or anything else, then he'd be a fool to try it without Juan's permission. If anyone laid a finger on a kid under Carlos's protection, they could expect a beating they'd never forget.

If Juan was small and didn't see too well, God had given him talents to make up for these disadvantages. He was lively, he was naturally kind, and

he was funny. It wasn't long before Carlos had decided that his little
cousin belonged under his wing. The gang adopted him as a kind of mascot. If Juan's mother wanted him to study at school, that was okay. What
else could a kid like that do? For the rest of his childhood, no one gave
Juan any trouble.

And Maria did want Juan to study at school. She was passionate about
it. "You want a better life, you get an education," she told him, time and
again. And maybe if Juan had been big and strong he wouldn't have listened to her so much, but a little voice inside him seemed to tell him she
was right. So though he played with the other kids in the street, he'd often
pretend to be more tired than he was and go back indoors to study.

Juan and his mother lived in two dingy rooms on Lexington Avenue,
near 116th street. Though there were Catholic schools, Juan, like most
Puerto Ricans, went to the public school. There were several kinds of kid
at his school, and depending who they were, one could usually predict
where they lived. The black kids lived west of Park, the Puerto Ricans
from Park to Pleasant, and the Italians, whose families had usually been in
Harlem longest, from east of Pleasant. There were Jewish kids in that
school too, and several of the teachers were Jewish.

Juan was very fortunate in his school, because if one chose to take
advantage of it, the teaching there was good, and Juan was happy enough.
He found that most of the work came to him easily, especially mathematics, for which he seemed to have a natural talent.

It didn't take him long to make friends, and one of the kids he spent
time with was a Jewish boy named Michael. And it was Michael who said
to him one day, "When I get out of here, my parents hope I can get to
Stuyvesant." Juan didn't know what Stuyvesant was, so Michael explained
to him that the three best high schools in the city for the public-school
kids were Hunter, Bronx Science and Stuyvesant down in the Financial
District. The schools were free, Michael said, but the exams for entry were
tough, and competition was high.

When Juan told his mother about Michael's plans for high school, he
didn't think such information applied to him. So he was astonished, and
rather embarrassed when, the very next day, Maria called at the school
and asked one of the Jewish teachers how her son could get to such a
place too.

The teacher had looked rather surprised, but a week later, he had taken
Juan to one side and asked him a lot of questions about how he liked it at

school, what subjects he enjoyed most, and what he hoped for in his future life. And since Juan wanted to please his mother, who worked so hard for him, he said that he really wanted to go to Stuyvesant.

The teacher had looked rather doubtful. At the time Juan had supposed that this was because his grades weren't high enough, but later he realized that the teacher had been worried because Stuyvesant wasn't known for taking black Puerto Ricans. "To have any hope," the teacher told him, "you'll have to get grades at least as good as your friend Michael."

After that, Juan worked as hard as he could, and his grades were as good as Michael's. He sensed also that some of the teachers were paying him a little extra attention, and sometimes they would be tough on him, or give him more work to do, but he figured they were trying to help him, so he didn't complain. And in due course, when they took the exam, both he and Michael were accepted into Stuyvesant. He was excited, naturally, but when his mother got the news, she broke down and wept.

So Juan Campos had gone to Stuyvesant. Luckily his cousin Carlos decided to treat this strange circumstance as a kind of victory for the gang. Their mascot was going to get an education and maybe become a lawyer, or something like that, and learn how to beat the white people at their own dirty game. During their years at Stuyvesant, he and Michael would take the subway together every morning and evening. During the vacations, he worked at any job he could find, delivering food for pizza parlors or restaurants mostly, down in Carnegie Hill, where the tips were good, to help pay for his keep at home.

But in his last year at school, Juan's life had changed.

"I suppose," he told Gorham years later, "I was really a child until then."

He'd come home one evening to find that his mother had had a fall and hurt her leg. The next day she hadn't been able to go to work. For several days she'd been laid up, and Juan had looked after her each evening when he'd got back from school. She didn't want to see a doctor, but finally the pain and swelling in her ankle got so bad that she agreed. And then the truth had come out.

"I think she had a good idea she was sick all along and she didn't want to know about it." When the doctor told Juan that his mother's ankle would be okay in a month, but that she had a bad heart, Juan's path had been clear.

There were scholarships available for Stuyvesant pupils to go to the Ivy

League schools, but it was obvious that wouldn't work. The City College up at West 137th Street, however, was free and the education was good. He could attend it from home, and look after his mother as well. For the next years, he'd studied at City College by day and worked nights and vacations to help support her. When Maria hadn't even been able to do the few light jobs she'd still retained, he'd taken time off from college so that he could work non-stop and put some extra savings by. It had been tough, but they'd managed.

Then, in his final year at City College, she had died. He knew very well that she'd wanted to go; she was in pain and had little energy—but she also wanted him to be free.

Until his mother's sickness, Juan had never paid much attention to his surroundings. He knew the rooms they lived in needed painting, and that the light in the hallway didn't work, and that the landlord said he'd fix things and never did. But his mother had always insisted that the household was her affair, and he should concentrate on his studies. Sometimes he'd dreamed of having a fine house one day—he didn't know where— and of marrying and having a big family, and looking after his mother. This was a dream that his hard work at school might one day realize. The present, in his mind, was only a temporary state.

But as Maria grew weaker, and he had to take charge, the harsh realities of the present had become very real indeed. There was the rent to be paid, and food to be bought. Some weeks, there wasn't enough money, and on more than one occasion, Juan had to ask the owner of the nearby corner store to let him have food on credit. The man was friendly with Maria, and he was kind. When Juan came in one afternoon with a few dollars he owed him, the man just said, "That's okay, kid. Pay me back when you get rich."

More difficult were his dealings with the landlord. Mr. Bonati was a small, bald, middle-aged man who'd owned the building for a long time, and who collected the rents himself. When Juan had to pay him late, he was understanding. "I know your mother a long time, now," he said. "She gives me no trouble." But when Juan tackled him about the dangerous broken stair, or the blocked drain, or any of the other things that made daily life a trial, Bonati always gave him some excuse, and did nothing. Finally, seeing the young man's exasperation, Bonati had taken Juan by the arm.

"Listen, I can see you're a smart kid. You're polite, you're going to college. Think about it—do you know any other kids on this block going to college? Most of them never finished high school. So listen to what I'm telling you. Your mother pays me a low rent. You know why? Because this building is rent-controlled. That's why I can't make any money out of it either. It's why I can't afford to do many repairs. But this is a good building, by comparison. Some of the buildings around here are falling apart. You know that." Mr. Bonati waved his hand toward the north-west. "Do you remember that building a few blocks away which burned down eighteen months ago?" That had been a huge fire, and Juan remembered it well. "The owner of that place couldn't make a thing out of it. So he stripped out most of the wiring and after the building burned down, he collected the insurance. Do you understand what I'm telling you?"

"You mean he burned it down?" Juan had heard a rumor.

"I didn't say that. Okay?" Bonati gave him a quick, hard look. "It's like that all over El Barrio, all over Harlem. There used to be decent neighborhoods up here. Germans, Italians, Irish. But now it's all changed. The place is falling apart, and nobody cares. The kids up here live in terrible housing, they don't have jobs or education. They haven't a hope, and they know it. It's the same in Chicago and other big cities. I'm telling you, the whole of Harlem is a ticking time bomb."

A few days later, some men came to fix the drain. But Bonati never did anything else. So Juan made inquiries about getting his mother a better place to live in one of the housing projects, but got nowhere.

"Don't you know, kid?" the man at the corner store said. "The housing projects favor whites and blacks, but Puerto Ricans, they don't want to know about. In some areas, they just want to push the Puerto Ricans out."

He went to some of the white welfare organizations, and found the people there treated him with ill-concealed contempt. He wasn't surprised, but he nonetheless felt rage, not just for himself and his mother, but that Puerto Ricans in general should be treated like this. And now he began to understand that his mother's vision was not only that he, her son, should escape from poverty and make a good life for himself in the world, but that he should accomplish something larger than that. When she spoke of Baroso, she didn't just mean a man of respect, but one who had done something big and important to help his people. And he loved her for this greater, nobler ambition all the more.

After she died, Juan, who had grown into a slim and decidedly good-looking young man, returned to college. He graduated with honors, and wished that his mother could have been there to see it. And from that day, he had set out on the long and arduous path that destiny, it seemed, had chosen for him.

···

Gorham Master found the tiny restaurant Juan had chosen without difficulty. He arrived there first, and sat down at a little table for four, taking a seat with his back to the wall. A good-looking redhead arrived just moments after him, and was put at the next table. She also sat against the wall, as she waited for her date.

Apart from the fact that Gorham always enjoyed seeing Juan, he was curious to see the new girlfriend his friend was bringing. Five minutes later, they arrived.

Juan was looking well. He'd grown a pencil-thin mustache since they'd last met. It gave his clever, handsome face a somewhat military look. He greeted Gorham with a big grin, and introduced his girlfriend.

Janet Lorayn, Gorham noted with admiration, was drop-dead gorgeous. She looked, and moved, like a younger version of Tina Turner. Giving Gorham a warm smile, she sat down opposite him, with Juan on her left. The tables were so small and close together that Juan was almost looking into the face of the redhead at the next table.

They exchanged a few words of greeting. Gorham complimented Juan on his mustache, and Juan said that Janet thought it made him look like a pirate. "She says she likes pirates," he added.

The waitress came and they ordered a bottle of white wine. Gorham glanced outside; the sky was darkening as it began to fill with clouds. After they had poured their wine and the waitress had told them the two choices, Janet turned her attention on Gorham.

"So you're a banker?" she said.

"That's right. And you?"

"I work in a literary agency at the moment. It's interesting."

"She just sold the serial rights of a new novel today," Juan informed him proudly.

"Congratulations—we'll drink to that. My father wrote a novel once."

"I heard," said Janet. "*Verrazano Narrows*. That was a big deal."

Juan had observed the redhead at the next table. She couldn't fail to hear their conversation, but was politely ignoring them, and glancing toward the door from time to time. At the mention of the famous book, however, she did steal a quick glance toward Gorham, out of curiosity.

"Janet's wondering whether to try to get into the television business, however," said Juan. "She has a friend who works in production in NBC."

It was one of the things Gorham loved about the city that, just as in his father's young days when the great men of letters sat at the Algonquin Round Table, the big publishing houses were still here, and the mighty *New York Times*, and leading magazines, from *Time* to the *New Yorker*. The great television networks had joined them too—all gathered within walking distance of each other in Manhattan's Midtown. But it seemed Janet didn't want to talk about her future in television just now.

"What I want to know," she said, "is how you two met."

"At Columbia Business School," Gorham told her. "That was the great thing about the MBA course. You had all kinds of people, from conventional banking types like me to really unusual guys like Juan. Plenty of the people I knew in the MBA program went into not-for-profit organizations, careers in charity, hospital administration, you name it."

Gorham had been very impressed with Juan and so had the admissions office at Columbia. By that time, Juan had already worked for Father Gigante, the priest and community leader who was helping the poor up in the South Bronx, and he'd spent another year in the South Bronx with the Multi-Service Center in Hunts Point. Before trying to use his experience in El Barrio, he'd been told he ought to try for an MBA program, to which he'd not only been accepted, but got grants to pay for everything.

"I'm sure Columbia reckoned that, with his background, Juan could become a leader in New York," Gorham said. Then he grinned. "Of course, I have even higher ambitions for him."

"Tell me," said Janet.

"First he'll revitalize El Barrio, and he'll have to get into politics to do that. Then he'll become mayor of New York—another La Guardia. Then he'll run for president. By that time I'll be a big-time banker and I'll raise funds for him, and then when he's president, Juan will reward me by sending me somewhere really nice as an ambassador."

"Sounds great," said Janet, with a laugh. "Where do you plan to go?"

"Maybe London, or Paris. I will accept either."

"London," said Juan firmly. He turned to Janet. "His French is terrible."

"I'm impressed, Gorham," said Janet. "You have your whole life worked out."

"It all depends on Juan, though."

"Did Juan ever take you round Harlem?"

"I took him round El Barrio several times," Juan said. "He asked me to. And it's not all bad in El Barrio—he got to like our music, and our food, didn't you, Gorham?"

"I did."

"Of course," Juan continued, with a twinkle in his eye, "if you want to see something really impressive, you have to see Gorham's apartment. He owns this big place, you know, on Park Avenue."

But though he said this to Janet, it was the redhead at the next table that he was watching out of the corner of his eye. And sure enough, as he had planned, she turned to look at Gorham again.

Outside, there was a rumble of thunder. Rain started to fall. Juan glanced at the door. There was a young couple there, hoping to get in, but all the tables were now occupied. He saw his chance, and leaned across to the redhead.

"Excuse me, but are you waiting for someone?"

"Yes," said the redhead tersely. And then, so as not to seem rude, she added: "My brother."

"Do you think he'll show up?"

Juan had such a charming way of being intrusive, that people usually forgave him.

"Maybe." She glanced at her watch. "Maybe not."

"I was just thinking," said Juan politely, "that if you came to our table, those poor people at the door could get in out of the rain."

The redhead stared at him coldly for a moment, glanced at the couple at the door, and then relented.

"And if my brother turns up?"

"I think," Juan smiled, "we could fit him on the end of our table."

The redhead shook her head with a wry amusement. "Okay," she conceded, "I'm Maggie O'Donnell." They introduced themselves. "I guess I already know what you all do, but I'm a lawyer."

The meal passed very pleasantly. They learned that Maggie worked for Branch & Cabell, and Gorham said: "That means you're going back to work after this, am I right?" And Maggie admitted that she was.

It wasn't long before Gorham decided that this B & C lawyer was rather attractive, and he tried to find out more about her. He managed to discover that she'd been to a meeting of the Historical Landmarks Commission at lunchtime, and that she was passionate about protecting the city's classic architecture, like Grand Central, from the relentless advance of the glass-box skyscrapers. His father would have approved of that—a point in her favor. But though Maggie was perfectly friendly, Gorham noticed that she had the lawyer's trick of evading questions she didn't want to answer.

Gorham wanted to know more about what Juan had been doing recently, so Juan told them how he'd been working with nearby Mount Sinai Hospital to provide health care in El Barrio, and how he was trying to improve the terrible housing there. He'd been working with some of the radical Puerto Rican activists in El Barrio as well, getting them to back these projects too.

Gorham was impressed. "That's good work, Juan," he said. "The link with Mount Sinai is brilliant." Maggie also listened intently, but the young lawyer seemed puzzled.

"How do you work with the radicals?" she asked. "From what I hear, some of these people are pretty dangerous."

Juan sighed. He knew what was troubling her. Back at the end of the sixties some of the younger Puerto Ricans had formed a group, called themselves the Young Lords, and demanded better conditions in El Barrio. For a while they'd made common cause with the Black Panthers of Chicago, for which they'd been reviled in the press. It was hardly surprising that a nice, white, middle-class lawyer like Maggie would find such people frightening.

"You have to understand, Maggie," he said, "that I was lucky. I got an education, and I was out of the gangs. Otherwise I might easily have been in prison by now, like my cousin Carlos. Illegal activities are natural in some communities." Maggie frowned—the lawyer in her didn't like that—but he pressed on. "Look, the problems of Harlem and the South Bronx are the same as those of other American cities. New York, Chicago, wherever: it's the same thing. You have poor populations who've suffered years of massive neglect, who have few if any chances of getting out of the mean streets where they live, and who believe, often rightly, that no one cares about them. When Puerto Ricans in El Barrio called themselves the Young Lords and organized free breakfasts and health clinics, that wasn't such a bad idea. They were demanding help for their people. So, in their way, were the Black Panthers in Chicago. When Puerto Ricans talked about self-determination, that wasn't so unreasonable either. Nobody else seemed to care about them.

"Some of them, in their rage, advocated violent demonstrations. I'm against that. And it's perfectly true there was an accompanying political philosophy. They claimed to be socialists or even communists—whatever that actually meant. Hoover and his FBI made a big deal of the communist thing. I'm certainly not a socialist, but I find their feelings understandable. When a society turns its back on one community, then people in that community may quite reasonably believe that life might be better under another system—it's human nature. So I try to alleviate the causes of that mistaken belief. Some people have worked hard to discredit the Young Lords and the Black Panthers, and they have largely succeeded, but the underlying problems that caused these groups to protest remain unsolved. If Harlem is still seething, it's for a reason, I promise you."

Juan realized he'd become a little heated, but he couldn't help it. He watched the redhead to see her reaction. He'd thought she might make a nice date for Gorham, but if she reacted badly to what he'd said, maybe he'd made the wrong choice.

"Interesting," she said.

Gorham laughed. "Typical lawyer," he said.

The conversation turned to people's childhoods after that. Janet had been brought up in Queens. "Black Catholic. My mom was very strict." Gorham described visits to his grandmother. Once or twice the conversation was interrupted by great crashes of thunder and lightning as the storm moved from south to north up Manhattan. Gorham learned that Maggie's grandfather had been brought up in a big house on lower Fifth Avenue. "Old Sean O'Donnell had money. He made it in the last century." She smiled. "We don't have it now."

"Lost in the crash and the Depression?" Gorham asked.

"Maybe some of it was. But I think we were just a big Irish family. Lots of children, for another three generations. It soon gets watered down. My father's worked all his life, and he still has a mortgage. What can I say?"

Once or twice toward the end of the meal, Maggie had discreetly glanced at her watch, obviously thinking about getting back to work. But the rain was falling so heavily that the chances of finding a taxi didn't look good. As they were having dessert, however, the storm withdrew to the north. The thunder could still be heard rolling up the Hudson, but the rain had slackened off. It was nearly nine thirty.

"Well," said Maggie, "this has been really nice, but I'll have to be getting back to work soon." A huge flash of lightning in the distance seemed to confirm the urgency of her mission.

"Won't you have coffee first?" said Gorham. "It'll help you work."

"Good idea," said Maggie.

And then all the lights went out.

It wasn't just in the little restaurant. The entire area abruptly went dark. There was a silence, followed by laughter. There were candles in little glass jars lighting the tables; after a few moments, the owner appeared from the kitchen and started lighting more. The coffee was already made, she told them, so they could have that, anyway.

"I expect it'll be over in a little while," said Gorham. "Con Ed has massive backup capacity."

"Or maybe it'll be like '65 again," said Juan. "A population explosion." It was a statistical fact that, nine months after the last big blackout, back in 1965, there had been a short, sharp increase in the local birth rate. Gorham turned to Maggie.

"I'm afraid you may have difficulty getting to work now."

"I'll find a taxi. It's not raining any more."

"But there's no light."

"Maybe the office has a backup generator."

"And if not?"

"I'll get some candles."

"What floor is your office on?"

"The thirty-second."

"You're going to walk up thirty-two floors?" Gorham asked. Maggie seemed to hesitate. "I guess this is how firms like Branch & Cabell test the commitment of their associates."

"Very funny," she said drily.

They drank their coffee. People passing in the street told them that every light in the city was out. Fifteen minutes went by and then Juan and Janet said they thought they'd be getting back. After Gorham and Juan had insisted they split the check between them, and Maggie had thanked Gorham, they all came out onto the sidewalk, and Juan and Janet turned northward.

"So," Gorham said, "are you really going to your office?"

Maggie stared south at the total blackness of Midtown. "I need to. But I guess not."

"Suggestion. We walk down Park toward my apartment, which is in the Seventies. If the lights come on, you can proceed. If not, I will give you a drink and then walk you safely home. Is that a good deal?"

"You are suggesting I enter a darkened building with a man I hardly know?"

"A Park Avenue co-op. One of the best."

"When has that ever protected a lady?"

"Never, as far as I know."

"Just a drink. You have candles? I'm not sitting in the dark."

"You have my word."

"What floor? The elevator won't be working."

"Third."

Twenty minutes later, she started laughing. "You said you were on the third floor."

"No I didn't, I said fifth. We're almost there. Look." He pointed the flashlight the doorman had given him. "Just ahead."

When they got into the apartment, he put her in the living room and returned a few moments later with a pair of handsome silver candlesticks. Placing these on a table and lighting them, he then went to the closet near the dining room and pulled out every one of the large number of silver candlesticks that Charlie had inherited from his mother. Soon the hall, kitchen, living room and dining room were filled with bright candlelight. Maggie sat on the sofa watching him.

"Nice apartment."

"Thank you. I inherited it. What would you like to drink?"

"Red wine." In the candlelight, Maggie's red hair took on a magical glow. Her face looked softer. Her manner seemed to relax a little, too. "Maybe you could whip up a little soufflé."

"I'm a terrible cook."

She got up and had a look around while he got the wine. Then she sat down, cradling the wine glass thoughtfully.

"So," she said with a smile, "this is your technique, is it? You invite the girl round for a drink, so she can see the beautiful apartment. Then you take her out for dinner telling her that you're too helpless to cook. By this time, she has decided that you and your apartment need her tender loving care."

"Absolutely inaccurate. If true, I'd be married by now."

"Poor defense."

They talked very easily. He told her how he'd always planned to live in the city since he was a little boy, and asked her why she had come there.

"Actually, it was my brother. He lives down in the Village, and one Sunday he took me out, and we walked into Soho. This was early in '73, when the World Trade Center towers had recently been completed. It was an overcast morning, but the sun was trying to break through the clouds. And there was this great, gray tower in the sky below Soho, kind of grainy, and as the sunlight caught it, the tower seemed to change its texture. It was one of the most magical moments in my life. That's when I decided I had to come to New York."

"I thought you didn't like that kind of architecture. The international style."

"I usually don't. But the towers are different somehow. It's the surface I guess, the play of the light."

"Is your brother married?"

"No. Actually, he's gay." She paused. "My parents don't know."

"That must be difficult. When did you find out?"

"Eight years ago. Martin and I are very close, and he told me. That was 1969, the year of the Stonewall riots after the police raided that gay bar in the Village. I was still at school."

"Isn't it time he told your parents?"

"Yes, but it won't be easy. It's going to be a big shock to Dad, because Martin's the only son, and Dad's relying on him to carry on the family name. Martin has to tell them sooner or later, but I'd better be around when he does. Everybody's going to need me. Especially Martin." She smiled. "I'm always there for my brother."

Gorham nodded. There was more to this attractive lawyer than he'd guessed.

"The family's a powerful thing. I feel this huge responsibility to restore my family to what it used to be, but I have to admit that I chose it. My father never did. Do you have anything like that?"

"I don't feel a duty to the past, but I do feel a duty toward myself. My mother was always very strong about that. She was forever telling me I could be anything I want, and that I should have a career. Get married, she said, but never be dependent on a husband. She's a schoolteacher."

"Has there been friction between her and your father?"

"No, they're devoted to each other. It's just what she believes in."

"I know quite a few women lawyers who did really well, but then stopped working when they had children."

"Not this girl."

"You think you can have it all?"

"Do it all, have it all. Sure. It's an article of faith."

"It may not be easy."

"Good organization will be critical—I'm a great organizer. But I'm afraid I'd be a terrible corporate wife."

"You'd better marry a lawyer, then. Someone who understands what you have to do."

She shook her head. "No way."

"Why?"

"Competition. There's always going to be competition in any profession. Somebody's going to win and somebody's going to lose. Put that in a marriage and I think it would be too difficult."

"You don't intend to lose?"

"Do you?"

"I guess not," said Gorham. "So what's your plan?"

"No plan. Just hope I meet Mr. Right. Someone who thinks life's an adventure. Someone who wants to keep on growing—professionally and personally."

Gorham considered a while. This lawyer was quite a challenge.

"What did you think of my friend Juan? You seemed to be noncommittal after he gave the big speech about the Young Lords and the Panthers."

"No, I was just thinking about what he said. I thought he was quite admirable actually."

Gorham nodded. He'd met plenty of women in New York who wanted successful careers. But in Maggie he sensed not only intelligence and determination, but a warmth that he found attractive. Behind her lawyer's caution, he realized, there was also a free spirit.

They were just sitting quietly when the telephone rang.

"Hi, Gorham." It was Juan. "Have you seen what's going on?"

"How do you mean?"

"I guess it's quiet down there on Park."

"Pretty much."

"Well, stay indoors, buddy. I discovered what happened, by the way. Lightning strikes destroyed some of the power grid—they have lights in New Jersey, but almost the entire five boroughs are down. Things are heating up in El Barrio, and if the lights don't come on soon, there's going to be a lot of action in Harlem tonight. I already saw one store broken into just up the street."

"You mean there's looting?"

"Of course there's looting. The stores are full of things people want, and nobody can see what's going on." His voice sounded almost cheerful about it. "Gorham, if you had a bunch of kids and no money, you'd be looting too. Anyway, I just wanted to tell you to stay indoors. This could spread downtown as well, the way things are looking."

"What are you going to do?"

"Well, I may go out and take a look. But this is home territory for me, if you know what I mean."

"Stay out of harm's way, Juan."

"Don't worry, Gorham, I will."

Gorham hung up, and told Maggie what Juan had said.

"Maybe you'd better stay here," he said. "There's a spare bedroom."

She gave him a cynical look. "Nice try."

In normal circumstances, he supposed he might have made some careful moves to see which way the evening would go. He was starting to get really interested in Maggie, but now wasn't the time.

"No," he said quietly, "much as I like your company, Maggie, I wasn't trying to make a move. What I am going to do, though, is take you safely to your door in a little while. If Juan thinks it could get rough out there, I'm not taking any chances."

"Okay. That's nice of you."

They talked for a short while after that. He asked if he could give her a call, and she said yes, and gave him her number. Then he said he'd take her home. Before doing so he gave Juan a call to find out the latest, but there was no reply.

There weren't any taxis on Park, so they started to walk up to Eighty-sixth. Everything was dark, and quiet, but staring up the wide avenue, they could see faint glows that suggested fires. They walked together without speaking, but when they got to Eighty-fourth, Maggie broke the silence.

"Something on your mind?"

"It's nothing. Kind of stupid."

"Let me guess. You were worried when Juan didn't pick up."

He turned to her in the darkness. He couldn't really see her face.

"Actually, I was. Which is absurd. He knows El Barrio like the back of his hand."

"Where does he live?"

"Right on Ninety-sixth and Lexington. It's actually a doorman building."

"After you leave me safe at Eighty-sixth, you're going to go up to his place, aren't you?"

"I was thinking of it, actually."

"So." She linked her arm in his. "Let's go up there together."

"You can't come."

"You can't stop me."

He looked at her in astonishment. "You are a strange woman, Miss O'Donnell."

"You better believe it."

When they got to the Ninety-sixth Street crossing, they had a view over a whole section of Spanish Harlem. The streets were quiet for the moment, but they could see several fires. They walked swiftly along to Juan's building. The doorman had shut the door, but after shining a flashlight to inspect them, he opened it, and Gorham explained his mission.

"Mr. Campos didn't go out again, sir, I can tell you that." Gorham expressed relief. "Did you come here to visit him once before?" the doorman asked. Gorham replied that he had. "Well"— the doorman evidently decided that Gorham and Maggie looked respectable—"some of the tenants went up on the roof. He may be up there. The intercom isn't working, but I can telephone his number if you have it, just in case he came back down."

This time Juan picked up. He was amazed to find that Gorham was at his building.

"I thought you might be hanging out with the pretty redhead."

"She's with me."

"You want to come up on the roof? There's a bunch of us up there, and we have beer. You'll have to walk up a dozen floors."

Gorham relayed the invitation to Maggie.

"We accept," she said.

There were quite a few people up on the roof. There was a good view over sections of Harlem; part of the skyline of Brooklyn, to the east, was also visible; and all over the area, fires had broken out.

The sound of fire engine sirens echoed across the night. After a while, from a few blocks up Lexington, there was a screech of tires followed by a resounding crash of glass, as if someone had driven a van through the windows of a store.

"That'll be the supermarket," said Juan calmly. Then, turning to Maggie, he added: "El Barrio. My people."

They sipped from cans of beer, and watched the fires spreading in the hot and humid night. After a time, over in Brooklyn, a huge fire started to develop. Half an hour passed, but it just kept spreading.

"It must stretch for twenty blocks," Gorham said.

"More, I think," said Juan.

And so, well into the early hours of the morning, they stayed on the roof, watching the great, divided city of New York express its tensions, its rage and its misery, by fire, and looting, and more fire.

Giving Birth

❈1987❈

GORHAM MASTER RACED around the apartment. He knew he shouldn't panic like this. In the bedroom, Maggie's bag was neatly packed, and had been for weeks. So why didn't he just grab it and run? Maggie was already on her way to the hospital, racing in a taxi through the November streets. She'd need him to be there with the bag, when she arrived.

Their first child. They'd waited a long time, and they'd both agreed that they should. Maggie had wanted to get more established in her career, and he'd wanted that for her too. And now at last the great day had come, and he was filled with panic.

Was Maggie ready for this? Was she going to be all right?

He'd thought she should stop work last week. But she'd assured him it was okay.

"Quite honestly, sweetie," she told him, "I'd rather have the work to distract me." He saw her point, of course. But had she gone too far? Now that the great moment had arrived, he was seized with fear. Should he have begged her not to go into work today? If, God forbid, something went wrong now, it would all be his fault.

She'd left the apartment at eight this morning. At eleven, in the middle of a meeting in one of the big, wood-paneled conference rooms in the ten floors of Branch & Cabell's Midtown offices, she had started to go into labor. She'd been very calm; he could just imagine it. She'd excused herself, called him to bring her bag, and gone down in the elevator to find a taxi to the hospital. It was uptown, but at this time of day, it shouldn't take her long. He needed to hurry.

"Bella," he called.

"Yes, Mr. Master." Bella was standing behind him already. Thank God for Bella. She always knew where everything was.

"Did I forget anything?"

Bella was a treasure. She came from Guatemala, and like so many of the domestics in New York, she had begun her career as an illegal immigrant, but her previous employers had managed to get her a green card. He and Maggie had employed her three years ago—after all, with two people working full-time, it was a lot easier if one had a housekeeper. When they had first engaged her, Gorham had been a little uncertain about the forms of address to be used nowadays, but Bella had solved that for them. She'd been working in a big Fifth Avenue apartment before and she sensed, quite correctly, that the people in the Park Avenue building expected everything to be formal. "Mr. and Mrs. Master," she called them, and they didn't argue.

But there was another tactic involved in employing Bella. In a little while, they'd planned to have children. Maggie wanted someone whom she could really trust already in place, as part of the family, before that happened. The understanding was that when they had a baby, she'd be the nanny too. Recently, though, Bella had been dropping hints about how much she had to do, and he could see the writing on the wall. Within a year, he reckoned, Bella's idea was that they'd be employing a nanny as well as a housekeeper. And this was not what they wanted to do. There might be a battle ahead there, he supposed.

"No, Mr. Master." Was there a hint in her tone that he was always looking for things? Maybe not. Anyway, she smiled. "Everything's going to be fine."

He told himself not to be foolish. Bella was right, of course. Maggie was in good condition. They'd seen the sonograms. The baby was fine. And it was a boy. Gorham Vandyck Master, Jr. The names had been Maggie's idea, not his, because she knew it would please him. She might not share his dynastic sense, but she was happy to go along with it. Well, it did please him. So if Maggie was okay with the idea, why fight it?

The baby was fine, and the doctor was fine as well. Caruso was a good doctor. Not everyone had the guts to go into obstetrics these days. If anything went wrong, everyone wanted to sue the obstetrician. The insurance premiums for obstetricians were so high that many medical students reckoned they just couldn't afford to get into the field. Caruso was only a few years older than he was, but Maggie had researched him and been impressed.

Dr. Caruso had turned out to be a nice man, as well. Gorham had happened to meet him one evening about six months ago, when the doctor was walking home. His surgery was only a few blocks down from them on Park Avenue, so they'd walked along together and had quite a chat. "I live over on the West Side," he'd told Gorham, "on West End Avenue. Unless the weather's bad, I walk to work and back across the park every day." He'd smiled. "Even doctors need to take exercise, you know."

"Were you brought up on the West Side?"

"Brooklyn. My father had a house in Park Slope. But I went to school here in the city." He named a private school that Gorham knew well.

"Great school. Did you enjoy it?"

"To tell you the truth, not really. The other boys mostly treated me like dirt."

"For living in Brooklyn?" It was true that the splendid brownstones of Park Slope had become rundown in the fifties, and most of the respectable folk had moved out. But in the sixties, a renewal had been under way. All kinds of people had moved into the area, many of them people who wanted to restore the houses for their own sake. The private-school kids probably didn't live there, but all the same . . . "I was brought up on Staten Island," Gorham said.

"Nice place. Brooklyn wasn't the problem, though."

"You were on scholarship? They were mean to you because you weren't rich? That's despicable."

"No—as a matter of fact, we weren't short of money at all. My father began his life as a bricklayer, and my mother's family ran a delicatessen. But then my father received a legacy from his uncle and became a developer. Small-time stuff—he bought up Brooklyn houses, restored them and sold them—but he did pretty well." Dr. Caruso paused. "No, the problem was nothing subtle. It was because I was Italian. Simple as that. Italian name. Dirt." He shrugged. "Now I'm their obstetrician."

"I hope you charge them top dollar," said Gorham drily.

"I live well. Actually, my son just started at private school, and he has no trouble at all."

Ethnic was fashionable nowadays, Gorham thought, and he was glad of it. He'd heard of Jewish families, for instance, people who'd anglicized their East European names a generation ago, recently deciding to return to the original ones. Attitudes were changing. His own blue-blood name only gave him pleasure because it was honestly derived, from historical roots. At least, that's what he told himself. "My view of ancestry is strictly postmodern," he liked to pronounce at dinner parties. "A harmless ornament, to be shared with one's friends." That was pretty good, he thought.

And was Caruso any relation of the famous tenor? he'd asked. The obstetrician's intelligent face was not unlike pictures of the great singer.

"Who knows?" said Dr. Caruso. "Way back, perhaps. My family knew him—they were very proud of that—and he always told them we were related." He smiled. "Caruso was a man of great kindness, you understand."

Gorham Master was glad that Dr. Caruso would be delivering his son.

✛

He grabbed Maggie's bag, told Bella to stay in the apartment in case they had to call her for anything, and took the elevator down to the lobby. The doorman hailed a taxi.

It wasn't a long journey. Across to Madison, then straight up to 101st, over to Fifth Avenue and you were at Mount Sinai Hospital. Dr. Caruso would meet them there.

The taxi driver went three blocks up Park before turning left. Only a block to Madison. Then he stopped.

"Is there a problem?"

"Yes. Problem." A heavy Russian accent. "Truck. He don't move."

"I have to get to the hospital." Maggie was probably already there now.

"Vot can I do if he don't move?"

Nothing. Should he get out and pick up a cab on Madison? If he did that, the minute he got to Madison, the blockage would clear. Then the Russian would go by and wouldn't stop if he hailed it again. Then there wouldn't be any more taxis on Madison. Such things had happened to him before. Gorham Master swore quietly to himself and closed his eyes. Patience. Clear his mind. Keep calm.

And try not to think of the other business. The business he hadn't told Maggie about.

❖

On the whole, during the last ten years, his life had still gone according to plan. He'd made VP years ago, and the bank seemed to think well of him. He'd shown a real talent for client relations, and he'd been shrewd in picking his corporate mentors. Several years he'd been awarded six-figure bonuses on top of his salary. This spring, he'd been made a senior vice president. That was important. But even more important was something else he'd been offered shortly afterward.

Stock options: the chance to buy bank stock at advantageous prices. Golden handcuffs, as they were known—for they were structured so that, to get the real benefit of the options, one needed to stay at the bank. A VP might get a promotion and a higher salary, but the only way to tell whether the bank really valued him was to follow the money. If the bank really wanted to keep him, it gave him stock options.

The city seemed to be prospering too. In 1977, just after the terrible arson and looting of the blackout, the new, feisty Mayor Koch was elected. The first thing he'd set out to do was restore the city's disastrous finances. And he'd been remarkably successful. In a few years, the city budget was even out of the red. In '81, Koch had actually been nominated by both the Democratic and Republican parties—such a thing had never happened before. "How am I doing?" the mayor would call out whenever he saw a crowd, and most of the time they told him he was doing pretty well.

And Gorham had married Maggie.

Their courtship had been typical of those where at least one of the partners is working a ninety-hour week. That certainly hadn't been in the original plan.

Sometimes Gorham Master wondered, did the big law firms and investment banks overdo it a bit with the hours? It showed the young associates were serious and committed, of course, but was there an element of sadistic pride in it, like pledging for a fraternity? But unlike the frat pledges, this went on for years, until one made partner.

Maggie did corporate work. Often, when she had big deals going through, he'd gone down to her offices at maybe nine or ten at night, taken her out for a quick dinner, then let her get back to work until two or three in the morning. Both their courtship and the first years of their marriage had been like that. Romance snatched at odd moments, leisure organized in little compartments of time. In a way it was exciting.

Wartime affairs and marriages, Gorham realized, must have been like this. But peace was a long time coming.

They had been having an affair for a year before he proposed to her. By that time he was completely crazy about her. If she wasn't a corporate wife, he didn't care. And she, for her part, not only loved him, but would sometimes say in wonderment: "I just can't believe that you put up with the terrible hours I have to keep." His fascination and her gratitude, Gorham reckoned, made a good cement in the building of their marriage.

"If you want to have it all, Maggie," he'd cheerfully remind her, "just remember that having it all includes me."

The marriage was at her parents' Catholic church in Norwalk, Connecticut. Her parents thought Gorham was perfect. They didn't even mind that he wasn't Catholic. As for Maggie, she didn't tell the priest, but she'd already assured Gorham that their children could attend any church he liked, or none.

Juan was best man—he'd married Janet by then—and Maggie's brother Martin was one of the ushers. Martin was a pleasant, rather intellectual fellow, and he and Gorham got along fine. At the end of the wedding, Maggie's father had quietly suggested to Martin that if he had no plans for ever marrying, perhaps he'd like to tell him about it some time.

The pattern of their lives changed only a little as they entered the 1980s. If Gorham needed Maggie to attend a business dinner with him in the city, she'd make great efforts to do so. Once, when Branch & Cabell hosted a weekend at a resort for all the partners, associates and their spouses, Gorham was amused, during the lawyers' business sessions, to be taken around and entertained with all the spouses. "I like being a spouse," he told Maggie with a grin. "I had twenty wives all to myself."

The only other necessary defining of their positions in the early eighties had been the newly popular social acronyms.

"I have always been a WASP," Gorham rightly declared. "And I guess I may be called a preppy. But Maggie is definitely a yuppie."

Even this changed in 1986, however, when Maggie was made a partner. "And a partner of Branch & Cabell," she insisted, "can no longer be called a yuppie."

"Not even a pretty young red-headed partner?"

"Nope. But I'll tell you something else about a partner in Branch & Cabell."

"What's that?"

"A partner in Branch & Cabell," she informed him with a smile, "might get pregnant."

Her pregnancy the next year had raised another issue.

They were happy in the apartment on Park. When they married, Maggie had done a little redecoration, and they'd had fun buying some new furniture together. The third year of their marriage, after he'd been awarded a handsome bonus, his Christmas present to her had been the money to install a new kitchen. That had been a big deal.

Maggie had made one other small improvement to the apartment. She'd opened a closet one day and found in there a carefully wrapped parcel that looked like a picture of some kind. Asked what it was, Gorham had confessed to his shame that it was the only gift he'd failed to deliver for Charlie, after his father's death. "And so much time has passed now that I'm embarrassed to give it to the rightful owner," he said.

"Can I see what it is?" she'd asked.

"I suppose so."

"My God, Gorham," Maggie exclaimed when she'd unwrapped the parcel, "it's a Robert Motherwell drawing. This thing is really valuable."

"I hardly know what to do about it," he admitted.

"Well, I'm putting it on the wall until you make up your mind." And there, adding a special elegance to their living room, it had remained ever since.

Now they were starting a family, however, they'd have to consider moving to a larger place. They could manage in the six-room with one child, who would have the second bedroom, but if another child came along, then they'd really need more space. They liked the building, so they decided to wait for a while to see if a larger apartment became available. With their two salaries, they could certainly finance a mortgage and the higher maintenance.

Taken all together, therefore, Gorham and Maggie had a very happy marriage. Only one thing had suffered, and they both felt it. Their friends. How long was it now since they'd had Maggie's brother come to supper? Three months at least. It was nobody's fault, there just never seemed to be any time. And what about Juan? They hadn't seen him for more than a year.

What made it worse was that Juan was having a bad time. Mayor Koch had done well by the city below Ninety-sixth Street, but not so well for the districts like Harlem, El Barrio and the South Bronx. Some people reckoned he didn't care that much. Others pointed out that, when the problems were so huge, even Koch couldn't do everything at once. Either way, Juan had been able to make very little progress. "Things in El Barrio are getting steadily worse, not better," he'd told them. He was so discouraged that he was thinking of taking a job in one of the big utilities, where at least he could use his business skills.

As soon as the baby was born, Gorham promised himself, he'd make it an occasion to call Juan and have him and Janet to supper.

Despite these regrets, which could certainly be remedied, Gorham should have counted himself a very fortunate man. And he would have, had it not been for one problem: good fortune wasn't enough.

It wasn't surprising. When one thought about it, Gorham considered, New York had always been a place for people who wanted more. Whether a poor immigrant or a rich merchant, people came to New York to get more. In bad times they came there to survive, in good times to prosper, and in boom times to get rich. Very rich. Fast.

And as the eighties progressed, New York had been booming.

It was the stock market that was booming. The market and all the service industries, including the law firms, that went with it. In '84, the market had experienced its first million share trading day. Traders, brokers, anyone dealing in shares or bonds had the opportunity to make a fortune. It was all beautifully summarized in Tom Wolfe's *Bonfire of the Vanities*, which had just hit the best-seller lists as Maggie's pregnancy began.

Greed was everywhere. Greed was exciting. Successful greedy men were heroes. Greed was good.

But Gorham had to ask himself: Had he been greedy enough?

Sometimes, sitting in his office, he'd take out the silver Morgan dollar his grandmother had given him and stare at it sadly. Would the Masters in times past, the merchants and owners of privateers, and speculators in property and land, would they have sat quietly in a corporate office and taken a salary—all right, a salary with bonus and stock options—but would they have been so cautious when others were making rapid fortunes? He didn't think so. New York was booming and he was sitting idly by, trapped by his own caution and respectability.

Was everyone of his own, old-money class doomed to mediocrity? No, some, like Tom Wolfe himself, had kicked over the traces.

Gorham hadn't kicked over the traces exactly, but he had begun some quiet trading of his own, and he had done well. He'd borrowed to invest, of course—that was the only way to make money fast, and the risk was not so great in a rising market. In fact, by the time of Maggie's pregnancy, he'd built up an impressive portfolio.

He hadn't told Maggie. He reckoned he would when he had put by enough to really impress her—and that would take some doing for a lawyer used to dealing with clients who had very substantial assets indeed. But he was working on it. Concealing his activities from her was perfectly easy, because they filed separate tax returns.

It had been her idea, right at the start of the marriage. He didn't know what she made, and she didn't know what he made. They kept tally of their living expenses, which were split evenly between them, and that was all they needed to know. Until Maggie made partner, he'd assumed that he made more money than she did. Now that she was a partner, he wasn't quite sure. Not that it really mattered, of course. But with the stock options and the bonuses he always earned, he reckoned that, yes, he probably still made more—though partners in the big law firms did awfully well. But when he finally cleaned up in the markets, he had thought with secret satisfaction, that was when he'd let her know.

And everything would have been all right, until the disaster last month.

For in October, the market had crashed. Not a crash like the Great Crash, but a vicious correction. The brokerage houses were in deep pain, and people were being laid off in large numbers. It didn't affect someone like himself in a commercial bank, and certainly not the lawyers, who always had work adjudicating every disaster. But his private holdings had suffered horribly. Two days ago he'd gone through what was left of his portfolio after he'd dealt with all the calls, and found that he was precisely back to where he'd started several years ago. So much for his performance. It was just as well they weren't looking to trade up to a larger apartment this year.

He hadn't told Maggie. No need to disturb her with such news when she was about to give birth. Not much point in telling her about it afterward, either. That was what every good trader did, he told himself. Cut your losses. Keep quiet, and move swiftly forward.

It was three days ago that the offer had suddenly been made. A telephone call from a banker he knew slightly. A discreet meeting, followed by further meetings with partners of the investment house in question. Then a tentative offer. Something for him to think about.

He'd been asked if he'd like to cross over into investment banking. It was a compliment, of course. The partners at the investment bank thought he had both the skills and the client relationships to be very useful to them, and having discussed the matter in some detail, he could see the force of their argument. The fit looked good, and he quite liked the people he'd be working with.

And as always in an investment bank, there would be excitement, the opportunity for creative initiatives of his own, the chance to make a lot of money. And considerably longer hours.

It could be that this was a big chance for him. Just the sort of thing, he supposed, that the Masters in the past would have gone for. The downside was that he'd lose a bunch of stock options, and probably see less of his little family than he'd been planning.

Was it the right thing to do? Did he have the confidence? Was he ready, after taking a beating in the market, to give up his security?

He didn't know. He wanted to discuss it with Maggie. But it wasn't exactly the subject to raise with your wife when she was in the middle of giving birth.

+++

They were moving. The truck driver had finished delivering, the Russian had sworn at him, the truck driver had sworn back and, with the Russian mumbling furiously to himself, they had raced up Madison. The lights were synchronized on Madison, thank God, instead of stopping you every eight or ten blocks, the way they did on Park. In minutes, they were at Mount Sinai, and he was racing in through the entrance to look for Maggie.

She had already been taken up to the fifth floor. When he got there, the first person he saw was Dr. Caruso.

"All is well," Caruso told him reassuringly. "I had her taken straight up—she's actually dilating pretty fast."

"She shouldn't have gone into the office, should she?"

The doctor shrugged. "You know your wife. Though unless there's a problem, active women often have babies with greater ease." He grinned. "I might have preferred a less hurried schedule than this."

"At least you didn't have to deliver the baby in the Branch & Cabell conference room. Be grateful for that."

"True. So, Maggie says you're coming into the delivery room."

"I have to."

"It's not obligatory."

"No, actually, I have to." Gorham smiled. "I'll explain later."

"We'll need to get you suited up then," said Caruso. "The nurse will give you the scrubs, and if you're wearing a watch, take it off. In the meantime, her room's just over there, second door."

As he looked at Maggie, a great wave of affection passed over him.

"Hi. I brought the bag. Are you okay?"

"I'm fine," Maggie said brightly. "No problem."

She was a little bit scared. But only he would have known it.

"Bit of an interruption to your meeting," he joked. "You couldn't ask the baby to reschedule?"

"I guess not." She smiled. "Obstinate like his mother."

"Did you call your mom and dad?" Her parents had retired to Florida recently.

"Yes. I promised to call again, afterward. And you?"

Gorham's mother lived in Florida too.

"I didn't have time yet."

A nurse appeared with pale blue scrubs. Gorham put them on. He wondered what to do with his watch. He didn't want to leave it in the room, he'd rather keep it with him. The scrubs had a pocket, so he put the watch in there.

Dr. Caruso came back and examined the patient. A big smile.

"Well, well. You don't waste any time. I'll return shortly."

Gorham went to Maggie's side and took her hand.

"All right?"

Maggie had refused an epidural. Typical Maggie. She was going to do it all herself, without help, in her own way.

"Okay," said Gorham. He went to the foot of the bed and looked at her severely. "I guess it's time you learned how to breathe."

❖

The first breathing lesson had taken place three months ago. Husbands and wives were supposed to go together, so that they could learn to practice as a team. It was all part of being a modern husband and father, and he was fine with that. They'd gathered in a little conference room at the hospital. He and another father got there first. The nurse who was giving the class arrived a couple of minutes afterward. Then they waited.

After five minutes, the nurse asked where their wives were. After ten she started to get cross. The other man, a small, balding guy of about his own age, sighed and looked at him.

"What's your wife do?"

"Lawyer. And you?"

"Mine's an investment banker."

They'd both turned to the nurse.

"We'd better start without them," they said.

Now that Maggie had made partner, the pressure wasn't quite so bad. But if anyone thought she was going to break off an important meeting to go to a breathing class . . .

And she hadn't. Not to the first, nor the second. The third time, she did turn up. The nurse hadn't been too happy, but Gorham didn't mind—he was getting pretty good at breathing by now.

"Okay," said the nurse, looking bleakly at Maggie. "The key is to get a rhythm going that helps you to relax. You're going to learn to breathe in, on RE . . . count one . . . two . . . three . . . four . . . and LAX . . . RE . . . one . . . two . . . three . . . LAX. As the contractions get a little closer, we may want to speed it up a bit. So, just follow your husband now while he gives you the time. And RE . . . one . . . two . . ."

The duty nurse's head appeared round the door. "There's a call for a Ms. O'Donnell," she said.

"Would you please tell them she'll call back later?" said the nurse.

"I'm afraid," said Maggie, "I'll have to take that." She started toward the door.

"Would you please sit down?" The nurse's voice was rising in anger.

"Sorry," said Maggie as she reached the door.

"This is your baby," screamed the nurse.

Maggie turned, glanced lovingly at Gorham, and gave the nurse a brilliant smile.

"Don't worry," she said. "We're a great team. He'll breathe, and I'll have the baby."

⁂

"Breathe . . . two . . . three . . . Push," said Gorham and the doctor. "Breathe . . . two . . . three . . . Push."

"Push now . . ." said the doctor. "Good girl . . . that's it . . . almost there . . . push . . . hard as you can . . ."

"Aagh," screamed Maggie.

Dr. Caruso wasn't talking now. He was busy. He was pulling the baby out.

"One more time," he called. Maggie gave another scream . . .

Gorham stared. Dr. Caruso took a step back. The baby cried out. Caruso smiled.

"Congratulations. You have a son."

So that was it.

A few minutes later the doctor remarked to them both: "I see you both went to the breathing classes. Good job."

Gorham looked at Maggie, and Maggie looked at Gorham.

"Absolutely," said Maggie.

⁘

So everything was all right. After a while Maggie wanted to rest for a few hours, so Gorham decided to go back to the apartment. He took off the scrubs and the nurse told him to drop them into the chute that went down to the laundry. He got his things together, and prepared to leave. He was just about to walk off the floor with Dr. Caruso when he realized what he'd done.

"Shoot. I left my watch in the pocket of the scrubs. It's gone down into the laundry."

"I'm sorry to hear that," said Caruso. "Was it a Rolex?"

"Oh no. Nothing expensive. All the same . . ."

"You can tell the nurse, and she'll let the laundry know. They might find it."

"Do you think this happens quite often?"

"Probably."

"Do they ever find the watches?"

"I couldn't say. I believe the jobs down there are quite popular."

"Right."

"Look at it this way," said Caruso cheerfully. "You may have lost a watch, but you've gained a son."

⁘

When he got home, Gorham called Maggie's parents and his mother. Then he opened a bottle of champagne, and made Bella have a drink with him to toast the birth, and told her she should come with him when he went back to the hospital, so that she could see the baby. He wanted Bella to bond with the baby too.

But first there was some time to kill. He was too excited just to sit down and look at television. He certainly couldn't do any work. He started to pace about the apartment.

Maybe he'd call Juan. That would be good.

But he put it off for a moment, and continued to pace. He hardly wanted to think about the subject, but he couldn't help himself.

What the devil was he going to do about that offer from the investment bank?

Millennium

T HE CRISIS IN the life of Gorham Master developed so gradually that, as the years passed, he himself could not have said when the process first began. Probably it was when he'd refused the offer to join the investment house at the time of young Gorham Junior's birth. At the time it had seemed for the best, and Maggie had agreed with his decision, too.

Since then, the flow of his life had been even. The stock market crash of '87 had quite soon become a memory, albeit a painful one, as it subsided into its proper place as one more of the cycles of market boom and bust that had been repeating regularly now between London and New York for about three hundred years.

It had been succeeded, however, by another recession, this time in the New York real estate market, which had been rather beneficial to the Master family. For soon after his second son, Richard, was born, an eight-room apartment in the building became available. "And the asking price is only seventy percent of what I reckon it would have been two or three years ago," he told Maggie. The financial logic was impeccable: trade up in a down market. It was an estate sale, too, and the trustees of the estate were glad to sell to a qualified buyer who was already in the building, so that there were no problems with getting the co-op board approval, and no need even to pay commission to a realtor. Gorham and Maggie were able to negotiate a highly advantageous price. They sold their six-room apartment, took out a joint mortgage for the difference, and bought the eight. The following year, Gorham had stood for election to the co-op board, and served on it for several years.

Even the eight-room, however, was soon full. For after the two boys, they both still wanted a daughter, and in 1992, Emma arrived. The two boys had to share the second bedroom, therefore, while Emma had the third. With an eight, there were two maids' rooms off the kitchen, and by the time Emma arrived, Bella the housekeeper had been joined there by Megan the nanny, a jolly girl from Wisconsin who lived with them for several years until she was succeeded by her cousin Millie. With this pleasant Upper East Side household, any reasonable person should have been well content.

Yet it was then, for the first time in his life, that Gorham had started to dream of living outside New York.

Not that there was so much wrong with the city. Indeed, for many people, New York was becoming a better place to live than it had been for years. Mayor Koch had been succeeded by Mayor Dinkins who, as an African American, had been perceived as more sympathetic to the troubles of Harlem and the other deprived areas. But the city had retained its reputation for crime, especially muggings, until nearly halfway through the nineties, when hard-line Mayor Giuliani had taken over. Like Giuliani or not, his "zero tolerance" policy on crime seemed to have worked. One could walk the streets nowadays with little fear of trouble.

The city felt cleaner, too. Behind the New York Public Library, where once the Crystal Palace had stood, the little green of Bryant Park had become a dismal enclave where rats scurried through the vegetation, and dope dealers plied their trade. Now it was made into an area where people from the nearby offices could sit and have a cappuccino. Along Forty-second toward Times Square, the dreary movie houses that purveyed hardcore porn were swept away. Downtown, Soho and the area next to it, known as Tribeca now, were becoming fashionable enclaves for people who liked to live in lofts. True, this gentrification and yuppification of the city might take away some of its older character, but on the whole Gorham thought the changes an improvement.

No, his desire to leave the city, at first anyway, was simply a desire for more physical space.

For large and handsome though the apartment was, there were times when all the family yearned for a place where they could spread out a bit.

The boys would have liked their own rooms. July and August in New York City could never be anything but punishing. Many of the commercial bankers that Gorham knew lived in the suburbs. Two of his friends, both SVPs like himself, had splendid houses in New Canaan, with two or four acres around them, tennis court, swimming pool. They got up early to commute into the city, but they reckoned it was worth it.

"They don't have working wives," Maggie very reasonably pointed out. "I can't be a mother and commute as well." She smiled. "Not even if we could afford a car and driver. Anyway," she added, "the city schools are better."

In 1997, however, they had found a useful compromise. A country house. It was maybe a tad inconvenient that they should both have fallen in love with a little farmhouse up in North Salem. A mile or two further and they'd have been in Putnam County, where the prices and property taxes were lower, while North Salem was just inside Westchester County, and had unusually high property taxes to pay for the local school. But they adored the house, and there it was.

Gorham was pretty happy. They went up there most weekends, and the children loved it. In the summer, he and Maggie quite often commuted from the house several days a week. It took an hour and fifteen minutes door to door whether they drove or took the train down to Grand Central. He felt as if he'd opened a window in his life.

And, it had to be confessed, it fitted into his plan for his life. Other people might like to have summer houses, or rent them out on Long Island; there was the rich crowd in the Hamptons who paid big money to be there. But there were many people who preferred the quieter, more rural surroundings of the big corridor, from Bedford in the middle of Westchester, northward up the Hudson Valley into fashionable Dutchess County. People who liked horses especially. North Salem might not be deep country, but it was hardly suburban. There was a local hunt, and several estates running into hundreds of acres. Like Bedford, it was a place where rich people went, and this pleased Gorham, for he could feel that the Master family was where it ought to be.

But was he?

It was sometime in the mid-nineties when Gorham had realized the truth, that he wasn't going any further in the bank. It wasn't that he'd failed—his job was safe and he was still valued—but there was a group of people of the same age as he who had just done a little better. Maybe they were better politicians. Maybe they had been lucky. But he was never going to be the CEO, or even one of the tiny cadre who really ran the bank. He was going to be the nice guy just below that level.

There was another, even more disturbing thought. It was a time of amalgamation. Banks were getting bigger. Like some vast game of financial Pac-Man, one bank was swallowing another and, many people said, only the biggest would survive. Their huge monetary power and lowered costs would crush all opposition. So far his bank had neither bought, nor been acquired, but if and when that happened, two things were likely to follow, one good and one bad. The good part of it was that his bank stock and options would probably be worth a lot more money. He might come out of such a deal a quite considerably richer man, but not more than that. It was the cadre just above him that had the big stock options. He'd known ordinary bank executives who'd made fifty, a hundred million or more in these corporate games. By getting stuck where he was on the corporate ladder, however, he'd miss out on the big rewards. He might hope to make a very few million at best, if he was lucky, but not more.

The bad side, however, depressed him deeply. For as he considered all the other banks, and all the executives he knew, he became almost certain of one thing. In every likely contingency he could envision, it would be his opposite number in the other bank who would be asked to stay, and he who would be asked to leave.

With his good name intact, of course. These departures happened all the time. Plenty of men would take their money and retire quite happily, and live well for the rest of their lives. But he'd wanted more than that. He'd wanted the top, the big time. He'd wanted to be the man who was honored at important functions in the city, and who was asked onto boards. That had been the plan.

Instead of that, he was going to be the spouse of B & C partner Maggie O'Donnell, the nice guy who'd been a banker until he was eased out. And this while his kids were still in school. It hadn't happened yet, but the prospect haunted him.

Even this might not have been so bad, however, if it hadn't been for what was happening all around him.

New money. Nineties money. Seventies and eighties money hadn't been so bad. When entrepreneurs had developed the technologies that became Silicon Valley, there had been something heroic about their enterprise. Technology wizards had mortgaged their houses and started working out of their garages; daring venture capitalists had had the vision to back them. Companies had been created that, in time, threw off huge amounts of cash and changed the world. In the process, some of the entrepreneurs had become vastly rich, but they had taken on few of the old-fashioned trappings of wealth. They led exciting lives of real quality. They created charities in which they became personally involved. Wealth was not about status, but about new ideas.

But nineties money, it seemed to Gorham, was different. The dot.com boom was about using the new technology to provide all kinds of services, so that new companies could be invented with such speed that he couldn't keep track of them. Some, he reckoned, had a chance of success. But others appeared to Gorham to be based on concepts so flimsy that it reminded him of the story he'd once read about a prospectus, issued before London's great South Sea Bubble market crash of 1720, which had announced that a company was to be formed "for a purpose yet to be discovered." Yet these companies were being formed, their initial public offerings were being oversubscribed, and making their founders instantly rich, often before there was even a smell of profit.

"The way I see it," he'd said to Maggie, "the process is similar to what happened in the nineteenth century with the railroads. In those days, competing companies fought for control of the route along which people and freight was to be carried. Dot.com companies are racing to gain control of an information highway, to build up a huge network before any significant traffic actually flows along it." He shrugged. "People are investing in expectations."

But people were investing, and getting hugely rich. The NASDAQ exchange was booming. Kids in their twenties were walking away with tens, even hundreds of millions, and buying huge lofts down in Tribeca because they thought the old-money crowd on Park and Fifth were boring. Private equity men who arranged these IPOs were making similar amounts. Wall Street traders were getting huge bonuses and buying multimillion-dollar apartments for cash.

Was his family benefiting from this explosion of money? Maggie was doing well—lawyers always did. Her brother Martin was now living with a man who, having sold a small dot.com company, had bought an entire building in Soho for use as a private residence and art gallery, in addition to the beach house he owned out on Fire Island.

Gorham, however, had failed to join the party. As he looked back now, he regretted that decision not to join the investment house in '87. He should have taken the high road—God knows what he'd be worth now if he'd done that. Most days, in the office, surrounded by commercial bankers like himself, he was too busy to let it prey upon his mind. But sometimes there would be sudden ugly reminders.

Going to watch the ball game at his children's private school, for instance, one couldn't fail to notice the limousines outside the gym from which some of the fathers, the Wall Street big hitters, had just stepped. Not that anything was ever said, of course, but while he winced at the school fees, these were the guys giving the million-dollar gifts to the school and going onto the board of trustees. He knew. The kids knew too. People always knew, in New York. The worst occasion, though, had been in the fall of '99, when he and Maggie had gone to dinner with Peter Codford.

Peter Codford had been at Columbia with Gorham. He had then gone into venture capital in California for a while, later setting up his own private equity operation in New York. He and Gorham hadn't seen each other for many years when they happened to meet at a conference, and Peter had invited Gorham to dinner.

Peter Codford was six feet four inches tall, with a spare, athletic build, and he still had the same full head of dark brown hair that he'd had when he got his MBA. Only the lines on his face had deepened. The effect was to add to the image of casual authority that he'd possessed even in his twenties. His wife Judy was lively and clever. It also turned out that she and Maggie had known each other at law school.

"I went on working for a while after Peter and I married," Judy told them. "But then Peter had to move, so I stopped, and I never went back to work again." She smiled. "I rather regret that."

The Codfords lived in a fifteen-room apartment near the Metropolitan on Fifth. It was a palace, and would have contained Gorham and Maggie's Park Avenue apartment more than twice. Peter also had a house in the Hamptons, on Georgica Pond, and another apartment, on Nob Hill in San Francisco.

The conversation was certainly easy. Both couples had the same background and outlook, as well as some shared memories. Gorham was interested that Peter was similarly cautious about the dot.com boom. "People have made a lot of money," he said, "but there has got to be a big correction." Peter also wanted some information about the politics of loan decisions at the commercial banks. Had it changed in the last year? He sketched a situation at a company in which he was a minority shareholder. What would be Gorham's advice if they wanted to approach a commercial bank for a loan?

They talked about their families, and Gorham and Maggie learned that Peter and Judy had lost a son.

They discussed the millennium bug. Were all the world's computers really going to crash when the date went to zero? "The bank has spent a fortune preparing for it," Gorham said, "but Maggie reckons nothing will happen at all." He was also curious to know what areas Peter was looking to invest in next. "America will continue to be our core business," Peter said, "Europe, less and less. We think the Far East will be the growth area for the future. In a couple of years, Judy and I may move to Hawaii, to be nearer the action."

It was a pleasant evening, and afterward Gorham and Maggie walked home down Fifth.

"I really enjoyed that," said Maggie. "It was a nice surprise to meet Judy again."

Gorham nodded, but said nothing. They walked on in silence for a block.

"What sort of money do you suppose Peter has?" he said at last.

"I've no idea."

"He must have a hundred million, at least."

A hundred million. Once upon a time, a million bucks was a lot of money. But the bar had been raised a long way since then, especially in the last two decades. For the truly successful, Gorham reckoned, for a man like Peter, in the new global economy, a hundred million was only entry-level rich. How many people in New York had a hundred million dollars these days? A lot, certainly. Rich with a capital R, these days, was a billion.

"What's the matter?" asked Maggie, when they'd gone another block.

"My life has been a total failure."

"Thank you so much. That's really nice to hear. Your wife and children count for nothing, I suppose."

"I don't mean that."

"Yes you do. We're your life, you know."

"Of course you are. But he and I did our MBAs together. Professionally he did it right, and I didn't."

"That's garbage. You did something different, that's all. Tell me something: when would you say you're most happy?"

"When I'm with you and the children, I guess."

"I'm really pleased to hear that. Did you notice that Peter told us he'd lost a son? And you really think he's more fortunate than you?"

"No, just more successful professionally."

"Be grateful for what you have, Gorham." They went on in silence for another minute. He could tell Maggie was really angry. "Juan Campos was at Columbia with you too," she suddenly said. "Are you trying to tell me Juan is some kind of failure? Because I don't happen to think he is."

Juan Campos had had a bad time for a number of years, when El Barrio and every other poor area of the city had fallen into ever greater neglect. But he'd come through it and was making a big success as an administrator in the community college system now. Gorham had a feeling that Juan's career might be developing into greater things.

"Okay," Gorham said. "You've made your point."

That weekend, they stayed in the city. Saturday was a bright, clear day. They went down to the South Street Seaport, and Gorham amazed his children by telling them that their ancestors had actually been merchants with counting houses down there. Then they all went to a movie together. On Sunday, Maggie made brunch, and they had friends round, and that evening he helped the kids with their homework. He felt better after that, and for several weeks he kept himself busy with his work and the children, and with Maggie of course, and he'd supposed that he was back to being his usual self, when he overheard Maggie having a telephone conversation with a friend.

"I just don't know what to do with him," she said. "It's really difficult." Then, when she saw him come into the room, she'd quickly ended the call.

"What was that about?" he asked.

"Just a client who's giving me some problems," she said. "I'd rather not talk about it."

But he suspected that she might have been talking about him.

❖

The new millennium began. The much-anticipated Y2K bug hardly materialized at all in the USA, or the UK, or the other countries that had prepared for it. But then it didn't seem to appear in the countries that had almost ignored it. That spring, the dot.com boom had reached its high point, then the NASDAQ index had started a wholesale retreat.

Early in April, Juan Campos had called, sounding very cheerful, and they'd met for lunch. Things were going well for Juan. Janet had made a documentary on his community college. "You can't make a dime with a documentary," Juan said, "but it has given her enormous satisfaction. She wants to show it to you herself sometime." Gorham was delighted to see his friend so upbeat, and promised to come up and visit them soon.

Only when Maggie asked him that evening how his lunch had gone, and suggested that they should all four of them go out to dinner together, did it cross Gorham's mind that maybe Juan's call to him might have been prompted by her. Did his wife really think that he was in such need of cheering up? He thought he seemed perfectly happy.

That summer they took the children to Europe. They went to Florence, Rome and Pompeii. The boys seemed quite interested, but little Emma was only eight, so maybe she was a little young, though she was very patient with the long lines, which they partly avoided by getting guides. Then they went to the beach for a few days, to make up for all the forced culture. It was one of the best holidays they'd had in years.

Back in New York, Gorham made a determined effort to keep his life on an even keel. He stood for the board of the building again, and was easily elected. He didn't much like some of the other people on the board, but that wasn't the point. He was determined to grasp everything about the life he had and hold onto it. He made a point of taking Maggie out to dinner, just the two of them, every other week at least. Time was compartmentalized in New York. At work, naturally, there was a schedule, but he tightened up his private life as well. Twice a week he played tennis at the Town Tennis Club near Sutton Place, or in the winter months on the covered courts under the Fifty-ninth Street Bridge. All through the rest of that year, he felt himself to be in control of the situation. Maggie seemed happy. His home life was exemplary. As the end of the year approached, Gorham was feeling rather proud of himself. So when the next blow struck, it took him by surprise.

It was at a cocktail party the week before Christmas, and Gorham found himself talking to a pleasant fellow who told him he was a historian at Columbia. They discussed the university a little, and then Gorham asked the man what work he'd been engaged in recently.

"I'm actually on a sabbatical," the fellow announced, "so that I can complete a book I've been working on for a few years. It's about Ben Franklin in London. Sets his life there in the context of everything that was going on in science, philosophy, politics."

"That sounds incredibly interesting."

"I think it is."

"Tell me more."

"Just stop me when you've had enough." The guy was about his own age, Gorham supposed. Medium height, round-faced and balding, he wore metal-rimmed glasses and a bow tie. He was friendly and unassuming, but as he talked about the world Ben Franklin had known, and the lively intellectual tradition Franklin represented, one could feel his intensity and enthusiasm. It was infectious. "Am I boring you?" he genially inquired after a few minutes.

"Absolutely not," said Gorham. And when the historian stopped and said he reckoned that was pretty much what his book was about and, with a twinkle in his eye, that maybe when it came out, Gorham would like to buy a copy, Gorham assured him: "I shall buy several and give them to friends. You have no idea," he added, "how much I envy you."

The man looked quite surprised. "You make far more money, and enjoy a lot more respect in the world than most authors do," he said mildly.

"But what about the mind?"

"Many of the bankers I know, besides being highly intelligent, have jobs that require a full use of their intellect. The challenges of running a business are quite as great as those of mastering a piece of history."

"I'm not sure that's true," said Gorham, "but even if it were, you'll have one thing I never will."

"Which is?"

"You will produce something that you can call your own. Your book will remain there, forever."

"Forever is a long time," the man responded with a laugh.

"Everything I do is ephemeral," said Gorham. "When the banks get together to make a big loan, they announce the fact in the newspaper with an ad describing the loan and listing all the main participating banks. We call it a tombstone. So I guess you could say that my life has been preparing a bunch of tombstones."

"They represent enterprises that wouldn't be there otherwise. I see birth in what you do, not death." The writer smiled. "An appropriate thought, as Christmas is approaching."

Gorham smiled too, and they parted. But alone that night, he asked himself: What have I done that I can put my hands on? What can I look back on in my career and say, "This is mine. This is what I created and left behind"? And he could find nothing, nor could he feel anything but a terrible, spiritual emptiness.

In January 2001, Gorham Master signed on with a headhunter. He told no one, not even Maggie. Perhaps the headhunter could find something for him that would make sense of his life, before it was too late.

The Board Game

GORHAM GLANCED AT his watch just as the telephone rang. It was time to go. If he and Maggie had privately quarreled the night before, no one seeing them now would have guessed it.

The boys were all excited: Gorham, Jr., Richard, and Gorham, Jr.'s, best friend Lee. Gorham was looking forward to it, too. They were going to a Yankee game, for God's sake.

"It's John Vorpal," said Maggie. Why the hell did Vorpal have to bother him now?

"Tell him I have to go to the game," said Gorham.

"Honey, he says he has to talk to you."

"He's coming to dinner this evening, damn it."

"He says it's private. Board business." Maggie gave him the phone.

Gorham muttered a curse. The truth was he didn't really like John Vorpal; however, they both served on the co-op board, so he had to make efforts to get along. But since Vorpal became chairman of the board, he and Jim Bandersnatch were doing a bunch of things that Gorham didn't approve of.

"John, I can't talk now."

"We need to discuss 7B. They want an answer. Are you around on Sunday?"

"No, I have to be up in Westchester."

"That's too bad, Gorham."

"After dinner tonight?"

Maggie gave him a dirty look. But what could he do? At least this might keep it brief.

"After dinner then." Vorpal wasn't pleased either.

But if John Vorpal insisted on having a private talk about 7B, which was already on the schedule for the meeting next Wednesday, well, to hell with him. He could stay after dinner.

There was only one problem. If John Vorpal was going to say what Gorham thought he was going to say, then he, Gorham Vandyck Master, was going to have a very serious disagreement with him. It could be a blazing row. And one really didn't want to have a blazing row with the chairman of the board of a Park Avenue building.

⁙

The game was due to start a little after 1 p.m. They really needed to get going.

"Come on," he said. "We're taking the subway."

"We are?" his son said, in astonishment.

Didn't anyone in this family use public transport? When the nanny took young Gorham, Jr., or his siblings to any of their appointments, she took a taxi. When Bella ran errands for Maggie, she probably took a taxi too. At least, he thought, it cost less than having your own car and driver, which several of the people in the building did.

The Masters kept just two cars. The Mercedes sedan in the garage round the corner, and a nice blue SUV for Maggie, which lived in the garage of the country house.

"Getting in and out of Yankee Stadium can be a hassle," he said firmly. "The subway will be quicker."

As they rode in the subway, Gorham looked at the three boys with affection.

Gorham Vandyck Master, Jr., a thirteen-year-old, fair-haired son of privilege; Richard, eleven years old, a thinner, wirier version of his brother; and young Gorham's best friend, Lee.

Gorham could never figure out Lee's Chinese name exactly, but it didn't matter, because everyone called him Lee. He had met Lee's parents one time when they had come to collect him from the apartment. They lived up in Harlem, hardly spoke a word of English; the father was a plumber or something. But their son was a genius.

It always seemed to Gorham Master that Lee was totally round. His friendly face, under a mop of black hair, was round. His body wasn't fat, just round. His temper was so easy that Master reckoned his psyche must somehow be round, so that everything bounced off it. Lee took the subway from Harlem each morning and, Master was convinced, just turned himself into a ball and rolled along the sidewalk from the station to the school.

But Lee wrote the best essays in his grade. He'd surely finish up at Harvard or Yale or some Ivy League place. And what did he want to be? Once, when they were all sitting in the kitchen, the boy had confessed that he'd like to be a senator. He also wanted to be a big collector of Chinese art. "And you know what," Master had told his son afterward, "he'll probably make it." And the thought filled Master with pride for his country and his city.

And how did this kid come to be at his son's fancy private school? With a scholarship, of course. Maybe twenty percent of the kids there were on scholarships.

If there was one thing New York private schools were good at, it was raising money. He'd no sooner paid the hefty tuition fees for Gorham, Jr.'s, first trimester in kindergarten when the parents' committee had hit him for a donation as well. They didn't waste any time. And before they even graduated, the kids in twelfth grade organized themselves to start donating as alumni. Just to get everybody into the habit. And the scale of giving was astounding. The parents' committees raised several million in donations every year; the accounts were so impressive they were scary.

But if the system was scary, it meant that those scholarship kids from poor homes got the best education available in America, and the rich parents were happy to pay for them. That was the American way. Of course, it didn't do any harm to the school's academic results, either.

Gorham, Jr., had plenty of friends, but Lee was the closest to him. Both kids were nice, both ambitious, both striving for excellence. He was proud of the friend his son had chosen.

They got to the game with time to spare.

꘏

Yankee Stadium, the Bronx. The House that Ruth Built, scene of Babe Ruth's greatest triumphs. The huge stadium was packed, the crowd expec-tant. The Yankees, the biggest sports franchise in America, were going for their fourth consecutive World Series in a row. That would also be a fifth in six years.

He had great seats—field level, on the third-base side. The boys were thrilled. And today, the Yankees were playing the Red Sox.

The Boston Red Sox. The ancient rivalry, so full of passion—and heartbreak, if you were a Red Sox fan.

At 1:15 the game began. And for the next three and a quarter hours, Gorham Vandyck Master enjoyed one of the happiest afternoons of his life. The game was wonderful. The crowd roared. He said to hell with dinner and his cholesterol, and ate three hot dogs. The boys assuredly ate more, but he didn't count.

What a game! The Yankees made seven runs in the sixth inning, and Tino Martinez hit two home runs, to defeat the Red Sox 9 to 2.

"Well, boys," he said, "that was a game to remember for the rest of our lives."

᛭

When they got back to the apartment, they found a scene of activity. The caterers had already arrived.

"You boys," said Maggie firmly, "get cleaned up and out of the way." And it was clear to Gorham that this referred to him as well.

Lee was sleeping over, because he and Gorham, Jr., were going to Greg Cohen's bar mitzvah. This would be the bar mitzvah year, and it was normal for the Jewish boys and girls having a bar or bat mitzvah to invite most of their class. Sometimes one went to the religious service as well, especially if it was a close friend, but Gorham, Jr., usually just went to the party later. And that was what the two boys were doing that evening.

Gorham went straight to the master bedroom, showered and changed into a suit for dinner. He was going to take the boys to the bar mitzvah, spend a few minutes there to say congratulations to the Cohens, and get back to the apartment before the guests arrived. It was a little tight, but he reckoned he could do it.

By 6:15, he was ready, and Maggie came into the bedroom to get ready herself. But he still had one important duty to perform before taking the boys. He went into the kitchen.

"Hi, Katie." He smiled with pleasure, and went to give the caterer a kiss.

Katie Keller Katerers. She'd asked them what they thought of the name when she started up two years ago. He and Maggie had both told her to go with it.

Gorham hadn't really known the Kellers until after his father's death. Charlie had still had the Theodore Keller photograph collection and, following his instructions, Gorham had gone to see the family to find out what they'd like him to do with it. It hadn't taken long for them to agree to find a dealer, who had quietly promoted and sold the collection down the years. He and the Kellers split the modest proceeds. They'd kept in touch, so Gorham had actually known Katie Keller her entire life, and he was delighted to do what he could to help someone whose family had such a long connection to his.

Katie was twenty-five now, though with her blonde hair tightly pulled back, and wearing her chef's outfit, he reckoned she looked more like eighteen, and adorable. It went without saying that whenever they needed catering, he and Maggie called upon her services.

Not that they entertained a lot. The occasional party. Once in a while, a sit-down dinner. Bella's cooking was fine, but not up to a formal dinner party, and they hadn't anyone to serve really, so like most people they knew, they used caterers for these occasions.

They'd be ten at dinner tonight, and Katie would produce a four-course meal. She had one full-time employee, Kent, supplemented by two young actors to serve and wash up afterward. Including his own wine, Gorham reckoned the entire evening would cost a little over a thousand dollars, which was less than you'd have to pay for ten people in a fancy restaurant.

But first he must deal with the wine.

Gorham didn't have a large wine cellar, but he knew quite a bit, and was proud of his modest collection. The storage cages down in the building's basement were about ninety-five degrees, so he kept his wine up at the country house, and for an occasion like this, he'd collect what he wanted from there and bring it down to the apartment, where he had a temperature-controlled unit. After the menu had been chosen last week, he'd selected some bottles of a French Chablis, an excellent Californian Pinot Noir he could trust, and a wonderful dessert wine, made in small quantities by a winery he'd discovered that was owned by a rich dentist in San Francisco.

He had some nice decanters that had come originally from the old

822   EDWARD RUTHERFURD

family house in Gramercy Park and he liked to use them. But one had to be careful with Pinot Noir and not decant it too early. Kent had a considerable knowledge of wines himself, so the two of them had an enjoyable five minutes discussing the wines and agreeing on the arrangements for serving them.

Then he turned to have a few words with Katie.

On the outside, especially when she was working, Katie seemed such a serious little person, everything neatly in place, her face scrubbed. She was as perfect as a Meissen doll. Yet underneath was a bright girl with a wicked sense of humor. He talked to her while she was unwrapping the hors d'oeuvres. She gave him a smile.

"Can I tell you something?" she asked.

"Sure."

"You're in my way."

"Sorry." He moved to one side. "How's Rick?" The boyfriend. The fiancé, now—they were getting married next year.

"He's fine. We've found a house."

"Where?"

"New Jersey."

"That's great."

"It is. If we can find the money."

"Think you can?"

"Probably. If my business goes well. And if . . ."

"What?"

"You get out of my way."

He laughed. "I'm off," he said. Young Rick, in his opinion, was a lucky man.

⁘

As he wanted to look in himself, he took a taxi with the boys to the party, rather than waste time parking the car. The party was in a big Midtown hotel, so it only took a few minutes to get there. A sign in the lobby directed them to a large elevator down a passage, and moments later they were emerging on an upper floor and entering the wonderful world of Greg Cohen's bar mitzvah party.

Mrs. Cohen had clearly decided she wanted this to be a very special occasion. She had chosen a theme, and even hired a designer who, by the look of things, had brought in an army of decorators, flower arrangers and scenery-makers. And so it was, this evening, that this vast Midtown hotel ballroom had been transformed, as though by magic, into a tropical island. Along the right-hand wall was a sandy beach, fringed with seagrass and even, here and there, a palm tree. On the left side was the dance floor, complete with DJ and professional dancers. There were fairground booths of every kind, offering prizes that you could take away too, in addition to the bag of party favors you'd get at the end. Still more impressive, the whole of the back of the room was filled with a reconstruction of a roller coaster. And in the center of everything, in pride of place and serving now, was a hot-dog stand.

"Wow," said the boys.

The girls in their Betsey Johnson dresses were already gathering in a big group. Gorham, Jr., Richard and Lee went to join the boys' group. It was funny how, in seventh and eighth grades, these modern kids still segregated themselves into single-sex groups at parties. One of the jobs of the professional dancers was to try to get them to dance together. By eleventh and twelfth grade that would have changed. Big time. When it came to his daughter, he wasn't sure he wanted to think about that. But for now, the girls just danced with each other, pretty much.

What had it cost? Gorham wondered. At least a quarter-million dollars. He'd been to parties that cost more. Over the top, in his opinion. Nothing like the old guard, that was for sure.

Or was it? As he gazed at the splendid scene, it suddenly struck Gorham that he was completely wrong. When the grand old New York plutocrats of the gilded age gave their magnificent parties, like the fellow who had about twenty gentlemen all dine on horseback, were they actually doing anything different? He knew a little history. What about the great parties of Edwardian England, or Versailles, or Elizabethan England, or medieval France, or the Roman Empire? They were all recorded in paintings and in literature. The identical story. Conspicuous consumption and display.

It had always been that way in New York, right back to the days when his ancestors had come here. The people who ran the city, whether they bribed an English governor or raised all the money for good causes, were always the rich. Astors, Vanderbilts, whoever, they all had their turn. He knew a fellow who'd started life driving a truck, and who lived in a thirty-thousand-square-foot mansion in Alpine, New Jersey, now. Gave great parties, too . . .

As for people like his own family, he thought, you know what they say: old money, no money. Old money was genteel and had nice manners, and he liked those things. It was fine to talk the talk; but at the end of the day, if you couldn't walk the walk, what were you? A little pretentious, perhaps, if the truth were told.

He caught sight of another parent, Mrs. Blum. Her daughter was at the party and she had promised Maggie that she'd give the boys a ride home with her. He went over, thanked her, and confirmed the ride.

That just left the Cohens. He saw them standing near the entrance. David Cohen, the father, was a nice guy. He liked to go deep-sea fishing in Florida.

"Congratulations. A terrific party."

"It was all Cindy's doing," said David with a smile, indicating his wife.

"You did an amazing job," Gorham said to Cindy.

"I had a great designer," said Cindy.

A gray-haired couple were standing beside them.

"Gorham, do you know my parents, Michael and Sarah?"

Gorham shook hands. David's mother seemed to be studying him.

"I didn't catch your name," she said.

"Gorham Master."

"Sarah Adler Cohen."

A signal. She was telling him she had a professional name. He thought quickly. She saved him.

"I have the Sarah Adler Art Gallery. And would you be the son of Charlie Master, who had the Keller photography collection?"

"Yes, I am."

And then he remembered, with a feeling of sinking horror. This was the lady he was supposed to deliver the Motherwell to. The drawing that still graced the living room in the apartment. Was she expecting it? Did she know that his father had told him to go and see her? A terrible feeling of guilt overcame him.

But the old lady was chatting to him quite happily. What was she saying?

"Well, when I was young, before I had my own place, your father came to the gallery where I worked and arranged a show of Theodore Keller's work there. And I was put in charge of it. The first show I ever did. So I got to meet your father. I was very sorry to hear he died."

"I never knew that. I'm so delighted to meet you," he stammered. She must be in her seventies, he supposed. She had a nice face, intelligent. She glanced at her husband and son, but they had been distracted by other guests.

"You like this party?" she asked.

"Of course. Don't you?"

She shrugged. "Too much conspicuous consumption for my taste." She looked at him thoughtfully, rather in the way, he supposed, that she might look at a painting she was appraising. "You should come by the gallery some time," she said. "I'm there most afternoons. Monday the gallery's closed, but I work there alone all day. Monday is a good day to call on me." She reached into her bag and pulled out a card. She glanced at her husband, but he was talking to someone else. "Actually," she said to Gorham quietly, "I have something of your father's I want to give you. Would you call me on Monday?"

"I'll do that," he promised, then saw the time. "I'm really sorry, I have to go—we have a dinner party."

"In that case, you're probably late already." Sarah Adler smiled. "Go. Go." But just before he turned, she added: "Promise to call me, Monday."

❖

She was right. He was late. He got an exasperated look from Maggie on his return. But fortunately only one of the couples had arrived, and these two were his favorites, Herbert and Mary Humblay. Herbert was a retired clergyman, and they lived in a nice old co-op on Sutton Place. The Humblays were good people to have at a dinner party. Their circle of friends in the city was huge, they had wide interests, and if there were any latent tensions between the dinner guests, their kindly presence seemed miraculously to defuse them.

So when he arrived, the Humblays were just asking to see Emma to say hello, and Mary Humblay was saying, "Now I hope you haven't made her get all dressed up just because we're here, because that would be a shame," and Herbert was remarking that it was as much as anyone could do to get their own granddaughter to clean up even to go to church. And Gorham felt himself relax, and was glad that it was the Humblays and not the Vorpals who'd arrived first, to set the tone of the evening.

Anyway, Emma came in with her friend Jane, who was there for a sleepover, and they were wearing similar dresses in pink and blue and looking very sweet. They brought the puppy with them.

Until a year ago the co-op had been a "no pets" building. Gorham couldn't remember why, but it had always been that way. Then Mrs. Vorpal had wanted to have a dog, so Vorpal had persuaded the board to change the rules.

The two girls had just started to talk to Mr. and Mrs. Humblay when the Vorpals arrived. Kent let them in and smoothly took their drink orders before ushering them into the living room. Mrs. Vorpal wanted a vodka martini; Vorpal took Scotch on the rocks.

"Well, good evening, Emma," said Vorpal, who pretended he liked children.

"Hi, Mr. and Mrs. Vorpal," said Emma.

Gorham introduced the Vorpals to the Humblays.

"We were just looking at this fine puppy," said Herbert.

The puppy, it had to be said, was cute. A tiny, fluffy white ball, peeping out with large eyes from beside Emma's cheek.

"You should thank Mr. Vorpal," said Maggie. "It's because of him that you're allowed to have a puppy."

"Thank you, Mr. Vorpal," said Emma.

Vorpal's sword-like face broke into a smile. "It was my pleasure. I just think it's nice for the children in the building to be able to have a pet."

"That's so nice," said Mary Humblay.

"Have to agree with you there," said Herbert.

"Okay, girls," said Maggie, "you can go if you want. But mind the noise, please."

The waiters brought the canapés round. The next guests, the O'Sullivans, arrived. He was a partner at a big law firm, quiet, judicious, but always good company; his wife Maeve was a slim, strikingly elegant Irishwoman who ran her own small brokerage house. Lastly came Liz Rabinovich and her boyfriend Juan. Liz was a speechwriter. She'd worked for some big-name politicians, though she had mostly corporate clients at present. But you never knew with Liz—she was something of a free spirit. As for Juan, he was a bit of a mystery man. Liz said he was Cuban. He'd once told Gorham that his mother's family was Venezuelan, but that their money was in Switzerland. Juan lived with Liz when he was in New York, but Liz said he had a spectacular apartment in Paris. Gorham didn't trust Juan. "Liz only likes men she doesn't trust," Maggie told him.

The dinner went well. Liz, who always had plenty of Washington gossip, had been seated next to O'Sullivan. O'Sullivan was discreet, but well informed, and he seemed to be enjoying Liz's company. Vorpal wanted to discover Juan's business, and Gorham enjoyed watching him get more and more frustrated. At one point, when they were discussing real estate, old Herbert Humblay explained to them how the ancient endowments of Trinity worked. Not only had the Trinity vestry been able, down the centuries, to found one church after another out of its huge rents, but to help the work of other churches all over the world. The value of its real estate holdings in the Financial District was absolutely huge. As Vorpal listened intently to what Humblay was saying, and calculating the numbers, he began to look at the clergyman with a new respect.

And then, of course, there was Maggie. Gorham gazed down the table toward her. His wife was looking stunning tonight—her red hair had been beautifully cut that afternoon, and she'd had a manicure as well. As she smiled down the table at him, only the faintest glint in her eye gave a hint of the quarrel they'd had last night.

⁜

It was his fault, he supposed. Perhaps if he'd shared more information with her, the conversation might have been different. But then again, it might not.

He'd never told her he'd gone to see the headhunter at the start of the year. Maybe because he felt that it was an admission that he wasn't reconciled to his life, even an admission of failure. Also, no doubt, because he was pretty sure she'd have told him to stick with the bank where he was and leave the headhunter alone. If he heard of any job he seriously wanted to consider, that would be the time to talk to Maggie about it.

Whatever the reason, Maggie had known nothing. She also did not know, therefore, that for nearly eight months, the headhunter had failed to come up with a single opportunity.

He knew the guy was good at what he did, when he called him from time to time, just to check in, he was always told the same thing.

"You have to be patient, Gorham. We're not talking about some middle-management position here. We are looking for a really significant opportunity, a top position, and a good fit. These things only come along once in a while."

Intellectually, Gorham understood. But he could not escape the feeling that nothing was happening, that nobody wanted him. He felt worse than ever. And his fraying temper had shown in countless small ways, mostly in a general moroseness, and occasional flashes of irritation with Maggie or the children.

So when, on Friday night, she had quietly sat him down and made her suggestion, it had come at the wrong time, and produced an unfortunate result.

"Honey," she'd said, "I really feel you're unhappy. And maybe it's your marriage, but I think it's your job."

"Everything's fine," he'd snapped.

"No it isn't, Gorham. Don't say that. You're not in good shape."

"Thank you so much."

"I just want to help, honey."

"In what way?"

"I just don't think you like what you do any more."

"And?"

"With what you've already saved, your stock and all that, plus what I make now, we really don't have to worry. You could quit if you want to and do something you really liked. You're a wonderful husband and a great father. We could have a perfect family life if you were just doing something that made you happy."

"You're telling me to retire?"

"No, I'm just saying why not do something you enjoy? The money isn't a problem."

So that was it. She didn't even need his income any more. He'd watched Maggie with admiration as she organized her career, the household, the kids' play dates, everything. Now it seemed she was planning to organize him as well. The final indignity. First he'd failed. Now he was going to be neutered.

"Go to hell," he'd said.

"That's not a fair response."

"It's the only one you're getting. You run your life, I'll run mine."

"We share our lives, Gorham."

"Some things we share, some things we don't. Get used to it."

They hadn't spoken any more that night.

❖

In Gorham's experience, at any dinner party, there was usually one thing somebody said that stuck in your mind afterward. This evening, it was Maeve O'Sullivan who provided it.

Gorham admired Maeve. By day she managed money, and did it brilliantly, but she didn't find it satisfied her intellect. She spoke four languages. She played the piano seriously well. And she read books. Lots of them.

They were discussing the long hours the young kids worked in the Financial District.

"You know," Maeve said, "I was reading Virginia Woolf the other day, and she remarked that at one period of her life, she was able to get so much done because she had three uninterrupted hours to work in every day. And I thought, what on earth is she talking about? Only three hours a day? And then I looked around the office at all the people working their fourteen-hour days, and I thought, how many of you actually spend three hours in real, creative, intellectual activity in a day? And I reckoned, probably not one." She smiled. "And there's Virginia Woolf achieving more than they ever will in their lives, on three hours a day. It makes you think. They might do better if they worked less."

"Mind you, she killed herself," said John Vorpal, and everybody laughed.

But Maeve was right, all the same. It was something to think about.

·‡·

The evening ended pleasantly, and one could tell the guests had enjoyed themselves. As he said good-bye to the last of them and went back into the living room to face John Vorpal, Gorham felt almost friendly toward him. There was just Vorpal—his wife had gone back to their apartment.

"Okay, Gorham," Vorpal said, pulling out the papers, "7B."

Gorham was sorry that the people in 7B were leaving, but a big job opportunity was taking them to California, so 7B was on the market. A good offer had been made. They wanted to take it. But of course, the prospective purchasers had to go before the board. Or to be precise, a committee of the board. This was the first time an apartment had been sold since Vorpal became chairman. The committee was due to meet, and then interview the applicants, that coming Wednesday. So if Vorpal wanted to talk to him now, that could only mean one thing. Trouble.

Maggie came into the room.

"May I join you?"

Gorham frowned. It was he who was on the board, not her. This was an unwarranted interference. But Vorpal looked up, and smiled.

"I wish you would." Vorpal liked Maggie. He supposed that, as a partner in Branch & Cabell, she'd agree with him, whereas he considered Gorham to be a little unreliable. He passed her a copy of the application. "I think we may have a problem with this. Jim Bandersnatch thinks so too."

"Dr. Caruso?" said Maggie.

"I think I'd better tell you that we know this man," said Gorham. "He delivered all three of our children. We like him."

Vorpal's face fell.

"Not," said Maggie quietly, "that Gorham would let that influence him in considering Dr. Caruso's suitability for this building."

Gorham stared at her. This was a deliberate undermining of his position. He kept his temper, however. He must remain calm.

"So what's the problem?" he asked.

"He lives on West End Avenue," said Vorpal.

"He has for years. Lots of good people live on West End."

"I'd have preferred Central Park West."

"There are some quite exclusive buildings on West End, you know."

"His isn't one of them," said Vorpal drily.

"His references look all right. Here's one from a trustee of Mount Sinai—those are very important people. This guy Anderson's a big hitter."

"Yes. As a professional reference, excellent. But as a social reference, not so good."

"Why?"

"Anderson lives in a town house. And Caruso's other social reference comes from out of town." Vorpal shook his head. "What we like to see is a reference from someone who lives in, and is preferably on the board of, a very good building. A building like ours. Someone who has the same fit."

"I see."

"I'm looking for clubs, Gorham, for people with a significant social presence in the city, for big charitable donations. And I don't see them—I don't see them at all. I don't even see a country club. This application lacks . . ." he searched for a word, "substance."

"I could write him a reference," said Gorham wickedly.

Vorpal's face suggested that, in his private estimation, that might not have been enough. But his answer was more clever.

"I find it significant that he didn't ask you, or one of his many patients like you, to do so."

"Anything else?" asked Master.

"There is the question of money."

"Okay."

"We have always been an all-cash building, of course."

Many buildings allowed you to have a mortgage for half the price of your apartment. That wasn't a bad idea. Financial stability was good. Lesser buildings might allow sixty or even seventy percent mortgages. By the time you got to ninety percent debt, you were really trash. But the top buildings, the ruthless enclaves, didn't allow any debt at all. If you needed to borrow money to buy your apartment, then you didn't belong. Go and take out a mortgage on your country house if that was the kind of thing you liked to do.

"There seems to be no problem with cash. The Carusos have plenty—I happen to know that his wife inherited money some years ago. Actually, their financial disclosures look pretty good."

As well as the usual bank references and tax returns, the co-op demanded more than usually detailed statements of assets. Prospective buyers couldn't fake them out. All the good co-op boards left applicants exposed when it came to their personal finances, but Vorpal and Bandersnatch wanted them totally naked.

"Hmm. Pretty good, but maybe not good enough. As you know, Gorham, the building has always looked for a comfortable margin here. On the basic level, we want to be quite sure there won't be any difficulty with the monthly maintenance, which for Caruso's apartment runs six thousand a month now, or with any assessments the board may need to impose. But we like evidence of solidness. We have for a long time now required that people can prove assets of maybe two or three times the value of the apartment they're buying."

"I've always thought that a little harsh."

"Well, I think, and Jim thinks, that in the current climate we can do a little better."

"Better?"

"What we're really looking for here is five times assets."

"You want Caruso to have twenty-five million dollars?"

"I think we can get that."

"Hell, John, I don't have twenty-five million dollars."

"Your family's been here seventy years. We like that."

"But you want the new people to have that kind of money?"

"Those are the kind of people we want."

"Do you have twenty-five million dollars, John?"

Maggie gave him a warning look. This question was a bad idea. But Gorham wasn't going to back down.

"John, do you know what Groucho Marx said about clubs? 'I don't want to belong to a club that takes people like me.' Are you sure we're not straying into Groucho Marx territory here?"

"Other buildings are the same, Gorham. You're out of date. There's at least one building on this avenue that insists on ten times assets."

"You mean, you'd need fifty million dollars before they let you in?"

"That's exactly what I mean. You should know that, Gorham."

Gorham said nothing. Actually, he did have some idea how things were going, though in fact he'd heard a story the other day of a grand building where things had gone the other way. Some twenty-five-year-old whiz kid from Wall Street had applied to a building and stated his newly earned assets. The chairman of the board was so furious that the kid was already so much richer than he was, that he turned him down. When asked why, he answered: "We're looking for old money here."

But he didn't remind Vorpal of that story.

"I hear what you say, John, and I'll think hard about it."

"I hope you will." Vorpal turned to Maggie. "Thank you for a lovely meal." And he was gone.

"I want Caruso in this building," Gorham said to Maggie.

Her face was a mask. "I'm not sure it can be done."

"Aside from Vorpal and Bandersnatch, there are two more members of the committee. I'll get to them."

"So will he."

"Thank you," he said drily, "for your support." And he turned away from her without another word.

❖

Early the next morning, he went up to the house in North Salem. The fencing needed fixing, to keep out the deer. He didn't return until evening.

The Towers

MAGGIE LEFT THE apartment early on Monday morning. Gorham stayed long enough to see the kids leave for the school bus. He was just about to go himself when Katie Keller came up the service elevator to the kitchen door with one of her crew. After a weekend dinner, she usually preferred to swing by first thing on Monday to pick up the containers and trays she'd left neatly stacked in one corner of the kitchen.

"Any big parties coming up?" he asked.

"Better than that, maybe," she said. "There's a company talking about a contract for a bunch of corporate entertaining—that could make a huge difference if I get it. I'm going to see them early tomorrow morning. They have offices downtown, in the Financial District."

"That's great. Good luck," he said.

Then he went to his office. He had a busy day ahead of him.

During the day on Sunday, he'd managed to speak to one of the other committee members about Dr. Caruso and had stressed to him that Caruso was a distinguished man. Not rich, admittedly, but financially solid, totally respectable. "Maggie and I have known him for nearly twenty years." A slight exaggeration. As soon as he got to his office, he tracked down the other member who promised: "We'll see him."

That at least was something. But he wondered whether to let Caruso know that there could be a problem. It might be a kindness. But there was probably no need. Vorpal would already have let the current owners of 7B know that he wasn't happy, and the realtor too, in the hope that he could kill the deal in advance. Better leave it alone. The business still offended him though.

⁘

The call from the headhunter came through at ten thirty. It only took a couple of minutes, and after it was over, Gorham canceled his midday meeting and told his assistant that he'd be out for lunch. Then, in some excitement, he closed the door of his office, and sat staring out of the window.

At 12:20, he left the office and took a taxi downtown. He did not get back until three in the afternoon.

⁘

It was four o'clock when he remembered the old lady. He silently cursed himself for promising to call her that day, but a promise was a promise, and besides, the days ahead were likely to be so filled that he'd better get his business with her over as soon as possible. He called the number of the gallery.

She sounded delighted to hear from him. "I was afraid you would forget to call."

"How could I forget?"

"I have something for you. Are you free this afternoon?"

"I'm afraid not," he told her. The interruption from the headhunter had left him with a backlog of work to clear. She sounded disappointed.

"I had a call from my daughter today. She needs me to come and help her later this week, and then I'm on holiday with my husband. I always believe in doing things at once, so that they don't get forgotten. Don't you agree?"

He thought wryly of the thirty-three years that he had now been holding on to the Motherwell drawing for her.

"I certainly do," he said.

"Do you get up early?" she asked.

"Quite often."

"I have a meeting tomorrow morning," she said. "But we could have an early breakfast, if you like."

"I have an eight thirty meeting myself, I'm afraid."

"Perfect—that's when my meeting is, too. Shall we say seven? They serve breakfast from seven at the Regency on Park. That's not far from your apartment, is it?"

He didn't know what to say. A woman in her seventies was hustling him into a breakfast at some ungodly hour, and she'd already cornered him. He could see how she ran her gallery.

"That would be fine," he heard himself saying.

He worked until six thirty, then gave Maggie a call to find out what time she'd be home. She said seven fifteen.

"After supper," he told her, "I need to talk to you alone."

"Oh?" She sounded tense. "What about?"

"Business," he said. "I can't tell you over the phone. Something's come up."

They ate with the children as usual and got them started on their homework. It was nine o'clock before they went into the bedroom and closed the door. Maggie was watching him cautiously, her face set.

"Okay," he said, "I got a call from a headhunter I know today. I went downtown to see him at lunchtime. There's a chance I could be offered a job."

"What sort of job?" She wasn't giving anything away.

"As COO of a bank, actually. A smaller bank, of course. But they have a very attractive package to offer me. Effectively, they'd buy me out of my bank, and offer me a very attractive performance-related contract. It could be worth quite a lot of money." He paused. "The idea is that in three or four years I would take over as CEO. They think I have the experience to build it up into a much more significant operation. From what I've learned, I think they're right."

But she'd already seen where this was going.

"Where's the bank?"

"Boston. I'd commute weekly. It could work."

"So we'd see you at weekends."

"Right."

"Maybe."

"I'd be here weekends."

"And how do you feel about that?"

"I'd rather it was here in New York, obviously. But I don't think that's going to happen. Professionally, this is what I've always wanted."

"But you have three children who need you. Are you really going to walk out on them, on me?"

"That is totally unfair. I wouldn't want to walk out on them, on you, and this would not be doing so."

"Maybe not in theory, not in your own mind as you see things now. But in practice that is exactly what you would be doing."

"It's not 'as I see things,' Maggie. There's no need to patronize me."

"Okay, I won't patronize you. If this was absolutely necessary, if this was the only way you could make a living to support us, that would be different. But it is totally unnecessary. We're fine as we are, and yet you are planning to walk out on your wife and family."

"I'm not fine as I am, Maggie. I have the chance to run a bank."

It was too much. She lost her temper.

"Big deal, Gorham. Great for your ego. Whether you would be so happy doing it is another matter. I'm not sure you actually like being a banker, if you really want to know."

"You mean I'm not that good at it."

"I guess you're okay at it." She was stepping into dangerous territory—she had to know that—but she was angry now. "I think you just have a vision of yourself as a banker. That isn't quite the same thing."

"Well, tomorrow morning I have a meeting down at the World Trade Center—that's where the headhunter's office is—with the chairman of the bank. If that goes well, and we sense a good fit, I'll be going up to Boston to meet a few more people early next week. And if I think it's a good idea to take that job, then that's what I'll be doing."

"And I'll also be considering what I'm going to do, Gorham. Because I think you may be putting just a little more strain on this marriage than it can bear. Maybe you'd like to think about that, too."

"You want to wreck our marriage? You want to do that to the children?"

"That's out of order."

"Is it? I wonder, Maggie. You've got the career and the lifestyle and the kids. Maybe you don't really need a husband now. You can take my place on the board of the building with John Vorpal, and live happily ever after."

"Spare me the more pathetic aspects of your midlife crisis."

"You know what, Maggie? You're right. You're always right. You are the perfect Branch & Cabell lawyer who always knows best. Maybe I should just enjoy my midlife crisis by myself. You never know, having a midlife crisis might even be something I have a real talent for. Perhaps it will make me a pile of money."

"I think this conversation should end."

"There we can agree."

⁜

Tuesday began as a clear, bright September day. Dr. Caruso left his apartment on West End Avenue early.

He'd heard that there might be trouble with the board at Park Avenue, and was a little hurt. "Is it because I have an Italian name?" he'd asked the realtor. The memories of his childhood were still quite keen.

"Absolutely not," she assured him. "They might have liked more social references, but there's a money issue, too. The new board chairman wants richer people."

Well, if that was all, Caruso wasn't too dismayed. At least, not for himself. He wasn't sure he wanted to have his wife humiliated and embarrassed, though. He'd thought of speaking to the Masters about it, but he didn't want to put them in an awkward position.

"I think we should go to the interview," he said to his wife. "I'll ask them what it is they want, and if they don't like us then fine, I shall tell them straight out that we don't want to be in the building. Politely of course. But I'm not going to take any crap from them."

He felt better after he said that.

Anyway, this morning he had a meeting scheduled with his insurance agent. There was an old term policy that the agent had been bugging him for years to convert. Finally he'd agreed to do it. Term policies were cheaper when you started, but the guy was right, they got expensive as time went on. He had an early meeting arranged so that he could still get back uptown to his surgery at the usual time.

It was a fine day. The insurance offices were quite a way up the World Trade Center's South Tower. The view from up there would be spectacular.

⁜

Katie Keller was quietly confident. You had to admit, her presentation book was fantastic. Maybe some of Theodore Keller's artistic genes had found their way down to her. Pictures of dinner parties and banquets, corporate lunches and buffets, beautifully displayed with menus and letters of thanks. She even had a shot showing a well-known financier giving a presentation with a table of her refreshments discreetly visible to one side.

She had photographs of the various teams, including one corporate lunch where she'd had to provide a dozen waiters and waitresses—actually the cast of an Off-Broadway musical. That had been a blast. And there were shots of her kitchen, looking almost unbelievably metallic. Okay, some of that was faked.

Oh, and the flower arrangements were also fantastic.

She had price lists, and bar charts, and a graph showing how her costs were rising just under those of the prevailing competition. The corporate accounts loved that kind of thing.

So she was happy. She was wearing a dress that looked both pretty and businesslike. Get them both ways.

Her fiancé Rick was driving. As they came over the George Washington Bridge, she could look both upriver past the Palisades, and down to the distant, glimmering waters of New York harbor. It was so beautiful.

As they came down the Henry Hudson Parkway alongside the river, she gazed at the water. They passed the yacht basin at Seventy-ninth Street, and in the low Fifties, they reached the big piers where the Cunard liners still came in.

On the left, big warehouse-like buildings prevailed. Katie knew enough of Theodore Keller's work to realize that down here somewhere he must have taken the famous shot of the men walking up the railroad tracks.

The traffic wasn't too bad, and soon the towers of the World Trade Center were looming impressively ahead.

Katie Keller loved those towers. She knew that when they first went up, thirty years ago, some people had said they were architecturally dull. But she didn't find them dull. Some of the gleaming glass rectangles that had started up since might be a little glitzy and lacking in character, but the towers were different. The broad horizontal bands softly divided their sheer verticality into sections that, strangely, gave them a tall intimacy. And the thin, silver-gray, vertical lines that ran down each face caught the altering light of the sky so that the towers' faces were as constantly changing as the wide waters of the harbor and the great northerly Hudson below. Sometimes they were gleaming softly silver, sometimes they were granular gray. Once in a while, even, for haunting moments, a corner would flash like a sword, as its long blade caught the bright arc of the sun.

She loved the way that, when you walked in Soho, they hovered over the line of the rooftops, graceful as the towers of a cathedral.

The World Financial Center was approaching on their right, and Liberty Street was just ahead. Rick slowed the car to drop her off.

❖

At 6:45 that morning, Gorham went into the living room. Spreading some wrapping paper on the floor, he carefully took the Motherwell drawing down from the wall, folded the paper around it, and taped it. Maggie was still in the shower. He wondered whether she'd notice it was gone before she left for the office. She mightn't be very pleased, but that was too bad. The drawing really didn't belong to them. Putting it under his arm, he left the building.

Sarah Adler was already waiting for him at the Regency, and they went straight into breakfast. She was looking very fresh and businesslike, wearing a cream-colored coat and skirt outfit, very simple and elegant, and carrying a briefcase.

She was going to see a small finance house, she explained, that wanted to start an art collection they could display on their office walls. Before considering the deal, she had to take a look at the space, and the partners.

"What will you be looking for?" he asked.

"Whether they are good enough for my artists," she answered firmly.

When he handed over the parcel and confessed with some embarrassment that the Motherwell had been gracing his living-room wall for more than thirty years, she was greatly amused.

"Of course you didn't want to part with it," she said. "I'm so glad that you liked it too. Did you know that it was I who gave it to your father originally?"

No, he admitted, he did not.

"And you know nothing about my relationship with your father?"

Again, he had to admit his ignorance.

"Do you remember the girl from Brooklyn in his book, *Verrazano Narrows*?"

"Certainly."

"Well, that was me."

It did not take Sarah long to tell him the story. "I've never told my husband. I have had a very happy marriage, but every woman likes to have her secrets. And then, after the book became so famous, I didn't want my husband's patients saying, 'Oh, his wife is the girl in that book.' Not in those days, anyway. Your father was very discreet, also. He was a good man."

"It seemed from the book that you were very close."

"He wanted to marry me, and I nearly accepted. I would have been your stepmother. What do you think of that?"

"I think it would have been wonderful."

"Maybe. It was difficult in those days." She looked thoughtful. "Your father was a remarkable man, in his way. For someone like Charlie to want to marry a girl from Brooklyn, from a family of Conservative Jews, even, in those days . . . Charlie was a man of large mind."

"I guess he was. I loved my father, but I suppose I was a little disappointed as well. I think he might have made more of his life. Perhaps if he'd married you he would have."

"Who can say?" Sarah Adler shrugged. "I have lived too long to believe you can predict what people will do. But your father's book will be read for a long time. He will be remembered. Do we remember any of your other ancestors?"

"Maybe not."

"You look like him, you know. You remind me of him."

"I think we're very different."

Sarah Adler reached down to her briefcase. She opened it and took something out.

"Do you know what this is?" she asked.

"Looks like an Indian belt of some kind."

"It is. A wampum belt." She spread it out. "Look at the design. Isn't it wonderful?" She gazed at it. "The design says something, of course—though we don't know what—but it's also a piece of pure abstract art. This was an heirloom in your family, you know. Yet Charlie gave it to me. He had it framed, but the frame's rather big, so I took it out to bring you this morning. I think you should have it."

"I couldn't take it from you—it must have such memories."

"It has, but I'd like you to have it. I'm returning it to the family, just as you are returning the drawing." She smiled. "The cycle is complete."

Gorham said nothing. He suddenly thought of the gap on the living-room wall where the Motherwell had been, and wondered if the wampum belt would go there. He didn't think so. Then it occurred to him that if his marriage fell apart, perhaps he wouldn't be seeing so much of that living-room wall anyway.

Sarah Adler was looking at Gorham carefully.

"You don't look happy. Something in your life is troubling you."

"Maybe."

"Would you like to tell me? After all, I was almost your stepmother."

Gorham supposed that if he was going to share the information with anyone, this clever older woman who'd loved his father was probably as good a person as he'd ever find. It didn't take him long to relate what had happened. After he had finished, Sarah was silent for a minute. Then she smiled at him.

"So," she said gently, "I see that Charlie failed."

"I always felt that, but I thought you told me he succeeded."

"No, I don't mean that Charlie failed to be a banker, or whatever you think he should have been. I mean that he failed to teach you anything." She sighed. "All those weekends he used to take you from Staten Island and show you New York. All that effort, and you never learned anything about the city at all. That's sad. Poor Charlie."

"I don't understand."

"All the richness of this city. All the life. The newspapers, the theaters, the galleries, the jazz, the businesses and activities of every kind. There's almost nothing you can't find in New York, and he wanted to introduce you to all of it. People come here from all over the world, there are communities and cultures of every kind, and you want none of it, except one little thing. To run a bank. That's not so interesting."

"I guess I've always wanted the financial success you find in New York. That's a powerful thing."

"You know there has been a dot.com boom—except that it's turning out to be a bubble."

"Probably."

"Don't you know that there's another bubble as well? An expectations bubble. Bigger houses, private planes, yachts . . . stupid salaries and bonuses. People come to desire these things and expect them. But the expectations bubble will burst as well, as all bubbles do."

"Then you won't be able to sell the big Picassos."

"Come to my gallery and I will sell you beautiful things at a more reasonable price. But the point is that they will have value. Things of real beauty, things of the spirit. That is art. New York is full of people like me, and you have missed us. You see only dollars."

"When I was a boy," said Gorham, "my grandmother gave me a silver dollar. I guess for me that was a symbol of all the family had been, when we had money. I keep it with me to this day, in my pocket, just to remind me what I come from. The old Master family, before my father's aberration. I suppose you think it foolish, but I feel as if my grandmother was passing that on to me, like a talisman."

"Really? That would be a Morgan dollar, I believe."

"Yes. But how did you know?"

"Because I was seeing your father at the time, and he told me about it. Your grandmother wanted to give you something and she asked Charlie for advice. So he gave her the dollar, which he'd bought from a collector, so that she could give it to you. Your silver dollar actually came from Charlie. The rest is your own construction."

Gorham was silent for several moments, then he shook his head. "You're telling me I'm deluded."

"People come to New York to be free, but you have constructed a prison for yourself." She sighed. "I loved your father, Gorham, but I'm glad I married my husband. And do you know how we've built up our marriage? Layer upon layer. Shared experience, children, loyalty. Layer upon layer. Until we have something of more value than anything I can imagine. And we've tried to pass that on to our children. That's all parents can do—try to teach their children how to live. I don't think you're doing that by going to Boston." She looked at her watch. "I have to go."

"I guess I do, too."

Sarah Adler stood up. "I've given you a lecture. Now I'll give you a present. I know you like it. I gave it to your father once, now I'm giving it to you." She handed him the Motherwell drawing. "Please go back to your family and have a good life, Gorham. That would make me very happy." She gave him a quick smile. "I'll let you pay for the breakfast."

Then she was moving swiftly away.

He was just waiting for the check when an idea occurred to him. He hurried out of the dining room.

Sarah Adler was just about to step into a taxi on Park when he caught up with her.

"I want to give you something too." He handed her the wampum belt.

"My father would have wanted you to keep it—I know he would—but you can consider it a present from me."

"Well, thank you." She fixed her eyes on his. "Think about what I said." Then, with a mischievous smile, she put it round her waist and tied it. "How do I look?"

"Adorable."

"Well, then I guess I am." She got into the taxi, and it moved away, as he turned back inside to pay the check.

"Where to?" the driver asked Sarah Adler, as the taxi started down Park.

"World Trade Center," she replied.

⁙

Gorham sat for several minutes alone at their table. He pondered what to do. He glanced at his watch. If he was going to turn up for the meeting at the headhunter's, he'd better get going. With the drawing under his arm, he went out onto Park, and moments later, he was being driven south.

It was an easy ride down FDR Drive. The taxi rounded the bulge of the Lower East Side by the Williamsburg Bridge. Manhattan Bridge came next, then the Brooklyn Bridge, and just after that, the South Street Seaport on the waterfront.

That was where he made his decision. As the taxi came onto South Street and made a right onto Whitehall, he took out his cellphone. He wouldn't be going to the meeting.

He didn't feel like going straight back to his office. He got out of the taxi and decided to call Maggie.

⁙

At approximately 7:59 on the morning of September 11, 2001, American Airlines Flight 11 from Boston to Los Angeles had taken off from Logan International Airport. The plane was a Boeing 767, with ninety-two people on board, including crew. Soon after 8:16, the plane, flying at 29,000 feet, deviated from its scheduled course and failed to respond to repeated calls from Boston Air Traffic Control. For a time, its whereabouts were unclear.

At 8:26 the plane turned south. By now BATC had heard the leading hijacker giving instructions to the passengers. At 8:37 the plane was spotted. It was flying south approximately along the line of the Hudson River. NORAD was informed and two F-15 fighters were prepared for take-off from the Otis base in Massachusetts.

At 8:43 the plane made a final turn toward Manhattan.

Very few people noticed the plane as it approached the city. For a start, there wasn't much time. Initially, the sight of a plane flying low toward Manhattan would not have seemed so strange. Plenty of planes, if not on quite this flight path, came in low over the city as they approached nearby La Guardia. As it passed over the city, few people in the narrow canyons of the streets would even have seen it. Those on the waterfront, or across the river in New Jersey, did see it, however. Though it did not seem out of control, it was now far too low. Some witnesses thought the pilot must be in trouble and was maybe hoping to crash-land in the Hudson.

Only at the last moment did the plane level out, appear to accelerate, and head straight for the northern face of the World Trade Center Number 1 Tower. It did not occur to people that this extraordinary flight path was deliberately chosen.

At 8.46 the plane smashed into the side of the North Tower just above the ninety-third floor and embedded itself deep into the building with a huge explosion. It was traveling at 404 knots and carried 10,000 gallons of fuel.

❖

At 8:35, Dr. Caruso had been ushered into the office. It was only in the twenties in the South Tower, but the view over the water was splendid. The insurance agent, Doug, an old friend, had told him he'd join him in a minute. Standing at the window, Caruso had glanced up.

The North Tower loomed just a short distance away. At the top of that tower, on the 106th and 107th floors, was the Windows on the World restaurant. It was a splendid establishment, and the highest grossing restaurant in the USA. When friends from outside the city came to visit New York, he liked to take them there. He probably did this a couple of times a year. And he never tired of it. You could walk round the bar area and look out over Brooklyn on one side, New Jersey the other, north up the Hudson or south across the harbor. You could see for twenty miles. Sometimes, low clouds even passed below you, cutting off sections of the city like a thin veil. He smiled.

Doug hurried into the room, apologizing for keeping him waiting.

NEW YORK   845

"I've got a bunch of stuff for you to look at," he said with a grin. "Then I'll tell you what I think you ought to do."

"Great," said Dr. Caruso as he sat down. "Let me make a suggestion. Why don't you tell me what to do first? Then after I've got the diagnosis, I'll look at the patient."

"Sounds good to me." And he launched into a quick appraisal of Caruso's life expectancy, from an actuarial point of view, and what that meant for his future premiums. Then he launched into a disquisition about how Caruso could save money—in the long run.

He'd just got going with his proposal, when he started, glanced up at the North Tower and then stared.

"What the hell is that?" he said.

✦

"Ms. O'Donnell's office."

"This is her husband. Is she there?"

"I'm sorry, Mr. Master. She's away at a meeting. You could try her cell, but she probably has it switched off just now. Is there a message?"

"Tell her I'll call later. Actually, tell her that I decided not to go to Boston. She'll understand."

He hung up. And he was just wondering whether to walk a few blocks before heading back to his office, when an extraordinary sound caused him to look up. High in the World Trade Center's North Tower, a huge fire had just broken out, and smoke was billowing from it.

"What happened?" he asked a man standing nearby.

"Looks like a bomb," said the man.

"A plane went smack into it," said a young woman. "I saw it. Must've gone out of control."

✦

"They say we have to evacuate," said Doug. "I don't know why. The fire's in the other building."

They went out toward the elevators. There was a crowd of people waiting by them already.

"Want to take the stairs?" asked Caruso.

"Twenty and some floors?" said Doug. "Not much."

"I guess we'd better be patient then," said Caruso. "Can we finish this meeting on the sidewalk?"

"I can finish a meeting in any space known to man," said Doug, "including numerous bars. But I'd prefer my office."

The elevators were all full. "I can't believe this is necessary," somebody said.

A couple of minutes later, a receptionist came out from a neighboring office.

"They just called to say we don't need to evacuate," she announced. "The building's fine. The building's secure. You can all get back to work."

With a collective sigh, everyone started to file back to their offices.

"Okay," said Doug, when they reached his office again, "let's get back to your life."

⁜

Gorham was still watching the fire in the North Tower when the second plane struck. A bang like a thunderclap came from the far corner of the building, high, maybe eighty floors up. At almost the same instant, a huge fireball burst out of the side of the building far above. Thinking quickly, Gorham hurled himself toward an entrance to avoid any falling debris.

He heard screams of fear. People who'd started evacuating the building earlier were coming out of one of the elevators. He was thinking hard.

This couldn't be an accident. Two coincidences like that? Impossible. Carefully, he stepped away from the entrance. Black smoke and flame were billowing from both buildings, making blood-colored, oily clouds against the pale blue sky.

He ran.

When he'd gone three or four hundred yards north up Church Street, he paused to consider the situation. It seemed to him there could be only one explanation: it was a terrorist attack. What else could it be? After all, back in 1993, terrorists had planted a truck bomb in the World Trade Center garage which had done huge damage, injured more than a thousand people, and might have brought the Twin Towers down. This looked like a similar attempt. And if so, what else was to come?

A stream of people were coming up the street. It seemed as if everyone was deciding to leave the area.

His cellphone rang.

"Mr. Master?" It was Maggie's assistant again. "Where are you?"

"Down near the World Trade Center. But I'm fine, I'm not in the building."

"We just saw what happened on the television. We just saw the second plane."

"I saw it too. Did you speak with my wife?"

"That's why I'm calling. I wondered if you did."

"No. She probably turned her cell off during her meeting."

"Only . . ." Maggie's secretary seemed to hesitate a moment. "Mr. Master, that's where she went."

"What do you mean? The meeting got moved to the World Trade Center?"

"That's what she told her paralegal just before she left. Oh, I'm so sorry, Mr. Master, I'm just so worried."

"Which tower?"

"We don't know."

"What's the name of the firm?"

"We're trying to check."

"For God's sake, you must know who she's meeting."

"We're checking that out right now. One of the other partners knows, but he's in a meeting."

"Well, interrupt the meeting. Right away. And call me back please." It was an order.

"Yes, Mr. Master."

"Call me back." Goddammit. His pulse was suddenly racing. If necessary, he would climb up the fireman's ladder or scale the sides of the building, but he was going to get Maggie out of there. No question. Only he had to know which building.

He tried Maggie's cell. Nothing. He started to walk back toward the World Trade Center. Minutes passed. More and more people were coming up the street. He'd give Maggie's office a couple more minutes, no more.

His cell went again.

"Daddy?" It was Emma.

"Hi, honey." He tried to sound unconcerned. "Aren't you in class?"

"I'm just going back in. Daddy, is everything all right? Are you anywhere near downtown? What's happening down there?"

"I'm out in the street, sweetie. There's some kind of fire in the World Trade Center. But I'm quite all right."

"Is it, like, bombs or something?"

"Could be."

"Where's Mommy?"

"In a meeting."

"She's not down there, is she?"

He hesitated, but only for a second. "Why ever would you think that?"

"I don't know. I called her cell and she didn't answer."

"You know she always turns her cell off when she's in big meetings."

"I know. I just . . ."

"She's in Midtown somewhere, honey. Everybody's fine, go back to class."

"Okay, Daddy."

She hung up. He redialed Maggie's office immediately.

"I'm sorry, Mr. Master, we're still trying to get that information."

"Now I want you to listen very carefully," Gorham said. "If any of the children call, nobody is to tell them that their mother is at the World Trade Center. This is really important. You have to tell them she's somewhere in Midtown. I can't have the kids going crazy at school, when there's probably no need. Do you understand?"

"Yes, Mr. Master. I get it," she said.

"Call me back with the information about where she is," he told her. "I need to know." Then he hung up.

But ten minutes passed, and still she didn't call.

⁘

Dr. Caruso was glad to be out of Doug's office. He'd changed his mind just a couple of minutes after he'd got back there. Not that he was worried about his safety, but it occurred to him that there must be a lot of people injured in the North Tower. No doubt the emergency services would cope efficiently, but he was still a doctor. All right, an obstetrician, but a doctor nonetheless. He'd decided to go down to see if there was anything he could do to help.

It hadn't taken him long to find a fire chief.

"Thank you, doctor. Would you stick around?"

"Sure." They were in the lower lobby.

"I'll get back to you."

The second plane had hit a moment later.

He'd been waiting quite a while now. Firemen came and went. They were brave fellows, but it looked as if this situation was presenting them with some huge problems. So far, he hadn't seen that fire chief again.

✥

It was 9:25 when his cellphone rang again. It was a number he didn't know. He took the call impatiently, wanting to get rid of it as quickly as possible.

"Honey? Can you hear me?"

"Maggie! Where are you?"

"I'm at the World Trade Center."

"I know. Which tower?"

"South. I'd have called you before but my damn cell cut out, and this nice guy let me use his. Where are you?"

"On Church Street, at Chambers. Maggie, I'm not going to Boston, okay? I was crazy. I love you."

"Oh thank God, Gorham. I love you too. I'm coming down the stairs, but it's kinda slow. Some of the building's got twisted around a little."

"I'm coming in to get you."

"Don't do that, honey. Please. I don't even know where I am. You'll never find me, and then we'll miss, and then I won't be able to find you. Just wait right there. I'm on my way. It's not like the building's going to fall down or anything."

"Just keep talking to me then."

"Honey, the guy needs his phone back. I'll call. Just wait there and give me a big hug when I get out."

"Okay. But Maggie—" The call had ended. "I love you," he said to the cellphone.

✥

By 9:40, Dr. Caruso reckoned that if he was going to be of any use to anybody, he'd better look around and make his own assessment. He was in the upper lobby when he heard the first thud. At first he didn't realize what it was. A few moments later, there came two more.

Bodies. They were coming from the North Tower. He understood what that meant. People must be trapped up there in heat which was becoming unbearable. So you had the choice: burn alive or jump. He'd read accounts of people jumping from buildings, but this was different— these bodies were falling a thousand feet. The math wasn't difficult. Accelerating at thirty-two feet per second, after falling a thousand feet, a body hits a hard surface very hard indeed. He wasn't sure if you'd be conscious just before impact, but death would be completely instantaneous. If these were his only options, he reckoned, he'd choose to jump. But the sound it made . . . He tried not to hear the sound it made.

"There's my doctor. You thought I'd forgotten you." The Irish face of the fire chief, looking a little red from exertion. "Like to do me a favor?"

"Of course."

"Well then, doc, what I'd like you to do is go over to Trinity Church. There may be some folks over there that need attention, and I believe some of my boys are there too. Would you do that?"

"I'm on my way."

He went outside onto Liberty and started south down Broadway, glad to have something to do. He'd better call his wife to let her know he was safe. She could call the office. And while she was at it, he suddenly thought, why not call the realtor and tell her they'd changed their minds about that damn Park Avenue building. He didn't want to live there any more.

❖

It was nearing ten o'clock. What could be taking her so long? Gorham stared at the tower. While the flames were still burning brightly up in the North Tower, the South Tower seemed to have settled into a smokier, more sullen mood. Several times he'd heard explosions from lower down in the towers. Stores of gas or electrical equipment? Or perhaps, he guessed, fuel from the planes might have run down the inside of the buildings, collected again, and suddenly exploded. Who knew? But whatever the causes of these other sounds, it was smoke rather than flame that was to be seen issuing from the South Tower now.

Almost ten o'clock. Surely she must appear any second now.

His cellphone rang.

"Hi, honey, it's me."

"Thank God."

"That was a bit of a journey down."

"Maggie . . ."

"What's up?"

His eyes were fixed on the upper part of the South Tower. Something was happening. The top seemed to be leaning, twisting.

"Maggie, where are you?"

Now the tower seemed to be righting itself, but only because further down, something had snapped or shifted. For suddenly the roof of the great tower was beginning to sink.

"It's okay, Gorham. I'm down, and—"

"Maggie—"

Nothing. Deadness. The top of the huge tower had started to travel downward. He had never seen anything like it, except in movies, or old newsreels. The controlled demolition of high-rise buildings. It was amazing how they could just sink, like a collapsing concertina. And that was what was happening now. The South Tower was falling in on itself.

But so slowly. He could not believe how slowly. Second by second, as if in slow motion, the tower was traveling down. One second, two seconds, three seconds, four . . . With majestic, deliberate, measured speed, the top was sinking while, at the bottom, with a slow roar, like a groaning waterfall, a huge, grayish cloud of dust was belching out.

"Maggie." No voice.

The ground was trembling now. He could feel the tremor underfoot. The billowing tidal wave of dust was rolling up the street toward him like a volcano's pyroclastic flow. He must back away and flee. He had no choice. He couldn't stand his ground. He backed into Chambers Street, hoping the dust wave would not sweep down over the rooftops and smother him. But the rumbling continued, for nine interminable seconds, as the tower fell, and the cloud of dust, as if it had acquired a life of its own, grew and roiled on itself, and grew again until, in all the streets around, you could not see the light at all.

He could hear people running northward, half choking, many of them. After a while, he unbuttoned the top of his shirt, pulled it up to use as a mask, and tried to make his way south into the dust storm. But it was no good. He was choking and he couldn't see. Finally, like everyone else, he retreated further up the street, and reaching a point where the air was somewhat clearer, he sat down on the sidewalk, and watched the gray-dusted figures as they passed, like Shades from Hades, in the forlorn hope that one of them, after all, might be his wife.

And then, after ten minutes, she came toward him.

"Hoped I might find you here," she said.

"I thought . . ."

"I'd only just left the building when it started coming down. I guess it broke the cell connection. Then a whole bunch of us went into a café to get out of the dust. But I came up the street as soon as I could. You look awful."

"And you look wonderful." He took her in his arms.

"I'm a little dusty."

"You're alive."

"I think we mostly got out. I'm not sure about the people higher up though, above the fire."

"Oh my God."

"What?"

"Katie Keller. She told me she was going to a meeting somewhere in the Financial District this morning. Do you have her cell number?"

"I think so."

"Let's try to call."

But there was no answer when they did.

⁘

As it moved to and fro that morning, still wrapped around the waist of Sarah Adler in the high room in the tower, the wampum belt had looked very well. Its little white and colored shells were as bright as on the day they were strung. To those who could read its message, woven with such love, it declared: "Father of Pale Feather."

And as the great burning rose, and the huge tower swayed, and then sank, so huge was the heat and so stupendous the pressure of that massive falling that, like everything around it, above and below, the wampum belt was atomized into a dust so fine it could scarcely be seen. For a short time it hovered around the base of the vanished tower. But then at last the wind, kinder than men, lifted it up in a cloud—high, high over the harbor waters, and the city, and the great river that led to the north.

Epilogue

T HEY SAT IN the café. It was a beautiful day. Gorham looked across at the Metropolitan Opera and smiled at his daughter. He could see that she was going to try something on him, but he waited for it to come.

She looked serious.

"Dad."

"Yes, my darling."

"I think I have ADD."

"Really? That's nice."

"No, Dad. I mean it. I really can't concentrate."

"Well, I'm certainly sorry to hear that. When did you discover this?"

"This year, I guess."

"You don't think it could have anything to do with all the parties you went to?"

"Dad, be serious."

"I am being serious. Listen, Emma, I have to tell you something. You can't have ADD."

"How do you know?"

"Listen, when I brought you over here this morning and made you look at those two huge Chagalls by the entrance to the Met, did you have trouble doing that?"

"Yes."

"I don't mean did you complain all the way across the park about having to look at the damned opera house—by the way, it's a very fine opera house and a damn sight better than the old one, but never mind that. I mean, were you able to stare at the Chagalls and take them in?"

"I had great difficulty."

"No you didn't. I watched you."

"That is so unfair. You're worse than Mommy."

"Wow. Impressive insult." He looked at her seriously. "Emma, you have to understand. Attention deficit disorder exists. A few people have it, and if they really do, it's no joke. But nowadays, half the kids in your school say they have it. Why's that?"

"You get extra time in exams."

"Right. It's a racket. The parents tell the doctors they think their kids have it, and the doctors go along with it, and soon everybody has it, so they can have extra time with their exams and improve their grades."

"Isn't that a good reason to have it?"

"No. And I also know the Ritalin racket."

"Meaning?"

"Ritalin is the drug usually prescribed for ADD. Ritalin helps concentration. It also has the useful property of letting you stay awake and mentally alert through a day and a night. If you have to pull an all-nighter on a college essay, it'll get you through. So the kids who claim to have ADD get prescribed the Ritalin, and then they sell it to the college kids. Do you think I don't know that?"

"So what's your point?"

"The fact that there's a secondary market in something doesn't make it right."

"Mommy doesn't say I haven't got ADD."

"What does she say?"

"She says she doesn't know."

"Your mother's a lawyer."

"You think you're so clever."

"I pay for your school fees. And I pay for your tutors. Last year you had a tutor for math, and another for science, and another to prepare you for your SATs. Shortly you will have a tutor to help you prepare for your college applications. Your mother will insist on that. You have so many damn tutors that I don't know why I pay for you to go to school. But I am not paying for ADD. That is final. And let me tell you something else. There are kids all over America who don't have all these fancy tutors, and who just sit down to do their SATs and applications, without any help at all."

"But they don't get into the best schools."

"Actually, you're wrong. I'm very glad that some of them do."

Gorham shook his head. You could say, of course, that he'd brought this upon himself. He'd raised the kids in pampered privilege precisely because he wanted the best for them, and now he'd got what he paid for. But it went beyond his kids, who were a little spoiled, but fundamentally sound. New York, it seemed to him, was just the pinnacle of a more general problem.

Look at what happened if one of the kids got sick. Antibiotics, right away. It wasn't just New York, or even America. He had friends in Europe who told him that the socialized doctors there did exactly the same thing. Give the child antibiotics and stay out of trouble. The only trouble was, did any of these children build up natural resistances? The new bugs that resisted antibiotics were going to come and get them one day.

There was never a downside. Nothing must be allowed to go wrong. You could find the tough old American spirit on the sports field. But was that enough?

"I can't believe you won't let me have ADD," Emma said.

Yet maybe deep down, he thought, she was pleased. Kids like it if you say no. He remembered his son once, when he was a little guy, saying something about another boy: "His parents don't care about him at all, Dad. They let him do anything he likes." There was wisdom in that.

"Let's walk back across the park," he suggested.

"Walk? Okay."

But a tiny detour first, he thought. Just up to Seventy-second Street. It was a grand street to walk across. As they came to Central Park West, he paused and pointed at the Dakota.

"You know who lived there."

"Tell me."

"John Lennon. The Beatles."

"Right. I knew that. He got shot there. And his wife Yoko Ono made a beautiful garden in the park opposite."

"Did you ever go in there?"

"I know you're going to take me anyway."

"Too right I am."

They crossed Central Park West and entered the park. He led Emma to the entrance of Yoko Ono's garden.

"It's called Strawberry Fields, after a famous Beatles song," he said.

"Okay."

"Now, look down at that plaque on the ground. What does it say?"

"It says, 'Imagine.' "

"Right. That's after a song too." He hummed a bit of it.

"You really shouldn't sing, Dad."

"It's about everybody in the world living in peace. Well, it's about quite a lot of things that I guess were important to John Lennon. But the real point is kind of existential. You can change the world if you're prepared to imagine something better. You have to imagine. Do you get it?"

"If you say so."

"Well, I do."

They strolled round it.

"There would have been deer here originally, of course."

"Like all over Westchester."

"Exactly. Manhattan was a big Indian hunting ground when the Dutch first came. Your ancestors, you know."

"Yes, Dad." She rolled her eyes, but with a smile. "I know. I'm descended from the Dutch and the English, and I don't know who else."

"Broadway, pretty much, was an Indian trail. And another trail went up somewhat east of Central Park."

"Great. Do I have to know all this?"

"I think so."

"Anything else?"

Gorham was silent. He was thinking.

"It's funny, this is called Strawberry Fields because of the song, but when it was in its native state, there could easily have been wild strawberries here. Have you ever eaten wild strawberries?"

"I don't think so."

"We must remedy that sometime. We ought to go camping and eat wild strawberries."

To his surprise, she seemed to like the idea.

"We could do that. Go camping together." She put her arm through his. "Can we do that? Promise?"

"I promise."

They walked across the park arm in arm. The sun was warm. He didn't try to preach to her any more, and she seemed quite happy just walking by his side.

His children were all right, he thought. All they needed was a challenge. Look at some of their friends—Lee, the Chinese boy, had got to Harvard. Or look at the people who had risen to be mayors of the city in recent decades. Fiorello La Guardia, Ed Koch, David Dinkins, Rudy Giuliani—Jewish, black, Italian, every one of them had come up from poverty the hard way. You might like this one or that, but what a story for a great city. Plenty of his kids' rich friends came from families who'd been on the Lower East Side two generations earlier. The American dream was not a dream; it was a reality. People came here for freedom and, hard though the way up might be, they found it. To make it, you needed the work ethic. And a good thing too.

He thought of Dr. Caruso. Caruso actually did a day a week unpaid at a clinic in the Bronx. Few people knew that. But the guy had also invested brilliantly in the stock market boom and then sold out at the peak in 2008. Bought himself a town house on Park which cost a serious amount of money. By chance, the very same month, the guy who'd finally bought 7B had been indicted for fraud.

"That's a first for the building," Gorham had remarked to Vorpal. "We never had an indictment before." He'd shaken his head. "And who'd have thought it? The guy had six times assets."

Fortunately, Vorpal had no idea that there was irony in these remarks.

⁂

It had taken two years, after the tragedy of 9/11, before Gorham Master had left the bank, and when the transition had come, it had seemed the most natural thing in the world. It happened one evening at dinner.

He and Maggie had been making a point of getting together with Juan and Janet every few months, and they had been at the Campos's apartment one Sunday brunch when Juan had remarked that of all the people in their MBA class at Columbia, the one he'd be curious to meet would be Peter Codford.

"That can be arranged," said Gorham, and later that year, when Peter was in town, Gorham and Maggie invited them all to dinner.

It had proved to be a delightful reunion for the three old friends. Peter had been particularly interested in the work Juan did. "I'm especially interested in what you say about El Barrio," he remarked over dessert, "because Judy and I are setting up a foundation whose focus is going to be on America's inner cities. We want to look at problems right across the country, and El Barrio is exactly the sort of area that would be of concern to us."

"Now I know that you are truly rich," said Juan with a laugh.

"If you've been financially successful, you have to decide how you're going to use the money. But my own contribution will only get the foundation started. Raising new money will be a crucial part of the foundation's ongoing task. We really need a banker as a CEO, I think."

"Maybe Gorham should do it," said Maggie.

"Really?" Peter turned to Gorham. "Would you be interested? I couldn't pay you the kind of money you make at the bank, but it could be a really interesting challenge." He glanced at Judy, who nodded and smiled. "I'd love to talk to you about it, if you might be interested."

Six months later, Gorham had become the first CEO of the Codford Foundation. Together with his income from his bank shares the foundation salary gave him enough to get by. Less than Maggie was making now, by far, but what did that matter?

And he'd been a brilliant success. His years as a banker certainly gave him many skills, but his genuine enthusiasm for what the foundation was doing made him a wonderful advocate for the cause, and he discovered that he had a genius for fund-raising. He'd never been happier in his life. A year ago, he'd even been honored at a big New York dinner.

"But I still have a long way to go," he told Maggie. "I shall never consider myself successful until I have secured a significant donation from Vorpal and Bandersnatch."

"We'll go to work on them together," she promised.

✦

When they got to their building, he gave Emma a kiss.

"Thank you for coming to see the Chagalls with me," he said.

"It was fun. Aren't you coming up?"

"I just have an errand to run. I'll be back inside half an hour."

"Okay, Dad." She smiled. "Thank you."

He turned down Park Avenue. He didn't really have an errand, he just needed to walk a little more. Park Avenue was looking its best. You wouldn't think times were hard—not so bad for lawyers, it had to be admitted, though the family assets had decreased substantially in the last eighteen months. But it was tough for a lot of people.

When you thought about it, though, the cycle of boom and bust, advance and recession, had been going on in the two biggest financial centers, New York and London, for centuries. Some busts were bigger than others—the Depression was huge. But this beautiful avenue still went on.

Poor immigrants still arrived and found the freedom they sought, and prospered.

And let's face it, when you thought of the riots, the brutality, even the prejudices of generations past, New York for all its faults was a far kinder place than ever before in its history.

The Big Apple. People thought that phrase came from the sixties. Actually it came from the late twenties and thirties, but what the hell? And what did it actually mean? Something you could take a big bite out of, he supposed. Some said it was the apple that tempted Adam. No doubt that too—New York was always materialist. But it was also the city of excellence, of art, music, of endless possibilities.

He passed a fashionable store and was surprised to see that in their window display they were using a Theodore Keller print. It looked terrific. That really pleased him.

And made him think of Katie. Katie Keller had done well.

As well as her catering business, she'd opened her own restaurant in northern Westchester County. He and Maggie often went there on summer weekends.

He remembered so well the moment of panic he'd had back on the terrible day the towers came down. She'd been in the Financial Center across the street, thank God, but it had been hours before they'd been able to make contact with her.

Only one person that he knew himself had died that terrible day. Old Sarah Adler. If it hadn't been for her, he'd have been in the headhunter's office in the World Trade Center himself. Whether he'd have been trapped and lost his life it was impossible to say. But whether or not she'd saved his life in a physical sense, she'd saved it in every other way.

Sarah Adler had gone. Along with more than a thousand others, she had left not a trace of her body that could be identified. An absolute and final loss.

Not absolute, perhaps. She was remembered. Whenever he looked at the great space in the sky where the towers had been, he always thought of her with gratitude, and affection. And thousands of others were remembered, in a similar fashion.

And he was glad that a new, Freedom Tower would arise to take the former towers' place, for it seemed to him that this was everything that New York stood for. No matter how hard things were, New Yorkers never gave up.

He continued walking. He came down past the Waldorf-Astoria, and the enclave of office buildings around the lovely, Byzantine-looking church of St. Bartholomew. As the lunch hour approached, a jazz band had started playing in the entrance of one of the bank buildings. People were gathering to stand or sit and listen to the music.

How delightful it was in the sun. Even here in New York, time could sometimes stand still.

And suddenly it came to him. That Strawberry Fields garden he'd come from, and the Freedom Tower he'd been thinking of: taken together, didn't they contain the two words that said it all about this city, the two words that really mattered? It seemed to him that they did. Two words: the one an invitation, the other an ideal, an adventure, a necessity. "Imagine" said the garden. "Freedom" said the tower. Imagine freedom. That was the spirit, the message of this city he loved. You really didn't need anything more. Dream it and do it. But first you must dream it.

Imagine. Freedom. Always.

Acknowledgments

During the course of researching this novel, I have consulted a great many books, articles and other sources. I should like in particular to record my thanks and appreciation as follows.

My warm thanks Professor Kenneth T. Jackson, for the most courteous and kindly overall guidance, and for *The Encyclopedia of New York City*, which sits in joint pride of place upon my desk, beside the magnificent *Gotham*, by Edwin G. Burrows and Mike Wallace.

I owe a thirty-year debt of thanks to the curators and staff of the New York Public Library, and thanks for kind help from all the staff at the Museum of the City of New York, the New-York Historical Society, the American Museum of Natural History, the American Indian Museum, South Street Seaport, the Lower East Side Tenement Museum, Ellis Island Immigration Museum, and further special thanks to Carol Willis for her help and guidance at the Skyscraper Museum.

One of the greatest joys of my professional life is the chance to work with distinguished historians, scholars and experts in the preparation of these books. The following have graciously read sections of my manuscript, in several cases hundreds of pages, made corrections and given invaluable counsel. I am therefore privileged to thank Graham Russell Hodges, Professor of Early American History at Colgate University; Edwin G. Burrows, Professor of History at Brooklyn College, City University of New York; Christopher Gray, Office for Metropolitan History, and "Streetscapes" Columnist, *The New York Times*; Barry Moreno, Curator, The Bob Hope Memorial Library at Ellis Island; Rabbi Robert Orkand, Temple Israel, Westport, CT; and Mark Feldman, of Weston, CT. Whatever shortcomings remain are mine alone.

Special thanks are also due to Dan McNerney for his invaluable research assistance. And though space does not permit a complete list of all the many kind people who have given help, support, and information during the gestation of this book, I should like in particular to mention: Theresa Havell Carter, Sam Delgado, Harry Morgan, Joan Morgan, Miles Morgan, Maria Pashby, Michele Kellner Perkins, Ed Reynolds, Winthrop and Mary Rutherfurd, Susan Segal, Tim Smith, and the late Isabella H. Watts.

My many thanks to Mike Morgenfeld for kindly preparing maps, and to Heidi Boshoff, once again, for preparing the manuscript with wonderful efficiency.

Finally, as always, I thank my agent Gill Coleridge, without whom I should be entirely lost, my wonderful editors, Oliver Johnson at Century and William Thomas at Doubleday, whose exemplary thoroughness and creative responses to problems have so hugely improved this manuscript, and Charlotte Haycock at Century and Melissa Danaczko at Doubleday for so kindly and patiently guiding the manuscript through its final stages.

PHOTO: © JEANNE MASOERO

Edward Rutherfurd is the author of six novels, including *London, Sarum, The Princes of Ireland,* and *The Rebels of Ireland.*